HOW FIRM A FOUNDATION

DAVID WEBER

TOR®

A TOM DOHERTY ASSOCIATES BOOK
NEW YORK

This is a work of fiction. All of the characters, organizations, and events portrayed in this novel are either products of the author's imagination or are used fictitiously.

HOW FIRM A FOUNDATION

Copyright © 2011 by David Weber

All rights reserved.

Maps by Ellisa Mitchell

A Tor Book
Published by Tom Doherty Associates, LLC
175 Fifth Avenue
New York, NY 10010

www.tor-forge.com

Tor® is a registered trademark of Tom Doherty Associates, LLC.

ISBN 978-0-7653-6125-7

First Edition: September 2011
First Mass Market Edition: August 2012

Printed in the United States of America

0 9 8 7 6 5 4 3 2 1

For Alice G. Weber, with love.
Hey, Mom! Look! I did it!

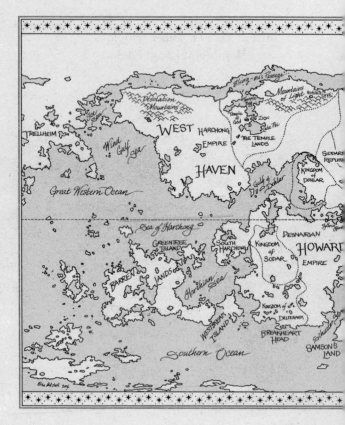

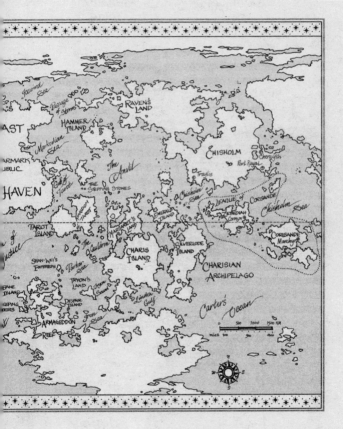

NORTH WATCH
Silkiah Bay
HOWARD HEAD
WIDOWS POINT
HOWARD ISLAND
GOOSE ISLAND
JAHRAS ISLAND
Howard Passage
TERRENCE POINT
Gulf of Jahras
Terrence Bay
SUMMER ISLAND
SPIDER CRAB ISLAND
SINGER ISLAND
PEARL POINT
SYLMAHN ISLAND
RAY ISLAND
Khairman Keep
DUCHY of KHOLMAN
Iythria
Kholman River
SPIDER CRAB ISLAND
SINGER ISLAND
Pilot Shoal
Outer Gate Channel
Iythria Bank
East Pass
West Roadstead
PEARL POINT
SYLMAHN ISLAND
Middle Ground
Ray Island Shoal
The Kettle
Sylmahn's Passage
RAY ISLAND
Kettle Bottom Shoal
Rocky Bank Shoal
Outer Roadstead
Sickle Shoal
North Gate
Triangle Shoal
West Gate
Inner Harbor
IYTHRIA
Kholman River

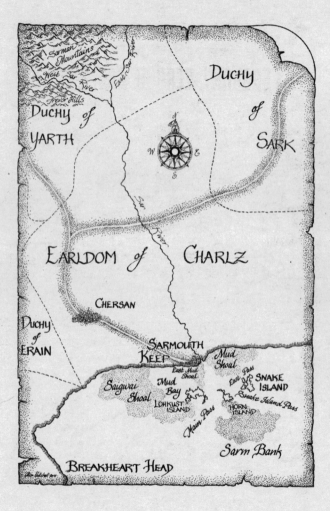

FEBRUARY, YEAR OF GOD 895

·✦·

Castaway Islands,
Great Western Ocean;
Imperial Palace,
City of Cherayth,
Kingdom of Chisholm;
and
Ehdwyrd Howsmyn's Study,
Delthak,
Kingdom of Old Charis

Nights didn't come much darker, Merlin Athrawes reflected as he stood gazing up at the cloud-choked, stormy sky. There were no stars, and no moon, through those clouds, and although it was summer in Safehold's southern hemisphere, the Castaway Islands were almost four thousand miles below the equator on a planet whose average temperature was rather lower than Old Terra's to begin with. That made "summer" a purely relative term, and he wondered again how the islands had come to be named.

There were four of them, none of which had ever been *individually* named. The largest was just under two hundred and fifty miles in its longest dimension; the smallest was barely twenty-seven miles long; and aside from a few species of arctic wyverns and the seals (which actually resembled the Terran species of the same name) which used their limited beaches, he'd seen no sign of life anywhere on any of them. He could well believe that any ship which had ever approached the barren, steep-sided volcanic peaks rising from the depths of the Great Western Ocean had managed to wreck themselves. What he couldn't figure out was why anyone would have been in the vicinity in the first place, and how there could have been any surviving castaways to name the islands afterward.

He knew they hadn't been named by the terraforming crews which had first prepared Safehold for human habitation. He had access to Pei Shan-wei's original maps, and these miserable hunks of weather and wind-lashed igneous rock, sand, and shingle bore no name on them. There were still quite a few unnamed bits and pieces of real estate scattered around the planet, actually, despite the detailed atlases which were part of the *Holy Writ* of the Church of God Awaiting. There were far fewer than there'd been when Shan-wei and the rest of the Alexandria Enclave were murdered, though, and he found it fascinating (in a historical sort of way) to see which of them had been christened only after dispersion had started shifting the colonists' descendants' Standard English into Safehold's present dialects.

He wasn't here to do etiological research on planetary linguistics, however, and he turned his back to the howling wind and examined the last of the emitters once more.

The device was about half his own height and four feet across, a mostly featureless box with a couple of closed access panels, one on each side. There were quite a few other similar devices—some quite a bit larger; most about the same size or smaller—scattered around the four islands, and he opened one of the panels to study the glowing LEDs.

He didn't really *have* to do it, of course. He could have used his built-in com to consult the artificial intelligence known as Owl who was actually going to be conducting most of this experiment anyway. And he didn't really need the LEDs, either; the storm-lashed gloom was daylight clear to his artificial eyes. There were some advantages to having been dead for a thousand standard years or so, including the fact that his PICA body was immune to little things like hypothermia. He'd come to appreciate those advantages more deeply, in many ways, than he ever had when a living, breathing young woman named Nimue Alban had used her PICA only occasionally, which didn't keep him from sometimes missing that young woman with an aching, empty need.

He brushed that thought aside—not easily, but with practiced skill—and closed the panel with a nod of satisfaction. Then he crunched back across the rocky flat to his recon skimmer, climbed the short ladder, and settled into the cockpit. A moment later, he was rising on countergrav, turbines compensating for the battering wind as he climbed quickly to twenty thousand feet. He broke through the overcast and climbed another four thousand feet, then leveled out in the thinner, far calmer air.

There was plenty of moonlight up here, above the storm wrack, and he gazed down, drinking in the beauty of the black and silver-struck cloud summits. Then he drew a deep breath—purely out of habit, not out of need—and spoke.

"All right, Owl. Activate phase one."

"Activating, Lieutenant Commander," the computer said from its hidden cavern at the base of Safehold's tallest mountain, almost thirteen thousand miles from Merlin's present location. The signal between the recon skimmer and the computer was bounced off one of the Self-Navigating Autonomous Reconnaissance and Communications platforms Merlin had deployed in orbit around the planet. Those heavily stealthed, fusion-powered SNARCs were the most deadly weapons in Merlin's arsenal. He relied on them heavily, and they provided him and the handful of human beings who knew his secret with communications and recon capabilities no one else on the planet could match.

Unfortunately, that didn't necessarily mean someone—or something—*off* the planet couldn't match or even exceed them. Which was, after all, pretty much the point of this evening's experiment.

Merlin had chosen the Castaway Islands with care. They were eleven thousand miles from the Temple, eighty-seven hundred miles from the city of Tellesberg, seventy-five hundred miles from the city of Cherayth, and just over twenty-six hundred miles from the Barren Lands, the closest putatively inhabited real estate on the entire planet. No one was going to see anything that happened here. And no one (aside from those arctic wyverns and seals) was going to get killed if things turned out . . . badly.

Not that it looked that way to the recon skimmer's sensors at the moment. Indeed, according to *them*, there were thousands of moving, human-sized thermal signatures scattered around the islands in half a dozen "towns" and "villages." One of those towns was centered on the device he'd just examined twenty-four thousand feet below the skimmer, which had just come to life as Owl obeyed his instructions. No one looking at it would have noticed anything, but the skimmer's sensors picked up the new heat source immediately.

Merlin sat back, watching the thermal signature as its temperature rose to approximately five hundred degrees on the Fahrenheit scale Eric Langhorne had imposed upon the brainwashed colonists almost nine hundred Safeholdian years ago. It held steady at that point, and if there'd still been any human (or PICA) eyes to watch, they would have noticed it was beginning to vent steam. Not a lot of it, and the wind snatched the steam plume to bits almost more quickly than it could appear. But the sensors saw it clearly, noted its cyclic nature. Only an artificial source could have emitted it in such a steady pattern, and Merlin waited another five minutes, simply watching his instruments.

"Have we detected any response from the kinetic platforms, Owl?" he asked then.

"Negative, Lieutenant Commander," the AI replied calmly.

"Initiate phase two, then."

"Initiating, Lieutenant Commander."

A moment later, additional heat sources began to appear. One or two of them, at first, then half a dozen. Two dozen. Then still more, scattered around the islands as individuals and in clusters, all in around the same temperature range, but registering in several different *sizes,* and all of them "leaking" those cyclical puffs of steam. The cycles weren't all identical and the steam plumes came in several different sizes and durations, but all of them were clearly artificial in origin.

Merlin sat very still, watching his instruments, waiting. Five more minutes crept past. Then ten. Fifteen.

"Any response from the kinetic platforms now, Owl?"

"Negative, Lieutenant Commander."

"Good. That's good, Owl."

There was no response from the computer this time. Merlin hadn't really expected one, although Owl did seem to be at least starting to develop the personality the operator's manual promised he would . . . eventually. The AI had actually offered spontaneous responses and interpolations on a handful of occasions, although seldom to Merlin. In fact, now that he thought about it, the majority of those spontaneous responses had been directed to Empress Sharleyan, and Merlin wondered why that was. Not that he expected he'd ever find out. Even back when there'd been a Terran Federation, AIs—even Class I AIs (which Owl most emphatically was not)—had often had quirky personalities that responded better to some humans than to others.

"Activate phase three," he said now.

"Activating, Lieutenant Commander."

This time, if Merlin had still been a flesh-and-blood human being, he would have held his breath as two-thirds or so of the steam signatures on his sensors began to move. Most of them moved fairly slowly, their paths marked by twists and turns, stopping and starting, turning sharply, then going straight for short distances. Several others, though, were not only larger and more powerful but moved much more rapidly and smoothly . . . almost as if they'd been on rails.

Merlin watched the slower moving heat signatures

tracing out the skeletal outlines of what could have been street grids in the "towns" and "villages" while the larger, faster-moving ones moved steadily between the clusters of their slower brethren. Nothing else seemed to be happening, and he made himself wait for another half hour before he spoke again.

"Still nothing from the platforms, Owl?"

"Negative, Lieutenant Commander."

"Are we picking up any signal traffic between the platforms and the Temple?"

"Negative, Lieutenant Commander."

"Good." Merlin's one-word response was even more enthusiastic this time, and he felt himself smiling. He leaned back in the flight couch, clasping his hands behind his head, and gazed up at the moon that never looked quite right to his Earth-born memories and the starscape no Terrestrial astronomer had ever seen. "We'll give it another hour or so," he decided. "Tell me if you pick up anything—anything at all—from the platforms, from the Temple, or between them."

"Acknowledged, Lieutenant Commander."

"And I suppose while we're waiting, you might as well start giving me my share of the flagged take from the SNARCs."

"Yes, Lieutenant Commander."

▼ ▼ ▼

"Well," Merlin said, several hours later as his skimmer headed northwest across the eastern reaches of Carter's Ocean towards the city of Cherayth, "I have to say, it looks promising so far, at least."

"You could've told us when you started your little test."

Cayleb Ahrmahk, Emperor of Charis and King of Old Charis, sounded more than a little testy himself, Merlin thought with a smile. At the moment, he and Empress Sharleyan sat across a table from one another. The breakfast plates had been taken away, although Cayleb continued to nurse a cup of chocolate. Another cup sat in front of Sharleyan, but she was too busy breast-feeding their daughter, Princess Alahnah, to do anything with it at the moment. Depressingly early morning sunlight came through the frost-rimed window behind Cayleb's chair, and Sergeant Edwyrd Seahamper stood outside the small dining chamber's door, ensuring their privacy.

Like them, Seahamper was listening to Merlin over the invisible, transparent plug in his right ear. Unlike them, the sergeant was unable to participate in the conversation, since (also unlike them) he didn't have any convenient sentries making sure no one was going to wander by and hear him talking to thin air.

"I did tell you I intended to initiate the test as soon as Owl and I had the last of the EW emitters in place, Cayleb," Merlin said now, mildly. "And if I recall, you and Sharleyan knew 'Seijin Merlin' was going to be 'meditating' for the next couple of days. In fact, that was part of the cover plan to free me up to conduct the test in the first place, unless memory fails me. And in regard to that last observation, I might point out that *my* memory is no longer dependent on fallible organic components."

"Very funny, Merlin," Cayleb said.

"Oh, don't be such a fussbudget, Cayleb!" Sharleyan scolded with a smile. "Alahnah was actually letting us sleep last night, and if Merlin was prepared to let us go on sleeping, *I'm* not going to complain. And frankly, dear, I don't think any of our councilors are going to complain if *you* got a bit more rest last night, either. You have been a little grumpy lately."

Cayleb gave her a moderately betrayed look, but she only shook her head at him.

"Go on with your report, Merlin. Please," she said. "Before Cayleb says something else *we'll* all regret, whether *he* does or not."

There was the sound of something suspiciously like a muffled laugh from the fifth and final party to their conversation.

"I *heard* that, Ehdwyrd!" Cayleb said.

"I'm sure I don't know what you're referring to, Your Majesty. Or, I suppose, I should say 'Your Grace' since you and Her Majesty are currently in Chisholm," Ehdwyrd Howsmyn replied innocently from his study in far-off Old Charis.

"Oh, of *course* you don't."

"Oh, hush, Cayleb!" Sharleyan kicked him under the breakfast table. "Go on, Merlin. Quick!"

"Your wish is my command, Your Majesty," Merlin assured her while Cayleb rubbed his kneecap with his right hand and waved a mock-threatening fist with his left.

"As I was saying," Merlin continued, his tone considerably more serious than it had been, "things are looking good so far. Everything I could see on the skimmer's sensors, and everything Owl can see using the SNARCs, looks exactly like a whole batch of steam engines either sitting in place and working or chugging around the landscape. They've been doing it for better than seven hours now, and so far neither the kinetic bombardment platform nor whatever the hell those energy sources under the Temple are seem to have been taking any notice at all. So if the 'Archangels' did set up any kind of automatic technology-killing surveillance program, it doesn't look like simple steam engines are high enough tech to break through the filters."

"I almost wish we'd gotten *some* reaction out of them, though," Cayleb said in a far more thoughtful tone, forgetting to glower at his beloved wife. "In a lot of ways, I would've been happier if the platforms had sent some kind of 'Look, I see some steam engines!' message to the Temple and nothing had happened. At least then I'd feel more confident that if there *is* some command loop to anything under the damned place, whatever the anything was, it wasn't going to tell the platforms to kill the engines. As it is, we can't be sure something's not going to cause whatever the anything might be to change its mind and start issuing kill orders at a later date about something else."

"My head hurts trying to follow that," Sharleyan complained. He gave her a look, and she shrugged. "Oh, I understood what you were saying, it's just a bit . . . twisty for this early in the morning."

"I understand what you're saying, too, Cayleb," Merlin said. "For myself, though, I'm just as glad it didn't happen that way. Sure, it'd be a relief in some ways, but it wouldn't actually prove anything one way or the other about the decision-making processes we're up against. And, to be honest, I'm just delighted we *didn't* wake up anything under the Temple with our little test. The last thing we need is to throw anything else into the equation—especially anything that might decide to take the Group of Four's side!"

"There's something to that," Cayleb agreed, and Sharleyan nodded feelingly.

None of them felt the least bit happy about the energy signatures Merlin had detected under the Temple. The native-born Safeholdians' familiarity with technology remained largely theoretical and vastly incomplete, but they were more than willing to take Merlin's and Owl's word that the signatures they were seeing seemed to indicate something more than just the heating and cooling plant and maintenance equipment necessary to keep the "mystic" Temple environment up and running. As Cayleb had said, it would be nice to know that whatever those additional signatures represented wasn't going to instruct the orbital kinetic platforms which had transformed the Alexandria Enclave into Armageddon Reef nine hundred years before to start killing the first steam engines they saw even after it had been told about them. On the other hand, if whatever was under the Temple (assuming there really was something and they weren't all just being constructively paranoid) was "asleep," keeping it that way as long as possible seemed like a very good idea.

"I agree with you, Merlin," Howsmyn said. "Still, as the person most likely to catch a kinetic bombardment if it turns out we're wrong about this, I have to admit I'm a little worried about how persistence might play into this from the platforms' side."

"That's why I said it looks good *so far*," Merlin replied with a nod none of the others could see. "It's entirely possible there's some kind of signal-over-time filter built into the platforms' sensors. I know it's tempting to think of all the 'Archangels' as megalomaniac lunatics, but they weren't all *totally* insane, after all. So I'd like to think that whoever took over after Commodore Pei killed Langhorne at least had sense enough to not order the 'Rakurai' to shoot on sight the instant it detected something which *might* be a violation of the Proscriptions. I can think of several natural phenomena that could be mistaken at first glance for the kind of industrial or technological processes the Proscriptions are supposed to prevent. So I think—or hope, at least—that it's likely Langhorne's successors would have considered the same possibility.

"For now, at least, what we're showing them is a complex of obviously artificial temperature sources moving around on several islands spread over a total area of roughly a hundred thousand square miles. If they look a little more closely, they'll get confirmation that they're 'steam engines,' and Owl will be turning them on and off, just as he'll be stopping the 'trains' at 'stations' at intervals." He shrugged. "We've got enough power to keep the emitters going literally for months, and Owl's remotes can handle anything that might come up in the way of glitches. My vote is that we do just that. Let them run for at least a month or two. If we don't get any reaction out of the platforms or those energy sources under the Temple in that long, I think we'll be reasonably safe operating on the assumption that we can get away with at least introducing steam. We're a long way from my even wanting to experiment with how they'll react to *electricity,* but just steam will be a huge advantage, even if we're limited to direct drive applications."

"That's for certain," Howsmyn agreed feelingly. "The hydro accumulators are an enormous help, and thank God Father Paityr signed off on them! But they're big, clunky, and expensive. I can't build the things up at the mine sites, either, and if I can get away with using steam engines instead of dragons for traction on the railways here at the foundry, it'll only be a matter of time—and not a lot of that—before some clever soul sees the possibilities where genuine railroads are concerned." He snorted in amusement. "For that matter, if someone else doesn't see the possibilities, after a couple of months of running them around the foundries it'll be reasonable enough for *me* to experience another 'moment of inspiration.' I'm developing quite a reputation for intuitive genius, you know."

His last sentence managed to sound insufferably smug, and Merlin chuckled as he visualized the ironmaster's elevated nose and broad grin.

"Better you than me, for *oh* so many reasons," he said feelingly.

"That's all well and good," Sharleyan put in, "and I agree with everything you've just said, Ehdwyrd. But that does rather bring up the next sticking point, too, I'm afraid."

"You mean how we get *Father Paityr* to sign off on the concept of steam power," Howsmyn said in a considerably glummer tone.

"Exactly." Sharleyan grimaced. "I really like him, and I admire and respect him, too. But this one's so far beyond anything the Proscriptions envision that getting his approval isn't going to be easy, to say the least."

"That's unfortunately true," Merlin acknowledged. "And pushing him so far his principles and beliefs finally come up against his faith in Maikel's judgment would come under the heading of a Really Bad Idea. Having him in the Church of Charis' corner is an enormous plus—and not just in Charis, either, given his family's prestige and reputation. But the flip side of that is that turning him *against* the Church of Charis would probably be disastrous. To be perfectly honest, that's another reason I've always figured keeping the emitters running for a fairly lengthy period doesn't have any downside. Now that we know—or if we *decide* we know—the bombardment platforms aren't going to kill us, we can start giving some thought about how we convince Father Paityr not to blow the whistle on us, as well."

"And if it turns out the bombardment platforms are going to kill the 'steam engines' after all," Cayleb agreed, "nothing but a bunch of thoroughly useless, uninhabited islands gets hurt."

"Useless, uninhabited islands so far away from anyone that no one's even going to realize 'Langhorne's Rakurai' has struck again if it happens," Sharleyan said with a nod.

"That's the idea, anyway," Merlin said. "That's the idea."

. II .

HMS *Destiny*, 54,
Gulf of Mathyas

"Well, Master Aplyn-Ahrmahk?" Lieutenant Rhobair Lathyk called through his leather speaking trumpet from the deck far below. "You *do* plan on making your report sometime today, don't you?"

Ensign Hektor Aplyn-Ahrmahk, known on social occasions as His Grace, the Duke of Darcos, grimaced. Lieutenant Lathyk thought he was a wit, and in Aplyn-Ahrmahk's considered opinion, he was half right. That wasn't something he was prepared to offer up as an unsolicited opinion, however. And, to be fair, whatever the lieutenant's failings as a wellspring of humor, he was one of the best seamen Aplyn-Ahrmahk had ever met. One might not think a young man not yet sixteen would be the best possible judge of seamanship, but Aplyn-Ahrmahk had been at sea since his tenth birthday. He'd seen a lot of sea officers since then, some capable and some not. Lathyk definitely fell into the former category, and the fact that he'd had an opportunity to polish his skills under Sir Dunkyn Yairley—undoubtedly the finest seaman under whom Aplyn-Ahrmahk had ever served—hadn't hurt.

Nonetheless, and despite all of Lieutenant Lathyk's sterling qualities, Aplyn-Ahrmahk thought several rather uncomplimentary thoughts about him while he struggled with the heavy spyglass. He'd heard rumors about the twin-barreled spyglasses which had been proposed by the Royal College, and he hoped half the tales about their advantages were true. Even if they were, however, it was going to be quite some time before they actually reached the fleet. In the meantime youthful ensigns still got to go scampering up to the main topmast crosstrees with long clumsy spyglasses and do their best to see through haze, mist, and Langhorne only knew what to straighten out a midshipman's confused report while impatient seniors shouted putatively jocular comments from the comfort of the quarterdeck.

The young man peered through the spyglass, long practice helping him hold it reasonably steady despite HMS *Destiny's* increasingly lively motion. A hundred and fifty feet long between perpendiculars, over forty-two feet in the beam, and displacing twelve hundred tons, the big, fifty-four-gun galleon was usually an excellent sea boat, but there seemed to be something about the current weather she didn't care for.

Neither did Aplyn-Ahrmahk, when he thought about it. There was a strange quality to the air, a sultry feeling that seemed to lie heavily against his skin, and the persistent, steamy haze over Staiphan Reach made it extraordinarily difficult to pick out details. Which was rather the point of Lieutenant Lathyk's inquiry, he supposed. Speaking of which. . . .

"I can't make it out, either, Sir!" He hated admitting that, but there was no point pretending. "I can barely make out Howard Island for the haze!" He looked down at Lathyk. "There's a couple of sail moving about beyond Howard, but all I can see are topsails! Can't say whether they're men-of-war or merchantmen from here!"

Lathyk craned his neck, gazing up at him for several moments, then shrugged.

"In that case, Master Aplyn-Ahrmahk, might I suggest you could be better employed on deck?"

"Aye, aye, Sir!"

Aplyn-Ahrmahk slung the spyglass over his back and adjusted the carry strap across his chest with care. Letting the expensive glass plummet to the deck and shatter probably wouldn't make Lathyk any happier with him . . . and that was assuming he managed to avoid braining one of *Destiny*'s crewmen with it. The way his luck had been going this morning, he doubted he'd be that fortunate.

Once he was sure the spyglass was secure, he headed down the shrouds towards the deck so far below.

"You say the haze is building?" Lathyk asked him almost before his feet had touched the quarterdeck, and Aplyn-Ahrmahk nodded.

"It is, Sir," he replied, trying very hard not to sound as if he were making excuses for an unsatisfactory report. "I'd estimate we've lost at least four or five miles' visibility since the turn of the glass."

"Um." Lathyk gave the almost toneless, noncommittal sound which served to inform the world that he was thinking. After a moment, he looked back up at the sky, gazing south-southwest down the length of Terrence Bay, into the eye of the wind. There was a hint of darkness on the horizon, despite the relatively early hour, and anvil-headed clouds with an odd striated appearance and black, ominous bases were welling up above that dark line. Back on a planet called Earth which neither Lathyk nor Aplyn-Ahrmahk had ever heard of, those clouds might have been called cumulonimbus.

"What's the glass, Chief Waigan?" Lathyk asked after a moment.

"Still falling, Sir." Chief Petty Officer Frahnklyn Waigan's voice was unhappy. "Better'n seven points in the last hour, and the rate's increasing."

Aplyn-Ahrmahk felt his nerves tighten. Before the introduction of the new Arabic numerals it had been impossible to label the intervals on a barometer's face as accurately as they could now be divided. What had mattered for weather prediction purposes, however, was less the actual pressure at any given moment than the observed rate of *change* in that pressure. A fall of more than .07 inches of mercury in no more than an hour was a pretty high rate, and he found himself turning to look the same direction Lathyk was looking.

"Master Aplyn-Ahrmahk, be kind enough to present my compliments to the Captain," Lathyk said. "Inform him that the glass is dropping quickly and that I don't like the looks of the weather."

"Aye, Sir. Your compliments to the Captain, the glass is dropping quickly, and you don't like the looks of the weather."

Lathyk nodded satisfaction, and Aplyn-Ahrmahk headed for the quarterdeck hatch just a bit more swiftly even than usual.

▼ ▼ ▼

Lieutenant Lathyk's sense of humor might leave a little something to be desired; his weather sense, unfortunately, did not.

The wind had increased dramatically, rising from a topgallant breeze, little more than eight or nine miles per hour, to something much stronger in a scant twenty minutes. The waves, which had been barely two feet tall, with a light scattering of glassy-looking foam, were three times that tall now, with white, foamy crests everywhere, and spray was beginning to fly. A seaman would have called it a topsail breeze and been happy to see it under normal conditions. With a wind speed of just under twenty-five miles an hour, a ship like *Destiny* would turn out perhaps seven knots with the wind on her quarter and all sail set to the topgallants. But that sort of increase in so short a period was most *un*welcome, especially with the barometer continuing to fall at an ever steeper rate. Indeed, one might almost have said the glass was beginning to plummet.

"Don't like it, Captain," Lathyk said as he and Captain Yairley stood beside the ship's double wheel, gazing down at the binnacle. The lieutenant shook his head and raised his eyes to the set of the canvas. "Don't usually see heavy weather out of the south*west* this time of year, not in these waters."

Yairley nodded, hands clasped behind him while he considered the compass card.

As the acting commodore of the squadron keeping watch over the Imperial Desnairian Navy's exit from the Gulf of Jahras, he had quite a few things to be worried over. Just for starters, his "squadron" was down to only his own ship at the moment, since *Destiny*'s sister ship *Mountain Root* had encountered one of the Gulf of Mathyas' uncharted rocks three days before. She'd stripped off half her copper and suffered significant hull damage, and while her pumps had contained the flooding and she'd been in no immediate danger of sinking, she'd obviously needed to withdraw for repairs. To make bad worse, HMS *Valiant,* the third galleon of his truncated squadron (every squadron had been "truncated" in the wake of the Markovian Sea action), had reported a serious freshwater shortage two days before that, thanks to leaks in no less than three of her iron water tanks, and Yairley had already been considering detaching *her* for repairs. Under the circumstances, little though any commander in his place could have cared for the decision, he'd chosen to send both damaged galleons back to Thol Bay in Tarot, the closest friendly naval base, for repairs, with *Valiant* escorting *Mountain Root* just in case her hull leaks should suddenly worsen in the course of the three-thousand-mile voyage.

Of course, a single galleon could scarcely hope to enforce a "blockade" of the Gulf of Jahras—Staiphan Reach was over a hundred and twenty miles across, although the shipping channel was considerably narrower—but he was due to be reinforced by an additional six galleons in another five-day or so, and that wasn't really his true task, anyway. It wasn't as if the Desnairian Navy had ever shown anything like a spirit of enterprise, after all. In point of fact, the Imperial Charisian Navy would have welcomed a Desnairian sortie, although it was highly unlikely the Desnairians would be foolish enough to give the ICN the opportunity to get at them in open water, especially after what had happened to the Navy of God in the Markovian Sea. If, for some inexplicable reason, the Duke of Jahras *did* suddenly decide to venture forth, it wasn't Yairley's job to stop him, but rather to report that fact and then shadow him. The messenger wyverns in the special below-decks coop would get word of any Desnairian movements to Admiral Payter Shain at Thol Bay in little more than three days, despite the distance, and Shain would know exactly what to do with that information.

In the extraordinarily unlikely eventuality that the Desnairians decided to move north, they'd have to fight their way through the Tarot Channel, directly past Shain's squadron. That wasn't going to happen, especially since Yairley's warning would ensure Shain had been heavily reinforced from Charis by the time Jahras got there. In the more likely case of his moving *south*, down the eastern coast of Howard to swing around its southern end and join the Earl of Thirsk, there'd be ample time for the ICN's far swifter, copper-sheathed schooners—once again, dispatched as soon as Admiral Shain received Yairley's warning—to carry word to Corisande and Chisholm long before the Desnairians could reach their destination.

In effect, his "squadron" was essentially an advanced listening post . . . and better than three thousand miles from the nearest friendly base. All sorts of unpleasant things could happen to a small, isolated force operating that far from any support—as, indeed, what had happened to *Mountain Root* and *Valiant* demonstrated. Under the circumstances, the ICN had scarcely selected that squadron's commander at random, particularly in light of the delicate situation with the Grand Duchy of Silkiah. Silkiah Bay opened off the Gulf of Mathyas just to the north of Staiphan Reach, and dozens of "Silkiahan" and "Siddarmarkian" merchantmen with Charisian crews and captains plied in and out of Silkiah Bay every five-day in barely sub-rosa violation of Zhaspahr Clyntahn's trade embargo. Anything so blatant as the intrusion of a regular Charisian warship into Silkiah Bay could all too easily inspire Clyntahn to the sort of rage which would bring a screeching end to that highly lucrative, mutually profitable arrangement, and Yairley had to be extraordinarily careful about avoiding any appearance of open collusion between his command and the Silkiahans.

In theory his single galleon was sufficient to discharge his responsibilities in the event of a Desnairian sortie, but in the real world, he was all alone, totally unsupported, and had no friendly harbor in which he could take refuge in the face of heavy weather, all of which had to be weighing on his mind as the implacable masses of angry-looking cloud swept closer. If he was particularly perturbed, he gave no sign of it, however, although his lips were pursed and his eyes were thoughtful. Then he drew a deep breath and turned to Lathyk.

"We'll alter course, Master Lathyk," he said crisply. "Put her before the wind, if you please. I want more water under our lee if this wind decides to back on us."

"Aye, Sir."

"And after you've got her on her new heading, I want the topgallant masts sent down."

Someone who knew Lathyk well and was watching him closely might have seen a small flicker of surprise in his eyes, but it was very brief and there was no sign of it in his voice as he touched his chest in salute.

"Aye, Sir." The first lieutenant looked at the boatswain's mate of the watch. "Hands to the braces, Master Kwayle!"

"Aye, aye, Sir!"

▼ ▼ ▼

The glass continued to fall, the wind continued to rise, and lightning began to flicker under the clouds advancing inexorably from the south.

Destiny looked oddly truncated with her upper masts struck. Her courses had been furled, her inner and middle jibs struck, storm staysails had been carefully checked and prepared, and single reefs had been taken in her topsails. Despite the enormous reduction in canvas, she continued to forge steadily northeast from her original position at a very respectable rate of speed. The wind velocity was easily up to thirty miles per hour, and considerably more powerful gusts were beginning to make themselves felt, as well. Large waves came driving towards the ship from astern, ten feet high and more and crowned in white as they rolled up under her quarter to impart a sharp corkscrew motion, and lifelines had been rigged on deck and oilskins had been broken out. The foul weather gear was hot and sweltering, despite the rising wind, although no one was optimistic enough to believe that was going to remain true very much longer. Their current position was less than three hundred miles above the equator, but those oncoming clouds were high and the rain they were about to release was going to be cold.

Very cold.

Aplyn-Ahrmahk would have been hard put to analyze the atmospheric mechanics of what was about to happen, but what he saw when he looked south from his station on *Destiny*'s quarterdeck was the collision between two weather fronts. A high pressure area's heavier, colder air out of the west was driving under the warmer, water-saturated air behind a warm front which had moved into the Gulf of Mathyas from the east three days earlier and then stalled. Due to the planet's rotation, winds tended to blow parallel to the isobars delineating weather fronts, which meant two powerful, moving wind masses were coming steadily into collision in what a Terran weatherman would have called a tropical cyclone.

Fortunately, it was the wrong time of year for the most violent form of tropical cyclone ... which was more commonly called "hurricane."

Ensign Aplyn-Ahrmahk didn't need to understand all the mechanics involved in the process to read the weather signs, however. He understood the consequences of what was about to happen quite well, and he wasn't looking forward to them. The good news was that Captain Yairley's preparations had been made in ample time and there'd been time to double-check and triple-check all of them. The bad news was that the weather didn't seem to have heard that this wasn't hurricane season.

Don't be silly, he told himself firmly. *This isn't going to be a* hurricane, *Hektor! Things would be getting worse even faster than they are if that were the case. I think.*

"Take a party and double-check the lashings on the quarter boats, Master Aplyn-Ahrmahk," Captain Yairley said.

"Aye, Sir!" Aplyn-Ahrmahk saluted and turned away. "Master Selkyr!"

"Aye, Sir?" Ahntahn Selkyr, another of *Destiny*'s boatswain's mates, replied.

"Let's check the lashings on the boats," Aplyn-Ahrmahk said, and headed purposefully aft while Selkyr mustered half a dozen hands to join him.

"Giving the lad something to think about, Sir?" Lieutenant Lathyk asked quietly, watching the youthful ensign with a smile.

"Oh, perhaps a little," Yairley acknowledged with a faint smile of his own. "At the same time, it won't hurt anything, and Master Aplyn-Ahrmahk's a good officer. He'll see that it's done right."

"Yes, he will, Sir," Lathyk agreed, then turned to look back at the looming mass of clouds rising higher and higher in the south. The air seemed thicker and heavier somehow, despite the freshening wind, and there was an odd tint to the light.

"I thought you were overreacting, to be honest, Sir, when you had the topgallant masts sent down. Now"—he shrugged, his expression unhappy—"I'm not so sure you were."

"It's always such a comfort to me when your judgment agrees with my own, Rhobair," Yairley said dryly, and

Lathyk chuckled. Then the captain sobered. "All the same, I don't like the feel of this at all. And I don't like the way the clouds are spreading to the east, as well. Mark my words, Rhobair, this thing is going to back around on us before it's done."

Lathyk nodded somberly. The predominant winds tended to be from the northeast in the Gulf of Mathyas during the winter months, which would normally have led one to expect any wind changes to veer further to the west, not to the east. Despite which, he had an unhappy suspicion that the captain was right.

"Do you think we'll be able to make enough easting to clear Silkiah Bay if it does back on us, Sir?"

"Now that's the interesting question, isn't it?" Yairley smiled again, then turned his back on the dark horizon and watched Aplyn-Ahrmahk and his seamen inspecting the lashings which secured the boats on the quarterdeck's davits.

"I think we'll probably clear the mouth of the bay," he said after a moment. "What I'm not so sure about is that we'll be able to get into the approaches to Tabard Reach. I suppose"—he showed his teeth—"we'll just have to find out, won't we?"

▼ ▼ ▼

Lightning streaked across the purple-black heavens like Langhorne's own Rakurai. Thunder exploded like the reply of Shan-wei's artillery, audible even through the wind-shriek and the pounding, battering fury of waves approaching thirty feet in height, and ice-cold rain hammered a man's oilskins like a thousand tiny mallets. HMS *Destiny* staggered through those heavy seas, running before the wind now under no more than a single storm jib, a close-reefed main topsail, and a reefed forecourse, and Sir Dunkyn Yairley stood braced, secured to a quarterdeck lifeline by a turn around his chest, and watched the four men on the wheel fight to control his ship.

The seas were trying to push her stern around to the

east, and he was forced to carry more canvas and more weather helm than he would have preferred to hold her up. It was officially a storm now, with wind speeds hitting better than fifty-five miles per hour, and not a mere gale or even a *strong* gale, and he suspected it was going to get even nastier before it was over. He didn't like showing that much of the forecourse, but he needed that lift forward. Despite which he'd have to take in both the topsail and the course and go to storm staysails alone, if the wind got much worse. He needed to get as far east as he could, though, and reducing sail would reduce his speed, as well. Deciding when to make that change—and making it before he endangered his ship—was going to be as much a matter of instinct as anything else, and he wondered why the possibility of being driven under and drowned caused him so much less concern than the possibility of losing legs or arms to enemy round shot.

The thought made him chuckle, and while none of the helmsmen could have heard him through the shrieking tumult and the waterfall beating of icy rain, they saw his fleeting smile and looked at one another with smiles of their own.

He didn't notice as he turned and peered into the murk to the northwest. By his best estimate, they'd made roughly twenty-five miles, possibly thirty, since the visibility closed in. If so, *Destiny* was now about two hundred miles southeast of Ahna's Point and four hundred and sixty miles southeast of Silk Town. It also put him only about a hundred and twenty miles south of Garfish Bank, however, and his smile disappeared as he pictured distances and bearings from the chart in his mind. He'd made enough easting to avoid being driven into Silkiah Bay—probably—if the wind did back, but he needed at least another two hundred and fifty miles—preferably more like three hundred—before he'd have Tabard Reach under his lee, and he didn't like to think about how many ships had come to grief on Garfish Bank or in Scrabble Sound behind it.

But that's not going to happen to my *ship*, he told himself, and tried to ignore the prayerful note in his own thought.

▼ ▼ ▼

"Hands aloft to reduce sail!"

The order was barely audible through the howl of wind and the continuous drumroll of thunder, but the grim-faced topmen didn't have to hear the command. They knew exactly what they faced . . . and exactly what it was going to be like up there on the yards, and they looked at one another with forced smiles.

"Up you go, lads!"

In the teeth of such a wind, the lee shrouds would have been a death trap, and the topmen swarmed up even the weather shrouds with more than usual care. They gathered in the tops, keeping well inside the topmast rigging, while men on deck tailed onto the braces.

A seventeen-mile-per-hour wind put one pound of pressure per square foot on a sail. At thirty-two miles per hour, the pressure didn't simply double; it *quadrupled,* and the wind was blowing far harder than that now. At the moment, *Destiny*'s forecourse was double-reefed, shortening its normal hoist of thirty-six feet to only twenty-four. Unlike a trapezoidal topsail, the course was truly *square,* equally wide at both head and foot, which meant its sixty-two-foot width was unaffected by the decrease in height. Its effective sail area had thus been reduced from over twenty-two hundred square feet to just under fifteen hundred, but the fifty-five-plus-mile-per-hour wind was still exerting over twelve tons of pressure on that straining piece of canvas. The slightest accident could turn all that energy loose to wreak havoc on the ship's rigging, with potentially deadly consequences under the current weather conditions.

"Brace up the forecourse!"

"Weather brace, haul! Tend the lee braces!"

The ship's course had been adjusted to bring the wind on to her larboard quarter. Now the foreyard swung as the larboard brace, leading aft to its sheave on the maintop and from there to deck level, hauled that end—the weather end—of the yard aft. The force of the wind itself helped the maneuver, pushing the starboard end of the yard around to leeward, and as the yard swung, the sail shifted from perpendicular to the wind's direction to almost parallel. The shrouds supporting the mast got in the way and prevented the yard from being trimmed as close to fore-and-aft as *Destiny* might have wished—that was the main reason no squarerigger could come as close to the wind as a schooner could—but it still eased the pressure on the forecourse immensely.

"Clew up! Spilling lines, haul!"

The clewlines ran from the lower corners of the course to the ends of the yards, then through blocks near the yard's center and down to deck level, while the buntlines ran from the yard to the foot of the sail. As the men on deck hauled away, the clewlines and buntlines raised the sail, aided by the spilling lines—special lines which had been rigged for precisely this heavy-weather necessity. They were simply ropes which had been run down from the yard then looped up around the sail, almost like another set of buntlines, and their function was exactly what their name implied: when they were hauled up, the lower edge of the sail was gathered in a bight, spilling wind out of the canvas so it could be drawn up to the yard without quite so much of a struggle.

"Ease halliards!"

The topmen in the foretop waited until the canvas had been fully gathered in and the yard had been trimmed back to its original squared position before they were allowed out onto it. Squaring the yard once more made it far easier—and safer—for them to transfer from the top to the spar. Under calmer conditions, many of those men would have scampered cheerfully out along the yard itself with blithe confidence in their sense of balance. Under *these* conditions, use of the foot rope rigged under the yard was mandatory.

They spread themselves along the seventy-five-foot-long spar, seventy feet above the reeling, plunging deck—

almost ninety feet above the white, seething fury of the water in those fleeting moments when the deck was actually level—and began fisting the canvas into final submission while wind and rain shrieked around them.

One by one the gaskets went around the gathered sail and its yard, securing it firmly, and then it was the main topsail's turn.

▼ ▼ ▼

"Keep her as close to northeast-by-east as you can, Waigan!" Sir Dunkyn Yairley shouted in his senior helmsman's ear.

Waigan, a grizzled veteran if ever there was one, looked up at the storm staysails—the triangular, triple-thickness staysails set between the mizzen and the main and between the main and the fore—which, along with her storm forestaysail, were all the canvas *Destiny* could show now.

"Nor'east-by-east, aye, Sir!" he shouted back while rainwater and spray ran from his iron-gray beard. "Close as we can, Sir!" he promised, and Yairley nodded and slapped him on the shoulder in satisfaction.

No sailing ship could possibly maintain a set course, especially under these conditions. Indeed, it took all four of the men on the wheel to hold *any* course. The best they could do was keep the ship on roughly the designated heading, and the *senior* helmsman wasn't even going to be looking at the compass card. *His* attention was going to be locked like iron to those staysails, being certain they were drawing properly, lending the ship the power and the stability she needed to survive the maelstrom. The senior of his assistants would watch the compass and alert him if they started to stray too far from the desired heading.

Yairley gave the canvas one more look, then swiped water from his own eyes and beckoned to Garaith Symkee, *Destiny*'s second lieutenant.

"Aye, Sir?" Lieutenant Symkee shouted, leaning close enough to Yairley to be heard through the tumult.

"I think she'll do well enough for now, Master Sym-kee!" Yairley shouted back. "Keep her as close to an east-erly heading as you can! Don't forget Garfish Bank's waiting for us up yonder!" He pointed north, over the larboard bulwark. "I'd just as soon it go on waiting, if you take my meaning!"

Symkee grinned hugely, nodding his head in enthusiastic agreement, and Yairley grinned back.

"I'm going below to see if Raigly can't find me something to eat! If the cooks can manage it, I'll see to it there's at least hot tea—and hopefully something a bit better, as well—for the watch on deck!"

"Thank you, Sir!"

Yairley nodded and started working his way hand-over-hand along the lifeline towards the hatch. It was going to be an extraordinarily long night, he expected, and he was going to need his rest. And hot food, come to that. Every man aboard the ship was going to need all the energy he could lay hands on, but *Destiny*'s captain was responsible for the decisions by which they might all live or die.

Well, he thought wryly as he reached the hatch and started down the steep ladder towards his cabin and Sylvyst Raigly, his valet and steward, *I suppose it sounds better put that way than to think of it as the captain being spoiled and pampered. Not that I have any objection to being spoiled or pampered, now that I think of it.*

And not that it was any less true, however he put it.

HMS *Destiny*, 54,
Off Sand Shoal,
Scrabble Sound,
Grand Duchy of Silkiah

"Master Zhones!"

The miserable midshipman, hunched down in his oilskins and trying as hard as he could not to throw up—again—looked up as Lieutenant Symkee bellowed his name. Ahrlee Zhones was twelve years old, more horribly seasick than he'd ever been in his young life, and scared to death. But he was also an officer in training in the Imperial Charisian Navy, and he dragged himself fully upright.

"Aye, Sir?!" he shouted back through the howl and shriek of the wind.

"Fetch the Captain!" Zhones and Symkee were no more than five feet apart, but the midshipman could barely hear the second lieutenant through the tumult of the storm. "My compliments, and the wind is backing! Inform him it—"

"Belay that, Master Zhones!" another voice shouted, and Zhones and Symkee both wheeled around to see Sir Dunkyn Yairley. The captain had somehow magically materialized on the quarterdeck, his oilskins already shining with rain and spray, and his eyes were on the straining staysails. Despite the need to shout to make himself heard, his tone was almost calm—or so it seemed to Zhones, at any rate.

As the midshipman watched, the captain took a turn of rope around his chest and attached it to one of the standing lifelines, lashing himself into place almost absently while his attention remained focused on the sails and the barely visible weathervane at the mainmast head. Then he glanced at the illuminated compass card in the binnacle and turned to Symkee.

"I make it south-by-west, Master Symkee? Would you concur?"

"Perhaps another quarter point to the south, Sir," Symkee replied, with what struck Zhones as maddening deliberation, and the captain smiled slightly.

"Very well, Master Symkee, that will do well enough." He turned his attention back to the sails and frowned.

"Any orders, Sir?" Symkee shouted after a moment, and the captain turned to raise one eyebrow at him.

"When any occur to me, Master Symkee, you'll be the first to know!" It was, of course, impossible for anyone to shout in a tone of cool reprimand, but the captain managed it anyway, Zhones thought.

"Aye, Sir!" Symkee touched his chest in salute and carefully turned his attention elsewhere.

▼ ▼ ▼

Despite his calm demeanor and deflating tone, Sir Dunkyn Yairley's brain was working overtime as he considered his ship's geometry. The wind had grown so powerful that he'd had no choice but to put *Destiny* directly before it some hours earlier. Now the galleon scudded along with huge, white-bearded waves rolling up from astern, their crests ripped apart by the wind. As the wind shifted round towards the east, the ship was being slowly forced from a northeasterly to a more and more northerly course, while the seas—which hadn't yet adjusted to the shift in wind—still coming in from the south-southwest pounded her more and more from the quarter rather than directly aft, imparting an ugly corkscrew motion. That probably explained young Zhones' white-faced misery the captain thought with a sort of detached sympathy. The youngster was game enough, but he was definitely prone to seasickness.

More to the point, the change in motion had alerted Yairley to the change in wind direction and brought him back on deck, and if the wind continued to back, they could be in serious trouble.

It was impossible even for a seaman of his experience to know exactly how far east he'd managed to get, but he strongly suspected it hadn't been far enough. If his estimate was correct, they were almost directly due south of the Garfish Bank, the hundred-and-fifty-mile-long barrier of rock and sand which formed the eastern bound of Scrabble Sound. Langhorne only knew how many ships had come to grief on the bank, and the speed with which the wind had backed was frightening. If it continued at the present rate, it would be setting directly towards the bank within the hour, and if that happened. . . .

▼ ▼ ▼

The wind did continue to swing towards the east, and its rate of change actually increased. It might—possibly—have dropped in strength, but the malice of its new direction more than compensated for that minor dispensation, Yairley thought grimly. The rapid change in direction hadn't done a thing for the ship's motion, either; *Destiny* was corkscrewing more violently than ever as the waves rolled in now from broad on her larboard quarter, and the pumps were clanking for five minutes every hour as the ship labored. The intake didn't concern him particularly—every ship's seams leaked a little as her limber hull worked and flexed in weather like this, and some water always found its way in through gunports and hatches, however tightly they were sealed—but the wild vista of the storm-threshed night's spray and foam was even more confused and bewildering than it had been before.

And unless he missed his guess, his ship's bowsprit was now pointed directly at Garfish Bank.

We're not going to get far enough to the east no matter what we do, he thought grimly. *That only leaves west. Of course, there are problems with that, too, aren't there?*

He considered it for a moment more, looking at the

sails, considering the sea state and the strength of the howling wind, and made his decision.

"Call the hands, Master Symkee! We'll put her on the larboard tack, if you please!"

▼ ▼ ▼

Sir Dunkyn Yairley stood gazing into the dark and found himself wishing the earlier, continuous displays of lightning hadn't decided to take themselves elsewhere. He could see very little, although with the amount and density of the wind-driven spray, it probably wouldn't have mattered if he'd had better light, he admitted. But what he couldn't see, he could still feel, and he laid one hand on *Destiny*'s bulwark, closed his eyes, and concentrated on the shocklike impacts of the towering waves.

Timing, a small corner of his brain thought distantly. *It's always a matter of timing.*

He was unaware of the white-faced, nauseated twelve-year-old midshipman who stood watching his closed eyes and thoughtful expression with something very like awe. And he was only distantly aware of the seamen crouching ready at the staysails' tacks and sheets in the lee of the bulwarks and hammock nettings, taking what shelter they could while they kept their eyes fixed on their officers. What he needed to accomplish was a straightforward maneuver, but under these conditions of wind and weather even a small error could lead to disaster.

The waves rolled in, and he felt their rhythm settling into his own flesh and sinew. The moment would come, he thought. It would come and—

"Starboard your helm!" he heard himself bark. His own order came almost as a surprise, the product of instinct and subliminal timing at least as much as of conscious thought. "Lay her on the larboard tack—as close to south-by-west as you can!"

"Aye, aye, Sir!"

Destiny's double wheel turned to the left as all four helmsmen heaved their weight on the spokes. The tiller ropes wrapped around the wheel's barrel turned the tiller to the right in response, which kicked the *rudder* to the left, and the galleon began turning to larboard. The turn brought her broadside on to the seas still pounding in from the south-southwest, but Yairley's seaman's sense had served him well. Even as she began her turn, one of the crashing seas rolled up under her larboard quarter at almost the perfect moment, lifting her stern and helping to force her around before the next wave could strike.

"Off sheets and tacks!" It was Lathyk's voice from forward.

Yairley opened his eyes once more, watching as his ship fought around through the maelstrom of warring wind and wave in a thunder of canvas and water and a groan of timbers. The next mighty sea came surging in, taking her hard on the larboard beam, bursting over the hammock nettings in green and white fury, and the galleon rolled wildly, tobogganing down into the wave's trough while her mastheads spiraled in dizzying circles against the storm-sick heavens. Yairley felt the lifeline hammering at his chest, heard the sound of young Zhones' retching even through all that mad tumult, but she was coming round, settling on her new heading.

"Meet her!" he shouted.

"Sheet home!" Lathyk bellowed through his speaking trumpet.

Destiny's bow buried itself in the next wave. White water exploded over the forecastle and came sluicing aft in a gray-green wall. Two or three seamen went down, kicking and spluttering as they lost their footing and were washed into the scuppers before their lifelines came up taut, but the sheets were hardened in as the ship came fully round on her new heading. Her bowsprit climbed against the sky, rising higher and higher as her bows came clear of the smother of foam and gray-green water, and Yairley breathed a sigh of relief as she reached the top of the wave and then went driving down its back with an almost exuberant violence.

Showing only her fore-and-aft staysails, she could actually come a full two points closer to the wind than she could have under square sails, and Yairley watched the swaying compass card as the helmsmen eased the wheel. It gimbaled back and forth as the men on the wheel picked their way through the tumult of wind and wave, balancing the thrust and set of her canvas against the force of the seas.

"South-sou'west's as near as she'll come, Sir!" the senior man told him after a minute or two, and he nodded.

"Keep her so!" he shouted back.

"Aye, aye, Sir!"

The ship's plunging motion was more violent than it had been running before the wind. He heard the explosive impact as her bow met each succeeding wave, and the shocks were harder and more jarring, but the corkscrew roll had been greatly reduced as she headed more nearly into the seas. Spray and green water fountained up over her bow again and again, yet she seemed to be taking it well, and Yairley nodded again in satisfaction then turned to look out over the tumbling waste of water once more.

Now to see how accurate his position estimate had been.

▼ ▼ ▼

The day which had turned into night dragged on towards day once more, and the wind continued to howl. Its force had lessened considerably, but it was still blowing at gale force, with wind speeds above forty miles per hour. The seas showed less moderation, although with the falling wind that had to come eventually, and Yairley peered about as the midnight murk turned slowly, slowly into a hard pewter dawn under purple-black clouds. The rain had all but ceased, and he allowed himself a cautious, unobtrusive breath of optimism as visibility ever so gradually increased. He considered making more sail—with the current wind he could probably get double- or triple-reefed topsails and courses on her—but he'd already added the main topgallant staysail, the main topmast staysail, and the mizzen staysail. The fore-and-aft sails provided less driving power than the square sails would have, but they let him stay enough closer to the wind to make good a heading of roughly south-southwest. The further south—and west, of course, but especially *south*—he could get, the better, and—

"Breakers!" The shout came down from above, thin and lost through the wail of wind. "Breakers on the starboard quarter!"

Yairley wheeled in the indicated direction, staring intently, but the breakers were not yet visible from deck level. He looked around and raised his voice.

"Main topmast, Master Aplyn-Ahrmahk! Take a glass. Smartly, now!"

"Aye, Sir!"

The youthful ensign leapt into the weather shrouds and went scampering up the ratlines to the topmast crosstrees with the spyglass slung across his back. He reached his destination swiftly, and Yairley looked up, watching with deliberate calm as Aplyn-Ahrmahk raised the glass and peered to the north. He stayed that way for several seconds, then reslung the glass, reached for a back stay, wrapped his legs around it, and slid down it to the deck, braking his velocity with his hands. He hit the deck with a thump and came trotting aft to the captain.

"I believe Master Lathyk will have something to say to you about the proper manner of descending to the deck, Master Aplyn-Ahrmahk!" Yairley observed tartly.

"Yes, Sir." Aplyn-Ahrmahk's tone was properly apologetic, but a devilish glint lurked in his brown eyes, Yairley thought. Then the young man's expression sobered. "I thought I'd best get down here quickly, Sir." He raised his arm and pointed over the starboard quarter. "There's a line of breakers out there, about five miles on the quarter, Captain. A long one—they reach as far as I could see to the northeast. And they're wide, too." He met Yairley's gaze levelly. "I think it's the Garfish Bank, Sir."

So the ensign had been thinking the same thing *he* had, Yairley reflected. And if he was right—which, unfortunately, he almost certainly was—they were substantially further north than the captain had believed they'd been driven. Not that there'd been anything he could have done to prevent it even if he'd known. In fact, if he hadn't changed heading when he had, they'd have driven onto the bank hours earlier, but still. . . .

"Thank you, Master Aplyn-Ahrmahk. Be good enough to ask Lieutenant Lathyk to join me on deck, if you would."

"Aye, aye, Sir."

The ensign disappeared, and Sir Dunkyn Yairley bent over the compass, picturing charts again in his mind, and worried.

▼ ▼ ▼

"You wanted me, Sir?" Rhobair Lathyk said respectfully. He was still chewing on a piece of biscuit, Yairley noted.

"I apologize for interrupting your breakfast, Master Lathyk," the captain said. "Unfortunately, according to Master Aplyn-Ahrmahk we're no more than five miles clear—at best—of the Garfish Bank."

"I see, Sir." Lathyk swallowed the biscuit, then bent to examine the compass exactly as Yairley had.

"Assuming Master Aplyn-Ahrmahk's eye is as accurate as usual," Yairley continued, "we're a good forty miles north of my estimated position and Sand Shoal lies about forty miles off the starboard bow. Which means Scrabble Sound lies broad on the starboard beam."

"Aye, Sir." Lathyk nodded soberly. The good news was that Scrabble Sound ran almost a hundred and twenty miles south to north, which gave them that much sea room before they ran into the eastern face of Ahna's Point or into Scrabble Shoal, itself. The bad news was that from their current position they couldn't possibly clear *Sand* Shoal at the western edge of Scrabble Pass, the mouth of the sound . . . and even if they had, it would only have been to allow the wind to drive them into Silkiah Bay instead of Scrabble Sound.

"Go about, Sir?" he asked. "On the starboard tack we

might just be able to hold a course across the sound for Fishhook Strait."

Fishhook Strait, roughly a hundred miles north of their current position, was the passage between Scrabble Sound and the northern reaches of the Gulf of Mathyas.

"I'm thinking the same thing," Yairley confirmed, "but not until we're past the southern end of the bank. And even then"—he met Lathyk's eyes levelly—"with this wind, the odds are we'll have to anchor, instead."

"Aye, Sir." Lathyk nodded. "I'll see to the anchors now, should I?"

"I think that would be an excellent idea, Master Lathyk," Yairley replied with a wintry smile.

▼ ▼ ▼

"I don't like this one bit, Zhaksyn," Hektor Aplyn-Ahrmahk admitted quietly several hours later. Or as quietly as he could and still make himself heard at the main topmast crosstrees, at any rate. He was peering ahead through his spyglass as he spoke, and the line of angry white water reaching out from the barely visible gray mass of the mainland stretched squarely across *Destiny*'s bowsprit. He had to hold on to his perch rather more firmly than usual. Although the wind had eased still further, Scrabble Sound was a shallow, treacherous body of water. Its wave action could be severe—especially with a southeasterly blowing straight into it—and the masts' motion was enough to make even Aplyn-Ahrmahk dizzy.

"Not much about it to like, if you'll pardon my saying so, Sir," the lookout perched at the crosstrees with him replied.

"No. No, there isn't." Aplyn-Ahrmahk lowered the glass with a sigh, then slung it over his shoulder once more. He started to reach for the back stay again, then stopped himself and looked at the lookout. "Best not, I suppose."

"Better safe nor sorry, Sir," Zhaksyn agreed with a grin. "Specially seeing as how the First Lieutenant's on deck."

"Exactly what I was thinking myself." Aplyn-Ahrmahk patted the seaman on the shoulder and started down the more sedate path of the shrouds.

"Well, Master Aplyn-Ahrmahk?" Captain Yairley asked calmly when he reached the quarterdeck. The captain's valet stood at his side, improbably neatly groomed even under these circumstances, and Yairley held a huge mug of tea between his hands. The steam from the hot liquid whipped away on the wind before anyone had a chance to see it, but its warmth felt comforting against his palms, and he raised it to inhale its spicy scent while he waited for Aplyn-Ahrmahk's report. The steep-sided crest of Ahna's Point was visible from deck level, however, which meant he already had an unfortunately good notion of what the ensign was about to say.

"White water clear across the bow, Sir," Aplyn-Ahrmahk confirmed with a salute. "All the way from the coast"—his left arm gestured in a northwesterly direction—"to a good five points off the starboard bow." His arm swung in an arc from northwest to east-northeast, and Yairley nodded.

"Thank you, Master Aplyn-Ahrmahk," he said in that same calm tone, and took a reflective sip of tea. Then he turned to Lieutenant Lathyk.

"The depth?"

"The lead shows twenty-four fathoms, Sir. And shoaling."

Yairley nodded. Twenty-four fathoms—a hundred and forty-four feet—accorded relatively well with the sparse (and unreliable) depths recorded on his less-than-complete charts. But *Destiny* drew just over twenty feet at normal load, and the leadsman was undoubtedly right about the decreasing depth. By all accounts Scrabble Sound shoaled rapidly, and that meant those hundred and forty-four feet could disappear quickly.

"I think we'll anchor, Master Lathyk."

"Aye, Sir."

"Then call the hands."

"Aye, Sir! Master Symmyns! Hands to anchor!"

"Hands to anchor, aye, aye, Sir!"

Bosun's pipes shrilled as the hands raced to their stations. Both of the bower anchors had been made ready hours ago in anticipation of exactly this situation. The canvas hawse-plugs which normally kept water from entering through the hawseholes during violent weather had been removed. The anchor cables, each just over six inches in diameter and nineteen inches in circumference, had been gotten up through the forward hatch, led through the open hawseholes, and bent to the anchors. A turn of each cable had been taken around the riding bitts, the heavy upright timbers just abaft the foremast, before fifty fathoms of cable were flaked down, and the upper end of the turn led down through the hatch to the cable tier where the remainder of the cable was stored. The anchors themselves had been gotten off of the forechannels and hung from the catheads, and a buoy had been made fast to the ring of each anchor.

Under the current circumstances, there was nothing "routine" about anchoring, and Yairley handed the empty mug to Sylvyst Raigly, then stood with his hands clasped behind him, lips pursed in a merely thoughtful expression while he contemplated the state of the bottom.

His charts for Scrabble Sound were scarcely anything he would have called reliable. The sound wasn't particularly deep (which helped to account for how violent the seas remained even though the wind had continued to drop), but the chart showed only scattered lines of soundings. He could only guess at the depths between them, and according to his sailing notes, the sound contained quite a few completely uncharted pinnacles of rock. Those same notes indicated a rocky bottom, with unreliable holding qualities, which wasn't something he wanted to hear about at this particular moment. Almost as bad, a rocky bottom posed a significant threat that his anchor cables would chafe and fray as they dragged on the bottom.

Beggars can't be choosers, Dunkyn, he reminded himself, glancing as casually as possible at the angry white confusion of surf where the heavy seas pounded the rocky, steeply rising beach below Ahna's Point or surged angrily above Scrabble Shoal. There was no way *Destiny* could possibly weather the shoal under these wind conditions. She was firmly embayed, trapped on a lee shore with no option but to anchor until wind and weather moderated enough for her to work her way back out.

Well, at least you managed to stay out of Silkiah Bay, he reminded himself, and snorted in amusement.

"All hands, bring ship to anchor!" Lathyk bellowed the preparatory order as the last of the hands fell in at his station, and Yairley drew a deep breath.

"Hands aloft to shorten sail!" he ordered, and watched the topmen swarm aloft.

"Stand by to take in topsails and courses! Man clew-lines and buntlines!"

Clewlines and buntlines were slipped off their belaying pins as the assigned hands tailed onto them.

"Haul taut! In topsails! Up foresail and mainsail!"

The canvas disappeared, drawing up like great curtains for the waiting topmen to fist it in and gasket it to the yards. Yairley felt *Destiny*'s motion change as she lost the driving force of the huge square sails and continued ahead under jib and spanker alone. She became heavier, less responsive under the weight of the pounding seas as she lost speed through the water.

"Stand clear of the starboard cable! Cock-bill the starboard anchor!"

The shank painter, which had secured the crown of the anchor to the ship's side, was cast off, letting the anchor hang vertically from the starboard cathead, its broad flukes dragging the water and threatening to swing back against the hull as the broken waves surged against the ship.

"Let go the starboard anchor!"

A senior petty officer cast off the ring stopper, the line passed through the ring of the anchor to suspend it from the cathead, and threw himself instantly flat on the deck as the anchor plunged and the free end of the stopper came flying back across the bulwark with a fearsome crack.

The cable flaked on deck went thundering through the hawsehole, seasoned wood smoking with friction heat despite the all-pervasive spray as the braided hemp ran violently out while *Destiny* continued ahead, "sailing out" her cable.

"Stream the starboard buoy!"

The anchor buoy—a sealed float attached to the starboard anchor by a hundred-and-fifty-foot line—was released. It plunged into the water, following the anchor. If the cable parted, the buoy would still mark the anchor's location, and its line was heavy enough that the anchor could be recovered by it.

"Stand clear of the *larboard* cable! Cock-bill the anchor!"

Yairley watched men with buckets of seawater douse the smoking starboard cable. Another moment or two and—

Destiny staggered. The galleon lurched, the men at the wheel were hurled violently to the deck, and Yairley's head came up as a dull, crunching shock ran through the deck underfoot. For a moment, she seemed to hang in place, then there was a second crunch and she staggered onward, across whatever she'd struck.

"Away carpenter's party!" Lieutenant Lathyk shouted, and the carpenter and his mates bolted for the main hatchway, racing below to check for hull damage, but Yairley had other things on his mind. Whatever else had happened, it was obvious he'd just lost his rudder. He hoped it was only temporary, but in the meantime . . .

"Down jib! Haul out the spanker!"

The jib disappeared, settling down to be gathered in by the hands on the bowsprit. Without the thrust of the rudder, Yairley couldn't maintain the heading he'd originally intended. He'd planned to sail parallel to the shore while he dropped both anchors for the widest purchase possible on the treacherous bottom, but the drag of the cable still thundering out of her starboard hawsehole was already forcing *Destiny*'s head up to the wind. The pounding seas continued to thrust her bodily sideways to larboard, though, and he wanted to get as far away from whatever they'd struck—probably one of those Shan-wei-damned uncharted rocks—as possible before he released the second anchor.

Fifty fathoms of cable had run out to the first anchor, and the ship was slowing, turning all the way back through the wind under the braking effect of the cable's drag. She wasn't going to carry much farther, he decided.

"Let go the larboard anchor!"

The second anchor plunged, and the pounding vibration of heavy hemp hawsers hammered through the ship's fabric as both cables ran out.

"Stream the larboard buoy!"

The larboard anchor buoy went over the side, and then the starboard cable came up against the riding bitt and the cable stoppers—a series of lines "nipped" to the anchor cable and then made fast to purchases on deck—came taut, preventing any more of it from veering. The ship twitched, but enough slack had veered that she didn't stop moving immediately, and the larboard cable continued running out for several more seconds. Then it, too, came up against its bitt and stoppers and *Destiny* came fully head to the wind and began drifting slowly to leeward until the tautening cables' counter-balanced tension could stop her. It looked as if she'd come-to at least two hundred yards from shore, and they could use the capstans to equalize the amount of cable veered to each anchor once they were sure both were holding. In the meantime. . . .

Yairley had already turned to the wheel. Frahnklyn Waigan was back on his feet, although one of his assistants was still on the deck with an unnaturally bent arm which was obviously broken. As Yairley looked, the petty officer turned the wheel easily with a single hand and grimaced.

"Nothin', Sir." He'd somehow retained a wad of chew-leaf, and he spat a disgusted stream of brown juice into the spittoon fixed to the base of the binnacle. "Nothin' at all."

"I see." Yairley nodded. He'd been afraid of that, and he wondered just how bad the damage actually was. If he'd simply lost the tiller or fractured the rudderhead, repair would be relatively straightforward . . . probably. That was the reason *Destiny* carried an entire spare tiller, after all. Even if the rudderhead had been entirely wrung off, leaving nothing to attach the tiller to, they could still rig chains to the rudder itself just above the waterline and steer with tackles. But he doubted they'd been that fortunate, and if the rudder was entirely gone. . . .

He turned as Lathyk arrived on the quarterdeck.

"Both anchors seem to be holding, Sir," the first lieutenant said, touching his chest in salute. "For now, at least."

"Thank you, Master Lathyk," Yairley said sincerely, although he really wished the lieutenant had been able to leave off his last four words. "I suppose the next order of business is—"

"Beg your pardon, Sir." Yairley turned his head the other way to face Maikel Symmyns, *Destiny*'s boatswain.

"Yes, Bosun?"

" 'Fraid the entire rudder's gone, Sir." Symmyns grimaced. "Can't be certain yet, but it looks to me as if the gudgeons've been stripped clean away, as well."

"Better and better, Bosun." Yairley sighed, and the weathered, salt-and-pepper-haired Symmyns smiled grimly. The boatswain was the ship's senior noncommissioned officer, and he'd first gone to sea as a ship's boy when he was only six years old. There was very little he hadn't seen in the ensuing fifty years.

"Beg pardon, Captain." Yet another voice spoke, and Yairley found one of the ship's carpenter's mates at his elbow.

"Yes?"

"Master Mahgail's compliments, Sir, and we're making water aft. Master Mahgail says as how it looks like we've started at least a couple of planks, but nothing the pumps can't handle. Most likely stripped a lot of the copper, though, and the rudder post's cracked clean through. And he asks if he can have a few more hands to help inspect the rest of the hull."

"I see." Yairley gazed at him for a moment, then nodded. "My compliments to Master Mahgail. Tell him I appreciate the report, and that I look forward to more complete information as it comes to him. Master Lathyk," he looked at the first lieutenant, "see to it that Master Mahgail has all the hands he needs."

"Aye, Sir."

"Very well, then." Yairley drew a deep breath, clasped his hands behind him once more, and squared his shoulders. "Let's be about it," he said.

. IV .

HMS *Destiny*, 54,
Off Scrabble Shoal,
Grand Duchy of Silkiah

"Pull, you lazy bastards!" Stywyrt Mahlyk, Sir Dunkyn Yairley's personal coxswain, shouted as the thirty-foot longboat porpoised its way through the confused waves and spray like a seasick kraken. Hektor Aplyn-Ahrmahk, crouching in the bow and hanging on for dear life while *Destiny*'s starboard sheet anchor weighted down the longboat's stern and accentuated the boat's . . . lively movement, thought Mahlyk, sounded appallingly cheerful under the circumstances.

"Think *this* is a blow?!" the coxswain demanded of the laboring oarsmen in scoffing tones as the boat's forward third went briefly airborne across a wave crest, then slammed back down again. "Why, you sorry Delferahkan excuses for sailor men! I've *farted* worse weather than this!"

Despite their exertion and the spray soaking them to the skin, one or two of the oarsmen actually managed a laugh. Mahlyk was amazingly popular with *Destiny*'s crew, despite his slave-driver mentality where Captain Yairley's cutter was concerned. At the moment, he'd traded in the cutter for the larger and more seaworthy longboat, but he'd brought along the cutter's crew, and there was no insult to which he could lay his tongue that didn't make them smile. In point of fact, his crew took simple pride in his ability to outswear any other member of the ship's company when the mood took him.

Which, alas, it did far more often than not, if the truth be known, especially when the captain wasn't about.

He and Aplyn-Ahrmahk were old friends, and the ensign remembered an incendiary raid on an Emeraldian port in which he and Mahlyk had torched a half-dozen warehouses and at least two taverns. They'd tossed incendiaries into three galleons, as well, as he recalled, but they hadn't been the only ones firing the ships, so they couldn't claim solo credit for them. Their current expedition was somewhat less entertaining than that one had been, but it was certainly no less *exciting*.

The longboat swooped up another steep wave, leaving Aplyn-Ahrmahk's stomach briefly behind, and the ensign turned to look back at the galleon. *Destiny* pitched and rolled to her bower anchors with all the elegance of a drunken pig, masts and yards spiraling crazily against the clouds. She looked truncated and incomplete with her upper masts struck, but she was still one of the most beautiful things he'd ever seen. More importantly at the moment, Lieutenant Lathyk stood on the forecastle, a semaphore flag tucked under his arm, watching the boat from under a shading palm while Lieutenant Symkee used one of the new sextants the Royal College had recently introduced as a successor to the old back staff to measure the angle between the longboat and the buoys marking the positions of the bower anchors. As Aplyn-Ahrmahk watched, Lathyk took the flag from under his arm and raised it slowly over his head.

"Ready, Mahlyk!" the ensign called.

"Aye, Sir!" the coxswain acknowledged, and reached for the lanyard with his left hand while his right fist gripped the tiller bar. Another minute passed. Then another. Then—

The flag in Lathyk's hand waved.

"Let go!" Aplyn-Ahrmahk shouted, and the longboat surged suddenly as Mahlyk jerked the lanyard which toggled the trigger and released the three-ton sheet anchor from the heavy davit rigged in the longboat's stern. It plunged into the water, well up to windward of the more weatherly of the two anchors *Destiny* had already dropped, and the longboat seemed to shake itself in delight at having shed the irksome load.

"Stream the buoy!" Aplyn-Ahrmahk ordered, and the anchor buoy was heaved over the side behind the sheet anchor.

Although the longboat moved much more easily without the anchor's hanging weight and the drag of the cable trailing astern, there were still a few tricky moments as Mahlyk brought it about. But the coxswain chose his moment carefully, using wind and wave action to help drive the boat around, and then they were pulling strongly back towards *Destiny*.

Aplyn-Ahrmahk sat on the bow thwart, looking aft past Mahlyk at the brightly painted anchor buoy, which got progressively smaller with distance, disappearing in the troughs of the waves, then bobbing back into sight. Boat work was always risky in blowing weather like this, but on a lee shore, with the entire rudder carried away and a bottom where anchors were known to drag, the notion of getting a third anchor laid out made plenty of sense to him. Of course, he did wonder how *he'd* ended up selected for the delightful task. Personally, he would cheerfully have declined the honor in favor of Tohmys Tymkyn, *Destiny*'s fourth lieutenant. But Tymkyn was busy with the galleon's pinnace, locating and buoying the spire of rock which had claimed the ship's rudder. He was having at least as exciting a time of it as Aplyn-Ahrmahk, and the ensign wondered if the two of them had been chosen because they were so junior they'd be less badly missed if one or both of them didn't make it home again.

I'm sure I'm doing the Captain a disservice, he told himself firmly, wiping spray from his face, and then smiled as he wondered how Sir Dunkyn was going to react to his upcoming little show of initiative. *I can always blame it on Stywyrt,* he thought hopefully. *Sir Dunkyn's known him long enough to realize what a corrupting influence he can be on a young and innocent officer such as myself.*

"*Pull!* Langhorne—I thought you were *seamen!*" Mahlyk bawled, as if on cue. "I've seen dockside doxies with stronger backs! Aye, and *legs,* too!"

Aplyn-Ahrmahk shook his head in resignation.

▾ ▾ ▾

Sir Dunkyn Yairley watched with carefully concealed relief as the longboat was swayed back aboard. The pinnace followed, nesting inside the longboat on the gallows of spare spars above the main hatch. The cutters on the quarter and stern davits would have been much easier to get out and in again, especially with the deck so cluttered with the yards and sails which had been sent down from above to reduce topweight, and they *probably* would have sufficed. But they might not have, either, in these sea conditions, and he was disinclined to take chances with men's lives, whether the rules of the game allowed him to show his concern or not.

And they definitely *wouldn't have sufficed for what that young idiot pulled after dropping the sheet anchor!* he thought sourly.

He considered reprimanding Aplyn-Ahrmahk. The ensign and that scapegrace ne'er-do-well Mahlyk had taken it upon themselves to sweep the seabed north of *Destiny* with a grappling iron-weighted trailing line which should (in theory, at least) have snagged on any rocks rising high enough to be a threat to the galleon even at low tide. As a result, Yairley now knew he had over a mile of rock-free clear water for maneuvering room to the north of his current position. They hadn't happened to ask permission for that little escapade, and they'd almost capsized twice before they'd finished, and the captain was severely torn between a warm sense of pride in a youngster who'd become one of his special protégés and anger at both of them for risking their lives and their entire boat's crew without authorization.

Well, time enough to make my mind up about that later, he decided. *And in the meantime, I'll just concentrate on putting the fear of Shan-wei into the young jackanapes.*

He paused long enough to give Aplyn-Ahrmahk a steely-eyed glare as a down payment, then turned back to the task of creating a jury-rigged rudder.

Maikel Symmyns had gotten a spare main topgallant yard laid across the quarterdeck so that its arms jutted out through the aftermost gunports on either side, supported with "lifts" to the mizzenmast and guys running forward to the main chains. Hanging blocks had been secured to either end of the spar, and the falls run forward from them through the fairleads under the wheel. Several turns had been taken around the barrel of the wheel, and then the free ends of the falls had been seized to the staple at the midpoint of the drum to anchor everything firmly.

"Here 'tis, Sir," Garam Mahgail said, and Yairley turned to face the ship's carpenter. The carpenter was a warrant officer, not a commissioned officer, and he was probably close to half-again Yairley's age and bald as an egg, but still brawny and calloused. At the moment, his bushy eyebrows were raised as he exhibited his craftsmanship for the captain's approval.

"Is this what you had in mind, Sir?" he asked, and Yairley nodded.

"That's *precisely* what I had in mind, Master Mahgail!" he assured the warrant officer, and beckoned Symmyns over. The boatswain obeyed the gesture, and the captain pointed at Mahgail's handiwork.

"Well, Bo'sun?"

"Aye, I think it'll work right well, Sir," Symmyns said with a slow smile of approval. "Mind you, it's going to be Shan-wei's own drag in a light air, Cap'n! Be like towing a couple of sea anchors astern, it will."

"Oh, not quite *that* bad, Bo'sun," Yairley disagreed with a smile of his own. "More like one sea anchor and a half."

"Whatever you say, Sir." Symmyns' smile turned into a grin for a moment, and then he turned back to his working party and started barking additional orders.

At Yairley's instructions, Mahgail had fitted a pair of gundeck water tubs with bridles on their open ends, and inhauls had been made fast to the bottoms. Now the captain watched as one of the tubs was secured to either end of the spar by a line run to the inhaul. Then the bitter end from the hanging block was secured to the bridle. With the wheel in the "midships" position, the inhauls would tow the tubs through the water a good fifty feet behind the ship with their bottoms up, but when the wheel was turned to larboard, the bridle rope from the tub on that side to the barrel of the wheel would be shortened, pulling the tub around to tow open-end first. The resultant heavy drag on that side of the ship would force the galleon to turn to larboard until the wheel was reversed and the tub went gradually back to its bottom-up position, where it would exert far less drag. And as the wheel continued turning to starboard, the *starboard* tub would go from the bottom-up to the open-end-forward position, causing the ship to turn to starboard.

There were drawbacks to the arrangement, of course. As Symmyns had pointed out, the drag penalty would be significant. Water was far denser than air, which explained how something as relatively tiny as a ship's rudder could steer something a galleon's size to begin with, and the resistance even with both tubs floating bottom-up would knock back *Destiny*'s speed far more than a landsman might expect. And whereas a rudder could be used even when backing a ship, the tubs were all too likely to foul their control lines—or actually be drawn *under* the ship—in that sort of situation. But Symmyns' initial diagnosis had been correct. The gudgeons, the hingelike sockets into which the pintle pins of the rudder mounted, had been completely torn out, and the rudder post itself was badly damaged and leaking. They had a pattern from which to build a complete replacement rudder, but there was nothing left to attach a replacement to, and his improvised arrangement should work once he got the ship underway once more.

Which isn't going to happen, of course, until the wind veers, he reflected sourly.

But at least he had three anchors out, so far they all seemed to be holding, and there was no sign anyone ashore had even noticed their presence. Under the circumstances, he was more than prepared to settle for that for the moment.

▼ ▼ ▼

"Oh, Pasquale, take me now!" Trahvys Saylkyrk groaned.

He was the oldest of *Destiny*'s midshipmen—in fact, he was two years older than Hektor Aplyn-Ahrmahk— and he didn't usually have any particular problem with seasickness. The last couple of days had pushed even his stomach over the edge, however, and he looked down at the stew in his bowl with a distinctly queasy expression. The ship's motion was actually more violent than it had been before she anchored, in some ways, as heavy, confused seas continued to roll in from the southeast. She lay with her head to the wind now, which meant she climbed each steep roller as it came in, then buried her nose and kicked her heels at the sky as it ran aft. And just to complete Saylkyrk's misery, the galleon threw in her own special little corkscrew with every third or fourth plunge.

"*Please* take me now!" he added as one of those corkscrews ran through the ship's timbers and his stomach heaved, and Aplyn-Ahrmahk laughed.

"I doubt he'd have you," he said. As an ensign, he was neither fish nor wyvern in a lot of ways. Although he was senior to any of the ship's midshipmen, he still wasn't a commissioned officer, and wouldn't be until his sixteenth birthday. As such, he continued to live in the midshipmen's berth and served as the senior member of the midshipmen's mess. Now he looked across the swaying mess table at Saylkyrk and grinned. "Archangels have standards, you know. He'd probably take one look at that pasty green complexion and pass."

"Fine for you to say," Saylkyrk said with a grimace. "There are times I don't think you *have* a stomach, Hektor!"

"Nonsense! You're just jealous, Trahvys," Aplyn-Ahrmahk shot back with a still broader grin. Some midshipmen might have resented being required to take the orders of someone so much younger than he was, but Saylkyrk and Aplyn-Ahrmahk had been friends for years. Now the ensign elevated his nose, turned his head to display his profile, and sniffed dramatically. "Not that I don't find your petty envy easy enough to understand. It must be difficult living in the shadow of such superhuman beauty as my own."

"Beauty!" Saylkyrk snorted and dug a spoon glumly into the stew. "It's not your 'beauty' I envy. Or that I *would* envy, if you had any! It's the fact that I've never seen you puking into the bilges."

"You would've if you'd been in my first ship with me," Aplyn-Ahrmahk told him with a shudder. "Of course, that was a galley—only about two-thirds *Destiny*'s size." He shook his head feelingly. "I was as sick as a . . . as a . . . as sick as Ahrlee over there," he said, twitching his head at the still-miserable Zhones.

"Oh, no, you weren't," Zhones replied feebly. "You couldn't've been; you're still alive."

The other midshipmen chuckled with the cheerful callousness of their youth, but one of them patted Zhones comfortingly on the back.

"Don't worry, Ahrlee. They say once your tonsils come up it gets easier."

"Bastard!" Zhones shot back with a somewhat strained grin.

"Don't pay any attention to him, Ahrlee!" Aplyn-Ahrmahk commanded. "Besides, it's not your tonsils; it's your toenails. After you bring your *toenails* up it gets easier."

Even Zhones laughed at that one, and Aplyn-Ahrmahk

smiled as he pushed his own chocolate cup across the table to the younger midshipman.

Hot chocolate was even harder to come by aboard ship than it was ashore, and it was expensive. With his allowance from his adoptive father, Aplyn-Ahrmahk could have afforded to bring along his own private store and enjoy it with every meal. Fortunately, he also had enough common sense to do nothing of the sort. He'd been born to humble enough beginnings to realize how throwing his newfound wealth into his fellows' faces would have been received, so instead he'd invested in a supply for the entire mess. By this point, they'd been away from port long enough it was running decidedly low, however, and the cook's mate assigned as the midshipmen's mess steward was rationing it out in miserly doses. But the Charisian naval tradition was that the ship's company was kept well fed, with hot food whenever possible, especially after a day and a night like *Destiny* had just passed. Despite Saylkyrk's obvious lack of enthusiasm for the stew in his bowl it was actually quite tasty (albeit a bit greasy), and their steward had made enough chocolate for everyone. For that matter, he'd even managed to come up with fresh bread. He'd expended the last of their flour in the process, but the result had been well worth it.

Unfortunately, poor Zhones clearly wasn't going to be able to keep the stew down. He'd contented himself by devouring his share of the precious bread one slow, savoring mouthful at a time, washing it down with the sweet, strong chocolate. Now he looked up as Aplyn-Ahrmahk's mug slid in front of him.

"I—" he began, but Aplyn-Ahrmahk shook his head.

"Consider it a trade," he said cheerfully, snagging Zhones' untouched stew bowl and pulling it closer. "Like Trahvys says, I've got an iron stomach. You don't. Besides, the sugar'll do you good."

Zhones looked at him for a moment, then nodded.

"Thanks," he said a bit softly.

Aplyn-Ahrmahk waved the gratitude away and scooped up another spoonful of the stew. It really was tasty, and—

"All hands!" The shout echoed down from the deck above. "All hands!"

By the time Aplyn-Ahrmahk's spoon settled into the stew once more, he was already halfway up the ladder to the upper deck.

▼ ▼ ▼

It took all the self-discipline Sir Dunkyn Yairley had learned in thirty-five years at sea to not swear out loud as his earlier thoughts about his improvised rudder ran back through his mind.

I suppose the good news is that we're still two hundred yards offshore, he told himself. *That gives us a little more room to play with . . . and if the spar's just long enough to keep the tubs out from under her, they may still work, anyway. Of course, they may* not, *too. . . .*

He watched *Destiny*'s company completing his highly unusual preparations with frenzied, disciplined speed, and he hoped there'd be time.

Of course there'll be time, Dunkyn. You've got a remarkable talent for finding things to worry about, don't you? He shook his head mentally, keeping himself physically motionless with his hands clasped behind him. *Just keep your tunic on!*

"Another six or seven minutes, Sir!" Rhobair Lathyk promised, and Yairley nodded, turning to watch the longboat fighting its way back towards the ship.

He'd hated sending Mahlyk and Aplyn-Ahrmahk back out, but they were clearly the best team for the job, as they'd just finished demonstrating. Two of the ensign's seamen had gone over the side while they struggled to get the bitter end of the spring nipped onto the buoyed anchor cable. Unlike most Safeholdian sailors, Charisian seamen by and large swam quite well, but not even the best of swimmers was the equal of waters like these. Fortunately, Aplyn-Ahrmahk had insisted on lifelines for every member of the longboat's crew, and the involuntary swimmers had been hauled back aboard by their fellows. From the looks of things, one of them had needed artificial respiration, but both of them were sitting up now, huddled in the half foot of water sloshing around the floorboards as the thirty-foot boat clawed its way back towards the galleon.

"Lines over the side, Master Lathyk," Yairley said, looking back at the first lieutenant. "There's not going to be time to recover the boat. Bring them up on lines and then cast it adrift." He bared his teeth. "Assuming any of us get out of this alive, we can always find ourselves another longboat, can't we?"

"Assuming, Sir," Lathyk agreed, but he also grinned hugely. It was the same way he grinned when the ship cleared for action, Yairley noted.

"Cheerful bugger, aren't you?" he observed mildly, and Lathyk laughed.

"Can't say I'm looking *forward* to it, Sir, but there's no point fretting, now is there? And at least it ought to be damned interesting! Besides, with all due respect, you've never gotten us into a fix yet that you couldn't get us back out of."

"I appreciate the vote of confidence. On the other hand, this is the sort of thing you usually only get one opportunity to do wrong," Yairley pointed out in a dry tone.

"True enough, Sir," Lathyk agreed cheerfully. "And now, if you'll excuse me, I'll go see about losing that longboat for you."

He touched his chest in salute and moved off across the pitching, rearing deck, and Yairley shook his head. Lathyk was one of those officers who grew increasingly informal and damnably cheerful as the situation grew more desperate. That wasn't Sir Dunkyn Yairley's style, yet he had to admit Lathyk's optimism (which might even be genuine) made him feel a little better.

He turned back to the matter at hand, trying not to worry about the possibility that one or more of the longboat's crew could still be crushed against *Destiny*'s side or fall into the water to be sucked under the turn of the bilge and drowned. It helped that he had plenty of *other* things to worry about.

The never-to-be-sufficiently-damned wind had decided to back still further, and it had done so with appalling speed after holding almost steady for over four hours. It was almost as if it had deliberately set out to lull him into a sense of confidence just to make the final ambush more disconcerting. For four hours, *Destiny* had lain to her anchors, bucking and rolling but holding her ground despite his sailing notes' warnings about the nature of Scrabble Sound's bottom. But then, in less than twenty minutes, the wind had backed another five full points—almost sixty degrees—from southeast-by-south to due east, and the galleon had weathervaned, turning to keep her bow pointed into it, which meant her stern was now pointed directly at Ahna's Point. The speed with which the wind had shifted also meant that the seas continued to roll in from the southeast, not the east, pounding her starboard bow, which had radically shifted the forces and stresses affecting her . . . and her anchors. Now the wind was driving her towards Ahna's Point; the seas were driving her towards Scrabble Shoal; and her larboard anchor cable had parted completely.

Must be even rockier than I was afraid of over there, Yairley thought now, looking at the bobbing buoy marking the lost anchor's position. *That was an almost new cable, and it was wormed, parceled, and served, to boot!*

"Worming" was the practice of working oakum into the contlines, the surface depressions between the strands of the cable. "Parceling" wrapped the entire cable in multi-ply strips of canvas, and the boatswain had served the entire "shot" of cable by covering the parceling, in turn, in tightly wrapped coils of one-inch rope. All of that was designed to protect the cable against fraying and chafing . . . and the rough-edged bottom had obviously chewed its way through all precautions anyway.

Fortunately, the cables to the starboard bower anchor and the sheet anchor Aplyn-Ahrmahk and Mahlyk had laid out hadn't snapped—yet, at least—but both of them were finally beginning to drag the way he'd been more than half afraid they would from the outset. It was a slow process, but it was also one which was gathering speed. At the present rate, *Destiny* would go ashore within the next two hours at the outside.

At least the tide's nearly full, he reminded himself. *It'd be better if we had the ebb to work with, but at least the current's slowed and we've got as much water under the keel as we're ever likely to have.*

He watched the longboat's crew struggling one-by-one up and through the bulwark entry port. Aplyn-Ahrmahk, of course, came last, and Yairley felt at least one of his worries ease as the young ensign scrambled aboard.

"Master Lathyk's compliments, Sir," Midshipman Zhones said, sliding to a stop in front of him and saluting, "and the boat crew's been recovered. And all preparations for getting underway are completed."

"Thank you, Master Zhones," Yairley said gravely. "In that case, I suppose we should make sail, don't you?"

"Uh, yes, Sir. I mean, aye, aye, Sir!"

"Very good, Master Zhones." Yairley smiled. "Go to your station, then."

"Aye, aye, Sir!"

The midshipman saluted again and dashed away, and Yairley glanced one more time around his command, mentally double-checking every detail.

The topgallant masts and topmasts were housed, but the topsail yards had been gotten back up to work on the topmast caps, and the topsails and foresails' gaskets had been stripped off and replaced with lengths of spun yarn so that they could be set instantly. The fore- and main-yards had been braced up for the larboard tack, and the spring Aplyn-Ahrmahk and Mahlyk had managed to make fast to the larboard anchor cable had been led in through an after gunport and made fast. Every eye was on the quarterdeck, and Yairley stepped slowly and calmly to his place by the wheel.

He looked back at his watching men. They could all very easily die in the next few minutes. If the ship took the ground in something as rocky as Scrabble Sound in this kind of sea, she was almost certain to break up, and the chances of making it to shore would be poor, at best. Yet as he surveyed all of those watching faces, he saw no doubt. Anxiety, yes. Even fear, here and there, but not doubt. They trusted him, and he drew a deep breath.

"Stand by the cables!"

Tymythy Kwayle, with a gleaming, broad-headed ax in hand, stood by the riding bitts where the sheet anchor cable crossed them. Boatswain Symmyns himself stood by the larboard cable with an identical ax, both of them waiting for the order to cut the hawsers. If everything went according to plan, the moment the anchor cables were cut, the spring attached to the larboard cable would become her new anchor cable, pulling her *stern,* rather than her bow, around into the wind. With her yards already braced, the instant the wind came two points forward of the beam she could cut the spring, as well, and make sail close-hauled on the larboard tack, which would put her roughly on a course of south-southeast. She ought to be able to hold that heading clean back out of Scrabble Sound the way she'd come, if only the wind held steady. Or, for that matter, if it chose to back still further east towards the north. Of course, if it decided to *veer* to the west, instead. . . .

Stop that, he told himself absently. *The wind isn't really trying to kill you, Dunkyn, and you know it.*

"Stand by to make sail! Lay aloft, topmen!"

The topmen hurried aloft, and he let them get settled into place. Then—

"Man halliards and sheets! Man braces!"

Everything was ready, and he squared his shoulders.

"Cut the cables!"

The axes flashed. It took more than one blow to sever a cable six inches in diameter, but Kwayle and Symmyns were both powerfully muscled and only too well aware of the stakes this day. They managed it in no more than two or three blows each, and the freed hawsers went whipping out of the hawseholes like angry serpents at virtually the same moment.

Destiny fell off the wind almost instantly, leaning over

to starboard as her stern came round to larboard. It was working, and—

Then the spring parted.

Yairley felt the twanging shock as the line snapped, simply overpowered by the force of the sea striking the ship. She hadn't turned remotely far enough yet, and the sea took her, driving her towards the rocky beach waiting to devour her. For a moment, just an instant, Yairley's brain froze. He felt his ship rolling madly, starting to drive stern-first towards destruction, and knew there was nothing he could do about it.

Yet even as that realization hammered through him, he heard someone else snapping orders in a preposterously level voice which sounded remarkably like his own.

"Let fall fore topsail and course! Up fore topmast stay-sail!"

The crewmen who'd realized just as well as their captain that their ship was about to die didn't even hesitate as the bone-deep discipline of the Imperial Charisian Navy's ruthless drills and training took them by the throat, instead. They simply obeyed, and the fore topsail and course fell, and the topmast staysail rose, flapping and thundering on the wind.

"Sheet home! *Weather* braces haul! Back topsail and course!"

That was the critical moment, Yairley realized later. His entire ship's company had been anticipating the order to haul taut the *lee* braces, trimming the yards around to take the wind as the ship turned. That was what they'd been focused on, but now he was *backing* the sails; trimming them to take the wind from directly ahead, instead. Any hesitation, any confusion in the wake of the unexpected change in orders, would have been fatal, but *Destiny*'s crew never faltered.

The yards shifted, the sails pressed back against the mast, and *Destiny* began moving through the water—not forward, but *astern*—while the sudden pressure drove her head still further round to starboard.

Destiny backed around on her heel—slowly, clumsily,

canvas volleying and thundering, spray everywhere, the deck lurching underfoot. She wallowed drunkenly from side to side, but she was moving astern even as she drifted rapidly towards the beach. Sir Dunkyn Yairley had imposed his will upon his ship, and he stared up at the masthead weathervane, waiting, praying his improvised anchor hadn't been fouled, judging his moment.

And then—

"Let fall the mizzen topsail!" he shouted the moment the wind came abaft the starboard beam at last. "Starboard your helm! Off forward braces! Off fore topmast staysail sheets! *Lee* braces haul! Brace up! Shift the fore topmast staysail! Let fall main topsail and main course! Sheet home! Main topsail and course braces haul!"

The orders came with metronome precision, as if he'd practiced this exact maneuver a hundred times before, drilled his crew in it daily. The mizzen topsail filled immediately, arresting the ship's sternward movement, and the forward square sails and fore topmast staysail were trimmed round. Then the main topsail and main course blossomed, as well, and suddenly *Destiny* was moving steadily, confidently, surging through the confused seas on the larboard tack with torrents of spray bursting above her bow. As she gathered way, the floating tubs of her improvised rudder settled back into their designed positions, and she answered the helm with steadily increasing obedience.

"*Done* it, lads!" someone shouted. "Three cheers for the Captain!"

HMS *Destiny* was a warship of the Imperial Charisian Navy, and the ICN had standards of discipline and professionalism other navies could only envy. Discipline and professionalism which, for just an instant, vanished into wild, braying cheers and whistles as their ship forged towards safety.

Sir Dunkyn Yairley rounded on his ship's company, his expression thunderous, but he found himself face-to-face with a broadly grinning first lieutenant and an ensign who was capering on deck and snapping the fingers of both hands.

"And what sort of an example is *this,* Master Lathyk?! Master Aplyn-Ahrmahk?!" the captain barked.

"Not a very good one, I'm afraid, Sir," Lathyk replied. "And I beg your pardon for it. I'll sort the men out shortly, too, Sir, I promise. But for now, let them cheer, Sir! They deserve it. By *God,* they deserve it!"

He met Yairley's eyes steadily, and the captain felt his immediate ire ease just a bit as the realization of what they'd just accomplished began to sink into *him,* as well.

"I had the quartermaster of the watch time it, Sir," Aplyn-Ahrmahk said, and Yairley looked at him. The ensign had stopped capering about like a demented monkey-lizard, but he was still grinning like a lunatic.

"Three minutes!" the young man said. "Three *minutes*—that's how long it took you, Sir!"

Aplyn-Ahrmahk's eyes gleamed with admiration, and Yairley gazed back at him for a moment, then, almost against his will, he laughed.

"Three minutes you say, Master Aplyn-Ahrmahk?" He shook his head. "I fear you're wrong about that. I assure you from my own personal experience that it took at least three *hours.*"

MARCH, YEAR OF GOD 895

·✦·

I

Ehdwyrd Howsmyn's Foundry,
Earldom of High Rock,
Kingdom of Old Charis

The blast furnace screamed, belching incandescent fury against the night, and the sharpness of coal smoke blended with the smell of hot iron, sweat, and at least a thousand other smells Father Paityr Wylsynn couldn't begin to identify. The mingled scent of purpose and industry hung heavy in the humid air, catching lightly at the back of his throat even through the panes of glass.

He stood gazing out Ehdwyrd Howsmyn's office window into the hot summer darkness and wondered how he'd come here. Not just the trip to this office, but to *why* he was here . . . and to what was happening inside his own mind and soul.

"A glass of wine, Father?" Howsmyn asked from behind him, and the priest turned from the window.

"Yes, thank you," he agreed with a smile.

For all his incredible (and steadily growing) wealth, Howsmyn preferred to dispense with servants whenever possible, and the young intendant watched him pour with his own hands. The ironmaster extended one of the glasses to his guest, then joined him beside the window, looking out over the huge sprawl of the largest ironworks in the entire world.

It was, Wylsynn admitted, an awesome sight. The furnace closest to the window (and it wasn't actually all *that* close, he acknowledged) was only one of dozens. They fumed and smoked like so many volcanoes, and when he looked to his right he could see a flood of molten iron, glowing with a white heart of fury, flowing from a furnace which had just been tapped. The glare of the fuming iron lit the faces of the workers tending the furnace, turning them into demon helpers from the forge of Shan-wei herself as the incandescent river poured into the waiting molds.

Howsmyn's Delthak foundries never slept. Even as Wylsynn watched, draft dragons hauled huge wagons piled with coke and iron ore and crushed limestone along the iron rails Howsmyn had laid down, and the rhythmic thud and clang of water-powered drop hammers seemed to vibrate in his own blood and bone. When he looked to the east, he could see the glow of the lampposts lining the road all the way to Port Ithmyn, the harbor city the man who'd become known throughout Safehold as "The Ironmaster of Charis" had built on the west shore of Lake Ithmyn expressly to serve his complex. Port Ithmyn was over four miles away, invisible with distance, yet Wylsynn could picture the lanterns and torches illuminating its never-silent waterfront without any difficulty at all.

If Clyntahn could see this he'd die of sheer apoplexy, Wylsynn reflected, and despite his own internal doubts— or possibly even because of them—the thought gave him intense satisfaction. Still. . . .

"I can hardly believe all you've accomplished, Master Howsmyn," he said, waving his wineglass at everything beyond the window. "All this out of nothing but empty ground just five years ago." He shook his head. "You Charisians have done a lot of amazing things, but I think this is possibly the most amazing of all."

"It wasn't quite 'nothing but empty ground,' Father," Howsmyn disagreed. "Oh," he grinned, "it wasn't a lot *more* than empty ground, that's true, but there was the village here. And the fishing village at Port Ithmyn. Still, I'll grant your point, and God knows I've plowed enough marks back into the soil, as it were."

Wylsynn nodded, accepting the minor correction. Then he sighed and turned to face his host squarely.

"Of course, I suspect the Grand Inquisitor would have a few things to say if *he* could see it," he said. "Which is rather the point of my visit."

"Of course it is, Father," Howsmyn said calmly. "I haven't added anything beyond those things you and I have discussed, but you'd be derelict in your duties if you didn't reassure yourself of that. I think it's probably too late to carry out any inspections tonight, but tomorrow morning we'll look at anything you want to see. I would ask you to take a guide—there are some hazardous processes out there, and I'd hate to accidentally incinerate the Archbishop's Intendant—but you're perfectly welcome to decide for yourself what you want to look at or examine, or which of my supervisors or shift workers you'd care to interview." He inclined his head in a gesture which wasn't quite a bow. "You've been nothing but courteous and conscientious under extraordinarily difficult circumstances, Father. I can't ask for more than that."

"I'm glad you think so. On the other hand, I have to admit there are times I wonder—worry about—the slash lizard you've saddled here." Wylsynn waved his glass at the fire-lit night beyond the window once more. "I know nothing you've done violates the Proscriptions, yet the sheer scale of your effort, and the . . . innovative way you've applied allowable knowledge is disturbing. The *Writ* warns that change begets change, and while it says nothing about matters of scale, there are those—not all of them Temple Loyalists, by any stretch—who worry that innovation on such a scale will inevitably erode the Proscriptions."

"Which must put you in a most difficult position, Father," Howsmyn observed.

"Oh, indeed it does." Wylsynn smiled thinly. "It helps that Archbishop Maikel doesn't share those concerns, and he's supported all of my determinations where your new techniques are concerned. I don't suppose that would make the *Grand Inquisitor* any more supportive, but it does quite a lot for my own peace of mind. And to be honest, the thought of how the Grand Inquisitor would react if he truly knew all you and the other 'innovators' here in Charis have been up to pleases me immensely. In fact, that's part of my problem, I'm afraid."

Howsmyn gazed at him for a moment, then cocked his head to one side.

"I'm no Bédardist, Father," he said almost gently, "but I'd be astonished if you didn't feel that way after what happened to your father and your uncle. Obviously, I don't know you as well as the Archbishop does, but I do know you better than many, I expect, after how closely we've worked together for the past couple of years. You're worried that your inevitable anger at Clyntahn and the Group of Four might cause you to overlook violations of the Proscriptions because of a desire to strike back at them, aren't you?"

Wylsynn's eyes widened with respect. It wasn't really surprise; Ehdwyrd Howsmyn was one of the smartest men he knew, after all. Yet the ironmaster's willingness to address his own concerns so directly, and the edge of compassion in Howsmyn's tone, were more than he'd expected.

"That's part of the problem," he acknowledged. "In fact, it's a very *large* part. I'm afraid it's not quite all of it, however. The truth is that I'm grappling with doubts of my own."

"We all are, Father." Howsmyn smiled crookedly. "I hope this won't sound presumptuous coming from a layman, but it seems to me that someone in your position, especially, would find that all but inevitable."

"I know." Wylsynn nodded. "And you're right. However," he inhaled more briskly, "at the moment I'm most interested in these 'accumulators' of yours. I may have seen the plans and approved them, yet there's a part of me that wants to actually see *them*." He smiled suddenly, the boyish expression making him look even younger than his years. "It's difficult, as you've observed, balancing my duty as Intendant against my duty as Director of the Office of Patents, but the Director in me is fascinated by the possibilities of your accumulators."

"I feel the same way," Howsmyn admitted with an an-

swering gleam of humor. "And if you'll look over there"—
he pointed out the window—"you'll see Accumulator
Number Three beside that blast furnace."

Wylsynn's eyes followed the pointing index finger and
narrowed as the furnace's seething glow illuminated a
massive brickwork structure. As he'd just said, he'd seen
the plans for Howsmyn's accumulators, but mere draw-
ings, however accurately scaled, couldn't have prepared
him for the reality.

The huge tower rose fifty feet into the air. A trio of blast
furnaces clustered around it, and on the far side, a long,
broad structure—a workshop of some sort—stretched
into the night. The workshop was two stories tall, its
walls pierced by vast expanses of windows to take advantage of natural light during the day. Now those windows
glowed with *internal* light, spilling from lanterns and interspersed with frequent, far brighter bursts of glare from
furnaces and forges within it.

"In another couple of months, I'll have nine of them
up and running," Howsmyn continued. "I'd like to have
more, honestly, but at that point we'll be getting close to
the capacity the river can supply. I've considered running
an aqueduct from the mountains to increase supply, but
frankly an aqueduct big enough to supply even one accumulator would be far too expensive. It'd tie up too
much manpower I need elsewhere, for that matter. Instead, I'm looking at the possibility of using windmills to
pump from the lake, although there are some technical
issues there, too."

"I can imagine," Wylsynn murmured, wondering what
would happen if the accumulator he could see sprang a
leak.

The use of cisterns and water tanks to generate water
pressure for plumbing and sewer systems had been part
of Safehold since the Creation itself, but no one had ever
considered using them the way Ehdwyrd Howsmyn was
using them. Probably, Wylsynn thought, because no one
else had ever had the sheer audacity to think on the scale
the ironmaster did.

Howsmyn's new blast furnaces and "puddling hearths" required levels of forced draft no one had ever contemplated before. He was driving them to unheard-of temperatures, recirculating the hot smoke and gases through firebrick flues to reclaim and utilize their heat in ways no one else ever had, and his output was exploding upward. And it was as if each new accomplishment only suggested even more possibilities to his fertile mind, like the massive new multiton drop hammers and the ever larger, ever more ambitious casting processes his workers were developing. All of which required still more power. Far more of it, in fact, than conventional waterwheels could possibly provide.

Which was where the concept for the "accumulator" had come from.

Waterwheels, as Howsmyn had pointed out in his patent and vetting applications, were inherently inefficient in several ways. The most obvious, of course, was that there wasn't always a handy waterfall where you wanted one. Holding ponds could be built, just as he'd done here at Delthak, but there were limits on the head of pressure one could build up using ponds, and water flows could fluctuate at the most inconvenient times. So it had occurred to him that if he could accumulate enough water, it might be possible to build his *own* waterfall, one that was located where he needed it and didn't fluctuate unpredictably. And if he was going to do that, he might as well come up with a more efficient design to use that artificial waterfall's power, as well.

In many ways, vetting the application in Wylsynn's role as Intendant had been simple and straightforward. Nothing in the Proscriptions of Jwo-jeng forbade any of Howsmyn's proposals. They all fell within the Archangel's trinity of acceptable power: wind, water, and muscle. True, nothing in the *Writ* seemed ever to have contemplated something on the scale Howsmyn had in mind, but that was scarcely a valid reason to deny him an attestation of approval. And wearing his hat as the Director of Patents, rather than his priest's cap, Wylsynn had been more than pleased to grant Howsmyn the patent he'd requested.

And tomorrow morning I'll inspect one of them with my own eyes, he reflected now. *I hope I don't fall into it!*

His lips twitched in an almost-smile. He was quite a good swimmer, yet the thought of just how much water a structure the size of the accumulator might hold was daunting. He'd seen the numbers—Dr. Mahklyn at the Royal College had calculated them for him—but they'd been only figures on a piece of paper then. Now he was looking at the reality of a "cistern" fifty feet tall and thirty-five feet on a side, all raised an additional thirty feet into the air. According to Mahklyn, it held close to half a *million* gallons of water. That was a number Wylsynn couldn't even have thought of before the introduction of the Arabic numerals which were themselves barely five years old. Yet all that water, and all the immense pressure it generated, was concentrated on a single pipe at the bottom of the accumulator—a single pipe almost wide enough for a man—well, a tall *boy*, at least—to stand in that delivered the accumulator's outflow not to a waterwheel but to something Howsmyn had dubbed a "turbine."

Another new innovation, Wylsynn thought, *but still well within the Proscriptions. Jwo-jeng never said a wheel was the only way to generate water power, and we've been using windmills forever. Which is all one of his "turbines" really is, when all's said; it's just driven by water instead of wind.*

Locating it *inside* the pipe, however, allowed the "turbine" to use the full force of all the water rushing through the pipe under all that pressure. Not only that, but the accumulator's design meant the pressure reaching the turbine was constant. And while it took a half-dozen conventional waterwheels just to pump enough water to keep each accumulator supplied, the outflow from the turbine was routed back to the holding ponds supplying and driving the waterwheels, which allowed much of it to be recirculated and reused. Now if Howsmyn's plans to pump water from the lake proved workable (as most of his plans seemed to do), his supply of water—and power—would be assured effectively year-round.

He's got his canals completed now, too, the priest reflected. *Now that he can barge iron ore and coal directly all the way from his mines up in the Hanth Mountains he can actually* use *all of that power. Archangels only know what that's going to mean for his productivity!*

It was a sobering thought, and the fresh increases in Delthak's output were undoubtedly going to make Ehdwyrd Howsmyn even wealthier. More importantly, they were going to be crucial to the Empire of Charis' ability to survive under the relentless onslaught of the Church of God Awaiting.

No, not the Church, *Paityr,* Wylsynn reminded himself yet again. *It's the Group of Four, that murderous bastard Clyntahn and the rest.* They're *the ones trying to destroy Charis and anyone else who dares to challenge their perversion of everything Mother Church is supposed to stand for!*

It was true. He *knew* it was true. And yet it was growing harder for him to make that separation as he watched everyone in the Church's hierarchy meekly bend the knee to the Group of Four, accepting Clyntahn's atrocities, his twisting of everything the Office of Inquisition was supposed to be and stand for. It was easy enough to understand the fear behind that acceptance. What had happened to his own father, his uncle, and their friends among the vicarate who'd dared to reject Clyntahn's obscene version of Mother Church was a terrible warning of what would happen to anyone foolish enough to oppose him now.

Yet how had he ever come to hold the Grand Inquisitor's office in the first place? How could Mother Church have been so blind, so foolish—so stupid and lost to her responsibility to God Himself—as to entrust *Zhaspahr Clyntahn* with that position? And where had the other vicars been when Clyntahn had Samyl and Hauwerd Wylsynn and the other members of their circle of reformers slaughtered? When he'd applied the Punishment of Schueler to vicars of Mother Church not for any error of doctrine, not any act of heresy, but for having the audacity to oppose *him*? None of the other vicars could have believed the Inquisition's preposterous allegations against their Reformist fellows, yet not one voice had been raised in protest. Not *one*, when Langhorne himself had charged Mother Church's priests to die for what they knew was true and right if that proved necessary.

He closed his eyes, listening to the shriek of the blast furnaces, feeling the disciplined energy and power pulsing around him, gathering itself to resist Clyntahn and the other men in far distant Zion who supported him, and felt the doubt gnawing at his certainty once again. Not at his faith in God. Nothing could ever touch that, he thought. But his faith in Mother Church. His faith in Mother Church's fitness as the guardian of God's plan and message to His children.

There were men fighting to resist the Group of Four's corruption, yet they'd been forced to do it outside Mother Church—in *despite* of Mother Church—and in the process they were taking God's message into other waters, subtly reshaping its direction and scope. Were they right to do that? Wylsynn's own heart cried out to move in the same directions, to broaden the scope of God's love in the same ways, but was *he* right to do that? Or had they all fallen prey to Shan-wei? Was the Mother of Deception using the Reformists' own better natures, their own yearning to understand God, to lead them into *opposition* to God? Into believing God must be wise enough to think the same way *they* did rather than accepting that no mortal mind was great enough to grasp the mind of God? That it was not their job to lecture God but rather to hear His voice and obey it, whether or not it accorded with their own desires and prejudices? Their own limited understanding of all He saw and had ordained?

And how much of his own yearning to embrace that reshaped direction stemmed from his own searing anger? From the rage he couldn't suppress, however hard he tried, when he thought about Clyntahn and the mockery he'd made of the Inquisition? From his fury at the vicars who'd stood idly by and watched it happen? Who even now acquiesced by their silence in every atrocity Clyntahn proclaimed in the name of his own twisted image of Mother Church, the Archangels, and God Himself?

And, terribly though it frightened and shamed him to ask the question, or even dare to admit he could feel such things, how much of it stemmed from his anger at God Himself, and at His Archangels, for *letting* this happen? If Shan-wei could seduce men through the goodness of their hearts, by subtly twisting their faith and their love for their fellow men and women, how much more easily might she seduce them through the dark poison of anger? And where might anger such as his all too easily lead?

I know where my heart lies, where my own faith lives, Paityr Wylsynn thought. *Even if I wished to pretend I didn't, that I weren't so strongly drawn to the Church of Charis' message, there'd be no point trying. The truth is the truth, however men might try to change it, but have I become part of the Darkness in my drive to serve the Light? And how does any man try—what right does he have to try—to be one of God's priests when he can't even know what the truth in his own heart is . . . or whether it springs from Light or Darkness?*

He opened his eyes once more, looking out over the fiery vista of Ehdwyrd Howsmyn's enormous foundry complex, and worried.

II

HMS *Royal Charis*, 58,
West Isle Channel,
and
Imperial Palace,
Cherayth,
Kingdom of Chisholm

The cabin lamps swung wildly, sending their light skittering across the richly woven carpets and the gleaming wood of the polished table. Glass decanters sang a mad song of vibration, planking and stout hull timbers groaned in complaint, wind howled, rain beat with icy fists on the skylight, and the steady cannon-shot impacts as HMS *Royal Charis*' bow slammed into one tall, gray wave after another echoed through the plunging ship's bones.

A landsman would have found all of that dreadfully alarming, assuming seasickness would have allowed him to stop vomiting long enough to appreciate it. Cayleb Ahrmahk, on the other hand, had never suffered from seasickness, and he'd seen heavy weather bad enough to make the current unpleasantness seem relatively mild.

Well, maybe a bit more than relatively mild, *if we're going to be honest,* he admitted to himself.

It was only late afternoon, yet as he gazed out through the stern windows at the raging sea in *Royal Charis*' wake it could have been night. True, by the standards of his own homeland, night came early in these relatively northern latitudes in midwinter, but this was early even for the West Isle Channel. Solid cloud cover tended to do that, and if this weather was merely . . . exceptionally lively, there was worse coming soon enough. The front rolling in across the Zebediah Sea to meet him was going to make *this* seem like a walk in the park.

"Lovely weather you've chosen for a voyage," a female voice no one else aboard *Royal Charis* could hear remarked in his ear.

"I didn't exactly *choose* it," he pointed out in reply. He had to speak rather loudly for the com concealed in his jeweled pectoral scepter to pick up his voice amid all the background noise, but no one was likely to overhear him in this sort of weather. "And your sympathy underwhelms me, dear."

"Nonsense. I know you, Cayleb. You're having the time of your life," Empress Sharleyan replied tartly from the study across the hall from their suite in the Imperial Palace. She sat in a comfortable armchair parked near the cast-iron stove filling the library with welcome warmth, and their infant daughter slept blessedly peacefully on her shoulder.

"He does rather look forward to these exhilarating moments, doesn't he?" another, deeper voice observed over the same com net.

"Ganging up on me, Merlin?" Cayleb inquired.

"Simply stating the truth as I see it, Your Grace. The painfully *obvious* truth, I might add."

Normally, Merlin would have been aboard *Royal Charis* with Cayleb as the emperor's personal armsman and bodyguard. Circumstances weren't normal, however, and Cayleb and Sharleyan had agreed it was more important for the immediate future that he keep an eye on the empress. There wasn't much for a bodyguard to do aboard a ship battling her way against winter headwinds across nine thousand-odd miles of salt water from Cherayth to Tellesberg. And not even a *seijin* who was also a fusion-powered PICA could do much about winter weather . . . except, of course, to see it coming through the SNARCs deployed around the planet. Cayleb could monitor that information as well as Merlin could, however, and he was just as capable of receiving Owl's weather predictions from the computer's hiding place under the far distant Mountains of Light.

Not that he could share that information with anyone

in *Royal Charis'* crew. On the other hand, the Imperial Charisian Navy had a near idolatrous faith in Cayleb Ahrmahk's sea sense. If he told Captain Gyrard he smelled a storm coming, no one was going to argue with him.

"*He* may not mind weather like this," a considerably more sour voice inserted. "Some of the rest of us lack the sort of stomachs that seem to be issued to Charisian monarchs."

"It'll do you good, Nahrmahn," Cayleb replied with a chuckle. "Ohlyvya's been after you to lose weight, anyway. And if you can't keep anything down, then by the time we reach Tellesberg you're probably going to waste away to no more than, oh, half the man you are today."

"Very funny," Nahrmahn half growled.

Unlike Cayleb, who was gazing out into the dark the better to appreciate the weather, the rotund little Prince of Emerald was curled as close as he could fold himself into a miserable knot in his swaying cot. He wasn't quite as seasick as Cayleb's rather callous remark suggested, but he was quite seasick enough to be going on with.

His wife, Princess Ohlyvya, on the other hand, was as resistant to motion sickness as Cayleb himself. Nahrmahn found that a particularly unjust dispensation of divine capriciousness, since she'd said very much the same thing the emperor just had to him that very morning. At the moment, she was sitting in a chair securely lashed to the deck, knitting, and he heard her soft chuckle over the com.

"I suppose it really isn't all *that* funny, dear," she said now. "Still, we all know you'll get over it in another five-day or so. You'll be just fine." She waited half a beat. "Assuming the ship doesn't sink, of course."

"At the moment, that would be something of a relief," Nahrmahn informed her.

"Oh, stop complaining and think about all the scheming and planning and skullduggery you'll have to keep you occupied once we get home again!"

"Ohlyvya's right, Nahrmahn," Sharleyan said, and her voice was rather more serious than it had been. "Cayleb's going to need you to help sort out the mess. Since I can't be there to help out myself, I'm just as happy you can be."

"I appreciate the compliment, Your Majesty," Nahrmahn said. "All the same, I can't help thinking how much more comfortable it would have been to provide all that assistance from a nice, motionless bedroom in Cherayth."

"Coms are all well and good," Sharleyan replied, "but he's going to need someone to obviously confer with instead of just listening to voices out of thin air. And having another warm body he can send out to *do* things isn't going to hurt one bit, either."

"I have to agree with that," Cayleb said. "Although trying to picture any Charisian's reaction to the notion of using Prince Nahrmahn of Emerald as an official representative and emissary a couple of years ago boggles the mind."

"I'm sure it boggles your mind less than mine," Nahrmahn replied tartly, and it was Cayleb's turn to chuckle. "On the other hand, it's worked out better—and a lot more satisfyingly—than several alternatives I could think of right offhand," the Emeraldian continued a bit more seriously.

"I'd have to agree with that, too," Cayleb acknowledged. "Although I wish to hell you and I didn't have to go home and assist each other with this mess."

"I wish you didn't have to either," Sharleyan agreed somberly, "but *this* mess is a lot less ugly than the one we could've had."

Cayleb nodded, his expression sober, at the accuracy of her remark.

The Navy of God had outnumbered the Imperial Charisian Navy by a terrifying margin when they met in the Gulf of Tarot barely two months ago. Of the twenty-five Charisian galleons who'd engaged, one had been completely destroyed, eleven had been reduced to near wrecks, five more had lost masts and spars, and only eight had emerged more or less intact. Charis had suffered over three thousand casualties, more than half of them fatal . . .

including Cayleb's cousin, High Admiral Bryahn Lock Island. Yet hideously expensive as the victory had been, it had also been overwhelming. Forty-nine of the Navy of God's galleons had been captured. Fourteen had been destroyed in action, another seventeen had been scuttled after their capture as too damaged to be worth keeping, and only nine had actually managed to escape. Forty-one Harchongese galleons had been captured, as well, and the blow to the Church's naval power had been devastating.

Cayleb Ahrmahk had never felt so useless as he had watching that titanic engagement through Merlin's SNARCs. He'd seen every moment of it, including his cousin's death, but he'd been the better part of eight thousand miles away, unable to do anything *but* watch the death and destruction. Almost worse, there'd been no acceptable way for him and Sharleyan even to know the battle had been fought. They'd had to pretend they knew nothing about it, had no idea how desperate it had been or how many men had died obeying their orders. Even when Admiral Kohdy Nylz had arrived with the reinforcements dispatched to Chisholm when they'd anticipated the Church was sending its ships west to join Admiral Thirsk in Dohlar instead of east to the Desnairian Empire, they'd been unable to discuss it with him in any way.

It had taken another full two-and-a-half five-days for a weather-battered schooner to arrive with Admiral Rock Point's official dispatches, and the only good thing was that their inner circle had had plenty of time by then to confer and make plans over their coms. Which was why Cayleb was already on his way back to Tellesberg, despite the fact that he and Sharleyan had been scheduled to remain in Cherayth for another month and a half. And it was also the reason Sharleyan wasn't headed back to Tellesberg with him.

One of them had to return. In theory, they could have used their coms to coordinate responses with Rock Point, Archbishop Maikel Staynair, Baron Wave Thunder, and the inner circle's other members in Tellesberg from

Cherayth. In fact, that's what they'd been doing, in many ways. But there were limits to what their subordinates could do on their own authority, which meant either Cayleb or Sharleyan had to be there in person. For that matter, the entire world would be *expecting* one or both of them to return to Old Charis after such a cataclysmic shift in naval power. They couldn't afford the sort of questions not returning might arouse, and the truth was that Cayleb *wanted* to be there. Not that he was going to get there in any kind of hurry. This time of year, they'd be lucky if *Royal Charis* could make the crossing in less than two months, although Cayleb expected they'd be able to shave at least a five-day or so off of the time anyone else might have managed.

Unfortunately, Sharleyan couldn't come with him. He was just as glad to spare Alahnah the roughness and potential hazards of this particular winter voyage, but that wasn't the main reason she and her mother had remained in Cherayth. Nor was it the reason Merlin had remained with them. Sharleyan would be making a voyage of her own soon enough, and Cayleb didn't envy the task *she* was going to face at the end of it.

Well, no one ever told you it was going to be easy . . . or pleasant, he reminded himself. *So stop thinking about how much you envy Nahrmahn and Ohlyvya for at least being together and concentrate on getting your job done. Sharley will handle her part of it just fine, and the sooner she does, the sooner she* will *be joining you.*

"I agree things could be a lot worse," he said in a deliberately more cheerful tone, then smiled wickedly. "For example, I could be just as bad a sailor as Nahrmahn!"

III

The Temple,
City of Zion,
The Temple Lands

*And aren't we four poor miserable looking sons-of-bitches
for the most powerful men in the world?* Vicar Rhobair
Duchairn thought sourly, gazing around the conference
chamber. None of the other faces were gazing back at him
at the moment, and all of them wore expressions which
mingled various degrees of shock, dismay, and anger.

The atmosphere in the sumptuously furnished, indirectly lit, mystically comfortable chamber was like an echo
of the bitter blizzard even then blowing through the streets
of Zion beyond the Temple's precincts. Not surprisingly,
given the message they'd just received . . . and the fact
that it had taken so long to reach them. Poor visibility
was the greatest weakness of the Church's semaphore
system, and this winter's weather seemed to be proving
worse than usual. It certainly was in Zion itself, as Duchairn was all too well aware. His efforts to provide the
city's poor and homeless with enough warmth and food
to survive had saved scores—if not hundreds—of lives so
far, yet the worst was yet to come and he knew he wasn't
going to save all of them.

At least this year, though, Mother Church was actually
trying to honor her obligation to succor the weakest and
most vulnerable of God's children. And seeing that she
did was eating up a lot of Duchairn's time. It was also
taking him beyond the Temple far more frequently than
any of his colleagues managed, and he suspected it was
giving him a far better perspective on how the citizens of
Zion really felt about Mother Church's jihad. Zhaspahr
Clyntahn's inquisitors circulated throughout the city and
Clyntahn had access to all of their reports, but Duchairn

doubted the Grand Inquisitor paid a great deal of attention to what Zion's poorest inhabitants were saying. Duchairn's own activities brought him into much more frequent contact with those same poor, however, and at least some of what they truly felt had to leak through the deference and (much as it distressed him to admit it existed) the *fear* his high clerical rank inspired. He might have learned still more if he hadn't been continually accompanied by his assigned escort of Temple Guardsmen, but that was out of the question.

Which says some pretty ugly things about how our beloved subjects regard us, doesn't it, Rhobair? He felt his lips trying to twist in a bitter smile at the irony of it all. All he really wanted to do was reach out to the people of Zion the way a vicar of God was supposed to, yet trying to do that without bodyguards was entirely too likely to get him killed by some of those same people. *And it would make sense from their perspective, I suppose. I don't imagine some of them are differentiating very much among us just now, and given Zhaspahr's idea of how to inspire obedience, somebody probably would put a knife in my ribs if only he had the chance. Not that there's any way Allayn and Zhaspahr would let me out without my keepers even if everyone loved and cherished all four of us as much as Charis seems to cherish Staynair.*

Duchairn knew perfectly well why Allayn Maigwair and Zhaspahr Clyntahn regarded Captain Khanstahnzo Phandys as the perfect man to command his bodyguard . . . and keep an alert eye on his activities. As the officer who'd thwarted the Wylsynn brothers' escape from the Inquisition—and personally killed Hauwerd Wylsynn when the "renegade" vicar resisted arrest—his reliability was beyond question.

Of course, these days things like reliability and loyalty were almost as subject to change as Zion's weather, weren't they? And not just where members of the Guard were concerned. All he had to do was glance at the ugly look Clyntahn was bending upon Maigwair to realize that.

"Tell me, Allayn," Clyntahn said now. "Can you and the Guard do *anything* right?"

Maigwair flushed darkly and started to open his mouth quickly. But then he stopped, pressing his lips together, and Duchairn felt a spasm of sympathy. As the Captain General of the Church of God Awaiting, Maigwair commanded all of her armed forces except the small, elite armed cadre of the Inquisition. That had made him responsible for building, arming, and training the Navy of God, and it had been commanded by Guard officers on its voyage to Desnair.

A voyage which, as the dispatch which had occasioned this meeting made clear, had not prospered.

"I think that might be a bit overly severe, Zhaspahr," Duchairn heard himself say, and the Grand Inquisitor turned his baleful gaze upon him. Clyntahn's heavy jowls were dark with anger, and despite himself, Duchairn felt a quiver of fear as those fuming eyes came to bear.

"Why?" the inquisitor demanded in a harsh, ugly tone. "They've obviously fucked up by the numbers . . . again."

"If Father Greyghor's dispatch is accurate, and we have no reason yet to believe it isn't, Bishop Kornylys clearly encountered a new and unexpected Charisian weapon . . . again." Duchairn kept his voice deliberately level and nonconfrontational, although he saw Clyntahn's eyes narrow angrily at the deliberate mimicry of his last two words. "If that weapon was as destructive as Father Greyghor's message suggests, it's hardly surprising the Bishop suffered a major defeat."

"*Major defeat,*" he thought. *My, what a delicate way to describe what must've been a massacre. It seems I have a gift for words after all.*

The fact that Father Greyghor Searose, the commanding officer of the galleon NGS *Saint Styvyn*, appeared to be the senior surviving officer of Bishop Kornylys Harpahr's entire fleet—that not a single *squadron* commander seemed to have made it to safety—implied all sorts of things Duchairn really didn't want to think about. According to Searose's semaphore dispatch, only seven other ships had survived to join *Saint Styvyn* in Bedard Bay. *Seven* out of a hundred and thirty. The fact that they'd been anticipating a very different message for five-days—the notification that Harpahr had reached his destination and united his forces and the Imperial Desnairian Navy into an irresistible armada—had only made the shock of the message they'd actually gotten even worse. No wonder Clyntahn's nose was out of joint . . . especially since he was the one who'd insisted on sending them to the Gulf of Jahras in the first place instead of to Earl Thirsk in Gorath Bay.

"Rhobair has a point, Zhaspahr," Zahmsyn Trynair put in quietly, and it was the inquisitor's turn to glare at the Church's Chancellor, the final member of the Group of Four. "I'm not saying things were handled perfectly," Trynair continued. "But if the Charisians somehow managed to actually make our ships *explode* in action, it's scarcely surprising we lost the battle. For that matter," the Chancellor's expression was that of a worried man, "I don't know how the people are going to react when they hear about exploding ships at sea! Langhorne only knows what Shan-wei-spawned deviltry was involved in *that!*"

"There wasn't any 'deviltry' involved!" Clyntahn snapped. "It was probably—"

He broke off with an angry chop of his right hand, and Duchairn wondered what he'd been about to say. Virtually all of Mother Church's spies reported to the Grand Inquisitor. Was it possible Clyntahn had received some warning of the new weapon . . . and failed to pass it on to Maigwair?

"I don't think it was deviltry, either, Zhasphar," he said mildly. "Zahmsyn has a point about how *others* may see it, however, including quite a few vicars. So how do we convince *them* it wasn't?"

"First, by pointing out that the *Writ* clearly establishes that Shan-wei's arts cannot prevail against godly and faithful men, far less a fleet sent out in God's own name to fight His jihad!" Clyntahn shot back. "And, secondly, by pointing out that nothing else these goddamned heretics have trotted out has amounted to actual witchcraft or deviltry. Pressing and twisting the limits of the Proscriptions till they squeal, yes, but so far all of it's been things our own artisans can duplicate without placing ourselves in Shan-wei's talons!"

That was an interesting change in perspective on Clyntahn's part, Duchairn thought. It had probably been brewing ever since the inquisitor decided Mother Church had no choice but to adopt the Charisians' innovations themselves if they hoped to defeat the heretics. Odd how the line between the acceptable and the anathematized started blurring as soon as Clyntahn realized the kingdom he'd wanted to murder might actually have a chance to win.

"Very well, I'll accept that," Trynair responded, although from his tone he still cherished a few reservations. "Convincing the common folk of it may be a little more difficult, however. And 'deviltry' or not, the shock of it—not to mention its obvious destructiveness—undoubtedly explains how Bishop Kornylys and his warriors were overcome."

"I think that's almost certainly what happened." Maigwair's voice was unwontedly quiet. The Group of Four's least imaginative member clearly realized how thin the ice was underfoot, but his expression was stubborn. "There's no way Harpahr could have seen this coming. *We* certainly didn't! And, frankly, I'm willing to bet the Harchongese got in the way more than they ever helped!"

Clyntahn's glare grew still sharper. The Harchong Empire's monolithic loyalty to Mother Church loomed large in the Grand Inquisitor's thinking. Harchong, the most populous of all the Safeholdian realms, formed an almost bottomless reservoir of manpower upon which the Church might draw and, geographically, it protected the Temple Lands' western flank. Perhaps even more important from Clyntahn's perspective, though, was Harchong's automatic, bone-deep aversion to the sort of innovations and social change which had made Charis so threatening in the Inquisition's eyes from the very beginning.

Despite which, not even he could pretend Harchong's contribution to Bishop Kornylys Harpahr's fleet had constituted anything but a handicap. Poorly manned, worse officered, and in far too many cases completely unarmed thanks to the inefficiency of Harchong's foundries, they must have been like an anchor tied to Harpahr's ankle when the Charisians swooped down upon him.

"I get a little tired of hearing about Harchong's shortcomings," the Grand Inquisitor said sharply. "I'll grant they aren't the best seamen in the world, but at least we can *count* on them . . . unlike some people I could mention." He made a harsh, angry sound deep in his throat. "Funny how Searose ended up in *Siddarmark* of all damned places, isn't it?"

Duchairn managed not to roll his eyes, but he'd seen that one coming. Clyntahn's aversion towards and suspicion of Siddarmark were just as deep and automatic as his preference for Harchong.

"I'm sure it was simply a case of Bedard Bay's being the closest safe port he could reach," Trynair said.

"Maybe so, but I'd almost be happier to see them on the bottom of the sea," the inquisitor growled. "The last thing we need is to have our Navy—our *surviving* Navy, I suppose I should say—getting contaminated by *those* bastards. The embargo's leaking like a fucking sieve already; Langhorne only knows how bad it'd get if the people responsible for enforcing it signed on with that pain in the ass Stohnar!"

"Zhaspahr, you know I agree we have to be cautious where Siddarmark is concerned," the Chancellor said in a careful tone. "And I realize Stohnar is obviously conniving with his own merchants and banking houses to evade the embargo. But Rhobair's right, too. At this moment, Siddarmark and Silkiah have the most prosperous economies of any of the mainland realms precisely *because* the embargo is 'leaking like a sieve' in their cases. You know that's true."

"So we should just sit on our asses and let Stohnar and the others laugh up their sleeves at Mother Church?" Clyntahn challenged harshly. "Let them flout Mother Church's legitimate authority in the middle of the first true jihad in history and get *rich* out of it?!"

"Do you think I like that any better than you do?" Trynair demanded. "But we've already got one slash lizard by the tail. One war at a time, please, Zhaspahr! And if it's all the same to you, I'd really like to take care of the one we're already fighting before we start another one with Siddarmark."

Clyntahn scowled, and Duchairn heaved a mental sigh. The Church had already lost the tithes from the scattered lands which had joined or been conquered by the Empire of Charis. That was a not insignificant slice of revenue in its own right, but of all the mainland realms, only the Republic of Siddarmark, the Grand Duchy of Silkiah, and the Desnairian Empire were managing to pay anything like their prewar tithes, and it was questionable how much longer that would be true in Desnair's case.

The only reason the Empire was making ends meet was the depth and richness of its gold mines, and that gold was running like water as the rest of the Desnairian economy slowed drastically. The result was a drastic rise in prices which was crushing the poor and the limited Desnairian middle class, and in the end, far more of the total tithe came from those two classes than from the aristocracy. If they could no longer make ends meet, if their incomes dropped, then so did their ability to pay their tithes, and Duchairn could already see the downward spiral starting to set in.

All of that made the fact that the Republic and the Grand Duchy *were* able to pay their full prewar tithes even more important. And the reason they were, as Trynair had just reminded Clyntahn, was precisely because they were the only two mainland realms continuing to carry on a brisk trade with Charis. In fact, even though the total level of their trade had dropped significantly because of the need to evade Clyntahn's prohibition of any commerce with Charis, Siddarmark in particular was actually *more* prosperous than it had been three years ago.

Everybody knows Siddarmark's always been the main conduit between Charis and the Temple Lands, whether Zhaspahr wants to admit it or not, the Treasurer thought disgustedly. *Their farmers have been cleaning up out of the need to provision all our armed forces, of course, but now that Charisian goods can't be imported legally into the Temple Lands—thanks to Zhaspahr's stupid embargo— Siddarmark's merchants and banking houses are making even more on the transaction. And it's still costing us less to buy Charisian than to buy anything manufactured here on the mainland. So if we break the Siddarmarkian economy, we break our own!*

He knew how much the situation infuriated Clyntahn, but for once the Grand Inquisitor had faced the united opposition of all three of his colleagues. They simply couldn't afford to kill the wyvern that fetched the golden rabbit—not when Mother Church was pouring so much gold into building the weapons she needed to fight her jihad. That was the argument which had finally brought him—grudgingly, dragging his heels the whole way—into accepting that he had no choice but to close his eyes to the systematic violation of his embargo.

And the fact that it's his embargo, one he insisted on decreeing without any precedent, only pisses him off worse, Duchairn thought. *Bad enough that they should defy God's will, but Langhorne forbid they should dare to challenge* Zhaspahr Clyntahn's *will!*

"I think we need to turn our attention back to the matter at hand," he said before Clyntahn could fire back at Trynair and back himself still further into an untenable corner. "And while I know none of us wanted to hear about any of this, I'd like to point out that all we have so far is Father Greyghor's preliminary *semaphore* report. Reports over the semaphore are never as detailed as couriered or wyvern-carried reports. I'm sure he dispatched a courier at the same time he handed his preliminary message to the semaphore clerks, but it's not going to get here for a while, given the weather, so I think it's probably a bit early for us to be trying to decide exactly what happened, or how, or who's to blame for it. There'll be time enough for that once we know more."

For a moment, he expected Clyntahn to launch a fresh verbal assault. But then the other man made himself inhale deeply. He nodded once, curtly, and thrust himself back in his chair.

"That much I'll give you," he said grudgingly. "If it does turn out, though, that all this resulted from someone's carelessness or stupidity, there *will* be consequences."

He wasn't looking at Maigwair as he spoke, but Duchairn saw the Captain General's eyes flicker with an anger of their own. It was just like Clyntahn to conveniently misremember who'd originally come up with a plan that hadn't worked out. The frightening thing, as far as Duchairn was concerned, was that he was almost certain the Grand Inquisitor honestly did remember things the way he described them. Not at first, perhaps, but given even a little time he could genuinely convince himself the truth was what he *wanted* the truth to be.

Which is how we all got into this mess in the first place, the Treasurer thought bitterly. *Well, that and the fact that not one of the rest of us had the guts, the gumption, or the mother wit to recognize where all four of us were headed and drag the fool to a stop.*

"Something we are going to have to think about, and quickly, though," he continued out loud, "are the *consequences* of what's happened. The purely military consequences are beyond my purview, I'm afraid. The fiscal consequences, however, fall squarely into my lap, and they're going to be ugly."

Trynair looked glum, Maigwair looked worried, and Clyntahn looked irritated, but none of them disagreed with him.

"We poured literally millions of marks into building those ships," Duchairn continued unflinchingly. "Now that entire investment's gone. Worse, I think we have to assume that at least a great many of the ships we've lost will be taken into Charisian service. Not only are we confronted with the need to replace our own losses, but we've just given the Charisians the equivalent of all that money in the hulls they're not going to have to build and the guns they're not going to have to cast after all. We still have the Desnairian and Dohlaran navies, but if the Charisians can find the crews to man all the galleons they have now, they'll have a crushing advantage over Desnair or Dohlar in isolation. In fact, they'll probably outnumber all our forces combined, even if we include our own unfinished construction and the ships Harchong hasn't finished yet. Frankly, I'm not at all sure we can recover from that position anytime soon."

"Then you'll just have to find a way for us to do it anyway," Clyntahn said flatly. "We can't get at the bastards without a fleet, and I think it's just become obvious we're going to need an even bigger fleet than we thought we did."

"It's easy to say 'find a way to do it anyway,' Zhaspahr," Duchairn replied. "Actually accomplishing it is a bit more difficult. I'm Mother Church's Treasurer. I *know* how deeply we've dipped into our reserves, and I know how our revenue stream's suffered since we've lost all tithes from Charis, Emerald, Chisholm, and now Corisande and Tarot." He carefully refrained from mentioning the subsequent importance of any places with names like Siddarmark or Silkiah. "I won't go so far as to say our coffers are empty, but I will say I can see their bottoms entirely too clearly. We don't have the funds to replace even what we've just lost, far less build 'an even bigger fleet.'"

"If we can't build a big enough fleet, Mother Church loses *everything*," Clyntahn shot back. "Do *you* want to face God and explain that we were too busy pinching coins to find the marks to save His Church from heresy, blasphemy, and apostasy?"

"No, I don't." *And I don't want to face the Inquisition because that's what you think I'm doing, either, Zhaspahr.*

"On the other hand, I can't simply wave my hands and magically refill the treasury."

"Surely you've been thinking about this contingency for some time, though, Rhobair?" Trynair put in in a pacific tone. "I know you like to be beforehand in solving problems, and you must've seen this one coming for some time."

"Of course I have. In fact, I've been mentioning it to all of you at regular intervals," Duchairn observed a bit tartly. "And I do see a few things we can do—none of which, unfortunately, are going to be pleasant. One thing, I'm afraid, is that we may find ourselves borrowing money from secular lords and secular banks instead of the other way round."

Trynair grimaced, and Maigwair looked acutely unhappy. Loans to secular princes and nobles were one of Mother Church's most effective means of keeping them compliant. Clearly, neither of them looked forward to finding that shoe on the other foot. Clyntahn's set, determined expression never wavered, however.

"You said that was one thing," Trynair said. "What other options have you been considering?"

He clearly hoped for something less extreme, but Duchairn shook his head almost gently.

"Zahmsyn, that's the *least* painful option open to us, and we're probably going to have to do it anyway, no matter what other avenues we turn to."

"Surely you're not serious!" Trynair protested.

"Zahmsyn, I'm telling you we've spent millions on the fleet. *Millions.* Just to give you an idea what I'm talking about, each of those galleons cost us around two hundred and seventy thousand marks. That's for the ships we built here in the Temple Lands; the ones we built in Harchong cost Mother Church well over three hundred thousand apiece, once we got finished paying all the graft that got loaded into the price."

He saw Clyntahn's eyes flash at the reference to Harchongese corruption, but there was no point trying to ignore ugly realities, and he went on grimly.

"Dohlaran and Desnairian-built ships come in somewhere between the two extremes, and that price doesn't include the guns. For one of our fifty-gun galleons, the artillery would add roughly another twenty thousand marks, so we might as well call it three hundred thousand a ship by the time we add powder, shot, muskets, cutlasses, boarding pikes, provisions, and all the other 'incidentals.' Again, those are the numbers for the ships we built right here, not for Harchong or one of the other realms, and between our Navy and Harchong's we've just lost somewhere around a hundred and thirty ships. That's the next best thing to forty million marks just for the *ships*, Zahmsyn, and don't forget that we've actually paid for building or converting over four hundred ships, including the ones we've lost. That puts Mother Church's total investment in them up to at least *a hundred and twenty million marks*, and bad as that number is, it doesn't even begin to count the full cost, because it doesn't allow for building the shipyards and foundries to build and arm them in the first place. It doesn't count workers' wages, the costs of assembling work forces, paying the crews, buying extra canvas for sails, building ropeworks, buying replacement spars. And it also doesn't count all the jihad's *other* expenses, like subsidies to help build the secular realms' armies, the interest we've forgiven on Rahnyld of Dohlar's loans, or dozens of others my clerks could list for us."

He paused to let those numbers sink in and saw shock on Trynair's face. Maigwair looked even more unhappy but much less surprised than the Chancellor. Of course, he'd had to live with those figures from the very beginning, but Duchairn found himself wondering if Trynair had ever really looked at them at all. And even Maigwair's awareness was probably more theoretical than real. No vicar had any real experience of what those kinds of numbers would have meant to someone in the real world, where a Siddarmarkian coal miner earned no more than a mark a day and even a skilled worker, like one of their own ship carpenters, earned no more than a mark and a half.

"We've had to come up with all that money," he continued after a moment, "and so far we've managed to. But at the same time, we've had to meet all Mother Church's other fiscal needs, and they haven't magically vanished. There's a limit to the cuts we can make in other areas in order to pay for our military buildup, and all of them together aren't going to come even close to making up the shortfall in our revenues. Not the way our finances are currently structured."

"So what do we do to change that structure?" Clyntahn demanded flatly.

"First, I'm afraid," Duchairn said, "we're going to have to impose direct taxation on the Temple Lands."

Clyntahn's face tightened further, and Trynair's eyes widened in alarm. The Knights of the Temple Lands, the secular rulers of the Temple Lands, were also the vicars of Mother Church. They'd never paid a single mark of taxes, and the mere threat of having to do so now could be guaranteed to create all manner of resentment. Their subjects were supposed to pay taxes to them, plus their tithes to Mother Church; *they* weren't supposed to pay taxes to anyone.

"They'll scream bloody murder!" Trynair protested.

"No," Clyntahn said harshly. "They won't."

The Chancellor had been about to say something more. Now he closed his mouth and looked at the Grand Inquisitor, instead.

"You were saying, Rhobair?" Clyntahn prompted, not giving Trynair so much as a glance.

"I think it's entirely possible we're going to have to begin disposing of some of Mother Church's property, as well." The Treasurer shrugged. "I don't like the thought, but Mother Church and the various orders have extensive holdings all over both Havens and Howard." In fact, as all four of them knew, the Church of God Awaiting was the biggest landholder in the entire world . . . by a huge margin. "We should be able to raise quite a lot of money without ever touching her main holdings in the Temple Lands."

Trynair looked almost as distressed by that notion as by the idea of taxing the Knights of the Temple Lands, but once again Clyntahn's expression didn't even waver.

"I'm sure you're not done with the bad-tasting medicine yet, Rhobair. Spit it out," he said.

"I've already warned all of our archbishops to anticipate an increase in their archbishoprics' tithes," Duchairn replied flatly. "At this time, it looks to me as if we'll have to raise them at a minimum from twenty percent to twenty-five percent. It may go all the way to thirty in the end."

That disturbed Trynair and Maigwair less than any of his other proposals, he noted, despite the severe impact it was going to have on the people being forced to pay those increased tithes. Clyntahn, on the other hand, seemed as impervious to its implications as he'd been to all the others.

"Those are all ways to *raise* money," he observed. "What about ways to *save* money?"

"There aren't a lot more of those available to us without cutting unacceptably into core expenditures." Duchairn met Clyntahn's eyes levelly across the conference table. "I've already drastically reduced subsidies to all of the orders, cut back on our classroom support for the teaching orders, and cut funding for the Pasqualate hospitals by ten percent."

"And you could save even more by cutting funding for Thirsk's precious 'pensions,'" Clyntahn grated. "Or by stopping coddling people too lazy to work for a living right here in Zion itself!"

"Mother Church committed herself to pay those pensions," Duchairn replied unflinchingly. "If we simply decide we're not going to after all, why should anyone trust us to meet any of our other obligations? And what effect do you think our decision not to provide for the widows and orphans of men who've died in Mother Church's service *after we've promised to* would have on the loyalty of the rest of Mother Church's sons and daughters, Zhaspahr? I realize you're the Grand Inquisitor, and I'll defer to your judgment if you insist, but that decision would strike at the very things all godly men hold most dear in this world: their responsibilities to their families and loved ones. If you threaten that, you undermine everything they hold fast to not simply in this world, but in the next."

Clyntahn's jaw muscles bunched, but Duchairn went on in that same level, steady voice.

"As for my 'coddling people too lazy to work,' this is something you and I have already discussed. Mother Church has a responsibility to look after her children, and it's one we've ignored far too long. Every single mark I've spent here in Zion this winter—every mark I might spend here *next* winter, or the winter after that—would be a single drop of water in the Great Western Ocean compared to the costs of this jihad. It's going to get lost in the bookkeeping when my clerks round their accounts, Zhaspahr. That's how insignificant it is compared to all our other expenses. And I've been out there, out in the city. I've seen how people are reacting to the shelters and soup kitchens. I'm sure your own inquisitors have been reporting to you and Wyllym about that, as well. Do you really think the paltry sums we're spending on that aren't a worthwhile investment in terms of the city's willingness to not simply endure but support what we're demanding of them and their sons and husbands and fathers?"

Their gazes locked, and tension hovered like smoke in the chamber's corners. For a moment, Duchairn thought Clyntahn's rage was going to push him over the line they'd drawn a year ago, the compromise which had bought Duchairn's acquiescence—his silence—where the Grand Inquisitor's pogroms and punishments were concerned. In Clyntahn's more reasonable moments, he probably did recognize it was necessary for the Church to show a kinder, more gentle face rather than relying solely on the Inquisition's iron fist. That didn't mean he liked it, though, and his resentment over the "diversion of resources" was exceeded only by his contempt for Duchairn's weakness. For the Treasurer's effort to salve his own conscience by showing his compassion to all the world.

If it came to an open confrontation between them, Duchairn knew exactly how badly it was going to end. There were some things he was no longer prepared to sacrifice, however, and after a moment, it was Clyntahn who looked away.

"Have it your own way," he grunted, as if it were a matter of no importance, and Duchairn felt his taut nerves relax ever so slightly.

"I agree there's no real point in cutting that small an amount out of our expenditures," Trynair said. "But do you think we'll be able to rebuild the fleet even if we do everything you've just described, Rhobair?"

"That's really a better question for Allayn than for me. I know how much we've already spent. I can make some estimates about how much it will cost to replace what we've lost. The good news in that respect is that now that we've got an experienced labor force assembled and all the plans worked out, we can probably build new ships more cheaply than we built the first ones. But Allayn's already been shifting the Guard's funding from naval expenditures to army expenditures. I don't see any way we're going to be able to meet his projections for things like the new muskets and the new field artillery if we're simultaneously going to have to rebuild the Navy."

"Well, Allayn?" Clyntahn asked unpleasantly.

"This all came at me just as quickly and unexpectedly as it came at any of the rest of you, Zhaspahr," Maigwair said in an unusually firm tone. "I'm going to have to look at the numbers, especially after we find out how accurate Searose's estimate of our losses really is. It's always possible they weren't as great as he thinks they were. At any rate, until I have some hard figures, there's no way to know how much rebuilding we're actually going to have to do.

"Having said that, though, there's no question that it's going to be the next best thing to impossible to push the development of the Guard's military support structure the way we originally planned. For one thing, field artillery's going to be in direct competition with casting replacement naval artillery for any new construction. A lot of the artisans and craftsmen we'll need to make rifled muskets and the new style bayonets are also going to be needed by the shipbuilding programs. As Rhobair says, we've planned all along on shifting emphasis once we got the shipbuilding program out of the way. In fact, I'd already started placing new orders and reassigning workers. Getting those workers back and shuffling the orders is going to be complicated."

"Should we just shelve land armaments in favor of replacing our naval losses?" Trynair asked.

"I think that's something we're all going to have to think about," Maigwair said. "My own feeling, bearing in mind that we don't have those definite numbers I mentioned, is that we'll have to cut back on the muskets and field artillery and shift a lot of emphasis back to the shipyards. I don't think we'll want to completely *cancel* the new programs, though. We need to at least make a start, and we need enough of the new weapons for the Guard to start training with them, learning their capabilities. Striking the balance between meeting that need and rebuilding the Navy is going to be tricky."

"That actually makes sense," Clyntahn said, as if the notion that anything coming out of Maigwair's mouth might do that astounded him. "On the other hand," he continued, ignoring the flash of anger in the Captain General's eyes, "at least it's not as if Cayleb and Sharleyan are going to be landing any armies on the mainland. Even adding the Chisholmian Army to the Charisians' Marines and assuming every outrageous report about their new weapons is accurate, they've got far too few troops to confront us on our own ground. Especially not when they've got to keep such hefty garrisons in Zebediah and Corisande."

"There's something to that," Maigwair conceded. "Doesn't mean they won't try hit-and-run raids, of course. They did that against Hektor in Corisande. And if they're willing to start that kind of nonsense on the mainland, our problem's going to be mobility, not manpower.

They can simply move raiding parties around faster by ship than we can march them overland, and the sad truth is that it doesn't really matter how good our weapons are if we can't catch up with them in the first place. That's one of the reasons I'm inclined to think we're going to have to place more emphasis on ships than muskets for the immediate future. We need to have enough of a navy to at least force them to make major detachments from their own fleet to support any operations along our coasts."

"And how realistic is that?" Clyntahn's question was marginally less caustic. "We're going to have to rebuild—there's no question of that, if we're ever going to take the war to them the way God demands—but how likely are we to be able to build enough of a replacement fleet quickly enough to keep them from raiding our coasts whenever they want?"

Maigwair's unhappy expression was answer enough, but Duchairn shook his head.

"I think Allayn may be worrying a bit too much about that, for the moment at least," he said. The others looked at him, and he shrugged. "They can probably raid the coast of Desnair if they really want to, but unless they go after one of the major ports—which would take more troops than they're likely to have—simple raids aren't likely to hurt us very much. The same is true of Delferahk." *Now, at least,* he added silently. *After all, Ferayd was the only "major port" Delferahk had, and it's gone now . . . thanks to you and your inquisitors, Zhaspahr.* "Dohlar is a long way from Charis and well protected, especially with Thirsk's fleet still intact to hold the Gulf of Dohlar. And even though I know you're not going to want to hear this, Zhaspahr, no one's going to be raiding Siddarmark or Silkiah as long as both of them are trading with Charis."

He paused, looking around their faces, then shrugged again.

"I agree we need to rebuild, but I also think we've got some time in hand before we're really going to *need* a fleet for anything except offensive operations. Just manning all the ships they've got now is going to be a huge drain on their manpower. As you say, Zhaspahr, they aren't going to be able to build an army large enough for any serious invasion of the mainland, so if their raids can only inconvenience us without really hurting us, I don't see any need to panic over the situation. Yes, it's serious, and we're going to have our work cut out for us to recover from it, but it's a long way from hopeless."

"That's sound reasoning," Clyntahn said after a moment, bestowing a rare look of approval on the Treasurer.

"Agreed." Trynair looked happier as well, and he nodded firmly. "Panic isn't going to help us, but clear thinking may."

"I agree, too," Maigwair said. "Of course, one thing we're going to have to do is figure out how this new weapon of theirs actually works. Until we know that and produce similar weapons of our own, meeting them at sea would be a recipe for disaster. And it's probably going to have a lot of implications for battles on *land*, too, for that matter." He looked at Clyntahn. "Do I have permission to begin work on that, Zhaspahr?"

"The Inquisition has no objection to your at least putting people to work thinking about it," the Grand Inquisitor replied, his eyes opaque. "I'll want to be kept closely informed, of course, and I'll be assigning one or two of my inquisitors to keep an eye on things. But as I said before, our own artisans have been able to accomplish many of the same things the heretics have done without violating the Proscriptions. I'm not prepared to say *they've* managed it entirely without violations, but we have, and I'm sure we'll be able to continue to do so."

Oh, I'm sure we will, too, Duchairn thought even as he and the other two nodded in grave agreement. *Your inquisitors are going to approve anything you tell them to, Zhaspahr, and you'll tell them to approve whatever Allayn comes up with even if it smashes right through the Proscriptions. After all, who's a mere Archangel like*

Jwo-jeng to place any limits on you *when it comes to smiting your enemies? In God's name, of course.*

He wondered once again where all this madness was going to end. And, once again, he told himself the one thing he knew with absolute certainty.

Wherever it ended, it was going to get far, far worse before it got better.

APRIL, YEAR OF GOD 895

✦

HMS *Dawn Star*, 58,
Chisholm Sea

Crown Princess Alahnah Zhanayt Naimu Ahrmahk wailed lustily as another sea rolled up under HMS *Dawn Star*'s quarter and sent the galleon corkscrewing unpleasantly. Despite her parentage, the infant crown princess was not a good sailor, and she obviously didn't care who knew it.

It was chilly in the large after cabin, despite the small coal stove securely affixed to the deck, and a warmly dressed Empress Sharleyan sat in a canvas sling-chair. The chair was adjusted so that its swinging movement could minimize the ship's motion as much as possible, and she cradled the blanket-cocooned baby on her shoulder, crooning to her.

It didn't seem to help a lot.

"Let me fetch Glahdys, Your Majesty!" Sairaih Hahlmyn, Sharleyan's personal maid, said yet again. "Maybe she's just hungry."

"While I'll admit this young monster is hungry *most* of the time, Sairaih, that's not the problem right now," Sharleyan replied wanly. "Believe me. I've already tried."

Sairaih sniffed. The sound was inaudible against the background noise of a wooden sailing ship underway in blowing weather, but Sharleyan didn't need to hear it. Glahdys Parkyr was Alahnah's wetnurse, and as far as Sairaih was concerned, that meant Mistress Parkyr should be the crown princess' *only* wetnurse. She'd made no secret of her opinion that Sharleyan had far too many pressing demands on her time to do anything so unfashionable as breast-feeding her daughter.

There were times Sharleyan was tempted to agree with her, and there were other times when she had no choice but to allow Mistress Parkyr to replace her. Sometimes that was because of those other pressing demands, but she'd also been forced to admit that her own milk production wouldn't have kept pace with Alahnah's needs without assistance. That bothered her more than she wanted to admit even to herself, which was one reason she was so stubborn about nursing the baby whenever she could.

In this case, however, that wasn't the problem. In fact, her breasts felt uncomfortably full at the moment and Alahnah was too busy protesting her universe's unnatural movement to care. Of course, Alahnah being Alahnah, dire starvation was going to redirect her attention sometime in the next half hour or so, Sharleyan thought wryly.

"You need your rest, Your Majesty," Sairaih said with all the stubbornness of an old and trusted retainer gamely refusing to give up the fight.

"I'm stuck aboard a ship in the middle of the Chisholm Sea, Sairaih," Sharleyan pointed out. "Exactly what do I need to be resting up *for*?"

The unfair question gave Sairaih pause, and she looked reproachfully at her empress for sinking so low as to actually use *logic* against her.

"Never mind," Sharleyan said after a moment. "I promise if I can't get her to settle down in a little bit, I'll let you get Glahdys or Hairyet to see what they can do. All right?"

"I'm sure whatever Your Majesty decides will be just fine," Sairaih said with immense dignity, and on that note, she swept a rather deeper curtsy than usual and withdrew from Sharleyan's cabin.

"Have you ever considered how the rest of your subjects would react to the knowledge of how ruthlessly you're tyrannized in your own household?" a deep voice asked in the empress' ear, and she chuckled.

"I have no idea what you're talking about," she replied

to the cabin's empty ear, and it was Merlin's turn to chuckle.

He stood alone on *Dawn Star*'s sternwalk, gazing out over the endless ranks of white-crested waves sweeping down on the ship from the northwest. There was enough flying spray, and the weather was cold enough, that no one seemed inclined to dispute his possession of the sternwalk at the moment. Of course, the fact that he was Emperor Cayleb's personal armsman and currently attached to Empress Sharleyan in the same role probably had as much to do with it as the weather did. Then there was that minor matter of his *seijin*'s reputation. Even most of those who knew him well were disinclined to crowd him when they didn't have to.

"No idea at all," he said now. "That's what you want me to believe?"

"I'll have you know, *Seijin* Merlin, that I rule my household with a will of iron," she told him firmly.

"Oh, of course you do." Merlin rolled his eyes. "I've seen the way they all jump to obey your orders in obvious terror."

"I should certainly hope so." She elevated her nose with a sniff Sairaih couldn't have bettered, but a sudden, renewed complaint from Alahnah spoiled her pose.

"There, baby," she murmured in the child's delicate ear. "Momma's here." She nuzzled the side of the little girl's neck, inhaling the scent of her while she patted her back gently.

Alahnah's protests died back to a more sustainable level, and Sharleyan shook her head.

"How much longer until that wind change gets here?" she asked.

"Another seven or eight hours yet, I'm afraid," Merlin replied, watching the real-time weather map from Owl's sensors.

"Wonderful," Sharleyan sighed.

"At least we've got better weather than Cayleb does," Merlin pointed out. At that moment, *Empress of Charis* was battling headwinds and high seas as she fought her way steadily westward. "And we'll be heading into even better weather in the next few days. Of course, it's going to get a lot hotter."

"Fine with me," Sharleyan said fervently. "Don't tell any of my Chisholmians, but this northern girl's been spoiled by Charisian weather."

"Would that have anything to do with the fact that the snow was three or four feet deep when we left Cherayth?" Merlin asked mildly.

"I think you can safely assume it factors into the equation."

"I thought it might. Still, you might want to remember that too much heat's as bad as too much cold, and the last time Cayleb and I were in Zebediahan waters, it was hot enough to fry eggs on a cannon's breech. I thought it was going to render that toad Symmyns down into candle fat right on the quarterdeck."

"And it would've saved all of us—including him—a lot of grief if it had," Sharleyan said, her voice and expression much grimmer than they had been. "That's another part of this trip I'm not looking forward to, Merlin."

"I know," Merlin agreed soberly. "And I know it probably doesn't help, but if anyone's ever had it coming, it's certainly him."

Sharleyan nodded. Tohmys Symmyns, Grand Duke of Zebediah, was presently ensconced in a reasonably comfortable cell in what used to be his own palace in the city of Carmyn. He'd been there for four months now, awaiting the arrival of Cayleb or Sharleyan, and he'd probably have preferred to go on waiting a lot longer. Facing the emperor or empress against whom one had committed high treason wasn't something to which most self-serving, treacherous schemers looked forward. Unfortunately for Symmyns, he was going to have the opportunity to do precisely that—briefly, at least—in another seven or eight days. And while Merlin knew Sharleyan wasn't looking forward to the meeting either, he also knew she would never flinch from what her duty required.

"I'm not looking forward to Corisande, either, for that matter," she said now. "Well, not most of it, anyway. But at least there'll be some good news to go along with the bad in Manchyr."

"Would it happen that Hauwyl's reaction is one of the things you *are* looking forward to?" Merlin inquired dryly.

"Absolutely," Sharleyan replied smugly.

"I still say it was a nasty trick for you and Cayleb to keep him entirely in the dark about it."

"We're cunning, devious, and underhanded heads of state engaged in a desperate struggle against an overwhelming foe," Sharleyan pointed out. "It's one of our responsibilities to keep our most trusted henchmen alert and on their toes, ready for anything which might come their way."

"Besides which you both like practical jokes."

"Besides which we both like practical jokes," she agreed.

. II .

Royal Palace,
City of Talkyra,
Kingdom of Delferahk

Thunder rumbled far out over Lake Erdan, and multi-forked tongues of lightning glared down the heavens. Heavy waves broke on the reed-grown shore far below the hanging turret, and Princess Irys Daykyn propped her elbows on the windowsill as she leaned out into the rough-armed wind. It slapped at her cheeks and whipped her hair, and she slitted her hazel eyes against its exuberant power.

The rain would be along soon. She could already smell its dampness and a hint of ozone on the wind, and her gaze searched the heavy-bellied clouds, watching them flash as more lightning danced above them without ever quite breaking free. She envied those clouds, that wind. Envied their freedom . . . and their power.

The air was chill, cool enough to be actively uncomfortable to her Corisandian-trained weather sense. March was one of the hot months in Manchyr, although the city was so close to the equator that seasonal variations were actually minimal. Irys had seen snow only two or three times in her entire life, on trips to the Barcor Mountains with her parents before her mother's death. Prince Hektor had never taken her back there after her mother died, and Irys wondered sometimes if that was because he'd had no heart to visit his wife's favorite vacation spot without her . . . or if he'd simply no longer been able to find the time. He'd been busy, after all.

Thunder crashed louder than before, and she saw the darkness in the air out over the lake where a wall of rain advanced slowly towards the castle and the city of Talkyra. It was rather like her life, she thought, that steadily oncoming darkness moving towards her while she could only stand and watch it come. This castle had been supposed to be a place of refuge, a fortress to protect her and her baby brother from the ruthless emperor who'd had her father and her older brother murdered. She'd never wanted to come, never wanted to leave her father's side, but he'd insisted. And it had been her responsibility, too. Someone had to look out for Daivyn. He was such a little boy, so young to be so valuable a pawn and have so many deadly enemies. And now the refuge felt all too much like a prison, the fortress too much like a trap.

She'd had time to think. In fact, she'd had entirely too much of it in the months she'd spent with her brother as "guests" of their kinsman, King Zhames of Delferahk. Months to wonder if they'd escaped one danger only to walk straight into one far worse. Months for her brain to beat against the bars of a cage only she could see. To think about why her father had sent her and Daivyn away. And, perhaps worse, to think about who and what her father had truly been.

She hated those thoughts, she admitted, gazing un-flinchingly into the heart of the oncoming storm. They felt disloyal, wrong. She'd loved her father, and she knew he'd loved her. There was no doubt in her mind about that. And he'd tutored her well in the arts of politics and strategy—as well as if it might have been possible for her to inherit his crown. Yet her very love for him had kept her from looking at him as clearly and fearlessly as she now contemplated the lightning and rain sweeping to-wards her across the enormous lake. He'd been a good prince in so many ways, but now, trapped in Delferahk, fearing for her brother's life, she realized there'd been a side of him she'd never seen.

Was it because I didn't want *to see it? Because I loved him* too *much? Wanted him to always be the perfect prince, the perfect father, I thought he was?*

She didn't know. She might never know. Yet once the questions were asked, they could never be unasked, and she'd begun to consider things she'd never considered be-fore. Like the fact that her father had been a tyrant. A be-nign tyrant in Corisande, perhaps, yet still a tyrant. And however benign he might have been within his own prince-dom, he'd been nothing of the sort outside it. She thought about his ruthless subjugation of Zebediah, his rivalries with King Sailys of Chisholm and King Haarahld of Cha-ris. His ambition for empire and his intrigues and relent-less drive to accomplish it. The bribes he'd paid to vicars and other senior churchmen to influence them against Charis.

None of that had made him a bad father. Oh, she could see now how the time he'd invested in his machinations had been stolen from his family. Was that one of the rea-sons her older brother had been such a disappointment to him? Because he'd been too busy building his realm to spend enough time in teaching the boy who would some-day inherit it to be the man capable of ruling it? Perhaps he'd spent so much more time with Irys because she was his daughter, and fathers doted on daughters. Or perhaps because she reminded him so much of her mother. Or perhaps simply because she was his firstborn, the child given to him before ambition had narrowed his horizons so sharply.

She'd never know about that, either. Not now. Yet she believed he'd truly done his best for his children. It might not have been exactly what they needed from him, but it had been the very best he could give them, and she would never question his love for her or her love for him.

Yet she'd come to the conclusion that she dared not allow love to blind her any longer. The world was a larger, and a more complex, and an infinitely more dangerous place than even she had realized, and if she and her brother—her rightful prince, despite his youth—were to survive in it, she could cling to no illusions about who might be her enemies, who might claim to be her friends, and why. She knew Phylyp Ahzgood, the man her father had chosen as his children's guardian and adviser, had always seen the world—and her father—more clearly than she. And she suspected he'd been trying as gently as possible to train her eyes to see as his did.

I'll try, Phylyp, she thought now as the first heavy raindrops pattered against the stonework and splashed her cheeks. *I'll try. I only hope we have the time for me to learn your lessons.*

▼ ▼ ▼

"Is she hanging out the window again, Tobys?" Phylyp Ahzgood, the Earl of 'Coris, asked wryly.

"Couldn't say as how she's *hanging* out the window, My Lord," Tobys Raimair replied in a judicious tone. He stroked his walrus mustache thoughtfully, bald head gleaming in the lamplight. "Might be she's closed it by now. Might be she hasn't, too." He shrugged. "Girl misses the weather, if you'll pardon my saying so."

"I know she does," Coris said, and smiled sadly. "You should've seen her in Corisande, Tobys. I swear she spent every minute she could on horseback somewhere. Either that, or sailing in the bay. It used to drive Prince Hektor's guardsmen crazy trying to keep an eye on her!"

"Aye?" Raimair cocked his head, still stroking his mustache, then chuckled. "Aye, I can believe that. Wish to Langhorne she could do the same thing here, too!"

"You and I both," Coris said. "You and I both. But even if the King would let her, *we* couldn't, could we?"

"No, I don't suppose we could, My Lord," Raimair agreed heavily.

They looked at one another in silence for several seconds. It would have been difficult to imagine a greater contrast between two men. Coris was fair-haired, of no more than average build, possibly even a bit on the slender side, aristocratically groomed and dressed in the height of fashion. Raimair looked like exactly what he was: a veteran of thirty years' service in the Corisandian Army. Dark-eyed, powerfully built, plainly dressed, he was as tough in both mind and body as he looked. He was also, as Captain Zhoel Harys had said when he recommended Raimair to Coris as Irys' bodyguard, "good with his hands."

And large and sinewy hands they were, too, Coris thought approvingly.

"Pardon me for asking, My Lord, and if it's none of my affair, you've only to say so, but is it my imagination or are you feeling just a mite more nervous of late?"

"Odd, Tobys. I never realized you *had* an imagination."

"Oh, aye, I've an imagination, My Lord." Raimair smiled thinly. "And it's been whispering to me here lately." His smile disappeared. "I'm not so very happy about what I'm hearing out of . . . places to the north, let's say."

Their eyes met. Then, after a moment, Coris nodded.

"Point taken," he said quietly. The Earl of Coris had learned long ago how risky it was to judge books by their covers. And he'd also learned long ago that a noncommissioned officer didn't serve as long as Raimair had without a brain that worked. Other people, including quite a few who should know better, forgot that all too often. They came to regard soldiers as little more than unthinking pawns, enforcers in uniform who were good for killing enemies and making certain one's own subjects were kept firmly in their places, but not for any tasks more mentally challenging than that. That blindness was a weakness Prince Hektor's spymaster had used to his advantage more than once, and he had no intention of forgetting that now.

"She's not discussed it with me, you understand, My Lord," Raimair said in an equally quiet voice, "but she's not so good as she thinks she is at hiding the way the wind's setting behind those eyes of hers. She's worried, and so are you, I think. So the thing that's working its way through my mind is whether or not the *lads* and I should be worried as well?"

"I wish I could answer that." Coris paused, gazing into the lamp flame and pursing his lips in thought for several seconds. Then he looked back at Raimair.

"She and the Prince are valuable game pieces, Tobys," he said. "You know that. But I've been receiving reports lately from home."

He paused again, and Raimair nodded.

"Aye, My Lord. I saw the dispatch from Earl Anvil Rock and this Regency Council when it arrived."

"I'm not talking about the Earl's *official* reports," Coris said softly. "He'll know as well as I do that any report he sends to Talkyra's going to be opened and read by at least one set of spies before it ever reaches me or the Princess. And don't forget—he's in the position of someone cooperating with the Charisians. Whether he's doing that willingly or only under duress, it's likely he'll bear that in mind whenever he drafts those reports he knows other people are going to read. The last thing he'd want would be for . . . certain parties to decide he's cooperating with Charis because he *wants* to. I'm not saying he'd lie to me or to Princess Irys, but there are ways to tell the truth, and then there are ways to tell the truth. For that matter, simply leaving things out is often the best way of all to mislead someone."

"But the Earl's her cousin, My Lord." Raimair sounded troubled. "Are you thinking he'd be looking to feather his own nest at her expense? Hers and the boy's? I mean, the Prince's?"

"I think it's . . . unlikely." Coris shrugged. "Anvil Rock was always sincerely attached to Prince Hektor and his children. I'm inclined to think he's doing the very best he can under the circumstances to look after Prince Daivyn's interests, and that's certainly the way his correspondence reads. Unfortunately, we're fourteen thousand miles as the wyvern flies from Manchyr, and a lot can change when a man finds himself sitting in a prince's chair, however he got there. That's why I left eyes and ears of my own behind to give me independent reports."

"And those would be the ones you're talking about now?" Raimair's eyes narrowed intently, and Coris nodded.

"They are. And they accord quite well with Earl Anvil Rock's, as a matter of fact. That's one of the things that worries me."

"Now you've gone and lost me, My Lord."

"I didn't mean to." Coris showed his teeth in a tight smile. "It's just that I'd rather hoped the Earl was putting a better face on things than circumstances really warranted. That there was more unrest—more resistance to the Charisians and, especially, to the 'Church of Charis'—than he's reported and that he was trying to cover his backside a bit in his dispatches to us here by understating it."

Raimair's eyebrows rose, and Coris shrugged.

"I don't want to hear about blood running in the streets any more than anyone else, Tobys. I'll admit a part of me would like to think Corisandians would be slow to accept foreign rulers they think had Prince Hektor assassinated, but I'd sooner not get anyone killed or any towns burned to the ground, either. You'll know better than I would how ugly suppressing rebellions can be."

Raimair nodded grimly, thinking about his previous prince's punitive campaigns to Zebediah, and Coris nodded back.

"Unfortunately, there are some people—the ones in the north you were just speaking of, for example—who aren't going to be happy to hear there's *not* widespread rebellion against Cayleb and Sharleyan. And they're going to be even less happy to hear the Reformists are making solid progress in the Church."

He paused again, unwilling even here, even with Raimair, to name specific names, but the ex-sergeant nodded once more.

"It's in my mind that those unhappy people will see any reports of cooperation and acceptance in Corisande as dangerous. They'll want as much as possible of the Charisians' manpower tied down back home, and any erosion of the Temple Loyalists' strength is going to be completely unacceptable to them. And there's not anyone they can reach *in Corisande* to change the way our people are beginning to think back home."

Raimair's eyes widened, then narrowed with sudden, grim understanding. He'd quietly assembled a tiny guard force—no more than fifteen men, plus himself—who were loyal not to King Zhames of Delferahk but to Princess Irys Daykyn and the Earl of Coris. He'd chosen them carefully, and the fact that Prince Hektor had established lavish accounts on the continents of Haven and Howard to support his espionage networks and that the Earl of Coris had access to them meant Raimair's men were quite comfortably paid. And not by King Zhames.

Or by Mother Church.

From the outset, Raimair's primary attention had been focused on the Delferahkans and any threat from the Charisians who'd assassinated Prince Hektor and his older son. Over the last couple of months, he'd begun to entertain a few doubts of his own about exactly who had assassinated whom, yet he'd never put together what Coris seemed to be suggesting now. But for all her youth, Princess Irys had a sometimes dismayingly sharp brain. The ex-sergeant never doubted for a moment that she'd already considered what he was considering now, whether she wanted to admit it even to herself or not.

And that would explain a lot about the brooding darkness he'd sensed within her, especially since the Grand

Inquisitor had begun his purge of the vicarate and the episcopate.

"It would be an awful shame if something were to happen to Prince Daivyn that led to all that rebellion back in Corisande after all, wouldn't it, My Lord?" he asked softly, and Coris nodded.

"It would indeed," he agreed. "So perhaps you *had* better have a word with the lads, Tobys. Tell them it's especially important to be on the watch for any Charisian assassins just now. Or, for that matter"—he looked into Raimair's eyes once more—"anyone *else's* assassins."

. III .

King's Harbor Citadel,
Helen Island,
Howell Bay,
Kingdom of Old Charis

Admiral Sir Domynk Staynair, Baron Rock Point, stood gazing out a familiar window at an incredibly crowded anchorage. His own flagship lay well out on the seventeen mile stretch of King's Harbor Bay, but dozens of other galleons were moored literally side-by-side all along the waterfront. Others lay to anchors and buoys while flotillas of small craft wended their way through the press.

From this high in the Citadel they looked like toy boats, growing smaller as the eye moved farther and farther away from the wharves and piers, and he'd never in his wildest imagination dreamed he might see that many warships anchored here.

They'd arrived over the last several weeks in fits and starts as the men who had originally crewed them were taken ashore or moved to one of the old ships which had been converted into prison hulks to accommodate them.

Under other circumstances, in another war, those men probably would have been paroled and repatriated to the Temple Lands and the Harchong Empire. In these circumstances, in *this* war, that was out of the question, and so the Kingdom of Old Charis had been forced to find places to put them.

Finding places to safely confine and guard upward of sixty thousand men, more than a few of whom were religious zealots perfectly prepared to die for what they believed God wanted of them, was a serious challenge. Safeholdian wars never produced POWs on a scale like that, and no realm had ever been prepared to accommodate them. The sheer expense of *feeding* that many prisoners, far less maintaining security and hopefully seeing to it that their living conditions were at least bearable, was one reason the practice of paroling honorably surrendered enemies was so universal. Perhaps Charis should have foreseen something like this, but it hadn't occurred to any of the native Safeholdians to even think about it. Nor, for that matter, had it occurred to Merlin Athrawes.

Rock Point had been inclined, when he first recognized the magnitude of the problem, to think Merlin *should* have seen it coming. After all, unlike Rock Point, Nimue Alban had been born and raised in the Terran Federation. She'd grown up learning about the long and bloody history of a planet called Old Terra, where prisoner hauls like this one had once been almost routine. But that was the point, he'd realized. It had been *history* to her . . . and there'd been no surrenders, no POWs, in the only war Nimue had actually fought, which explained why Merlin hadn't anticipated the problem either.

Oh, quit bitching, Rock Point told himself now. *The problem you've got is one hell of a lot better than the* alternative *would've been!*

Which was undoubtedly true, however inconvenient things might seem at the moment.

Most of the ships closer to shore still flew the imperial Charisian flag above the green, scepter-badged banner of the Church of God Awaiting. A handful still showed red and green banners with the crossed scepter and saber of the Harchong Empire, instead, but most of those were moored farther out, or in one of the other anchorages. King's Harbor was more concerned with the ships which had been fully armed, and surveyors and petty officers swarmed over those vessels like locusts. Their reports would tell Rock Point how quickly the prize vessels could be put into Charisian service . . . assuming he could find crews for them, of course.

And with Bryahn Lock Island's death, that decision would be his, at least until Cayleb could get home.

An embarrassment of riches, that's what it is, he thought. *Thank God the* Church *doesn't have them anymore, but what the hell am I going to do with all of them?*

He shook his head and turned back from the window to the two officers he'd actually come here to see.

Commodore Sir Ahlfryd Hyndryk, Baron Seamount, stood before one of the slate sheets which covered his office's walls. As always, the cuffs of his sky-blue uniform tunic were dusted with chalk and the fingers of his good hand were stained with ink. The short, plump Seamount was about as far removed from the popular imagination's image of a sea officer as it would be possible to get, yet his fertile brain and driving energy were one of the primary reasons all those prize ships were anchored in King's Harbor this sunny summer afternoon.

The rail-thin, black-haired commander standing respectfully to one side was at least ten or twelve years younger than Seamount. He radiated all the intensity and energy people tended not to notice just at first in his superior officer, and his left hand was heavily bandaged.

"It's good to see you, Ahlfryd," Rock Point said. "I apologize for not getting out here sooner, but—"

He shrugged, and Seamount nodded.

"I understand, Sir. You've had a lot to do."

The commodore's eyes dropped to the enormous rottweiler lying quietly beside his desk. Rock Point had inherited the acting rank of high admiral from Bryahn Lock Island, but Seamount had inherited Keelhaul. Frankly, the commodore was more than a little surprised the big, boisterous dog had survived his master's death. For the first couple of five-days, he'd been afraid Keelhaul was going to grieve himself to death, and he still hadn't fully regained the exuberance which had always been so much a part of him.

"Yes, I have." Rock Point inhaled deeply, then crossed to one of the office's armchairs. His peg leg thumped on the stone floor, the sound quite different from the sound his remaining shoe made, and he seated himself with a sigh of relief.

"Yes, I have," he repeated, "but I've finally managed to steal a couple of days away from all the reams of paper-work. So why don't the two of you dazzle me with what you've been up to while I've been away?"

"I don't know if 'dazzle' is exactly the right word, Sir," Seamount replied with a smile. "I do think you're going to be impressed, though. Pleased, too, I hope."

"I'm always *impressed* by your little surprises, Ahl-fryd," Rock Point said dryly. "Of course, sometimes I'm not so sure I'm going to survive them."

"We'll try to get you back to *Destroyer* undamaged, Sir."

"I'm vastly reassured. Now, about those surprises?"

"Well, there are several of them, actually, Sir."

Seamount crossed to the slate wall and reached for a piece of chalk. Rock Point watched him a bit warily. The commodore was a compulsive sketcher who had a tendency to illustrate his points enthusiastically.

"First, Sir, as you . . . suggested last time you were both here," Seamount continued, "I've had Commander Mahndrayn and the Experimental Board finishing up the work on the rifled artillery pieces. Master Howsmyn's provided us with the first three wire wound pieces, and they've performed admirably. They're only twelve-pounders—although the shot weight's actually closer to twenty-four pounds, given how much longer it is in proportion to its diameter—but as proof of the concept, they've been completely satisfactory. Master Howsmyn is confident he could go to production on much heavier weapons if and when you and Their Majesties should determine the time is right."

"That's excellent news, Ahlfryd!" Rock Point's smile of pleasure was completely genuine, even though he'd already known what Seamount was going to report. Ehdwyrd Howsmyn had kept him fully informed. Unfortunately, Seamount wasn't part of the inner circle, which meant explaining how Rock Point could have come by his knowledge would have been a trifle difficult.

"I'm not sure how our sudden acquisition of so many galleons is going to affect that decision," he continued. "On the one hand, we've already revealed the existence of the shell-firing *smoothbores*, and I'm sure that bastard Clyntahn is going to provide dispensations right and left while the Church works on duplicating them. I still don't see the additional theoretical range being all that valuable in a sea fight, what with the ships' relative motion, but I'm beginning to think that if Ehdwyrd has the capacity available it might not be a bad idea to begin manufacturing and stockpiling the rifled pieces. That way they'd be available quickly if and when, as you say, we decide to shift over to them."

"I'll look into that, Sir," Seamount said, chalk clacking as he turned to make a note to himself on the waiting slate. "It'll probably mean he needs to further increase his wire-drawing capacity, as well, so the additional lead-time would almost certainly be a good thing."

Rock Point nodded, and Seamount nodded back.

"Second," he continued, "at that same meeting you suggested Commander Mahndrayn give some thought to the best way to *protect* a ship from shellfire. He's done that, and discussed it with Sir Dustyn Olyvyr, as well. We don't have anything like a finished plan yet, but a few things have become evident to us."

"Such as?" Rock Point prompted, and Seamount gestured for Mahndrayn to take over.

"Well," the commander said in the soft, surprisingly melodious tenor which always sounded just a bit odd to

Rock Point coming out of someone who seemed so intense, "the first thing we realized was that wooden armor simply won't work, Sir. We can make the ships' sides thicker, but even if they're too thick for a shell to actually smash *through* them, we can't make them thick enough to guarantee it won't penetrate *into* them before it detonates. If that happens, it would be almost as bad as no 'armor' at all. It could even be worse, given the fire hazard and how much worse the splinters would be. Another objection to wood is its weight. It's a lot more massive for the same strength than iron, and the more we looked at it, the more obvious it became that iron armor that prevented shells from penetrating at all or actually broke them up on impact was the only practical answer."

"Practical?" Rock Point asked with a faint smile, and Mahndrayn chuckled sourly.

"Within limits, Sir. Within limits." The commander shrugged. "Actually, Master Howsmyn seems to feel that with his new smelting processes and the heavier hammer and rolling mills those 'accumulators' of his make possible he probably can provide iron plate to us in useful thicknesses and dimensions within the next six months to a year. He's not sure about quantities yet, but my observation's been that every one of his estimates for increased productivity has erred on the side of conservatism. And one thing's certain—we haven't seen any evidence that *anyone* on the other side would be in a position to match his production for years to come."

"That's true enough," Rock Point conceded. In fact, it was even truer than Mahndrayn realized, although that didn't mean enough small foundries couldn't produce at least some useful quantities of armor, even using old-fashioned muscle power to hammer out the plates.

"Assuming Master Howsmyn can manufacture the plate, and that we can come up with a satisfactory way of securing it to the hull, there are still going to be weight considerations," Mahndrayn continued. "Iron gives better protection than wood, but building in enough protection out of *anything* to stop shellfire is going to drive up displacements. That's one of the problems I've been discussing with Sir Dustyn.

"I understand Doctor Mahklyn at the College is also working with Sir Dustyn on mathematical ways to predict displacements and sail power and stability. I'm afraid I'm not too well informed on that, and neither is Sir Dustyn, for that matter. He's a practical designer of the old school, but he's at least willing to give Doctor Mahklyn's formulas a try once they're finished. In the meantime, though, it's obvious hull strength is already becoming an issue in our current designs. There's simply an upper limit on the practical dimensions and weights which can be constructed out of a material like wood, and we're approaching them rapidly. Sir Dustyn's been working on several ways to reinforce the hull's longitudinal strength, including diagonal planking and angled trusses between frames, but the most effective one he's come up with uses iron. Basically, he's boring holes in the ships' frames, then using long iron bolts between adjacent frames to stiffen the hull. Obviously, he hasn't had very long to observe the approach's success at sea, but so far he says it looks very promising.

"When I approached him about the notion of hanging iron armor on the outside of the ship, however, he told me immediately that he didn't think a wooden hull was going to be very practical. I'd already expected that response, so I asked him what he thought about going to a ship that was wooden-planked but iron-framed. Frankly, I expected him to think the notion was preposterous, but it turns out he'd already been thinking in that direction, himself. In fact, *his* suggestion was that we should think about building the *entire* ship out of iron."

Rock Point's eyes widened, and this time his surprise was genuine. Not at the notion of iron or steel-hulled vessels, but at the discovery that Sir Dustyn Olyvyr was already thinking in that direction.

"I can see where that would offer some advantages," he said after a moment. "But I can see a few drawbacks, too. For example, you can repair a wooden hull almost anywhere. A shattered iron frame member would be just a bit more difficult for the carpenters to fix! And then there's the question of whether or not even Master Howsmyn could produce iron in quantities like that."

"Oh, I agree entirely, Sir. I was impressed by the audacity of the suggestion, though, and the more I've thought about it, the more I have to say I believe the advantages would vastly outweigh the drawbacks—assuming, as you say, Master Howsmyn could produce the iron we needed. That's for the future, however. For the *immediate* future, the best we're going to be able to do is go to composite building techniques, with iron frames and wooden planking. And the truth is that that'll still give us significant advantages over all-wooden construction."

"I can see that. At the same time, I'd be very reluctant to simply scrap all the ships we've already built—not to mention the ones we've just captured—and start over with an entirely new construction technique."

"Yes, Sir. As an intermediate step, we've been looking at the possibility of cutting an existing galleon down by a full deck. We'd sacrifice the spar deck armament and completely remove the forecastle and quarterdeck. That should save us enough weight to allow the construction of an iron casemate to protect the broadside guns. We'd only have a single armed deck, but the guns would be much better protected. And we've also been considering that with shell-firing weapons we could reduce the number of broadside guns and actually increase the destructiveness of the armament. Our present thinking is that we might completely remove the current krakens and all the carronades from a ship like *Destroyer*, say, and replace them with half as many weapons with an eight- or nine-inch bore. The smaller gun would fire a solid rifled shot somewhere around a hundred and eighty to two hundred pounds. The shell would probably be about half that, allowing for the bursting charge. In an emergency, it could fire a sixty-eight-pound round shot, which would still be more destructive than just about anything else currently at sea."

"Rate of fire would drop significantly with that many fewer guns," Rock Point pointed out, and Mahndrayn nodded.

"Absolutely, Sir. On the other hand, each hit would be enormously more destructive. It takes dozens of hits, sometimes hundreds, to drive a galleon out of action with solid shot. A handful of hundred-pound exploding shells would be more than enough to do the job, and just to indicate how the weapons would scale, a rifled thirty-pounder's shot would weigh about *ninety* pounds, which would give you a shell weight of only forty-five or so, so you can see the advantage the larger gun has. Of course, the smoothbore thirty-pounder's shell is only around twenty-five pounds, and its bursting charge is proportionately lighter, as well. And if both sides start armoring their vessels with iron, anything much lighter than eight inches probably won't penetrate, anyway."

"That sounds logical enough," Rock Point acknowledged. "We'll have to think about it, of course. Fortunately it's not a decision we're going to have to make anytime soon."

"I'm afraid we might have to make it sooner than you may be thinking, Sir," Seamount put in. Rock Point looked at him, and the commodore shrugged. "You're talking about the possibility of beginning production and stockpiling weapons, Sir," he reminded his superior. "If we're going to do that, we're going to have to decide which weapons to build, first."

"Now that, Ahlfryd, is a very good point," Rock Point agreed. "Very well, I'll be thinking about it, and I'll discuss it with the Emperor as soon as possible."

"Thank you, Sir." Seamount smiled. "In the meantime, we have a few other thoughts that should be more immediately applicable to our needs."

"You do?"

"Yes. You may have noticed Commander Mahndrayn's hand, Sir?"

"You mean that fathom of gauze wrapped around it?" Rock Point asked dryly.

"Exactly, Sir." Seamount held up his own left hand, which had been mangled by an explosion many years before. "I think Urvyn was trying to do me one better. Unfortunately, he failed. All of *his* fingers are still intact . . . more or less."

"I'm relieved to hear it. Exactly what bearing does that have on our present discussion, however?"

"Well, what actually happened, Sir," Seamount said more seriously, "is that we've been experimenting with better ways to fire our artillery. The flintlocks we've gone to are far, far better than the old slow match-and-linstock or heated irons we used to use. That most of our new prizes' guns are still using, for that matter. But they still aren't as efficient as we could wish. I'm sure you're even better aware than we are here at the Experimental Board of how many misfires we still experience, especially when there's a lot of spray around or it's raining. So we've been looking for a more reliable method, and we've found one."

"You have?" Rock Point's eyes narrowed.

"Actually, we've come up with two of them, Sir." Seamount shrugged. "Both work, but I have to admit to a strong preference for one of them over the other."

"Go on."

"Doctor Lywys at the College gave us a whole list of ingredients to experiment with. One of them was something called 'fulminated quicksilver,' which is very attractive, on the face of it. You can detonate it with a single sharp blow, and the explosion is very hot. It would reduce lock time significantly, as well, which would undoubtedly improve accuracy. The problem is that it's very corrosive. And another difficulty is that it's too sensitive. We've experimented with ways of moderating its sensitivity by mixing in other ingredients, like powdered glass, and we've had some success, but any fuses using fulminated quicksilver are going to tend to corrode over time, and according to Doctor Lywys, they'll lose much of their power as they do. For that matter, she says at least some of them would probably detonate spontaneously if they were left in storage long enough. They do have the advantage that they're effectively impervious to damp, however, which would be a major plus for sea service."

"I can see where that would be true," Rock Point agreed.

"We've pushed ahead with developing those fuses—for the moment we're calling them fulminating fuses, after the quicksilver, although Urvyn is pushing for calling them 'percussion' fuses, since they're detonated by a blow—but I decided we should explore some other possibilities, as well. Which brought me to 'Shan-wei's candles.'"

Rock Point nodded. "Shan-wei's candles" was the name which had been assigned to what had once been called "strike-anywhere matches" back on Old Terra.

"Well, basically what we've come up with, Sir, is a tube—we're using the same sort of quills we've been using with the artillery flintlocks at the moment, although I think it's going to be better to come up with a metallic tube in the long run; probably made out of copper or tin—filled with the same compound we use in one of Shan-wei's candles. It's sealed with wax at both ends, and we insert a serrated wire into it lengthwise. When the wire is snatched out, friction ignites the compound in the tube, and that ignites the main charge in the gun. As far as we can tell, it's as reliable as the fulminating fuses even in heavy weather, as long as the wax seals are intact before the wire's pulled. It's less corrosive, as well, and it lets us dispense with hammer lock mechanisms, completely. For that matter, we could easily go directly to it on existing guns which are already designed to take the quills we're using with the flintlocks."

"I like it," Rock Point said with unfeigned enthusiasm. "In fact, I like it a lot—especially the 'easily' part." He grinned, but then he raised one eyebrow. "Exactly how do the Commander's damaged fingers figure into all this, though? Did he burn them on one of the 'candles'?"

"Not . . . precisely, Sir." Seamount shook his head. "I said I prefer the friction-ignited fuses for artillery, and

I do. But Urwyn's been exploring other possible uses for the *fulminating* fuses, and he's come up with a fascinating one."

"Oh?" Rock Point looked at the commander, who actually seemed a little flustered under the weight of his suddenly intense gaze.

"Why don't you go get your toy, Urwyn?" Seamount suggested.

"Of course, Sir. With your permission, High Admiral?"

Rock Point nodded, and Mahndrayn disappeared. A few minutes later, the office door opened once more and he walked back in carrying what looked like a standard rifled musket.

"It occurred to us, Sir," he said, holding the rifle in a rough port arms position as he faced Rock Point, "that the Marines and the Army were going to need reliable primers for their artillery, as well. And that if we were going to provide them for the guns, we might as well see about providing them for small arms, as well. Which is what this is."

He grounded the rifle butt on the floor and reached into the right side pocket of his tunic for a small disk of copper which he extended to Rock Point.

The high admiral took it a bit gingerly and stood, moving closer to the window to get better light as he examined it. It wasn't the flat disk he'd thought it was at first. Instead, it was hollowed on one side—a cup, not a disk—and there was something inside the hollow. He looked at it for a moment longer, then turned back to Mahndrayn.

"Should I assume the stuff inside this"—he held up the disk, indicating the hollow side with the index finger of his other hand—"is some of that 'fulminating quicksilver' of yours?"

"It is, Sir, sealed with a drop of varnish. And this"—Mahndrayn held up his bandaged hand—"is a reminder to me of just how sensitive it is. But what you have in your hand is what we're calling a 'primer cap,' at least for now. We call it that because it fits down over this"—he raised the rifle and cocked the hammer, indicating a raised nipple which had replaced the priming pan of a regular flintlock—"like a cap or a hat."

He turned the weapon, and Rock Point realized the striking face of the hammer wasn't flat. Instead, it had been hollowed out into something a fraction larger than the "cap" in his hand.

"We discovered early on that when one of the caps detonates it tends to spit bits and pieces in all directions," Mahndrayn said wryly, touching a scar on his cheek which Rock Point hadn't noticed. "The flash from a regular flintlock can be bad enough; this is worse, almost as bad as the flash from one of the old matchlocks. So we ground out the face of the hammer. This way, it comes down over the top of the nipple, which confines the detonation. It's actually a lot more pleasant to fire than a flintlock."

"And it does the same thing for reducing misfires, and being immune to rain, you were talking about where artillery is concerned, Ahlfryd?" Rock Point asked intently.

"Exactly, Sir." Seamount beamed proudly at Mahndrayn. "Urwyn here and his team have just found a way to increase the reliability of our rifles materially. And the conversion's fairly simple, too."

"*Very* good, Commander," Rock Point said sincerely, but Seamount raised one hand.

"He's not quite finished yet, Sir."

"He's not?" Rock Point looked speculatively at the commander, who looked more flustered than ever.

"No, he's not, Sir. And this next bit was entirely his own idea."

"Indeed? And what else do you have to show me, Commander?"

"Well . . . *this*, Sir."

Mahndrayn raised the rifle again and Rock Point suddenly noticed a lever on its side. He'd overlooked it when he examined the modified lock mechanism, but now the commander turned it. There was a clicking sound, and the acting high admiral's eyebrows rose as the breech of the rifle seemed to break apart. A solid chunk of steel, perhaps an inch and a half long, moved smoothly back and down, and he could suddenly see into the rifle's bore. The rifling grooves were clearly visible against the brightly polished interior, and Mahndrayn looked up at him.

"One of the things we've been thinking about in terms of the new artillery is ways to speed rate of fire, Sir," he said. "Obviously if we could think of some way to load them from the breech end, instead of having to shove the ammunition down the barrel, it would help a lot. The problem is coming up with a breech mechanism strong enough to stand the shock, quick enough to operate in some practical time frame, and one that seals tightly enough to prevent flash from leaking out disastrously every time you fire the piece. We haven't managed to solve those problems for *artillery*, but thinking about the difficulties involved suggested this to me."

"Exactly what is 'this,' Commander?" Rock Point asked warily, not quite able to believe what he was seeing. The possibility of breech-loading artillery, far less a breech-loading *rifle*, was one after which he'd hungered ever since gaining access to Owl's records, but he'd never imagined he might be seeing one this quickly. Especially without having pushed its development himself.

"Well," Mahndrayn said again, "the way it works is like this, Sir."

He reached back into his pocket and extracted a peculiar-looking rifle cartridge. It was a bit larger than the ones riflemen carried in their cartridge boxes, and there were two oddities about its appearance. For one thing, the paper was a peculiar grayish color, not the tan or cream of a standard cartridge. And for another, it ended in a thick, circular base of some kind of fabric that was actually broader than the cartridge itself.

"The cartridge's paper's been treated with the same compound we use in Shan-wei's candles, Sir," Mahndrayn said. "It's not exactly the same mix, but it's close. That means the entire cartridge is combustible, and it's sealed with paraffin to damp-proof it. The paraffin also helps to protect against accidental explosions, but with the new caps, the flash from the lock is more than enough to detonate the charge through the coating. And because the pan doesn't have to be separately primed, the rifleman doesn't have to bite off the bullet and charge the weapon with loose powder. Instead, he just slides it into the breech, like this."

He inserted the cartridge into the open breech, pushing it as far forward as it would go with his thumb, and Rock Point realized a slight lip had been machined into the rear of the opened barrel. The disk of fabric at the cartridge's base fitted into the lip, although it was thicker than the recess was deep.

"Once he's inserted the round," Mahndrayn went on, "he pulls the lever back up, like this"—he demonstrated, and the movable breech block rose back into place, driving firmly home against the fabric base—"which seals the breech again. There's a heavy mechanical advantage built into the lever, Sir, so that it actually crushes the felt on the end of the cartridge into the recess. That provides a flash-tight seal that's worked perfectly in every test firing. And after a round's been fired, the rifleman simply lowers the breech block again and pushes the next round straight in. The cartridges have stiffened walls to keep them from bending under the pressure, and what's left of the base from the *previous* round is shoved into the barrel, where it actually forms a wad for the next round."

Rock Point stared at the young naval officer for several seconds, then shook his head slowly.

"That's . . . brilliant," he said with the utmost sincerity.

"Yes, it is, Sir," Seamount said proudly. "And while it isn't quite as simple as changing a flintlock out for one of the new percussion locks, fitting existing rifles with the new breech mechanism will be a *lot* faster than building new weapons from scratch."

"You've just doubled or tripled our Marines' rate of fire, Commander," Rock Point said. "And I'm no Marine, far less a soldier, but it would seem to me that being able to load your weapon as quickly lying down as standing up would have to be a huge advantage in combat, as well."

"I'd like to think so, Sir," Mahndrayn said. His usually

intense eyes lowered themselves to the floor for a moment, then looked back up at Rock Point, dark and serious. "There are times I feel pretty useless, Sir," he admitted. "I know what Commodore Seamount and I do is important, but when I think about what other officers face at sea, in combat, I feel . . . well, like a slacker. It doesn't happen very often, but it *does* happen. So if this is really going to help, I'm glad."

"Commander," Rock Point rested one hand on Mahndrayn's shoulder and met those dark and serious eyes straight on, "there's not a single man in Their Majesties' uniform—not me, not even Admiral Lock Island and all the other men who died out on the Markovian Sea—who's done more than you've done here with Commodore Seamount. Not one. Believe me when I tell you that."

"I . . ." Mahndrayn faltered for a moment, then nodded. "Thank you, Sir."

"No, thank *you*, Commander. You and the Commodore have come through for us again, just as I expected you to. And because you have"—the admiral smiled suddenly, eyes glinting with deviltry—"I'll be coming up with another little challenge for you . . . as soon as I can think of it."

. IV .

Siddarmark City,
Republic of Siddarmark

"One would have expected God's own, personal navy to fare better than that, wouldn't one?" Madam Aivah Pahrsahn remarked, turning her head to look over one shapely shoulder at her guest.

A slender hand gestured out the window at the broad, gray waters of North Bedard Bay. Madam Pahrsahn's tastefully furnished apartment was on one of the better streets just outside the city's Charisian Quarter, only a block or so from where the Siddarmark River poured into the bay. Its windows usually afforded a breathtaking view of the harbor, but today the normally blue and sparkling bay was a steel-colored mirror of an equally steel-colored sky while cold wind swept icy herringbone waves across it.

A bleaker, less inviting vista would have been difficult to imagine, but that delicate, waving hand wasn't indicating the bay's weather. Instead, its gesture took in the handful of galleons anchored well out from the city's wharves. They huddled together on the frigid water, as if for support, managing to look pitiful and dejected even at this distance.

"One would have hoped it wouldn't have been necessary for God to build a navy in the first place," her guest replied sadly.

He was a lean, sparsely built man with silver hair, and his expression was considerably more grave than hers. He moved a little closer to her so that he could look out the window more comfortably, and his eyes were troubled.

"And while I can't pretend the Charisians deserve the sort of wholesale destruction Clyntahn wants to visit upon them, I don't want to think about how he and the others are going to react to what happened instead," he continued, shaking his head. "I don't see it imposing any sense of *restraint*, anyway."

"Why ever should they feel 'restraint,' Your Eminence?" Madam Pahrsahn asked acidly. "They speak with the very authority of the Archangels themselves, don't they?"

The silver-haired man winced. For a moment, he looked as if he wanted to argue the point, but then he shook his head.

"They *think* they do," he said in a tone which conceded her point, and her own eyes softened.

"Forgive me, Your Eminence. I shouldn't take out my

own anger on you. And that's what I'm doing, I suppose. Pitching a tantrum." She smiled slightly. "It would never have done in Zion, would it?"

"I imagine not," her guest said with a wry smile of his own. "I wish I'd had more of an opportunity to watch you in action, so to speak, then. Of course, without knowing then what I know now, I wouldn't truly have appreciated your artistry, would I?"

"I certainly hope not!" Her smile blossomed into something very like a grin. "It would have meant my mask was slipping badly. And think of your reputation! Archbishop Zhasyn Cahnyr visiting the infamous courtesan Ahnzhelyk Phonda? Your parishioners in Glacierheart would have been horrified!"

"My parishioners in Glacierheart have forgiven me a great deal over the years, 'Aivah,'" Zhasyn Cahnyr told her. "I'm sure they would have forgiven me that, as well. If anyone had even noticed a single lowly archbishop amongst all those vicars, that is."

"They weren't all venal and corrupt, Your Eminence," she said softly, sadly. "And even a lot of the ones who were both those things were more guilty of complacency than anything else."

"You don't have to defend them to me, my dear." He reached out to touch her forearm gently. "I knew them as well as you did, if not in precisely the same way."

He smiled again, squeezed her arm, and released it, then gazed out the window at those distant, anchored ships once more. As he watched, a guard boat appeared, rowing in a steady circle around them, as if to protect them from some shore-based pestilence.

Or, perhaps, to protect the shore from some contagion *they* carried, he thought grimly.

"I knew them," he repeated, "and too many of them are going to pay just as terrible a price as our friends before this is all ended."

"You think so?" The woman now known as Aivah Pahrsahn turned to face him fully. "You think it's going to come to that?"

"Of course it is," he said sadly, "and you know it as well as I do. It's inevitable that Clyntahn, at least, will find more enemies among the vicarate. Whether they're really there or not is immaterial as far as that's concerned! And"—his eyes narrowed as they gazed into hers—"you and I both know that what you and your agents are up to in the Temple Lands will only make that worse."

"Do you think I'm wrong to do it, then?" she asked levelly, meeting his eyes without flinching.

"No," he said after a moment, his voice even sadder. "I hate what it's going to cost, and I have more than a few concerns for your immortal soul, my dear, but I don't think you're wrong. There's a difference between not being wrong and being *right*, but I don't think there *is* any 'right' choice for you, and the *Writ* tells us no true son or daughter of God can stand idle when His work needs to be done. And dreadful as I think some of the consequences of your efforts are likely to prove, I'm afraid what you're set upon truly is God's work."

"I hope you're right, Your Eminence. And I think you are, although I try to remember that that could be my own anger and my own hatred speaking, not God. Sometimes I don't think there's a difference anymore."

"Which is why I have those concerns for your soul," he said gently. "It's always possible to do God's work for the wrong reasons, just as it's possible to do terrible things with the best of all possible motives. It would be a wonderful thing if He gave us the gift of fighting evil without learning to hate along the way, but I suspect only the greatest and brightest of souls ever manage that."

"Then I hope I'll have your prayers, Your Eminence."

"My prayers for your soul and for your success, alike." He smiled again, a bit crookedly. "It would be my pleasure, as well as my duty, to commend a soul such as yours to God under any circumstances. And given the debt I owe you, it would be downright churlish of me not to."

"Oh, nonsense!" She struck him gently on the shoulder.

"It was my pleasure. I only wish"—her expression darkened—"I'd been able to get more of the others out."

"You snatched scores of innocent victims out of Clyntahn's grasp," he said, his tone suddenly sterner. "Women and children who would have been tortured and butchered in that parody of justice of his, be they ever so blameless and innocent! Langhorne said, 'As you have done unto the least of God's children, for good or ill, so you have done unto me.' Remember that and never doubt for one moment that all that innocent blood will weigh heavily in your favor when the time comes for you to face him and God."

"I try to remember that," she half-whispered, turning back to the window and gazing sightlessly out across the bay. "I try. But then I think of all the ones we had to leave behind. Not just the Circle, Your Eminence, *all* of them."

"God gave Man free will," Cahnyr said. "That means some men will choose to do evil, and the innocent will suffer as a result. You can't judge yourself guilty because you were unable to stop *all* the evil Clyntahn and others chose to do. You stopped all it was in your power to stop, and God can ask no more than that."

She stared out the window for several more moments, then drew a deep breath and gave herself a visible shake.

"You're probably right, Your Eminence, but I intend to do a great deal more to those bastards before I'm done." She turned back from the window, and the steel behind her eyes was plain to see. "Not immediately, because it's going to take time to put the pieces in place. But once they are, Zhaspahr Clyntahn may find wearing the Grand Inquisitor's cap a lot less pleasant than he does today."

Cahnyr regarded her with a distinct sense of trepidation. He knew very few details of her current activities, and he knew she intended to keep it that way. Not because she distrusted him, but because she was one of the most accomplished mistresses of intrigue in the history of Zion. That placed her in some select company. Indeed, she'd matched wits with the full suppressive power of the Office of Inquisition, and she'd won. Not everything she'd wanted, perhaps, and whatever she might say—or he might say *to* her—she would never truly forgive herself for the victims she hadn't managed to save. Yet none of that changed the fact that she'd outmaneuvered the Grand Inquisitor on ground of his own choosing, from the very heart of his power and authority, and done it so adroitly and smoothly he still didn't know what had hit him.

Or who.

The woman who'd contrived all of that, kept that many plots in the air simultaneously without any of them slipping, plucked so many souls—including Zhasyn Cahnyr's—from the Inquisition's clutches, wasn't about to begin letting her right hand know what her left hand was doing now unless she absolutely had to. He didn't resent her reticence, or think it indicated any mistrust in his own discretion. But he did worry about what she might be up to.

"Whatever your plans, my dear," he said, "I'll pray for their success."

"Careful, Your Eminence!" Her smile turned suddenly roguish. "Remember my past vocation! You might not want to go around writing blank bank drafts like that!"

"Oh," he reached out and touched her cheek lightly, "I think I'll take my chances on that."

▼ ▼ ▼

"Madam Pahrsahn! How nice to see you again!"

The young man with auburn hair and gray eyes walked around his outsized desk to take his visitor's subtly perfumed hand in both of his. He bent over it, pressing a kiss on its back, then tucked it into his elbow and escorted her across the large office to the armchairs facing one another across a low table of beaten copper.

"Thank you, Master Qwentyn," she said as she seated herself.

A freshly fed fire crackled briskly in the grate to her right, noisily consuming gleaming coal which had probably come from Zhasyn Cahnyr's archbishopric in Glacierheart, she thought. Owain Qwentyn sat in the chair facing hers and leaned forward to personally pour hot chocolate into a delicate cup and hand it to her. He poured more chocolate into a second cup, picked it up on its saucer, and leaned back in his chair, regarding her expectantly.

"I must say, I wasn't certain you'd be coming today after all," he said, waving his free hand at the office window. The previous day's gray skies had made good on their wintry promise, and sleety rain pounded and rattled against the glass, sliding down it to gather in crusty waves in the corners of the panes. "I really would have preferred to stay home myself, all things considered," he added.

"I'm afraid I didn't have that option." She smiled charmingly at him. "I've got quite a few things to do over the next few five-days. If I started letting my schedule slip, I'd never get them done."

"I can believe that," he said, and he meant it.

The House of Qwentyn was by any measure the largest, wealthiest, and most powerful banking house in the Republic of Siddarmark and had been for generations. It hadn't gotten that way by accident, and a man as young as Owain Qwentyn wouldn't have held his present position, family connections or no, if he hadn't demonstrated his fitness for it. He'd been trusted with some of the house's most sensitive accounts for the last five years, which had exposed him to some fascinating financial strategists, yet Aivah Pahrsahn was probably the most intriguing puzzle yet to come his way.

Her primary accounts with the House of Qwentyn had been established over two decades ago, although he wouldn't have said she could possibly be a day past thirty-five, and her balance was enviable. In fact, it was a lot better than merely "enviable," if he wanted to be accurate. Coupled with her long established holdings in real estate and farmland, her investments in half a dozen of the Republic's biggest granaries and mining enterprises, and her stake in several of Siddar City's most prosperous merchant houses, that balance made her quite possibly the wealthiest woman Owain had ever met. Yet those transactions and acquisitions had been executed so gradually and steadily over the years, and spread between so many apparently separate accounts, that no one had noticed just how wealthy she was becoming. And no member of the House of Qwentyn had ever met her, either; every one of her instructions had arrived by mail. By *courier,* in point of fact, and not even via the Church's semaphore system or even wyvern post.

It had all been very mysterious when Owain finally looked at her accounts as a whole for the first time. He might not have noticed her even now if the somnolent, steady pace of her transactions hadn't suddenly become so much more active. Indeed, they'd become almost hectic, including a series of heavy transfers of funds since the . . . difficulties with Charis had begun, yet despite the many years she'd been a customer of his house, no one seemed to know where she'd come from in the first place. Somewhere in the Temple Lands, that much was obvious, yet where and how remained unanswered questions, and the House of Qwentyn, for all its discretion, was accustomed to knowing everything there was to know about its clients.

But not in this case. She'd presented all the necessary documentation to establish her identity on her arrival, and there was no question of her authority over those widespread accounts. Yet she'd simply appeared in Siddar a month or so ago, stepping into the capital city's social and financial life as if she'd always been there. She was beautiful, poised, obviously well educated, and gracious, and a great many of the social elite knew her (or weren't prepared to admit they *didn't* know Polite Society's latest adornment, at any rate), but Owain had been unable to nail down a single hard fact about her past life, and the air of mystery which clung to her only made her more fascinating.

"I've brought the list of transactions with me," she said now, reaching into her purse and extracting several sheets of paper. She extended them across the table to him, then sat back sipping her chocolate while he unfolded them and ran his eyes down the lines of clean, flowing script.

Those eyes widened, despite his best efforts to conceal his surprise, as he read. He turned the first page and examined the second just as carefully, and his surprise segued into something else. Something tinged with alarm.

He read the third and final sheet, then folded them back together, laid them on the tabletop, and looked at her intently.

"Those are . . . an extraordinary list of transactions, Madam Pahrsahn," he observed, and she startled him with a silvery little chuckle.

"I believe you'll rise high in your house's service, Master Qwentyn," she told him. "What you're really wondering is whether or not I'm out of my mind, although you're far too much the gentleman to ever actually say so."

"Nonsense," he replied. "Or, at least, I'd never go that far. I do wonder how carefully you've considered some of this, though." He leaned forward to tap the folded instructions. "I've studied the records of all your investment moves since our House has represented you, Madam. If you'll forgive my saying so, these instructions represent a significant change in your established approach. At the very least, they expose you to a much greater degree of financial risk."

"They also offer the potential for a very healthy return," she pointed out.

"Assuming they prosper," he pointed out in response.

"I believe they will," she said confidently.

He started to say something else, then paused, regarding her thoughtfully. Was it possible she knew something even he didn't?

"At the moment," he said after a minute or two, "the shipping arrangements you're proposing to invest in are being allowed by both the Republic and Mother Church. That's subject to change from either side with little or no notice, you realize. And if that happens you'll probably—no, almost certainly—lose your entire investment."

"I'm aware of that," she said calmly. "The profit margin's great enough to recoup my entire initial investment in no more than five months or so, however. Everything after that will be pure profit, even if the 'arrangements' should ultimately be disallowed. And my own read of the . . . decision-making process within the Temple, let us say, suggests no one's going to be putting any pressure on the Republic to interfere with them. Not for quite some time, at any rate."

She'd very carefully not said anything about "the Group of Four," Owain noticed. Given the fact that she clearly came from the Temple Lands herself, however, there was no doubt in his mind about what she was implying.

"Do you have any idea how long 'quite some time' might be?" he asked.

"Obviously, that's bound to be something of a guessing game," she replied in that same calm tone. "Consider this, however. At the moment, only the Republic and the Silkiahans are actually succeeding in paying their full tithes to Mother Church. If these 'arrangements' were to be terminated, that would no longer be the case." She shrugged. "Given the obvious financial strain of the Holy War, especially in light of that unfortunate business in the Markovian Sea, it seems most unlikely Vicar Rhobair and Vicar Zahmsyn are going to endanger their strongest revenue streams."

He frowned thoughtfully. Her analysis made a great deal of sense, although the financial and economic stupidity which could have decreed something like the embargo on Charisian trade in the first place didn't argue for the Group of Four's ability to recognize logic when it saw it. On the other hand, it fitted quite well with some of the things his grandfather Tymahn had said. Although. . . .

"I think you're probably right about that, Madam," he said. "However, I'm a bit more leery about some of these other investments."

"Don't be, Master Qwentyn," she said firmly. "Foundries are always good investments in . . . times of uncertainty. And according to my sources, all three of these are experimenting with the new cannon-casting techniques. I realize they wouldn't dream of putting the new guns into *production* without Mother Church's approval, but I feel there's an excellent chance that approval will be forthcoming, especially now that the Navy of God needs to replace so many ships."

Owain's eyes narrowed. If there was one thing in the entire world of which he was totally certain it was that the Church of God Awaiting would never permit the Republic of Siddarmark to begin casting the new model artillery. Not when the Council of Vicars in its role as the Knights of the Temple Lands had been so anxious for so long over the potential threat the Republic posed to the Temple Lands' eastern border. Only a fool, which no member of the House of Qwentyn was likely to be, could have missed the fact that Siddarmark's foundries were the only ones in either Haven or Howard which had received *no* orders from the Navy of God's ordnance officers. Foodstuffs and ship timbers, coal and coke and iron ore for other people's foundries, even ironwork to build warships in other realms, yes; artillery, no.

Yet Madam Pahrsahn seemed so serenely confident. . . .

"Very well, Madam." He bent his head in a courteous, seated bow. "If these are your desires, it will be my honor to carry them out for you."

"Thank you, Master Qwentyn," she said with another of those charming smiles. Then she set her cup and saucer back on the table and rose. "In that case, I'll bid you good afternoon and get out of your way."

He stood with a smile of his own and escorted her back to the office door. A footman appeared with her heavy winter coat, and he saw an older woman, as plain as Madam Pahrsahn was lovely, waiting for her.

Owain personally assisted her with her coat, then raised one of her slender hands—gloved, now—and kissed its back once more.

"As always, a pleasure, Madam," he murmured.

"And for me, as well," she assured him, and then she was gone.

▼ ▼ ▼

"So what do you make of Madam Pahrsahn, Henrai?" Greyghor Stohnar asked as he stood with his back to a roaring fireplace, toasting his posterior.

"Madam Pahrsahn, My Lord?" Lord Henrai Maidyn, the Republic of Siddarmark's Chancellor of the Exchequer, sat in a window seat, nursing a tulip-shaped brandy glass as he leaned back against the paneled wall of the council chamber. Now he raised his eyebrows interrogatively, his expression innocent.

"Yes, you know, the mysterious Madam Pahrsahn." The elected ruler of the Republic smiled thinly at him. "The one who appeared so suddenly and with so little warning? The one who floats gaily through the highest reaches of Society . . . and hobnobs with Reformist clergymen? Whose accounts are personally handled by Owain Qwentyn? Whose door is always open to poets, musicians, milliners, dressmakers . . . and a man who looks remarkably like the apostate heretic and blasphemer Zhasyn Cahnyr? That Madam Pahrsahn."

"Oh, *that* Madam Pahrsahn!"

Maidyn smiled back at the Lord Protector. Here in the Republic of Siddarmark, the Chancellor of the Exchequer was also in charge of little matters like espionage.

"Yes, that one," Stohnar said, his tone more serious, and Maidyn shrugged.

"I'm afraid the jury's still out, My Lord. Some of it's obvious, but the rest is still sufficiently obscure to make her *very* interesting. She's clearly from the Temple Lands, and I think it's equally clear her sudden appearance here has something to do with Clyntahn's decision to purge the vicarate. The question, of course, is precisely *what* it has to do with that decision."

"You think she's a wife or daughter who managed to get out?"

"Possibly. Or even a mistress." Maidyn shrugged again. "The amount of cash and all those deep investments she had tucked away here in Siddar were certainly big enough to represent someone important's escape fund. It could have been one of the vicars who saw the ax coming, I suppose, although whoever it was must have been clairvoyant to see *this* coming." He grimaced distastefully. "If someone did see a major shipwreck ahead, though, whoever it was might have put it under a woman's name in an effort to keep Clyntahn from sniffing it out."

"But you don't think that's what it is," Stohnar observed.

"No, I don't." Maidyn passed the brandy glass under his nose, inhaling its bouquet, then looked back at the Lord Protector. "She's too decisive. She's moving too swiftly now that she's here." He shook his head. "No, she's got a well-defined agenda in mind, and whoever she is, and wherever she came from originally, she's acting on her own now—for herself, not as anyone's public front."

"But what in God's name is she *doing*?" Stohnar shook his head. "I agree her sudden arrival's directly related to Clyntahn's purge, but if that's the case, I'd expect her to keep a low profile like the others."

The two men looked at one another. They'd been very careful to insure that neither of them learned—officially— about the refugees from the Temple Lands who'd arrived so quietly in the Republic. Most of them had continued onward, taking passage on Siddarmarkian-registry merchant vessels which somehow had Charisian crews . . . and homeports. By now they must have reached or nearly reached the Charisian Empire and safety, and personally, Stohnar wished them well. He wished *anyone* that unmitigated bastard Clyntahn wanted dead well.

A handful of the refugees, however, had remained in Siddarmark, seeking asylum with relatives or friends. At least two of them had found shelter with priests Stohnar was reasonably certain nourished Reformist tendencies of their own. All of them, though, had done their very best to disappear as tracelessly as possible, doing absolutely nothing which might have attracted attention to them.

And then there was Aivah Pahrsahn.

"I doubt she'd spend so much time gadding about to the opera and the theater if it wasn't part of her cover," Maidyn said after a moment. "And it makes a sort of risky sense, if she *is* up to something certain people wouldn't care for. High visibility is often the best way to avoid the attention of people looking for surreptitious spies lurking in the shadows.

"As to what she might be up to that the Group of Four wouldn't like, there are all sorts of possibilities. For one thing, she's investing heavily in the Charisian trade, and according to Tymahn, her analysis of why Clyntahn's letting us get away with it pretty much matches my own. Of course, we could both be wrong about that. What I find more interesting, though, are her decision to buy into Hahraimahn's new coking ovens and her investments in foundries. Specifically in the foundries Daryus has been so interested in."

Lord Daryus Parkair was Seneschal of Siddarmark, which made him both the government minister directly responsible for the Army and also that Army's commanding general. If there was anyone in the entire Republic who Zhaspahr Clyntahn trusted even less (and hated even more) than Greyghor Stohnar, it had to be Daryus Parkair.

Parkair was well aware of that and fully reciprocated Clyntahn's hatred. He was also as well aware as Stohnar or Maidyn of all the reasons the Republic had been excluded from any of the Church's military buildup. Which was why he had very quietly and discreetly encouraged certain foundry owners to experiment—purely speculatively, of course—with how one might go about producing the new style artillery or the new rifled muskets. And as Parkair had pointed out to Maidyn just the other day, charcoal was becoming increasingly difficult to come by, which meant foundries could never have too much coke if they suddenly found themselves having to increase their output.

"I don't think even that would bother me," Stohnar replied. "Not if she wasn't sending so much money back *into* the Temple Lands. I'd be willing to put all of it down to shrewd speculation on her part, if not for that."

"It *is* an interesting puzzle, My Lord," Maidyn acknowledged. "She's obviously up to something, and my guess is that whatever it is, Clyntahn wouldn't like it. The question is whether or not he *knows* about it? I'm inclined to think not, or else the Inquisition would already have insisted we bring her in for a little chat. So then the question becomes whether or not the Inquisition is going to *become* aware of her? And, of course, whether or not we—as dutiful sons of Mother Church, desirous of proving our reliability to the Grand Inquisitor—should bring her to the Inquisition's notice ourselves?"

"I doubt very much that anything could convince Zhaspahr Clyntahn you and I are 'dutiful sons of Mother Church,' at least as *he* understands the term," Stohnar said frostily.

"True, only too true, I'm afraid." Maidyn's tone seemed remarkably free of regret. Then his expression sobered. "Still, it's a move we need to consider, My Lord. If the Inquisition becomes aware of her and learns we *didn't* bring her to its attention, it's only going to be one more log on the fire where Clyntahn's attitude is concerned."

"Granted." Stohnar nodded, waving one hand in a brushing-away gesture. "Granted. But if I'd needed anything to convince me the Group of Four is about as far removed from God's will as it's possible to get, Clyntahn's damned atrocities would've done it." He bared his teeth. "I've never pretended to be a saintly sort, Henrai, but if Zhaspahr Clyntahn's going to Heaven, I want to know where to buy my ticket to Hell now."

Maidyn's features smoothed into non-expression. Stohnar's statement wasn't a surprise, but the Lord Protector was a cautious man who seldom expressed himself that openly even among the handful of people he fully trusted.

"If Pahrsahn *is* conspiring against Clyntahn and his

hangers-on, Henrai," Stohnar went on, "then more power to her. Keep an eye on her. Do your best to make sure she's not doing something *we'd* disapprove of, but I want it all very tightly held. Use only men you fully trust, and be sure there's no trail of breadcrumbs from her to us. If the Inquisition does find out about her, I don't want them finding any indication we knew about her all along and simply failed to mention her to them. Is that clear?"

"Perfectly, My Lord." Maidyn gave him a brief, seated bow, then leaned back against the wall once more. "Although that does raise one other rather delicate point."

"Which is?"

"If we should happen to realize the Inquisition *is* beginning to look in her direction, do we warn her?"

Stohnar pursed his lips, unfocused eyes gazing at something only he could see while he considered the question. Then he shrugged.

"I suppose that will depend on the circumstances," he said then. "Not detecting her or mentioning her to the Inquisition is one thing. Warning her—and being *caught* warning her—is something else. And you and I both know that if we do warn her and she's caught anyway, in the end, she *will* tell the Inquisitors everything she knows." He shook his head slowly. "I wish her well. I wish *anyone* trying to make Clyntahn's life miserable well. But we're running too many risks of our own as it is. If there's a way to warn her anonymously, perhaps yes. But if there isn't, then I'm afraid she'll just have to take her chances on her own."

. V .

King's Harbor,
Helen Island,
Kingdom of Old Charis

Seagulls screamed and wyverns whistled shrilly, swooping and stooping above the broad expanse of King's Harbor. The winged inhabitants of Helen Island could hardly believe the largesse a generous nature had bestowed upon them. With so many ships cluttering up the waters, the supply of flotsam and plain old drifting garbage exceeded their most beatific dreams of greed, and they pounced upon it with gleeful abandon.

Oared barges, water hoys, sheer hulks, and a dozen other types of service craft made their ways in and around and through the press of anchored warships beneath that storm of wings. Newly mustered—and still mustering—ships' companies fell in on decks, raced up and down masts, panted under the unrelenting demands of their officers, and cursed their leather-lunged, hectoring petty officers with all the time-honored, tradition-sanctified fervency of new recruits the universe over, yet that represented barely a fraction of the human energy being expended throughout that broad harbor. Carpenters and shipfitters labored to repair lingering battle damage. Dockyard inspectors argued vociferously with working party supervisors. Pursers and clerks counted casks, barrels, crates, and bags of supplies and swore with weary creativity each time the numbers came up wrong and they had to start all over again. Sailmakers and chandlers, gunners and quartermasters, captains and midshipmen, chaplains and clerks, flag lieutenants and messengers were everywhere, all of them totally focused on the tasks at hand and utterly oblivious to all the clangor and rush going on about them. The sheer level of activity was staggering, even for the Imperial Charisian Navy, and the squeal of sheaves as heavy weights were lifted, the bellow of shouted orders, the thud of hammers and the clang of metal resounded across the water. Any casual observer might have been excused for assuming the scene was one of utter chaos and confusion, but he would have been wrong.

Amidst that much bustling traffic, one more admiral's barge was scarcely noticeable, Domynyk Staynair thought dryly, easing the peg which had replaced his lower right leg. It had been skillfully fitted, but there were still times the stump bothered him, especially when he'd been on his feet—well, *foot* and peg, he supposed—longer than he ought to have been. And "longer than he ought to have been" was a pretty good description of most of his working days since stepping into Bryahn Lock Island's shoes.

Shoe, *I suppose I mean,* he reflected mordantly, continuing his earlier thought, then looked up as the barge slid under the overhanging stern of one of the anchored galleons. Her original name—*Sword of God*—was still visible on her transom, although the decision had already been taken to rename her when she was commissioned into Charisian service. Of course, exactly what that new name would be was one of the myriad details which *hadn't* been decided upon just yet, wasn't it?

"In oars!" his coxswain shouted, and the oarsmen brought their long sweeps smartly inboard in a perfectly choreographed maneuver as he swung the tiller, sending them curving gracefully into *Sword of God*'s dense shadow and laying the barge alongside the larger ship.

"Chains!" the coxswain shouted, and the seaman perched in the bow reached out with his long boat hook and snagged the galleon's main chains with neat, practiced efficiency.

"Smartly done, Byrt," the admiral said.

"Thank'ee, My Lord," Byrtrym Veldamahn replied in a gratified tone. Rock Point wasn't known for bestowing empty compliments, but he *was* known for honest praise when a duty or an evolution was smartly performed.

The barge's other passengers remained seated as Rock

Point heaved himself upright. Tradition made the senior officer the last to board a small boat and the first to debark, and as a junior officer, Rock Point had subscribed to the theory that the tradition existed so that a tipsy captain or flag officer's dutiful subordinates could catch him when he tumbled back into the boat in a drunken heap. He'd changed his mind as he grew older and wiser (and more senior himself), but there might just be something to the catching notion in his own case, he reflected now. He'd actually learned to dance again, after a fashion at least, since losing his leg, but even a boat the size of his barge was lively underfoot, and he balanced carefully as he reached out for the battens affixed to the galleon's side.

If I had any sense, I'd stay right here on a thwart while they rigged a bo'sun's chair for me, he told himself dryly. *But I don't, so I'm not going to. If I fall and break my fool neck, it'll be no more than I deserve, but I'll be damned if they're going to hoist me aboard like one more piece of cargo!*

He reached up, caught one of the battens, balanced on his artificial leg while he got his left foot ready, then pushed himself upward. He could feel his subordinates watching him, no doubt poised to rescue him when his foolishness reaped the reward it so amply deserved. At least King's Harbor's water was relatively warm year-round, so if he missed the boat entirely he wasn't going to freeze . . . and as long as he didn't manage to get crushed between the barge and the galleon or pushed down under the turn of the bilge, he wouldn't drown, either. Not that he had any intention of allowing his illustrious naval career to be terminated quite that humiliatingly.

He heaved, and he'd always been powerfully muscled. Since the loss of his leg, his arms and shoulders had become even more powerful and they lifted him clear of the curtsying barge. He got the toe of his remaining foot onto another batten, clear of the barge's gunwale, then drew his peg up and wedged it carefully beside his foot before he reached upward once more. Climbing the side of a galleon had never been an easy task even for someone with the designed number of feet, and he felt himself panting heavily as he clambered up the battens.

This really isn't worth the effort, he thought, baring his teeth in a fierce grin, *but I'm too stubborn—and too stupid—to admit that to anyone. Besides, the day I stop doing this will be the day I stop being* able *to do it.*

He made it to the entry port and bo'sun's pipes squealed in salute as he hauled himself through it onto the deck of what had once been Bishop Kornylys Harpahr's flagship. If the truth be known, the identity of its previous owner was one of the reasons he'd selected it to become one of the first prizes to be commissioned into Charisian service.

That possibly ignoble (but profoundly satisfying) thought passed through his mind as the side boys came to attention and a short, compact officer in the uniform of a captain saluted.

"High Admiral, arriving!" the quartermaster of the watch announced, which still sounded a bit unnatural to Rock Point when someone applied the title to him.

"Welcome aboard, Sir," the captain said, extending his hand.

"Thank you, Captain Pruait." Rock Point clasped forearms with the captain, then stepped aside and turned to watch as three more officers climbed through the entry port in descending order of seniority.

The bo'sun's pipes shrilled again as another captain, this one on the tall side, stepped aboard, followed by Commander Mahndrayn and Lieutenant Styvyn Erayksyn, Rock Point's flag lieutenant. Erayksyn was about due for promotion to lieutenant commander, although Rock Point hadn't told him that yet. The promotion was going to bring a sea command with it, of course. That was inevitable, given the Imperial Charisian Navy's abrupt, unanticipated expansion. Even without that, Erayksyn amply deserved the reward of which every sea officer worth his salt dreamed, and Rock Point was pleased for young Styvyn. Of course, it was going to be a pain in the ass finding and breaking in a replacement who'd suit the high admiral half as well.

Pruait greeted the other newcomers in turn, then stepped back, sweeping both arms to indicate the broad, busy deck of the ship. It looked oddly unfinished to any Charisian officer's eyes, given the bulwarks' empty rows of gunports. There should have been a solid row of carronades crouching squatly in those ports, but this galleon had never carried them. In fact, that had quite a bit to do with Rock Point's current visit.

The most notable aspect of the ship's upper works, however, were the bustling work parties. Her original masts had been retained, but they were being fitted with entirely new yards on the Charisian pattern, and brand-new sails had already been sent up the foremast, and more new canvas was ascending the mainmast as Rock Point watched. Her new headsails had already been rigged, as well, and painting parties on scaffolding slung over her side were busy converting her original gaudy paint scheme into the utilitarian black-and-white of the Imperial Charisian Navy.

"As you can see, High Admiral, we've more than enough to keep us busy until you and Master Howsmyn get around to sending us our new toys," Pruait said. "I'd really like to get her coppered, as well, but Sir Dustyn's . . . explained to me why that's not going to happen."

The captain rolled his eyes, and Rock Point chuckled. Unlike the ICN's purpose built war galleons, the Navy of God's ships used iron nails and bolts throughout, which made it effectively impossible to sheath their lower hulls in copper. Rock Point wasn't about to try to explain electrolysis to Captain Pruait, and he was confident Sir Dustyn Olyvyr's "explanation" had been heavy on "because it won't *work*, damn it!" and considerably lighter on the theory.

"We may have to bite the bullet and go ahead and dry-dock her eventually to pull the underwater iron and refasten her with copper and bronze so we *can* copper her," he said out loud. "Don't go getting your hopes up!" he cautioned as Pruait's eyes lit. "It'd cost a fortune, given the number of prizes we're talking about, and Baron Ironhill and I are already fighting tooth and nail over the Navy's budget. But if we're going to keep her in commission, it'd probably be cheaper in the long run to protect her against borers rather than replacing half her underwater planking every couple of years. And that doesn't even consider how much slower the prizes are going to be without it."

Pruait nodded in understanding. The recent Charisian innovation of coppering warships below the waterline did more than simply protect their timbers from the shellfish who literally ate their way (often with dismaying speed) into the fabric of a ship. That would have been more than enough to make the practice worthwhile, despite its initial expense, but it also enormously reduced the growth of weeds and the other fouling which increased water resistance and *decreased* speed. The swiftness Charisian ships could maintain was a powerful tactical advantage, but if Rock Point was forced to operate coppered and uncoppered ships together, he'd lose most of it, since a fleet was no faster than its slowest unit.

On the other hand, Rock Point thought, *we've captured enough ships that we could make up entire squadrons— hell, fleets!—of ships without coppered bottoms. They'd be slower than other squadrons, but all the ships in them would have the same basic speed and handling characteristics. Still wouldn't do anything about the borers, though. And the truth is, these prize ships are better built in a lot of ways than ours are, so it'd make a lot of sense— economically, not just from a military perspective—to take care of them. The* designs *aren't as good as the ones Olyvyr's come up with, but the Temple obviously decided it might as well pay for the very best. We had to use a lot of green wood; they used only the best ship timbers, and they took long enough building the damned things they could leave them standing in the frame to season properly before they planked them.*

Charis hadn't had that option. They'd needed ships as quickly as they could build them, and one of the

consequences was that some of those improperly seasoned ships were already beginning to rot. It was hardly
a surprise—they'd known it was coming from the
beginning—and it wasn't anything they couldn't handle
so far. But over the next couple of years (assuming they
had a couple of years available) at least half of their
original war galleons were going to require major rebuilding or complete replacement, and wasn't that going
to be fun?

"While you and Sir Dustyn were discussing why you're
not going to get coppered, did you happen to discuss armaments and weights with him?" Rock Point asked out
loud, cocking his head at Pruait.

"Yes, Sir." Pruait nodded. "According to his weight
calculations, we can replace the original upper deck long
guns with thirty-pounder carronades on a one-for-one
basis without putting her overdraft or hurting her stability. Or we can replace them on a two-for-three basis with
fifty-seven-pounders. If we do that, though, we'll have to
rebuild the bulwarks to relocate the gunports. And he's
less confident of her longitudinal strength than he'd really like; he's inclined to go with the heavier carronades
but concentrate them closer to midships to reduce weights
at the ends of the hull and try to head off any hogging
tendencies."

"I see."

Rock Point turned, facing aft towards one of the distinctly non-Charisian features of the ship's design. While
the towering forecastle and aftercastle which had been
such a prominent feature of galley design had been omit-
ted, *Sword of God* was still far higher aft than a Charisian galleon because she boasted a poop deck *above* the
quarterdeck. It was narrow, and the additional height
probably made the ship considerably more leewardly than
she would have been without it, but it was also a feature
of all of the Navy of God's galleon designs, so the Temple
presumably thought it was worth it. Rock Point wasn't at
all certain he agreed with the Church, but he wasn't certain he *disagreed*, either.

"Did the two of you discuss cutting her down aft?" he asked, twitching his head in the poop deck's direction.

"Yes, Sir, we did." Pruait followed the direction of the high admiral's gaze and shrugged. "Cutting her down to quarterdeck level would reduce topweight. That would probably help her stability at least a bit, and Sir Dustyn's of the opinion it would make her handier, as well. But he doesn't think the weight reduction would have any significant effect on the weight of guns she could carry, and to be frank, I'm of the opinion that the overhead protection from enemy musket fire for the men at the wheel is probably worth any handling penalty. Although," he admitted, "some of the other new captains question whether the protection's worth the reduced visibility for the helmsmen."

"I think that's one of those things that could be argued either way," Rock Point said thoughtfully. "And it's probably going to come down to a matter of individual opinions, in the end. Funny how sea officers tend to be that way, isn't it?" He smiled briefly. "But since we don't have time to do it now, anyway, it looks like you're going to get the opportunity to experiment with that design feature after all."

Pruait didn't exactly look heartbroken, the high admiral noted, and shook his head. Then he indicated the other officers who'd followed him aboard.

"I know you've met Lieutenant Erayksyn," he said, "but I don't know if you've met Captain Sahlavahn and Commander Mahndrayn?"

"I've never met the Commander, Sir," Pruait admitted, nodding to Mahndrayn courteously as he spoke. "Captain Sahlavahn and I have known each other for quite some time now, though." He extended his hand to the captain and they clasped forearms. "I haven't seen you in too long, Trai."

"Baron Seamount and Baron Ironhill have been keeping me just a little busy, Tym," Sahlavahn replied wryly. "Oh, and High Admiral Rock Point, too, now that I think about it."

"The reward for doing a difficult job well is to be ordered to turn around and do something harder," High Rock observed. "And no good deed goes unpunished." He fluttered his right hand in a waving away gesture. "And other clichés along those lines."

"I believe I've heard something to that effect before, Sir," Pruait acknowledged, then looked back at Sahlavahn, and his expression sobered. "How's your sister, Trai?"

"As well as can be expected." Sahlavahn shrugged and waved at Mahndrayn. "I think Urvyn's actually had a letter from her since I have, though."

"I got one a couple of five-days ago," Mahndrayn acknowledged. He and Sahlavahn were second cousins, although Sahlavahn was more than ten years his senior, and Mahndrayn had always been close to Sahlavahn's younger sister, Wynai. "From what she has to say, things are getting pretty damned tense in the Republic, but there's no way she's going to convince Symyn to relocate to Charis." He shook his head. "Apparently he's making money hand-over-fist at the moment, and even though he's just about the most rabidly Siddarmarkian Siddarmarkian you're ever going to meet, his family does come from the Temple Lands. His various aunts and uncles 'back home' are already pissed off at him for living in the Charisian Quarter in Siddar City; Langhorne only knows what they'd say if they realized how enthusiastically he was helping violate Clyntahn's stupid embargo!"

Pruait snorted in understanding, and Rock Point reclaimed control of the conversation.

"Commander Mahndrayn's here in his role as liaison between Baron Seamount and Master Howsmyn," he said, "and Captain Sahlavahn was a member of Baron Seamount's Ordnance Board. He's been promoted to other duties since then—in fact, he's assumed command of the Hairatha powder mill—but he's still thoroughly familiar with most of our usual ordnance concerns, and he happens to have sailed down from Big Tirian for a conference with the Baron. So I thought I'd bring both of them along."

"I see, Sir," Pruait said with a nod. "And I'm glad to see them, because frankly, I'm not sure what our best solution is."

Rock Point scowled in agreement.

In many ways, the problem came under the heading of "an embarrassment of riches," he thought once more. The prize ships they'd captured carried literally thousands of artillery pieces, although a lot of those guns, especially the ones from Harchongian foundries, left a lot to be desired. The bronze pieces were probably acceptably safe; he wouldn't have trusted a Harchongian *iron* gun with a full powder charge if his life had depended upon it.

The Temple Lands' foundries had done a better job, and they'd also cast almost exclusively bronze guns. He wasn't overly concerned about *those* guns from a safety standpoint, but none of them used the same shot as the standard Charisian pieces, which meant no Charisian ammunition would fit them. Their smaller bores also meant their shot were lighter and less destructive, of course, which was another consideration.

"For the moment, we're going to leave you with your present gundeck guns," the high admiral said. "I know it's not an ideal solution, but in addition to all of the artillery pieces, we've captured several hundred thousand round shot for them. We're not going to have the manpower to put all the prize ships into commission anytime soon, whatever we'd like to do, so what we're going to do in the short term is to raid the shot lockers of the ships we can't man for ammunition for the ships we *can* man—like yours, Captain Pruait."

"I see, Sir."

It would have been unfair to call Pruait's tone unhappy, but he obviously wasn't delirious with joy, either, Rock Point observed.

"I said that's what we're going to do in the *short term*, Captain," he said, and smiled at Pruait's expression. "Exactly what we decide to do in the long term is going to have to wait until Master Howsmyn, Baron Seamount, and Commander Mahndrayn have had the opportunity to kick the question around for a while. To be honest, we've captured enough guns that it might very well make sense to begin casting shot to fit them. On the other hand, Master Howsmyn's production lines are all set up around our standard shot sizes. And then there's the question of what we do about *shells* for non-standard bore sizes. Do we manufacture shells for the captured guns, too?"

"How much of a problem would that present, High Admiral?" Pruait asked. Rock Point raised an eyebrow, and the captain shrugged. "I don't really know very much about these new 'shells,' Sir," he admitted. "I've talked about them with as many of the officers who were with you and High Admiral Lock Island in the Markovian Sea as I could, but that's not the same thing as really understanding them or how they differ from solid shot in terms of manufacture."

"I'm afraid you're hardly alone in that," Rock Point said wryly. "It was all very closely held before we were forced to commit the new weapons to action. Even Captain Sahlavahn and the Ordnance Board were left in the dark, as a matter of fact. Baron Seamount, the Experimental Board, and Master Howsmyn and a handful of his artisans did all the real work on them.

"And in answer to your question, Captain Pruait, I don't have the foggiest notion how much of a problem it would be to manufacture shells to fit the captured guns. Commander Mahndrayn and I will be leaving shortly to go discuss that very point with Master Howsmyn. We'll drop Captain Sahlavahn off at Big Tirian on our way, but I wanted to have his expertise available for our discussion here before we left."

"I'm afraid it's going to be mostly *background* expertise, Tym," Sahlavahn said dryly. "As the High Admiral says, I actually know relatively little about the exploding shells even now. I understand"—his tone got even dryer—"that I'm going to be learning more shortly, though. Baron Seamount tells me we're going to be filling quite a few shells, and the Hairatha Mill's going to be called upon to provide the powder for most of them."

"Oh, we'll be filling a *lot* of them, all right, Captain," Rock Point assured him with a hungry smile. "We're going to have a use for them sometime soon now. And we're counting on that efficiency of yours to help smooth out some of the bottlenecks to make sure we've got them when we need them."

Sahlavahn nodded. Although he'd commanded a galley under King Haarahld at the Battle of Darcos Sound, he'd served strictly in shoreside appointments since. He was nowhere near the gifted technocrat his younger cousin, Mahndrayn, had proven to be, however. In fact, he was inclined in the opposite direction, with a conservative bent that was occasionally frustrating to his superiors. But if it was occasionally frustrating, it was far more often valuable, the sort of conservatism that had an irritating, maddening ability to point out the flaws in the latest and greatest brilliant inspiration of his more innovative fellows. Even more to the point, he was at least as gifted as an administrator as Mahndrayn was as an innovator. The commander would have been hopelessly ill suited for the task of commanding the Hairatha powder mill on Big Tirian Island. His mind worked in leaps and jumps, thriving on intuition and incessantly questioning the known and accepted in pursuit of the unknown and the unconventional. Sahlavahn, on the other hand, had already expedited three production bottlenecks in the Imperial Charisian Navy's third-largest gunpowder production center by approaching them from his usual pragmatic, unflappable, *conservative* perspective.

"The main point," Rock Point continued, striding aft towards *Sword of God*'s poop deck as he spoke, "is to provide each of the ships with the most effective armament we can in the shortest time frame. At the moment, I'm thinking in terms of a work in progress in which we'll go immediately to an effective 'conventional' armament without worrying about explosive shells. That's what I meant about a short-term solution, Captain Pruait.

"The next stage of the work in progress will be to provide all of you with appropriate carronades. At this point, probably the thirty-pounders, since that won't require us to relocate gunports. And we can provide them with the same explosive shells the long thirties fire, which will give you a shell-firing capability at shorter ranges. Eventually, though, we're going to have to decide whether to melt down the captured guns and recast them as standard thirty-pounders so your entire armament can use the standardized shells, or to produce molds to cast shells to fit their existing bores."

He reached the taffrail and leaned on it, bracing his arms against it while he gazed out across the harbor. He stood for a moment, breathing the salt air deep, then turned back to Pruait, Sahlavahn, Mahndrayn, and Erayksyn.

"Suppose we do this Navy fashion," he said and turned a broad smile on Mahndrayn. "Since Styvyn doesn't know any more about the technical aspects of this than I do, we'll let him sit this one out. But that makes *you* the junior officer present with something to contribute, Commander Mahndrayn. Which means you get the opportunity to express your views first, before any of us crotchety seniors get out there and express something that might cause you to change your mind or not suggest something you think might piss one of us off. Of course, I've observed how . . . inhibited your imagination gets under these circumstances, but I believe you'll manage to bear up under the strain."

Pruait chuckled. Sahlavahn, on the other hand, laughed out loud, and Mahndrayn smiled back at the high admiral.

"I'll do my best, Sir," he said.

"I know you will, Commander." Rock Point turned to brace the small of his back against the taffrail, folded his arms across his chest, and cocked his head. "And on that note, why don't you begin?"

Archbishop's Palace,
City of Tellesberg,
Kingdom of Old Charis

Winter in Tellesberg was very different from winter in the Temple Lands, Paityr Wylsynn reflected as he stepped gratefully into the shaded portico of Archbishop Maikel's palace. Freezing to death wasn't much of an issue here. Indeed, the hardest thing for him to get used to when he'd first arrived had been the fierce, unremitting sunlight, although the climate did get at least marginally cooler this time of year than it was in summer. The locals took the heat in stride, however, and he loved the exotic sights and sounds, the tropical fruits, the brilliant flowers, and the almost equally brilliantly colored wyverns and birds. For that matter, he'd acclimated well enough even to the heat that the thought of returning to Temple Lands' snow and sleet held little allure.

Especially these days, he thought grimly. *Especially these days.*

"Good morning, Father," the senior of the guardsmen in the white-and-orange of the archbishop's service said.

"Good morning, Sergeant," Paityr replied, and the other members of the guard detachment nodded to him without further challenge. Not because they weren't fully alert—the attempt to assassinate Maikel Staynair in his own cathedral had put a conclusive end to any complacency they might once have felt—but because they'd seen him here so often.

And I'm not precisely the easiest person to mistake for someone else, either, I suppose, he reflected wryly, looking down at the purple sleeve of his cassock with its sword and flame badge. *I doubt there are half a dozen Schuelerites left in the entire Old Kingdom by now, and most of them are Temple Loyalists hiding in the deepest holes they can find. Besides,* I'd *stand out even if I were a Bédardist or a Pasqualate.*

"Welcome, Father Paityr. Welcome!"

The solemn, senior, and oh-so-superior servants who'd cluttered up the Archbishop's Palace under its previous owners had become a thing of the past. The palace was vast enough to require a fairly substantial staff, but Archbishop Maikel preferred a less supercilious environment. Alys Vraidahn had been his housekeeper for over thirty years, and he'd taken her with him to his new residence, where she'd proceeded to overhaul the staff from top to bottom in remarkably short order. A brisk, no-nonsense sort of person, Mistress Vraidahn, but as warmhearted as she was shrewd, and she'd adopted Paityr Wylsynn as yet another of the archbishop's unofficial sons and daughters. Now she swept him a curtsy, then laughed as he leaned forward and planted a kiss on her cheek.

"Now then!" she scolded, smacking him on the shoulder. "Don't you be giving an old woman the kind of notions she shouldn't be having over a young, unattached fellow such as yourself!"

"Ah, if only I could!" he sighed. He shook his head mournfully. "I'm not very good at darning my own socks," he confided.

"And are you saying that idle layabout Master Ahlwail can't do that just fine?" she challenged skeptically.

"Well, yes, I suppose he can. Poorly," Paityr said, shamelessly maligning his valet's sewing skills as he hung his head and looked as pitiable as possible. "But he's not a very good cook, you know," he added, actually getting his lower lip to quiver.

"Comes of being a foreigner," she told him, eyes twinkling. "Not but what you don't look like he's managed to keep a little meat on your bones." Paityr sniffed, looking as much like his starving seminarian days as he could manage, and she shook her head. "Oh, all right. All right! You come around to my kitchen before you leave. I'll have a little something for you to take back to your pantry."

"Bless you, Mistress Ahlys," Paityr said fervently, and she laughed again. Then she turned her head and spotted one of the footmen.

"Hi, Zhaksyn! Run and tell Father Bryahn Father Paityr's here to see His Eminence!"

Anything less like the protocol in a typical archbishop's residence would have been all but impossible to imagine, Paityr thought. Of course, so would the footman in question. The lad couldn't be much older than sixteen or seventeen years old, his fuzzy beard (which needed shaving) just into the wispy silk stage, and his head came up like a startled prong buck's as the housekeeper called his name.

"Yes, Mistress Vraidahn!" he blurted and disappeared at a half run.

Not, Paityr noticed, without darting an even more startled look at him. And not just because of his Schuelerite cassock, he felt sure.

Paityr had always been more than a little amused by the typical mainlanders' perspective on the provincialism of the "out islands" as they dismissively labeled Charis, Chisholm, and Corisande. Tarot (which was the *least* cosmopolitan of the lot, in Paityr's opinion) got a pass from mainland prejudices because it was so close to the mainland. Still, the Tarot Channel was over three hundred miles wide, and more than one mainland wit had been heard to observe that good cooking and culture had both drowned trying to make the swim.

And what made that so amusing to him was that Charisians were actually far more cosmopolitan than the vast majority of Safeholdians . . . including just about every mainlander Paityr had ever met. The ubiquitous Charisian merchant marine guaranteed that there were very few sights Charisians hadn't seen, and not just their sailors, either. Every nationality and physical type in the entire world—including the Harchongese, despite the Harchong Empire's insularity—passed through Tellesberg eventually. Despite which, Paityr Wylsynn still got more than his share of double takes from those he met.

His fair skin had grown tanned enough over the years

of his service here in Old Charis to almost pass for a native Charisian, but his gray eyes and bright red hair—touched to even more fiery brilliance by all that sunlight—marked his northern birth forever. There'd been times he'd resented that, and there were other times it had simply made him feel very far from home, homesick for the Temple Lands and the place of his birth. These days he didn't feel homesick at all, however, which had more than a little to do with the reason for this visit.

"Paityr!" Father Bryahn Ushyr, Archbishop Maikel's personal secretary, walked briskly into the entry hall holding out his hand. The two of them were much of an age, and Paityr smiled as he clasped forearms with his friend.

"Thank you for fitting me into his schedule on such short notice, Bryahn."

"You're welcome, not that it was all that much of a feat." Ushyr shrugged. "You're higher on his list than a lot of people, and not just because you're his Intendant. It brightened his day when I told him you wanted to see him."

"Sure it did." Paityr rolled his eyes, and Ushyr chuckled. But the secretary also shook his head.

"I'm serious, Paityr. His eyes lit up when I told him you'd asked for an appointment."

Paityr waved one hand in a brushing away gesture, but he couldn't pretend Ushyr's words didn't touch him with a glow of pleasure. In a lot of ways, whether Archbishop Maikel realized it or not, Paityr had come to regard him even more as a second father since his own father's death.

Which is also *part of the reason for this visit*, he reflected.

"Well, come on," Ushyr invited, and beckoned for Paityr to accompany him to the archbishop's office.

▼ ▼ ▼

"Paityr, it's good to see you."

Maikel Staynair rose behind his desk, smiling broadly, and extended his hand. Paityr bent to kiss the archbishop's ring of office, then straightened, tucking both his own hands into the sleeves of his cassock.

"Thank you, Your Eminence. I appreciate your agreeing to see me on so little notice."

"Nonsense!" Staynair waved like a man swatting away an insect. "First, you're my Intendant, which means I'm always *supposed* to have time to see you." He grinned and pointed at the armchair facing his desk. "And, second, you're a lively young fellow who usually has something worth listening to, unlike all too many of the people who parade through this office on a regular basis."

"I do try not to bore you, Your Eminence," Paityr admitted, sitting in the indicated chair with a smile.

"I know, and I really shouldn't complain about the others." Staynair sat back down behind his desk and shrugged. "Most of them can't help it, and at least some of them have a legitimate reason for being here. Fortunately, I've become increasingly adroit at steering the ones who don't off for Bryahn to deal with, poor fellow."

The archbishop tipped back in his swivel chair, interlacing his fingers across his chest, and cocked his head to one side.

"And how are your mother and the rest of your family?" he asked in a considerably more serious tone.

"Well, Your Eminence. Or as well as anyone could be under the circumstances." Paityr twitched his shoulders. "We're all grateful to God and to Madam Ahnzhelyk and *Seijin* Merlin's friend for getting so many out of Clyntahn's grasp, but that only makes us more aware of what's happened in the Temple Lands. And I suppose it's a bit difficult for them—for all of us—not to feel guilty over having managed to get here when so many others didn't."

"That's a very human reaction." Staynair nodded. "And it's also a very irrational one. I'm sure you realize that."

"Oh, I do. For that matter, Lysbet and the others do, too. But, as you say, it's a very human reaction, Your Eminence. It's going to be a while before they manage to get past that, I'm afraid."

"Understandable. But please tell Madam Wylsynn my

office and I are at her disposal if she should have need of us."

"Thank you, Your Eminence." Paityr smiled again, gratefully. The offer wasn't the automatic formula it might have been coming from another archbishop, and he knew it.

"You're welcome, of course," Staynair said. "On the other hand, I don't imagine that's the reason you wanted to see me today?"

"No," Paityr admitted, gray eyes darkening. "No, it wasn't, Your Eminence. I've come to see you on a spiritual matter."

"A spiritual matter concerning what? Or should I say concerning *whom*?" Staynair's dark eyes were shrewd, and Paityr sat back in his chair.

"Concerning *me,* Your Eminence." He drew a deep breath. "I'm afraid my soul isn't as tranquil as it ought to be."

"You're scarcely unique in that, my son," Staynair pointed out somberly, swinging his chair from side to side in a slow, gentle arc. "All of God's children—or all of them whose minds work, at any rate—are grappling with questions and concerns more than sufficient to destroy their tranquility."

"I realize that, Your Eminence, but this is something that hasn't happened to me before. I'm experiencing doubt. Not just questions, not just uncertainty over the direction in which I ought to be going, but genuine *doubt*."

"Doubt over what?" Staynair asked, eyes narrowing. "Your actions? Your beliefs? The doctrine of the Church of Charis?"

"I'm afraid it's more fundamental than that, Your Eminence," Paityr admitted. "Of course I have the occasional evening when I lie awake wondering if it was my own hubris, my own pride in my ability to know better than Mother Church, that led me to obey Archbishop Erayk's instructions to remain here in Charis and work with you and His Majesty. I'm neither so stupid nor so self-righteous as to be immune to that sort of doubt, and I hope I never will be. And I can honestly say I've experienced very little doubt over whether or not the Church of Charis has a better understanding of the mind of God than that butcher Clyntahn and his friends. Forgive me for saying this, but you could scarcely have *less* understanding!" He shook his head. "No, what I'm beginning to doubt is whether or not I have a true vocation after all."

Staynair's chair was suddenly still and silence hovered in the office. Then the archbishop tilted his head to one side and pursed his lips.

"I imagine no priest is ever fully immunized against that question," he said slowly. "However clearly we may have been called by God, we remain mortals with all the weaknesses of any mortal. But I have to tell you, Father, that of all the priests I've known, I can think of none whose vocation seemed clearer to *me* than your own. I realize another's opinion is scarcely armor against one's own doubts, and the truth of a priest's vocation is ultimately between him and God, not him and anyone else. Despite that, I must tell you I can think of no one into whose hands I would be more willing to entrust God's work."

Paityr's eyes widened. He deeply admired and respected Maikel Staynair and he'd known Staynair was fond of him. That he'd become one of the archbishop's protégés. Yet Staynair's words—and especially the serious, measured tone in which they'd been spoken—had taken him by surprise.

"I'm honored, Your Eminence," he replied after a moment. "That means a great deal to me, especially coming from you. Yet the fact of my doubt remains. I'm no longer certain of my vocation, and can a true priest—one who had a true vocation to begin with—ever lose it?"

"What does the Office of Inquisition teach?" Staynair asked in reply.

"That a priest is a priest forever," Paityr responded. "That a true vocation can never be lost, else it was never a *true* vocation to begin with. But if that's true, Your Eminence, did I ever have that true vocation to begin with?"

"That *is* what the Inquisition teaches, but as you may have noticed," Staynair said a bit dryly, "I've found myself in disagreement with the Office of Inquisition on several minor doctrinal matters lately."

Despite Paityr's own concern and genuine distress, the archbishop's tone drew an unwilling chuckle out of him, and Staynair smiled. Then his expression turned serious once more.

"All humor notwithstanding, my son, I believe the Inquisition has been in error in many ways. You know where most of my points of disagreement with the Grand Inquisitor lie, and you know it's my belief that we serve a loving God who desires what's best for His children and also desires that those children come to Him in joyous love, not fear. I can't believe it's His will for us to be miserable, or to be crushed underfoot, or to be driven into His arms by the lash.

"You and I have differed on occasion on the extent to which the freedom of will and freedom of choice I believe are so critical to a healthy relationship with God may threaten to confuse and disorder our right understanding of God's will for us and for all of His world. Despite that, I've never doubted for a moment that you've looked upon the task of disciplining the children of Mother Church with the love and compassion a true parent brings to that duty. I've never seen a malicious act, or a capricious decision. Indeed, I've seen you deal patiently and calmly with idiots who would have driven one of the Archangels themselves into a frothing madness. And I've seen the unflinching fashion in which you've stood fast for the things in which you believe without ever descending into the sort of mental and spiritual arrogance which know that anyone who disagrees with them must be completely and unequivocally wrong. That's the priest I see when I consider whether or not you have a true vocation, Father Paityr, and I ask you to remember that it's the *Writ* which says a priest is a priest forever and the *Inquisition* which has *interpreted* that as meaning that a priest who loses his vocation was therefore never in fact a true priest at all. Search the *Writ* as you will, my son, but you will never find those words, that statement, anywhere in it."

He paused, letting silence lie over the two of them once more, yet Paityr knew the archbishop wasn't done yet. So he sat, waiting, and after a moment Staynair continued.

"I'm a Bédardist. My order knows more about the ways in which the human mind and the human spirit can hurt themselves than most of us wish we'd ever had to learn. There's no question that we can convince ourselves of literally anything we wish to believe, and there's also no question that we can be far more ruthless—far more cruel—in punishing ourselves than any other reasonable person would ever be. We can—and we *will*, my son, trust me in this—find innumerable ways in which to doubt and question and indict ourselves for things only we know about, supposed crimes only *we* realize were ever committed. There are times when that truly is a form of justice, but far more often it's a case of punishing the innocent. Or, at the very least, of punishing our own real or imagined misdeeds far more severely than we would ever punish anyone else for the same offense.

"I'm not going to tell you that's what you're doing. I could point out any number of factors in your life which could account for stress, for worry, for outrage, even for the need to punish yourself for surviving when your father and your uncle and so many people you've known all your life have been so cruelly butchered. I believe it would be completely valid to argue that all of those factors combined would be enough to push anyone into questioning his faith, and that's the basis of any true vocation, my son. Faith . . . and love.

"But I don't believe your faith *has* wavered." Staynair shook his head, tipping his chair further back. "I've seen no sign of it, and I know your love for your fellow children of God is as warm and vital today as it ever was. Still, even the most faithful and loving of hearts may not hold a true priest's vocation. And despite what the Office of Inquisition may have taught, I must tell you I've known men who I believe had true and burning vocations who *have* lost them. It can happen, however much we may wish it couldn't, and when it does those who have lost them are cruelest of all in punishing themselves for it. Deep inside, they believe not that they've lost their vocation, but that it was taken from them. That they proved somehow inadequate to the tasks God had appointed for them, and that because of that inadequacy and failure He stripped away that spark of Himself which had drawn them into this service in the joy of loving Him.

"Only it doesn't work that way, my son."

Staynair let his chair come forward, planting his elbows wide apart on his desk blotter and folding his hands while he leaned forward across them.

"God does not strip Himself away from anyone. The only way we can lose God is to walk away from Him. That is the absolute, central, unwavering core of my own belief . . . and of yours." He looked directly into Paityr's gray eyes. "Sometimes we can stumble, lose our way. Children often do that. But as a loving parent *always* does, God is waiting when we do, calling to us so that we can hear His voice and follow it home once more. The fact that a priest has lost his vocation to serve *as a priest* doesn't mean he's lost his vocation to be one of God's children. If you should decide that, in fact, you are no longer called to the priesthood, I will grant you a temporary easing of your vows while you meditate upon what it would then be best for you to do. I don't think that's what you need, but if *you* think so, you must be the best judge, and I'll go that far towards abiding by your judgment. I implore you, however, not to take an irrevocable step before that judgment is certain. And whatever you finally decide, know this—you are a true child of God, and whether it be as a priest or as a member of the laity, He has many tasks yet for you to do . . . as do I."

Paityr sat very still, and deep inside he felt a flicker of resentment, and that resentment touched the anger which was so much a part of him these days. It was like the breath of a bellows, fanning the fire, and that shamed him . . . which only made the anger perversely stronger. It was irrational of him to feel that way, and he knew it. It was also small-minded and childish, and he knew that, too. But he realized now that what he'd really wanted was for Staynair to reassure him that he couldn't possibly have lost his vocation. That when the *Writ* said a priest was a priest forever it meant a true vocation was just as imperishable as the Inquisition had always insisted it was.

And instead, the archbishop had given him this. Had given him, he realized, nothing but the truth and compassion and love . . . and a refusal to treat him as a child.

The silence stretched out, and then Staynair sat back in his chair once more.

"I don't know if this will make any difference to what you're thinking and feeling at this moment, my son, but you're not the only priest in this room who ever questioned whether or not he had a true vocation."

Paityr's eyes widened, and Staynair smiled crookedly.

"Oh, yes, there was a time—before you were born; I'm not as young as I used to be, you know—but there *was* a time when a very young under-priest named Maikel Staynair wondered if he hadn't made a horrible mistake in taking his vows. The things going on in his life were less cataclysmic than what you've experienced in the last few years, but they seemed quite cataclysmic enough for his purposes. And he was angry at God." Their eyes met once more, and Paityr felt a jolt go through his soul. "Angry at God the same way the most loving of children can be angry at his father or his mother if that father or mother seems to have failed him. Seems to have let terrible things happen when he didn't have to. That young under-priest didn't even realize he was angry. He simply thought he was . . . confused. That the world had turned out to be bigger and more complex than he'd thought it was. And because he'd been taught it was unforgivable to be angry at *God*, he internalized all that anger and aimed it at himself in the form of doubts and self-condemnation."

Paityr's jaw tightened as he felt the echo of that young Maikel Staynair's experience in himself. Until this moment, he wouldn't have thought Staynair could ever have felt what the archbishop was describing to him now. Maikel Staynair's faith and love burned with a bright, unwavering flame. That flame, that shakable inner serenity, was the reason he could walk into a hostile cathedral in a place like Corisande and reach out even to people who'd been prepared to hate and revile him as a heretic. Not only reach out to them but inspire them to reach back to *him* in response. It was who and what he *was*. How could a man like that, a *priest* like that, ever have been touched with the darkness and corrosion Paityr felt gnawing at his own soul?

"What . . . May I ask what that young under-priest did, Your Eminence?" he asked after a long, aching moment, and to his own surprise, he managed to smile. "I mean, it's obvious he managed to cope with it somehow after all."

"Indeed he did." Staynair nodded. "But he didn't do it by himself. He reached out to others. He shared his doubts and his confusion and learned to recognize the anger for what it was and to realize it's the people we love most—and who most love us—who can make us angriest of all. I wouldn't want to say"—the archbishop's smile became something suspiciously grin-like—"that he was a *stubborn* young man, but I suppose some people who knew him then might have leapt to that erroneous conclusion. For that matter, *some* people might actually think he's *still* a bit stubborn. Foolish of them, of course, but people can be that way, can't they?"

"I, ah, suppose they can, Your Eminence. Some of them, I mean."

"Your natural and innate sense of tact is one of the things I've always most admired in you, Father Paityr," Staynair replied. Then he squared his shoulders.

"All jesting aside, I needed help, and I think you could use some of that same help. For that matter, I think you're probably less pigheaded and stubborn about availing yourself of it than I was. As your Archbishop, I'm going to strongly suggest that before you do anything else, before you make any decisions, you retire for a retreat at the same monastery to which I retreated. Will you do that for me? Will you spend a few five-days thinking and contemplating and possibly seeing some truths you haven't seen before, or haven't seen as clearly as you'd thought you had?"

"Of course, Your Eminence," Paityr said simply.

"Very well. In that case, I'll send a message to Father Zhon at Saint Zherneau's and tell him to expect you."

. VII .

HMS *Dawn Star*, 58,
Hannah Bay,
and
Ducal Palace,
Carmyn,
Grand Duchy of Zebediah

It was even hotter than the first time he'd been to Hannah Bay, Merlin thought. And while that might be of primarily theoretical interest to a PICA, it was of rather more pressing relevance to the flesh-and-blood members of *Dawn Star*'s still breathing ship's company. Particularly to those—like Empress Sharleyan herself—who'd been born Chisholmians and not Old Charisians.

"Dear God," Sharleyan said, fanning herself as she stepped out onto the awning-shaded quarterdeck with Sergeant Seahamper, "you warned me it would be hot, Merlin, but *this*—!"

"I'll admit I didn't expect it to be quite this warm," Merlin said. "On the other hand, you *are* almost directly on the equator, Your Majesty."

"A point which has been drawn rather sharply to my attention," she replied tartly.

"At least you're not the only one suffering from it," Merlin offered helpfully, eliciting a glare of truly imperial proportions.

Crown Princess Alahnah had been a happier baby since the stormy weather had eased, but it would appear she had not yet developed her father's tolerance for warm temperatures. "Cranky" was a frail description of her current mood, as Sharleyan was better aware than most.

"Perhaps I'd better rephrase that, Your Majesty," he said, and heard something suspiciously like a chuckle from Seahamper's direction. He glanced at the grizzled sergeant, but Seahamper only smiled back at him blandly.

"Perhaps you had," Sharleyan agreed pointedly, reclaiming his attention from her personal armsman. "Unless *you'd* care to go see if you can get your goddaughter into a more cheerful mood yourself, that is."

"It's always my honor to undertake even the most difficult of tasks in your service, Your Majesty," Merlin replied with a bow. "*Impossible* tasks, however, are beyond the abilities even of *seijins*."

"Don't I know it!" Sharleyan said feelingly.

The empress walked to the rail and the officers and seamen whose station was the quarterdeck moved back to give her space as she stood gazing out across the bay's blue waters. They looked seductively cool as they sparkled and flashed in the relentless, brilliant sunlight, and she wished fervently that she could take advantage of that coolness. Unfortunately, she had other things to deal with, and her mouth tightened as she looked at the six Imperial Charisian Navy galleons anchored in company with *Dawn Star*. Twenty more galleons—transports flying the imperial banner—lay between them and shore, with lighters and longboats ferrying their cargo of Imperial Army troops ashore. She doubted very much that those reinforcements were going to be necessary, given Tohmys Symmyns' unpopularity with the people of Zebediah. In fact, she'd argued against bringing them along, but that wasn't an argument Cayleb or the Duke of Eastshare, the Army's commander, had been willing to entertain, and

Merlin had voted with them. Rather enthusiastically, in fact, if her memory served.

"I hope none of the Zebediahans are going to take the wrong message from this," she said now, quietly enough that only Merlin's ears could hear her.

"I'm not sure there *is* a wrong message they could take from it," he replied sub-vocally from behind her, and she smiled slightly as she heard his voice over the com earplug. "I think it's as important for the lesser nobility and the commoners to understand you and Cayleb aren't going to put up with any more nonsense as it is for any of Zebediah's more nobly born confidants to get the same message. Nobody in a place like Zebediah is going to stick his neck out in support of what may be a simply transitory regime. Unless they're pretty sure you plan to hang around—and to enforce the new rules—people are likely to keep their heads down. Especially when you add in the fact that coming out in favor of Charisian rule is going to get them on the wrong side of the Inquisition and Mother Church, as well."

"I know," she murmured back. "I just can't help thinking about Hektor's efforts. These people haven't had a lot of good experiences with foreign troops, Merlin."

"No," he agreed, enhanced vision watching the first squads of Army troops debarking onto Carmyn's wharves. "It's time we changed that, though, and Kynt is just the man to make a good start in that direction."

Sharleyan nodded. Kynt Clareyk, the Baron of Green Valley, was an ex-Marine. Although only a recent addition to the inner circle, he'd cherished his suspicions for some time where *Seijin* Merlin's role in the innovations which had made Charis' survival possible were concerned. He was also one of the new Imperial Army's most highly regarded officers. Even his Chisholmian-born fellows, who tended to regard Marines as excellent for boarding actions and smash and grab raids but fairly useless for extended campaigns, listened very carefully to anything Green Valley had to say.

"I can't help wishing we had something which more

immediately demanded his talents, though," she said after a moment. "Or perhaps I should say I hope nothing happens *here* which immediately demands his talents."

"Until we figure out how somebody with an army our size invades something the size of the mainland, I think this is probably the best use for his talents we're likely to find," Merlin said philosophically. "Thank God. For a while there I was afraid we might really need him in Corisande after all."

"That could still happen," Sharleyan pointed out.

"Not with Koryn Gahrvai and his father sitting on the situation," Merlin disagreed. "The only real chance Craggy Hill's lot had was to convince the Duke of Margo and the Temple Loyalists to support them against the Regency Council's 'traitorous ambition to replace our rightful Prince with their own tyrannical despotism in the service of traitors, blasphemers, and heretics.' When that appeal fell flat, I knew we had them. For now, at least."

"I wish you hadn't felt compelled to add the qualifier," she said dryly.

"To quote a truly ancient aphorism from Old Terra, 'Nothing's sure but death and taxes,' Your Majesty." Merlin smiled as the empress' straight, slender shoulders quivered with suppressed laughter, then cleared his throat.

"Excuse me, Your Majesty," he said out loud, "but I believe Master Pahskal is trying to attract your attention."

"Thank you, Merlin," she said, turning from the rail and smiling at the sandy-haired young midshipman who'd been shifting his weight uneasily from one foot to the other.

Faydohr Pahskal had just turned thirteen and he was the son of a family of Cherayth fishermen who'd never imagined he might come into such proximity of his queen and empress. He'd clearly been torn between whatever instructions he'd received from Captain Kahbryllo and an acute uncertainty over the wisdom of disturbing Empress Sharleyan when everyone else had obviously withdrawn to the far side of the quarterdeck to give her privacy.

"Should I assume the Captain's sent you with a message, Master Pahskal?" she asked with a smile.

"Ah, yes, Your Majesty. I mean, he has." Pahskal blushed hotly, although it was difficult to tell, thanks to how severely his fair skin had burned under the last couple of days' intense sunlight. "I mean," he continued, rushing the words a bit desperately, "Captain Kahbryllo sends his compliments and asks if you would be pleased to go ashore in about one hour, Your Majesty."

"That would suit me quite well, Master Pahskal," Sharleyan said gravely. "Thank you."

"You're welcome, Your Majesty!" Pahskal half blurted, touched his chest in salute, and dashed away, obviously relieved at having discharged his mission without being incinerated by the imperial disfavor.

"It's hard to believe Hektor was even younger than that at Darcos Sound," Sharleyan said, her smile turning a bit sad, and Merlin nodded.

"It is, although I doubt even Master Pahskal seems quite that young when it's simply a matter of life or death, Your Majesty."

"Am I really that terrifying?"

"To a thirteen-year-old?" Merlin laughed. "Your Majesty, the thought of facing you and Cayleb can turn strong men's knees to water. When a mere midshipman finds himself trapped between the doomwhale of his captain's instructions and the deep blue sea of an empress' potential unhappiness, the only thing he wants to be is somewhere else. Preferably as quickly as possible."

"Do you think he'll get over it eventually?" Sharleyan asked, trying very hard not to laugh herself.

"Oh, probably, Your Majesty. If he spends enough time in your vicinity, that is. In fact, I wouldn't be surprised if that was why Captain Kahbryllo sent him instead of coming to speak to you himself."

"You may be right," Sharleyan said. Then she snapped her fingers and gave her head a half-shake.

"What is it, Your Majesty?" Merlin asked.

"I should have asked young Pahskal to pass the word to Spynsair and Father Neythan, as well."

"I doubt Captain Kahbryllo forgot to include your personal clerk and your senior law master in the message queue, Your Majesty."

"No, but I should have made certain."

"Will it put your mind at ease if I go and personally bend all the sinister power of my fearsome reputation on making certain they got the word too, Your Majesty?" Merlin inquired, sweeping her a deep bow, and she giggled. Unmistakably, she giggled.

"I suppose that's not *really* necessary, Captain Athrawes," she said gravely, then sighed, her expression much less humorous than it had been a moment before. "And I also suppose I'm thinking about minor details as a way to avoid thinking about more momentous ones."

"It happens, Your Majesty," Merlin said with a small shrug. "But I've noticed you usually get around to facing up to all of them in the end. It seems to be a habit you share with Cayleb."

"I'd better!" she said in a considerably tarter tone. "And I imagine I'd better go and get ready for a boat trip, too. Under the circumstances, though, I think it would be wiser to leave Alahnah on board with Sairaih and Glahdys. Assuming of course"—she rolled her eyes—"a mere empress can convince Sairaih to stay aboard herself!"

▼ ▼ ▼

"Welcome, Your Majesty."

Baron Green Valley went down on one knee and bowed very formally as Sharleyan stepped into the throne room of the palace which had once belonged to Tohmys Symmyns, and fabric rustled as every other man—and the handful of women—followed his example. Only the sentries standing against the huge chamber's walls and the Imperial Guardsmen following at Sharleyan's heels remained upright. Especially the grim-faced sergeant at her side and the tall, sapphire-eyed captain at her back, with one hand resting lightly on the hilt of his sword. She rather doubted any of those kneeling Zebediahans were unaware of *his* presence, which was the main reason he was here, and she turned her head, regarding them all regally.

She let silence hover for almost a full minute, listening to a stillness so intense that the zinging flight of one of the local insects was clearly audible. Then, confident she'd made her point, she reached down and laid one slim hand on Green Valley's shoulder.

"Thank you, General Green Valley," she said, projecting her voice clearly and choosing his military title with malice aforethought. "We could wish the journey had been a little less tempestuous, but it's good to be here . . . and to see such an old and trusted friend again."

No one with a working brain would ever have imagined that she and Cayleb would have sent someone they *didn't* trust to handle the delicate task of arresting a grand duke, yet she could almost physically feel the way attention clicked in Green Valley's direction. It never hurt to make it publicly clear who enjoyed the Crown's trust—and had the Crown's ear, if it came to that. Which was also the reason—or one of them, at least—she'd used the imperial "we."

"Rise, please," she said, tugging gently on his shoulder, and smiled as he rose to tower over her. He was tall for a Charisian, within a few inches of Merlin's own height, and he smiled back at her.

"We realize we have a great many details to which we must attend," she continued, turning to look past him and let her eyes sweep the assemblage of notables. Every senior Zebediahan noble, and a great many of the lesser nobility, as well, were present in that throne room. It was almost claustrophobically full as a consequence, although her guardsmen maintained an open bubble at least four yards across around *her* at all times.

Wide enough to stop an assassin with cold steel, at any rate, she thought. *A bit more problematic where muskets are concerned, I suppose, but getting one of those past Merlin and the SNARCs wouldn't be the easiest thing in the world. And then there's the fact that every stitch I'm wearing, aside from my lingerie, is made out of antiballistic smart fabric. If somebody does get a shot at me, he's going to be very surprised when the miraculous favor of the Archangels comes to my rescue.* She suppressed an urge to smile. *Now that I think about it, that might not be such a bad thing. It'd certainly give Clyntahn and the Temple Loyalists conniptions!*

"Yet first and foremost among those details," she continued out loud, keeping her voice womanfully level despite her devilish amusement as she imagined Clyntahn's reaction to her miraculous deliverance, "is our duty to thank you for the exemplary fashion in which you have performed your duties here. We and the Emperor have read your reports with great interest and approval. And while we deeply regret the necessity which impelled us to send you here in the first place, it seems evident to us that not only you but many of the loyal members of the Zebediahan nobility, faithful to their sworn word, have done all we might ask of any man in these difficult and troubling times."

She sensed the slight rustle of relief which went through the still-kneeling aristocrats as her tone registered, and she was hard-pressed not to smile sardonically.

Of course they're relieved by your attitude, Sharley. More than half of them probably expected you to come in snorting fire and breathing brimstone! That would have been Hektor's *approach, at any rate. Now they're at least provisionally ready to believe they're not all going to be tainted in your eyes by past associations with Zebediah.* Despite herself, her lip curled ever so slightly. *I suppose it would probably be a good idea not to mention how many of them you know were toying with the idea of supporting him this time around.*

It had been tempting to make a clean sweep of those who'd come closest to throwing in their lot with Symmyns and the Northern Conspiracy down in Corisande. Some of them had come *very* close, as a matter of fact, which didn't augur well for their continued future loyalty to Charis. Still, as Cayleb and Staynair had pointed out, thinking about an act was a very different thing from actually *committing* it. People dedicated to the concept of freedom of thought could scarcely go around lopping off heads just because possibly treasonous thoughts might have rattled around inside them at one point or another. Besides, knowing who the weak links were offered the opportunity to *strengthen* them in the future.

And in the meantime, it lets us know who to keep an eye on.

"I thank you for those kind words, Your Majesty," Green Valley said, bowing once more.

"They're no more than you deserve of us, General," she said sincerely, inclining her own head to him ever so slightly. "And now, of your courtesy, would you be so kind as to escort us?"

"It would be my honor, Your Majesty," he replied, offering her his arm.

She tucked her hand into it and allowed him to escort her ceremonially to the throne awaiting her . . . and that sapphire-eyed Guardsman followed silently at her back.

▼ ▼ ▼

"Well, that went about as well as it could have, I think," Sharleyan said several hours later.

She sat in the luxurious bedchamber which had once belonged to the man now sitting in a far more humble chamber in one of the palace's more securely guarded towers. The bedchamber was actually rather more luxurious than she would have preferred, and she'd already made a mental note to have its more ostentatious furnishings removed. If nothing else, it would probably give her enough space to walk in a straight line for more than three feet at a time, she thought tartly.

"And at least you're sitting in a nice warm—and still—palace," Cayleb replied sourly over her earplug.

His passage back to Old Charis wasn't setting any records after all. Despite having left Cherayth almost two five-days before Sharleyan had, he still hadn't cleared the

Zebediah Sea. In fact, he was barely more than twelve hundred miles from Carmyn even as he spoke, and *Royal Charis* was plunging wildly as she fought her way through the Mackas Strait in the teeth of a full storm roaring its way eastward from the East Chisholm Sea with what the old Beaufort scale would have called Force Ten winds, approaching sixty miles per hour. She shuddered and bucked her way through waves almost thirty feet high, with long overhanging crests. Foam blew in dense white streaks and great gray patches along the direction of the wind; everywhere the eye looked, the surface of the sea was white and tumbling; and the galleon's stout timbers quivered under the heavy impacts slamming into them.

"What's this? The *Charisian* seaman with the cast-iron stomach upset over a little rough weather?"

Sharleyan put considerably more humor into the question than she actually felt. She'd spent enough time aboard ship by now herself to realize *Royal Charis* wasn't really in desperate straits, despite the violence of her motion. Still, even the best found ship could founder.

"It's not the motion, it's the temperature," Cayleb shot back. "*You* may be accustomed to freezing your toes off, dear, but I'm a Charisian boy. And my favorite hot water bottle happens to be in Zebediah at the moment!"

"Trust me, if it weren't for the motion I'd trade places with you in a heartbeat," she said feelingly. "I've learned to love the weather in Tellesberg, but this is ridiculous!"

She wiped a sheen of perspiration from her forehead. The bedchamber's open windows faced the harbor, and the evening sea breeze was just beginning to make up. It was going to get better soon, she told herself firmly.

"Nahrmahn would trade with you, too, Your Majesty," Princess Ohlyvya said. "I don't believe I've ever seen him more miserable. I think he was bringing up the soles of his shoes this afternoon."

The Emeraldian princess's tone mingled amusement, sympathy, and at least some genuine concern. In fact, her worry over her husband was clearly helping to divert her from any qualms she might feel herself in the face of such weather, and Sharleyan smiled.

"I wondered why he hadn't had anything to say," she said.

"He got the healer to prescribe golden berry tea with an infusion of sleep root, and he's been sleeping ever since," Ohlyvya told her. "Should I try to wake him?"

"Oh, no! If he can sleep, let him."

"Thank you," Ohlyvya said sincerely.

"At the moment, I find myself envying him," Cayleb remarked only half humorously. "But since I'm awake and not asleep, was there anything we particularly needed to discuss?"

"I don't really think so. To be honest, I just needed to hear your voice more than anything else," Sharleyan admitted. "I think we got off on the right foot today, and Kynt played his part wonderfully. There are a couple of people I'd like Nahrmahn to keep a little closer eye on than we'd discussed. Now that I've personally met them, I'm a bit less optimistic about their fundamental reliability than I was. Aside from that, though, I really do think it's going well so far. I'm just not looking forward to tomorrow, I suppose."

"I don't blame you." Cayleb's tone was more sober than it had been. "Mind you, I don't think it would bother me as much as I think it's bothering you. Probably because I've already had the questionable pleasure of meeting him. In a lot of ways, I wish I could have taken this one off your shoulders, but—"

He shrugged, and Sharleyan nodded. They'd discussed it often enough, and the logic which had sent her here was at least half her own. The world—and especially the Empire of Charis—needed to understand she and Cayleb genuinely were *corulers* . . . and that his was not the only hand which could wield a sword when it was necessary. She'd demonstrated that clearly enough to her own Chisholmians, and as a very young monarch ruling in Queen

Ysbet's shadow she'd learned that sometimes the sword *was* necessary.

And when it is, flinching is the worst thing—for everyone—you can possibly do, she thought grimly. *I learned that lesson the hard way, too.*

"Well, you can't take it off me," she told him philosophically. "And it's later here than it is where you are, and your daughter has gotten over her snit over the local temperature and is about to begin demanding her supper. So I think it's probably time I went and saw to that minor detail. Good night, everyone."

▼ ▼ ▼

Sharleyan Ahrmahk sat very still as the prisoner was brought before her. He was neatly, even soberly, dressed, without the sartorial magnificence which had graced his person in better days, and he looked acutely nervous, to say the least.

Tohmys Symmyns was a man of average height and average build, with thinning dark hair, a prominent nose, and eyes that reminded Sharleyan of a dead kraken's. He'd grown a beard during his incarceration, and it didn't do a thing for him. The smudges of white in his hair and the strands of white in the dark beard made him look even older than his age but without affording him any veneer of wisdom.

Of course, that could be at least partly because of how much she knew about him, she reflected grimly.

She sat in the throne which had once been his, her crown of state on her head, dressed in white and wearing the violet sash of a judge, and his muddy eyes widened at the sight of that sash.

Idiot, she thought coldly. *Just what did you expect was going to happen?*

He wasn't manacled—she and Cayleb had been prepared to make that much concession to his high rank—but the two Army sergeants walking behind him wore the expressions of men who devoutly wished he'd give them an excuse to lay hands on him.

At least he wasn't that stupid, and he came to a halt at the foot of the throne room's dais. He stared at her for a moment, then fell to both knees and prostrated himself before her.

She let him lie there for long, endless seconds, and as she did, she felt a sort of cruel pleasure which surprised her. It shamed her, too, that pleasure, yet she couldn't deny it. And the truth was that if anyone deserved the torment of uncertainty and fear which must be pulsing through him at that moment, Tohmys Symmyns was that anyone.

The silence stretched out, and she felt the tension of the nobles and clerics who'd been summoned to bear witness to what was about to happen. They lined the walls of the throne room, there to observe, not speak, and that was another reason she let him wait. He himself would have no opportunity to learn from what happened here this day; others might.

"Tohmys Symmyns," she said finally, and his head snapped up as she used his name and not the title which had been his for so long, "you have been accused of treason. The charges have been considered by a jury of the lords secular and temporal of the Empire and of the Church of Charis. The evidence has been carefully sifted, and you have been given the opportunity to testify in your own defense and to name and summon any witnesses of your choice. That jury's verdict has been rendered. Is there anything you would wish to say to us or to God before you hear it?"

"Your Majesty," his voice was more than a little hoarse, a far cry from the silky, unctuous instrument it once had been, "I don't know why my enemies have told you such lies! I swear to you on my own immortal soul that I'm innocent—*innocent!*—of all the crimes charged against me! Yes, I corresponded with Earl Craggy Hill and others in Corisande, but never to conspire against you or His Majesty! These were men I'd known and worked with for years, Your Majesty. Men whose loyalty to you and His Majesty I knew was suspect. I sought only to discover their plans, to ferret out any plots they might be hatching in order to bring them to your attention!"

He rose on his knees, extending both arms in a gesture of supplication and innocence.

"You know what pressures have been brought to bear on all of us to renounce our oaths to you and to the Crown, Your Majesty. You know the Temple and the Temple Loyalists insist those oaths cannot bind us in the face of the Grand Vicar's pronunciation of excommunication against you and His Majesty and interdict against the entire Empire. Yet I swear to you that I *have* observed every provision of my oath, given to His Majesty aboard ship off this very city when I swore fealty to your Crown of my own free will, in the face of no threat or coercion! Whatever others may or may not have done, *I* have stood firm in the Empire's service!"

He fell silent, staring at her imploringly, and she looked back with no expression at all. She let the silence linger once more, then spoke.

"You speak eloquently of your loyalty to us and Emperor Cayleb," she said then, coldly, "but the documents in your own hand which have come into our possession speak even more eloquently. The testimony of the Earl of Swayle further indicts you, and so do the recorded serial numbers of the weapons which were delivered here, in Zebediah, into your own possession . . . yet ended in a warehouse in Telitha. Weapons which would have been used to kill Soldiers and Marines in our service had the conspirators in Corisande succeeded in their aims. No witness you have called has been able to refute that evidence, nor have you. We are not inclined to believe your lies at this late date."

"Your Majesty, *please!*"

He shook his head, beginning to sweat. Sharleyan was vaguely surprised it had taken this long for those beads of perspiration to appear, but then she realized Nahrmahn had been right. Even at this late date Symmyns hadn't quite believed he wouldn't be able to fast talk his way out yet again.

"You were given every opportunity to demonstrate your loyalty to us and to Emperor Cayleb," she said flatly. "You chose instead to demonstrate your *dis*loyalty. We cannot control what passes through the minds and hearts of our subjects—no merely mortal monarch can hope to do that, nor would we even if it were within our power. But we can reward faithful service, and we can and must—and *will*—punish treachery and betrayal. Recall the words of your oath to His Majesty. To be our 'true man, of heart, will, body, and sword.' Those were the words of the oath you swore 'without mental or moral reservation.' Do you recall them?"

He stared at her wordlessly, his lips bloodless.

"No?" She gazed back at him, and then, finally, she smiled. It was a thin smile, keener than a dagger, and he flinched before it. "Then perhaps you remember what he swore to you in return, in his name and in our own. 'We will extend protection against all enemies, loyalty for fealty, justice for justice, fidelity for fidelity, and punishment for oath-breaking. May God judge us and ours as He judges you and yours.' You chose not to honor your oath to us, but we most assuredly *will* honor ours to you."

"Your Majesty, I have a wife! A *daughter!* Would you deprive her of a *father?!*"

Despite herself, Sharleyan winced internally at that reminder of her own loss. But there was a difference this time, she told herself, and no sign of that wince was allowed to touch her expression.

"We will grieve for your daughter," she told him in a voice of iron. "Yet our grief will not stay the hand of justice."

He wrenched his gaze from hers, staring around the throne room as if seeking some voice which might speak in his defense or issue some plea for clemency even at this late date. There was none. The men and women most likely to have allied themselves with him were the ones *least* likely to risk their own skins on his behalf, and the last color drained out of his face as he saw the opaque eyes looking back at him.

"The jury which has inquired into your guilt or innocence has found you guilty of each and every charge against you, Tohmys Symmyns, once Grand Duke of Zebediah." Sharleyan Ahrmahk's voice was chipped flint, and his eyes snapped back to her face like frightened rabbits. "You are stripped of your position and attainted for treason. Your wealth is forfeit to the Crown for your crimes, and your lands and your titles escheat to the Crown, to be kept or bestowed wherever the Crown, in its own good judgment, shall choose. And it is the sentence of the Crown that you be taken from this throne room to a place of execution and there beheaded and buried in the unconsecrated ground reserved for traitors. We will hear no plea for clemency. There will be no appeal from this decision. You will be permitted access to clergy of your choice so that you may confess your sins, if such is your desire, but it is our command that this sentence shall be executed before sundown of this very day, and may God have mercy upon your soul."

She stood, a slender dark-haired flame in white, slashed by that violet stole, rubies and sapphires glittering like pools of crimson and blue fire in her crown of state, gazing down at the white-faced, stricken man she had just condemned to death.

And then she turned, Merlin Athrawes a silent presence at her back, and walked out of that throne room's ringing silence without another word.

Monastery of Saint Zherneau,
City of Tellesberg,
Kingdom of Old Charis

It was raining—gently, for a Tellesberg afternoon—as Father Paityr Wylsynn knelt in the kitchen garden of the Monastery of Saint Zherneau. He felt his plain, borrowed habit growing progressively heavier with moisture as the blowing mist washed over him, but he didn't care. In fact, he treasured it. It wasn't a cold, drenching rain, after all. More like a caress, possibly even a kiss from God's world, he thought with a touch of whimsy as his muddy hands extracted weeds from neat rows of staked tomato vines and the warm, earthy, *growing* smell of wet leaves and rich, moist soil rose about him like the Archangel Sondheim's incense.

It had been too long since he'd done simple work, he thought. He'd been so wrapped up in his duties and his responsibilities—his probably arrogant belief that so many critical things depended upon *him*—that he'd forgotten even the greatest and holiest man imaginable (which he most decidedly was not) was only one more worker in a far greater Worker's garden. If Saint Zherneau's had done no more than remind him of that simple fact, he would still have owed Archbishop Maikel and Father Zhon enormous thanks.

But that wasn't all Saint Zherneau's had done.

He moved forward a few feet to reach a fresh batch of weeds and raised his face to the tiny, delicate fingertips of the rain. He had two more rows of tomatoes to do, and then the squash. That was going to be more of a penance, since if there was one vegetable he detested, it was squash.

I suppose it's proof of the Archangels' workmanship that they created people to be different enough that there's somebody to like every edible plant, he thought. *I'm not too sure why they wasted the effort on squash, but I'm sure it was part of God's plan. I'm not so sure a taste for* brussels sprouts *was, though, come to think of it.*

He smiled and raised a clod of wet earth in his fingers. He looked down at it and squeezed gently, compressing it into a smooth oval, and for the first time in far too long he felt another, far greater hand shaping his own life.

▼ ▼ ▼

"Well, what do you think?" Father Zhon Byrkyt asked.

He sat gazing out the window at the red-haired, youthful priest pulling weeds in the monastery's garden. The young man seemed oblivious to the gently falling rain, although Byrkyt doubted that was the case. In fact, from how slowly and carefully Father Paityr was working, Byrkyt suspected he was actually enjoying it.

"You know my opinion," Father Ahbel Zhastrow said. "I was inclined in his favor before he ever arrived, and I've seen nothing to change that opinion."

Father Ahbel was the Abbot of Saint Zherneau's, a title Byrkyt had held until fairly recently. Age was paring away Byrkyt's strength, however. In fact, he was fading visibly, although he seemed less aware of the process—or less concerned *by* it, at any rate—than anyone else. He'd been forced to give up his duties as abbot because of failing health, but he retained the office of librarian, which was arguably of even greater importance and responsibility, given the . . . peculiarities of the Order of Saint Zherneau.

"I've come to think highly of him myself," Brother Bahrtalam Fauyair said. The almoner, in charge of feeding the poor in Saint Zherneau's neighborhood, was brown-haired and brown-eyed, broad-shouldered and powerfully built, with a battered, pugilist's face which hinted only too accurately of his youthful life as a waterfront loanshark's enforcer before he heard God's call. Now that face wore an anxious expression, and he shook his head slowly.

"I've come to think *very* highly of him," he continued,

"but I can't quite forget he's an inquisitor. Everything I've ever heard of him, far less what we've seen while he's been here, shouts that he's nothing at all like Clyntahn or Rayno. But he's still an inquisitor—raised and trained as a Schuelerite—and we've *never* admitted a Schuelerite to the inner circle. There was a reason for that, and I just can't convince myself we should set that rule aside if we don't absolutely have to."

"Bahrtalam has a point," Brother Symyn Shaumahn said. As the monastery's hosteler, charged with serving the needs of the homeless and seeing to the well-being and comfort of Saint Zherneau's guests, he and Fauyair worked closely together every day. They didn't look very much alike, though. Shaumahn was gray-haired, slender, and at least fifteen or twenty years older than Fauyair, with a thin face and a scholarly look.

"He has a point," he repeated. "Oh, there was never a hard and fast *rule* about Schuelerites, but there was certainly agreement!" He made a wry face, and Byrkyt chuckled. "All the same, Bahrtalam," Shaumahn turned from the window to face Fauyair fully, "we've discarded a lot of other rules, including rules which *were* hard and fast, over the last couple of years. We haven't set any of them aside without good reason, yet set them aside we have. I'll agree that the mere thought of letting an *inquisitor* anywhere near the journal is enough to set my teeth on edge, but I'm inclined to support Zhon and Ahbel on this one."

"You are?" Fauyair looked surprised, and Shaumahn shrugged.

"Not without someone showing me a very good reason to, I assure you! But I think Maikel's almost certainly right about this young man. For that matter, I'll remind all of us that Maikel's judgment of someone's character is usually frighteningly acute. Everything I've seen of Father Paityr only confirms what Maikel's told us in his case, at any rate, and Maikel and the others are absolutely correct about the huge advantages inherent in bringing this particular inquisitor over to the truth."

"But those very advantages would become equally huge disasters if it turns out Maikel isn't right in his case after all," Sister Ahmai Bailahnd pointed out.

If Sister Ahmai—more properly Mother Abbess Ahmai—was perturbed by the fact that she was the only woman present, it wasn't apparent. For that matter, she'd been a frequent visitor at Saint Zherneau's over the years. The Abbey of Saint Evehlain was Saint Zherneau's sister abbey, although it had been founded almost two hundred years after Saint Zherneau's. Sister Ahmai was a petite, slender woman with delicate hands, an oval face, brown hair, and a strong nose. She limped from a left leg which had been badly broken when she'd been younger, and damp weather (like today's) made it worse. Her brown eyes were shadowed with more than the aching discomfort of her leg as she looked out the window with the others, however.

"Trust me, Ahmai, we're all painfully aware of that," Brother Tairaince Bairzhair, Saint Zherneau's treasurer, said wryly. His brown hair was sprinkled with white, and he rubbed the scar on his forehead with one finger, brown eyes intent as he too watched the oblivious young priest working in the garden. "The fact that, unlike so many other intendants, he's never been capricious, that he's always been fair and compassionate, would be enough to give him a commanding stature all by itself." Bairzhair snorted. "After all, we're all so unaccustomed to that sort of behavior out of any Schuelerite, and especially out of an intendant!

"But then there's the fact that Schuelerite or no—*inquisitor* or no—I've never heard anyone accuse him of speaking a harsh word, and all of Old Charis has seen the faith that carried him through the silence about his family after his father's death. Then add in the fact that the Wylsynn family's always had a reputation for piety, *and* the fact that he's now the son and nephew of two vicars who were martyred by that bastard Clyntahn, and you get a package that could do us all incredible damage if we tell him the truth and he doesn't believe it."

"It could be even worse than that, Tairaince," Fauyair pointed out. "What if he *does* believe the truth . . . and it destroys his faith in God completely?"

All of them looked at one another silently, then Byrkyt nodded.

"We've been lucky in that respect so far," he said heavily, "but sooner or later, we're going to be *un*lucky. We all know that. That's the reason we've recommended against telling so many candidates we know are good and godly people, and we all know that, too. And whether any of us wants to talk about it or not, we also know what Cayleb and Sharleyan—and Merlin—will find themselves forced to do if it turns out we've told someone and it was a mistake."

He leaned back against the wall, regarding all of them steadily.

"I'm an old man. I won't be party to making these decisions very much longer, and I imagine I'm going to be giving account to God for the decisions I have helped make sooner than the rest of you are. But none of us can pretend we don't recognize the stakes we're playing for, or that Cayleb and Sharleyan can afford to be anything but ruthless if it turns out we've told someone who will use that knowledge against us. And let's be honest, simple outrage—the kind of outrage the best of men are most likely to feel—would be all the reason anyone would need to proclaim the truth from the highest mountain. Of course, it would probably get him killed very quickly, but how likely is that to be a factor in the thinking of someone like that? So as I see it, the real question here isn't whether or not Father Paityr is a compassionate, loving servant of God, but whether we want to take the chance of being responsible for the *death* of a compassionate, loving servant of God if it should happen that his outrage upon learning the truth makes him a threat to everything we're trying to accomplish?"

The others looked back at him in fresh silence, and then—as one—they turned to look back out the window at the young man kneeling in the borrowed habit pulling weeds in the rain.

▼ ▼ ▼

"You weren't joking when you said you liked salad, were you?"

Paityr Wylsynn looked up from his second large serving of salad and smiled at Brother Bahrtalam.

"Oh, I've always liked it," he said cheerfully. "I've discovered that when I'm personally responsible for exterminating the weeds and beating off the attacks of one bug or another the tomatoes taste even better, however. And your brothers make one of the best balsamic dressings I've ever tried. Has the monastery ever considered marketing it? I'm sure you could raise quite a bit of revenue, and I've never heard of a monastery that couldn't use more funds for charitable works!"

"That's true enough," Brother Tairaince put in. Saint Zherneau's had no rule of silence, especially at meals, and the treasurer chuckled as he sat back on the bench running down the other side of the long, brilliantly polished refectory table. "And Saint Zherneau's is no exception to the rule, either. You may have noticed we're not exactly swimming in charitable bequests, Father."

"As a matter of fact, I *had* noticed," Paityr replied. He looked around the large, lovingly maintained and painstakingly clean dining room, then back at Bairzhair. "I don't believe I've ever seen a more beautiful monastery, Brother, and I've seen evidence enough of the good you do in this neighborhood, but if you'll forgive me it's obvious the monastery could use some improvements and overdue repairs."

"Well, I'm sure you've also noticed that unlike most monasteries, we're very small," Bairzhair responded. "Our opportunities to engage in revenue-generating crafts, or even to support ourselves with something larger than our kitchen garden, are limited, to say the least. And, alas, our 'neighborhood,' as you put it, lacks the resources to support even itself, much less us." He smiled gently. "That, after all, is the reason we're here."

"That and to provide a place where any of our brethren who need it can find a spot to catch his breath," Father Ahbel said, entering the conversation and smiling at Paityr. "Or, for that matter, where someone *recommended* by one of our brethren can catch his breath. To be totally honest, that's really the primary reason for our existence, Father. Oh, the work we do is eminently worth doing, and the people among whom we do it are as worthy—and as needful—as any of God's children. But the truth is that in some ways Saint Zherneau's is actually . . . well, *selfish* would probably be too strong a word, but it's headed in the right direction. We offer a place where people who get too caught up in the breathless, everyday race of trying to see to God's business in His world can step back and put their hands to His *work* for a time, instead. Where they can participate in the simple pastoral duties that called them to God's service in the first place. That's one reason the brethren of Saint Zherneau make no distinction between the other orders. We're open to Bédardists, Pasqualates, Langhornites . . ." He shrugged. "I'm sure you've seen representatives of almost every order during even your relatively brief stay with us."

"Yes, I have, Father," Paityr replied, but his eyes had narrowed, and he sounded like a man picking his words—possibly even his thoughts—with care. "I've noticed, and I've also noticed that I've seen no Schuelerites."

"No, you haven't." If Zhastrow was taken aback by Paityr's observation, he showed no sign of it. Instead, he cocked his head to one side and smiled gently at the younger priest. "However, Father Paityr, you've probably seen many more Schuelerites than I have. I mean no disrespect, but do you really think the majority of them would find the atmosphere of Saint Zherneau's . . . congenial?"

"Probably not," Paityr acknowledged, and shook his head sadly. "I think my father and Uncle Hauwerd would have, but you're right about most of the order, I'm afraid. Which rather leads me to the question of why Archbishop Maikel thought this would be a good place to send *me*, I suppose."

"I won't presume to speak for the Archbishop," Zhastrow replied, "but it might be because you're not very much like the majority of Schuelerites. Again, I mean no disrespect to your order, Father, but it seems to me there's a rather authoritarian mindset to much of what it does. I'm inclined to think that's probably inevitable, given the nature of the Inquisition's duties, of course. But I hope you'll forgive me for pointing out that you—and from what I've heard, your father—believe the basis of true discipline has to be love, and that it must be tempered by compassion and gentleness. And from what I've seen of you during your visit with us, that's almost certainly what drew you into the priesthood in the first place. For that matter," he looked directly into Paityr's eyes, "it's also the reason you were so angry when you first came to us, isn't it?"

The question came so gently it took Paityr almost completely unawares, and he found himself nodding before he'd even truly digested it.

"Yes, it is," he admitted. "Archbishop Maikel recognized that before I was willing to admit it even to myself. And you and Father Zhon—all the brothers—have helped me to realize just how foolish that was of me."

"Well, now I suppose that depends in part on the reasons for your anger," Byrkyt said.

The librarian had come into the room from behind Paityr, and the intendant turned on his bench as Byrkyt made his slow and creaky way across the floor, leaning heavily on a cane. Paityr started to get up to offer his own place, but the librarian rested a gnarled hand on his shoulder and shook his head.

"Oh, stay where you are, youngster! If I decide I need somewhere to sit, I'll move one of these other idle layabouts out of my way. In fact—"

He poked Fauyair with the end of his cane, and the far larger and far younger almoner rose with a chuckle.

"*I* have to check the kitchen," he said, elevating his nose. "Which, of course, is the only reason I will so meekly yield my place."

"Oh, we all know how 'meek' *you* are!" Byrkyt said. "Now run along. I need to talk to young Paityr."

"The *Writ* devotes a great deal of attention to the tyranny of power," Fauyair observed to no one in particular. "I wonder why it gives so much less attention to the tyranny of old age?"

"Because it's *not* tyranny. It's just an excess of common sense."

Fauyair laughed, touched Byrkyt affectionately on the shoulder, and took his leave as the librarian settled his increasingly frail bones into the vacated spot.

"As I was about to say," he continued, turning back to Paityr, "whether it's foolish to be angry or not depends on the reasons for the anger. And who it's directed at, of course. Being angry at God *is* fairly foolish, when you come down to it, which I suppose is the reason all of us spend so much time doing it, whether we realize it or not. But being angry at those who pervert God's will, or who use the cover and excuse of God's will to impose their own wills on others?" He shook his head, ancient eyes bright as they gazed into Paityr's. "There's nothing foolish in that, my son. Hatred is a poison, but *anger*—good, honestly-come-by anger, the kind that stems from outrage, from the need to protect the weak or lift the fallen or stop the cruel—that's not poison. That's *strength*. Too much of it can *lead* to hatred, and from there it's one slippery step to self-damnation, but never underestimate the empowering strength of the right *sort* of anger."

The others were listening now, more than one of them nodding in silent agreement, and Paityr felt himself nodding back.

"You're in a unique position, Father," Byrkyt said after a moment. "Of course, all of us are in unique positions. It comes with being unique human beings. But the consequences of your position—or, rather, of the actions of someone *in* your position—are going to be greater and affect far more people more profoundly than most priests ever have the opportunity to accomplish. You're aware of that. In fact, I'm fairly confident that your awareness of it was one of the things helping to get your own spiritual balance *out* of balance. You've been spending too much of your time and strength trying to *shoulder* your responsibilities, trying to reach ahead and figure out what those responsibilities were, rather than simply letting God *show* you. He does that, you know. Sometimes directly, by laying His finger on your heart, and sometimes by sending others of His children to pull you out of the ditch you've fallen into. Or to point you in a direction which wouldn't have occurred to you on your own."

"I know." Paityr smiled at the old man, then turned his head, allowing his smile to take in all the brethren seated about them. "I know. But do you think He sent me to you simply to be pulled out of the ditch, or to be pointed in another direction, as well? You wouldn't happen to have any spiritual road maps in your library, would you, Father Zhon?"

"Now that's a profound sort of question, the sort of thing I might have expected out of a Schuelerite!" Byrkyt smiled back and cuffed the younger priest gently on the side of his head. "And, like any profound question, I'm sure it has a profound answer . . . somewhere. But only time will tell, I suppose." His smile turned softer, and the hand which had smacked Paityr's head so lightly moved to cup the side of his face, instead. "Only time will tell."

MAY, YEAR OF GOD 895

·✦·

.I.

The Temple,
City of Zion,
The Temple Lands

"Well, you were right, Rhobair," Zhaspahr Clyntahn said caustically. "I know *I* feel a whole lot better now that we've gotten the complete report. Don't you?"

The Grand Inquisitor's sarcasm was even more biting than usual . . . not that it came as a surprise. In fact, if Rhobair Duchairn was surprised by anything it was that Clyntahn wasn't throwing a full-fledged tantrum.

Of course there's time for that still, he reminded himself. *We're only just getting started. Langhorne knows where he's going to go before we get* finished *this afternoon!*

"No, Zhaspahr," he said as calmly as he could. "It doesn't make me feel much better. It does confirm some things, though . . . including the fact that Allayn's plan to misdirect the Charisians seems to have worked. I can't believe someone like Cayleb would have sent less than thirty of his ships to intercept a *hundred* and thirty of our own if he hadn't been caught completely on the wrong foot."

"Why not?" Clyntahn demanded bitterly. "Their 'less than thirty' seem to've kicked our hundred and thirty's ass pretty damn thoroughly." He glared at Maigwair. "They didn't *need* to send any more ships than they did. God! It's *pathetic!*"

"Zhaspahr," Duchairn said, "you can't blame men for losing a battle when they suddenly come up against a weapon that causes their own ships to blow up under them. Especially when they didn't have any idea it was coming! I don't know about you, but if I expected some-one to be firing round shot at *me* and instead they were firing some kind of ammunition that *exploded* the min-ute it hit my ship, I'd find that fairly disconcerting. In fact, I'd find it downright *terrifying!*"

"The fucking cowards were supposed to be Temple Guardsmen!" Clyntahn snarled, his face darkening dan-gerously. He seemed even angrier than the failure of one of his plans usually made him feel. "They're God's own warriors, damn it, not little children seeing *fireworks* for the first time!"

Duchairn started to fire back a quick, angry response, but he caught himself in time. Pushing Clyntahn over the brink would do nothing but get someone killed. Still. . . .

"Perhaps you're right about that," the Treasurer said instead of what he'd started to say. "At the same time, do you think it would really have made a lot of difference if Harpahr had tried to fight to the last ship?" Clyntahn looked at him incredulously, and Duchairn held up both hands. "All right, I'll give you that if they had, the Chari-sians wouldn't have gained all the ships that surrendered. I have to say, though, that reading Searose's report, I don't see how Harpahr could have kept his ships from striking their colors however hard he'd tried. I'm not condoning their cowardice, Zhaspahr. I'm simply saying that human nature being human nature, Harpahr *couldn't* have stopped it. Not when the Charisians' new weapons came as a total surprise."

"I am getting damned sick and tired of every fucking new Charisian weapon coming 'as a total surprise,'" Clyntahn grated.

"If it's any consolation, I think this one must've been pretty close to a surprise for the Charisians, too," Duchairn replied.

"What the hell are you talking about now?" Clyntahn demanded.

"I think it's pretty obvious they haven't had it for very long," Duchairn said. "If they had, we'd have already seen it in action. For that matter, they wouldn't have tried something as desperate as a point-blank engagement in the middle of the night. If they had the ability to stand off and fire these explosive shot or whatever they are, why should they have closed? They sailed right into the middle of our ships—so close they were fighting old-fashioned *boarding actions*, Zhaspahr. It's right here in Searose's report."

"So what?" Clyntahn waved a dismissive hand.

"Rhobair has a point," Allayn Maigwair said. The Grand Inquisitor rounded on him, but Maigwair stood his ground. "I've read the reports, too, Zhaspahr. Everything the Charisians have done from Armageddon Reef and Crag Reach on has been built around artillery, not boarding actions. Oh, there've been boardings in most of the engagements, but they were the exceptions. Either that or they were the 'tidying up,' taking prizes which had already been battered into effective surrender with the guns. And the main reasons that's been the case are that the Charisians are more experienced than almost anyone else they've fought and that they have less manpower than we do. However good they may be in boarding melees, the last thing they want to do is to come to us in the kind of fight that lets us trade casualties one-for-one with them, and they've built all their tactics around *avoiding* that kind of battle. But that's exactly what they were doing against Harpahr's fleet."

"Sure it was . . . until they turned around and blew the shit out of him!" Clyntahn said impatiently.

"That's not what Allayn's trying to tell you, Zhaspahr." Somehow Duchairn managed to keep his frustration out of his tone. "What he's telling you is that an *outnumbered* Charisian fleet fought *our* kind of battle . . . until it managed to get the bulk of Harpahr's fleet into artillery range. They didn't switch to this new weapon until then, and they have to have taken serious casualties before they did. That suggests that whatever it is they were using, they didn't have a lot of it. They decided they had to make every shot count, and the only way to do that was to come to us—take their licks on the way in and hope they could finish us off with one or two good, heavy punches once they got inside our reach."

Clyntahn glowered at him, but from the Grand Inquisitor's expression, there was at least a possibility his brain was beginning to work. It might even be beginning to work well enough to overcome his ire, although Duchairn wouldn't have cared to bet on the possibility.

"I think Rhobair's right, Zhaspahr," Maigwair said now. "There's no way we can know how much they actually had of whatever special ammunition they were using, but the indications are that they didn't have anywhere near as much of it as they would've liked. From Searose's report, it's obvious he doesn't know what percentage of their total fleet had it, but he says he personally saw at least four of their galleons which were still firing normal round shot even after our ships had started to explode. As a matter of fact, I was impressed by the fact that he was able to keep his wits about himself well enough to notice that."

"And that's one reason I think Allayn's misdirection with the sailing orders actually worked," Duchairn said, piling on while the piling was good. "If they only had a handful of ships which were able to use this weapon, for whatever reason, then they would *certainly* have concentrated as many as possible of their regular galleons to support that handful. They didn't. To me, that seems to indicate their spies did pick up Harpahr's original orders to sail west. They must have sent a major portion of their fleet east in response to that. It's the only explanation for why they didn't close in on Harpahr with everything they had."

"What about that blockade of theirs?" Clyntahn challenged in a marginally calmer tone. "According to Jahras and Kholman they must have had at least forty galleons off the Gulf of Jahras. Maybe *that's* where your missing ships were."

"It could've been, but I don't think it was," Maigwair said. "I've been going over their reports, too, and they never actually saw the majority of those 'war galleons' at all. What they saw were masts and sails on the horizon, and don't forget the way Haarahld used merchant galleons to convince Black Water that Cayleb's galleons were with his fleet in the Sea of Charis when they were actually off ambushing Malikai off Armageddon Reef. I think this may have been more of the same, and I don't really see how anyone can blame them for being fooled under the circumstances."

"Maybe," Clyntahn said grudgingly.

"It works with what we know of the timing," Duchairn said, nodding at Maigwair. "Their spy network's obviously as good as we thought it was. We fooled them with Allayn's original orders, and that drew their main fleet out of position. But then their spies realized we'd misled them and reported Harpahr's real sailing orders in time for them to realize what was happening. Only they still didn't have time to get recall orders to the ships they'd already sent off, so they put together a 'fleet' of merchant galleons to convince Jahras and Kholman they couldn't fight their way out to sea while they scraped up everything they had—including the handful of ships they could equip with their new weapon—and threw them directly into Harpahr's teeth. If their weapon hadn't worked, we would've had them, Zhaspahr. It's that simple, and that's how close we came to accomplishing exactly what you originally proposed to do."

For a moment, he was afraid that last sentence had been too blatant an appeal to Clyntahn's ego. But then he saw the Grand Inquisitor nodding slowly and more thoughtfully. Clyntahn didn't look one bit less angry, but at least he'd lost some of the dangerous, saw-toothed rage which had been riding him with spurs of fire.

"All right," he said, "but even if you're right, the fact remains that we've suffered yet another defeat at the hands of heretics and apostates. The way we seem to keep stumbling from one disaster to another is bound to have an impact on even the most faithful if it goes on long enough. In fact, my inquisitors' reports indicate that that process may already have begun."

"That's a serious concern," Zahmsyn Trynair said, entering the conversation for the first time. Duchairn tried not to glare at the Chancellor, but he supposed it was better Trynair should come late to the party than stay home entirely.

"That's a *very* serious concern," Trynair repeated now. "What do you mean the 'process' may already have begun, Zhaspahr?"

"We're not seeing a sudden upsurge in heresy, if that's what you're worried about," Clyntahn said. "Aside, of course," he darted a venomous look at Duchairn and Trynair, "from the increasing number of 'Reformists' surfacing in Siddarmark, that is. But what we *are* seeing is what I suppose it would be fairest to call demoralization. People are seeing that despite the fact that we hugely outnumber the heretics, they keep winning battle after battle. Despite our best efforts, the casualty and prisoner totals from this latest debacle are going to get out, you know, and when they do, people are going to compare them to how little *we've* had to show for our efforts to date. Don't think for a moment that it isn't going to encourage the weak-hearted to feel even more despondent. In fact, it's likely to start undermining support for the jihad in general. At the very least"—he paused for a moment, letting his eyes circle the table—"it's going to begin to undermine confidence in the jihad's *direction*."

Duchairn felt Trynair and Maigwair settle into sudden, frozen stillness. There was no mistaking Clyntahn's implication.

"I scarcely think," the Treasurer said into the silence, choosing his words with excruciating care, "that anyone within the vicarate is likely to challenge our direction of the jihad."

After all, he added silently, *you've slaughtered anybody who might have the courage or the wit to breathe a word about how thoroughly we've bungled things, haven't you, Zhaspahr?*

"I'm not talking about the vicarate." There was something smug—and ugly—about the Grand Inquisitor's assurance, Duchairn thought, but then Clyntahn continued. "I'm worried about people *outside* the vicarate. I'm worried about all the bastards in Siddarmark and Silkiah who're going their merry way violating the embargo every day. I'm worried about the upsurge in 'Reformist' propaganda that's turning up in Siddarmark . . . and other realms, according to my inquisitors. Places like Dohlar and Desnair, for example—even the Temple Lands! And I'm worried about people who are going to lose heart because Mother Church seems unwilling to reach out her hand and smite the ungodly."

"We've been *trying* to smite the ungodly," Duchairn pointed out, trying to disguise the sinking sensation he felt. "The problem is that it hasn't been working out very well despite our best efforts."

"The *problem*," Clyntahn said, his tone and expression both unyielding, "is that we haven't reached out to the ungodly we *can* reach. The ungodly right here on the mainland."

"Like who, Zhaspahr?" Trynair asked.

"Like Stohnar and his bastard friends, for one," Clyntahn shot back. His lips twisted, but then he made them untwist with a visible act of will. "But that's all right, I understand why we can't touch them right now. The three of you have made that *abundantly* clear. I won't pretend it doesn't piss me off, and I won't pretend I don't think it's ultimately a mistake. But I'm willing to concede the point—for now, at least—where Siddarmark and Silkiah are concerned."

Duchairn's heart plunged as he realized where Clyntahn was headed. He couldn't even pretend it was a surprise, despite the sickness in his belly.

"I'm talking about those prisoners Thirsk took last year," Clyntahn went on flatly. "The ones he's somehow persistently managed not to hand over to the Inquisition or send to the Temple. They're *heretics*, Zahmsyn. They're rebels against God Himself, taken in the act of rebellion! My God, man—how much more evidence do you *need*? If Mother Church can't act against *them*, then who *can*

she act against? Do you think there aren't thousands—
millions—of people who aren't asking themselves that
very question right this moment?"

"I understand what you're talking about, Zhaspahr,"
Maigwair said cautiously, "but Thirsk and Bishop
Staiphan have a point, as well. If we deliver men who
surrender to us to the Inquisition to suffer the Question
and the Punishment of Schueler as they ought, then what
happens to *our* men who try to surrender to *them*?"

"Mother Church and the Inquisition cannot allow
themselves to be swayed from their clear duty by such
concerns," Clyntahn said in that same flat, unyielding
tone. "Should the heretics choose to mistreat our warriors, to abuse the true sons of God who fall into their
power, then that blood will be on *their* hands, not ours.
We can only do what *The Book of Schueler* and all the
rest of the *Writ* call upon us to do and trust in God and
the Archangels. No one ever told us that doing God's will
would be easy, but that makes it no less our duty and responsibility to do it. In fact, we ought—"

He stopped, clapping his mouth shut, and Duchairn
felt the despair of defeat. Maigwair wasn't going to support him, despite what he'd just said. Not when a part of
him agreed with Clyntahn to begin with, and especially
not when the Grand Inquisitor had just made his fury
over what had happened in the Markovian Sea so abundantly clear. And Trynair wasn't going to argue with
Clyntahn, either. Partly because he, too, agreed with the
inquisitor, but even more because of what Clyntahn had
just stopped short of saying.

*He's offering a quid pro quo where Siddarmark and
Silkiah are concerned*, Duchairn thought bitterly. *He's
not putting it into so many words, but Zahmsyn understands him just fine, anyway. And without at least one of
them to back me, I can't argue with him either. If I try, I'll
lose, and all I'll accomplish will be to burn one more
bridge with him.*

It was true, every word of it, and the Treasurer knew it,
just as he knew the demand for the Charisian prisoners

to be shipped to Zion would be sent out that very after-noon. But somehow knowing he couldn't have stopped it even if he'd tried didn't make him feel one bit less guilty and dirty for not trying after all.

▼ ▼ ▼

"May I ask how the meeting went, Your Grace?" Wyllym Rayno, Archbishop of Chiang-wu, inquired a bit cautiously.

He was almost certainly the only person in Zion who would have dared to ask that question at all, given the rumors circulating through the Temple about Greyghor Searose's written report. He was also, however, the adjutant of the Order of Schueler, which made him the Grand Inquisitor's second-in-command in both the order and the Office of Inquisition. The two of them had worked closely together for almost two decades, and if there'd been one person in the world whom Clyntahn had truly been prepared to trust, that person would have been Rayno.

"Actually," Clyntahn said with a smile which would have astonished any of his fellows among the Group of Four, given the tone of the meeting which had just ended, "it went well, Wyllym. Quite well."

"We'll be able to move against the heretic prisoners in Gorath, then, Your Grace?" Rayno's tone brightened, and Clyntahn nodded.

"Yes," he replied, then grimaced. "I had to go ahead and more or less promise—again—to keep our hands off Siddarmark and Silkiah." He shrugged. "We knew going in that that was going to happen. Of course, my esteemed colleagues don't have to know *everything* we're up to, now do they?"

"No, Your Grace," Rayno murmured.

He wondered how many of the rest of the Group of Four realized the extent to which Clyntahn used his well-earned reputation for bullheaded refusal to compromise and fiery temper to manipulate them. It had taken even Rayno years to discover that at least half that reputation was a weapon the Grand Inquisitor had crafted deliberately, with careful forethought. Its true effectiveness depended on the reality of the fury hiding so close beneath its wielder's surface, of course, but on his bare-knuckled climb to the Grand Inquisitorship, Zhaspahr Clyntahn had discovered that while intolerance and ambition might make him hated, it was his passionate temper which made him *feared*. He'd learned to use that temper, not simply to be used by it, to batter opponents into submission, and the technique had served him well. It was a brute force approach, but it was also only one of the many weapons in his arsenal, as one unfortunate victim after another had discovered.

"What can you tell me about this new weapon Searose is blathering about?" Clyntahn asked with one of the abrupt changes of subject for which he was famous.

"Our agents in Charis continue to . . . fare poorly." Rayno didn't like admitting that, yet there was no use pretending otherwise. "Wave Thunder's organization obviously has Shan-wei's own luck, but I'm afraid there's no point pretending he isn't extremely competent, Your Grace, as well. Every effort to build an actual network, even among the Loyalists in Old Charis, has failed."

"That wasn't the question I asked," Clyntahn pointed out.

"I realize that, Your Grace," Rayno responded calmly. "It was more in the nature of a prefatory remark."

Clyntahn's lips twitched on the brink of a smile. He was well aware of the extent to which Rayno "managed" him, and he was perfectly content to go right on being managed . . . within limits, and as long as Rayno produced results.

"What I was going to say," the archbishop continued, "is that our original hypothesis appears to be correct. According to one of the very few agents we have in place, the Charisians are casting what amounts to hollow round shot and filling the cavities with gunpowder. What he hasn't been able to confirm is how they're getting them to explode, although he's offered a couple of theories which sound to my admittedly untrained ear as if they make sense."

Neither of them chose to mention the fact that Clyntahn had somehow failed to keep Allayn Maigwair informed of those agents' reports.

"What are the chances of having him dig more deeply into the matter?"

"I would advise against that, Your Grace. The agent we're talking about is Harysyn."

Clyntahn's grunt was an acceptance of Rayno's advice.

"Harysyn" was the codename they'd assigned to one of their tiny handful of sources within the Kingdom of Old Charis. As Rayno had pointed out, every effort to establish a formal network in Old Charis—indeed, almost anywhere in the accursed Empire of Charis—had run into one stone wall after another. Sometimes it was almost enough to make Clyntahn truly believe in demonic interference on the other side. As a result of that unending sequence of failures, however, the sources which *were* available to them were more precious than jewels. That was why they'd been assigned codenames which Clyntahn insisted on using even in his conversations with Rayno. In fact, he'd made a point of never learning what the sources' actual names might be, on the theory that what he didn't know, he couldn't disclose even by accident.

While he hated to admit it, Maigwair and that gutless fool Duchairn did have a point about the apparent effectiveness of *Charisian* spies. He didn't believe any of them were managing to operate within the Temple itself, but they had to be operating—and operating effectively—throughout the Temple Lands. It was the only explanation for how so many clerics—or their families, at least—could have escaped the Inquisition when he broke the Wylsynns' group. Or how the Charisians could have discovered that Kornylys Harpahr's fleet was actually going east, instead of west, for that matter. And that being the case, he wasn't going to take a chance on *anyone's* learning the identities of those precious sources of information.

All their surviving sources had been strictly ordered to recruit no other agents. That reduced their "reach," since it meant each and every one of those agents could report only what he or she actually saw or heard. It also meant each of them required his or her individual conduit back to the Temple, which made the transmission of anything they learned even slower and more cumbersome than it would already have been across such vast distances. Unfortunately, as Rayno had just said, every agent who *had* attempted to recruit others, to build any sort of true network, had been pounced on within weeks. It had taken a while for the Inquisition to realize that was happening, but once it had become evident, the decision to change their operational patterns had virtually made itself. And onerous as the restrictions might be, anything which made the spies they had managed to put—or keep—in place less likely to attract Wave Thunder's attention was thoroughly worthwhile.

Harysyn was a special case even among that tiny handful of assets, however. He hadn't been placed in Charis at all; he'd been born there. A Temple Loyalist horrified by his kingdom's heresy, he'd found his own way to communicate with the Inquisition, and virtually all those communications flowed only in one direction—from him to the Temple. He'd established his own channels, including one which would let them communicate back to him in an excruciatingly slow and roundabout fashion, although he'd also cautioned them that it could be used only sparingly, if there was no other choice. He was prepared to provide all the information he could, he'd told them from the outset, but if they expected him to avoid the detection which had befallen so many other agents and Loyalists, they would have to settle for what he could tell them and for *his* maintaining control of their communications.

That had been more than enough to make Clyntahn and Rayno suspicious initially, since both of them were well aware of how much damage a double agent could do by feeding them false information. But Harysyn had been reporting for almost three years now without their detecting a single falsehood, and he'd been promoted by his superiors twice during that time, giving him better and better access. Besides that, he was crucial to one of Clyntahn's central strategies.

That was the main reason he'd been given the codename "Harysyn," after one of the greatest mortal heroes of the war against Shan-wei's disciples at the dawn of Creation.

"Did he have anything else for us in the same report?" the Grand Inquisitor asked. "Anything specific to what happened to Harpahr?"

"Not specific to that, no, Your Grace." Rayno shook his head. "There's no mention at all of that battle in his message. I judge it was probably composed before the battle was even fought—or before any report of it had reached Harysyn, at any rate. He does say Mahndrayn's been in discussions about ship design with Olyvyr, though. And he's heard rumors Seamount and Mahndrayn are working with Howsmyn on further improving these new projectiles—'shells,' they're calling them—as well as continuing to experiment with new cannon founding techniques. Whatever they're up to, though, they're keeping the information very confidential, and Harysyn's promotion means he's no longer in a position to see any of their internal correspondence."

Clyntahn grunted again, less happily this time. Harysyn's sketches of things like the new Charisian hollow-based bullets, flintlock mechanisms, and artillery cartridges had been of immense value. He'd managed to provide the formula for the Charisians' gunpowder (which not only caused less fouling but was rather more powerful than Mother Church's had been) and the new techniques for producing granular powder, as well. Of course, the Inquisition had been forced to take great care in how it made that information available to the Temple Guard and the secular lords, lest it betray the fact that it had an agent placed to obtain it in the first place. It had, however, given Clyntahn invaluable advance notice on the innovations he had to justify under the Proscriptions of Jwo-jeng.

"And that insufferable bastard Wylsynn?" he growled now as the thought of the Proscriptions drew his mind into a familiar groove.

"Harysyn has seen very little of him personally."

Rayno kept his tone as clinical as possible; Clyntahn's hatred for the Wylsynn family had become even more obsessive over the last year. Bad enough that Samyl and Hauwerd Wylsynn, the two men he'd hated most in all the world, had escaped the Question and the Punishment by dying before they could be taken into custody. Worse that Samyl's wife and children had escaped the Inquisition completely. Yet worse than any of that, except in a purely personal sense, of course, was *Paityr* Wylsynn's desertion to the heresy. He'd actually agreed to continue serving as Maikel Staynair's Intendant, and not content with that, he'd even assumed direction of the Charisians' Shan-wei-spawned "Patent Office." A member of Clyntahn's own order was actively abetting the flood of innovations that had allowed the renegade kingdom to escape the justly deserved destruction the Grand Inquisitor had decreed for it in the first place!

"He has managed to confirm, however, that Madam Wylsynn and her children have reached Tellesberg, Your Grace," Rayno added delicately, and Clyntahn's face turned dangerously dark.

For a moment, it looked as if the Grand Inquisitor might launch into one of his more furious tirades. But he stopped and controlled himself, instead.

"I suppose we'll just have to hope he's in his office at the wrong time," he said. Then he shook his head. "Actually, I hope he *isn't*. I don't want that son of Shan-wei slipping through our hands the way his father and his uncle did. He has far too much to atone for by simply dying on us."

"As you say, Your Grace," Rayno murmured with a slight bow.

"Very well." Clyntahn's nostrils flared as he inhaled, then he shook himself. "The Sword of Schueler?"

"That operation is slightly behind schedule, Your Grace. I'm afraid it's taking a bit longer—partly because the winter was so severe—to lay the groundwork properly. We're also encountering more delays than we'd anticipated in finding the . . . properly receptive sons of Mother Church. We're making steady progress now, however. The organization is going well, and I hope to be able to have everything in place in the next month or two. In the meantime, our inquisitors have confirmed that Cahnyr, at least, is in Siddar City. They're not certain how he got there, and no one's figured out how he managed to get out of Glacierheart in the first place, but he's increasingly visible in Reformist circles."

"And our *good* friend Stohnar remains blissfully unaware of his presence, I suppose?" Clyntahn sneered.

"So it would appear, Your Grace." Rayno smiled thinly. "For such a successful ruler, the Lord Protector appears to be singularly ill-informed about events in his own realm. Or perhaps I should say he appears *selectively* ill-informed. Archbishop Praidwyn is still en route to Siddar, but Bishop Executor Baikyr reports that he's pointedly drawn Lord Protector Greyghor's attention to the growing boldness of Reformist heretics in the Republic. In return, the Lord Protector has assured the Bishop Executor that his guardsmen are doing all they can to assist the Inquisition in dealing with the regrettable situation."

His eyes met Clyntahn's, and they grimaced almost in unison.

"Unfortunately," Rayno continued, "all of his efforts to assist Bishop Executor Baikyr have failed. Despite his guard's very best efforts, even fairly notorious Reformists seem to slip away before they can be taken into custody. Indeed, it's almost as if they were being warned—by someone—that they're about to be arrested. And so far, despite the persistent reports of Cahnyr's presence in the capital, he continues to elude the authorities."

Clyntahn made a harsh sound deep in his throat. The Inquisition had always relied heavily on secular rulers to assist in the suppression of heresy. Not even Mother Church could produce sufficient manpower to police all of Safehold against such dangerous thoughts and movements, and the system had worked well over the centuries. Yet that neatly summed up the problem they faced now, the Grand Inquisitor thought grimly, because it was no *longer* working . . . and no Grand Inquisitor, including him, had seen the current breakdown coming. He'd been caught as unawares by it as anyone, and though he was expanding the Order of Schueler as rapidly as he could, it took years to properly train an inquisitor. In the meantime, he continued to have no choice but to rely on the secular authorities, and too many of those authorities were clearly more interested in hampering the Inquisition than in aiding it.

"Perhaps Archbishop Praidwyn will be able to inspire the Lord Protector to be of somewhat greater assistance," he said, then smiled. "And if he can't, there's always the Sword of Schueler, isn't there?"

"Indeed, Your Grace," Rayno agreed with an answering smile.

"And Operation Rakurai?"

"The men have been selected," Rayno said in a much graver voice. "All of them have been carefully examined and vetted, Your Grace, and I have their dossiers for you to consider at your convenience. The arrangements to deliver them are almost complete, as well. Once you've made your final selections, we'll be able to move rapidly to put them in place."

"You're satisfied with them?"

"With *all* of them, Your Grace," Rayno replied firmly. "We haven't told any of them exactly what Rakurai will entail, of course. I've tried to provide you with at least twice the number of recruits you requested in order to give you the greatest possible latitude in making your final choices. In addition, of course, I'm sure we'll be able to find . . . other uses for men with such deep faith and fervor. But as you've so rightly stressed from the beginning, security is of critical importance, for this mission especially. We can't afford to have anyone not directly involved in it privy to any of its details."

"But you're confident all of them will be willing to undertake the mission when the time comes?"

"I'm certain of it, Your Grace. These men are truly committed to the will of God and to the Archangels' service and Mother Church, and they know abomination when they see it." The archbishop shook his head. "They won't flinch in the face of Shan-wei herself, Your Grace, far less the prospect of any mortal foe."

"Good, Wyllym," Zhaspahr Clyntahn said softly. "Good."

. II .

HMS *Royal Charis*, 58,
and
Archbishop's Palace,
City of Tellesberg,
Kingdom of Old Charis

"Thank God," Nahrmahn Baytz said with quiet, heartfelt fervor as he watched the Tellesberg waterfront creep steadily (if slowly) closer. "I've come to the conclusion, all of Nahrmahn Gareyt's dreadful novels about buccaneer kingdoms notwithstanding, that while I may be an *island* prince, I am *not* a swashbuckling one."

"Don't worry," Cayleb Ahrmahk reassured him. "I doubt anyone's going to expect you to be one. In fact, the mind boggles at the thought."

"Oh?" Nahrmahn looked at his emperor with raised eyebrows. "Are you implying that I cut a less than romantic figure, Your Majesty?"

"Heavens, no!" Cayleb looked shocked at the suggestion. "As a matter of fact, I think you cut a much more romantic figure than you did before we left Cherayth. Or a considerably thinner one, anyway."

"Don't tease him, Your Majesty," Princess Ohlyvya scolded. "And as for you, Nahrmahn, you cut quite romantic enough a figure for me. And I'd better not catch you cutting romantic figures for anyone else!"

"Somehow I don't think you're saving him from being teased, Ohlyvya," Cayleb pointed out.

"I didn't say I was trying to. With all due respect, Your Majesty, I was simply pointing out that he belongs to *me*. If there's any teasing to do, I'll do it."

Cayleb smiled, although it was true Nahrmahn had dropped quite a few pounds during the long, strenuous voyage. He didn't doubt for a moment that the Emeraldian could scarcely wait to get his feet on dry land once more.

If the truth be told, Cayleb was more anxious than usual to get ashore himself. The trip from Chisholm had been the most exhausting voyage he could remember, with one ugly storm after another, and his role as a mere passenger had kept him effectively confined below decks the entire time. For some reason, Captain Gyrard seemed to object to having his sovereign on the quarterdeck when everyone had to be lashed into place with lifelines. After the first couple of real blows, Cayleb had discovered he lacked the heart to overrule the captain's obviously sincere (and worried) objections and accepted his banishment below. Not that the captain hadn't had a valid point, he supposed. The mountainous seas had frequently reared as high as twenty-five or thirty feet, and their power had been mind-numbing. The unending succession of impacts had left *Royal Charis*' crew and passengers feeling as if they'd been beaten black and blue, and the ship's carpenter had been kept busy dealing with a host of minor repairs. The boatswain had been kept busy, as well, as sails and gear carried away aloft, and one of their escorting galleons had disappeared for three days. If not for the imagery from Merlin's SNARCs, Cay-leb would have assumed she'd gone down, and at one point, as his flagship had driven before the wind under nothing but bare poles, giving up heartbreaking miles of her hard-won western progress, he hadn't been at all sure *Royal Charis* wasn't going to founder herself—a point he'd been very careful not to discuss with Sharleyan at the time.

The main reason he wanted off the ship, though, had nothing to do with all of that and everything to do with the tasks awaiting him. One of them, in particular, prom-ised to be especially ticklish, and the timing window for it was going to be interesting.

He watched the oared galleys that served as tugs row-ing strongly out to meet his flagship and heard the cheers of welcome rising from their companies and his smile grew a bit broader.

"Just be patient, Nahrmahn," he said soothingly. "We'll have you ashore in no time. Unless one of those tugs ac-cidentally rams us and sinks us, of course."

▼ ▼ ▼

Sir Rayjhis Yowance, Earl of Gray Harbor, was generally recognized as the First Councilor of the Empire of Cha-ris, although the title tended to change off with Baron Green Mountain when the court was in Cherayth. Now he stood watching the galleys nudge *Royal Charis* closer to the stone quay and felt a vast surge of relief. Throwing lines flew ashore, followed by thick hawsers that dropped over the waiting bollards. The ship took tension on the mooring hawsers with her own capstans, fenders squeaked and groaned between her and the quay's tall side, and a gangplank went across to her bulwark-level entry port.

Gray Harbor had commanded his own ship in his time, and he recognized the signs of heavy weather when he saw them. Much of the galleon's paint had been stripped away to expose patches of raw wood; sea slime streaked her hull; one of her quarter boats was missing, the falls lashed tightly across the davits where the sea had stove in the vanished boat; the railing of her sternwalk had been badly damaged; two of her topsails had the newer, less stained look of replacement canvas; and one of her forward gunport lids had been replaced by the ship's carpenter. The bare, unpainted wood looked like a missing tooth in the neat row of the galleon's gunports, and as he looked at the other four galleons of her escort, he saw equal or worse signs of how hard their voyage had been.

I know that boy has an iron stomach, the earl reflected, *but I'll bet even he had his anxious moments on this one. Thank God I didn't know anything about it until he got here! I've got gray hairs enough as it is.*

Gray Harbor knew he tended to worry about what Cayleb airily called "the details" of keeping the Empire running. That was his job, when it came down to it, and he was well aware that whatever Cayleb might *call* them, the emperor knew exactly how important they truly were. Nonetheless, there were times he felt a distinct temptation to say "I told you so," and looking at the battered ship at quayside was definitely one of those moments.

I don't care how much sense it made from a diplomatic perspective, he thought now, sourly, *this nonsense about their spending half the year here in Tellesberg and the other half in Cherayth is just that—nonsense! Ships sink— even the best of them, sometimes, damn it—and if anyone should've known that, it's Cayleb Ahrmahk. But, no, he had to throw that into the marriage proposal, too. And then he and Sharley—and Alahnah—go sailing back and forth on the* same *damned ship. So if it sinks, we lose all three of them!*

He knew he was being silly, and he didn't really care. Not at the moment. And he didn't feel any particular responsibility to be rational, either. Certainly, this time Sharleyan was on a different ship . . . but that only meant she'd have the opportunity to sink on her *own* on the way back from Corisande. Assuming, he reminded himself, HMS *Dawn Star* hadn't already sunk somewhere in the Chisholm Sea, taking Empress and Crown Princess with her.

Oh, stop that!

He shook his head, feeling his disapproving frown disappearing into a grin as Cayleb Ahrmahk came bounding down the gangplank in complete disregard of the careful formality of an emperor's proper arrival in his capital city. The trumpeters, as surprised as anyone by Cayleb's diversion from the anticipated order of disembarkation, began a belated fanfare as the youthful monarch's feet found the quay. Half the assembled courtiers looked offended, another quarter looked surprised, and the remainder were roaring as lustily with laughter as any of the galleon's seamen or watching longshoremen.

You're not going to change them . . . and even if you could, you know you really wouldn't, Gray Harbor told himself. *Besides, it's part of the magic. And*—his expression sobered—*it's part of their* legend. *Part of what makes this whole thing* work, *and they wouldn't have it if God hadn't given it to them. So why don't you just do what they* obviously do and trust God to go on getting it right?

"Welcome home, Your Maj—" he began, starting a formal bow, only to be interrupted as a pair of powerful arms which were obviously as unconcerned with protocol as the rest of the emperor enveloped him in a huge hug.

"It's good to *be* home, Rayjhis!" a voice said in his ear. The arms around him tightened, two sinewy hands thumped him once each on the back, hard, and then Cayleb stood back. He laid those hands on Gray Harbor's shoulders, looking into his face, and smiled that enormous, infectious Ahrmahk smile.

"What say you and I get back to the Palace out of all this racket"—he twitched his head to take in the cheering crowds who were doing their best to deafen everyone in Tellesberg—"and find ourselves some tall, cold drinks while we catch each other up on all the news?"

▼ ▼ ▼

"Thank you for joining us, Paityr," Archbishop Maikel Staynair said as Bryahn Ushyr ushered Paityr Wylsynn into his office once again.

The intendant began to smile in acknowledgment, but

then his face went suddenly neutral as he realized Hainryk Waignair, the elderly Bishop of Tellesberg, and Emperor Cayleb were already present.

"As you can see," Staynair continued, watching Wylsynn's expression, "we've been joined by a couple of additional guests. That's because we have something rather . . . unusual to discuss with you. Something which may require quite a lot of convincing, I'm afraid. So, please, come in and have a seat. You, too, Bryahn."

Ushyr seemed unsurprised by the invitation, and he touched Wylsynn's elbow, startling the young Schuelerite back into motion. The two of them crossed to Staynair's desk to kiss his ring respectfully, then settled into two of the three still unoccupied chairs arranged to face the archbishop and his other guests.

"Allow me to add my thanks to Maikel's, Father," Cayleb said. "And not just for joining us today. I'm well aware of how much my House and my Kingdom—the entire Empire—owe to your compassion and open-mindedness. To be honest, that awareness is one of the reasons for this meeting."

"I beg your pardon, Your Majesty?" Wylsynn's expression was a combination of surprise and puzzlement.

The emperor had arrived back in Tellesberg only yesterday afternoon, and with all that had happened since he and the empress had left Old Charis for Chisholm, there must have been a virtual whirlwind of details and decisions requiring his attention. So what was he doing anywhere except the halls of Tellesberg Palace? If he wanted to meet with Archbishop Maikel or any of the rest of them, he could easily have summoned them to the palace rather than meeting them here. For that matter, how had he gotten to Archbishop Maikel's office without anyone noticing it? And where were the Imperial Guardsmen who should be keeping an eye on him?

"In answer to one of the several questions I'm sure are swirling around inside that active brain of yours," Cayleb said, "there's a tunnel between Tellesberg Palace and the Cathedral. It's been there for the better part of two centuries now, and I'm not the first monarch who's made use of it. Admittedly, we're using it quite a bit more now than we used to, and we never made use of the tunnel between the Cathedral and the Archbishop's Palace before the, um, recent change in management." He smiled infectiously. "I wouldn't be a bit surprised to discover there were similar tunnels between a lot of cathedrals and a lot of palaces. Prince Nahrmahn's confirmed that there's one in Eraystor, at any rate."

"I see, Your Majesty." Wylsynn knew his voice still sounded puzzled, and Cayleb chuckled.

"You see *that* much, you mean, Father," he said. "You're still *at* sea about the rest of it, though, aren't you?"

"I'm afraid so, Your Majesty," Wylsynn admitted.

"All will become clear shortly, Father. In fact," the emperor's expression sobered suddenly, "a great *many* things are about to become clear to you. Before we get into that, however, Maikel has a few things to say to you."

Cayleb sat back in his chair, passing the conversation over to the archbishop, and Wylsynn turned to look at the head of the Church of Charis.

"What we're about to tell you, Father," Staynair's voice was as sober as the emperor's expression, "is going to come as a shock. In fact, even someone with your faith is going to find parts of it very difficult to believe . . . or to *accept,* at least. And I know—know from personal, firsthand experience, believe me—that it will completely change the way in which you look at the world. The decision to tell you wasn't lightly made, nor was it made solely by the men you see in this room at this moment. The truth is that I sent you to Saint Zherneau's for more than one reason, my son. I did send you there because of the spiritual crisis you faced, and I was absolutely honest with you when I told you I'd experienced a similar crisis many years ago and found answers to it at Saint Zherneau's.

"What I didn't tell you at that time was the way in which what I learned at Saint Zherneau's *changed* my faith. I believe it broadened and deepened that faith, yet honesty compels me to say it might just as easily have destroyed my belief forever, had it been presented to me in even a slightly different fashion. And the second reason I sent you to Father Zhon and Father Ahbel was to give them the opportunity to meet you. To come to know you. To be brutally honest, to *evaluate* you . . . and how you might react to the same knowledge."

Wylsynn sat very still, eyes fixed on the archbishop's face, and somewhere deep inside he felt a taut, singing tension. That tension rose, twisting higher and tighter, and his right hand wrapped its fingers around his pectoral scepter.

"The reason for this meeting tonight is that the Brethren decided it would be best to share that same knowledge with you. Not the safest thing to do, perhaps, and not necessarily the wisest, but the best. The Brethren feel—as I do—that you deserve that knowledge, yet it's also a two-edged sword. There are dangers in what we're about to tell you, my son, and not just spiritual ones. There are dangers for us, for you, and for all the untold millions of God's children living on this world or who may *ever* live upon it, and I fear it may bring you great pain. Yet I also believe it will ultimately bring you even greater joy, and in either case, I would never inflict it upon you if not for my deep belief that one of the reasons God sent you to Charis in the first place was to receive exactly this knowledge."

He paused, and Wylsynn drew a shaky breath. He looked around the other faces, saw the same solemnity in all of them, and a part of him wanted to stop the archbishop before he could utter another word. There was something terrifying about the stillness, about those expressions, and he realized he believed every word Staynair had already said. Yet behind his terror, beyond the fear, lay something else. Trust.

"If your purpose was to impress me with the seriousness of whatever you're about to tell me, Your Eminence, you've succeeded," he said after a moment, and felt almost surprised his voice didn't quiver around the edges.

"Good," Cayleb said, reclaiming the thread of the conversation, and Wylsynn's eyes went to the emperor. "But before we get any further into this, there's one other person who needs to be party to the discussion."

Wylsynn's eyebrows rose, but before he could frame the question, even to himself, the door between Staynair's spacious office and Ushyr's much more humble adjoining cubicle opened and a tall, blue-eyed man in the cuirass and chain mail of the Imperial Guard stepped through it.

The intendant's eyes widened in shock and disbelief. Everyone in Tellesberg knew Merlin Athrawes had been sent to Zebediah and Corisande to protect Empress Sharleyan and Crown Princess Alahnah. At that moment, he was almost seven thousand miles from Tellesberg Palace as a wyvern might have flown. He couldn't possibly be *here!*

Yet he was.

"Good afternoon, Father Paityr," Merlin said in his deep voice, one hand stroking his fierce mustachios. "As I told you once in King Haarahld's presence, I believe in God, I believe God has a plan for all men, everywhere, and I believe it's the duty of every man and woman to stand and contend for Light against the Darkness. That was the truth, as you confirmed for yourself, but I'm afraid I wasn't able to tell you *all* the truth then. Today I can."

▼ ▼ ▼

Paityr Wylsynn's face was ashen, despite his deeply tanned complexion.

Twilight had settled beyond the windows while Merlin, Cayleb, and Staynair took turns describing the Journal of Saint Zherneau. The blows to Wylsynn's certainty had come hard and fast, and he knew now why Merlin was present. It was hard enough to believe the truth—even to accept that it might *be* the truth—with the *seijin* sitting there watching his face in the archbishop's office when Wylsynn had *known* he was thousands of miles away.

Of course, the fact he's here doesn't necessarily prove everything they've just told you is *the truth, Paityr, does it?* his Schuelerite training demanded. *The* Writ *tells us there are such things as demons, and who* but *a demon could have made the journey Merlin claims to have made in this "recon skimmer" of his?*

Yet even as he asked himself that, he knew he didn't believe for a moment that Merlin was a demon. In many ways, he wished he did. Things would have been so much simpler, and he would never have known his deep and abiding faith had been built entirely upon the most monstrous lie in human history, if only he'd been able to believe that. The priest in him, and the young seminarian he'd been even before he took his vows, cried out to turn away. To reject the lies of Shan-wei's demon henchman before they completed the corruption of his soul—a corruption which must have begun well before this moment if he could accept even for an instant that Merlin *wasn't* a demon.

And he couldn't reject them as lies. That was the problem. He *couldn't.*

And not just because of all those examples of "technology" Merlin's just demonstrated, either, he thought starkly. *All those doubts of yours, all those questions about how God could have permitted someone like Clyntahn to assume such power. They're part of the reason you believe every single thing these people have just told you. But all the things they've said still don't* answer *the questions! Unless the answer is simply so obvious you're afraid to reach out and touch it. If it's all truly a lie, if there truly are no Archangels and never were, then what if God Himself* was *never anything but a lie? That would explain His permitting Clyntahn to murder and kill and maim in His name, wouldn't it? Because He wouldn't be doing anything of the sort . . . since He never existed in the first place.*

"I'm sorry, Father," Merlin said softly. "I'm sorry we've had to inflict this on you. It's different for me. One thing my experience here on Safehold has taught me is that I'll never truly be able to understand the shock involved in having all that absolute, documented certainty snatched out from under you."

"That's . . . a very good way to describe it, actually, *Seijin* Merlin. Or should I call you Nimue Alban?"

"The Archbishop and I have an ongoing argument about that," Merlin said with an odd, almost whimsical smile. "To be honest, Father, I still haven't decided exactly what I really am. On the other hand, I've also decided there's no option but to continue on the assumption that I *am* Nimue Alban—or that she's a part of me, at any rate—because the life or death of the human species depends on the completion of the mission she agreed to undertake."

"Because of these . . . Gbaba?" Wylsynn pronounced the unfamiliar word carefully.

"That's certainly the greatest, most pressing part of it," Merlin agreed. "Sooner or later, humanity *is* going to encounter them again. If we do that without knowing what's coming, it's highly unlikely we'll be fortunate enough to survive a second time. But there's more to it than that, too. The society created here on Safehold is a straitjacket, at best. At worst, it's the greatest intellectual and spiritual tyranny in history. We—*all* of us, Father Paityr, including this PICA sitting in front of you—have a responsibility, a duty, to break that tyranny. Even if there is no God, the moral responsibility remains. And if there *is* a God, as I believe there is, we have a responsibility to Him, as well."

Wylsynn stared at the PICA—the machine—and he felt a sudden almost irresistible need to laugh insanely. Merlin wasn't even alive, and yet he was telling Wylsynn *he* believed in God? And what was *Wylsynn* supposed to believe in now?

"I know what you're thinking at this moment, Paityr," Staynair said quietly.

Wylsynn's gray eyes snapped to him, wide with disbelief that *anyone* could truly know that, yet that incredulity faded as he gazed into the archbishop's face.

"Not the exact words you're using to flagellate yourself, of course," Staynair continued. "All of us find our own ways to do that. But I know the doubts, the sense of betrayal—of *violation*. All these years, you've deeply and sincerely believed in the *Holy Writ*, in *The Testimonies*, in Mother Church, in the Archangels, and in God. You've *believed,* my son, and you've given your life to that belief. And now you've discovered it's all a lie, all built on deliberate fabrications for the express purpose of preventing you from ever reaching out to the truth. It's worse than being physically violated, because you've just discovered your very soul was raped by merely mortal men and women, *pretending* to be gods, who died centuries before your own birth."

He paused, and Wylsynn looked at him silently, unable to speak, and Staynair shook his head slowly.

"I can't and won't try to dictate the 'right way' to deal with what you're feeling at this moment," the archbishop said quietly. "That would violate my own most deeply held beliefs. But I will ask you to think about this. The Church of God Awaiting wasn't created by God. It was built by men and women ... men and women who'd seen a more terrible tragedy than anything you and I could possibly imagine. Who'd been broken and damaged by that experience, and who were prepared to do anything—*anything at all*—to prevent it from happening again. I believe they were terribly, horribly mistaken in what they did, yet I've come to the conclusion over the years since *I* first discovered Saint Zherneau's journal—and even more in the time since I've known Merlin, and gained access to Owl's records of pre-Safeholdian history—that for all their unspeakable crimes, they weren't really monsters. Oh, they did monstrous *things* in plenty, and understanding the why can't excuse the *what* of their actions. I'm not trying to say it could, and I'm sure they did what they did for all the flawed, personal motives we could imagine, as well, including the hunger for power and the need to control. But that doesn't change the truth of the fact that they genuinely believed the ultimate survival of the human race depended upon their actions.

"Do I think that justifies what they did? No. Do I think it makes the final product of their lie any less monstrous? No. Am I prepared to close my eyes, turn away and allow that lie to continue unchallenged forever? A thousand times no. But neither do I think they acted out of pure evil and self-interest. And neither do I believe anything *they* might have done indicts God. Remember that they built their lie not out of whole cloth, but out of bits and pieces they took away from the writings and the beliefs—and the *faith*—of thousands of generations which had groped and felt their way towards God without benefit of the unbroken, unchallenged—and *untrue*—scripture and history which *we* possess. And so I come to my final rhetorical question. Do I believe the fact that men and women made unscrupulous by desperation and terror misused and abused religion and God Himself means God doesn't exist? A *million* times no, my son.

"I can no longer prove that to you by showing you the incontrovertible, inviolable word set down by the immortal Archangels. I can only ask you to reach inside yourself once more, to seek the wellsprings of faith and to look at all the wonders of the universe—and all the still greater wonders which are about to become available to you—and decide for yourself. Merlin and I had a discussion about this very subject the night he and I first told Cayleb the truth. I wasn't aware then that I was following in the footsteps of another, far more ancient philosopher when I asked him what I could possibly *lose* by believing in God, but now I ask you the same question, Paityr. What do you lose by believing in a loving, compassionate God Who's finally found a way to reach out to His children once more? Will it make you an evil man? Lead you into the same sort of actions that ensnared the real Langhorne and the real Bédard? Or will you continue to reach out in love to those about you? To do good, when the opportunity to do good comes to you? To reach the end of your life knowing you've truly labored to leave the world and all in it a better place than it might otherwise have been?

"And if there *is* no God, if all there is beyond this life is a dreamless, eternal sleep—only nothingness—what will your faith have cost you then?" The archbishop smiled suddenly. "Do you expect to feel cheated or swindled when you realize there was no God waiting beyond that threshold? Only two things can lie on the other side of death, Paityr. It's what Merlin or Owl might describe as 'a binary solution set.' There's either nothingness, or some sort of continued existence, whether it leads us to what we think of now as God or not. And if it's nothingness, then whether or not you were 'cheated' is meaningless. And if there is a continued existence which doesn't contain that Whom I think of as God, then I'll simply have to start over learning the truth again, won't I?"

Paityr gazed at him for several more seconds, then drew a deep breath.

"I don't know what to believe at this moment, Your Eminence," he said finally. "I never imagined I could feel such turmoil as I'm feeling right now. Intellectually, I believe you when you say you've experienced the same things, and I can see you truly have found a way for your faith to survive those experiences. I envy that . . . I think. And the fact that I don't know whether I truly envy your certainty or resent it as yet another manifestation of the lie sums up the heart of my confusion. I'll need time, and a great deal of it, before I can put my spiritual house back in order and say 'Yes, *this* is where I stand.'"

"Of course you will," Staynair said simply. "Surely you don't think anyone *else* has ever simply taken this in stride and continued without missing a step!"

"I don't really know *what* I think right now, Your Eminence!" Wylsynn was astonished by the note of genuine humor in his own response.

"Then you're about where everyone is at this point, Father," Merlin told him, and smiled with a bittersweet crookedness. "And believe me, I may not have had to grapple with the knowledge that I'd been lied to all my life, but waking up in Nimue's Cave and realizing I'd been dead for the better part of a thousand years was just a *little* difficult to process."

"I can believe that," Wylsynn said, yet even as he spoke his eyes had darkened, and his expression turned grim.

"What is it, Paityr?" Staynair asked quickly but softly, and the intendant shook his head hard.

"It's just . . . ironic that Merlin should mention 'a thousand years,' " he said. "You see, not *everything* about the Archangels and Mother Church was set forth in the *Writ* or *The Testimonies* after all, Your Eminence."

. III .

A Recon Skimmer, Above Carter's Ocean

Merlin Athrawes leaned back in his flight couch, gazing up through the canopy at the distant moon. The waters of Carter's Ocean stretched out far below him like an endless black mirror, touched with silver highlights. The stars were distant, glittering pinpricks overhead, but ahead of him lay a wall of cloud, the back edge of a massive weather front moving steadily eastward across Corisande.

It all seemed incredibly peaceful, restful even. It wasn't, of course. The winds along the leading edge of that front were less powerful than those which had battered Cayleb further north, but they were quite powerful enough. And they were going to catch up with *Dawn Star* in the next few hours. The galleon and her escorts were passing through Coris Strait, about to enter South Reach Sound southeast of Corisande before looping back westward through White Horse Reach to the Corisandian capital of Manchyr, and Merlin wondered if the bad weather was going to be his ally or his comeuppance. Getting on and off a sailing ship in the middle of the ocean without being detected was a nontrivial challenge, even for a PICA. As it was, he'd officially retreated to his cabin to "meditate," and Sharleyan and the rest of her guard detail would see to it that he wasn't disturbed. He'd even left a rope trailing helpfully from the galleon's sternwalk so he could shinny back aboard, hopefully unnoticed. After so long, it had become almost a well-established routine.

Except, of course, that if the weather's as bad as it looks like being tonight, there're going to be people keeping an anxious watch on little things like rigging and sails or rogue waves . . . any one of whom might just happen to notice the odd seijin *climbing up a rope out of the ocean in the middle of the night.*

His lips twitched at the thought, yet he wasn't really worried about it. He'd be able to spot any lookout before the lookout could spot him, and a PICA could easily spend an hour or two submerged in the ship's wake, clinging to a rope and waiting patiently until the coast was clear. Not only that, but he'd be back aboard several hours before local dawn, with plenty of darkness to help cover his return. In fact, that was the real reason for the timing of the conference with Father Paityr. They'd had to make sufficient allowance for Merlin's transit, and he'd had to plan on both departing and returning under cover of night if he wanted to be certain he wasn't observed.

And that's exactly what you're going to be doing, he told himself. *So why don't you stop worrying about that and start worrying about what Father Paityr just told you, instead?*

His brief almost-smile disappeared, and he shook his head.

I guess fair's fair. You've cheerfully torn lots of other people's worlds apart by telling the truth about Langhorne and Bédard. It's about time somebody returned the compliment.

He closed his eyes and his perfect PICA's memory replayed the conversation in Maikel Staynair's office.

▼ ▼ ▼

"What do you mean 'Not everything about the Archangels and Mother Church was set forth in the *Writ* or *The Testimonies*,' my son?" Staynair asked, his eyes narrowing with concern as Paityr Wylsynn's tone registered.

"I mean there's more than one reason my family's always been so deeply involved in the affairs of Mother Church, Your Eminence."

Wylsynn's face was tight, his voice harrowed with mingled bitterness, anger, and lingering shock at what he'd already been told. He looked around the others' faces and drew a deep breath.

"The tradition of my family's always been that we were directly descended from the Archangel Schueler," he said harshly. "All my life, that's been a source of great joy to me—and of a pride I've struggled against as something unbecoming in any son of Mother Church. And, of course, it was also something Mother Church and the Inquisition would flatly have denied could have been possible. That's one of the reasons my family was always so careful to keep the tradition secret. But we were also specifically *charged* to keep it so—according to the tradition—when certain knowledge was left in our possession."

Merlin's molycirc nerves tingled with sudden apprehension, but he kept his face expressionless as he cocked his head.

"May I assume your possession of the Stone of Schueler was part of that tradition and knowledge, Father?"

"Indeed you may." The bitterness in Wylsynn's tone was joined by corrosive anger. "All my life I've believed this"—he lifted his pectoral scepter, the disguised reliquary which concealed the relic his family had treasured for so long—"had been left as a sign of God's approval of our faithfulness." He snorted harshly. "Except, of course, that it's nothing of the sort!"

"I don't know why it was left with you, Father," Merlin said gently. "I'm pretty sure whoever handed it to your ancestors—and it may actually have been Schueler, for all we know—didn't have any particular faith in God. From what I've heard about your history, though, that hasn't kept your family from believing in Him. As for what the 'Stone of Schueler' actually is, it's what was called a 'verifier.' Once upon a time, it might've been called a 'lie detector,' instead. And however it came into your possession, Father, it truly does do what your ancestors were told it did. It tells you whether or not someone is telling you the truth. In fact," he smiled wryly, "it's a full-spectrum verifier, which means it can also tell when a *PICA* is telling you the truth. Which required a certain . . . circumspection when I answered the questions you once put to me in King Haarahld's throne room."

"Given what you've just told me about Safehold's true history, I'd say that was probably an understatement," Wylsynn replied with the first thing like a true smile he'd produced in the last hour or two.

"Oh, it was!" Merlin nodded. "At the same time, what I told you then was the truth, exactly as it insisted."

"I believe that," Wylsynn said quietly. "What I'm struggling with is whether or not I should believe anything *else* I once thought was true."

There was silence for a moment, then the young man in the Schuelerite cassock shook himself.

"I'm going to have to deal with that. I know that. But I also understand why you have to be leaving shortly, Merlin, so I suppose I'd better get on with it."

He drew a deep breath, visibly bracing himself, then sat back in his chair and folded his hands in his lap.

"When I was a boy, my father and Uncle Hauwerd told me all the tales about our family's history and the role we'd played in the vicarate and in Mother Church's history. Or I thought they told me *all* the tales, at any rate. It was enough to make me realize we had a special, joyous duty, and it helped me understand why my family had stood for reform, held tight to the truth, for so many centuries. Why we'd made so many enemies as corruption set deeper and deeper into the vicarate. The voice of conscience seldom makes comfortable hearing, and never less comfortable than to those who know deep in their hearts how far short of their duties and their responsibilities they've fallen. All of the orders teach that, and it was enough—I thought then—to explain everything.

"Yet it wasn't until I'd graduated from seminary and been ordained that Father told me the *complete* truth about our family and our traditions. That was when he showed me the Stone of Schueler and the Key."

He paused, and Merlin's eyebrows quirked. He looked quickly at the others and saw the same expression looking back at him. Then all of them returned their attention to the young priest.

"The 'Key,' Father?" Merlin prompted.

"According to the secret history Father showed me, the Key and the Stone were both left in our possession by the Archangel Schueler himself. The Stone you know about. The Key must be another piece of your 'technology,' *Seijin* Merlin, although it's less spectacular at first glance than the Stone. It's a small sphere, flattened on one side and about this far across"—he held up thumb and forefinger, perhaps two inches apart—"which looks like plain, polished steel." His lips flickered in a small smile. "In fact, it's so plain generations of Wylsynns have hidden it in plain sight by using it as a paperweight."

There was a ghost of genuine humor in his voice, and Merlin felt himself smiling back, but then Wylsynn continued.

"By itself, the Key really is nothing but a paperweight," he said soberly, "but in conjunction with the Stone, it becomes something else. The best way I can describe it is as a . . . repository of visions."

Merlin straightened in his chair, his expression suddenly intent.

"Father, I never had the opportunity to actually examine the Stone. I just assumed that it filled only a small section of your scepter's staff. But it doesn't, does it?"

"No, it doesn't," Wylsynn confirmed. "It fills almost the full length of the staff, and it can be removed. When it is, it mates to the Key. Its lower end clings unbreakably to the flat face of the Key, as if they've become one, and they can be released from one another only by someone who knows the proper command." His eyes watched Merlin carefully. "Should I assume you know how it works and why?"

"I'd have to examine both of them to be certain," Merlin replied, "but I'm reasonably sure that among the instructions your family was left was a ritual which regularly exposed the Stone to direct sunlight?" Wylsynn nodded, and Merlin shrugged. "What that was doing, Father, was to charge—to empower—the Stone. In time, you'll understand exactly what I'm talking about. For the moment, simply accept that there's nothing demonic or divine in the process; it's a simple matter of physics.

"At any rate, what you're calling the Key is a memory module, a solid chunk of molecular circuitry. You could fire it out of a cannon without hurting it, and that single sphere you've described could easily contain all the knowledge in all the libraries of the entire Charisian Empire with space left over. The problem is getting it out, and for that you need a power source. So I'm reasonably sure that when you remove the Stone entirely from the scepter, the length of it that 'mates to the Key' doesn't glow the way the rest of it does, right?"

"Correct." Wylsynn nodded.

"Of course it doesn't." Merlin shook his head. "That's the adapter, Father. It takes the energy you've stored in the Stone and feeds it to the memory module. And when it does, the module projects images, doesn't it?"

"That's precisely what it does," Wylsynn said grimly, "and if you hadn't demonstrated your 'com' and its ability to generate 'holograms,' I would never have believed a word any of you told me. Because, you see, I've *seen* the image of the 'Holy Schueler' himself. I've heard his voice. Until this very day, I've believed—deeply and truly believed—that my family and I had been directly touched by the very finger of God. And I'd *still* believe that . . . if you hadn't just shown me exactly the same sort of 'vision' which has lied to my family for nine centuries."

Merlin sat silent for a long, still moment. It had never occurred to him that anyone associated with the Temple might possess such an artifact. Yet now that he knew, he also realized the blow the truth had delivered to Paityr Wylsynn was even crueler than anything it had done to anyone else. The young Schuelerite's faith had been so sure, so total, because he'd *known* he'd been in the very presence of God . . . or in the presence of one of God's Archangels, at least. Now he knew how bitterly betrayed he and all his family had actually been—knew his father and uncle had gone to their deaths seduced and lied to by the very vision which had lied to *him*, as well.

In that moment, Merlin's own soul cried out against what had been done—what *he'd* done—to Paityr Wylsynn. How could any mortal being be expected to deal with something like this? How could any faith, any belief, not be twisted into something bitter and cold and hateful after the realization of a betrayal so profound, so complete, and so personal?

"My son," Maikel Staynair said quietly into the silence, his expression sad, "I understand the reasons for your pain. I doubt I can truly imagine its *depth*, but I understand its cause. And I believe I can at least imagine the extent to which you must now question all you ever knew or ever believed—not just about the Church, and not just about the 'Archangels,' but about everything. About yourself, about God, about how much of the vocation you've felt was solely the result of deception. About how you could have been so stupid as to be deceived, and how so many generations of your family could have dedicated themselves—*sacrificed* themselves—to the lie you've just discovered. It can be no other way."

Wylsynn looked at him, and the archbishop shook his head gently.

"My son—Paityr—I will never fault you if you decide *all* of it was a lie, and that God does not and never did exist. After discovering a deception such as this, it would *take* an archangel not to lash out in the bitterness and the fury it's so justly awakened within you. And if that happens, you must never blame yourself for it, either. If you decide—if *you* decide—God doesn't exist, then you must not punish yourself in the stillness of your own mind for turning away from all you were taught to believe and revere. I hope and pray that won't happen. The depth and strength of the faith I've seen out of you is too great for me to want to see it cast away for any reason. But I would rather see it discarded cleanly than see you trying to *force* a life into it when it no longer has pulse or breath of its own. Do you understand what I'm saying to you?"

Wylsynn looked back at the archbishop for several seconds, then nodded slowly.

"I think so, Your Eminence," he said slowly. "And I'm not sure what's going to happen. You're right that I now know the faith which has carried me so far has been only the shadow cast by a direct and personal lie. Yet that's true of all of us, I suppose, isn't it? *My* lie's been more spectacular than that of others, but all of us have been lied to. So in the final analysis, what I have to determine is whether it's the way in which the lie is transmitted or the lie itself which truly matters . . . and whether a lie can still contain even the tiniest grain of truth."

"If it's any consolation, my son," Staynair said with a crooked smile, "the *Writ* wasn't the first holy book to say that faith grows like a mustard seed. God works from tiny beginnings to great ends."

"I hope you're right, Your Eminence. Or I *think* I do. It's going to be a while before I can decide whether or not I *want* my faith to survive, I'm afraid."

"Of course it is," Staynair said simply.

Wylsynn nodded, then turned back to Merlin.

"At any rate, Merlin, your description of how the Key works was accurate. When Father showed it to me, it projected images, visions—holograms—of the Archangel Schueler himself, instructing us in our family's responsibilities." He frowned thoughtfully. "I sometimes think that was one reason my family's always supported a . . . gentler approach for the Inquisition. The Schueler of the

Key isn't the grim and terrible Schueler who prescribed the Question and the Punishment. Stern, yes, but without the demeanor of someone who could demand such hideous punishment for a child of God who was merely mistaken."

"I never knew the real Schueler," Merlin said. "Nimue may have met him, but if so, it was after she'd recorded ... me." He smiled sadly. "Because of that, I've never seen any reason not to assume *The Book of Schueler* was written by the 'Archangel Schueler,' but we really don't have confirmation of the authorship of *any* of the books of the *Writ*, when you come down to it. For that matter, *The Book of Schueler* wasn't part of the original, early copy of the *Writ* Commodore Pei left in Nimue's Cave. The entire thing was extensively reworked after Langhorne took out the Alexandrian Enclave—inevitably, I suppose—and *The Book of Schueler* and *The Book of Chihiro* were both added. I don't know if it's any consolation, Father, but it really is possible the actual Schueler never wrote the book credited to him. And if he didn't, then he isn't the author of the Question and the Punishment, either."

"I would like to believe that was the case," Wylsynn said softly after a moment. "I'd like to believe not *everything* I thought I knew was a lie. And if it's true my family actually is descended from the real Schueler, it would ease my heart to know he wasn't capable of decreeing such hideous penalties in defense of a 'religion' he knew was nothing but a lie."

He was silent again for a moment. Then he gave himself a shake.

"However that may be," he continued more briskly, "what my family's referred to as 'the Vision of the Archangel Schueler' for as long as we can remember instructs us not simply in our duty to keep Mother Church untainted, without stain, focused on her great mission in the world, but also charges us with a special responsibility. A Key within the Key, as it were."

"I beg your pardon?" Merlin asked.

"There's a chamber under the Temple," Wylsynn told him. "I've never actually been there, but I've seen it in 'the Vision.' I know the way to it, and I can picture it in my mind's eye even now. And within that chamber is an altar, one with 'God lights' set into its surface. There are also two handprints, one each for a right and a left hand, on either side of a small, circular recess. According to 'the Vision,' if one truly dedicated to God and His plan places the Key in that recess and his hands in those imprints and calls upon Schueler's name, the power of God Himself will awaken to defend Mother Church in her hour of need."

Merlin felt the heart he no longer had stop beating.

"According to 'the Vision,' it may be done only once, and only in the hour of Mother Church's *true* need," Wylsynn continued. "Knowing Father and Uncle Hauwerd, there's no way they would have viewed the Reformist movement as a genuine threat to Mother Church. The Church of Charis has made no demands which actually conflict with the *Writ* in any way, and they would have realized that as well as I do. I'm sure the schism distressed them deeply, and that both of them were profoundly concerned about the implications for the unity of God's church and plan, but the Temple would have had to be threatened with actual physical invasion before either of them would have felt the time had come to awaken God's power in the Church's defense. There's no doubt in my mind that both of them agreed with the Reformists' indictments of the vicarate and believed the Reformists were truer sons of God than the Group of Four could ever be. I don't know where that would have led them in the end, but there's no way they would have presumed to beseech God to strike down men and women they believed were simply attempting to live the lives and the faith God had ordained for them from the beginning."

The others were all looking at Merlin, and Cayleb cleared his throat.

"Is that 'altar' what I'm afraid it is?" he asked carefully.

"I don't know . . . but it certainly could be," Merlin said unhappily. "I don't know what would happen if someone obeyed Schueler's commands. It might simply trigger some sort of reaction out of the bombardment platform. Or, for that matter, one of the things I've been afraid of for some time is that Langhorne—or whoever built the Temple after Langhorne was dead—could have included an AI in the master plan. Something like Owl, but probably with more capacity. Only I'd decided that couldn't be the case, because if there were an AI monitoring what the vicarate's been up to for the last two or three centuries, it probably would've already intervened. But if there's something like that down there that's on standby, waiting for a human command to wake it up. . . ."

His voice trailed off, and Cayleb, Staynair, and Waignair looked at one another tautly.

"I have far too little grasp of this 'technology' you've described to even guess whether or not there's an 'AI' involved," Wylsynn said. "I only know that if 'the Vision' is telling the truth and the ritual is properly performed, *something* will respond."

"But no one beyond your family even knows about the ritual?" Cayleb asked, and Wylsynn shrugged.

"To the best of my knowledge, no, Your Majesty. On the other hand, so far as I know, none of the other families in the vicarate were aware of what *my* family knew, either. We always believed on the basis of what 'the Vision' told us that we'd been chosen, singled out, as the only guardians of that chamber and altar, but there may have actually been others. The Stone's existence was known, of course, although most people believe it was lost forever at Saint Evrahard's death. So far as we knew, no one else had ever been informed of the Key's existence, although, in more recent years, Father came to fear from some things he'd heard that perhaps someone else *did* know at least something about the Key and the Stone's continued existence. He never said who that someone might be, but I know he was concerned by the possibility of one or both of them falling into hands which might well misuse them."

"I wish *we* could get our hands on that damned Key!" Merlin said forcefully, and Wylsynn surprised him with a chuckle.

"What?" Merlin's eyes narrowed. "I said something funny?"

"No," Wylsynn said. "But when I said Father and Uncle Hauwerd wouldn't have petitioned God to strike the Reformists, I suppose I should really have said they *couldn't* have. When Father suggested I should take the post as Archbishop Erayk's intendant here in Charis, he sent me on my way at least in part to keep certain things out of Clyntahn's reach. With the Stone, of course, but also with a family keepsake. A paperweight."

"The 'Key' is here in *Charis*?" Cayleb demanded.

"Sitting on the corner of my desk in the Patent Office, Your Majesty," Wylsynn confirmed.

"With your permission, Father, I'd like to have one of Owl's remotes collect that from you and take it back to Nimue's Cave where we can examine it properly," Merlin said, watching Wylsynn's face carefully.

"Of course you have my permission . . . not that I imagine there's much I could do to stop you," Wylsynn replied with a half smile. Then his expression sobered once more. "Just as I'm reasonably confident that if it turns out you were . . . ill-advised to tell me the truth about the Church and the Archangels, there wouldn't be much I could do to stop you from correcting your error."

The silence was sudden and intense, lingering until Wylsynn himself broke it with a small, dry chuckle.

"I'm an inquisitor, a Schuelerite," he said. "Surely you didn't imagine I could hear what you've told me and not recognize what you'd have to do if you thought I might betray you? I'm sure all of you—especially you, Your Eminence—would deeply regret the necessity, but I'm also sure you'd do it. And if you're telling me the truth, which I believe you are, you'd have no choice."

"I hope you won't be offended by this, Father, but at this particular moment you remind me rather strongly of Prince Nahrmahn," Merlin said.

"Yes, I'm sure it would've occurred to the Prince, as well," Wylsynn said thoughtfully.

"And to his wife, too," Cayleb said. "I think she's just as smart as he is, and she hasn't lived with him that long without recognizing necessity when she sees it."

"All I can tell you is that at this moment I feel no inclination to betray your confidence, Your Majesty." Wylsynn shrugged. "Obviously, I'm still in something of a state of shock. I don't know how I'm going to feel about it tomorrow, or the next day. I will promise this, however. Archbishop Maikel's always extended me his trust, and I won't abuse that now. With your permission, Your Eminence, I request permission to withdraw to Saint Zherneau's again for the next five-day or so. I truly do need to spend some time in meditation and thought, for obvious reasons." He grimaced. "But I'd also like the opportunity to examine Saint Zherneau's journal for myself, and to spend some additional time speaking with Father Zhon and the rest of the Brethren who've grappled with the same issues rather longer than I have. That should keep me out of the public eye while I do some grappling of my own, which will also spare you the necessity of returning me to the genteel confinement I enjoyed immediately after Archbishop Erayk's departure for the Temple."

"It was never my intention to lock you up while you considered all the implications, Father," Staynair said.

"With all due respect, Your Eminence, it *should* have been," Wylsynn said bluntly. "You've taken chances enough letting a convinced and believing Schuelerite so close to you and to the levers of power here in the Empire. Until you know—until we *all* know, including myself—which direction the *disillusioned* Schuelerite is going to go, you really can't afford to take any more chances. The amount of damage I could do to your cause with a few careless words, far less if I choose to lash out in my anger—and I *am* angry, Your Eminence; never doubt it—would be incalculable."

"I'm afraid he has a point, Maikel," Cayleb said. "I have to admit I'm a lot happier with the notion of a voluntary . . . let's call it 'seclusion' instead of 'confinement' on his part than I'd be with the notion of clapping him into a cell somewhere, but he does have a point."

"Very well, my son," Staynair said heavily.

"And I'm sure those 'remotes' of yours will keep an eye on me as well, *Seijin* Merlin," Wylsynn said wryly.

"But not when you're closeted with Father Zhon or any of the others, Father," Merlin murmured, and the young priest laughed.

"I'll bear that in mind," he said. Then his expression sobered once more.

"You asked whether there might be another Key, or its equivalent, and I said I thought not. I still think that's probably the case. And if it is, then presumably you don't have to worry about someone deliberately awakening whatever might lie under the Temple. But there's a reason I said your comment about having been dead for 'almost a thousand years' was ironic, Merlin."

"And that reason was?" Merlin asked slowly.

"Because according to the 'Vision of Schueler,' " Wylsynn said softly, "the Archangels themselves will return a thousand years after the Creation to be sure Mother Church continues to serve the true plan of God."

▼ ▼ ▼

Merlin blinked as his memory finished replaying the conversation, and the same chill ran through him once again.

He'd always been afraid of those power sources under the Temple. He'd thought he wanted nothing more than to discover the truth about them. Now he realized the reality might be even worse than he'd allowed himself to imagine.

The Archangels will return, he thought. *What the* hell *does that mean? Were those lunatics crazy enough to put a batch of "Archangels" into cryo under there? Were they actually willing to trust the cryo systems to keep them going that* long? *And even if they were,* could *the systems stand up for that many years?*

So far as he knew, no one had ever used the cryo suspension systems for a period greater than thirty or forty years. Theoretically, they were supposed to be good for up to a century and a half. But *nine* centuries?

But maybe that's not what it is after all. Maybe it is *an AI. It could be that they didn't trust an AI to run continuously but were willing to let it come up* periodically. *Only if that's the case, why wait a thousand years before it makes its first check? Unless the "Vision of Schueler" is lying and whatever it is has actually been popping up for a look every fifty or sixty years, I suppose. Except that it's pretty evident the vicarate's been departing from the image of the Church laid down in the* Holy Writ *for at least two or three hundred years, so if there's an AI down there that's supposed to be making midcourse adjustments, why's it kept its mouth shut? Unless it's broken, and that doesn't seem likely, given how many of the Temple's other systems still seem to be up and running. I can't imagine they'd've built the place without making certain something as critical as a monitoring AI would be the* last *thing to go down, not the first!*

He grimaced, then froze as another thought struck him.

I'm the only PICA Commodore Pei *and the others had access to,* an icy mental voice said. *But what if I'm not the only PICA that came to Safehold after all? What if* that's *what's down there? The only reason I'm capable of long-term operation is because Doctor Proctor hacked my basic software. It's possible they could have brought along—hell, even built after they got here, despite Langhorne's anti-technology lunacy!—a PICA or two of their own. And if they didn't have Proctor's fine touch on the software, their PICAs could be limited to the "legal" ten days of autonomous operation before their personalities and memories automatically dump. So maybe, if that's the case, it* would *make sense for them to only spin up once every thousand years or so. They get up, spend a day or two looking around, and if everything's humming along, they go back into shutdown immediately. For that matter, they could have* multiple *PICAs stashed down there in the cellar. One of them wakes up and looks around, and if there's a problem, he's got reinforcements he can call up. Hell, for that matter if they* did *have more than one PICA down there and it was keyed to the same person, could he* bootstrap *himself back and forth between them to get around the ten-day limit?!*

He didn't know the answer to his own question. Under the Federation's restrictions on Personality Integrated Cybernetic Avatars, each PICA had been unique to the human being who owned it. It had been physically impossible for anyone else to operate it, and just as it had been illegal for a PICA to operate for more than ten days in autonomous mode, it had been illegal for an individual even to *operate*, far less own, more than a single PICA, except under strenuously controlled circumstances which usually had to do with high-risk industrial processes or something similar. So far as he was aware, no one had ever attempted to simply shuttle someone's memories and personality back and forth between a pair of identical PICAs keyed to the same owner/operator. He had no idea how the software's built-in restrictions would react to that, but it was certainly possible it would represent a lower-risk solution than Proctor's hack of his own software. Assuming one had access to multiple PICAs, of course.

And didn't *that* lead to an interesting speculation?

"Owl?"

"Yes, Lieutenant Commander Alban?" the distant AI replied.

"Could we use the fabrication unit in the cave to build another PICA?"

"That question requires refinement, Lieutenant Commander Alban."

"What?" Merlin blinked at the unexpected response. "What sort of 'refinement'? List the difficulties."

"Theoretically, the fabrication unit could construct a PICA," the AI said. "It would deplete certain critical elements below the minimum inventory level specified in my core programming, which would require human override authorization. In addition, however, it would require data not available to me."

"What sort of data are we talking about?"

"I do not have detailed schematics or design data on PICAs."

"You don't?" Merlin's eyebrows rose in surprise.

"No, Lieutenant Commander Alban," Owl replied, and Merlin reminded himself not to swear when the AI stopped there, obviously satisfied with its response.

"Why not?" he asked after a moment.

"Because it was never entered into my database."

Merlin began reciting the names of the Federation's presidents to himself. *Obviously* it had never been entered into Owl's database. Of course, that wasn't the "why" he'd had in mind when he posed the question!

"*Why* was it never entered into your database?" he asked finally. "And if you don't have a definitive answer, speculate."

"I do not have a definitive answer, Lieutenant Commander Alban. However, I would speculate that it was never entered because the construction of PICAs was a highly specialized enterprise attended by a great many legal restrictions and security regulations and procedures. It would not be something that would be found in a general database. Certainly it would not be part of a tactical computer's database, nor, apparently, part of the library database downloaded from *Romulus*."

"Damn. That *does* make sense," Merlin muttered.

Owl, predictably, made no reply.

Merlin grimaced, but he was actually just as happy to be left to his thoughts for the moment.

The possibility of building additional PICAs had never occurred to him before. On the other hand, if he could, and if the additional PICAs' software duplicated his own, he could create clones of himself, which would be hugely helpful. Not only would it allow him to be in more than one place simultaneously, it would give him the advantage of redundancy if one of him inadvertently did something to which some high-tech watchdog system might take exception.

And if Wylsynn's right about something "returning" in a thousand years, I may just need all the reinforcements I can get, he thought grimly. *This is the year 895, but they've numbered their "Years of God" from the end of "Shan-wei's Rebellion," from the time the Church of God turned into the Church of God Awaiting. The Day of Creation was seventy years—Standard Years, not Safeholdian ones—before that. And that makes this year 979 since the Creation. Which means we've got twenty years, give or take, before whatever's going to happen happens.*

Twenty years might sound like a lot, but not when it was all the time they had to break not simply the Church of God Awaiting's political supremacy but also its stranglehold on Safehold's religious and technological life. They'd been working on it for five years already, and all they'd really managed so far was to stave off defeat. Well, they'd begun gnawing away at the Proscriptions of Jwo-jeng—slowly and very, very cautiously—but they certainly hadn't found a way to take the war to the Church and the Group of Four on the mainland! And even if they managed that, simply defeating the Group of Four militarily wasn't going to miraculously undo ten centuries' belief in the *Holy Writ* and the Archangels. That fight was going to take far longer . . . and it was likely to involve even more bloodshed than the current conflict.

Perhaps still worse, if there was something—"Archangel," AI, or PICA—waiting to "wake up" under the Temple, he had to assume any technological advancement beyond the simple steam engines which still hadn't attracted the bombardment system's attention to the Castaway Islands *was* going to be noticed by its sensors and reported to the Temple. At which point it was entirely possible the wake-up's schedule might be rather drastically revised.

"Owl, could analysis of this PICA give you the data you'd require to build additional ones?"

"Probability of success would approach unity assuming a complete analysis of software and hardware," the AI replied.

"And would such an analysis constitute a risk to *this* PICA's continued operation?"

"Preliminary analysis indicates a sixty-five to seventy percent probability it would be rendered permanently inoperable," Owl said calmly.

"Why?"

"Most probable cause would be failure of the unit's software. There is a significant probability that the necessary analysis would trigger a reboot, which would wipe the unit's current memory and personality."

"What if it were possible to reload the memory and personality from another source?"

"In that case the probability of rendering the current unit inoperable would drop to approximately twenty-eight percent."

"Still that high?" Merlin frowned. "Why?"

"In the event of a reboot, standard protocols would reinstall original program and system defaults, Lieutenant Commander. The software alteration which permits this unit's indefinite operation lies far outside those defaults and would be eliminated in such an eventuality, thus restoring the ten-day limitation on autonomous operation."

Merlin grimaced. That made sense, he supposed, and twenty-eight percent was still unacceptably high. Under the current circumstances, at least. But if circumstances *changed*. . . .

"Do you have the capability out of existing resources to build both a Class II VR and a recording unit?" he asked.

"Affirmative, Lieutenant Commander Alban."

"In that case, get started on both of them immediately. I assume you can run up the recording unit first?"

"Affirmative, Lieutenant Commander Alban."

"Then send it out to me as soon as it's finished." He grimaced again. "I might as well get myself recorded as soon as possible."

"Acknowledged, Lieutenant Commander Alban."

JUNE, YEAR OF GOD 895

✦

Siddar City,
Republic of Siddarmark

"Don't be such a greedy guts!" Byrk Raimahn scolded as the wyvern swooped down and snatched the morsel of fresh bread from his fingers. "There's plenty if you just behave yourselves!"

The triumphant wyvern only whistled smugly at him and flapped its way back up onto the green-budded branch of the apple tree from which it had launched its pounce. It seemed remarkably unmoved by his appeal to its better nature, Byrk reflected, and tore another piece from the loaf. He shredded it into smaller pieces, scattering them across the flagstone terrace for the less aggressive of his winged diners, then picked up a wedge of sharp cheddar cheese from the plate beside the bowl of grapes. He leaned back in his rattan chair, propping his heels on the matching chair which faced him on the other side of the table, and nibbled as he enjoyed the cool northern sunlight.

It wasn't much like home, he thought, gazing out across the sparkling waters of North Bedard Bay. The locals (a label which he still had trouble applying to himself) usually called it simply North Bay, to distinguish it from the even larger Bedard Bay to the south. This far north of the equator, the seasons stood on their heads and even late spring and early summer were almost uncomfortably cool to his Charisian blood. Trees were much later to leaf, flowers were later to bloom (and less colorful when they did), and ocean water was far too cold for a Charisian boy to swim in. Besides, he missed Tellesberg's livelier waterfront, sharper-edged theaters, and heady, bustling air of intellectual ferment.

Of course, that intellectual ferment was the main reason he was sitting here on his grandfather's Siddar City terrace feeding bread to greedy wyverns and squabbling seagulls. It wasn't like—

"So, here you are!" a familiar voice said, and he looked over his shoulder, then rose with a smile of welcome for the silver-haired, plump but distinguished-looking woman who'd just stepped out of the mansion's side door behind him.

"I wasn't exactly *hiding*, Grandmother," he pointed out. "In fact, if you'd opened a window and listened, I'm sure you could have tracked me down without any trouble at all."

He pulled one of the chairs away from the table with one hand while the other gestured at the guitar lying in its open case on the bench beside him.

"For that matter, if you'd only *looked* out the window, the fleeing birds and the small creatures running for the shrubbery with their paws over their ears would have pinpointed me for you."

"Oh, nonsense, Byrk!" She laughed, patting him on the cheek before she seated herself in the proffered chair. "Your playing's not *that* bad."

"Just not *that* bad?" he teased, raising one eyebrow at her. "Is that another way of saying it's *almost* that bad?"

"No, that's what your grandfather would call it·if *he* were here," Sahmantha Raimahn replied. "And he'd mean just as little of it as I would. Go ahead and play something for me now, Byrk."

"Well, if you insist," he said in a long-suffering tone.

She made a face at him, and he laughed as he picked the guitar back up. He thought for a moment, picking random notes as he considered, then struck the opening chord of "The Way of the Widow-Maker," one of the very first ballads he'd learned to play sitting on Sahmantha's lap. The sad, rich notes spilled across the terrace while the sunlight struck chestnut highlights in his brown hair and the wind ruffled that hair, sighed in the branches of the ornamental fruit trees, and sent the shrubbery's sprays of blossoms flickering in light and shadow.

He bent his head, eyes half-closed, giving himself to the ballad, and his grandmother drew her steel thistle silk wrap closely about her shoulders. She knew he thought of his music as a rich young man's hobby, but he was wrong. It was far more than that, and as she watched him play her own eyes lost some of their usual sparkle, darkening while the lament for lost sailors spilled up from his guitar strings to circle and curtsy around the terrace. It was a haunting melody, as lovely as it was sad, and she remembered how he'd insisted she teach it to him when he'd been barely seven years old.

The year before his parents' deaths had sent him to her more as her youngest son than her oldest *grandson*.

"I don't suppose you could've thought of anything *more* depressing, could you?" she teased gently when the final note had faded away, and he shrugged.

"I don't really think of it as depressing," he said, laying the guitar back in the case and running a fingertip gently down the bright strings. He looked back up at her. "It's sad, yes, but not *depressing,* Grandmother. There's too much love for the sea in it for that."

"Perhaps you're right," she conceded.

"Of course I am—*I'm* the poet, remember?" He smiled infectiously. "Besides," his smile turned warmer, gentler, "I love it because of who it was that taught it to me."

"Flatterer." She reached out and smacked him gently on the knee. "You got that from your father. And *he* got it from your grandfather!"

"Really?" He seemed astounded by the notion and gazed thoughtfully out across the gleaming blue water for several seconds, then nodded with the air of someone who'd just experienced a revelation. "So *that's* how someone with the Raimahn nose got someone as good-looking as you to marry him! I'd always wondered about that, actually."

"You, Byrk Raimahn, are what was known in my youth as a rapscallion."

"Oh, no, Grandmother—you wrong me! I'm sure the term you'd really have applied to me would've been *much* ruder than that."

She laughed and shook her head at him, and he offered her the bowl of grapes. She selected one and popped it into her mouth, and he set the bowl down in front of her.

"Somehow the hothouse grapes just aren't as good," he commented. "They make me miss our vineyards back home."

He glanced back out across the bay as he spoke and missed the shadow that flitted through her eyes. Or he could pretend he had, at least.

"I think they have a lower sugar content," she said out loud, no sign of that shadow touching her voice.

"That's probably it," he agreed, looking back at her with another smile.

She returned the smile, plucked another grape, and leaned back, cocking her head to one side.

"What's this about you being off to Madam Pahrsahn's again this evening?" she asked lightly. "I hear you have at least a dozen rivals for her affections, you know."

"Alas, too true!" He pressed the back of his wrist to his forehead, his expression tragic. "That cretin Raif Ahlaixsyn offered her a sonnet last night, and he actually had the gall to make it a *good* one." He shook his head. "Quickly, Grandmother! Tell me what to do to recover in her eyes!"

"Oh, I'm sure you'll come about." She shook her head at him. "Although, at the rate she seems to attract fresh suitors, you may yet find yourself crowded out."

"Grandmother," he looked at her affectionately, "I enormously admire Madam Pahrsahn. I also think she's one of the most beautiful women I've ever met, and bearing in mind my paternal grandmother's youthful beauty that's a pretty high bar for anyone to pass. Even more important, I've never met anyone more brilliant and cultured than she is. But she's also somewhere around twice my age, and I think she regards me more in the light of a puppy who hasn't yet grown into his ears and feet than anything remotely like a paramour. I promise I'm on my very best behavior at her soirées."

"Of course you are. I know that," she said, just that bit too quickly, and he laughed and shook a finger under her nose.

"Oh, no, you *don't* know it!" he scolded. "What a fibber! You're worried your darling grandson is going to be so enamored of the gorgeous, sophisticated older woman that he's going to commit some indiscretion with her." He shook his head, brown eyes glinting devilishly. "Trust me, Grandmother! When *I* commit youthful indiscretions, I'll take great care to make certain you know nothing about them. That way *you'll* be happy, and *I'll* remain intact."

"You're right, 'rapscallion' is definitely too polite a term for you, young man!"

Her lips quivered as she fought to restrain a smile, and he laughed again.

"Which is why you're afraid of those youthful indiscretions of mine," he observed. "A charming, unprincipled rogue and general, all-round ne'er-do-well is far more likely to succeed in being indiscreet, I imagine."

"That must be it," she agreed. "But you are going to be out again this evening?" He looked a question at her, and she shrugged. "Your grandfather and I have invitations to the theater tonight—they're presenting a new version of Yairdahn's *Flower Maiden*—and I just wanted to know whether we should include you in the party."

"It's tempting," he said. "That's always been my favorite of Yairdahn's plays, but I think I'll pass, if you and Grandfather won't be offended. I don't think it's going to be up to the Royal Company's production. Remember the last time we saw it at the Round? I doubt they'll be able to match that here in Siddar City."

"Perhaps not." She shrugged lightly. "It is an easy play to get wrong, I'll admit," she went on, deliberately not addressing his reference to the Round Theatre, the epicenter of the performing arts back home in Tellesberg. "And your grandfather and I won't be at all offended by the thought that you prefer a younger, livelier set of companions for the evening. Go have a good time."

"I'm sure I will. And I promise—no indiscretions!"

He gave her a wink, closed the guitar case, kissed her cheek, and headed off into the townhouse whistling.

She watched him go with a smile, but the smile faded as his whistling did, and she looked back out across the bay with a far more pensive expression.

Despite Aivah Pahrsahn's indisputable beauty, Sahmantha Raimahn had never cherished the least fear Byrk might become amorously involved with her. For that matter, she wouldn't have been terribly concerned if he had. Madam Pahrsahn was as cultured as she was lovely. If anyone would have known how to take a young lover's ardor, treat it with gentleness, and send it on its way undamaged in the fullness of time, it would be she. And she was also wealthy enough for Sahmantha to be certain she couldn't possibly cherish any designs upon the Raimahn family fortune. In fact, Sahmantha would actually have preferred for her grandson's interest in her to have been far more . . . romantically focused than she feared it was.

She hadn't been entirely honest with Byrk about her husband's probable reaction to his destination for the evening, either. Claitahn Raimahn hadn't shaken the dust of Tellesberg from his feet lightly when he moved his entire household—and all of his business investments—from Charis to the Republic of Siddarmark. Claitahn was a Charisian to his toenails, but he was also a man who took his principles seriously and a devout son of Mother Church. When it came time to choose between heretical Crown and orthodox Church, principles and belief alike had driven the inevitable outcome.

His stature among Charis' mercantile elite, his wealth, and the fact that he'd sacrificed so much of that wealth in the process of moving it from Tellesberg to Siddar City's Charisian Quarter gave him a standing second to none in the Charisian émigré community, yet he himself remained trapped between his two worlds. Despite his horror at the Church of Charis' open break with the Grand Vicar, he remained too much a Charisian not to argue that the Kingdom had been grievously provoked. One sin couldn't justify another in his view, but neither would he condemn Charis' initial reaction to a totally unprovoked and unjustified onslaught. He'd fully supported King Haarahld's decision to fight in self-defense; it was *King Cayleb's* actions he could not condone.

Not that he blamed Cayleb entirely. Haarahld's premature death had brought Cayleb to the throne too early, in Claitahn's view, and the new king had found himself in a desperately dangerous position. It had been his job to protect his people—no one could dispute that—and he'd been too young, too susceptible to the pressures of his advisers and councilors when it came to doing that job. The true culprits were Maikel Staynair and the Earl of Gray Harbor, who'd pushed Cayleb into supporting open schism instead of at least trying to make a respectful appeal to the Grand Vicar's justice first. From there to the creation of the new, bastard "Empire of Charis" had been only a single, inevitable step, in Claitahn's opinion, and he could not support it. But by the same token, he was quick and fierce to defend Charis, as opposed to the *Church* of Charis, when tempers flared.

His and Sahmantha's surviving children had accompanied them into voluntary exile, and he encouraged them to continue thinking of themselves as Charisians. Sahmantha lacked the heart to tell him, yet her own advice was quite different. In fact, she'd encouraged them to find homes outside the Charisian Quarter and do their very best to integrate into the *Siddarmarkian* community.

She loved her homeland as much as Claitahn ever had, but unlike him, she was able to admit—and too self-honest to deny—that the Church of Charis wasn't going away. Claitahn would never see his dreamed-of, longed-for peaceful reconciliation with the Temple. If the heretical church was brought down, it would fall only to the sword, and the carnage—and retribution—would destroy the kingdom he remembered so lovingly. The ashes would poison the ground and bear bitter fruit for generations to come, and she would not see her family poisoned in turn by clinging to an identity which was doomed. Better, far better, for them to recognize reality and become the Siddarmarkians into which fate and their faith in God had transformed them. She and Claitahn would die here in Siddar City, be buried in the Republic's alien soil, still dreaming of the past they could never hope to reclaim, and she would never even hint to him that she'd realized that hope could never have been *more* than a dream.

But not every Charisian living in the Republic shared that attitude. The fracture lines within the rapidly growing Charisian community here in Siddar City grew deeper—and uglier—with every passing day. Over a third of its members were here not because they'd fled Charis out of religious principle but because this was where trade and commerce had brought them long before the current warfare had erupted. The swelling influx of newcomers were as much Temple Loyalist as she and Claitahn could ever be, yet even a growing fraction of them were being attracted to the Reformist elements within the *mainland* Church, and nowhere were those Reformist elements stronger than here in the Republic. Many a Siddarmarkian—and even many of the Charisian émigrées who'd turned their backs in horror on the open schism of the Church of Charis—found the condemnations of clerics like Maikel Staynair resonating with their own disappointment in what the vicarate and the Church had become in the hands of men like Zahmsyn Trynair and Zhaspahr Clyntahn. Schism they would not condone; Reform they were prepared to respectfully demand.

Sahmantha Raimahn was a shrewd, clear-eyed observer, determined to protect her family, and the shadows were growing darker, even here in the Republic. Claitahn sensed it, too, and despite his own sympathy for much of the Reformist argument, he resolutely refused to embrace it. Neither would Sahmantha, for she'd seen only too clearly the horrors of which Zhaspahr Clyntahn's Inquisition was capable. She recognized the danger hovering in the Reformist label, even here in the Republic, where the Inquisition's writ ran less deeply, and that was the true reason she longed to pry her grandson gently away from Aivah Pahrsahn. She'd begun picking up whispers that the brilliant, witty, wealthy beauty who'd taken Siddar City's society by storm looked with favor upon the Reformist movement. As always, Madam Pahrsahn spoke gently and calmly, championing *peaceful* reform, condemning violence, couching her murmured arguments in terms of love and compassion. No reasonable soul could possibly have accused her of the least impropriety . . . but these were not the times for reasonable souls.

Be careful, Byrk, she thought after the grandson she'd raised. *Oh, be* careful, *my love! You're too much like your grandfather. You try to hide it, but beneath that surface you show the world, you feel too deeply and there's too much integrity for times like these. Forget you're a Charisian and remember to be cautious. Be* Siddarmarkian, *please!*

▼ ▼ ▼

Thwap!

Sailys Trahskhat stiffened as the well-rotted apple smacked him squarely between the shoulder blades and then oozed down his back in trickles of brown pulp and slime. His head whipped around, looking for the hand which had thrown it, but no guilty expression gave away the culprit. Indeed, *no one* seemed to be looking his way . . . which said a great deal.

His fists clenched at his side, but he managed—somehow—to keep the fury he felt out of his expression. It wasn't the first time something like that had happened. It wouldn't be the last, either, he thought grimly. He was just lucky it had been an apple instead of a rock.

And at least this time the bastard didn't shout *anything*, he thought. *Fucking coward! Brave enough when he doesn't have to actually* face *someone, isn't he?* Then he gave himself a mental shake. *Just as well, too. If he had* said *anything, pointed himself out, I'd've had to do something about it, and Langhorne only knows where* that *would've ended!*

He bent back to his task, hoisting another bag of Emeraldian cocoa beans onto his shoulder and rejoining the line of longshoremen carrying them into the waiting warehouse. It didn't pay all that much, but it was better than the soup kitchens, and he was lucky to have the work. Enough people didn't, and in his calmer moments he realized that was part of the reason for the hostility he encountered every day. But still. . . .

"See who it was?" a voice asked quietly as he entered the warehouse's dim cavern. He hefted his bag down on a pallet, then turned towards the speaker, and Franz Shumahn, his shift foreman, raised an eyebrow at him. Shumahn was Siddarmarkian, but he was also a decent man, and he looked concerned.

"Nope." Trahskhat shook his head and smiled, deliberately making light of it. "Just as well, I guess. Last thing we need is a riot down here on the docks just because some stupid bastard needed his head ripped off and shoved up his ass. Probably wouldn't have done me any good with the Guard, either, now that I think about it."

"Probably putting it lightly," Shumahn acknowledged with a chuckle. He seemed genuinely amused, but there was a note of warning in it, too, Trahskhat thought. Not that it was necessary.

"As long as they stick to *rotten* fruit, it's not going to cost anything but another washing day for Myrahm," Trahskhat said as philosophically as he could. "If they start throwing rocks, like they did at the fish market last five-day, though, it's going to get ugly, Franz."

"I know." Shumahn looked worried. "I'll have a word with the boss. See if we can't get a little more security down here. A couple of big bruisers with cudgels'd probably cut down on this shit a lot."

Trahskhat nodded. It might. It might not, too. A lot would depend on whether the troublemakers thought the "big bruisers with the cudgels" were there to help Trahskhat or *them*.

It's not just about you, you know, he reminded himself. *There's other Charisians down here on the docks, too. And you're lucky Shumahn's thinking about getting someone down here to break the troublemakers' heads instead of how much simpler it would be to just fire your ass!*

"I'm asking Horahs and Wyllym to keep an eye out for the rest of this shift," Shumahn added. "Anybody else tries something, they'll spot him. And if he works for us, his ass is history. The boss doesn't like this kind of shit."

"Thanks," Trahskhat said with quiet sincerity, and headed back for the next bag.

The work was hard, often brutally so, and the job was a huge step down for a man who'd once been the Telles-berg Krakens' starting first baseman. The pay was no more than two-thirds of what he'd have been making back in Tellesberg even for the same work, either. Worse yet, it cost more to live here in Siddar City than it ever had back home. His wife, Myrahm, actually made more than he did, but she was a skilled weaver. The Charisian community living in Siddarmark had always been heavily represented in the textile trade, and she'd been fortunate enough to find a job working for fellow Charisians. He was pretty sure her employers had embraced the Church of Charis, at least in private, but they were still good people, and he was glad Myrahm had found employment with them. He didn't want to think about her having to face the kind of daily harassment *he* encountered down here on the docks.

It wasn't fair, but the *Writ* had never promised life would be fair, only that God and the Archangels would be just and compassionate at its end. That was enough for any man, when it came down to it. But it was hard. Hard when the rotten apples came flying from anonymous hands. Hard when he had to face his older son Mahrtyn and try to explain why so many people hated him simply for being Charisian. And especially hard when someone shouted "Heretic!" or "Blasphemer!" from the cover of darkness as they passed outside the tiny apartment which was all he and Myrahm could afford, even here in the Quarter.

If they'd been heretics, they'd still be in Tellesberg, he thought grimly. Still with the neighbors they'd grown up with, not estranged from their own families. They'd come to Siddar City because they couldn't be party to the schism, couldn't stand by and watch while God's own Church was torn apart. No, they didn't like everything about the current situation in Zion. In fact, in the privacy of his own mind, Sailys regarded Zhaspahr Clyntahn as an abomination, an indelible stain on the sanctity of Mother Church. But the *Writ* and *The Commentaries* made it abundantly clear that the Church was greater than those who served her. Their sins could not diminish her authority, nor could they absolve her children from their obedience to her. They had the right to protest, to seek redress, when her servants fell short of their responsibilities. Indeed, they had a duty to *insist* her priesthood be worthy of their offices and the God they served. But that wasn't the same thing as throwing defiance into the Grand Vicar's own face! And it certainly wasn't the same thing as setting up the judgment of a mere provincial archbishop as superior to that of the Archangels themselves!

He felt the rage building in him again and forced himself to let go of it. It wasn't his business to judge other men. It was his job to make sure he met his own responsibilities and didn't help others avoid theirs. Those responsibilities included standing up for what he knew was right, and they included putting up with idiots who didn't understand, as well. As long as he did what *he* knew was right, he could leave final judgments to Langhorne and God.

He picked up another sack, settled it on his shoulder, and turned back towards the warehouse.

▼ ▼ ▼

Fucking heretic, Samyl Naigail thought bitterly. *Should've thrown a damned rock. Hell,* his lips drew back in an embittered snarl as he stood in the alley between the warehouses, glaring out at the busy scene, *I should've thrown a fucking knife!*

Naigail was only seventeen, but he knew what was going on. He knew who was to blame. His father had been a sailmaker, and a good one, but never a *prosperous* one. That was the fucking Charisians' fault, too. Bad enough when everyone had "known" Charisians built the best ships in the world, whether they really did or not. The shipbuilders here in Siddar City had at least managed to keep their heads above water, and at least there'd been *some* work those days. But then the bastards had introduced their damned "schooner rig," and things had gotten even worse. Everybody had to have one of the new damned ships, and if you didn't know how the sails were cut, then you were just fucking out of luck as far as new orders went, weren't you? Besides, who could match the quality of the canvas coming out of Charis these days? And who could afford to *buy* the quality of canvas coming out of Charis?

Nobody, that was who! And as if *that* weren't enough, then the goddamned heretics had to launch their fucking schism against Mother Church! Of course they'd driven the Grand Inquisitor into declaring an embargo against trade with them. What else had they expected? But they'd had an answer for that, too, hadn't they? Them and their buddies the fat, sand maggot bankers. Hell, half of *them* were Charisians, too, weren't they? And they got their sodomite friends in the Lord Protector's government to go along with it.

So now everyone was using Charisian ships, with Charisian crews, financed by Charisian money, and pretending they were Siddarmarkian. Everybody knew better, but did it *matter*?

No, of course it didn't! Whatever the registration papers might say, they were Charisian ships, and the Charisian privateers knew it. So they got safe passage while everyone *else's* shipping got wiped off the face of the ocean. The shippers and the warehouses and the longshoremen were still doing just fine, them and their fucking Charisian friends. But the honest workers—the honest *Temple Loyalist* workers—who couldn't find jobs as carpenters or sailmakers or chandlers or in the ropewalks, *they* were starving to death! Unless they wanted to go crawling to one of the soup kitchens, at least. But a man had his pride, and it wasn't right. It wasn't *right* for good, hard-working, believing Siddarmarkians to be thrown out of work and forced to accept charity just to survive.

His father hadn't been able to face it. They could say what they liked about accidents, but Samyl knew better. His father had always liked his beer, yes, but he'd never have gotten so drunk he staggered *accidentally* off the end of the wharf in the middle of winter and drowned, assuming he hadn't frozen to death first. And he'd been careful to arrange an apprenticeship with his older brother for Samyl first. No, it hadn't been an accident. He'd made it *look* like one so Mother Church would agree to bury him in holy ground, and he'd done what he could to take care of his boy first. It wasn't his fault Uncle Byrt's sail loft had collapsed into bankruptcy as well.

Samyl felt the hot tide sweeping up inside him again, but he fought it down. This wasn't the time. Master Bahzkai and Father Saimyn were right about that. If they started actually attacking Charisians, really *hurting* the bastards the way they deserved, they were likely to actually generate some kind of sympathy for them. The very idea seemed impossible, but the city authorities were letting the damned heretics stay right here in Siddar City, weren't they? If they were willing to whore themselves out for Charisian gold to that extent, then who knew where they'd be willing to go in the end?

No, he thought, turning away and shoving his hands into his tunic pockets as he stamped angrily down the narrow, noisome alley, the time might come, but it hadn't come yet. Father Saimyn promised God and the Archangels would smite the Charisians in the fullness of time, and for now—at least—Samyl Naigail would wait to see that happen.

But if it didn't, he wasn't going to wait forever.

▼ ▼ ▼

"Good evening, Madam Pahrsahn," Tobys Suwyl said. He knew he sounded more than a little stuffy, but he couldn't help it. Pahrsahn was just as charming, witty, beautiful, and wealthy as all her champions claimed, but he caught the stink of Reform from her.

"Good evening yourself, Master Suwyl," Pahrsahn replied, smiling at him and extending one slim hand. Appearances had to be maintained, and he bent over it, brushing it with his lips. "I hadn't expected to see you tonight," she continued as he straightened.

"When my wife heard Sharghati would be performing at your party, she simply had to be here," he said.

"Ah." Pahrsahn's smile broadened and turned impish. "I'd rather hoped it would have that effect," she confided. "And I have to admit any excuse to listen to her sing was worthwhile."

Suwyl nodded. And she was right. Ahlyssa Sharghati was the most highly sought-after soprano in all of Siddarmark. She'd traveled all the way to the Harchong Empire to study voice, and even the most sturdily Siddarmarkian critic had to acknowledge opera still attained its highest expression in the Empire. She could command any venue—or fee—she chose, and the fact that this was the second party of Pahrsahn's she'd graced said a great deal about the woman's wealth.

Either that, or it may say some unappetizing things about Sharghati's own religious leanings, he thought, looking around the assembled guests.

"Well, I do hope you and your charming wife will enjoy yourselves this evening," Pahrsahn said to him. "In the meantime, however, I see the Seneschal's wife has just come in. I'm afraid I'm going to have to meet my social obligations and greet her. If there's anything you need, please don't hesitate to ask one of my servants to see to it for you."

She swept him a stylish half-curtsy with all the polished elegance only to be expected from someone who'd come from Zion itself. Then she moved away, smiling and gracious, strewing conversational tidbits in her wake, and Suwyl watched her go with a sense of relief.

If he was going to be honest, his dislike for her stemmed far less from religious principles than from the threat she represented. Personally, Suwyl didn't really care who ran the Temple. As far as he was concerned, that was God's business, and God would get around to straightening it out eventually if He wasn't happy about it. In the meantime, however, one of Mother Church's responsibilities was to see that people behaved themselves. And when people behaved themselves, there weren't things like wars and violence. And when there weren't things like wars and violence, simple bankers could engage in honest, gainful trade without having to worry about what the lunatics on either side were going to tear down, burn to the ground, or blow up next.

Suwyl considered himself as Charisian as the next man, but he'd lived here in Siddar City for almost thirty years. He was part of the city, a known man, respected and listened to throughout the business community, not just in the Quarter, with contacts at the highest level of the government. Or at least he was for now. There was no telling how long it would continue to be true, though, and it was the maniacs like Staynair and "Emperor" Cayleb who were to blame.

Remember what the healers keep telling you about your temper, Tobys, he reminded himself. *The last thing you need is to work yourself into an apoplectic fit over things you can't do anything about anyway.*

He drew a deep breath, held it, and then exhaled slowly. His wife Zhandra had taught him the technique, and it actually worked. Sometimes, anyway.

Fortunately, this was one of the sometimes, and he felt his anger ease. A business colleague nodded to him in passing, and he managed to nod back with a genuine smile. Then he accepted a goblet of wine from one of Pahrsahn's servants and sipped.

At least the woman's taste in wine is as good as her taste in music, he reflected morosely. *That's something, if I'm going to be stuck here all night anyway.*

He took another sip and began easing his way through the crowd, looking for his wife.

▼ ▼ ▼

"Good evening, Aivah," a quiet voice said, and Aivah Pahrsahn turned to smile at the silver-haired man who didn't happen to be wearing a cassock this evening.

"And good evening to you, too, Zhasyn," she said, tactfully avoiding any last names or ecclesiastic titles. "You are aware the Seneschal and his wife are both attending tonight, aren't you?" she added teasingly.

"I assure you, I'll stay out of Lord Daryus' way," he replied with a smile. "Although according to my sources, he'll probably be going pretty far out of his way himself to avoid noticing me. May I ask if your . . . negotiations with him have prospered?"

"Oh, I'm sure both the Republic and I will be making a great deal of money, Zhasyn," she assured him. "And it really won't hurt for Hahraimahn's foundries to get a small infusion of capital at a time like this."

"Small?" He raised his eyebrows in polite incredulity, and she laughed.

"Perhaps not so small on the scale of individuals," she acknowledged, "but still relatively small on the scale of entire realms. Indeed," her smile faded slightly, "small enough I think there's an excellent chance none of Clyntahn's eyes or ears will realize it's even been made. For a while, at least."

Zhasyn Cahnyr nodded, although his eyes were worried. "Madam Pahrsahn's" investment was nowhere near so cut and dried as she chose to pretend, and she was playing a more dangerous game than she was willing to admit. He was less certain than she that the Inquisition wouldn't get wind of a "private investment" which amounted to the purchase of several thousand rifled muskets and bayonets. More than that, he was more than a little frightened of exactly what she intended to do with them once she had them.

Perhaps it's just as well she hasn't enlightened you on that particular point, he told himself dryly. *You'd probably worry even more if you* did *know what she was going to do with them!*

"You have made it clear to your 'special guests' that there's a degree of risk involved here, haven't you?" he asked now, changing the subject.

"Of course I have, Zhasyn." She smiled and touched his cheek gently. "I admire and respect you, my friend, but I'm not going to throw any lambs to the slash lizards without due consideration. I'm very careful about who I approach with your invitation, and after the initial flirtation—I'd be tempted to say 'seduction' if it wouldn't seem too much like a bad jest, given my previous vocation—I'm very careful to warn them about the dangers. And that's why I send them to you only one or two at a time. We can't avoid letting you and me know who they are, but we can at least protect their identities from anyone else."

"Forgive me." He smiled back and cupped his left hand lightly over the fingers on his cheek. "I forget sometimes how long you've been doing this sort of thing. I should know better than to try to teach such a mistress of her art."

"'Mistress of her art'?" She shook her head, eyes dancing. "And here I went to such lengths to avoid any double entendres!"

"My dear, I know it amuses you to try, but you're really not going to shock me or offend me by throwing your past into my face," he pointed out.

"I know. But you're right, it does amuse me. And it probably says something unfortunate about me, as well." She shook her head, still smiling. "My initial involvement in this sort of thing was what you might call a reaction against the high clergy, you know. I can't quite seem to forget that even though you're not like the vast majority of your ecclesiastic brethren, you *are* an archbishop. I think that's why I feel such a compulsion to keep trying."

"As long as it amuses you," he said, then looked across the room. "Not to change the subject—although that's really exactly why I'm doing it—who's that youngster with Sharghati?"

She turned to follow the direction of his glance.

"Which one? The younger of the two is Byrk Raimahn. He's Claitahn Raimahn's grandson, and I strongly suspect him of harboring Reformist thoughts. In fact, I'm not so sure he'd be happy stopping short of Church of Charis-style thinking if he had his druthers, although he's far too astute and too well informed to come out and say anything of the sort. The fellow with him is Raif Ahlaixsyn. He's about ten years older than young Raimahn and a Siddarmarkian. I've met his father. The family's got money, and I think they'd really prefer to sit on the sidelines, but I'm not sure about Raif. Not yet." She frowned thoughtfully. "I think there's some potential there, but given his family connections, I'm being particularly cautious about exploring it." She shrugged. "In the meantime, he's really quite a good poet and making him a more or less permanent fixture at my parties is something of a social coup."

"You actually enjoy this, don't you?" he asked. She looked back at him, and he shrugged. "I mean *all* of it. The scheming, outwitting your enemies, laying the evil low, the dancing on the edge of the sword blade—not just all of that, but the parties and the gaiety, too. You do, don't you?"

"Of course I do, Zhasyn!" She seemed surprised by the question. "It's what I do. Oh," her eyes hardened, although her smile never wavered, "don't think for one moment that I'm not going to dance in that pig Clyntahn's blood the day Cayleb and Sharleyan take his head. And string up the rest of the Group of Four, and the entire damned *vicarate*—what's left of it—for that matter. Never underestimate that side of me, Zhasyn, or you may get hurt. But the rest?" The hardness disappeared and her eyes danced once more. "It's the grandest game in the world, my friend! Beside this, anything else would be only half alive."

He gazed at her for a moment, then shook his head, and she laughed.

"Take yourself off to the private salon now, Zhasyn," she told him. "Your first meeting's scheduled to begin in about ten minutes. And in the meantime," she smiled brilliantly, "I have to go have a word with the Seneschal."

. II .

The Prison Hulks,
and
HMS *Chihiro*, 50,
Gorath Bay,
Kingdom of Dholar

"How is he this morning, Naiklos?" Sir Gwylym Manthyr asked, turning his back on the vista of Gorath Bay.

"Not as well as he pretends, Sir," Naiklos Vahlain replied.

The slight, dapper valet joined the admiral at the forecastle rail and stroked his mustache gently as he, too, looked out across the bay. The sky was a blue bowl overhead, dotted with white cloud puffs, and a brisk breeze—cool, but without the bitter bite of the winter just past—blew across the deck. Wyverns and seabirds rode the breeze, their cries and whistles faint, and three-foot waves gave the deck underfoot a slight pitch as the ship's anchor held her head to the wind.

Not that the roofed-over obsolete coastal galley was much of a ship, anymore, Manthyr reflected, gazing once more across the bay at the hateful sight of the city of Gorath's tall stone walls. He'd had altogether too much opportunity to examine those walls over the last seven months. He'd spent endless hours picturing how vulnerable they would be to modern artillery . . . and regretting the fact that he'd never have the chance to see that vulnerability demonstrated.

He turned away from the familiar lava-flow anger of that thought, not that the contemplation of his remaining "command" was any more appealing. Lywys Gardynyr, the Earl of Thirsk, had done his best for his prisoners—better, to be honest, than Manthyr had anticipated, after the unyielding terms then-Crown Prince Cayleb had inflicted upon *him* after the Battle of Crag Reach—but he'd faced certain limitations. The greatest of which was that he appeared to be the only Dohlaran aristocrat with anything remotely resembling a sense of honor. The others were too busy hating all Charisians for the crushing humiliation of the Battles of Rock Point and Crag Reach. Either that, or they were Temple Loyalists too busy sucking up to the Inquisition—or both—to worry about little things like the proper treatment of honorably surrendered prisoners of war.

Manthyr knew his own sense of failure and helplessness when he contemplated the probable future of the men and officers he'd commanded only made his bitterness worse. But when he looked around the moldering old galleys which had been converted into prison hulks to house his personnel, when he considered how grudgingly their needs were met, how meager their rations were, how little concern even the Order of Pasquale had demonstrated for his wounded and sick, it was hard to feel anything *except* bitterness.

Especially when you know the only thing standing between your people and the Inquisition is Thirsk and—who would have believed it?—a Schuelerite *auxiliary bishop,* he thought.

He wasn't the only Charisian that bitterness was poisoning, he reminded himself. He and his surviving officers did all they could to maintain morale, but it was hard. Charisian seamen by and large were far from stupid, and even the youngest surviving ship's boy could figure out what was going on. Penned up in the drab, damp, barren sameness of their floating prisons day after day; denied the right to so much as send letters home to tell their families they were still alive (so far, at least); poorly fed; without exercise; with no warm clothing against a winter which had been numbingly cold for men from their semi-tropical homeland, it was scarcely surprising when even Charisians found it difficult to pretend to one another that they couldn't see what was coming.

Which is one reason we've got so much sickness in the hulks, Manthyr told himself bitterly. *Not that there aren't plenty of other reasons. Aside from Thirsk and Maik none of these people give a good goddamn about whether or not heretic Charisians are covered by Pasquale's Law. Hell, most of them probably figure "heretics" don't have any right to worry about Pasquale's commands! They're sure as hell not bothering themselves to provide the proper diet his law decrees, anyway. No wonder we're actually seeing scurvy among the men! And when you crank that kind of so-called food into the living conditions—such as they are—and the despair, it's a wonder everyone isn't down sick!*

His jaw muscles ached, and he forced himself to deliberately unclench them. None of their chaplains had survived the final battle, which was probably just as well, since the Inquisition would most certainly have demanded (and received) possession of any heretical priests who fell into their hands. Manthyr liked to think that at least some of the Dohlaran clergy would have been interested in meeting the spiritual needs of his men, but they'd been forbidden to by Wylsynn Lainyr, the Bishop Executor of Gorath, and Ahbsahlahn Kharmych, his intendant. If the rumor mill was to be believed, Bishop Staiphan Maik, the Dohlaran *Navy's* special intendant, had attempted to get that ruling overturned, but if he'd tried, he hadn't succeeded. Bishop Executor Wylsynn was willing to grant access to clergy for Charisians who were prepared to renounce—and *admit*—their heresy and the blasphemous rites in which they had participated in the worship of Shan-wei, but that was as far as he was prepared to go.

Which, since we haven't had any "blasphemous rites" or "worshipped" Shan-wei, would be just a bit difficult for any of them to do honestly. And all of us know from what happened to those poor bastards the Inquisition got hold of after the Ferayd Massacre how Clyntahn would use any "confessions" against Charis. Not to mention the fact that "admitting" any such thing would make whoever "confessed" automatically subject to the Punishment of Schueler. And only a drooling idiot would believe someone like Clyntahn wouldn't get around to applying it sooner or later, no matter what Lainyr might promise first.

Despite that, some of his men—a few; no more than a couple of dozen—had "recanted" their heresy and been "received back into the bosom of Mother Church" . . . for now, at least. Or so their fellows had been told, at any rate. Manthyr had his doubts about how long *that* was going to last, and the constancy of the rest of his people in the face of what they all knew awaited them eventually had been one of his few sources of consolation over the past months.

Yet even that consolation had been flawed with bitterness, and the despair was always there for everyone. It combined with all those other factors to drive down the men's ability—and willingness—to resist disease, and by his latest estimate, at least a third of his remaining personnel were currently ill. It had been worse over the winter months, in some ways, but malnutrition and privation hadn't yet reduced their resistance then. Now that spring's milder temperatures had arrived, the sick list should have been shrinking; instead, it was climbing, and they were losing three or four men every five-day.

Men who were forbidden burial in consecrated ground as the "spawn of Shan-wei" they were. Instead, their bodies were to be taken ashore on Archbishop Trumahn's personal order and cast into pits in the fields where the Dohlaran capital buried its garbage. Its *other* garbage, as the holy archbishop had put it. Which was why Manthyr and his officers had taken to dropping their dead quietly and reverently over the side under cover of night, weighted with whatever they could find for the job and accompanied by the murmured words of the burial service any captain remembered only too well.

The numbers were going to get worse. He was almost certain of that, and he was desperately worried about young Lainsair Svairsmahn, HMS *Dancer*'s only surviving midshipman. Svairsmahn had lost his left leg just below the hip during the final, desperate hour of the action which had hammered four of Manthyr's ships into wrecks before they finally struck. The boy had been barely twelve and a half when they took off his leg, yet his courage had almost broken Manthyr's heart. He and Vahlain had cared personally for Svairsmahn over the bitter winter just past, nursing him through his recovery, slipping him extra food from their own meager rations (and denying they were doing anything of the sort whenever he asked). There'd been times, especially right after the amputation, when Manthyr had been afraid they were going to lose the boy anyway, as he'd lost so many other officers and men. But Svairsmahn had always pulled through.

Which only made his current illness even more heartbreaking to both of them, he admitted, looking back out across the bulwark, watching the guard boats row steadily, methodically around the prison hulks in their endless, unceasing circles. Not that even a Charisian seaman was going to try to swim ashore in water still fanged with winter cold from a hulk anchored the better part of a mile and a half from shore.

"I think his temperature may have come down a little, Sir Gwylym," Vahlain offered, and Manthyr glanced at him. The valet shrugged. "I know we both want to *believe* that, Sir, but I really think it may be true in this case. If he just hadn't been so weakened already. . . ."

His voice trailed off, and Manthyr nodded. Then he laid one hand on Vahlain's shoulder.

"We've gotten him this far, Naiklos. We're not going to lose him now."

"Of course not, Sir!" the valet agreed gamely, and both of them tried to pretend they truly believed they weren't lying.

▼ ▼ ▼

"My Lord, this is an act of murder," Lywys Gardynyr said flatly.

He stood with his back to the stern windows of HMS *Chihiro*, his face like carven stone, and his eyes were hard. Not a large man, the Earl of Thirsk, but at that moment he seemed to fill the day cabin.

"That isn't for you to judge, Lywys," Auxiliary Bishop Staiphan Maik replied. His own expression was set, his eyes grim, yet his voice was remarkably gentle for a Schuelerite, under the circumstances.

"My Lord, you *know* what's going to happen!" Despair flickered behind the hardness in Thirsk's eyes.

"We're both sons of Mother Church," Maik said in a sterner tone. "It's not up to us to judge her actions, but rather to obey her commands."

This time, Thirsk's eyes flashed, but he bit back an angry retort. He'd come to know the auxiliary bishop well—too well for either of their comfort and good, he sometimes thought—and he knew Maik was no happier with this command than he was. At the same time, the cleric had a point. It *wasn't* their place to judge the Church's actions, even if at this moment in time her policies were being decided by bloody-handed murderers.

God, the earl demanded harshly in the stillness of his own mind, *how can You be letting this happen? Why are You letting this happen?! This is* wrong. *I know it, Bishop Staiphan knows it, yet both of us are going to watch it happen anyway because* Your *Church commands it. What are You* thinking?

A part of him cringed from the impiety of his own

questions, yet he couldn't stop thinking them, couldn't stop wondering what part of the inscrutable mind of God could let someone like Zhaspahr Clyntahn attain to the Grand Inquisitor's chair. It made no sense to him, no matter how hard he tried to force it into some kind of order, some sort of pattern he could understand and accept.

But if I can't understand why it's happening, he thought, shoulders slumping, *I damned well understand* what's *happening.*

He wheeled away from the auxiliary bishop, staring out the opened stern windows with his hands gripped together white-knuckled behind him while he fought his anger and tried to throttle his despair. He'd already put Maik into an invidious, even a dangerous, position and he knew it. Just as he knew all the reasons he shouldn't have done it. There were limits to what even the most broad-minded Schuelerite could overlook at a time like this, and he'd come perilously close to that limit. Which was particularly reprehensible when the Schuelerite in question was trying so hard to do what he knew was decent despite the all too real danger into which that plunged him.

"You're right, My Lord," the earl said at last, still facing the panorama of the harbor beyond the windows. "We *are* sons of Mother Church, and we have no choice but to obey the commands of her vicarate and the Grand Inquisitor. Nor is it our place to question those commands. Yet speaking purely as a layman, and as the commander of one of Mother Church's fleets"—*and the only* effective *fleet she has left,* he added silently—"I must express my concern about the future implications of this decision. I'd be derelict in my duty if I didn't, and—"

"Stop, my son," Maik interrupted, cutting him off before he could continue. Thirsk looked over his shoulder at him, and the auxiliary bishop shook his head.

"I know what you're about to say, and based purely on military logic and the reasoning of the world, I agree with you. This is going to create a situation the heretics are only too likely to seize upon as an excuse for carrying out atrocities against the loyal sons of Mother Church, and I fully realize the way in which it's likely to . . . adversely affect the other side's willingness to grant our soldiers and sailors quarter in the first place. From that perspective, I can't argue with a single thing you're about to say. But as the Grand Inquisitor has reminded all of us"—his eyes stabbed Thirsk's—"the logic of the world, even the mercy natural to any man's heart, must sometimes give place to the letter of God's law. That law sets one penalty, and only one, for the unregenerate, unrepentant heretic. As Schueler teaches, for the good of their souls, for the possibility of reclaiming them even at the very last moment from Shan-wei and the Pit, the Inquisition dares not relent lest the transitory illusion of mercy in *this* world lead to their utter damnation in the next. And as the Grand Inquisitor has also reminded us, at a time when God's Own Church stands in such peril, we dare not ignore the requirements of His law as set forth by the Archangel Schueler."

Thirsk's jaw clenched, but he heard the warning, and he understood. Understood not only that Maik was telling him further protest, however logically and reasonably couched, would be unavailing and almost certainly dangerous, but that the auxiliary bishop would be unable to protect him if he drew the Grand Inquisitor's ire down upon his own head.

"Very well, My Lord," the earl said finally. "I understand what you're saying, and I accept that I must obey the instructions we've been given. As you say, the Church stands in peril and this"—he emphasized the last word ever so slightly—"is not the time to question the Grand Inquisitor. Or the rest of the vicarate, of course."

Maik winced. It was almost imperceptible, but Thirsk saw it anyway, and he responded with an almost equally tiny nod. The auxiliary bishop raised one hand and started to say something, then visibly changed his mind and shifted subjects.

"Turning from our instructions to the rest of the dispatch, what did you think of Vicar Allayn's analysis of what happened, my son?" he asked instead.

"I thought it was cogently reasoned," Thirsk replied, smiling faintly and without humor as he recognized Maik's quest for a less volatile topic. He shrugged. "Obviously, the Charisians"—he seldom used the word "heretic" any longer in his conversations with Maik; probably another dangerous habit he was getting into—"have found some way to load their round shot with gunpowder, exactly as the Captain General is suggesting. I hadn't considered the possibility myself, and I'll have to have a word with the foundry masters before I could hazard a guess as to how difficult it might be to cast hollow shot that don't simply break up when you fire them, but it's obvious the Charisians have figured it out. How they manage to get the things to explode when they want them to is another matter, of course."

He frowned thoughtfully, his brain and professional curiosity engaged almost despite himself.

"It's got to be some sort of fuse," he half murmured, "but how do they *light* it? The barrel's too long to reach down and light it after they've loaded the gun, unless they're firing them only from carronades, and that doesn't seem possible given the weight of fire Father Greyghor reported. Hmmmmm. . . ." His frown deepened. "Muzzle flash? Is that what they're using? And if it is, how do they manage it without blowing the fuse into the shell and setting it off early?"

Staiphan Maik breathed a mental sigh of relief as Thirsk was diverted from his dangerous anger. It was only going to be temporary—the auxiliary bishop knew that— but he needed to back the admiral off before his stubborn sense of integrity dug in any deeper and left him no path of retreat. Lywys Gardynyr was too good a man to be allowed to deliver himself into the Inquisition's hands because of the very things that *made* him such a good man. And even if he hadn't been, Mother Church couldn't afford to lose the one admiral she had who seemed to be capable of meeting the Charisians on their own terms.

"Assuming Father Greyghor's reports are accurate," he said out loud, "what can we do in the face of such a weapon?"

"Nothing, My Lord." Thirsk raised both eyebrows, his tone surprised. "If they can make their cannon shot explode inside our ships, their combat advantage becomes effectively absolute. Presumably we could still get close enough to at least damage their ships, but only at the cost of coming into range at which they'll be able to *destroy* ours."

"So there's *nothing* we can do?" Maik couldn't hide his anxiety, and the earl shrugged.

"For now, My Lord, the only response I see is to attempt to learn how to make the same sorts of hollow shot for ourselves. Until we can respond in kind, we dare not meet them in battle. In some ways, however, this may actually work to our advantage. Once we've learned how to make the same weapon for ourselves, I mean." He grimaced. "I don't see how any ship could survive more than a very few hits from something like this. And that, I fear, means sea battles are about to become affairs of mutual annihilation, which will ultimately favor us, since we have so much more manpower and so much greater capability to build replacement ships. We can trade two ships, possibly even three, for each of theirs in the fullness of time. The cost in both money and lives will be atrocious, but it's one we can pay in the end, and they can't."

He obviously disliked saying that, and Maik's face tightened as he heard it. Unfortunately, it wasn't anything the auxiliary bishop hadn't already thought.

"It's probably not a bad thing that we're going to have to spend some time trying various approaches to the problem of producing and fusing hollow shot, really," Thirsk continued. "We're going to have to rebuild the Navy of God before we could even think about engaging the Charisians at sea again, especially given how the prizes they've added to their fleet will increase their own numbers. In fact, it looks to me—"

He broke off suddenly, eyes intent as they gazed at something Maik couldn't see. He stayed that way for several seconds, then blinked twice, slowly.

"You've thought of something, haven't you?" Maik challenged. The earl looked at him, and the auxiliary bishop chuckled. "I've seen that blink of yours before, my son. Out with it!"

"Well, I don't know how practical it might be, but one possible solution to this new weapon of theirs might be to find a way to prevent it from exploding inside our ships."

"Prevent it from exploding? How?" Maik's expression was perplexed, and Thirsk shook his head.

"Forgive me, My Lord. I should have phrased that more clearly. What I meant is that we have to find a way to prevent it from exploding *inside* our ships. To prevent it from *penetrating* our ships in the first place."

"And how might we do that?"

"I'm not certain," Thirsk acknowledged. "At the moment the only answer that suggests itself to me would be to somehow armor the sides of our vessels. I don't think we could do it simply by increasing the thickness of their scantlings, though. That would seem to leave only some kind of protective layer—a sheath of iron, perhaps—applied to the outside of the planking."

"Would that be possible?" Maik asked, his expression fascinated, and Thirsk shrugged again.

"That's a question to ask the ironmasters, My Lord. What I can already tell you from our experience with arming our galleons, though, is that producing that much iron would be—if you'll pardon the expression—hellishly expensive. I'm not at all sure what it would do to stability, either. Nonetheless, it's the only solution that suggests itself to me at this point."

"Expensive or not, it sounds to me as if you might be onto something here, my son." Maik nodded enthusiastically. "Write up your thoughts on this for Vicar Allayn, please. I'd like to send them off to the Temple with my next dispatch."

"Of course, My Lord," Thirsk said, but the enthusiasm had vanished from his voice once more at the mention of dispatches to the Temple, and Maik cursed himself for having brought them up. Not that he had much choice. Sooner or later he was going to *have* to talk about reports to the Temple, and Thirsk was going to have to *provide* those reports.

The auxiliary bishop stood for a moment, looking at the man whose loyalty to Mother Church he was charged to safeguard. Then he inhaled deeply.

"My son," he said carefully. "Lywys. I know you're unhappy about the orders concerning your prisoners." Thirsk's eyes narrowed, but Maik went on in that same careful, deliberate tone. "I know the logical arguments in support of your position, and I've already acknowledged you have a point in that regard. But I also know one reason for your unhappiness is how deeply it goes against your sense of honor, your integrity, to deliver those who surrendered to you and to whom you offered quarter to someone else's justice."

Those narrowed eyes glittered icily at the word "justice," but Maik allowed no answering reaction to cross his own sternly expressionless face.

"You're a good man, Lywys Gardynyr. One of whom I feel—I *know*—God approves. And a good father. Your daughters are godly women, their children are beautiful, and your sons-in-law are men much like you—men of integrity and honor. But Shan-wei's most dangerous snares appeal not to the evil side of our natures, but to the *good* side. She can—and will—use your goodness against you if you give her the opportunity. And if that happens, the consequences of *The Book of Schueler* await you. I know you're a man of courage. You've faced battle—and death—scores of times without letting that danger dissuade you, and I very much doubt a man such as you would allow *any* threat to dissuade you from doing what you believe is the right and honorable thing. But think carefully before you set out on a course such as that. The consequences you might face at the end of your journey would affect far more people than simply yourself."

Rage glowed at the backs of Thirsk's eyes, flaring like a furnace and no longer icy, at the unmistakable implication, but Maik continued unhurriedly.

"I'm a bishop of Mother Church, my son. I have no choice but to obey the ecclesiastic superiors I swore to obey the day I took my priest's vows. You're a layman, not a priest, yet it's your duty to obey Mother Church as well, although"—his eyes bored suddenly into Thirsk—"I'm fully aware you've taken no personal vow, as I have, to obey the Grand Inquisitor's instructions. Obviously, even though you've sworn no oath"—he emphasized the last three words ever so slightly—"you'd be bound by duty and integrity to obey him anyway. And if, as I do not anticipate for a moment, you might be tempted not to obey him at some point, that would not absolve you of your responsibility to consider the consequences for everyone else who might be affected by your actions and to be certain the innocent do not find themselves drawn into those consequences. Recall what the Holy Bédard said in the opening verses of the sixth chapter of her book. I commend her thought to you as you grapple with the heavy and complex burden God and the Archangels have laid upon your shoulders at this time."

The anger vanished from Thirsk's eyes, although the rest of his expression never even flickered. Silence hovered between them for several seconds as the earl looked back at the auxiliary bishop. Then he bowed slightly.

"I appreciate your concern," he said quietly and sincerely. "And your advice. I assure you, My Lord, that I'll think long and hard before I allow anything to affect my duty to Mother Church. And I'll bear your advice—and the Holy Bédard's—in mind at all times."

"Good, my son." Bishop Staiphan touched him on the shoulder. "Good."

▼ ▼ ▼

Much later, after Maik had departed for shore once more, Lywys Gardynyr crossed to his desk. He picked up his well-thumbed copy of the *Holy Writ* from his blotter, opened it, and leafed to the first three verses of the sixth chapter of *The Book of Bédard*. He didn't really need to read the words; like any dutiful son of Mother Church, he knew his Scripture well. Yet he read them anyway, eyes moving across the beautifully printed and illustrated page.

Behold and heed, you who are mothers and you who are fathers. Let not your actions or inactions bring calamity and evil upon your children. Be instead a roof over their heads, be walls about their safety.

The time will come when they will become parents to you in your old age, but that time is not yet. Now is the time to teach, and to nurture—to love and to guard.

When peril approaches, go forth to meet it far from them, lest it threaten them, as well. When duty calls you into danger, put them first in a place of safety. And when the threat of the ungodly draws nigh, set them beyond evil's reach before you ride out to battle, and do not let the hand of the wicked fall upon them.

Oh, yes, My Lord, he thought, gazing down at those words, *I'll bear your advice in mind.*

. III .

Imperial Palace,
City of Tellesberg,
Kingdom of Old Charis,
and
HMS *Dawn Star*, 58,
Off Round Head,
White Horse Reach,
Princedom of Corisande

"I hate this."

Sharleyan Ahrmahk sat on HMS *Dawn Star*'s stern-walk, Crown Princess Alahnah sleeping on her shoulder, and gazed out across the galleon's bubbling wake at blue water sparkling under a brilliant afternoon sun. Her canvas sling-chair moved gently under her with the ship's motion, rocking her and the baby; a pleasant following breeze stirred errant strands of the long, black hair braided loosely down her back; and the green, smooth hills of Round Head rose out of White Horse Reach to her left. She was less than a hundred and fifty miles from the end of her wearisome voyage to Manchyr, and she could comfortably expect to reach it before tomorrow's dawn.

None of which had anything to do with the wounded, sorrowful fury in her grim brown eyes.

"We all do," Merlin said. He stood with his hands braced on the sternwalk rail, leaning over it as he, too, looked out across the calm emptiness of the reach. "And I think we hate it most of all because we've seen it coming for so long."

"And because there's so damned little we can do about it," Cayleb agreed harshly from far distant Tellesberg.

It was much earlier in the morning there, and the skies were cloudier, with a promise of heavy rain as he sat looking out a palace window across the table set with a breakfast of which he'd eaten remarkably little. He was scheduled to meet with Earl Gray Harbor and Baron Ironhill, Keeper of the Purse for Old Charis and Chancellor of the Exchequer for the Charisian Empire. He wasn't looking forward to that meeting, and it had nothing to do with what he expected either of them to tell him. Trying to concentrate on their reports was going to be harder than usual, but he'd have to pretend there was nothing distracting him. He certainly couldn't tell them *what* was distracting him, at any rate, and that made it immeasurably worse, since both of them were Sir Gwylym Manthyr's friends, too.

"I'm afraid you're both right," Maikel Staynair said from his office. "I wish to God there were something we could do, but there isn't."

"There *has* to be something," Domynyk Staynair protested. He'd known Manthyr longer—and better—than any of the others, and anguish tightened his voice. "We can't just let that butcher Clyntahn. . . ."

He trailed off, and the others' faces stiffened. They knew exactly what was going to happen to any Charisian—especially any Charisian who'd been taken in the act of armed resistance to the Group of Four—who was dragged to Zion.

And as Cayleb had said, there was nothing they could do about it.

"I *could* take the skimmer," Merlin said after a moment.

"And do *what?*" Cayleb demanded even more harshly. Domynyk Staynair might have known Manthyr longer, but Sir Gwylym had been Cayleb's flag captain at Rock Point, Crag Reach, and Darcos Sound, the man who'd sunk his own ship in his desperate effort to reach Cayleb's father in time.

"What are you going to do?" the emperor continued in that same unyielding voice. "Not even *Seijin* Merlin's going to be able to rescue a couple of hundred sick, wounded, half-starved men in the middle of an entire continent! It's a coin-toss whether they're going to send them by road or by ship, and you know it, but say they choose the overland route. Even if you managed to singlehandedly slaughter every single guard, how do you get them out of East Haven before the rest of the damned Temple Guard and the Dohlaran Army catch up with you? Not to mention the little fact that you'd leave scores of witnesses to something which would be flat out impossible even for a *seijin*!

"And even if they decide to send them by sea, how are you going to help them? Blow the transports out of the water? That would at least keep them out of the Inquisition's hands, give them a clean death—and don't think I don't realize what a blessing that could be, Merlin! But if Father Paityr's right and there really are 'Archangels' sleeping under the Temple, don't you think the possibility of using advanced weapons that close to the Temple is likely to wake them up?"

"That's a valid point, but we can't just let ourselves be paralyzed worrying about it from here on out, either," Merlin replied.

"Merlin, I understand how badly you want to help our people," Archbishop Maikel said. "But Cayleb's right about the risk, too, and you know it."

"Of course I do!" Merlin's tone came far closer to snapping at Staynair than anyone was accustomed to hearing from him. "But Domynyk's got a point, too. Like Cayleb says, better to at least send them to the bottom of the ocean cleanly than let Clyntahn torture them to death for some kind of spectacle!"

"Merlin." Sharleyan's voice was soft, and she reached out to rest one hand on his mailed forearm. "None of us wants to see that happen. And any one of us would do anything we could to prevent it. But Cayleb's right that we'd never be able to get them off the mainland if they choose the overland route to Zion. And if they send them over-water, instead, what do you think would happen if all their transports sank in clear, calm weather? Do you really think anyone would accept that as some kind of freak co-incidence?" She shook her head as he turned to look down at her. "Everybody would know it wasn't that. So what would Clyntahn and the others do if it happened?"

"They'd proclaim Shan-wei had claimed her own," Domynyk Staynair put in harshly. "Which is exactly what they're going to claim after they torture them all to death, anyway!"

"But this time they'd have a clearly 'miraculous' disaster to back up their claim," his older brother pointed out. "It wouldn't make a lot of difference to any of our people, but it would be fodder for the Group of Four's propaganda mill."

"Frankly, that wouldn't stop me for a moment," Cayleb said. He picked up his chocolate mug and drained it, then set it down beside his still well-laden plate with considerably more force than usual. "My problem is that I can't get those 'sleeping Archangels' out of my brain. Merlin would have to use the skimmer's weapons, Domynyk. It'd be the only way he could put them down. And if I'd been the paranoid setting up something like Father Paityr's suggested is under the Temple, I'd damn well have everything within hundreds of miles of my bedroom covered with sensors that could hardly miss *energy* fire."

"I'm afraid he's right, Domynyk," Merlin sighed. "It may be plain blind dumb luck I haven't already triggered some kind of detection wandering around Haven and Howard the way I have. I'm inclined to think it's more likely because nothing I've done so far's crossed any threat thresholds they may've established. The skimmer's electronic and thermal signatures are actually a lot weaker than the ones from the regular air cars the 'Archangels' were flying around in at the time of the 'Creation.' It was designed to be extremely stealthy against first-line tactical sensors, and they weren't. I suspect that if anyone did set up some sort of sensor perimeter, the skimmer's signatures don't reach whatever level they established as representing a threat. But energy weapons?" He shook his head. "If they've got a sensor net up at all, they couldn't miss that."

"Couldn't we cobble up something else?" Ehdwyrd Howsmyn asked. The ironmaster stood on the balcony of his office, gazing sightlessly out across the sprawl of his huge and growing complex. "Surely you've got some missiles in inventory in the cave, Merlin! Couldn't we use *them*?"

"The only heavy projectile weapons in my cave are kinetic energy weapons," Merlin said. "Their drives would be just as detectable as energy weapons. They might even be *more* detectable, frankly, depending on what thresholds they set up. Owl might be able to 'cobble up' something cruder and less efficient. In fact, he probably could. But anything he came up with would look even more like the Rakurai . . . and still might cross the line."

"But if they *don't* have a sensor net up, Gwylym and all the others are going to die—under the Question and the Punishment—when we could've saved them . . . or at least killed them cleanly," Domynyk said flatly. "We owe him—we owe *all* of them—at least that much!"

"Are you prepared to take that risk when the first thing we'll know—if there is a net and we 'cross the line,' as Merlin put it—is when whatever the hell is under that obscene mausoleum in Zion wakes up?" Cayleb demanded, his voice even flatter—and harder—than Rock Point's. "I know he's your friend, Domynyk. He's my friend, too, and I'm his Emperor; his oaths were sworn to *me*, not you, and I swore oaths to *him* in return. If there's a single human being on the face of this planet—including *you!*—who wants to save him more than I do, I can't imagine who it is. But pretend for just a moment that you didn't even know him and the decision was solely up to you. Would you truly risk sounding an alarm that brings a genuine 'Archangel' *with control of Langhorne's Rakurai* back to the Group of Four's aid?"

Silence sang and crackled over the com for endless seconds. Then—

"No," Domynyk Staynair said, his voice almost inaudible. "No, I wouldn't, Cayleb."

"Churchill and Coventry, Merlin," Cayleb said almost

as softly, and Merlin winced. Sharleyan looked up at him, one eyebrow raised, and he shrugged.

"An episode from World War Two back on Old Terra," he said. "It was an example I used with Cayleb once in Corisande."

"And it's still a good one," Cayleb put in. "I don't like it. Like Sharley, I hate it. But somebody's got to make the call, and for better or for worse, it's me. And ugly as this is, as much as it's going to stick in my craw and choke me, I don't see another option. For that matter, Domynyk, if we could tell Gwylym the entire truth, what do you think *he'd* recommend?"

"Exactly what you just have, Your Majesty." Staynair spoke with unwonted formality, yet there was no trace of doubt in his voice.

"That's what I think, too," Cayleb said sadly.

.III.

Weavers Guildhall
and
Royal Palace,
City of Manchyr,
Princedom of Corisande

Paitryk Hainree stood on the walkway around the water tower cistern atop the Weavers Guildhall. The tower's façade was a kaleidoscope of sheep, angora lizards, spinning maidens, and busy looms, all carved into the Barcor Mountain granite of which it was made. It was one of the best known tourist attractions in Manchyr, but Hainree didn't care about that as he gazed out across the city of his birth and swore with vicious, silent venom while the galleons flying the black, blue, and white banner of the Empire of Charis edged delicately towards the Manchyr wharves. The sun was barely up, the air was still cool, with that smoky blue edge that comes just after dawn, the wind-powered pump which kept the cistern filled squeaked softly, almost musically behind him, and the air was fresh from the previous evening's gentle rain. It was going to be a beautiful day, he thought rancorously, when it should have been ripped by tornadoes and hurricanes.

His hands clenched on the walkway railing, forearms quivering with the force of his grip, eyes burning with hatred. Bad enough that that bitch "empress" should be visiting Corisande at all, but far worse to see the city draping itself with bunting, decorating its streets and squares with cut greenery and flowers. What did the idiots think they were *doing*? Couldn't they see where this was *heading*? Perhaps it looked for now as if the accursed Charisians were succeeding, but they'd set their puny, blasphemous wills against *God*, damn it! In the end, there could be only one outcome for mortal men vain and stupid enough to do that.

The air began to thud and the harbor fortresses blossomed with spurts of smoke as their guns thundered in formal salute to the arriving Empress of Charis. The waterfront was the better part of a mile from Hainree's vantage point, yet even from here he could hear the cheers go up from the packed wharves. For a moment, his entire body quivered with a sudden urge to fling himself over the railing. To plummet down to the paving below and put an end to his own fury. But he didn't. He wouldn't let the bastards be shed of him that easily.

He stared at the incoming galleons for another moment, then turned his back resolutely and started towards the ladder. He had a final inspection to make before he could sign off on his current assignment, and then he had his own preparations to see to.

He descended the ladder with the confidence and ease of practice. There was little left of the silversmith he'd once been as he swung down the rungs. That Paitryk Hainree had disappeared forever fourteen months ago when

Father Aidryan Wayman was arrested by the Charisians' Corisandian flunkies. Fortunately, before that happened, Hainree had taken Father Aidryan's advice to heart and established an escape plan all his own, one no one else had known anything about. And because he had, he'd managed to elude the terrifyingly efficient sweep of Sir Koryn Gahrvai's guardsmen. He still wasn't certain how he'd accomplished that, especially since they'd been hunting him by name and with a damnably accurate description, but if he'd needed any evidence that God Himself was watching out for him, he'd certainly had it as Father Aidryan's entire organization was smashed to flinders in a matter of days . . . and he wasn't.

And the other thing he'd had evidence of was that the only way to avoid arrest was to operate completely independently. To trust and recruit *no one*. At least a dozen other efforts to organize resistance against the occupation and the abomination of the Church of Charis had foundered in the last year. It was as if Gahrvai's guard had eyes everywhere, ears listening to every conversation. The only way to avoid them was to say nothing to anyone, and so Hainree had found new employment with the city of Manchyr's construction and maintenance office. He'd grown a beard, cut his hair differently, changed the way he dressed, gotten a colorful tattoo on his right cheek and the side of his neck, and found himself a room on the other side of the city where no one had ever seen or known him. He'd gone to ground and become someone else, who'd never heard of Paitryk Hainree the rabble-rouser.

But he hadn't forgotten Paitryk Hainree, and neither had he forgotten his duty to God and his murdered prince. They'd taken everything he'd ever been from him when they forced him to flee with a price on his head, yet that had simply added to his anger and his determination. Perhaps he was only one man, but one man—properly motivated—could still change an entire princedom.

Or even an empire, he thought as he neared the ground. *Or even an empire.*

▼ ▼ ▼

"Her portraits don't do her justice, do they?" Sir Alyk Ahrthyr murmured in Koryn Gahrvai's ear. "I hadn't realized she was so good-looking!"

"Alyk," Gahrvai whispered back, "I love you like a brother. But if you say *one* word to Her Majesty. . . ."

He let the sentence trail off, and Ahrthyr chuckled. The dashing Earl of Windshare found beautiful women irresistible. And, unfortunately, all too many beautiful women returned the compliment. By Gahrvai's count, Ahrthyr had fought at least eight duels with irate brothers, fiancés, fathers, and husbands. Of course, those were just the ones he knew about, and since Prince Hektor had outlawed public duels over ten years ago—officially, at least—there were probably more that Gahrvai *didn't* know about.

So far the earl had managed to survive all of them, and done it without killing anyone (and getting himself outlawed) in the process. How long he could keep that up was open to question. Besides, Gahrvai had met Cayleb Ahrmhak. Any woman he'd married was going to be more than a match for Windshare, and that didn't even consider what would happen if *Cayleb* found out about it.

"Ah, there's no poetry in your soul, Koryn!" the earl said now. "Anyone who could look on that face—and that figure, too, now that I think of it—and not be stirred is a confirmed misogynist." Ahrthyr paused, cocking his head to one side. "That wouldn't be the reason your father still isn't a *grand*father, would it, Koryn? Is there something you've never told me?"

"I've never told you I was about to kill you . . . until now," Gahrvai returned repressively. "That's subject to change if you don't *shut up*, though."

"Bully," Windshare muttered. "And party pooper, too, now that I think of it." Gahrvai's elbow drove none too gently into the earl's sternum and he "oofed" at the impact. "All right," he surrendered with a grin, rubbing his chest. "You win. I'll shut up. See, this is me not saying a thing. Very peaceful, isn't it? I don't believe you've ever had such a restful afternoon with me arou—"

The second elbow strike was considerably more forceful than the first.

▼ ▼ ▼

Sharleyan paced calmly up the crimson runner of carpet towards the throne. It was the first time she'd ever been in Manchyr, although she'd studied this very throne room many times since she'd gained access to Owl's SNARCs. It was rather more impressive in person, though, and much as she'd hated Hektor Daykyn, she had to admit he'd had far better taste than the late Grand Duke of Zebediah. Sunlight spilled through tall, arched windows down its long western wall, puddling on the polished parquet floor's inlaid marble medallions and geometric patterns. The wall itself was plastered and coffered, with the personal seals of the last half-dozen princes of Corisande worked into the recesses between the window embrasures in vibrant color, and banners hung from the high, spacious ceiling Manchyr's near-equatorial climate imposed on local architecture. That vaulted ceiling was also coffered, with polished, richly gleaming wooden beams framing painted panels decorated with incidents from the House of Daykyn's history, and the entire eastern wall consisted of latticed glass doors opening onto a formal garden glowing with tropical blossoms and glossy greenery.

At the moment she had rather less attention to spare than the architecture and landscaping probably deserved, however, and she concentrated on maintaining her confident expression as she processed towards the dais where the Earl of Anvil Rock, the Earl of Tartarian, and the other members of Prince Daivyn's Regency Council waited to greet her formally.

The remaining *members of the Regency Council, at any rate,* she reminded herself a bit tartly. Although, to be fair, Sir Wahlys Hillkeeper, the Earl of Craggy Hill, was still *technically* a member. Changing that—permanently— was one of the purposes of her visit.

It was extraordinarily quiet, quiet enough for her to hear the distant sound of surf through the glass doors which had been opened onto the garden. She had no doubt there were dozens of soft, hushed side conversations all about her, but these were courtiers. They'd learned how to have those conversations without drawing attention to themselves, and most of them were probably downright eager to avoid drawing *her* attention at this particular moment.

She felt her lips quiver with amusement and suppressed the thought firmly, continuing her stately, not to say implacable progress along the carpet. She wasn't as ostentatiously surrounded by bodyguards as she'd been in Zebediah, although no one was going to crowd her here, either. Sir Koryn Gahrvai's guardsmen lined the throne room's walls, bayoneted muskets grounded, and an honor guard of Imperial Charisian Marines had escorted her from the docks to the palace. She'd wanted to insist on a smaller, less obvious and lower-keyed presence, but she'd known better. There was no point pretending this was Chisholm or Charis. Not that there'd never been an attempt to kill her in Charis, now that she thought about it.

That reflection carried her to the end of the carpet, Merlin Athrawes pacing respectfully at her heels while Edwyrd Seahamper kept a king wyvern's eye on the rest of her personal detail, and Sir Rysel Gahrvai bowed formally to her.

"On behalf of Prince Daivyn, welcome to Manchyr, Your Majesty," he said.

"Thank you, My Lord," she replied. "I wish my visit might have come under happier circumstances, yet the welcome I've received—not just from you, but from so many of Manchyr's people—has been far warmer than I'd anticipated."

He bowed again at the compliment, although there'd been a slight double edge to it. For that matter, there'd been a double edge to his greeting. The exact status of Prince Daivyn remained what diplomats referred to as "a gray area," and for all the genuine spontaneity of the cheers which had greeted Sharleyan, not everyone in the greeting crowds had been cheering. Indeed, she suspected that no more than half of them had, and quite a few of those who hadn't cheered had been stonefaced and grimly silent, instead.

"May I escort you to your throne, Your Majesty?" Anvil Rock asked, and she inclined her head in gracious assent before she laid the fingertips of her right hand on his forearm. He assisted her carefully (and completely unnecessarily) up the five steps to the top of the dais and she smiled at him before she turned and seated herself.

She looked out across the throne room, seeing the faces, trying to sample the emotional aura. It was difficult, despite all the hours she'd spent poring over the SNARCs' reports from this very city. She felt confident she'd assessed Manchyr's attitude accurately, at least in general terms, and she knew far more about the aristocrats and clerics thronging this room than any of them could possibly imagine. Yet these were still human beings, and no one could predict human behavior with total assurance.

A throat cleared itself quietly to her right, and she looked up at Archbishop Klairmant Gairlyng. He looked back at her gravely, and she smiled and pitched her voice to carry.

"Before we begin, would you be kind enough to thank God for me for my safe arrival here, Your Eminence?"

"Of course, Your Majesty," he agreed with a small bow, then straightened and gazed out across the throne room himself.

"Let us pray," he said. Heads bowed throughout the vast room, and he raised his voice. "Almighty God, the high and mighty ruler of the universe, we thank You for the safety in which You have brought our royal visitor to this court. We beseech You to smile upon her and so to show her Your favor that she walks always in Your ways, mindful of Your commands and the dictates of Your justice. Guide, we beseech You, all the nations of this Your world into the way of Your truth and establish among them that peace which is the fruit of righteousness, that they may be in truth Your Kingdom and walk in all the ways You have prepared for them. And we most especially beseech You to look down from Your throne and bless Your servant Daivyn and all who advise, guide, and guard him. Bring him, too, safely back to us, and so resolve and compose the differences between Your children that all rulers of clean heart and good intent may gather in the amity Your plan has decreed for all men. We ask this in the name of Your servant Langhorne, who first declared Your will among men to the glory of Your Name. Amen."

That was an interesting choice of phrasing, Sharleyan thought wryly as she joined the others in touching fingertips first to her heart and then to her lips. The tightrope here in Corisande was more complicated than almost anywhere else in the youthful Empire of Charis, and Gairlyng clearly understood that. He'd managed to avoid calling Sharleyan Corisande's ruler, and she'd noticed the "royal visitor," as opposed to the possible "imperial visitor." At the same time, he'd adroitly avoided calling her an interloper, either, and no one could very well take offense at his request for God's blessing on young Daivyn. And the "resolve and compose the differences between Your children" was straight out of the Church of God Awaiting's most ancient liturgy. Of course, the people who'd written that liturgy had never envisioned a situation quite like this one.

The stir and shuffle of feet, the rustle of clothing and clearing of throats, which always followed a moment of prayer in Sharleyan's experience whispered through the throne room. Then Anvil Rock turned towards her and bowed, wordlessly offering her the opportunity to speak without any awkward little formalities which might have conceded—or denied—her authority to do so.

"I thank you for the welcome I received at dockside this morning," she said, and saw one or two people look up sharply when she avoided the royal "we." Well, there'd be time enough for that later.

"A Charisian monarch—and such I find I've become,

much though the idea would have astounded me as little as three years ago"—she smiled and a chuckle ran through the watching courtiers—"appreciates a welcoming port, especially at the end of a winter voyage which took rather longer than I might have wished. More than that, I realize how many difficult issues remain between the Princedom of Corisande and the Crown of Charis, and I take it as a favorable sign that so many turned out to wish me well upon my arrival here.

"At the same time," she allowed her expression and her tone to become more serious, "it's obvious not everyone here in Manchyr was equally happy to see me." She shook her head. "Under the circumstances, I can scarcely blame anyone who might continue to cherish reservations about the future, and it's only natural such reservations should express themselves in reservations about *me*, and about Emperor Cayleb. One of the reasons for Cayleb's visit here last year was to attempt to put some of those reservations to rest. That's also part of the reason for my visit this year. Of course"—her expression became grimmer—"there are other and less happy reasons, as well."

It was very quiet in the throne room, and she turned her head, surveying them all and letting them see her level eyes and firm mouth.

"It's never pleasant to be required to yield to force of arms," she said quietly. "Cayleb and I understand that. At the same time, I believe any fair-minded person must admit we were left very little choice. When five princedoms and kingdoms—including, I would remind all of us, my own—were required by 'the Knights of the Temple Lands' to league together against Old Charis, even though that kingdom had committed no crimes or offenses against any of them, Charis had no choice but to defend herself. And when it became evident that the corrupt vicars who'd seized control of Mother Church intended to continue their efforts to exterminate not just the Kingdom of Charis but any vestige of freedom of thought, the *Empire* of Charis had no choice but to carry the war to its enemies. And so that war came to your shores behind the banners of my Empire."

The quiet grew more intense, and she met it squarely, her shoulders straight.

"I won't pretend Chisholm lacked its own reasons for enmity with the House of Daykyn. I'm sure everyone in this throne room knows what they were and why they existed. But I will say that my enmity—and Cayleb's—was directed against the *head* of that house, and it stemmed from his actions, not from any ingrained hatred of Corisande or all things Corisandian. We had specific reasons to confront Prince Hektor on the field of battle, and so we did, openly and directly, with none of the diplomatic fictions, lies, and masks the 'Knights of the Temple Lands' had employed to hide their crimes."

She saw shoulders tighten as she took the bull firmly by the horns.

"I realize many continue to believe Cayleb ordered Hektor's assassination, and I suppose I can even understand why that belief should have gained such currency. But my husband is not a stupid man, my lords and ladies. Do any of you believe for one instant that the son of Haarahld of Charis could have failed to understand how Prince Hektor's murder on the very eve of his surrender would poison the hearts and minds of Corisandians against him? Can any of you think of an action better calculated to make the peaceful, orderly inclusion of Corisande in the Empire of Charis more difficult? Having sailed thousands of miles, having won his cause on the field of battle with one overwhelming victory after another, what could possibly have motivated anyone but a bloodthirsty monster to have not only Prince Hektor but his elder son murdered?"

She paused once more, for only a heartbeat this time. Then—

"You've had the opportunity to see the policies General Chermyn has administered here on our behalf, and you know that at the core of those policies lies our desire to demonstrate that the Empire of Charis respects the rule of law and has no desire to rule through terror and the iron fist of oppression. Many of you have had the opportunity to meet personally with Emperor Cayleb, and those who have must surely realize that however resolute he may be, however dangerous in battle, he is not and never has been a man who relishes the shedding of human blood. I ask you to ask yourselves if the Crown which dictated those policies and the Emperor you met would have resorted to the murder of a foe who had been vanquished and was prepared to offer honorable surrender. An honorable surrender which would have been of far more value to the Empire politically, both here in Corisande and abroad, than his murder—his martyrdom—could ever have been."

A half-heard susurration, like a sharp breeze across a sea of reeds, ran through the throne room as more than one of those nobles and prelates realized exactly what she was implying. No one dared speak out in open rejection, however, and she sat silently, letting the thought sink home for a full ten seconds before she resumed.

"I fully realize that the Group of Four has excommunicated both me and Cayleb and laid the entire Empire of Charis under the interdict," she said then. "As such, in the eyes of Temple Loyalists, any oaths you may swear to us or to the Church of Charis have no force. Obviously, we disagree, and we have no option but to hold those who swear to the terms of that to which they have sworn. No ruler, even in time of peace, can accept anything less; no ruler, even in time of war, has the right to demand anything more.

"I'm here in Corisande, in no small part, because of that. All of you know what I refer to when I say that. I regret that such a reason should have brought me here, and I regret that many whose only crime was loyalty to Corisande, to the House of Daykyn, and to the clergy they'd been taught to revere were caught up in the treachery and plotting of a handful of individuals who saw the opportunity to take power into their own hands for their own uses and their own purposes. I have no choice— Charis has no choice—but to exact justice, yet I will endeavor as Charis has always endeavored to mitigate justice with mercy wherever that may be possible."

She paused yet again, the quiet so intense she could hear the surf once more, and the instincts developed in so many years on a throne tried to parse the mood of the people in the throne room. At least some of them seemed to be genuinely trying to reserve judgment, she thought. Others, however assiduously they might try to hide it, had clearly made up their minds already and weren't about to be swayed by anyone's words ... especially hers. She couldn't tell how many fell into which camp, but it seemed to her that the balance was tilted ever so slightly against those who had already committed themselves to hostility.

"We've made it clear we aren't prepared to cavalierly strip Prince Daivyn of his birthright and inheritance," she said finally. "Obviously, when a minor prince is in exile in a foreign court, far from his own lands, we can't simply resign into his hands that which we've won on the field of battle. By the same token, we can understand why Prince Daivyn and those who genuinely have his best interests at heart should hesitate to deliver him back into the power of those many believe had his father and older brother murdered. Whether we did or not, simple prudence would dictate that he not be brought back into our reach until those responsible for guarding his life and well-being are fully satisfied it would be safe to do so. I don't pretend we like the situation, yet I'm also well aware no one here in *Corisande* likes it, either.

"It was the need to bear all of those factors in mind which led Emperor Cayleb to recognize the Regency Council as representing *Prince Daivyn*, not the Charisian Crown. Obviously, the Regency Council must accommodate itself to the demands of Charis, just as Prince Daivyn would be required to do were he here and ruling in his own right. That, unfortunately, is the way things work in a world where disputes between realms are too often settled upon the field of battle. It's our hope that in the fullness of time, and preferably sooner rather than later, all these issues will be resolved without further bloodshed here in Corisande, and we earnestly desire to find in that resolution a way to finally end the anger and distrust, the hostility, which has lain between Charis, Chisholm, and Corisande for so long. In the meantime, we have no intention of expropriating Prince Daivyn's lands, whether as Prince or as Duke of Manchyr. Aside from the abolition of serfdom, we have no intention of interfering with Corisande's traditional law or the traditional rights of her aristocracy or her commons. And aside from those actions necessary to purge Mother Church of the corruption which has infected and poisoned her, the lies which have been told in her name, we have no quarrel with her, either . . . and certainly not with God.

"And that, my lords and ladies, is what I've come here to Corisande to demonstrate for all to see. I will make no deals in secret. There will be no secret arrests and executions, just as there have been none yet. We will not torture confessions out of those we suspect of wrongdoing, and if we must inflict the death penalty, it will be carried out quickly and cleanly, without the torture in which Zhaspahr Clyntahn delights.

"In the end, you—as all of God's children—have a choice to make. You may choose to align yourself with the Empire and Church of Charis against the evil threatening to twist Mother Church and all we believe in into something vile and dark. You may choose to stand with Corisande and the rightful Prince of Corisande, and it's our hope that in the fullness of time Prince Daivyn will choose to stand with us. You may choose to reject the Empire and Church of Charis and fight them with all your power and all your heart, and that, too, is a choice only you can make. No Charisian monarch will ever seek to dictate your final choice to you, but we will do whatever we must to protect and nurture the things in which *we* believe, the causes for which *we* choose to fight and, if necessary, die. If our choices bring us into conflict, then so be it. Charis will not flinch, will not yield, and will not retreat. As my husband has said, 'Here we stand; we can do no other,' and stand we will, though all the forces of

Hell itself should come against us. Yet whether you make yourselves our friends or our foes, I will promise you this much."

The stillness was absolute, and she swept the listening throng with that level brown gaze yet again.

"We may fight you. We may even be forced to slay you. But we will never torture or terrify you into betraying your own beliefs. We will never convict without evidence. We will never ignore your right to trial and your right to defend yourself before God and the law, never capriciously sentence men and women to die simply because they disagree with us. And we will never dictate to your conscience, or murder you simply for daring to disagree with us, or torture you vilely to death simply to terrify others into doing our will, and call that the will of God."

She looked out at those silent, listening faces, and her voice was measured, each word beaten out of cold iron as she dropped her sworn oath into the silence.

"Those things are what the Group of Four does," she told them in that soft, terrible voice, "and we will *die* before we become them."

. V .

Imperial Palace,
City of Tellesberg,
Kingdom of Old Charis

"I'm going to strangle that parrot," Cayleb Ahrmahk said conversationally. "And if I weren't afraid it would poison me, I'd have the cook serve it for dinner."

The parrot which had just stolen a pistachio out of the silver bowl on the wrought-iron table landed on a branch on the far side of the terrace, transferred the stolen nut from its beak to its agile right foot, and squawked raucously at him. Obviously no respecter of imperial dignities, it proceeded to defecate in a long gray and white streak down the lime tree's bark, as well.

There were quite a few similar deposits decorating the terrace, Cayleb noticed. In fact, there were enough of them for at least two heroic sculptures. Probably even three, unless they were *equestrian* sculptures.

"With all due respect, Your Majesty," Prince Nahrmahn said, reaching out and scooping up a handful of the same pistachios, "first you'd have to catch it."

"Only if I insist on *strangling* it," Cayleb retorted. "A shotgun ought to do the job permanently enough, if a little more messily. It might even be more satisfying, now that I think about it."

"Zhanayt would be less than amused with you, Your Majesty," Earl Gray Harbor pointed out from his seat beside Nahrmahn. The first councilor shook his head. "She's turned that dratted bird into her own personal pet. That's why it's bold enough to swoop down and steal your nuts. She's been hand-feeding them to it for months now to get it to ride on her shoulder when she comes into the garden and it thinks it owns all of them. She'll pitch three kinds of fits if you harm a single feather on its loathsome little head."

"Wonderful."

Cayleb rolled his eyes while Nahrmahn and Gray Harbor chuckled. Princess Zhanayt's sixteenth birthday would roll around in another few five-days. That meant she was about fourteen and a half Old Terran years old, and she was entering what her deceased father would have called her "difficult stage." (He'd used a rather stronger term when it had been his older son's turn, as Cayleb recalled.)

Prince Zhan, her younger brother, was only two years behind her, but his engagement to Nahrmahn's daughter Mahrya seemed to be blunting the worst of his adolescent angst. Cayleb wasn't certain it was going to last, but for now at least the assurance that he would in just over three years' time be wedding one of the most lovely young women he'd ever met appeared to be giving him a level of confidence the mere fact that his brother was an emperor (and that he himself stood third in the line of succession) wouldn't have. Despite the inescapable political logic of the move, Cayleb had had his doubts about betrothing his baby brother to someone almost eight Safeholdian years older than he was, but so far, it was working out well. Thank God Mahrya took after her mother—physically, at least—rather than her father! And it didn't hurt that Zhan was far more inclined to be bookish than Cayleb had ever been. Nahrmahn's genetic contribution was obvious in Mahrya's keen wits and love affair with the printed page, and she'd been subtly guiding Zhan's choice of books for almost three years. He was even reading *poetry* now, which made him pretty nearly unique among fourteen-year-old males of Cayleb's acquaintance.

"Oh, come now!" Gray Harbor scolded the emperor. "I remember *you* as a teenager, Your Majesty. And I remember your father's description of you just before he sent you off on your midshipman's cruise."

"And that description would have been what?" Cayleb asked suspiciously.

"I believe his exact words were 'A stubborn, stiff-necked young hellion ripe for hanging,'" the earl replied with a smile. "I could be wrong about that, though. It might have been 'obstinate,' not stiff-necked."

"Why did everybody who knew me then persist in thinking of me as stubborn?" Cayleb's tone was plaintive. "I've always been one of the most reasonable people I know!"

Gray Harbor and Nahrmahn looked at one another, then back at their liege lord without saying a word, and he snorted.

"All right, *be* that way." He selected one of the roasted, salted pistachios, peeled the shell, and popped the nut into his mouth. He picked up another while he was chewing and tossed it at the parrot, which ignored the assault on its dignity with lordly disdain. The emperor shook his head and turned his attention back to Gray Harbor with a more thoughtful expression.

"So you think Coris is seriously contemplating some sort of an arrangement with us?" he asked, carefully projecting a note of skepticism. He couldn't very well tell Gray Harbor he'd been looking over Coris' shoulder—or that one of Owl's remotes had been, at any rate—at the very moment the Corisandian earl wrote the message Gray Harbor had received.

"I'd say he's definitely *contemplating* an arrangement, Your Majesty," Gray Harbor replied soberly. "Whether he actually wants to consummate anything of the sort is another matter, of course."

"You're saying you think this is in the nature of a sheet anchor?" Nahrmahn put in.

"Something like that, Your Highness." Gray Harbor nodded. "Whatever else he may have been, Coris was never a fool. I've come to the conclusion that he underestimated *you* rather badly, Your Highness, but then so did everyone else. And while he doesn't come right out and say so in his note, it has to be obvious to someone as astute and as well informed as him that it would've made absolutely no sense to assassinate Hektor and his son."

"I'm not sure I'd go quite that far, My Lord," Nahrmahn said thoughtfully. "About its making absolutely no sense, I mean. It would have been uncommonly stupid to have had him assassinated at that particular *moment,* I'll grant you, but I'm sure quite a few of the world's rulers wouldn't have shed any tears if an enemy like Hektor were to suffer a fatal accident after he'd sworn fealty . . . and before he could get around to violating that oath."

"All right, that's true enough." Gray Harbor nodded again. "But my point about the actual assassination stands. Not only that, but he has to realize how . . . convenient Hektor's murder was from the Group of Four's perspective. Assuming he's genuinely committed to young Daivyn's well-being, or simply to preserving his own future access to power in Daivyn's eventual court, he's got to be worried about someone like Clyntahn's deciding that Daivyn's death might be as helpful as his father's was. So as far as that goes, yes, I'm inclined to think he truly is looking for a way out of Delferahk if one should become necessary."

"But you don't think he's going to make a move in our direction unless he *does* decide it's necessary?" Cayleb asked.

"No, I don't. And to be fair, why should he? It's not as if we've done anything that would endear us to him, and for the moment at least it's entirely reasonable for his loyalty to Mother Church as well as whatever personal loyalty he feels towards Daivyn and Irys to push him towards staying out of our grasp. He was never as precipitous as Hektor, and I don't see any reason for that to change now. Especially when he knows that until he's actually *forced* to turn to us, he's in a far better bargaining position in Talkyra than he'd be in Tellesberg."

"So how do you think we should respond?"

"I've discussed that with Bynzhamyn and also with Ahlvyno," Gray Harbor replied, and Cayleb nodded. Bynzhamyn Raice wasn't simply Old Charis' spymaster and Ahlvyno Pawalsyn wasn't simply its finance minister; they were also two of Gray Harbor's oldest friends and most trusted colleagues.

"Both of them agree this is an opening that's far too valuable to pass up," the earl continued. "Obviously, we can't know where it's going to lead, but there's always the possibility it really will end up with Coris forced to seek asylum with us. From a political perspective, it would be impossible to overestimate the advantage of getting our hands—metaphorically speaking—on Irys and Daivyn. Whether we'd be able to convert that into any sort of willing cooperation on their part is another matter entirely, of course, and given Princess Irys' obvious influence with her younger brother and her evident conviction you did have her father and her older brother murdered, Cayleb, I'd say the chances were probably less than even. On the other hand, from all reports she's smart enough to recognize that whether we're her favorite people in the world or not, her brother probably has no option but to cooperate with us, at least officially. Especially if Coris does believe Clyntahn had Prince Hektor killed and he's managed to convince her of that."

"Well," Cayleb selected another pistachio and cracked it open, "I'm inclined to go along with you, Bynzhamyn, and Ahlvyno. So the next order of business is how we go about moving this courtship along, I suppose."

"I expect the biggest difficulty's going to be simply communicating back and forth," Nahrmahn said thoughtfully. "This isn't exactly something we can discuss with him over the Church's semaphore system, and speaking from the perspective of an experienced intriguer, that could be a real problem, especially in a case like this. How long did it take his message to get here, My Lord?"

"The better part of three months." Gray Harbor's sour tone acknowledged Nahrmahn's point. "I can't know what route it followed, but assuming it went downriver from Talkyra to Ferayd or Sarmouth before it found a ship to bring it to Tellesberg, it had over fifteen thousand miles to travel. Which means it actually made excellent time to get here as quickly as it did."

"But that's the sort of delay that introduces all sorts of potential 'cooling-off periods' into the courtship," Nahrmahn said. "And to be honest, the sort of thing that's most likely to force Coris' hand is also likely to come up in a much shorter time window than that. If he suddenly discovers Daivyn's in active danger from Clyntahn, for example, taking three months to get a message to us would make it all but impossible to coordinate any effective response with us. A six-month two-way communications time?" The Emeraldian shook his head. "That may work for the normal political seduction, but it won't in any sort of emergency situation."

"That's true, of course," Gray Harbor admitted. "We're still better off than we were, though, Your Highness."

"Oh, I agree!" Nahrmahn nodded vigorously. "It's just

that I think we might be able to . . . speed up message times. From his end to us, at least."

"And just how might we accomplish that?" Cayleb asked, sitting back and looking rather intently at the no longer quite so plump prince.

"Well, it occurs to me, Your Majesty, that I may have forgotten to mention one small capability of my erstwhile anti-Charisian intelligence service," Nahrmahn said with a charming smile. "As I'm sure you're aware, Emerald's always been famous for its racing, hunting, and messenger wyverns."

"I *do* seem to recall something about a wyvern salesman right here in Tellesberg, as a matter of fact," Cayleb replied somewhat repressively.

"Yes, that *was* one of our better cover arrangements, I thought," Nahrmahn agreed reminiscently. "It worked quite well for years."

"And the reason for this trip down memory lane?" Cayleb inquired.

"As it happens, Your Majesty, our royal wyvern breeders have been attempting to improve our messenger wyvern stock for quite a long time now, and not simply to help our wyvernries' sales. Some years ago—during my father's reign, as a matter of fact—we got a rather unexpected result when we crossed the Dark Hill line from Corisande with our own Gray Pattern line."

"Surely you're not proposing sending Earl Coris messenger wyverns, Your Highness," Gray Harbor said.

"That's precisely what I'm proposing, My Lord," Nahrmahn replied, and even Cayleb looked at him in disbelief.

Messenger wyverns had been a part of Safehold's communications system since the Creation. Now that he had access to Owl, Cayleb also knew the original messenger wyverns had been genetically engineered by Pei Shanwei's terraforming teams to deliberately enhance the various breeds' natural capabilities for the specific purpose of creating a low-tech means to help tie the original, scattered enclaves together. Bigger, stronger, and much tougher than Old Terran carrier pigeons, the wyverns Shan-wei had designed had fallen into two main categories, either of which could carry considerably heavier messages than their tiny Old Terran counterparts. They could even be used to carry small packages, although it wasn't the most reliable possible way to deliver them.

The short-range breeds were faster, smaller, and more maneuverable than their larger brethren. Capable of speeds of up to sixty miles per hour (although some of the racing breeds had been clocked at over a hundred miles per hour in a sprint), their maximum effective flight range was mostly under six hundred miles, which meant they could deliver a message to their maximum range in as little as ten or eleven hours, on average. They were the most commonly used breeds, in large part because the logistics meant there was little call for ranges longer than that. Like carrier pigeons, they were a one-way communications system, since they returned only to the wyvernry they recognized as "home," wherever that might be, which meant they had to be transported from their home to their point of release. Shuttling them back and forth by wagon or on lizardback over distances much greater than six hundred miles simply wasn't practical for most people, although the Church and some of the larger mainland realms maintained special relay systems to supplement and back up the semaphore towers. In addition— and unlike carrier pigeons—they could be relatively quickly imprinted with another "home" wyvernry. In fact, it was necessary to take precautions to prevent that from happening inadvertently.

The longer-range wyverns were slower, but they also were capable of flights of up to four thousand miles. Indeed, there were rumors of legendary flights of up to five thousand, although substantiation for such claims was notoriously thin on the ground. Because they were slower—and because they had to stop to hunt and roost on the way—they were capable of no more than seven hundred and fifty miles per day under average conditions, but even that meant they could deliver a message over a four-thousand-mile transit in less than six days. That was slower than the semaphore (under good visibility conditions, anyway), but faster than any other means of communications available . . . at least to those who didn't have the advantage of communicators and satellite relays.

"As Rayjhis just pointed out, it's fifteen thousand miles from here to Talkyra by ship and boat," Cayleb said. "I realize it's shorter than that in a direct line, but it's still close to seven thousand miles even for a wyvern, Nahrmahn!"

"Yes, it is," Nahrmahn agreed. "And it just happens I have at my disposal a breed of messenger wyvern capable of making flights at least that long."

"I find that difficult—not *impossible*, Your Highness; just difficult—to believe," Gray Harbor said after a moment. "If we really do have wyverns with that kind of range, however, I'm entirely in agreement with you. The question becomes how we get them to Earl Coris in the first place."

"I've been thinking about that, too, My Lord," Nahrmahn said with a smile, "and I think I know just the messenger, assuming we can contact him."

He glanced at Cayleb, who raised his eyebrows.

"And exactly who were you thinking about calling upon?" the emperor inquired politely.

"It just occurred to me, Your Majesty, to wonder if you might have some means of getting into contact with *Seijin* Merlin's friend Master Zhevons." Nahrmahn smiled toothily at Cayleb's expression. "He did so well at . . . motivating King Gorjah, and he's obviously at home operating on the mainland. It just seems appropriate, somehow, to get him into touch with Earl Coris, as well. Who knows?" His smile faded suddenly, his eyes meeting Cayleb's levelly. "It might just turn out that this is another situation that requires his special talents, Your Majesty."

. UI .

City of Gorath,
Kingdom of Dohlar,
and
Royal Palace,
Princedom of Corisande

"They're here, My Lord," Lieutenant Bahrdailahn said quietly.

"Thank you, Ahbail," Lywys Gardynyr said. He inhaled deeply, squared his shoulders, and turned to face the cabin door. "Show them in, please."

"Yes, My Lord." The flag lieutenant bowed considerably more deeply than usual and disappeared. A moment later, he returned.

"Admiral Manthyr, Captain Braishair, and Captain Krugair, My Lord," he announced unnecessarily, and Gardynyr bobbed his head to the newcomers.

"Gentlemen," he said.

"Earl Thirsk," Gwylym Manthyr replied for himself and his subordinates.

"I very much regret the necessity to summon you to this particular meeting," Thirsk said levelly, "but in the name of what honor remains to me, I have no choice. Admiral Manthyr, you surrendered your ships and personnel to me after a most gallant and determined defense—one which still commands my admiration and professional respect. At that time, I promised you honorable treatment under the laws of war. I regret that I face you as a man forsworn."

Bahrdailahn shifted slightly, face tightening in silent protest, but Thirsk continued in the same measured tone.

"I'm sure you recognized, as did I, that any promise on my part was subject to violation or outright revocation by my superiors or by Mother Church. As a loyal son of

Mother Church it's not my place to criticize or dispute her decisions; as an officer of the Royal Dohlaran Navy, I am ashamed."

He looked directly into Manchyr's eyes, hoping the Charisian saw the truth in his own.

"Your men have been badly enough abused in Dohlaran custody. The fact that I've done everything in my power to alleviate that abuse is no excuse for my failure to change it, nor will anything remove the stain of that abuse from the honor of my Navy. I once thought harshly of your Emperor and the terms he enforced upon my men; had I known then how you and your men would one day be treated by my own service, I would have gone down on my knees before him to thank him for his leniency."

He stopped speaking, and silence lingered in the wake of his final sentence. Several seconds passed, and then Manthyr cleared his throat.

"I won't pretend I'm not angry over the way my people have been treated, My Lord." He held Thirsk's gaze, and his eyes were as hard as his tone was flat. "God alone knows how many of those who died in the hulks would've lived if they'd been given proper food and even minimal medical care. And that doesn't even consider the fact that now your Navy is prepared to turn us over to the Inquisition in full knowledge of what will happen."

He saw Thirsk wince, but the Dohlaran admiral refused to look away or evade his flinty eyes, and after a moment, it was the Charisian who nodded ever so slightly.

"I won't pretend I'm not angry," he repeated, "and I won't pretend I don't agree that this is going to be an indelible stain on the honor not just of the Dohlaran Navy but of your entire Kingdom. The time will come, My Lord, when you and all Dohlarans will rue the way in which my men have been treated. I won't be here to see it, but as surely as the sun rises in the east, my Emperor will see justice done in our names, just as he did in Ferayd. It might be well for your King to remember that day, because this time there will be no question as to where the final responsibility lies.

"Yet while all of that's true, and while I have no doubt history will besmirch *your* name as surely as that of the Duke of Fern or King Rahnyld, I also know you personally did everything humanly possible to honor your word to me and see my men decently and honorably treated. I can't forgive you for the cause you serve, but I can and will say you serve it as honorably as any man living could."

"It's not given to us to choose the kings we're born to serve," Thirsk replied after a moment, "and honor and duty sometimes lead us places we wish we'd never had to go. This is one of those places and one of those times, Admiral Manthyr, yet I *am* a Dohlaran. I can't change the decisions which have been made by my King, and I won't break my oath to him. But neither can I hide behind that oath to evade my responsibility or hide my shame from myself or from you. And that's also the reason I asked you here this morning so that I might apologize to you personally, and through you to all of your men. I know it means very little, but it's all I have to give and the least I *can* give."

A part of Sir Gwylym Manthyr wanted to spit on the deck. Wanted to curse in Thirsk's face for the sheer uselessness of *words* against the scale of what was going to happen to his men. Words were cheap, apologies cost nothing, and neither of them would save a single one of his men from a single second of the agony waiting for them. And yet. . . .

Manthyr drew a deep breath. Perhaps Thirsk's apology was no more than a gesture, yet both of them knew how dangerous a gesture it was. There was no way the Inquisition could fail to learn of this meeting, and given Thirsk's efforts to protect his Charisian prisoners while they were in his custody, the inquisitors were unlikely to look kindly upon it. For the moment, at least, Thirsk was too important—probably—to the Church's jihad to find himself the Inquisition's guest, but that was always subject to change, and both of them knew how long a memory Zhaspahr Clyntahn had. So gesture though it might be, it was scarcely as empty as some might think.

"I'm no nobleman, My Lord," the Charisian said bluntly. "I don't understand all the ins and outs of a noble code of conduct. But I do understand duty, and I do know you've truly done all you could. I can't absolve you of the guilt you obviously feel. I don't know if I would if I could. But I do accept your apology in the spirit in which it's offered and I hope that when the bill finally comes due for what your Kingdom and the Inquisition are about to do, your efforts to do the right and honorable thing will be considered in your favor."

"You may not have been born a nobleman, Admiral, but at the moment I think that's a mark in your favor." Thirsk smiled humorlessly. "Perhaps if I weren't quite so pigheaded, we—"

He broke off, waving one hand, then glanced at the clock on the cabin bulkhead, and his jaw tightened.

"I'm not supposed to know, Admiral, but you have approximately four hours before your 'escort' arrives." He saw Manthyr's face turn to stone but went on unflinchingly. "Lieutenant Bahrdailahn will return you to the prison ships. If any of you wish to send a last letter home, I give you my word I'll personally see it delivered somehow to Charis. Please see to it that any letters are completed at least a half hour before the Navy is required to transfer you to your escort. Leave them aboard ship when you depart, and I'll have them collected in a day or two."

After the Inquisition's taken you all away and I can do it without having my own men and me sent to join you, he didn't say out loud, but Manthyr and his two captains heard it anyway.

"I thank you for that, My Lord." For the first time emotion softened the flint of the Charisian's voice. "I . . . hadn't expected it."

"I only wish I'd thought—" Thirsk began, then stopped. "I only wish I'd found the courage to *make* the offer sooner, Admiral," he admitted. "Now go, and whatever the Inquisition may think, may God be with you."

▼ ▼ ▼

"So, you're *Admiral* Manthyr," the Schuelerite upper-priest sneered.

Sir Gwylym Manthyr only gazed at him wordlessly, eyes contemptuous.

It was an almost obscenely beautiful day, given what was happening. The air was cool, the breeze refreshing, and the solid quay underfoot seemed to undulate gently. After so long in the hulks, it was going to take him some time to get his land legs back.

Seabirds and sea wyverns swooped about in their unending sweeps of Gorath Bay. There was always some interesting bit of garbage, some piece of flotsam, some unwary fish or the eyes of some drifting Charisian corpse, to attract their attention, and he realized he was going to miss their antics once they'd left the harbor behind. Funny. He hadn't thought there was *anything* he'd miss about Gorath Bay, but that was before the coin had finally dropped.

"Proud and silent, are you?" the Schuelerite observed, and spat on the ground just in front of Manthyr's feet. "We'll see how 'silent' you are when you reach Zion, heretic!"

The upper-priest was in his forties, Manthyr estimated, with dark hair and a close-cropped beard, and a coiled whip hung at his side. His brown eyes were hard, dark, and hating, which was scarcely a surprise. Zhaspahr Clyntahn would have handpicked the man responsible for delivering his latest victims.

"The Grand Inquisitor wants you in Zion in one piece," the Schuelerite continued. "Personally, I'd just as soon shoot all of you and leave you in the ditch like the carrion you are, but that's not my decision. What is my decision is how . . . discipline will be maintained on our journey. I'd advise you all to remember my patience is short and the men under my command understand how to deal with Shan-wei's get. Take that as all the warning you'll be given."

Manthyr simply looked back at him, refusing to flinch or look away yet able to picture the thin, wasted, raggedly dressed officers and men standing behind him on the quay. He and the Schuelerite both knew they'd heard every word, but he felt their angry, hopeless defiance at his back.

The Schuelerite glared at him for another minute, then turned his head.

"Captain Zhu!" he barked.

"Yes, Father Vyktyr?" a shortish, blocky officer in the uniform of the Temple Guard replied.

Captain Zhu was obviously Harchongian, with the strongly pronounced epicanthic fold of his people. He looked to be in his late thirties, with black hair, and his Guard uniform bore the sword-and-flame of the Order of Schueler as a shoulder patch. That indicated that while he was a Guard officer, he'd been seconded to the Inquisition, which probably made sense. The Inquisition had its own small, highly trained military force, but it specialized in enforcement, not in field exercises. For an overland journey this long, they'd want someone with experience handling troops in the field.

"Put this garbage in its cages." Father Vyktyr gestured contemptuously at the Charisians. "And I don't see any need to be overly gentle with them."

"As you say, Father," Zhu agreed with an unpleasant smile, and turned to the weathered-looking, squatly muscular sergeant at his heels. "You heard the Father, Sergeant Zhadahng. Get them moving."

"Yes, Sir."

▼ ▼ ▼

Well, I suppose this settles what I can—and can't—do, after all, Merlin Athrawes thought grimly, lying back in his borrowed bed in Manchyr's Royal Palace and watching through the SNARCs as the Charisian prisoners were driven aboard the wagons prepared to receive them.

The Temple Guardsmen were equipped with heavy, massive, old-style matchlocks, not the newer flintlocks which were beginning to trickle into the Temple's service, and they plied their musket butts freely. He watched Charisian seamen stagger as those musket butts slammed home between their shoulder blades or drove into their rib cages. More than one man went to his knees, to be kicked and beaten until he managed to claw his way back to his feet, and if any of his comrades tried to help him, they received the same treatment.

Merlin's sapphire eyes opened in the early morning darkness, hard with fury, as a young, one-legged midshipman fell. No one had struck him; he simply tripped as he tried to move fast enough to satisfy their captors on his single foot and obviously jury-rigged crutch. It didn't matter. The guards closed in, battering and kicking while the boy curled in a desperate, protective knot, trying to protect his head with his arms, and Merlin's jaw clenched as Sir Gwylym Manthyr deliberately stepped into that ring of sadistic blows. He watched the muscular admiral taking the musket butts on his own back and shoulders, never raising a hand against his assailants as he was battered to his hands and knees across the boy's body, only using his own body to protect that fallen midshipman.

Then there was another man inside that circle, one in what was left of the uniform of a Charisian captain. And another man, slightly built, with a waxed mustache, who Merlin recognized as Naiklos Vahlain. The guards beat and kicked them harder than ever, but a handful of seamen joined them. More than one of them went down, only to rise again, faces bloodied, bodies bruised, taking those blows with silent defiance until Manthyr could climb back up from his own knees and take that semi-conscious young body in his arms. Another musket crashed into the admiral's kidneys and he stumbled forward, face twisted with pain, but he refused to drop the midshipman.

One of the guards raised his musket high in both hands, obviously aiming a murderous butt stroke at Manthyr's head, and the admiral glared at him, eyes of fire hard in a blood-streaked face, daring him to strike. The blow started forward, only to stop in midair—stop so abruptly the Guardsman staggered—as an auburn-haired Guard lieutenant shouted an order.

The entire scene froze, and then, grudgingly, the Guardsmen stepped back and allowed the fallen to rise. There were still blows, still shouted obscenities, still sneering promises of worse to come, but at least Manthyr was allowed to carry that slight, fallen body to the waiting transport wagons.

The wagons were big enough for fifteen or twenty men to be crammed aboard with room for perhaps six of them to lie down at any given moment. They were heavy framed, without shock absorbers, springs, or anything resembling seats, sided with iron bars and roofed with iron gratings. They were basically dungeon cells on wheels, and the only overhead cover was in the form of canvas tarps which were currently tightly rolled and stowed behind the drivers' tall seats. Each wagon was drawn by two hill dragons, the size of terrestrial elephants but with longer bodies and six powerful legs each. They were capable of a surprising turn of speed and possessed excellent endurance.

The wagon doors were slammed and locked. Orders were shouted, and the convoy lurched into motion. There was no reason those wagons had to have been built without springs, Merlin knew. They'd been built that way deliberately, with only one object in view: to make any prisoners' journey as unpleasant as possible . . . and to show any witnesses how unpleasant that journey was.

Which is the entire reason they decided not to send them by water after all, Merlin reflected bitterly. *They're sending them the long way, by land, so they can stop in every town to display their prizes, give every village the chance to watch them roll through on their way to the Temple and the Punishment of Schueler. They're too damned valuable an* object lesson *for Clyntahn to waste sending them by sea . . . and God knows how many of them are going to die on the way. And there's not one damn thing I can do about it. I can't even sink them at sea to spare them from what's waiting.*

He watched that clumsy procession of iron-barred wagons lurching slowly northward from the city of Gorath and hated his helplessness as he'd seldom hated anything in Nimue Alban's life or his own. Yet while he watched, he made himself one solemn promise.

Sir Gwylym Manthyr was right. What had happened to the city of Ferayd was nothing compared to what was going to happen to the city of Gorath.

. UII .

Royal Palace,
City of Manchyr,
Princedom of Corisande

It wasn't the throne room this time.

In many ways, Sharleyan would have preferred that venue, but there were traditions to break. Prince Hektor's notion of judicial procedure had been to see to it that the accused got the proper sentence, not to worry about any pettifogging legal details like proving guilt or innocence. Trials were an inconvenient, messy formality which sometimes ended with the accused actually getting off entirely, which was scarcely the reason he'd had the culprit arrested in the first place! Far more efficient and direct to simply have him hauled in front of the throne and sentenced without all that unnecessary running around.

To be fair, the majority of Hektor's subjects had considered his justice neither unduly capricious nor unnecessarily cruel. He'd maintained public order, prevented the nobility from victimizing the commoners too outrageously, supported the merchants and bankers' property rights and general prosperity, and seen to it that most of his army's killing had been done on someone else's territory. Theoretically, there'd always been the appeal to the Church's judgment, although it had been resorted to only infrequently . . . and usually unsuccessfully. But by and large, Corisandians had assumed anyone Prince Hektor wanted to throw into prison or execute probably deserved it. If not for the crime of which he stood accused, for one he'd committed and gotten away with another time.

What that also meant, unfortunately, was that being hauled in front of the prince had been tantamount to being punished. And what that meant, in turn, was that if Sharleyan dispensed justice from the throne room which had once been Hektor's, those being brought before her would automatically assume they were simply there to learn what fate had already been decreed for them . . . and that "justice" actually had very little to do with the process. All of which explained why she was, instead, sitting in the magnificently (if darkly) paneled Princess Aleatha's Ballroom.

Sharleyan couldn't imagine anyone voluntarily holding a ball in the room. Only one wall had any windows at all, and they were small. Not only that, but more recently constructed portions of the palace cut off most of the light they would have taken in, anyway. She supposed the vast, gloomy chamber would have looked much more imposing with its dozen massive bronze chandeliers all alight, but the heat from that many candles would have been stifling, especially in Manchyr's climate.

Probably just that northern blood of yours talking, she thought. *As far as* these *people are concerned, it might simply have been comfortably warm. Maybe even bracingly cool!*

No, she decided. Not even Corisandians could have done anything but swelter under those circumstances.

She was dithering, she told herself, looking out across the rows of benches which had been assembled to face the dais upon which she sat. The main reason she'd chosen Princess Aleatha's Ballroom—aside from the fact that it *wasn't* the throne room—was its size. It was stupendous, bigger than any other chamber in the palace complex, and almost five hundred people sat looking back at her across the open space cordoned off by Sir Koryn Gahrvai's Guardsmen. There were nobles, clerics, and commoners in that crowd, chosen to make it as representative a mix of the population as possible, and some of them (not all commoners, by any means) seemed acutely uncomfortable in their present surroundings.

Perhaps some of that might have been due to the six members of the Charisian Imperial Guard who stood between them and her dais on either side of Edwyrd Seahamper. Or, for that matter, to the way Merlin Athrawes loomed silently, somberly, and very, very intimidatingly at her back.

The dais raised her throne approximately three feet, and it was flanked by only slightly less ornate chairs in which the members of Prince Daivyn's Regency Council were seated. Two more chairs (remarkably plebeian compared to the Regency Council's) sat directly before the dais at a long table placed just behind the line of Guardsmen and piled with documents. Spynsair Ahrnahld, her bespectacled, youthful secretary, sat in one of those chairs; Father Neythan Zhandor—bald head shining above its rapidly retreating fringe of brown hair, even in the ballroom's subdued light—occupied the other.

Archbishop Klairmant was also present, but he'd chosen to stand to Sharleyan's right rather than be seated himself. She wasn't certain why he'd made that choice. Perhaps it was to avoid giving the impression he, too, was seated to give judgment ex cathedra, adding the Church's imprimatur to whatever judgments she rendered. Yet his position might also lead some to think he was standing as her advisor and councilor.

And he's going to get damned tired before the day is over, she thought grimly. *Still, I suppose we'd best get to it.*

She raised one hand in a small yet regal gesture, and a shimmering musical note rang through the enormous room as Ahrnahld struck the gong on one end of the document-piled table.

"Draw nigh and give ear!" a deep-voiced chamberlain—a *Charisian* chamberlain—bellowed. "Give ear to the Crown's justice!"

Utter silence answered the command, and Sharleyan felt the stillness radiating outward. Many of the people seated on those rows of benches would normally have been chattering away behind their hands, eyes bright as they exchanged the latest, delicious gossip about the spectacle they were there to see. But not today. Today, they sat waiting tensely until the double doors of the ballroom's main entrance swung wide and six men were marched through them, surrounded by guards.

The prisoners were richly dressed, jewels sparkling about their persons, immaculately groomed. Yet despite that, and even though they held their heads high, there was something beaten about them. And well there should be, Sharleyan reflected grimly. They'd been arrested over six months ago. Their trials had been concluded before a combined panel of prelates, peers, and commoners two five-days before she ever arrived in Manchyr, and they could be in little doubt about the verdicts.

They halted in front of her, and to their credit (she supposed) five of them looked her squarely in the eye. The sixth, Sir Zher Sumyrs, the Baron of Barcor, refused to raise his own eyes and she saw the gleam of perspiration on his forehead.

Ahrnahld pushed back his chair and stood, taking the top folder from the stack in front of him and opening it before he looked at Sharleyan.

"Your Majesty," he said, "we bring before you, accused of treason, Wahlys Hillkeeper, Earl of Craggy Hill; Bryahn Selkyr, Earl of Deep Hollow; Sahlahmn Traigair, Earl of Storm Keep; Sir Adulfo Lynkyn, Earl of Black Water; Rahzhyr Mairwyn, Baron of Larchros; and Sir Zher Sumyrs, Baron of Barcor."

"Have these men been given benefit of trial? Have all of their rights under the law been observed?" Her voice was chill, and Zhandor stood beside Ahrnahld.

"They have, Your Majesty," he replied, his deep voice grave. "As the law requires, their cases were heard before a court of Church, Lords, and Commons which determined their guilt or innocence by secret ballot so that none might unduly influence the others. Each had benefit of counsel; each was allowed to examine all the evidence against him; and each was permitted to summon witnesses of his choice to testify on his behalf."

There was no hesitation or question in that voice, and Sharleyan heard one of the accused—Barcor, she thought—inhale sharply. Father Neythan Zhandor wasn't just any law master. He'd been picked by Maikel Staynair for this mission because of his reputation. A Langhornite, like most law masters, he was (or had been, before the schism, at least) widely acknowledged as one of Safehold's two or three most knowledgeable masters of admiralty and international law. If Father Neythan said all of their rights had been observed, that was that.

"Upon what grounds were they accused of treason?"

"Upon the following specifications, Your Majesty," Zhandor said, opening a folder of his own. "All stand accused of violating their sworn oaths of fealty to Prince Daivyn. All stand accused of violating their sworn oaths to the Crown of Charis, freely given after Corisande's surrender to the Empire. All stand accused of raising personal armies in violation of their oaths to the Crown of Charis and also in violation of the law of Corisande limiting the number of armed retainers permitted to any peer of the realm. All stand accused of trafficking and conspiring with the condemned Tohmys Symmyns of Zebediah. All stand accused of plotting insurrection and armed violence against Prince Daivyn's Regency Council and against the Crown of Charis. In addition, Earl Craggy Hill stands accused of violating his personal oath and abusing and betraying his authority and position as a member of the Regency Council in the furtherance of their conspiracy and his own quest for power."

Stillness crackled in the ballroom, and Barcor licked his lips. Craggy Hill glared at Sharleyan, but it was an empty glare, little more than surface deep, for something darker and far less defiant lived behind it.

"And has the court which heard their cases reached a verdict?"

"It has, Your Majesty," Ahrnahld said. He turned the top page in the folder before him.

"Wahlys Hillkeeper, Earl of Craggy Hill, has been adjudged guilty of all charges brought against him," he read in a flat, carrying voice. Then he turned a second page as he had the first.

"Bryahn Selkyr, Earl of Deep Hollow, has been adjudged guilty of all charges brought against him."

Another page.

"Sahlahmn Traigair, Earl of Storm Keep, has been adjudged guilty of all charges brought against him."

Another whisper of turning paper.

"Sir Adulfo Lynkyn, Earl of Black Water, has been adjudged guilty of all charges brought against him."

"Rahzhyr Mairwyn, Baron of Larchros, has been adjudged guilty of all charges brought against him."

"Sir Zher Sumyrs, Baron of Barcor, has been adjudged guilty of four of the five charges brought against him, but acquitted of the charge of personally trafficking and conspiring with Tohmys Symmyns."

The last page turned and he closed the folder. Then he turned and looked up at Sharleyan.

"The verdicts have been signed, sealed, and mutually witnessed by every member of the court, Your Majesty."

"Thank you," Sharleyan said and sat back in her throne, laying her forearms along the armrests as she gazed at the men before her. The ballroom's tension crackled higher now that the formalities were out of the way, and she felt the witnesses' focused attention like the rays of the sun captured and concentrated by a magnifying glass. But not quite like the sun, for this focus was cold and sharp as a Cherayth icicle, not fiery.

It ought *to be fiery,* she thought. *I ought to feel passionate satisfaction and justification at seeing these men brought to the end they deserve. But it isn't, and I don't.*

She didn't know precisely what she *did* feel, and it didn't matter. What mattered was what she had to *do.*

"You've heard the charges against you," she said in a voice of ice. "All of you have heard the verdicts. All of you have had ample opportunity to see the massive weight of evidence which was brought to bear against each of you. No honest-minded man or woman on the face of this world will ever be able to dispute the proofs of your crimes, and the records of your trials are open to all. Every step of the process which brings you here this day has been in accordance with the law of your own princedom, as well as the law of Charis. We will entertain no pleas or protests against the justice of the court which tried you or of the scrupulous observation of the law, your rights, or the verdicts. If any of you have anything you wish to say before sentence is passed upon you, how-ever, now is the time."

Craggy Hill and Storm Keep only glared, helpless fury burning in their eyes. Deep Hollow's facial muscles quiv-ered, although Sharleyan couldn't have said what emotion woke those spasms. He pressed his lips together without speaking, however, and her eyes moved to Black Water. The earl's face was dark with anger and curdled with hate, yet she actually felt a flicker of sympathy in his case. His father's death at Darcos Sound was what had brought him into the conspiracy. At least he had the excuse of honest anger, honest outrage, not solely the cynical ambition which had served Craggy Hill and Deep Hollow.

"I wish to speak," Baron Larchros said after a mo-ment, and Sharleyan nodded to him.

"Then do so."

"I can't speak for all of my fellows," he replied, raising his chin and looking her in the eye, "but I did what I did because I will never acknowledge the authority of the craven lickspittles of this 'Regency Council' of traitors you and your husband have foisted upon this Princedom. It was their willingness to sell themselves to you Chari-sians for personal power and advantage, not ambition on *my* part, which brought me to resist them! You may call it 'treason' if you please, but I say the treason was theirs, not mine, and that no man of conscience can be held to any oath sworn to traitors, regicides, heretics, and ex-communicates!"

A stir went through the witnesses, and Sharleyan gazed back down at him for several seconds without speaking. Then she nodded slowly.

"You speak clearly, Baron of Larchros," she said then. "And you speak with courage. You may even speak truthfully of your own motives, and we grant you their sincerity. Yet you did swear the oaths you violated. You did grant your allegiance to the Regency Council—the legally selected Regency Council, chosen by your own Parliament—as Prince Daivyn's representatives and the guardians of his interests and prerogatives here in Corisande. And you did violate the laws of Corisande, as well as conspiring to unleash warfare here in the heart of your own Princedom. We may concede that you acted out of what you believe to have been the best of motivations. We will *not* concede that your motivations justify your actions, nor will we retreat one inch from the authority which is ours under the accepted law of nations by right of victory, fairly and openly won upon the field of battle, and by acknowledgment of your own Parliament following that victory. We will say this much—you, more than any of your fellows, have our respect, but respect cannot stay the demands of justice."

Larchros' jaw clenched. He seemed to hover on the brink of saying something more, but he stopped himself and simply stood meeting her gaze with hot-eyed defiance.

"Please, Your Majesty!" Barcor said suddenly into the silence. "I was carried away by patriotism and loyalty to Mother Church—I admit it! But as the court itself determined, I was never party to the core of this conspiracy! I—"

He broke off as Sharleyan looked at him with undisguised contempt. His eyes fell, and she smiled coldly.

"The fact that cowardice prevented you from openly declaring yourself as Baron Larchros did is no defense," she said flatly. "You were prepared to take your share of the spoils when Craggy Hill and Storm Keep divided the new 'Regency Council' between themselves. You preferred to spend gold instead of blood or steel, perhaps, but you cannot separate yourself so easily from 'the core of this conspiracy,' My Lord. I told you we would hear no pleas, no protests of innocence. Have you anything further to say?"

Barcor's lips trembled. His face was ashen, and his head swiveled, eyes imploring the members of the Regency Council to intervene in his behalf. There was no response, and he swallowed convulsively as his eyes came back to Sharleyan.

She waited another measured thirty seconds, but none of the convicted men spoke again, and she nodded. It was time to end this, and she could at least give them the mercy of swiftness.

"It is our judgment that, for the crimes of which you stand convicted, you be taken from this place immediately to a place of execution and there beheaded. You will be granted access to clergy of your choice, but sentence will be carried out within this very hour, and may God have mercy on your souls."

. VIII .

City Engineer's Office
and
Royal Palace,
Princedom of Corisande

"That was a good job you did on the Guildhall, Bahrynd," Sylvayn Grahsmahn said as Bahrynd Laybrahn (who didn't look a thing like Paitryk Hainree) stepped into his office. "That cistern's been nothing but a pain in the ass for as long as I can remember."

"It wasn't hard once I realized the pump casing had to be leaking," Hainree replied. He shrugged. "Actually finding the leak and getting to it was a bitch, but fixing it once I found it was pretty routine, really."

"Well, I've been sending people over to look at it for the better part of half a year now," Grahsmahn grumbled, "and you're the first one to find the problem. I know you're still new, Bahrynd, but if the Master Engineer will go along with me, you're going to be a supervisor by this time next month."

"I appreciate the vote of confidence," Hainree said, although he was fairly certain the promotion wouldn't come through. "I just try to do my job."

He gazed out of Grahsmahn's office window. Dusk was coming on quickly, and he and the supervisor should already have left for the evening. In fact, they would have if Hainree hadn't gone to some lengths to arrange otherwise. He'd known Grahsmahn would want a detailed report on how he'd solved the problem, and he'd manipulated his own schedule to ensure he'd be late getting back to the large, rambling block of buildings on Horsewalk Square which housed the city engineer's offices. Grahsmahn had waited for him in order to get his report firsthand, and the supervisor had listened carefully as Hainree ran through everything he'd had to do to fix it.

The truth was that he'd enjoyed the challenge, and it had been the biggest job he'd been assigned since he'd started working his way up in the city's engineering and maintenance services. He'd begun as little more than a common laborer—a necessity, if he wanted to be certain no one asked any questions about his previous employers. It wasn't as if the work were exceptionally difficult, however, especially for a man who'd run his own business for so many years. And the Guildhall plumbing system's mysterious water losses had at least offered a puzzle sufficient to distract him from the future rushing rapidly towards him.

As he'd told Grahsmahn, figuring out what had to be wrong hadn't been hard.

The city reservoir, just northwest of Manchyr's walls, was fed by the Barcor River before the river flowed on through the city itself (becoming distinctly less potable in the process, and not just from storm runoff), and feed pipes from the reservoir flowed under the city itself. Unfortunately, there wasn't enough head pressure in the system to move water higher than the first floor of most of the city's buildings, which was one reason for the picturesque windmills spinning busily away on the rooftops of so many of the taller buildings all across the capital. They powered pumps which lifted water from the low-pressure mains to rooftop or water tower cisterns high enough for gravity-feed systems to develop reasonable pressure throughout the city.

The problem at the Weavers Guildhall was that the cistern level had been far below design specifications and still dropping. Obviously, there was a problem somewhere between the main and the cistern, but the pump itself had been operating perfectly. It was an ancient design, with an endless chain of flat, pivoted links traveling in a loop through a pair of shafts. Lifters—bronze saucers closely fitted to the diameter of the shafts—were set every foot or so along the chain, which traveled between the water main and the cistern. Water flowed into the inlet chamber at the bottom, which was slightly larger in diameter than the lifters. The lifters, however, formed a sort of moving cylinder inside the outflow shaft, capturing and lifting water as they moved through the inlet chamber and upward. With a good head of wind, a large enough windmill, and a wide enough pump shaft the system could move hundreds of gallons of water very quickly. Floats in the cisterns raised interrupter rods to disengage the windmill's steadying vanes when the holding tanks were full, letting the windmills pivot off the wind and go idle to prevent the pumps from raising too much water and simply wasting it, and most of the cisterns were large enough to meet demand in their buildings for at least a couple of windless days in a row.

It was a simple, reliable arrangement whose greatest vulnerability was the possibility that the chain might break. The gearing needed a change of lubricating oil about once a year, but aside from that the only other real maintenance concern was the durability of the flexible gaskets fitted to the edge of each lifter to ensure a good seal with the sides of the lift shaft. The gaskets were made from the sap of the rubber plant with which the Archangel Sondheim had gifted mankind at the Creation (and whose cultivation was a major income source for Corisande) and wore out only slowly, but eventually they did have to be replaced.

The Guildhall pump had shown no signs of excessive wear, however, even though it was delivering progressively less water despite running almost constantly. So the answer had to be that the water was escaping somewhere between the inlet and the cistern, but where? A diligent search had revealed no obvious leaks, but Hainree had known there had to be one, so he'd persevered until he finally found it. What had made it so difficult was that it was quite high, yet there'd been no signs of leakage . . . because the break in the shaft wall had occurred where it passed through a stone wall directly adjacent to the roof drainage system. Given the intensity of the rainstorms which frequently smote Manchyr, the Guildhall's downspouts and gutters were designed to handle a *lot* of water, and at the point where the break had appeared one of the main drain channels had been separated from the shaft only by a single relatively thin layer of cement. Once the shaft started leaking through the dividing cement, it had simply discharged itself down the drain, where no one ever saw it and there was no telltale seepage on any walls or gathering in the cellars.

It had also happened to be one of only two sections of the shaft which couldn't be eyeballed in a routine inspection, which ought to have suggested something to someone, since "routine inspections" had so singularly failed to find the problem. Hainree had been forced to lower himself down the outer edge of the building, pry loose two large building blocks, and then chip his way through the drainage channel's inch-thick wall before he could confirm his suspicions. Actually getting to the problem and fixing it had been relatively straightforward after that, although that didn't mean it hadn't still required plenty of hard work and sweat. In fact, he damned well deserved Grahsmahn's praise.

"Well, I just wish more of our people tried as hard to do their jobs as you do," the supervisor said now. "We'd be in a lot better shape, let me tell you! Not that we're having much luck getting the budget we need out of the Regency Council." He shook his head disgustedly. "We need someone on the Council who understands engineering problems—the kind that keep cities like Manchyr running and not just the ones that go into making newfangled weapons!"

Hainree nodded vigorously. It was one of Grahsmahn's recurrent refrains, and the supervisor probably had a point, although Hainree's own problems with the Regency Council focused on rather different concerns. However. . . .

"I meant to ask you for your impression of this Empress Sharleyan," he said, forcing himself to speak the hated name in an almost normal tone.

"I think she's . . . impressive." Grahsmahn leaned back in his chair, scratching the back of his neck, and shook his head slowly. "Somebody said she was beautiful, but me, I'm not so sure. She's a handsome woman, I'll give her that, but beautiful?" He shook his head again. "Too much nose, and those eyes of hers . . . Trust me, Bahrynd—she's got a temper that would make a slash lizard run for cover!"

"So was she ranting and raving?" Hainree asked.

"No, no, she wasn't." Grahsmahn stopped scratching the back of his neck and looked up at Hainree, his eyes unfocused with memory. "In fact, that's the reason she's so impressive, if you ask me. It's not natural for a young woman that age, and one who's hated the House of Daykyn so long, to *not* lose her temper at a time like this. I mean, here she's in a perfect position to *hammer* us after what those idiots tried to pull, and she's cool as a cucumber. Not wishy-washy, don't misunderstand me. I think she was madder than Shan-wei's Hell at Craggy Hill, at least. But she didn't scream, she didn't shout, and she just ordered them beheaded. Didn't have them tortured, didn't send their family members after them on general principle, didn't even have them hanged. Just a short, sharp appointment with an ax and it was all over." He shook his head again. "I'll be honest with you, Bahrynd, I can't see the Old Prince letting them off that easy. I'd say she's got a short way with people who cross her, but she's not going out of her way to be any nastier about it than she has to."

"You sound as if you actually admire her." Hainree couldn't quite keep the disapproval out of his voice, and Grahsmahn's eyes refocused as the supervisor looked up at him.

"Didn't say that," he said a bit testily. "Mind you, I'm of the opinion we could do worse, if only her damned husband hadn't had Prince Hektor murdered. For that matter, if young Daivyn were to come home—and assuming the Regency Council could keep his head on his shoulders when he did—I don't think she'd go out of her way to be nasty to *him,* either. Not so long as he didn't cross her, leastways."

"Maybe." Hainree shrugged. "And I'm no noble, or a member of Parliament, either. All the same, Master Grahsmahn, it seems to me that sooner or later there'd come a time when Prince Daivyn would have to 'cross her' if he was going to be true to Corisande. And from what you're saying. . . ."

He let his voice trail off, and Grahsmahn nodded unhappily.

"I'm inclined to think you've got a point," he sighed. "Hopefully, though, it's not anything that's going to happen soon, and if I were young Daivyn, I'd be staying far, far away from Corisande until Mother Church gets done sorting out what's going to happen with this Empire of Charis and Church of Charis."

It was Hainree's turn to nod, although he'd come to suspect Grahsmahn was at least mildly Reformist at heart himself. Perhaps that was why he wasn't as outraged as

Hainree at Sharleyan Ahrmahk's presence here in Manchyr.

"You're probably right," he said. "Are you looking forward to tomorrow?"

"Not really." Grahsmahn's expression was troubled. "I mean, I know it's an honor and everything, but I don't really like watching men being sentenced to death. Langhorne knows they spent long enough on the trials. If they weren't doing their best to be sure everything was done right and proper, they sure used up a lot of time doing something else! And I didn't hear any of them yesterday claiming they hadn't been given a fair trial, except maybe that sorry piece of shit Barcor. But I still don't like watching. Funny thing is, I don't think *she* likes being there any better than I do!" He gave a brief laugh. "I guess she's got even less choice about it than I do, though."

Hainree nodded again, though he doubted "Empress Sharleyan" was as bothered by all of this as Grahsmahn seemed to think. The supervisor really didn't have a choice, though. He was one of the randomly selected city professionals who'd been chosen to witness what happened, and attendance wasn't optional. Sharleyan and the Regency Council seemed determined to make certain there were plenty of eyes to see—and tongues to tell—what happened to whoever dared to raise his hand against their tyranny and treason.

"Well, Master Grahsmahn," he said now, "it may be you won't have to be there tomorrow after all. Things can change, you know."

"I wish it would," Grahsmahn said feelingly, pushing his chair back and starting around the end of his desk. "I've got enough other things I could be doing, and like I say, I don't like watch—"

His eyes widened in stunned horror as Hainree's right hand came up from his side and the short, keen-edged dagger drove home at the base of his throat. His voice died in a horrible gurgle and his hands reached up, clutching at Hainree's wrist. But the strength was flowing out of him with the flood of his blood, and Hainree twisted the blade as he drew it sideways. The flood became a torrent, and he stepped back as Grahsmahn thudded to the office floor with his eyes already glazing.

"I'm sorry," Hainree said. He knelt beside the body for a moment and signed Langhorne's Scepter on the supervisor's forehead. "You weren't a perfect man, but you deserved better than this. I'm about God's work, though, so perhaps He'll forgive both of us."

He patted Grahsmahn on the shoulder, then started going through the dead man's pockets. He needed only a handful of minutes to find what he sought, and he stood once more. He gazed down at the body again briefly as he slipped the ornately engraved summons into his pocket, then turned and stepped out of the office and used the key he'd also taken from Grahsmahn to lock the office door before he started down the stairs. He went the back way, reasonably confident he wouldn't be running into anyone this late. He'd managed to avoid most of the blood spray, anyway, and once he got out into the settling gloom the few drops he *hadn't* been able to avoid shouldn't be very noticeable.

If he was spotted before he got clear, or if someone should enter Grahsmahn's office despite the locked door between now and morning, that would be the end of his plan, but he knew in his heart of hearts it wouldn't happen. As he'd told Grahsmahn, he was about God's work, and unlike mortal men, God did not suffer His work to go undone.

▼ ▼ ▼

Sharleyan Ahrmahk sat once again on the dais in Princess Aleatha's Ballroom. They'd gotten an earlier start today, and even less sunlight came in through the ballroom's windows, so lamps had been lit in niches around the walls. Despite their brightly polished reflectors, they didn't shed a great deal of light, so stands of candles had been placed at either end of the document table for Spynsair Ahrnahld and Father Neythan's use. Once the sun finally cleared the roof of the palace wing shading the windows things should get better, she told herself, then nodded to Ahrnahld to strike the gong.

"Draw nigh and give ear!" the same chamberlain called as the musical note vibrated its way back into silence. "Give ear to the Crown's justice!"

The double doors opened once more, and four men—or perhaps three men and a boy, since one of them was clearly not yet out of his teens—were ushered through it. One of the older men wore the subdued finery of a minor noble, or at least a man of substantial wealth. The second looked as if he was probably a reasonably well-off city merchant, and the third—the oldest of the group, with iron-gray hair and a spade beard—was clearly an artisan of some sort, possibly a blacksmith, from his weathered complexion and powerfully muscled arms. The youngest was very plainly clothed, but someone—his mother, perhaps—had seen to it that plain though his garments might be, they were scrupulously clean and neat.

She studied their expressions as the guards ushered them—firmly, but without brutality—to their place in front of the dais. Despite the dimness of the light, she could see them quite clearly, thanks to the multi-function contact lenses Merlin and Owl had provided her, and she recognized the apprehension in their faces only too plainly.

I don't blame them for that in the least, she thought grimly. *And I hadn't realized how badly yesterday was going to depress me, either. I know it had to be done, and I knew it was going to be bad, but even so. . . .*

Her own expression was serene and calm with years of discipline and training, but behind that mask she saw again the previous day's unending procession of convicted traitors. Craggy Hill and his companions had received the "honor" of appearing before her first, but twenty-seven more men and six women had followed them. Followed them not simply before Sharleyan's dais, but to the executioner.

Thirty-nine human beings in a single day—the first *day,* she thought, trying not to dwell on how many days of this were yet to go. *Not many compared to the number that get killed on even a small battlefield, I suppose. And unlike the people who get killed in battles, every single one of them had earned conviction and execution. But I'm the one who pronounced their sentences. I may not have swung the ax, but I certainly wielded the sword.*

Her own thoughts before her arrival in Zebediah came back to her, and the knowledge that she'd been right then was cold comfort now.

But at least I don't have to send them all to death, she reminded herself, squaring her shoulders as the quartette of prisoners halted before her.

Spynsair Ahrnahld stood and opened another of those deadly folders, then turned to Sharleyan.

"Your Majesty," he said, "we bring before you, accused of treason, Zhulyis Pahlmahn, Parsaivahl Lahmbair, Ahstell Ibbet, and Charlz Dobyns."

"I attest that all of them were tried before a court of Church, Lords, and Commons and that all rights and procedures were carefully observed," Father Neythan added. "Each had benefit of counsel and was allowed to examine all the evidence against him and each was permitted to summon witnesses of his choice to testify on his behalf."

It was obvious the Langhornite was repeating a well-rehearsed formula, Sharleyan thought, yet it wasn't a *routine* formula. He and his two assistants actually had examined each of the court dockets and case records individually.

"Upon what grounds were they accused?"

"Upon the following specifications, Your Majesty," Ahrnahld said, consulting yet another folder. "Master Pahlmahn stands accused of extending letters of credit upon his banking house and of contributing his personal funds to the raising, equipping, and training of armsmen in the service of Earl Craggy Hill's conspiracy. He also had personal knowledge of the Earl's plans to assassinate Earl Anvil Rock and Earl Tartarian as the first step of their coup.

"Master Lahmbair stands accused of allowing ships

and freight wagons owned and employed by him to transport pikes, swords, muskets, and gunpowder for the purpose of arming the forces with which Earl Craggy Hill's conspiracy intended to seize control of the city of Lian in the Earldom of Tartarian.

"Master Ibbet stands accused of joining the armed band intended to seize control of Lian. He is also accused of lending his smithy as a place in which to conceal weapons and of assuming the acting rank of captain in the band being raised in that place.

"And Master Dobyns stands accused of helping to plan, organize, and train the individuals who, in accordance with Bishop Executor Thomys Shylair's instructions, were to attack the garrison from within in a 'spontaneous uprising' here in Manchyr should Craggy Hill's forces approach the city."

Sharleyan sat for a moment, looking at all four of them. Ibbet and Pahlmhan looked back at her with hopeless but unyielding defiance. Lahmbair seemed sunk in resignation, his eyes fixed on the floor, his shoulders sagging. Dobyns, the youngest of the three by a good fifteen years or more, looked frankly terrified. He was fighting to conceal it, that much was obvious, but she could see it in the taut shoulders, the hands clenched into fists at his sides, the lips tightly compressed to keep them from trembling.

"And has the court which heard their cases reached a verdict?" she asked.

"It has, Your Majesty," Ahrnahld replied. "All of them have been adjudged guilty of all charges brought against them." He extracted a thin sheaf of documents from his folder. "The verdicts have been signed, sealed, and mutually witnessed by every member of the court, Your Majesty."

"Thank you," Sharleyan said, and silence echoed as she swept her brown eyes once again across all four of those faces.

"One of a monarch's duties is to punish criminal actions," she said finally. "It's a grim duty, and one not lightly to be embraced. It leaves its weight here." She touched her own chest. "Yet it may not be shirked, either. It must be dealt with by any ruler worthy of the crown he or she wears. The courts here in your own Princedom have weighed the evidence against you and found all of you guilty of the crimes charged against you. And, as all of you are painfully aware by this time, the sentence for your crimes is death. There is no lesser sentence we may impose upon you, and so we sentence you to die."

Lahmbair's shoulders twitched, and young Dobyns closed his eyes, swaying slightly, but Ibbet and Pahlmahn only looked back at her. Clearly the sentence had come as no surprise to any of them.

"Yet having passed that sentence," Sharleyan said after a moment, "we wish to make a brief digression."

Lahmbair's gaze rose from the floor, his expression confused, and Dobyns' eyes popped open in surprise. The other two looked less confused than Lahmbair, but the wariness in their expressions only intensified.

"Father Neythan has reviewed every case, every verdict, to be brought before us for the sad duty of rendering sentence. Yet *we* have reviewed these cases, these verdicts, as well, and not simply with the eye of a law master whose duty it is to see that all the stern requirements of the law he serves have been faithfully observed. And because we've reviewed those cases, we know, Master Ibbet, that you joined the rebellion against the Regency Council not simply because of your religious beliefs—which are deeply and sincerely held—but because your brother and your nephew died in the Battle of Darcos Sound, your eldest son died in Talbor Pass . . . and your youngest son died in the Battle of Green Valley."

Ibbet's strong, weathered face seemed to crumple. Then it solidified into stone, yet Sharleyan's aided vision saw a tear glimmer in the dim light as she reminded him of all he'd lost.

"As for you, Master Pahlmahn," she continued, turning to the banker, "we know you asked *nothing* from Craggy Hill or the other conspirators when you provided them with the money they sought from you. We know you ruined yourself providing those funds, and we know you did it because you are a devout Temple Loyalist. But we also know you did it because your son Ahndrai was a member of Prince Hektor's personal guard who gave his life saving his Prince from an assassin's arbalest bolt . . . and that you believe that assassin was sent by Charis. He wasn't." She looked directly into Pahlmahn's eyes. "We give you our word—*I* give you my word, as Sharleyan Ahrmahk, not as an empress—that that assassin was *not* sent by Charis, yet that doesn't change the fact that you believed he was.

"And you, Master Lahmbair." The greengrocer's gaze snapped to her face. "You aided the conspirators because they needed your wagons and your barges and they took steps to see they had them. Your sister and her family—and your parents—live in Telitha, do they not?" Lahmbair's eyes flared wide. "And Earl Storm Keep's agents told you what would happen to them if you chose not to cooperate?" Lahmbair nodded convulsively, almost as if it were against his will, and she tilted her head to one side. "That was what you told the court, yet there wasn't a single witness to confirm it, was there? Not even your sister, as much as she longed to. For that matter, we very much doubt Earl Storm Keep, for all the crimes of which he was most assuredly guilty, would truly have murdered an elderly couple, their daughter, their son-in-law, and their grandchildren simply because you refused to cooperate. Yet we believe the threat *was* made, and there was no way you might have known it hadn't been made in all sincerity."

She looked into Lahmbair's face, seeing the shock, the disbelief, that anyone—especially she—might actually have believed his story. She held his gaze for several seconds in the dim light, and then turned to Dobyns.

"And you, Master Dobyns."

The young man twitched as if she'd just touched him with a hot iron, and despite the gravity and grimness of the moment, she felt her lips try to smile. She crushed the temptation and looked sternly down at him from her throne.

"You lost no one in battle against Charis, Master Dobyns," she told him. "You lost no one to an assassin's bolts, and no one threatened your family. For that matter, we rather doubt your religious convictions run so deep and so fiercely as to have compelled you to join this conspiracy. Yet it's obvious to us that the true reason for your complicity, the true flaw which brings you to this place this day, is far simpler than any of those: stupidity."

Dobyns jerked again, his expression incredulous, and for a moment the entire ballroom seemed frozen in place. Then someone cracked a laugh, and others joined him, unable not to, be the moment ever so grim. Sharleyan smiled herself, briefly, but then she banished the expression and leaned forward slightly.

"Do not mistake us, Master Dobyns," she said coldly through the last ripples of amusement. "This is no laughing matter. People would have *died* had you succeeded in the task the Bishop Executor had assigned you, and you knew it. But we believe you'd also strayed into dark and dangerous waters before you truly understood what you were doing. We believe that thoroughly though your actions merit the sentence we've passed upon you, your death will accomplish nothing, heal nothing—have no effect but to deprive you of any opportunity to learn from your mistakes."

She sat back in the throne, looking down at all four of them, then looked beyond them to the watching spectators.

"It's a monarch's duty to judge the guilty, to sentence the convicted, and to see to it that punishment is carried out," she said clearly. "But it's also a monarch's duty to temper punishment with compassion and to recognize when the public good may be served as well by mercy as by severity. In our judgment, all of you—even *you*, Master Dobyns—did what you did in the sincere belief that God *wanted* you to. It's also our belief that none of you acted out of ambition, or calculation, or a desire for power. Your actions were crimes, but you committed them out of patriotism, belief, grief, and what you genuinely believed duty required. We can't excuse the crimes you committed, but we can—and we do—understand *why* you committed them."

She paused once more, and then she smiled again. It was a thin smile, but a genuine one.

"We would like for you and everyone to believe that we understand because of our own saintliness. Unfortunately, while we may be many things, a saint is not one of them. We try as best we may to live as we believe God would have us live, yet we must also balance that desire against our responsibilities and the practical considerations of a crown. Sometimes, however, it becomes possible for those responsibilities and practical considerations to march with the things we believe God would have us do, and this is one of those moments."

She watched hope blossom on four faces, newborn and fragile, not yet able—or willing—to believe in itself.

"We must punish those responsible for evil, and we must show to all the world that we *will* punish our enemies," she said softly, "yet we must also prove—*I* must prove—that we are not the mindless slaves to vengeance who currently hold Mother Church in their grasp. Where we may exercise mercy, we will. Not because we are such a wonderful and saintly person, but because it is the right thing to do and because we realize that while we may destroy our foes with punishment, we can win friends and hearts only with *mercy*. It's our belief that all four of you would make better friends and subjects than enemies, and we wish to find out if our belief is accurate. And so we commute your sentences. We grant you pardon for all those crimes of which you were convicted and bid all four of you go, return to your lives. Understand us: should any of you ever stand before us again, convicted of *new* crimes, there will be no mercy the second time." Her brown eyes hardened briefly, but then the hardness passed. "Yet we do not think we will see you here again, and we will pray that the hurt and the fear and the anger which drove you to your actions will ease with the passage of time and God's love."

▼ ▼ ▼

Grahsmahn had been wrong, Paitryk Hainree decided. Empress Sharleyan *was* a beautiful woman, and not simply because of the magnificence of her clothing or the crown of state glittering on her head under the lamplight. Hate churned in his belly whenever he looked at her, yet he couldn't deny the simple truth. And physical beauty, when it came down to it, was one of Shan-wei's most deadly weapons. It was easy for a young and beautiful queen to inspire loyalty and devotion where some twisted crone whose physical envelope was as ugly as her soul would have found it far more difficult.

She had a commanding presence, too. Despite her youthfulness, she was clearly the dominant figure in the huge ballroom, and not simply because every witness knew she was there to send those brought before her to the headsman. Hainree had learned more than a few of the orator's and politician's tricks building his resistance movement here in Manchyr, and he recognized someone who'd mastered those skills far more completely than he had.

Especially now.

Total silence had fallen as she told the foursome in front of her to simply go home. No one had expected it, and her knowledge of each of the four convicted men had startled everyone. She'd consulted no notes, needed no memorandums; she'd known what each of them had done and, even more, she'd known *why* he'd done it. Corisandians were unaccustomed to monarchs or nobles or clerics who looked that deeply into the lives of those brought before them for judgment. And then she'd pardoned them. Their guilt had been proven, the sentence had been passed . . . and she'd exercised an empress' prerogative and *pardoned* them.

Even Hainree, who recognized a cynical political maneuver when he saw one, sat stunned by the totally unanticipated turn of events. But the silence didn't linger. He didn't know who started it, but the single pair of clapping hands somewhere among the benches of witnesses was joined in a rippling, swelling torrent by more. Then more. Within seconds Princess Aleatha's Ballroom was filled with the thunder of applause, and Paitryk Hainree made himself come to his own feet, sharing that applause even as he cringed inside when someone so deceived by Sharleyan's ploy actually shouted "God save Your Majesty!"

It took the guardsmen stationed throughout the ballroom several minutes to even begin restoring order, and Hainree took advantage of the confusion to change his position. Still clapping, obviously lost in his enthusiasm for Empress Sharleyan's compassion and mercy, he stepped forward, shouldering his way through other applauding witnesses. He'd been seated three benches back; by the time the applause began to die away, he'd reached the front row.

The thunder of clapping hands faded, not instantly and quickly but into smaller clusters that gradually slowed and then ceased, and Paitryk Hainree's right hand slid into the formal tunic which had cost him every one of the hard-earned marks he'd managed to save up over the past six months. It was probably better than any the real Grahsmahn had owned, but it had been worth every mark he'd paid. Coupled with Grahsmahn's summons to attend, his respectable garb had gotten him waved past the sentries stationed outside the ballroom. The sergeant who'd checked his summons had actually nodded respectfully to him, unaware of the way Hainree's heart had hammered and his palms had sweated.

Yet there was no sweat on those palms now, and he felt a great, swelling surge of elation. Of accomplishment. God had brought him to this time and this place for a reason, and Paitryk Hainree would not fail Him.

▼ ▼ ▼

Merlin Athrawes stood at Sharleyan's back, watching the crowd. Owl had deployed sensor remotes at strategic points, as well, but even with the AI's assistance there were too many people for Merlin to feel comfortable. There were simply too many bodies packed into the ballroom.

I wish Edwyrd and I had argued harder against this entire idea, he thought as the clapping and cheers began to die away. *Oh, it's a masterstroke, no question! But this is a damned* nightmare *from a security perspective. Still, it looks like—*

▼ ▼ ▼

"*Death to all heretics!*" Hainree shouted, and his hand came out of his tunic.

▼ ▼ ▼

Merlin might no longer be human, but he felt his heart freeze as the shrill shout cut through the fading cheers. Even a creature of mollycircs, with a reaction speed far greater than any flesh-and-blood human, could be paralyzed—however briefly—by shock. For the tiniest sliver of an instant, he could only stand there, his head snapping around, eyes searching for the person who'd shouted.

He saw the bearded man standing in the front row, well dressed but obviously not an aristocrat. Then he saw the man's right hand, and his own hand flashed towards the pistol at his side even as he leapt forward and his other hand reached for Sharleyan.

But that instant of shock had held him just too long.

▼ ▼ ▼

The double-barreled pistol in Hainree's hand had been made in Charis. He'd found that grimly appropriate when one of his original followers ambushed and murdered a Marine officer and brought him the weapon as a trophy.

It had been surprisingly difficult to acquire any sort of accuracy with the thing, and he'd quickly used up all of the ammunition which had been captured with it. A silversmith had no problem preparing the mold he needed to cast his own bullets, however, and he'd practiced hard even before Sir Koryn Gahrvai had arrested Father Aidryan and broken Hainree's own organization. He'd also sawed two inches off its barrel in order to make it more easily concealable and he'd devised a canvas scabbard to carry it under his left arm, hidden inside his generously cut tunic. There'd been times he'd wondered why he'd bothered, and why he'd kept a weapon which would automatically have convicted him of treason against the Regency Council if it had been found in his possession.

Now, as the heel of his left hand cocked both locks in a single, practiced swipe, his right hand raised the weapon, and he squeezed the trigger.

▼ ▼ ▼

Flame flashed from the pistol's priming pan and Merlin heard the distinctive "chuff-CRACK!" of a discharging flintlock in the instant before he reached Sharleyan.

His own pistol fired in the same fragment of time. It all happened far too quickly, too chaotically, for even a PICA to sort out. The two shots sounded as one, the assassin's second barrel discharged into the floor, Merlin's fingertips touched Sharleyan's shoulder . . . and he heard her sudden sharp grunt of anguish.

▼ ▼ ▼

Impossible.

The single word had time to flash through Paitryk Hainree's mind before the sapphire-eyed Imperial Guardsman's bullet exploded through his right lung a quarter inch from his heart. No human being could move that quickly, *react* that quickly!

Then the agony ripped him apart. He heard himself cry out, felt the pistol buck in his hand as the second barrel fired uselessly, felt himself going to his knees. He dropped the smoking weapon, both hands clawed at the brutal chest wound, he felt blood spraying from his mouth and nostrils in a choking, coppery tide, and a sudden terrible fear roared through him.

It wasn't supposed to be like this. He'd come here

knowing he was going to his death, succeed or fail, so what was *wrong* with him? Why should the actual approach of death terrify him this way? What had happened to his faith, his belief? And where was God's comfort and courage when he needed Him most?

There were no answers, only the questions, and he felt even them pouring out of him with his blood as he swayed and then toppled weakly from his knees.

But I did it, he told himself, his cheek pressed into the floor in the hot pool of his own blood as the blackness came for him. *I did it. I killed the bitch.*

And somehow, in that last bitter moment of awareness, it meant nothing at all.

. IX .

Sir Koryn Gahrvai's Townhouse
and
Royal Palace,
City of Manchyr

"So what do you think of her *now*, Alyk?"

Koryn Gahrvai sat back in his comfortable chair, listening to rain drum on the roof. The lanterns illuminating the garden at the heart of the square-built townhouse were barely visible through the pounding raindrops, and thunder rumbled intermittently, still somewhere to the south but rolling steadily closer.

"I'd ask her to marry me, if she weren't already married to an emperor," Alyk Ahrthyr said. He reached out to the punch bowl on the table and stirred it gently with the silver ladle, then snorted. "And if she didn't scare me to death!" he added.

"Now why should she do a thing like that?" Gahrvai's father asked sardonically. He sat at the head of the table, in the chair which would normally have been his son's, nursing a glass of Chisholmian whiskey. "It's not like she's done anything extraordinary lately, now is it?"

All five of the men sitting around that table looked at one another as a louder peal of thunder grumbled its way across the heavens. Lightning flickered, and Gahrvai raised his own glass in an acknowledging salute to his father before he looked at the Earl of Tartarian and Sir Charlz Doyal.

"Did either of you see that coming?" he asked.

"Which 'that' did you have in mind?" Tartarian inquired dryly. "Her performance, the assassination attempt, *Seijin* Merlin, or the fact that she survived?"

"How about all the above?" Gahrvai retorted.

"*I* didn't see any of it coming, at any rate," Doyal admitted. "Just for starters, she certainly hadn't discussed any pardons that I knew of."

He raised his eyebrows at Earl Anvil Rock and Earl Tartarian, but both of the older men shook their heads.

"Not with us," Anvil Rock said. "And I had a word with Archbishop Klairmant afterward, too. She hadn't mentioned anything about it to him, either."

"I didn't think she had," Doyal said. "And something I find almost as interesting is that she didn't ask anyone for a copy of their trial transcripts, either. Despite which she seemed to know more about all of them than *we* did."

"That might actually be the most easily explained part of it," Tartarian observed. Doyal looked at him with an expression of polite incredulity, and the earl chuckled. "Don't forget, it was *Seijin* Merlin's agents here in Corisande that put us onto the plot in the first place, and we still don't have any idea how they gathered some of the information they gave us." He shrugged. "All we *do* know is that every bit of that information checked out when we investigated. I think it's entirely possible they may have kept back some facts and suspicions they figured couldn't be proven in a court, and I don't imagine Merlin would have many reservations about sharing something like that with Empress Sharleyan."

"I suppose that could explain it," Doyal said in a tone which implied he believed nothing of the sort, and Tartarian pointed an index finger at him.

"Don't you go shooting holes in my perfectly good theory unless you've got one to replace it with, young man," he said severely. Doyal, who wasn't that many years Tartarian's junior, laughed, and Tartarian shook his head. But then his expression sobered. "And don't go shooting holes in my theory until you've got an explanation that won't scare the shit out of me when you come up with it, either."

"She really *is* more than a little frightening, isn't she?" Gahrvai said into the small silence Tartarian's last sentence had produced. Lightning flashed again overhead, close enough this time that the thunderclap seemed to rattle the opened garden windows in their frames.

"I'm not sure frightening is exactly the right word," his father objected, but Tartarian made a moderately rude noise in his throat.

"It'll do until we can come up with a better one, Rysel," he said.

"I think a lot of it was Archbishop Maikel's fault," Doyal put in. The others looked at him and he raised his right hand, palm uppermost as if he were releasing an invisible bird. "Remember how he reacted after that assassination attempt in Tellesberg Cathedral. According to the reports, he didn't even hesitate—just went ahead and celebrated mass with the assassins' blood and brains splashed all over his vestments. Frankly, I had my doubts about the stories at the time; now I'm starting to think it must be something in the water in Charis!"

"You may be righter about that than you think you are, Charlz," Gahrvai said ruefully. Doyal raised an eyebrow, and Gahrvai shrugged. "Don't forget, before he celebrated mass, he also rebuked the members of his congregation who wanted to go out and start stringing up Temple Loyalists in revenge. Does that remind you of anything?"

Doyal gazed at him for a moment, then nodded, and

Gahrvai nodded back while his mind replayed the chaos and confusion of the assassination attempt.

The only thing he'd been able to think when the would-be killer shouted was that Cayleb Ahrmahk would never forgive Corisande for allowing his wife to be murdered on her very throne. There'd been *no way* the man could miss, not from a range of no more than fifteen feet. Gahrvai would have been one of the first to admit that it was far harder to fire a pistol accurately than most people probably believed, especially when someone was gripped by the excitement and terror of a moment like that. Still, at that range? The man could almost have reached out and *touched* her with the pistol's muzzle before he pulled the trigger!

But his fears—like the assassin, apparently—had failed to reckon with Merlin Athrawes. Despite all the stories Gahrvai had heard, and despite the things he knew first-hand were true, he would never have believed any mortal man could move that quickly. The *seijin* clearly hadn't seen anything coming before the assassin produced his weapon. Despite that, the first two shots had sounded as one, and his bullet had hit the man who'd been identified as Bahrynd Laybrahn (although Gahrvai sincerely doubted that had been his true name) before "Laybrahn" could fire his second shot. The smear of lead where Laybrahn's second bullet smashed into the marble floor was barely two feet in front of where his body had fallen, and Spynsair Ahrnahld's left shoulder had been grazed by the ricochet before it buried itself in the ceiling.

Gahrvai had been in more than his fair share of chaotic, violent situations. He knew how impressions could blur, how a man could be absolutely positive of what he'd seen . . . and yet absolutely wrong about what had actually happened. And Merlin had reacted so quickly, moved with such speed once he did see the weapon, that he'd seemed almost to have been teleported by a wizard's spell out of some children's tale. But still, granting all of that, it simply didn't seem possible Sharleyan could have been missed.

Yet when Captain Athrawes rolled aside, coming up on one knee from where he'd covered her protectively with his own body, she'd been unhurt. Well, perhaps not totally *unhurt*, which certainly shouldn't surprise anyone. Merlin had been more concerned with protecting her from assassins than gentleness, and the weight of an armored man his size coming down that hard would have been enough to knock the breath out of anyone.

From Sharleyan's expression and the tightness of her shoulders when Merlin assisted her to her feet, Gahrvai had been certain for one heart-stopping moment that she *had* been hit. She'd leaned to her left, left hand pressed hard against her ribs, and her face had been pale and strained. But then she'd straightened, drawn an obviously cautious breath, and shaken her head—hard—at something Merlin must have said into her ear.

Shouts and screams had still filled the huge chamber, and no one else had been close enough to hear what the *seijin* might have said, anyway, but Gahrvai had no doubt at all what Merlin had advised. Unfortunately, even *seijins* had their limits, and one of those limits, clearly, was Sharleyan Tayt Ahrmahk.

"Be seated!" she'd shouted, and somehow she'd managed to pitch her voice so that it could be heard. Not by very many people at first, but those closest to her first stared at her in disbelief and then started repeating her command at the top of their lungs. In less than two minutes, by some sorcery Gahrvai didn't come close to understanding, she'd actually managed to restore something like order as she stood almost straight, one hand still pressed to her side.

Merlin Athrawes had stood beside her, his pistol still in his right hand, merciless sapphire eyes scanning the witness-filled benches, and Sergeant Seahamper had stood on her other side with an expression which could only be described as murderous. Gahrvai hadn't blamed either of them at all. God only knew if there was *another* assassin out there. It didn't seem possible, but then Gahrvai wouldn't have believed the first one could have gotten in unchallenged. And if there *was* another assassin, the slender white-and-blue-clad figure who'd lost her crown and whose long hair had come tumbling down about her shoulders would be a perfect target.

She'd seemed unaware of that, however, just as she'd seemed unaware of the bruise already darkening her left cheek. She'd simply stood there, exposed to any follow-up shot, *willing* the Corisandians back onto their benches. Only after the last of them sat had she seated herself once more, sitting very erect, her left elbow beside her and her upper arm still pressed against those ribs.

"Thank you," she'd said in a calm voice whose normality seemed utterly bizarre under the circumstances. Then she'd actually managed a smile, and if it was a bit shaky and passed quickly, who should blame her? She'd reached up with her right hand, tucking a strand of that fallen, glorious sable hair behind her ear and shaken her head.

"I deeply regret that this should have happened," she'd said, looking down at the body in the pool of blood as four of Gahrvai's guardsmen prepared to remove it. Her eloquent brown eyes had been shadowed, and she'd shaken her head sadly. "Surely God weeps to see such violence loosed among His children."

Stillness had seemed to flow outward from her. The scraping sound of the corpse's heels as the guardsmen picked up the body had seemed shockingly loud in the silence, and the empress had turned her head, watching as the man who'd tried to kill her was carried from her presence. A trail of blood droplets had followed him, dark in the lamplight as the guardsmen and their burden vanished through the double doors, and she'd gazed at those doors for a handful of heartbeats before she'd turned once more to look out at the assembled witnesses.

"There are times," she'd told them quietly, almost softly, "when all the killing and all the hatred strike me to the heart. When I wonder what sort of world my daughter will inherit? What kind of men and women will decide how the people of that world live? What they're allowed to believe?"

Gahrvai's eyes had widened as he realized she'd abandoned the royal "we." And they'd gone even wider as he saw those benches filled with Corisandians leaning towards a Chisholmian queen who was also a Charisian empress and listening intently. She'd no longer been a conquering monarch dispensing justice and retribution; she'd been something else. A young mother worried about her own child. A young woman who'd just survived a murder attempt. And a voice of calm when she should have been demanding vengeance upon those who had allowed such a thing to happen.

"Is this what we truly wish?" she'd asked in that same quiet voice. "To settle our differences with murder? For those of us on one side to leave those on the other no option but to kill or to be killed? It grieves my soul to know how many people—some of them known personally to me, some of them beloved friends and kinsmen, and far more who I never met but who were *someone's* kinsmen or kinswomen or beloved—have already died, yet the death toll is only starting. Yesterday I sat here in front of you and sent thirty-nine people to the headsman. Tomorrow and the next day I'll send still more, because I have no choice, and those decisions, those confirmations of the sentences of those brought before me, will live with me for the rest of my own life. Do you think any sane woman *wants* to order the deaths of others? Do you truly believe I wouldn't rather—*far* rather—pardon, as I've just pardoned Master Ibbet, Master Pahlmahn, Master Lahmbair, and young Dobyns? Despite anything the Group of Four may say, God does *not* call us to exult in the blood and agony of our enemies!"

She'd paused, her expression sad, her eyes dark in the shadows yet lit by the lamplight while the stink of blood and voided bowels and the brimstone reek of gunsmoke drifted like Shan-wei's perfume, and then she'd shaken her head.

"I wish I had some magic wand that could make all this go away, but I don't, and I can't. The only 'peace' someone like Zhaspahr Clyntahn will ever accept is the destruction of everything I know and love and hold dear. The only 'agreement' he will ever tolerate is one in which his own twisted, vicious perversion of God's will rules each and every one of God's children. Charis didn't *start* this war, my friends; Charis simply *survived* the war someone else launched at her like a slash lizard crazed by blood. And Charis will continue to do what she must to go on surviving, because that's what she owes to her own people, to her own children, and to God Himself.

"Which is what brings me to this throne in this room, delivering and confirming sentences of death. Many of these people amply deserve those sentences. For others the case is less clear-cut, however clear the law itself may be. And in still other cases, what the law decrees is neither true justice nor what compassion and mercy require. I must err on the side of caution in the cause of protecting that which I'm charged to protect, but where I can, where the chance exists, I'll grant that mercy whenever and however I may. I won't be able to do that as often as I wish, or as often as *you* could wish, but I'll do it as often as I *can*, and I'll ask God's help to live with the many times when I cannot."

A ripping sound had been loud in the stillness as Edwyrd Seahamper tore open Spynsair Ahrnahld's sleeve and applied a dressing of fleming moss from the emergency case each of her Imperial Guardsmen carried at his belt. She'd looked down, watching her secretary's pale face as the bandage was adjusted, then cocked her head at him.

"Can you continue, Spynsair?" she'd asked him, and Ahrnahld's hadn't been the only eyebrows which rose in astonishment at her question.

"Yes—I mean, of course, Your Majesty. If that's your wish," he'd said after a moment.

"Of course it's my wish," she'd replied with a crooked smile, that elbow and upper arm still pressed against her ribs. She'd sat very erect, but she'd also sat very still, and Gahrvai suspected it had hurt her to breathe. Yet if that was so, she'd allowed no sign of it to cross her expression or shadow her voice.

"We have much still to do today," she'd told her secretary, her eyes rising across the puddle of her assailant's blood to include the gathered witnesses in the same statement. "If we refuse to let Clyntahn and the Group of Four stop us, then we won't allow this to, either. Let us proceed."

▼ ▼ ▼

And proceed she had, Koryn Gahrvai thought now. For another four hours, until lunch. She'd seemed unaware her hair was steadily tumbling into looser and looser falls about her shoulders, just as she'd seemed unaware when Merlin Athrawes picked up the crown which had fallen from her head and stood holding it in the crook of his left arm like a paladin's helmet. There'd been the slightest, barely perceptible breathlessness in her voice, like a catch of pain, yet it was so faint Gahrvai suspected most of those watching her never heard it at all.

Seventeen more people were sent to execution that morning . . . but another six were pardoned. And in each case, Empress Sharleyan—still without notes—had recited the extenuating circumstances which led her to grant mercy in those cases. She'd continued unhurriedly, calmly, as if no one had ever attempted to harm her at all, and by the end of that morning, she'd held that audience of Corisandian witnesses in the palm of one slender hand.

The bell announcing the end of the morning session had sounded at last, and the empress had looked up with a wry smile.

"We trust no one will be disappointed if we adjourn for the day at this time," she'd said. "Under the circumstances, we believe it might be excusable."

There'd actually been an answering mutter of laughter, and her smile had grown broader.

"We'll take that as agreement," she'd told them, and stood.

She'd stepped down from the dais, and Gahrvai's eyes

had narrowed as she took Merlin Athrawes' left arm. She'd swayed slightly, and her nostrils had looked pinched as she'd seemed to stumble for a moment. Her elbow had still pressed against her ribs, and there'd been a certain fragility to her normally graceful carriage, yet she'd smiled graciously at him and at the others who bowed as she passed them.

And then she'd been gone.

▼ ▼ ▼

"How many women do you know who could've done what she did today?" Gahrvai asked now, looking around at his father and the others.

"Shan-wei!" Anvil Rock retorted. "Ask me how many *men* I know who could've done what she did today!"

"Either way, men or women, the answer is damned few," Tartarian said. "And don't think for a moment all those witnesses didn't realize it, too. Oh, I'm sure a lot of it was political calculation. She had to know how it would affect all of us. But even if that's true, she managed to *do* it, and I think it was at least as sincere as it was calculated. Probably more, to be honest."

"I think you're right," Gahrvai said. "And I have to ask myself whether or not those reports about her being 'uninjured' are truly accurate."

"Her ribs, you mean?" Windshare asked. Gahrvai nodded, and the dashing young earl shrugged. "I noticed that, too. Not that surprising, I suppose, with Merlin landing on top of her that way! Must've bruised the hell out of her."

"I think they were more than just bruised," Doyal said quietly. "I think it's entirely possible they were broken."

"Nonsense!" Anvil Rock objected. "I'm as impressed with her as any of you, but let's not get too carried away. Broken ribs are no joke, I've had my share of them over the years, by God! If she'd had that on top of almost being killed, not even *she* would have just sat there."

"With all due respect, My Lord," Doyal replied, "don't forget that this isn't the first time she's almost been killed.

Think about that affair at Saint Agtha's. According to my reports, she picked up her dead Guardsmen's rifles and killed at least a dozen of the attackers herself!" He shook his head. "Whatever else Sharleyan Ahrmahk may be, she's no hothouse flower. In fact, I'm coming to the opinion that she's even tougher than we thought she was."

Gahrvai started to say something, then changed his mind and sat back in his chair. His father didn't seem to notice, but one of Tartarian's eyebrows quirked slightly. He looked a question at the younger Gahrvai, but Sir Koryn only shook his head with a smile and listened while Earl Anvil Rock disposed of the notion that even Empress Sharleyan would have continued to dispense justice with broken ribs.

Tartarian let the moment pass, and Gahrvai was just as happy he had. After all, there was time to double-check his men's report in the morning. The would-be assassin's first bullet *had* to have gone somewhere, and the fact that no one had been able to find it—yet!—proved nothing. He'd been certain they were going to find it embedded in the massive throne somewhere, but they hadn't, which meant it had to have hit the rear wall, instead, didn't it? Of course it did!

Still, probably better to keep his mouth shut until they did manage to find it. If his father found Doyal's notion that Sharleyan had managed to go right on with broken ribs ridiculous, he would have found the suggestion that perhaps—just perhaps—that bullet hadn't completely missed its mark after all ludicrous.

Because it is *ludicrous, Koryn,* Gahrvai told himself firmly. Absolutely *ludicrous!*

▼ ▼ ▼

"I never want to hear another word about how stubborn *Cayleb* is," Merlin Athrawes said severely as he helped Sharleyan across her bedchamber. The rush of pouring rain and the rumble of thunder half drowned his voice, but she heard him and looked up with a battered, bruised, but still game smile.

He was glad to see it, but he'd been less than amused when he'd first gotten her back here.

The adrenaline, determination, and sheer willpower which had carried her from Princess Aleatha's Ballroom to her own suite had deserted her once she crossed the threshold. She'd virtually collapsed into Merlin's arms, and Sairaih Hahlmyn had fluttered around the *seijin* in shocked dismay as he'd scooped her up, carried her to her sleeping chamber, and deposited her gently on the enormous bed.

Sairaih's dismay had turned into something very like outrage as Merlin began calmly unbuttoning and unlacing the empress' gown.

"*Seijin* Merlin! What do you think you're *doing?*"

"Oh, hush, Sairaih!" Sharleyan had said weakly, her voice much thinner and breathless than usual. "The *seijin*'s a healer as well as a warrior, you ninny!"

"But, Your Majesty—!"

"I am *not* going to have a Corisandian healer in here examining me," Sharleyan had said flatly, sounding much more like her usual self for a moment. "The last thing we need is some wild rumor about how I was actually shot after all, and you *know* that's what would happen if word got out that I'd summoned healers to my bedchamber. By Langhorne's Watch, they'd have me on my death-bed!"

"But, Your Majesty—!"

"There's no point arguing with her, Sairaih," Merlin had said in a resigned voice. "Trust me, if there *is* any serious damage, Edwyrd and I will have a healer in here in a heartbeat, whatever she says. But she's probably right about the rumor potential, so if it's only bruising. . . ."

"But, Your Majesty—!"

The third attempt had been little more than pro forma, and Sharleyan had actually smiled as she shook her head.

"I won't say I'm as stubborn as Cayleb, no matter what Merlin thinks," she'd said. "But I am stubborn enough to win this argument, Sairaih. So why don't you just concentrate on brewing me some tea with *lots* of sugar? Trust me, I could use it."

"Very well, Your Majesty." Sairaih had finally conceded defeat. She'd given Merlin one last, moderately outraged look, then marched out past Sergeant Seahamper. The sergeant had looked at Sharleyan for a moment, shaken his head with a pronounced air of resignation, and moved his gaze to Merlin.

"Good luck getting her to see reason," he'd said a bit sourly. Then he'd tapped the ear holding his own com earplug. "And somehow I don't think His Majesty's going to hold off on yelling at her very much longer, even if it is the middle of the night in Tellesberg."

"Maybe we can at least get Owl to give them a private channel," Merlin had said hopefully. Seahamper had snorted, given Sharleyan one last look, then closed the door.

"It's not like I'm a complete idiot," the empress had said plaintively, then gasped as Merlin lifted her gently into a sitting position to peel the gown down from her shoulders. "Even if there'd been another one of them out there, it's not like I was running the kind of risk Maikel ran in the Cathedral."

"There shouldn't have been *any* of them," Merlin had said through his teeth. "How in God's name did they get a damned *pistol* past Gahrvai's guards?"

"I've been checking the record from the SNARCs' sensors," Seahamper had said over the com from the other side of the bedchamber's closed door. "Owl's managed to pick up the moment he was admitted. He was carrying the real Grahsmahn's summons; Grahsmahn was on the list from the first session; and it never occurred to any of us to tell them to look for firearms concealed inside someone's tunic because it hadn't occurred to us that anyone could *fit* one inside his tunic. And if you want something to make you feel even better, Merlin, Owl's run the imagery through his facial recognition software. Underneath all that beard and the tattoo, it was none other than our elusive friend Paitryk Hainree."

The sergeant's tone had been almost conversational, and Merlin had known he was almost certainly right about the confluence of factors which had allowed the gunman to get past Gahrvai's guardsmen. No one on Safehold had ever heard of a "photo ID," so unless Hainree had run into someone who'd remembered the real Grahsmahn from the previous session, there was precious little way anyone could have spotted the deception. Besides, if Owl was right and it had been Hainree, they'd already had ample evidence he was (or had been, at any rate) fiendishly good at getting into (and out of) places where he wasn't supposed to be. But Seahamper's calm tone hadn't fooled him. The sergeant was probably even more upset with himself than Merlin was with *himself*. This was exactly the sort of thing they were supposed to prevent.

"Don't the two of you pick on yourselves over this!" Sharleyan had scolded as Merlin gently eased down her chemise. "In a crowd that size? One man? And a man who had the exact documentation he was supposed to have?" She'd shaken her head. "Ideally, maybe you and the SNARCs should have spotted him. In fact, though, it's not at all surprising to me that someone managed to get past you. For that matter, Merlin, you and Edwyrd argued against this approach from the beginning exactly because you were afraid of something like this. So why aren't you simply saying 'I told you so' and letting it go at that?"

"Because you damn near got yourself *killed* this morning!" Merlin had snapped. He'd paused, looking down into her face, his sapphire eyes dark. "I've lost too many of you already, Sharley. I'm not about to lose any more!"

"Of course you're not," she'd said softly, laying one hand on his mailed forearm. "And I didn't mean to sound flip. But that doesn't make anything I just said untrue, does it? Besides," she'd smiled impishly, "at least we've just demonstrated that Owl's tailoring works!"

"More or less," Merlin had conceded, and grimaced as he ran his fingertips lightly across the huge discolored bruise on Sharleyan's rib cage. "On the other hand, it didn't spread the kinetic energy as well as I could have wished. You've got at least two broken ribs here, Sharley. Probably three. I'm seriously tempted to whisk you off to the cave tonight and let Owl's auto doc take a look at you."

"I don't think that's going to be nec—*Ow!*"

Sharleyan had flinched as he'd pressed just a bit harder. He'd shaken his head in apology, and she'd sucked in a deep breath.

"I don't think that's going to be necessary," she'd said. "Even if they're broken, I mean. Isn't this one of the reasons you inoculated us with the medical nanotech?"

"It'll help you heal *faster*; what it *won't* do is heal this overnight," Merlin had retorted. "And it's not going to help much with the pain, either. If you think this is bad now, you just wait till you wake up and try to move in the morning!"

"I know," she'd said glumly. "This isn't the first time I've broken them."

"You and that damned pony," Seahamper had muttered over the com, and she'd giggled, then gasped in pain.

"Exactly," she'd said, and looked up at Merlin. "I'm perfectly prepared to be 'indisposed' in the morning, at least as long as I can get to breakfast with the Regency Council without looking too much like I've been beaten with a stick. I figure they'll expect at least a little morning-after reaction out of me. So if we just strap up my ribs tightly, I can get through that much, I think. Then I *promise* I'll come straight back here and spend the day resting while all those busy little nanites work on fixing me."

"What do *you* think, Edwyrd?" Merlin had asked.

"Unless you're ready to knock her on the head, that's probably as close to a reasonable attitude as you're likely to get out of her," Seahamper had said sourly. "Besides," he'd gone on a bit grudgingly, "it might not be a very good idea to have her 'incommunicado' after something like this. I doubt anyone's going to come calling in the middle of the night, but the two of you would be gone for hours, and if something *does* come up I won't be able to fob people off the way I might get away with in Cherayth. 'I'm sorry, the Empress is unavailable' isn't going to cut it after something like this morning."

"You're probably right," Merlin had sighed, then looked down at Sharleyan and shaken his head. "Too bad current Safeholdian fashion doesn't include corsets," he'd said with a lurking smile. "They're probably the most fiendish device this side of the Inquisition, but just this once they'd actually come in handy! Since we don't have them, though, let's get you the rest of the way out of your clothes and see what we can do about strapping up those ribs."

▼ ▼ ▼

That had been the better part of six hours ago, and Seahamper had been right about Cayleb's reaction. The emperor had, indeed, gotten Owl to give him a private connection to Sharleyan, but her side of the conversation had been remarkably monosyllabic, consisting primarily of "Yes" or "No" interspersed with an occasional "Of course I won't" and even a single "Whatever you say." It had all been most unlike her, and it probably said a great deal about how deeply she'd been shaken, however composed she might have seemed on the surface.

Now Merlin helped her the last few feet from the bathroom. She made two or three false starts on getting herself turned around and folding down to sit on the bed, then gasped as Merlin scooped her up and effortlessly laid her down again.

"Thank you." She smiled tightly up at him as lightning whickered beyond her window, briefly etching his profile against the panes, and thunder crashed. "As a matter of fact, this is quite a bit worse than the falling-off-the-pony episode."

"You don't say?" Merlin replied dryly, then sighed, looking down at the ugly bruise on the left side of her face. His elbow had done that, he knew, and it was almost as dark as the one on her rib cage, he thought as he touched it with a gentle fingertip. They were lucky he hadn't broken her cheekbone, as well.

"Sorry about that," he said with a sad little smile.

"Why? For saving my life the second time?" She reached up and caught his hand, holding it for a moment. "This seems to be getting to be quite a habit for you where Ahrmahks are concerned, doesn't it? Look—there's even a thunderstorm! Do you think you could get over it by the time Alahnah grows up?"

"I'll try, Your Majesty. I'll certainly try. And when she's a bit older," Merlin reached into his belt pouch, "maybe she'd like a little memento of her first trip to Corisande with you."

"Memento?" Sharleyan repeated, then looked down as he laid something small and heavy in the palm of her hand. The pistol bullet was an ugly, flattened lump that gleamed dully in the light from her bedside lamp.

"Sure." Merlin looked into her eyes again. "It's not every mother who's already survived two separate assassination attempts before her first child's even a year old. But you know, it's all pretty fatiguing for us poor bodyguards, so let's try not going for number three until Alahnah's at least, oh, seven, let's say. All right?"

. X .

Tellesberg Palace,
City of Tellesberg,
Kingdom of Old Charis

King Gorjah of Tarot was not a large man.

He was a little taller than Prince Nahrmahn (not a difficult achievement) but far less . . . substantial. Of course, he was also considerably younger, only a few years older than Caleb himself, and he hadn't spent as many years in self-indulgence as Nahrmahn had. He was exquisitely tailored, his steel thistle silk tunic rustling as he moved, and his "kercheef," the traditional headwear of Tarot, was beautifully embroidered and glinted with the scattered flash of faceted gems. All in all, he was the perfect dictionary illustration of a well-groomed, wealthy young monarch perfectly turned out for an important social occasion. He was not, needless to say, the sartorial equal of the waiting emperor, whose crown of state flashed blue and red fire from rubies and sapphires, and whose ornate, embroidered, jeweled (and infernally hot) robes of state were trimmed with the winter-white fur of the mountain slash lizard.

Still, Cayleb had to give him what Merlin would have called "points for style," especially under the present circumstances. He'd obviously taken great pains to get his appearance exactly right for the occasion.

At the moment, however, he also had the look of a man who was distinctly nervous but doing surprisingly well at concealing it. He'd entered the throne room behind the chamberlain who'd announced his arrival, and he walked sedately towards the paired thrones at its end, ignoring the clusters of courtiers, councilors, and clerics who'd been assembled for his arrival.

It couldn't have been easy to do that, Cayleb reflected, watching Gorjah come. Of the five realms which had attacked Charis at the beginning of the war, Tarot was the only one who'd ever been a Charisian ally. As a matter of fact, Gorjah had been bound by a solemn mutual defense treaty to come to Charis' aid, and what he'd actually done was to pretend he intended to do exactly that even as he sent his own navy to rendezvous with the Dohlaran galley fleet sailing to complete Charis' ruin.

Needless to say, the Kingdom of Tarot—and its monarch—were less than universally beloved in Tellesberg.

At least the Guard's managed to keep anyone from throwing rotten vegetables at him, Cayleb thought dryly. *Under the circumstances, that's doing pretty well, given the . . . fractiousness of Charisians in general. And then there's probably the odd Temple Loyalist who'd love the opportunity to stick a knife in his ribs for turning around and "betraying" Clyntahn in turn by signing back up with us! Poor bastard can't win for losing, can he?*

Actually, the emperor found it difficult to blame Gorjah. Not that he intended to admit anything of the sort until he was positive the Tarotisian monarch would never even contemplate reprising his treason.

Which is one place where Clyntahn's reputation's actually going to work for us, Cayleb thought with considerably less amusement. *Only a frigging idiot would even think about coming back into his reach after crossing him this way!*

Gorjah reached the foot of the dais, stopped, and bowed deeply.

"Your Majesty," he said.

Cayleb allowed the silence to stretch out for four or five seconds, letting Gorjah remain bent in his formal bow, then cleared his throat.

"King Gorjah," he replied at last. "Until quite recently, I hadn't anticipated the possibility of your visiting here in Tellesberg."

"Ah, no, Your Majesty." Gorjah straightened and coughed delicately. "I don't suppose either of us expected to see one another again quite so soon."

"Oh, I'd anticipated visiting *you* very soon now," Cayleb assured him with a pointed smile, and Gorjah's expression wavered for a moment. Then he squared his shoulders and nodded.

"I suppose I deserved that," he said with what Cayleb privately thought was admirable calm. "And while I won't pretend I would have enjoyed the sort of visit you had in mind, Your Majesty, I doubt any reasonable man could have quibbled with your motivation."

"Probably not," Cayleb agreed, sitting back in his throne and wishing Sharleyan was in the empty throne beside him rather than stretched out on a sofa in her suite in Manchyr nursing her broken ribs.

"But you're here now," he continued, "and it would be

churlish to treat you discourteously. Or, for that matter, to pretend you had a great deal of choice when the Group of Four sent you your marching orders. After all," he reached out and touched the arm of that empty throne, "not even Queen Sharleyan saw a way to refuse the 'Knights of the Temple Lands'' demands. What matters are the present and the future, not the past." He nodded at where Nahrmahn Baytz, the golden chain of an imperial councilor around his neck, stood watching. "What's done is done, and past enmities are something none of us can afford in the face of the threat we all face."

"I agree, Your Majesty." Gorjah met his gaze levelly. "And while I'm not pretending things, I won't pretend the thought of openly defying Mother Church isn't frightening. Leaving aside the spiritual aspects of all this, the Church's power in the mortal world is enough to give anyone pause. But I've seen the other side from inside the belly of the beast, as it were." He shook his head, his expression grim, and Cayleb saw nothing but sincerity in his brown eyes. "If I'd ever doubted Clyntahn was mad, his purges and executions and his autos-da-fé have proven he is. Whatever he may have thought when he started this, by now he's convinced that anyone who's not totally subservient to him—to *him*, not to Mother Church or God—has no right even to exist. Confronting someone who thinks that way and controls all the power of the Inquisition is enough to terrify anyone, but the thought of what this world will become if someone like him *wins* is even more terrifying."

Cayleb looked back at him in silence, letting his words settle into the corners of the throne room. He thought the Tarotisian was sincere, although he also knew Gorjah was less than pleased, to put it mildly, at the present turn of events. It was true he couldn't realistically have resisted the Group of Four's demand that he betray Charis, but it was equally true he hadn't even been tempted to try. He'd always resented that treaty, the way in which he'd felt it turned Tarot into little more than a dependency of the Kingdom of Charis. And now he found himself forced to make formal submission, to turn his kingdom into a mere province of the *Empire* of Charis. That had to stick in his craw like fish bones, and perhaps that was the most fitting vengeance of all for his "treachery." Especially since there was no possible path back from the step he was about to take as long as the Group of Four breathed.

"In that case, King Gorjah," he said, "I suppose we should get on with it."

"Of course, Your Majesty."

Gorjah bowed again, then waited while a page placed an elaborately embroidered cushion on the uppermost step of the dais before Cayleb's throne. The page bowed to him and walked backwards away from the throne, and Gorjah knelt gracefully. Archbishop Maikel stepped forward on Cayleb's right and held out the gold and gem-clasped copy of the *Holy Writ*, and the king kissed the book, then laid his right hand upon it and looked up at Cayleb.

"I, Gorjah Alyksahndar Nyou, do swear allegiance and fealty to Emperor Cayleb and Empress Sharleyan of Charis," he said, his voice unflinching, if not joyous, "to be their true man, of heart, will, body, and sword. To do my utmost to discharge my obligations and duty to them, to their Crowns, and to their House, in all ways, as God shall give me the ability and the wit so to do. I swear this oath without mental or moral reservation, and I submit myself to the judgment of the Emperor and Empress and of God Himself for the fidelity with which I honor and discharge the obligations I now assume before God and this company."

Cayleb reached out and laid his right hand atop Gorjah's and met the kneeling king's eyes levelly.

"And we, Cayleb Zhan Haarahld Bryahn Ahrmahk, in our own name and in that of Sharleyan Ahdel Alahnah Ahrmahk, do accept your oath. We will extend protection against all enemies, loyalty for fealty, justice for justice, fidelity for fidelity, and punishment for oath-breaking. May God judge us and ours as He judges you and yours."

They stayed that way for a handful of seconds, hands touching, eyes meeting, and then Cayleb withdrew his hand and nodded.

"And that's that," he said with an off-center smile. "So now that we've got it out of the way," he stood, waving one hand in invitation to his newest vassal as he started down from the dais, "why don't we get down to work . . . and let me get out of this damned outfit?"

. XI .

Ship Chandler Quay,
City of Manchyr,
Princedom of Corisande

It was rather different from her arrival, Sharleyan Ahrmahk thought as the carriage rolled down Prince Fronz Avenue towards Ship Chandler Quay behind its escort of Corisandian cavalry. Then the cheers had been undeniably tentative—loud enough, but uncertain. The southeastern portion of Corisande had settled into firm loyalty to the Regency Council months earlier, and it had accepted that the Charisian occupation forces were genuinely doing their best to be no more repressive than they must. But the House of Ahrmahk was still saddled in all too many minds with the blood guilt for Hektor Daykyn's murder, and all the world knew how bitterly Sharleyan of Chisholm had hated the man and—by extension—the princedom she blamed for her father's death.

Those cheers of greeting had come from people who'd been grateful for the restoration of order and stability and the relative gentleness of the Charisian occupation . . . so far, at least. That wasn't remotely the same as being resigned to permanent Charisian domination, or becoming loyal Charisian subjects, but it had reflected their willingness to at least wait and see.

At the same time, there'd been an undeniable dread of what the late Prince Hektor's most deadly enemy might have in mind for his princedom, since he himself was beyond her vengeance. In light of her reputation, and even more in light of the way Hektor's propagandists had emphasized her hostility to his subjects, it had been no surprise the Corisandians had hoped, even prayed, Emperor Cayleb had meant his promises that there would be no violent repression, no unnecessary or casual reprisals, and that the rule of law would be respected. And, for that matter, that Sharleyan would consider herself bound by anything Cayleb might have promised. After all, she was his coruler, and no one in Corisande had any way of knowing exactly how the two of them thought that worked. She and Cayleb had *said* all the right things, but still. . . .

The fact that those accused of treason had been tried in Corisandian courts, before the peers and clergy of Corisande, rather than hauled before a Charisian occupation court, had been hopeful, yet everyone behind those cheers of greeting and the banners hung out to welcome her had known that if she chose, Sharleyan Ahrmahk could have decreed whatever fate she chose to order.

And that was what was different about today's cheers. She *could* have decreed whatever fate she chose . . . and she'd chosen to abide by the law, as her husband had sworn Charis would. No secret arrests, no condemnations on the basis of tortured confessions, no secret accusers who never had to face the accused, open trials and open verdicts openly arrived at. True, virtually all those verdicts had been guilty, yet even that was different in this case, because the evidence—the proof—had been overwhelming and utterly damning. No one doubted for a moment that anyone accused of treason against Prince Hektor would also have been found guilty, but neither did anyone doubt that Hektor would have seen little reason to worry about things like evidence and proof.

True, she *had* set aside some of those verdicts, yet unlike Hektor, it hadn't been to condemn those who'd been acquitted. Instead, almost a quarter of those who'd been *convicted* had been pardoned. Not because there'd been any question about their guilt, but because she'd *chosen* to pardon them. It wasn't even the general blanket, prison-emptying amnesty some rulers proclaimed as a grand gesture on assuming the throne, or for a wedding, or for the birth of an heir. No, she'd pardoned specific *individuals*, and in every instance she'd personally enumerated the reasons she'd chosen to show mercy.

And she'd gone right on doing it despite the attempt to murder her on her very throne.

Corisande wasn't used to that. For that matter, virtually *no* Safeholdian realm was used to that, and Corisande still didn't know what to make of it. But Corisande knew one thing—Sharleyan Ahrmahk, the archenemy and arch-hater of Corisande, was a very different proposition from someone like Zhaspahr Clyntahn or even Hektor Daykyn. Perhaps she was still—technically, at least—an enemy, and certainly she remained one of the foreign potentates who'd conquered their own princedom, but she'd conquered something else during her visit to Manchyr, as well.

She'd conquered their hearts.

▼ ▼ ▼

"I wouldn't have believed it if I hadn't seen it with my own eyes, Your Majesty," General Hauwyl Chermyn said, looking out the window of the carriage. He'd wanted to accompany Sharleyan on horseback as part of the security escort, but she'd insisted on his joining her in the carriage, instead. Now he shook his head and waved one hand at the cheering crowds who lined the streets all the way from the palace to quayside. "I remember what these people were like right after Hektor was killed. I wouldn't have given a Harchong copper for your life if you'd come to Manchyr then."

The weathered-looking Marine's expression was grim, and Sharleyan smiled fondly at him. There were lines in Chermyn's face that hadn't been there before Cayleb installed him as the Empire's viceroy general here in

Corisande. His dark hair had gone entirely iron-gray during his stay, as well, and his bushy mustache had turned almost entirely white. Yet his brown eyes were as alert as ever, and his heavyset, muscular body was still undeniably *solid*-looking, she thought. And well it should be, because if she'd had to come up with a single word to encapsulate Hauwyl Chermyn, it would have been "solid."

"Well, from all the reports I've seen, we owe a lot of the improvement to *you*, General," she said, then winced as the carriage hit an uneven paving stone and sent a stab of pain through her still knitting ribs.

"And if I'd done my job a bit better, Your Majesty," he growled, obviously not having missed her wince, "I'd have had that bastard Hainree—begging your pardon for the language—before he ever came that close to killing you." His face was briefly as iron-like as his hair color. "His Majesty'd never have forgiven me for letting something like that happen!"

"What you mean is you'd never have forgiven *yourself*," Sharleyan said, leaning forward to pat him on the knee as they sat facing each other. "Which would have been foolish of you, since no one could possibly have done a better job than the one you've done, but that wouldn't have changed a thing, would it?" It was her turn to shake her head. "You're not exactly a reasonable man where your own duty is concerned, General."

"Good of you to say so, anyway, Your Majesty," Chermyn said, "but you're being too kind. Letting me off too easily, too, for that matter. If not for *Seijin* Merlin, he'd have had you. For that matter, I thought at first he *had* hit you, and so did nearly everyone else, I understand."

"Cayleb and I both owe Merlin a great deal," Sharleyan agreed. "It's not the sort of debt you can really pay, either."

"Not the sort of debt you're *supposed* to pay, Your Majesty," Chermyn replied. "That's what duty's all about. The only way you can 'repay' that sort of service—the only service that really matters, if you'll pardon my saying so—is by being worthy of it. And I'd say"—he looked directly into her eyes—"that so far you and His Majesty have done a pretty fair job of that."

"As you say, General, 'Good of you to say so, anyway,' " Sharleyan said demurely and watched his lips twitch on the edge of a smile under the overhanging mustache.

Sharleyan glanced out the window again. They were approaching Ship Chandler Quay at last, and she saw *Dawn Star* moored against the fenders. She would really have preferred going out to her galleon by boat—somehow it seemed the proper "Charisian" way to do things—but Merlin, Seahamper, and Sairaih Hahlmyn had flatly refused to contemplate it. So had General Chermyn, for that matter, although the disapproval of a mere viceroy general had scarcely counted compared to *that* trio's united front! As Merlin and Sergeant Seahamper had pointed out, the trip in an undoubtedly pitching barge, followed by the journey up the ship's side, even in a bosun's chair, would have risked reinjuring the ribs which still had more than a little healing to do. And as Sairaih had unscrupulously thrown into the mix, it would be far safer for Crown Princess Alahnah to be carried from the carriage across a nice, solid stone quay and up a sturdy gangplank than to subject the child to all the risks of a boat trip.

I suppose someone who used to be your nurse really does know all the levers to pull, Sharleyan reflected now. *And it was damned underhanded of her to actually be right about it, too!*

She reached across to the bassinet in Sairaih's lap and touched her daughter's incredibly soft cheek. Alahnah's eyes were bright and wide, and she reached happily for her mother's hand. She was such a *good* baby—most of the time, anyway—and she was taking the carriage trip nicely in stride. Of course, she was probably going to make her sense of outraged betrayal loudly apparent the first time *Dawn Star* hit a patch of rough weather on the trip to Tellesberg.

Definitely your mother's *daughter, not your father's, in that regard, aren't you, love?* Sharleyan thought.

She looked up to see Chermyn smiling at her, and she smiled back at him.

"Been a while, Your Majesty," the general said with a twinkle, "but I still remember what the first one was like."

"And I understand you and Madam Chermyn are about to become grandparents?"

"Aye, that we are, Your Majesty. My oldest boy, Rhaz, is expecting his first. In fact, unless Pasquale's changed the rules, the baby's already arrived. I'm sure Mathyld's letter's on its way to tell me all about it."

"Are you hoping for a boy or a girl?"

"Doesn't matter to me, Your Majesty. As long as the baby's healthy and got all the right number of arms and legs and what-have-you, I'll be a happy man. Although," he looked down at Alahnah who was still hanging on to her mother's hand and cooing, "I guess if I had to be *completely* honest, I think I'd like a girl. Mathyld and I had the three boys, and they've been joys—most of the time, anyway." He rolled his eyes. "But I think most men, if they'll be honest about it, want at least one daughter or granddaughter to spoil. And"—his smile faded slightly— "I've three sons in harm's way. I could wish I had at least one daughter who wasn't."

"I can understand that." Sharleyan touched his knee again. "But it's sons like yours who stand between everyone's daughters and men like Zhaspahr Clyntahn, General. Be proud of them, and tell them, the next time you have the chance, how grateful Cayleb and I are for all *four* of you."

"I will, Your Majesty," Chermyn said a bit gruffly, then cleared his throat.

"I see we're almost at shipside, Your Majesty," he said in a deliberately brisker voice, and she nodded.

"So we are. Well, I suppose it's time for all of the ridiculous departure ceremony."

"I'd as soon miss it myself, truth be told," Chermyn admitted. "And I don't envy you and His Majesty for having to put up with so much of it. To be honest," he looked at her with an undeniably hopeful expression, "I'd like to think it might be possible for someone else to take over as viceroy general and let me get away from all the fuss and folderol and back to being an honest Marine. Or even transfer to the Army."

"I don't know, General," Sharleyan said, furrowing her brow pensively while she tried not to chuckle out loud at the opening he'd given her. "You've done so well here. And while I know the situation's improved, it's still going to be . . . delicate for quite some time to come."

"I know, Your Majesty," Chermyn sighed. He obviously hadn't expected to convince her.

"Still," Sharleyan said, drawing out the word as the carriage came to a halt and Merlin Athrawes and Edwyrd Seahamper swung down from their horses beside it. "I suppose I *can* think of one other duty Cayleb and I really need a good, experienced military officer and proven administrator to deal with. I'm afraid it's not a combat assignment, although for all I know there may be some fighting entailed, but it *would* get you out of Corisande," she ended hopefully, raising her eyebrows at him.

"I'd be honored to serve you and His Majesty in any way I could, Your Majesty," Chermyn said, although he couldn't quite hide his disappointment at the words "it's not a combat assignment."

"Well, I suppose in that case we could send Baron Green Valley down here to replace you, at least temporarily," Sharleyan said.

"Are you certain about that, Your Majesty?" Chermyn sounded a little startled. "I understood the Baron was going to be fully occupied in Zebediah for quite some time."

"Oh, he's been doing a very good job there," Sharleyan agreed with a nod. "And Duke Eastshare wants him back in Maikelberg, of course, so we may not be able to send *him* as your replacement, after all. Still, I'm sure we'll be able to find someone. In fact, now that I've thought about it for a moment, I think your Colonel Zhanstyn could probably hold the fort for you, possibly even on a semi-permanent or a permanent basis. But as far as Baron

Green Valley is concerned, he was never going to be our permanent viceroy in Zebediah."

"He wasn't?" Chermyn looked at her in surprise as Seahamper moved to open the carriage door and let down the steps while Merlin stood facing outward, eyes scanning the crowd. She cocked her head at the Marine, and he half raised one hand. "I'm sorry, Your Majesty. I must have misunderstood."

"The Baron's a very good man, General, but he was only there to keep a lid on the island until we could decide who to name to succeed Symmyns as grand duke. That was hardly an easy decision, of course. We needed a man of proven ability and loyalty. Someone we knew we could absolutely rely upon, and to be honest, someone who deserved the recognition and the rewards which were going to come along with all the undeniable pains of straightening out the mess Symmyns left behind. Trust me, the position's not going to be a sinecure for a long time to come, General!"

Chermyn nodded in understanding, and she shrugged.

"And once we did make up our mind who to choose, naturally we'd have to notify the new grand duke before we could even think about recalling Baron Green Valley . . . which I've just done, now that I think about it, Grand Duke Zebediah."

Her timing was perfect, she thought delightedly. The door opened right on cue as Chermyn suddenly stopped nodding and stared at her in stupefied shock. He opened his mouth, but no words came out, and Sharleyan nodded at Sairaih, who looked as if her grin were about to split her face in two as she gathered up Princess Alahnah's bassinet and diaper bag.

"Well, I see we're here, Your Grace, if I may be a little premature," Empress Sharleyan Ahrmahk said, bestowing a brilliant smile on the thunderstruck Marine, and then she held out her hand to Seahamper and descended the carriage steps into a hurricane of cheers, trumpets, and the thud of saluting guns.

JULY, YEAR OF GOD 895

·✦·

. I .

Hospice of the Holy Bédard
and
The Temple,
City of Zion,
The Temple Lands

"Langhorne bless you, Your Grace. Langhorne bless you!"

"Thank you, Father," Rhobair Duchairn said. "I appreciate the sentiment, but it's not as if I've been working as hard at this as you have. Or"—the vicar's smile carried an odd edge of bitterness—"for as long, either."

He laid a hand on Father Zytan Kwill's frail shoulder. The Bédardist upper-priest was far into his eighties and growing increasingly fragile with age, yet he burned with an inner intensity Duchairn could only envy.

"That may be true, Your Grace," Kwill replied, "but this winter . . ." He shook his head. "Do you realize we've had only thirty dead reported in the Hospice this winter from all causes? Only *thirty!*"

"I know." Duchairn nodded, although he also knew considerably more than thirty of Zion's inhabitants had perished over the previous winter. Yet Kwill had a point. The Order of Bédard and the Order of Pasquale were responsible for caring for Zion's poor and indigent. Well, technically all Mother Church's orders had that duty, but the Bédardists and the Pasqualates had shouldered the primary responsibility centuries earlier. They jointly administered the soup kitchens and the shelters, and the Pasqualates provided the healers who were supposed to see that the most vulnerable of God's children had the medical care to survive Zion's icy cold.

The problem, of course, was that they hadn't been doing that.

Duchairn looked out the window of Kwill's spartan office. The Hospice of the Holy Bédard was in one of Zion's older buildings, and the office had a spectacular view over the broad blue waters of Lake Pei, but it was as bare and sparsely furnished as an ascetic's cell in one of the meditative monasteries. No doubt that reflected Father Zytan's personality, but it was also because the priest had poured every mark he could lay hands on into his hopeless task for the last forty-seven years. With so many desperate needs, the thought of spending anything on himself would never even have crossed his mind.

And in all that time, Mother Church has never supported him the way she should have, the Treasurer thought grimly. *Not once. Not a single time have we funded him and the others the way we ought to have.*

The vicar crossed to the window, clasping his hands behind him, looking out at the leaves and blossoms which clothed the hills striding down from Zion to the huge lake. A cool breeze blew in through the opening, touching his face with gentle fingers, and the sails of small craft, barges, and larger merchant ships dotted the sparkling water under the sun's warm rays. He could see fishing boats farther out, and perfectly formed mountains of cloud sailed across the heavens. On a day like this, it was easy even for Duchairn, who'd spent the last thirty years of his life in Zion, to forget how savage north central Haven's winters truly were. To forget how the lake turned into a blue and gray sheet of ice, thick enough to support galleon-sized ice boats. To forget how snow drifted higher than a tall man's head in the city's streets. How some of those drifts, on the city's outskirts, climbed as much as two or even three stories up the sides of buildings.

And it's even easier for those of us who spend our winters in the Temple to forget that sort of unpleasantness, he acknowledged. *We don't have to deal with it, do we?*

*We have our own little enclave, blessed by God, and we
don't venture out of it . . . except, perhaps, on the milder
days when the wind doesn't howl and fresh blizzards
don't go screaming around our sanctified ears.*

He wanted to believe that was the reason for his own
decades of inactivity. Wanted to think he'd been so busy,
so focused on his manifold responsibilities that he'd simply gotten distracted. That he'd honestly forgotten to actually look out his window and see what was happening
to those outside the Temple's mystically heated and
cooled environment because he'd been so preoccupied
with his personal duties and obligations. Oh, *how* he
wanted to think that!

You were "preoccupied," all right, Rhobair, he told
himself, filling his lungs with the cool air, inhaling the
scent of the blossoms in the planter under Father Zytan's
window. *You were preoccupied with fine wines, gourmet
cooking, charming feminine companionship, and all the
arduous tasks of counting coins and managing your alli-
ances within the vicarate. Pity you didn't stop to think
about what the Archangels themselves told you were any
priest's true obligations and duties. If you had, Father Zytan might've had the money and the resources he needed
to actually do something about* those *responsibilities.*

"I'm overjoyed we lost so few . . . *this* winter, Father,"
he said, not looking away from the window. "I only regret that we lost so many the winter before, and the winter before that."

Kwill looked at the vicar's back, silhouetted against the
bright window, and wondered if Duchairn realized how
much pain rested like an anchor in the depths of his own
voice. The vicar was a Chihirite, like the majority of
Mother Church's administrators, without the trained insight into feelings and emotional processes that Kwill's
own order taught. Perhaps he truly didn't understand his
own feelings . . . or how clearly his tone communicated
them, at any rate.

Or how dangerous they could be to him under the
present circumstances.

"Your Grace," the upper-priest said, "I've spent considerably better than half my life feeling exactly that same regret every spring." Duchairn turned his head to look at him, and Kwill smiled sadly. "I suppose we should grow inured to it when it happens again and again, but every body we find buried in the snow, every child who becomes an orphan, every soul we can't somehow cram into the Hospice or one of the other shelters when the temperature drops and the wind comes screaming in off the lake— every single one of those deaths takes its own tiny piece of my soul with it. I've never learned to accept it, but I've had to learn to *deal* with it. To admit to myself that I truly did do everything I could to minimize those deaths . . . and to absolve myself of the guilt for them. It isn't easy to do that. No matter how much I've done, I'm always convinced I could—that I *should*—have done still more. I can *know* here"—he touched his temple gently—"that I truly did all I could, but it's hard to *accept* that here."

He touched his chest, and his sad smile grew gentler.

"I've had more practice trying to do that than you have, Your Grace. Partly because I'm the next best thing to thirty-five years older than you are. And I realize most people here in Zion and even in my own order seem to think I've been doing what I do since the Creation itself. The truth is, though, I was past forty before it even occurred to me that this should be my life's work. That it was what God had in mind for me to do." He shook his head. "Don't think for a moment all the years I wasted before I heard His voice don't come back to haunt me every winter, reminding me of all those earlier winters when I did nothing at all. I realize there are those who think of me as some sort of saintly paragon—those that don't think I'm an ornery old crackpot, at any rate!—but I was a much duller student than those people think. We hear Him when we hear Him, and it's up to Him to judge us. It's not up to others, and our own judgment is sometimes the least reliable of all, especially where our own actions are concerned."

"You're probably right, Father," Duchairn said after a long, silent moment, "yet if we *don't* judge ourselves, if we don't hold ourselves accountable, we turn our backs not just on our responsibilities but on ourselves. I've discovered guilt makes a bitter seasoning, but without it it's too easy to lose ourselves."

"Of course it is, Your Grace," Kwill said simply. "But if God says *He's* willing to forgive us when we recognize our faults and genuinely seek to amend our lives, then shouldn't *we* be willing to do the same thing?"

"You truly are a Bédardist, aren't you, Father?" Duchairn shook his head wryly. "And I'll try to bear your advice in mind. But the *Writ* says we're supposed to make recompense, to the best of our ability, to those we realize we've wronged. I'm afraid it's going to take me a while to accomplish that."

Kwill crossed the office to stand beside him at the window, but the priest didn't look out across the lake. Instead, he stood for several seconds regarding the vicar intently, gazing into his eyes. Then he reached out and laid a hand thinned by a lifetime's labors on Duchairn's chest.

"I think this is in a better state and far, far deeper than even you realize, Your Grace," he said softly. "But be careful. Even the greatest of hearts can accomplish nothing in this world after it ceases to beat."

Duchairn laid his hand across the priest's for a moment and inclined his head in what might have been agreement or simple acknowledgment. Then he inhaled deeply and stepped back.

"As always, Father Zytan, it's been both a joy and a privilege," he said more briskly. "And I'm pleased with your report, especially since I've managed to free up the funding to acquire or build additional shelters for the coming winter. Depending on where we place them, it would probably be cheaper to purchase and refurbish existing structures, and if we're going to be forced to build, it would be a good idea to get started as quickly as possible. So please give some thought to where the housing will be most urgently required. I'd like to have your recommendations for three or four new sites within the next couple of five-days."

"Of course, Your Grace. And thank you." Kwill smiled broadly. "We can always use additional roofs when the snow flies."

"I'll do my best, Father. Just as I'll do my best to bear your advice in mind." Duchairn extended his hand, and Kwill bent to brush his ring of office with his lips, then straightened. "Until next time, Father."

"May the Holy Bédard bless and keep you, Your Grace," Kwill murmured in response.

Duchairn nodded and left the office. His escort of Temple Guardsmen was waiting for him, of course. They didn't like letting him out of their sight even for his meetings with Father Zytan, and despite their discipline, it showed in their expressions.

Of course, there's more than one reason for that unhappiness at having me off doing Langhorne knows what, Duchairn thought with bitter amusement.

"Where to now, Your Grace?" the officer in command of his personal security detachment inquired politely.

"Back to the Temple, Major Phandys," Duchairn said to the man Zhaspahr Clyntahn and Allayn Maigwair had personally selected as his keeper. Their eyes met, and the vicar smiled thinly. "Back to the Temple," he repeated.

▼ ▼ ▼

"Major Phandys is here, Your Eminence."

"Thank you, Father. Send him in."

"Of course, Your Eminence."

The secretary bowed and withdrew. A moment later, Major Khanstahnzo Phandys entered Wyllym Rayno's office. He crossed to the archbishop and bent over his extended hand to kiss his ring.

"You sent for me, Your Eminence?" the major said as he straightened.

Technically, as a Temple Guardsman, he ought to have saluted instead of kissing Rayno's ring. Since the botched arrest of the Wylsynn brothers, however, Major Phandys had become considerably more than a simple Guardsman. It was scarcely his fault that arrest had gone so radically wrong, and the Inquisition had always had a keen eye for talent that could be co-opted without *officially* becoming part of the Order of Schueler.

"Yes, I did, Major." Rayno sat back down behind his desk, tipped his chair back, and surveyed Phandys thoughtfully. "I've read your latest report. As always, it was complete, concise, and to the point. I could wish more of the reports which crossed my desk were like it."

"Thank you, Your Eminence," Phandys murmured when the archbishop paused, obviously expecting some response. "I strive to offer Mother Church—and the Inquisition—my best effort."

"Indeed you do, Major." Rayno smiled with unusual warmth. "In fact, I've been considering whether or not I might be able to find an even more effective use for a man of your talents and piety."

"I'm always prepared to serve wherever Mother Church can best make use of me, Your Eminence," Phandys replied. "Have you someone in mind for my current responsibilities?"

"No, not really." Rayno's smile faded. "No, I'm afraid I don't, Major. That's one reason I called you in. Can you think of anyone else in the Guard suitable for the position?"

Phandys frowned for several seconds, hands clasped respectfully behind him while he considered.

"Off the top of my head, no, I'm afraid, Your Eminence." He shook his head regretfully. "I can think of several whose loyalty and devotion would make them suitable, but none who have the rank to serve as Vicar Rhobair's senior Guardsman. Of those who do have the rank, I'm afraid I'd have . . . reservations about recommending most of them. There *might* be one or two of sufficient rank and seniority, but none who could be assigned to him without a series of transfers to make them the logical choices. I can give you their names, if you like, Your Eminence, although I'd strongly recommend you interview them personally before you consider them for my current assignment."

"Your reasons?" Rayno's tone was honestly curious, and Phandys shrugged.

"I'd hesitate to recommend anyone I don't know personally and reasonably well, Your Eminence, but I doubt anyone ever knows someone as well as he thinks he does. And the fact that most of them are friends, or at least close acquaintances, would tend to make me suspect my own judgment. I'd simply feel more comfortable if someone with a more . . . detached perspective decided whether or not they'd be suitable for the duty."

"I see."

Rayno considered that for a moment. For a rather long moment, in fact. As he'd already suggested, the Inquisition always had far too many demands for men of talent and ability, and that was especially so these days. Phandys was already young for his current rank, but Rayno could easily have him promoted to colonel or even brigadier. Yet deciding whether or not to do that represented something of a balancing act. While the higher rank would give him greater seniority and authority, it would also make him even more of a marked man among his fellows. It was sadly true that the more closely identified with the Inquisition an officer became, the less his fellows tended to confide in him. Besides. . . .

"Please do provide me with those recommendations, Major," he said at length. "Even if I decide to leave you in your present assignment, it never hurts for the Inquisition to know where to lay its hand on Mother Church's dutiful sons when she needs them worst."

"Of course, Your Eminence." Phandys bowed slightly. "I'll have them for you by tomorrow afternoon, if that will be soon enough?"

"That will be fine, Major," Rayno said, and waved one hand in dismissal.

▼ ▼ ▼

"Well?" Zhaspahr Clyntahn said as Wyllym Rayno entered his office. "What's our good friend Rhobair been up to lately?"

"According to all my sources, Your Grace, he's been doing precisely what he said he was going to do. He paid another visit to Father Zytan yesterday, and he's scheduled a meeting next five-day with the senior Pasqualates from all five major hospitals to discuss the coordination of healers with his shelters and soup kitchens for next winter." The archbishop shrugged. "Apparently he wants to be better organized than he was this winter."

Clyntahn rolled his eyes. He didn't have anything against a practical, reasonable level of charitable works, but the vicars of Mother Church weren't supposed to allow themselves to be distracted from their own responsibilities. At a time like this, the Church's chief financial officer had dozens of concerns upon which he might more profitably spend his time than worrying about a winter which was still months away.

The Grand Inquisitor leaned back, the fingers of his right hand drumming an irritated tattoo on his desk. Duchairn's excessive, gushy piety was becoming more and more exasperating, yet all the old arguments against allowing the Group of Four's potential enemies to suspect a genuine division in their ranks remained, although those arguments were growing weaker as the example he'd made of the Wylsynns' circle of pro-Reformist traitors sank fully home. If not for that, he'd cheerfully contemplate jettisoning Duchairn. Unfortunately, if he purged Duchairn, he'd have to come up with someone else to do the man's job, and the unpalatable fact was that no one else could do it as well as he did. That consideration was especially pointed given Mother Church's current straitened financial condition.

No, he concluded yet again, regretfully, he couldn't get rid of Duchairn yet, however much the man's softhearted, mushy-brained sanctimony sickened him. Of course, the *reasons* he couldn't—those same straitened financial conditions—only made the other vicar's obsession with "providing for the poor" even more maddening. Still, if Clyntahn had no choice anyway, he might as well look at the bright side. Judging by the tenor of his own agents' reports, Duchairn's demand that the Group of Four show a "kinder, gentler face" truly was helping to bolster morale here in Zion. That sort of bought-and-paid-for "loyalty" was always a perishable commodity, far less reliable than the instant obedience instilled by the Inquisition's discipline, but it was probably useful in the short term, at least.

"What about Phandys?" he asked, and Rayno considered his response carefully.

The major had become one of Zhaspahr Clyntahn's favorites, although that outcome might not have been assured, given the way he'd deprived the Grand Inquisitor of one of his most anticipated prizes. Even Clyntahn had accepted that that was scarcely his fault when he'd found himself face-to-face with Hauwerd Wylsynn in personal combat, however, and without Phandys, the Wylsynns might actually have managed to get out of Zion. They wouldn't have gotten *far,* but the fact that they'd had the chance to run at all would have undermined the Inquisition's aura of invincibility. The Grand Inquisitor had chosen to look on the bright side, which explained how Captain Phandys had become *Major* Phandys.

"I understand your desire to make the best and fullest use of Major Phandys, Your Grace," the archbishop said after a moment. "And I'm looking into possible replacements for him in his current assignment. With all due respect, however, at this time I think it would be wisest to leave him where he is."

"Why?" Clyntahn asked tersely, and Rayno shrugged.

"As the Major himself pointed out to me this afternoon, Your Grace, finding someone equally reliable to replace him as Vicar Rhobair's chief guardian would be difficult. He's prepared to recommend some potential candidates, but Vicar Allayn would be forced to juggle assignments rather obviously to put one of them into Major Phandys' present position. And, to be totally honest, the more I've thought about it the more convinced I am that we really do need to keep one of our best and most observant people in charge of Vicar Rhobair's security."

The Grand Inquisitor scowled, yet the point about

keeping an eye on Duchairn was well taken, at least until they could find someone to replace him as Treasurer. Duchairn clearly knew Phandys was spying on him for the Inquisition, but he seemed resigned to the fact, and the major had demonstrated a surprising degree of tact. He went out of his way to avoid stepping on Duchairn's toes, and it was always possible the Treasurer actually appreciated his courtesy. As for Rayno's other argument, personally, Clyntahn wouldn't have given a damn if Maigwair had to rearrange assignments to put someone else into Phandys' position, but there was still that pestiferous, irritating need to preserve the fiction that the Group of Four remained fully united. If it became *too* obvious Clyntahn and Maigwair were assigning their own men to spy on Duchairn and Trynair, some of the currently cowed vicars might find themselves dangerously—or at least inconveniently—emboldened. And truth to tell, Duchairn was less predictable in many ways than Trynair, given the Chancellor's predictable—and manipulable—pragmatism and self-interest.

Rayno was right, he decided. Better to keep one of their best men right where he was until the time finally came to be shut of Duchairn entirely.

"All right," he growled. "I hate wasting someone of his abilities as a glorified nursemaid, but I suppose you have a point."

He frowned for another few seconds, then shrugged.

"All right," he said again, in a very different tone, changing subjects with his accustomed abruptness. "What's this we hear from Corisande?"

"Obviously our latest information is sadly out-of-date, as always, Your Grace," Rayno said a bit cautiously, "but according to my current reports, all of those arrested last year have now been tried. Formal sentencing is awaiting the arrival of either Cayleb or Sharleyan—probably Sharleyan—but all indications are that the overwhelming majority of those arrested"—even the redoubtable Rayno paused almost imperceptibly to brace himself—"have been found guilty."

Clyntahn's expression hardened and his jowls darkened, yet that was all. Some people might have been relieved by his apparent lack of reaction, but Rayno knew the Grand Inquisitor better than that.

"I don't suppose," Clyntahn said in an icy tone, "that anyone in that traitorous bastard Gairlyng's 'Church' raised a single voice in protest?"

"So far as I know, no, Your Grace." Rayno cleared his throat. "According to our sources, Gairlyng appointed clerics to the courts hearing the accusations as part of the farce that all the required legal procedures had been followed."

"Of course he did." Clyntahn's jaw muscles quivered for a moment. "We already knew that son-of-a-bitch Anvil Rock and his catamite Tartarian were willing to whore for Cayleb and his bitch any way they asked. So of course the 'Church of Charis' is going to just stand by and watch the judicial murder of Mother Church's loyal sons and daughters! What else could we *expect*?"

His face darkened steadily, and Rayno braced himself. But then, to the archbishop's surprise, the Grand Inquisitor wrapped his hands tightly together on his desk, hunched his shoulders, and visibly fought his rage back under control. It didn't come easily, and he didn't manage it quickly, but he did manage it in the end.

"You say formal announcement of the verdicts is awaiting Sharleyan's arrival?" he asked at last in a hard, tight voice.

"Yes, Your Grace. In fact, if she's kept to the schedule which was reported to us, she's already there. She may actually be ready to depart by now."

"So what you're saying is that they *have* been announced by now. And, presumably, *carried out*, as well." Clyntahn bared his teeth. "The bitch isn't going to leave without the satisfaction of seeing them all killed, now is she?"

"Presumably not, Your Grace."

"Do we have any indication of how the population in general's responding to all of this?"

"Not . . . really, Your Grace." Rayno twitched his shoulders unhappily. "So far there haven't been any indications of organized protest or outrage, but, again, all our reports are months out of date by the time they get here. It's always possible people have been waiting for confirmation of the verdicts before they reacted."

"And it's always possible they're just going to sit on their asses and let it happen, too," Clyntahn said flatly.

"I'm afraid so," Rayno admitted.

"Then it may be time to stiffen their spines." Clyntahn's expression was ugly. "What's the situation with Coris?"

"Nothing seems to have changed in that regard, Your Grace. As you know, I've got one of our best men planted on him, and Bishop Mytchail has his own agent in King Zhames' household, as well. Both of them agree Coris is doing what he was told to do."

"And that he *will* do what we need him to do?"

"Almost certainly, Your Grace."

"Only *almost?*" Clyntahn's eyes narrowed.

"I doubt he'd hesitate for a moment, Your Grace, if it weren't for the fact that everyone knows he was Hektor's spymaster—the man who managed Hektor's assassins, among other things. He has a reputation for personal ambition, and it might occur to him that if anyone was going to be blamed as Cayleb's tool in Daivyn's assassination, it would be him. Under the circumstances, I think he'd probably prefer not to give any additional credence to that kind of charge. That assessment is based at least in part on reports from Master Seablanket, our agent in his household."

"Hmmmmm." Clyntahn frowned, stroking his chin meditatively, eyes half-closed, for several seconds. "You know," he said thoughtfully, "that might not be such a bad idea. Letting Coris carry the blame for it, I mean." He smiled thinly. "He and Anvil Rock and Tartarian all worked together with Hektor, after all. Saddling him with responsibility—because he saw it as an opportunity to buy Cayleb's favor the same way they have, no doubt—would smear the two of them by association, too, wouldn't it?"

"It certainly might, Your Grace."

"Do you think Seablanket could handle it?"

"I think he *could,* but I'd rather not use him, Your Grace."

"Why not, especially if he's already in position?"

"Because he's too valuable, Your Grace. If I'm following your logic properly here, we need for the assassin—or for *an* assassin, at any rate—to be taken or killed after the boy is dead. Preferably killed, I should think, if we don't want any inconvenient interrogations. I'd hesitate to use up someone as capable as Seablanket if we don't absolutely have to."

"So who would you use instead?"

"My thought at this moment is that we might use a team from the Rakurai candidates you approved but haven't assigned, Your Grace. I'm sure we could select men who would be prepared to see to it that they weren't taken alive. In fact, we have several more native-born Charisians available."

Clyntahn cocked his head, then nodded slowly.

"That would be a nice touch, wouldn't it?" He smiled unpleasantly. "Of course, it would tend to direct suspicion away from Coris."

"Only in the sense that it wasn't actually his hand on the dagger, Your Grace," Rayno pointed out. "As you suggested, even if he didn't strike the blow himself, he might have connived with Cayleb. In fact, we might be able to help that perception along a little bit. At the appropriate time, we could instruct him to . . . creatively weaken Daivyn's security to let our assassins in. Seablanket's in a perfect position to pass him the message when we need to, and it won't hurt a thing at that point for Coris to realize we've been watching him more closely than he thought. And after the fact, if we decide to throw Coris to the slash lizard, the fact that he *did* let the assassins—the *Charisian-born* assassins—into Daivyn's presence would be the crowning touch. And if we decided *not* to throw him to the slash lizard after all, we simply wouldn't have to mention what he did."

"I like it." Clyntahn nodded. "All right, pick your team. We'll see how public opinion in Corisande reacts to Sharleyan's executions before we actually order them to proceed, but it won't hurt to have the pieces in position when the time comes."

. II .

Twyngyth,
Duchy of Malikai,
Kingdom of Dohlar

Sir Gwylym Manthyr's eyes opened as the hand shook his shoulder.

On the face of it, it was ridiculous that such a gentle summons could rouse him. Over the last five-day and a half, he'd learned to sleep despite the bone-jarring, jouncing, swaying, rumbling, grating progress of their mobile prison. Just the mind-numbing sound of steel-shod wooden wheels grinding over the hard surface of the royal high road should have been enough to make anything like sleep impossible, but Manthyr was a lifelong seaman. He'd learned to steal precious moments of sleep even in the teeth of a howling gale, and sheer exhaustion made it easier than it might have been otherwise. He'd never been so tired, so worn to the bone, in his entire life, and he knew it was even worse for many of his men.

He looked up into Naiklos Vahlain's face and opened his mouth, but he had to stop and swallow twice before he could moisten his vocal cords enough to speak.

"What is it, Naiklos?"

"Begging your pardon, Sir, but we're coming into a town. A big one. I think it's Twyngyth."

"I see." Manthyr lay still for another moment, then reached up and grabbed one of the wagon's iron bars and used it to haul himself to his feet. He balanced there, despite the shock waves which exploded up his legs and jolted painfully in his spine with the wagon's motion.

It was odd, a corner of his mind thought. Charis' highways were adequate to the kingdom's needs, but nothing like most of the mainland realms boasted. The reason for that, of course, was Howell Bay. Charis didn't *need* the sort of road network the mainlanders required, because water transport was always available and far more economical and speedy than even the best of road systems. Despite himself, Manthyr had been impressed by the sheer engineering ability and years of labor it must have taken to build the Dohlaran royal high roads, and their surfaces were hard and smooth, made of multiple layers of tamped gravel rolled out and then covered with slabs of cement.

And that was what was odd. One wouldn't have thought a surface that smooth could still be uneven, yet judging from the prison wagon's painful progress, it obviously could.

He rubbed his aching, gummy eyes and peered through the bars.

Naiklos was right; they were approaching a sizable town or city. Once upon a time, Manthyr had been accustomed to judging the size of the cities he encountered by comparison to Tellesberg, yet he'd discovered there were others which were larger still. Cherayth, in Chisholm, for example, or Gorath here in Dohlar. *This* town was much smaller than that—barely a third the size of Tellesberg—but it boasted fortified, bastioned walls at least twenty or thirty feet tall, and there was obviously artillery atop those walls, which argued for a certain importance. And if Manthyr's memory of the maps of Dohlar were correct (which it might well not be, since he'd been primarily interested in Dohlar's *coasts*), this almost certainly was Twyngyth.

And won't that *be fun*, he thought grimly, knees flexing as his weary body anticipated the jolts. It wasn't like being at sea, but there were some similarities. *You had to go and help His Majesty kill that asshole Duke Malikai off*

*Armageddon Reef, didn't you, Gwylym? I'll bet his lov-
ing family's been just praying for the opportunity to entertain you on your way through.*

▼ ▼ ▼

"Keep the crowd moving, Captain," Father Vyktyr Tahrlsahn said. "I'm sure everyone wants to see these bastards,
and I want to make sure everyone *gets* to see them, too.
See them from close enough they can smell the vermin's
stink!"

"Aye, Sir." Captain Walysh Zhu touched his breastplate
in salute, but behind that façade of stolid acknowledgment, his brain was busy.

Over the last several days, Zhu had realized Tahrlsahn
was even more . . . zealous than the captain had originally thought. Zhu was as orthodox and conservative as
only a Harchongese could be, and he saw no reason heretics should be accorded the protections of *honorable*
prisoners of war. Anyone who gave his allegiance to
Shan-wei deserved whatever came his way, after all. On
the other hand, Zhu took no particular pleasure from
seeing them abused without some specific reason. He'd
ordered his Guardsmen to show them why they'd be wise
to cooperate that very first day, but there'd been a *purpose* to that beating, a way to establish discipline without
actually killing anyone. And, if he was going to be honest, there *had* been a certain personal satisfaction in it, as
well. Payback for what their bastard friends had done to
the Navy of God and the Imperial Harchongese Navy in
the Markovian Sea, if nothing else.

But Tahrlsahn sometimes seemed to have trouble remembering they were supposed to deliver their prisoners
intact to the Temple. Personally, Zhu estimated they were
likely to lose perhaps one in five from sheer exhaustion
and privation even under the best of conditions. But they
weren't *getting* the best of conditions, were they? They'd
been scrawny as skinned wyverns when he'd collected
them from the prison hulks in Gorath, and Tahrlsahn
wasn't going out of his way to fatten them up since. Zhu

suspected there was sickness among them, as well, helping to gnaw away at their reserves of strength, but Tahrlsahn had endorsed Bishop Executor Wylsynn's ban on providing the "malingering bastards" with healers. And the prison wagons' jarring ride was far more debilitating than Tahrlsahn seemed to realize.

Now they were coming into Twyngyth, the biggest city they'd passed through yet, and Tahrlsahn's instructions made him a little nervous. It had been bad enough in some of the other villages and small towns. Zhu remembered the village where twenty or thirty men and adolescent boys had jogged along beside the prison wagons, pelting the Charisians with stones picked up from the roadside. At least one prisoner had lost an eye, and another had gone down unconscious when a rock hit him in the head. Zhu didn't know how much the blow to his skull had to do with it, but the same man had gone berserk the next afternoon and attacked a Guardsman with his bare hands when he and his fellows were released from their wagon for a latrine break. Tahrlsahn would just as soon have left them to foul the wagons with their own wastes, but Father Myrtan, his second-in-command, had convinced him that at least the rudiments of Pasquale's laws of hygiene had to be observed if they didn't want the Guardsmen to come under the Archangel's curse, as well.

Zhu didn't know about that, but he had a pretty fair notion how foul the prison wagons would smell to anyone unfortunate enough to be escorting them from downwind. That was more than enough to put him on Father Myrtan's side of that debate, although Tahrlsahn had almost changed his mind and prohibited the stops after all when the screaming Charisian got both hands around a Guardsman's throat and started beating the man's head on the ground. Three more Charisians had turned on their captors, as well—less from any real hope of achieving anything, Zhu thought, than out of pure instinct to aid their fellow—and despite the prisoners' half-starved condition, it had taken over forty guardsmen to subdue the single unlocked wagon's twenty Charisians.

When it ended, two Guardsmen were seriously injured and the first Charisian and one of his companions were dead. Two more had died over the next day and a half, and six more had received broken bones ... not all of them *before* they were subdued. Sergeant Zhadahng came from the Empire's Bedard Province in far western West Haven. *Nobody* was more orthodox than someone from Bedard, especially someone who'd been born a serf like Zhadahng. And no one was more accustomed to receiving—and meting out—brutality than a Bedard serf. There was no doubt in Zhu's mind that Zhadahng had seen to the administration of a little additional "discipline" on his own initiative.

The captain had chosen not to make an issue out of it in this instance. First, because a little extra emphasis for the prisoners probably wouldn't hurt anything ... except the prisoners, who were heretics and deserved it anyway. And, second (and more to the point), because he had no doubt Tahrlsahn would have supported the sergeant's actions. He'd certainly brushed aside Father Myrtan's earlier efforts to convince him to make at least some improvements in the prisoners' condition. The argument had become heated—dangerously so, Zhu thought—before Father Vyktyr sharply ordered Father Myrtan to be silent. He was hardly likely to support Zhu if he disciplined Zhadahng for something as minor as beating a heretic or two to death. And Tahrlsahn was one of the Grand Inquisitor's favorites.

Yet what worried him at the moment was less what Zhadahng or his own men might do than what the good citizens of Twyngyth might take it into *their* minds to do. The convoy's progress was slow—deliberately so, to make sure there was time for crowds to gather properly in the towns along its route—and that meant there was plenty of time for broadsheets and posters to go up along the way. Literacy was much more common in Dohlar than in Harchong, and even the most ill-educated villager could always find someone to read the latest broadsheet to him. Which meant there'd also been ample opportunity for everyone along the route to discuss all the inequities of the Charisian heretics about to be found—briefly—in their midst. And as they'd drawn gradually closer to Twyngyth, Zhu had noticed a steadily rising level of vituperation and hatred in the broadsheets nailed to the milestones they'd passed along the way.

I wonder how much of that is the Ahlverez family's doing? he thought. *From everything I've heard, they wanted the Dohlarans to string these bastards up for what happened to Duke Malikai at Rock Point! And they know we've got our hands on* "Emperor" *Cayleb's flag captain from that battle, too. I'll bet they really* want *to get their hands on him! Stupid of them, of course—nothing they could do to him would be a patch on what the Inquisition's got waiting in Zion. But none of these damned Dohlarans seem overly blessed with logic.*

On the other hand, the Inquisition wanted to make sure *it* got its hands on Gwylym Manthyr. It wouldn't thank Tahrlsahn—or Captain Walysh Zhu—if it didn't, and Zhu rather suspected the Grand Inquisitor himself would make his displeasure known if that happened, even if Tahrlsahn *was* one of his favorites.

"Forgive me, Father Vyktyr," he said after a moment, "but I'm a little concerned over the prisoners' security." He'd started to use the word "safety" but stopped himself in time.

"What do you mean?" Tahrlsahn's eyes narrowed.

"Twyngyth is a larger city than any we've stopped in so far, Father," Zhu said in his calmest, most reasonable tone. "The crowds will be a lot thicker, and we'll be inside the city proper, surrounded by buildings and narrow streets."

"And your point is, Captain?" Tahrlsahn prompted impatiently.

"As I'm sure you're aware, Father, the natural anger heresy always arouses seems to be burning especially high here in Malikai. I imagine that has a lot to do with what happened to *Duke* Malikai at the Battle of Rock Point. What I'm afraid of is that someone carried away by that anger might feel compelled to take God's justice into his own hands."

"What do you mean 'carried away'? Carried away how?"

Zhu wasn't even tempted to roll his eyes, but he found himself wishing—for far from the first time—that Father Myrtan was in command of the convoy. Tahrlsahn's burning hatred for any heretic seemed to get in the way of his logical processes from time to time.

Like every time he thinks about them at all! the captain thought dryly.

"Father, it's my understanding that we're supposed to deliver the heretics alive and intact to the Inquisition in Zion." Zhu's rising inflection and raised eyebrows made the statement a politely phrased question, and Tahrlsahn nodded impatiently.

"What I'm afraid of, Father, is that feelings are running so high here in Twyngyth that someone's likely to stick a knife into one of them if he gets the opportunity. And in a built-up area like a city, there's a lot better chance that if some kind of mob mentality builds, they'd be able to rush my men and get through to the heretics. In that case, we could lose *dozens* of them, Father, in addition to the ones we're losing from . . . natural attrition. We've already lost eight since leaving Gorath; at that rate, we'll be lucky to get twenty of them as far as Zion to face the Inquisition." Zhu was afraid he might be being dangerously blunt, but he saw no other option. "I simply don't want to lose any of them here by allowing the crowds to get too dense or too close to the wagons."

Tahrlsahn glared at him for a moment, but then his eyes narrowed, and Zhu could almost see the wheels inside his brain beginning to turn at last. Apparently the captain had finally found an argument Father Myrtan's appeals to *The Book of Pasquale* and the *Holy Writ* had failed to present.

"Very well, Captain Zhu," the upper-priest finally said. "I'll leave the security arrangements in your hands. Mind you, I want the Dohlarans to have ample opportunity to bear witness to what happens to heretics! I'm firm on that point. But you're probably right that letting them too close to the wagons would constitute an unnecessary additional risk. I'll send a messenger ahead to tell the city authorities we need to clear one of their larger market squares as a place to bivouac overnight. Then we'll set up a perimeter of—What? Fifteen yards? Twenty?—around the wagons themselves."

"With your approval, Father, I'd feel more comfortable with twenty."

"Oh, very well!" Tahrlsahn waved an obviously irritated hand. "Make it twenty, if you think that's necessary. And remember what I said about keeping the crowd moving, so everyone gets his chance to see them!"

"Of course, Father. I assure you that everyone in Twyngyth will have ample opportunity to see what happens to the defilers of Mother Church."

. III .

HMS *Destiny*, 54,
and
HMS *Destroyer*, 54,
King's Harbor,
Helen Island,
Kingdom of Old Charis

" 'Vast heaving! Avast heaving!" Hektor Aplyn-Ahrmahk shouted, and the capstan stopped turning instantly.

The new-model kraken hung suspended above HMS *Destiny*'s deck, gleaming in the sunlight, and its shadow fell across the youthful ensign. He stepped across the bar taut fall leading back through the deck-level snatch block to the capstan, then stood, hands on hips, and glared up at the three-ton hammer of the gun tube suspended from the mainmast pendant and the forecourse's yardarm. He stood that way for several seconds before he shook his head and turned to the boatswain's mate who'd been supervising the operation with a disgusted expression.

"Get that gun back down on the dock and rig that sling properly, Selkyr!" he snapped, raising his right hand and jabbing an index finger skyward.

The boatswain's mate in question was at least twice Aplyn-Ahrmahk's age, but he looked up, following the ensign's pointing finger, then cringed. The rope cradle secured around the gun's trunnions had managed to slip badly off-center. The iron tube had begun to twist sideways, pulling hard against the steadying line rigged from its cascabel to the hook of the winding-tackle's lower block and threatening to slide completely free of the sling.

"Aye, aye, Sir!" he replied. "Sorry, Sir. Don't know how that happened."

"Just get it back down and straighten it out," Aplyn-Ahrmahk said in calmer tones. Then he grinned. "Somehow I don't think the Captain would thank us for dropping that thing down the main hatch and out the bottom when the dockyard still hasn't turned us loose!"

"No, Sir, that he wouldn't," Selkyr agreed fervently.

"Then see to it," Aplyn-Ahrmahk said. "Because he's not going to be very happy if we don't get finished on time, either."

"Aye, Sir." Selkyr saluted in acknowledgment and turned back to his working party.

Aplyn-Ahrmahk stood back, watching as the men on the capstan began cautiously turning it the other way, leaning back against the capstan bars now to brake its motion as they slackened the fall. The hands tending the guidelines and manning the forebraces swung the yardarm back outboard, and the gun descended once more to the dock beside which *Destiny* lay moored.

Selkyr was an unhappy man, and he made his displeasure known to the working party as it set about rerigging the sling properly, yet there was a certain restraint in his manner, and Aplyn-Ahrmahk gave a mental nod of approval. The boatswain's mate was clearly more concerned with seeing to it that his men got the problem fixed and learned not to let it happen again than with pounding whoever had made the mistake this time. A good petty officer—and Ahntahn Selkyr was just that—preferred correction to punishment whenever possible, and that was especially important given the number of green hands currently diluting *Destiny*'s normally proficient and well-trained company.

The ship had been required to give up a sizable draft of experienced seamen and petty officers during her stint in dockyard hands. In fact, she'd been raided even more heavily than many of the other ships which were losing trained personnel to form the cadres of new ships' companies. Aplyn-Ahrmahk suspected *Destiny*'s crew quality had something to do with the reason she'd been forced to give up so many more of her people than those other ships had, and he couldn't help resenting it more than a little.

They probably figure the Captain can always train more, he thought sourly. *And I guess it's a compliment, in a backhanded sort of way. They need good people, and the Captain produces good people . . . so obviously the thing to do is reward him by taking them all away from him and making him go produce still more of them! It's just harvesting the natural increase.*

He was being unfair to the Navy, and in his calmer moments he knew it. He understood the frantic efforts the Navy was making to man its recently acquired galleons, and he couldn't quibble with the need to provide the most experienced possible cadres for the newly inducted men going into their crews. The Imperial Charisian Navy had consisted of just over ninety galleons prior to the Battle of the Markovian Sea; now it had over two hundred, courtesy of its construction programs . . . and the Navy of God and the Imperial Harchongese Navy. Manning even half those new prizes had required an enormous increase in manpower, and manpower was the Empire of Charis' greatest weakness in its confrontation with the Church of God Awaiting and the huge populations of the mainland realms. It simply didn't have enough warm bodies to go around.

For the first time in its history, Old Charis faced the threat of being forced to resort to the sort of impressment other navies had routinely employed for centuries. The Crown had always had the *authority* to impress seamen, but the House of Ahrmahk had been careful not to use it, and for good reason. The fact that the Royal Charisian Navy's galleys had been manned solely by volunteers built around solid cores of long-service, highly experienced regulars had been its most telling advantage, and they'd been willing to accept a smaller fleet than they could have built in order to maintain that qualitative edge.

With every mainland realm united against the Empire, however, that was a luxury the *Imperial* Charisian Navy couldn't afford. It needed as many hulls as it could get, and while galleons didn't require the hundreds of rowers galleys did, they were far bigger than even Charisian galleys had been and much more heavily armed. Providing them with gun crews and enough trained seamen to manage their powerful sail plans drove the size of their companies up rapidly, and completely filling the "establishment" crew for a galleon like *Destiny* required approximately four hundred men. With the prizes being put into commission, the Navy's galleon strength would rise to two hundred and eleven . . . which would require over eighty-four thousand men. And that didn't even consider all of the schooners, brigs, and other light warships and dispatch vessels. Or the competition for the strength to man the Navy's shoreside establishments. Or the requirements of the Marine Corps, or the Imperial Army. Or the fishing fleet. Or the merchant marine upon which the Empire's prosperity and very survival depended. And while the Crown was finding—somehow—all the men it needed for *those* requirements, the manufactories producing both the sinews of war and the goods fueling the steadily growing economy—not to mention the farms feeding the Empire's subjects—still had to be provided for somehow.

So far, enlistment was managing—barely—to meet demands, but an increasing percentage of the Navy's strength was Emeraldian or Chisholmian, and even the native Old Charisians coming forward boasted a lower percentage of experienced seamen. From what Aplyn-Ahrmahk had seen, the basic quality of the new men was just fine; they were simply less well trained and hardened to the demands of life at sea than the Navy was accustomed to. And even with the newcomers, *Destiny*'s official four-hundred-man company was forty-three men short.

Well, he thought, watching the gun begin to rise once more, *I guess having too many ships and too few experienced men is a lot better problem to have than the other way around!*

▼ ▼ ▼

Sir Domynyk Staynair leaned back in the window seat, one arm stretched along the top of its cushioned back and his truncated right leg stretched out in front of him, the padded peg resting on a footstool. It was almost the turn of the watch, and the cabin's skylight was open, admitting the sounds of King's Harbor and the closer, quieter voices of the officer of the watch and his senior quartermaster as they discussed HMS *Destroyer*'s log entry. The more distant cries of gulls and sea wyverns drifted down through it, as well, and wavery patterns of bright light reflected into the cabin through the quarter and stern windows, gleaming on polished bookshelves, sideboards, and tables. It sparkled from the cut crystal of decanters, sending rainbow ripples across the cabin as the galleon stirred gently, and the portraits of Emperor Cayleb and Empress Sharleyan faced each other across the deck's thick carpets. Those carpets had been a gift from Empress Sharleyan, and their deep-toned color went just a bit oddly with the gayer fabric of the chair coverings Rock Point favored. The table at the center of the cabin was buried under charts, dividers, and compasses, and Zhastrow Tymkyn, his new secretary, sat at his small desk to one side, pen scratching as he annotated his minutes of the high admiral's last conference.

The cabin door opened, and Rock Point's even newer flag lieutenant ushered another officer through it.

Lieutenant Haarlahm Mahzyngail had stepped into Lieutenant Erayksyn's position less than two five-days earlier, and he still seemed out of place aboard a Charisian warship. Not because of any lack of competency, but because his fair hair, blue eyes, and pronounced Chisholmian accent remained such a novelty here in Old Charis. They were becoming more commonplace, though, as more and more Chisholmians enlisted in the Navy. It was surprising, really. Given the Royal Army's traditional prestige in Chisholm, Rock Point would have expected any adventurous young lad from that island to have been army mad, not drawn to a naval career. As things were working out, though, he'd actually received an only half-humorous protest from the Duke of Eastshare, the Imperial Army's commander, about the Navy's "poaching" on his private preserve.

Probably has something to do with the fact that we've kicked the Loyalists' asses at sea every time we've crossed swords, he thought. *Except,* he corrected himself much more grimly, *where Thirsk is concerned, of course.*

That thought hit harder than usual as the overland convoy carrying Gwylym Manthyr and his men crept steadily towards Zion. Grief for a friend and anger at his own helplessness seethed just below the surface for a moment, but he made himself push those emotions back into the depths. It felt disloyal, yet there wasn't anything he could do to change what was going to happen, and Gwylym wouldn't have thanked him for letting friendship distract him from his own duties and responsibilities.

"Captain Yairley, High Admiral," Mahzyngail announced, and Rock Point nodded. The young Chisholmian was still feeling his way into his duties, although one might not have supposed that from his confident demeanor. He wasn't yet as familiar with his admiral's professional and personal relationships as he might have been, however, and he'd decided—wisely, in Rock Point's opinion—to err on the side of formality until he got them all straightened out in his own mind.

"So I see," Rock Point said, and smiled at the young man. "For future reference, Haarlahm, Sir Dunkyn is an old acquaintance. I know him well. So be sure you keep an eye on the silverware when he's around."

Mahzyngail's nod of acknowledgment bobbled noticeably on the last sentence. He froze for just a moment, then completed the movement.

"I'll strive to bear that in mind, Sir," he said, and Rock Point chuckled.

"See you do," he said, then held out his right hand to Yairley. "I'm going to stay moored right where I am. Rank has its privileges and I'll be damned if I'll clump around when I don't have to. Sit."

He pointed with his left hand while the two of them clasped arms, and Yairley settled into the indicated chair with a small smile of his own. He was a naturally less demonstrative man than Rock Point, and more than one of his fellows had put him down as a dour, fussy worrier. There might actually be some accuracy in that, the high admiral thought, but only a very *small* accuracy.

"How's *Destiny* coming?" he demanded, coming straight to the point.

"The dockyard says I can have her back Thursday." Yairley shrugged. "I'll believe *that* when I see it, but I think we probably will be able to warp her out to the roadstead sometime in the next five-day or so. We're taking her gundeck guns back onboard this afternoon, the carronades will come back aboard tomorrow morning, and I'm reasonably satisfied with her repairs. The sail loft's running behind, though. That's why I'm doubtful about Thursday. Once they get the new canvas delivered, though, we'll be in reasonably good shape."

"Careless of you to break her that way in the first place," Rock Point said with a broad smile, and Yairley smiled back with considerably less amusement.

"So you'll be ready to take her back to sea before the end of the month?" the high admiral continued.

"I don't think we'll be anything like properly worked up by then, but, yes, Sir." Yairley's shoulders shrugged very slightly. "I've got a lot of inexperienced men and outright landsmen to turn into trained seamen somehow, and getting them to sea's probably the best way to be about it."

"You're not the only one with *that* problem, believe me!" Rock Point said sourly. He looked out the quarter windows at the busy panorama of King's Harbor. "The only thing worse than figuring out where to get the men we need is figuring out how to *pay* them once we've got them." He grimaced. "I used to think it was funny watching Bryahn and Ironhill arm wrestling over the budget. Somehow it's not so humorous anymore."

He gazed at the anchorage for another moment, then turned back to Yairley.

"Did you go over those notes I sent you about Ahlfryd's new 'high-angle' guns?"

"Yes, Sir. Very interesting stuff, although I was a bit at a loss as to why you were telling *me* about them." Rock Point raised an eyebrow and Yairley shrugged. "It was pretty obvious he must've been working on them for some time, especially if they're as close to ready to deploy as your memo suggested. Since I hadn't heard a whisper about them—and no one else had, either, as far as I know—I have to assume they were another one of Baron Seamount's 'Top Secret, Cut Your Own Throat After Reading' projects. Not the sort of thing a galleon captain would really need to know about, I'd've thought."

"No?" Rock Point smiled a bit oddly. "Well, you did a good job convincing Jahras to stay in port when Harpahr and Sun Rising came calling last year, Dunkyn," he went on in an obvious non sequitur. "And even with that little . . . excitement of yours in Scrabble Sound, you've done even better, since. So I'm afraid I'm taking *Destiny* away from you, in a manner of speaking."

"I beg your pardon, Sir?" Yairley's tone was considerably sharper than he usually allowed himself, and Rock Point smiled slightly.

"I said 'in a manner of speaking,'" he pointed out.

"Which is my way of telling you you've been promoted to rear admiral. Congratulations, Dunkyn."

Yairley's eyes widened, and the high admiral chuckled.

"I hate to say this, but you didn't get your streamer just because we need flag officers so badly with all this sudden expansion. You also got it because you damned well deserve it. Frankly, it's overdue, but we also need good galleon captains, and you're one of the best we've got. As a matter of fact, I actually hesitated about submitting your name to His Majesty. Not because of any reservations on my part, but because I'm only too well aware of how badly we're going to need those same good captains to lick all these newcomers into shape."

"I'm honored, Sir," Yairley said after a moment, "although I'm going to hate giving up *Destiny*. If I may, Lieutenant Lathyk's overdue for promotion and he—"

"To repeat myself, I *did* say you'd be giving her up 'in a manner of speaking,' Dunkyn. I assumed that given your choice of flagships, you'd probably pick her. Was I correct?"

"Yes, Sir. Of course!"

"Well, unless I'm mistaken, it's still a flag officer's privilege to request the flag captain of his choice. Now I'd assumed someone of your well-known demanding disposition wouldn't have put up with someone like Lathyk unless he was at least marginally competent. If I was wrong, if you really want him promoted to, say, commander and given one of the new brigs instead, I suppose I could go back to His Majesty and change my current recommendation."

"And that recommendation would be precisely what, Sir?" Yairley regarded his superior with a distinctly suspicious expression.

"That he be promoted to captain immediately and assigned as HMS *Destiny*'s commanding officer."

"Upon mature consideration, Sir, I see no reason you should put yourself to the trouble or inconvenience His Majesty by changing your recommendation."

"I thought that was how you'd see it." Rock Point

chuckled, then heaved himself to his feet. "Come take a look at the chart."

He crossed to the table, Yairley at his side, and the two of them gazed down at the huge chart of the Gulf of Mathyas and much smaller Gulf of Jahras. Rock Point leaned over and thumped an index finger on Silkiah Bay.

"As you'll know better than most, we've got an awful lot of 'Silkiahan' galleons moving in and out of Silk Town with Charisian cargoes," he said. "Now, I've never been one for subordinating military decisions to economic ones, but in this case we're talking about a big enough piece of our total trade to make anyone nervous. To be honest, that's one reason we've stayed away from"—his fingertip slid down to the southwest and tapped once—"Desnair and the Gulf of Jahras. We're not certain why Clyntahn hasn't made a bigger push to shut down the Silkiahans' and the Siddarmarkians' defiance of his embargo, and we haven't wanted to do anything to draw his attention to Silk Town or change his mind in that regard. It's not just good for our own manufactories and merchant marine, Dunkyn. It's steadily undermining the Group of Four's authority in both the Republic and the Grand Duchy, and it's simultaneously drawing more and more Siddarmarkians and Silkiahans into our arms, whether they realize it or not.

"Nonetheless," he tapped the city of Iythria, "it's time we did something about the Desnairian fleet. Even after the Battle of the Markovian Sea, we actually don't have much better than parity with the combined Desnairian and Dohlaran fleets. I'd like better numbers than that, of course, but while Gorath Bay and Iythria are barely thirteen hundred miles apart in a straight line, they're damned near seventeen *thousand* miles apart as a ship sails. That's just a *tad* far for them to be supporting one another if we should decide to concentrate our strength in order to overwhelm one of them in isolation, wouldn't you say?"

He raised his eyebrows, and Yairley heard something suspiciously like a snort of amusement from Zhastrow Tymkyn's direction.

"Yes, Sir. I think I'd agree with that," the newly promoted admiral replied.

"I'm glad to hear that. Because, next month, you're going to help me take advantage of that little fact. In fact, you're going to be carrying my dispatches to Admiral Shain ahead of the rest of the fleet . . . and I'm sending some new ships with you. Which is why you got that memo about the high-angle guns you were wondering about."

Rock Point smiled, and this time there was no humor at all in the expression.

. IU .

Royal College,
Tellesberg Palace,
City of Tellesberg,
Kingdom of Old Charis

Dr. Rahzhyr Mahklyn looked up as someone knocked on his office door.

"Yes?"

"Father Paityr is here, Doctor," his senior assistant, Dairak Bowave, announced through the closed door.

"Ah! Excellent, Dairak! Please show the Father in!"

Mahklyn stood behind his desk, beaming as Bowave escorted Paityr Wylsynn into his office. It was the first time the intendant had actually visited the Royal College, and Mahklyn knew most of his colleagues were a little nervous about his decision to do so now. They'd skirted the edge of what Mother Church deemed acceptable knowledge for so long that having the official keeper of the Inquisition in Old Charis actually in their midst was . . . disconcerting.

Of course, those worried colleagues of his didn't know everything *he* knew about Paityr Wylsynn.

"Come in, Father!" Mahklyn held out his right hand. "It's an honor to welcome you."

"And it's a privilege to be here, Doctor." Wylsynn took the proffered hand, and Mahklyn surveyed the younger man's expression carefully. Wylsynn was obviously aware of his intense regard, but he only looked back, meeting the older man's eyes levelly. "I've been away from my own office too long," he continued, "but there are times when anyone needs a bit of a sabbatical. A retreat to think things through and settle oneself back down, you might say."

"I understand entirely, Father. Please, have a seat."

Mahklyn escorted Wylsynn to the armchairs arranged across a small table from one another near one of the large office's windows. They sat and Bowave set a tray on the table between them. It held two tall, delicate glasses and a crystal pitcher beaded with moisture, and Wylsynn's eyebrows rose as he beheld it.

"A sinful luxury, I know, Father," Mahklyn said wryly. "For decades I was perfectly happy living a properly ascetic scholarly existence in the old College down by the docks. Then it burned to the ground and His Majesty *insisted* we relocate to the Palace. Little did I realize that would be just the first crack in my armor of austerity!"

He poured chilled lemonade into the glasses, and ice—actual ice, Wylsynn realized—tapped musically against the inside of the pitcher.

"His Majesty insists we take advantage of his hospitality," the doctor continued, handing a glass to his guest, "which includes the royal icehouse. I tried manfully, I assure you, to resist the temptation of that sinful luxury, but my younger granddaughter Eydyth discovered its existence and I was doomed. Doomed, I tell you!"

Wylsynn laughed and accepted the glass, then sipped gracefully. Ice and icehouses had been much more easily come by in the cool northern land of his birth than in excessively sunny Charis. There was ice on the very tallest mountains even here in Charis and even in summer, but getting to it was far more difficult, and there were no conveniently frozen winter lakes from which it might be harvested, either. That made it a scandalously pricey luxury in Tellesberg.

"Will there be anything else, Doctor?" Bowave inquired, and Mahklyn shook his head.

"No, Dairak. I think the Father and I will manage just fine. If I do need anything, I'll call, I promise."

"Of course." Bowave bobbed a bow in Mahklyn's direction, then bowed rather more formally to Wylsynn. "Father Paityr," he said, and withdrew, closing the door behind him.

"This is good," Wylsynn said, taking another swallow of lemonade. "And I do appreciate the ice, although it's really too expensive to be wasting on me."

"That's what I told Eydyth when she discovered it," Mahklyn said dryly. "Unfortunately, young Zhan was in the vicinity at the time." He rolled his eyes. "I think Princess Mahrya's a very good influence on him in most ways, but he's acquiring the habit of largesse, especially when she's looking and he can impress her with it. Mind you, she *isn't* impressed by it—she's too much her parents' daughter for that sort of nonsense—but he doesn't realize that yet, and he's a teenager who's discovered just how attractive his fiancée actually is. So when he heard me telling Eydyth I thought it would be a bad idea, he *insisted* we make use of it. And, to be fair, if you pack it in enough sawdust you can actually ship ice all the way from Chisholm to Tellesberg in the middle of summer and get here with as much as half of your original cargo. Which, given the price in Tellesberg, is enough to make a *very* healthy profit!"

"I suspect there's going to be an even stronger market for ice-makers in Charis than there is for air-conditioning, when the time finally comes," Paitryk said, looking across at his host.

Mahklyn sat very still for a moment, looking back at him thoughtfully. Then he gave a slow nod.

"I imagine there is, Father. And we could probably actually get away with a compressed-air plant to manufacture it without worrying about the Proscriptions. I'm sure Edwyrd could even power it with one of his waterwheels."

"Please, Doctor." Wylsynn closed his eyes and shuddered theatrically. "I can already hear the Temple Loyalists' outrage! Much as I like cold drinks, I'd really prefer to avoid that battle if we can. After all," his eyes opened again, meeting Mahklyn's, "we're going to have so many others to fight first."

"True." Mahklyn nodded again. "May I ask how you feel about that, Father?"

"About kicking over the traces where the Proscriptions are concerned?" Wylsynn gave a short, sharp crack of laughter. "That doesn't bother me at all, trust me! Not now. But if you mean how do I feel about discovering the truth about the Church and the 'Archangels,' that's a bit more complicated. There's still a part of me that expects the Rakurai to come crashing through the window any minute now for my daring to even question, far less reject, the will of Langhorne. And there's another part of me that wants to march straight into the Cathedral next Wednesday and proclaim the truth to the entire congregation. And there's another part of me that's just plain pissed off at God for letting all this happen."

He paused, and then sat back in his chair and laughed again, far more gently, as he saw Mahklyn's expression.

"Sorry, Doctor. I imagine that was a little more answer than you really wanted."

"Not so much more than I wanted as more than I *expected*, Father. I'm relieved to hear you're angry, though. It certainly beats some other reactions I could think of . . . as long as the anger's directed at the right targets, of course."

"It took me a while to accept that same conclusion, Doctor, and I won't pretend I'm as comfortable as I was back in the days of my blissful ignorance. But I've also discovered at least a shadow of Archbishop Maikel's serenity lurking in the depths of my own soul, although it's going to be a while yet before I can be as . . . tranquil about all of this as he is. On the other hand, I realized I wouldn't be as angry at God as I am unless I still believed in Him, which was something of a relief. And along the way, I've also discovered my belief is even more precious, in some ways, because it no longer rests upon the incontrovertible proof of the historical record. I almost suspect that that's the true secret of the Archbishop's faith."

"In what way?" Mahklyn asked with genuine interest. He'd found himself slipping into what Owl's library records would have described as a Deist mindset, and he didn't know whether or not to envy Maikel Staynair's fiercer, more personal faith.

"The real secret of the strength of Archbishop Maikel's faith is almost absurdly simple," Wylsynn told him. "In fact, he's explained it to us dozens of times in sermons, every time he tells us there comes a point at which any child of God has to decide what he truly believes. *Decide* what he believes, Doctor. Not simply accept, not simply never bother to question, based on 'what everyone knows' or on *The Testimonies* or 'the Archangel Chihiro's' *Holy Writ*, but decide for *himself*." The young man who'd been a Schuelerite shrugged. "It's that simple and that hard, and I'm not quite there yet."

"Neither am I," Mahklyn confessed.

"I suspect very few people in history, whether here on Safehold or back on Old Terra, have ever matched our Archbishop's personal faith," Wylsynn pointed out.

"A personal faith which, thank God, doesn't prevent him from being one of the most pragmatic men I've ever met," Mahklyn said.

"As long as we're not talking about something which would compromise his own principles, at least," Wylsynn agreed.

"And you feel the same way?" Mahklyn asked quietly.

"And I'm trying very *hard* to feel the same way." Wylsynn quirked a brief smile. "I'm afraid I haven't quite decided where my principles are going to settle now that I've learned the truth. In fact, I'm afraid I'm discovering that I have very few principles—or hesitations, at least—when it comes to considering things to do to those bastards in Zion."

"I can work with that," Mahklyn said with an answering and far colder smile. "Of course, I've been thinking about it for a while longer than you have."

"True, but I have a very personal motivation for seeing every one of them dangling at the end of a rope, just like those butchers in Ferayd."

"By the oddest turn of fate, I believe that's precisely what Their Majesties and Captain Athrawes have in mind, Father."

"In that case, why don't we see what we could do to expedite that moment?" Wylsynn's naturally warm eyes were as cold as the gray ice of Hsing-wu's Passage in winter. "I've been giving some thought to Commander Mahndrayn and Baron Seamount's more recent ideas, and even more to Master Howsmyn's. I don't believe the Baron's notions are going to present any serious problems, but Master Howsmyn's getting close to the Proscriptions' limits. I can probably cover his interest in hydraulics by an extension of my attestation for his accumulators, but his proposed steam engines clearly cross the line into exactly the sort of knowledge Jwo-jeng and Langhorne wanted to make certain we'd never go anywhere near."

"I was afraid you'd say that."

"In my present mood, that's actually a powerful recommendation for building the things tomorrow," Wylsynn said dryly. "Nonetheless, we're obviously going to have problems if we don't prepare the ground carefully. Fortunately, all the years I spent condemning intendants and inquisitors who connived at getting around the Proscriptions in return for the proper considerations gave me all sorts of examples of logic-chopping when I approached my new task, and it occurred to me that if I simply borrowed a page from their book, the steam engine problem might not be so insurmountable as I'd first thought."

"Indeed?" Mahklyn leaned back and raised his eyebrows hopefully.

"Of course not!" Wylsynn assured him. "It's very simple, Doctor! We've used steam and pressure cookers since the Creation in things like food preparation and preservation. There's nothing new or tainted about generating *steam*! Who could possibly object to someone's doing that? And when you come right down to it, producing steam the way Master Howsmyn is proposing is simply a way of generating wind pressure on demand, isn't it? Of course it is! And we've used windmills since the Creation, too. For that matter, wind is one of Jwo-jeng's allowable trinity of wind, water, and muscle! So except for the novel notion of making wind where and how it's most urgently required, I see no barrier under the Proscriptions to the development of Master Howsmyn's new device."

He leaned back in his own chair and smiled broadly at his host.

"Do you?" he asked.

.V.

King's Harbor,
Helen Island;
Navy Powder Mill #3,
Big Tirian Island;
and
Tellesberg Palace,
City of Tellesberg
Kingdom of Old Charis

"Have you got those new fuse notes for Master Howsmyn, Urvyn?"

"Right here, Sir," Urvyn Mahndrayn said patiently, tapping the leather briefcase clasped under his left arm with his right forefinger. "And I also have the improved high-angle gun sketches, and the memoranda High Admiral Rock Point wants me to deliver, and the memo from

Baron Ironhill, *and* your invitation for him to dine with you when he visits Tellesberg next month." He smiled at his superior and raised his eyebrows innocently. "Was there anything else, Sir?"

"You," Sir Ahlfryd Hyndryk, Baron Seamount, said severely, swivel chair squeaking as he leaned back, the better to contemplate the commander, "are an insubordinate young whelp, aren't you?"

"Never, Sir!" Mahndrayn shook his head, expression more innocent than ever. "How could you possibly think such a thing?"

"After working with you for the last couple of years?" Seamount snorted. "Trust me, it's easy."

"I'm shocked to hear you say that, Sir," Mahndrayn said mournfully.

"Disappointed if I didn't, more likely!"

Mahndrayn only grinned, and Seamount chuckled.

Sunlight poured into the baron's office. He had a marvelous view out over King's Harbor from his windows, although some people might have felt just a little uncomfortable knowing that the fortress' main powder magazine was directly underneath them. The slate wall panels were covered with their usual smudgy chalked notations, at least a quarter of which were in Mahndrayn's handwriting, not Seamount's. Stacks of memos and folders of correspondence littered the baron's desk in seeming confusion, although Mahndrayn knew they were actually carefully organized.

"Are you sure my absence isn't going to knock anything off schedule, Sir?" the commander asked more seriously, and Seamount shrugged.

"I realize this may come as another shock to you, Commander, but I'd been looking after myself on my own for quite some time before you happened along. I imagine I'll be able to fumble through somehow until you get back," he said dryly.

Mahndrayn nodded, although he and Seamount both knew he'd been gradually assuming more and more responsibilities as Seamount's assistant and executive officer—what High Admiral Lock Island had called a "chief of staff." And a trip to Ehdwyrd Howsmyn's massive foundry complex wasn't exactly a jaunt to Tellesberg, either; it was well over eight hundred miles, which would take a full five-day each way. That was going to take a serious bite out of Mahndrayn's usual schedule, and a lot of additional work was going to end up dumped back on Seamount's desk while he was away.

"I think we've got everything covered," the baron went on, more serious now. "I won't pretend it's not going to be a pain, and I don't want you away any longer than you have to be, but we've been letting stuff that needs to be handed off to Master Howsmyn pile up too long because both of us were too busy to make the trip. If we're going to meet High Admiral Rock Point's schedule, we can't afford to let that go on. Which means one of us has to go, since no one else is cleared for all of this material, and I just plain can't. Which is why—"

He gestured at the briefcase under Mahndrayn's arm, and the commander nodded again.

"Yes, Sir. I think Master Howsmyn and I can probably cover everything in one day. And I promise I'll get back here as quickly as I can."

"Quickly is good, but the whole point of this trip is to give Master Howsmyn the chance to ask any questions he needs to face-to-face. Don't rush your meeting with him. Better to take an extra day, or even two or three, than for one of us to have to make the same trip again."

"I understand, Sir."

"I'm sure you do. And give your cousin my regards."

"I will, Sir."

"Good. Now go." Seamount pointed at the office door, and Mahndrayn smiled, saluted, and obeyed the command.

▼ ▼ ▼

"Urvyn! This is a surprise," Trai Sahlavahn said as the yeoman ushered his cousin into his office. "I didn't know you were coming!"

"I'm on my way to see Master Howsmyn," Mahndrayn explained, crossing the office to clasp Sahlavahn's offered forearm. "Big Tirian's not very far out of the way, so I thought I'd drop by."

"I see."

Sahlavahn tilted his head to one side, regarding his cousin speculatively. Mahndrayn's intensity and energy frequently fooled people into thinking he was impetuous, or at least impulsive, but Sahlavahn knew better. While he might be prone to rushing off in two or three directions at once, the commander had a remarkable ability to keep everything he was doing organized, balanced, and far more tightly scheduled than anyone else realized. The term "multi-tasking" was one of many which had been lost on Safehold, but if there'd been anyone on the planet it applied to, it would have been Urvyn Mahndrayn. That was something he had in common with Baron Seamount, which was one of the many reasons the two of them complemented one another so well.

But it was also the reason Sahlavahn rather doubted his cousin had "just decided" to drop in on him. True, Big Tirian Island did lie about midway between Helen Island and Port Ithmyn, but Mahndrayn wasn't the sort to take time off for personal visits when he was on official business. Besides, he and Sahlavahn exchanged letters on a regular basis, so it wasn't as if they had a lot of private family matters to catch up on.

"Are you going to be here overnight?" he asked, leading the way to the windows overlooking Eydyth Sound, the channel between Big Tirian and the mainland portion of the Duchy of Tirian.

Although Sahlavahn's command—officially, Navy Powder Mill #3, but more generally known as the Hairatha Mill—was officially part of the port city of Hairatha, it was actually located over a mile north of the main port. For fairly obvious reasons, really, given the nature of what it produced and the quantities in which it produced it. At any given moment, there was a minimum of several hundred tons of gunpowder in the Hairatha

Mill's storage magazines, and no one wanted those magazines too close to a major city. Then there was the minor fact that Hairatha was one of the Navy's main bases and dockyards. Losing that would have been just a trifle inconvenient, as well, he supposed.

"Probably not overnight," Mahndrayn said, following him to the window and gazing across the twenty-six-mile-wide sound at the green blur of the mainland. "I've got a lot to discuss with Master Howsmyn, and Baron Seamount needs me back at King's Harbor as quickly as I can get there."

"I see," Sahlavahn said again, and turned to face him. "So why do I have the feeling you didn't come four or five hours out of your way just for a family visit with one of your favorite cousins?"

"Because I didn't," Mahndrayn half sighed.

"Then why did you come? Really?" Sahlavahn raised an eyebrow, and Mahndrayn shrugged.

"Because I came across a discrepancy I hope is just a clerical error," he said.

"You *hope* it's a clerical error?"

"Well, if it's not, then I think we may have a fairly significant problem."

"You're beginning to make me nervous, Urvyn," Sahlavahn said frankly, and Mahndrayn shrugged again. Then he set his briefcase on the window ledge in front of him, opened it, extracted a sheet of paper, and handed it across.

Sahlavahn accepted the sheet, tipped it slightly to catch the better light from the window, and squinted nearsightedly as he looked at it. Then he raised his eyes to his cousin's face with a perplexed expression.

"This is what you came to see me about?" He waved it gently. "Last month's production return and shipping summary?"

"Yes," Mahndrayn said flatly, and Sahlavahn frowned.

"I don't understand, Urvyn. What about it?"

"It's wrong."

"Wrong?" Sahlavahn's frown deepened. "What are you talking about? What's wrong with it?"

"There's a discrepancy, Trai," Mahndrayn said. "A forty-five-*ton* discrepancy."

"*What?*" Sahlavahn's frown disappeared and his eyes widened abruptly.

"The amount you shipped doesn't match the amount you delivered. Look at the numbers for the June fifteenth shipment." Mahndrayn tapped the top of the sheet. "You loaded one thousand and seventy-five tons of powder in a total of six shipments, but when the individual quantities of each shipment are totaled, they only come to one thousand and *thirty* tons." He tapped the foot of the sheet. "There's forty-five tons missing, Trai."

"That's ridiculous!" Sahlavahn said.

"That's what I thought, too," Mahndrayn replied. "So I checked the numbers three times, and they came out the same way each time." He shrugged and smiled crookedly. "You know how I am. I couldn't get my brain to turn loose of it, so I pulled the detail sheets and went over the numbers in each shipment's individual consignments one by one. And I found the problem right here, I think." He leaned over the sheet and found the specific entry he wanted. "Right here. Somebody dropped a decimal point. I think this was supposed to be a fifty-ton consignment, but it's listed as only *five* tons."

"So somebody just made a mistake, is what you're saying?"

"Like I said, I hope it's just a clerical error. But this shipment was supposed to come to King's Harbor, Trai. So I went and checked . . . and five tons is exactly what we received. So either you have an extra forty-five tons of gunpowder still in inventory here at Hairatha, or else we have forty-five tons of unaccounted for gunpowder floating around somewhere."

"Langhorne!" Sahlavahn looked at his cousin, face pale. "I hope to God you're right about its being a clerical error! Give me just a second."

He crossed to his desk, sat, and pulled a pair of thick ledger books from one of its drawers. He picked up the reading glasses from the corner of his blotter, perched them on the tip of his nose, and consulted the sheet of paper Mahndrayn had handed him. Then he set aside the topmost ledger book, opened the bottom one, and ran his finger down one of the neatly tabulated columns.

"According to the manifest, your 'missing' gunpowder came out of Magazine Six," he said, looking up over the tops of his glasses. His color was a little better, but his expression remained drawn. "Assuming it's a clerical error and the additional forty-five tons was never loaded, that's where it should still be. I assume Baron Seamount would like me to go see whether or not it's still there?"

He managed a wan smile, and Mahndrayn chuckled.

"Actually, I haven't discussed it with the Baron yet," he said. "To be honest, I'm almost certain it really is a simple error—we'd certainly only requested five tons, not *fifty!*—but I figured this was the sort of thing I should make sure about. And since I was going to be headed up this way, it seemed simplest to discuss it with you personally. Assuming it *is* an error, you're the one in the best position to straighten it out. And on the off chance that it *isn't* an error, that somebody's playing clever-buggers with our powder shipments, the less attention we draw to it until we've figured out what's going on, the better."

"Langhorne, Urvyn—you didn't even *mention* this to Baron Seamount?" Sahlavahn took off his glasses and shook his head at his cousin. "If someone's 'playing clever-buggers' with something like this, we need to get him and Baron Wave Thunder informed as quickly as possible! That's a *lot* of gunpowder!"

"I know. I just wanted to make sure it really was missing before I started running around screaming," Mahndrayn said. "I mean, clerical error's far and away the most likely answer, and I didn't want the Baron—*either* of the Barons, now that I think about it—to think I was getting hysterical over nothing."

"Well, I suppose I can understand that."

Sahlavahn closed the ledger and stood, resting one hand on its cover for a moment while he frowned down at it, his eyes anxious. His face remained pale and drawn, and he seemed to be thinking hard, Mahndrayn noticed, and it was hard to blame him. As he'd said, forty-five tons *was* a lot of gunpowder—enough for almost ten thousand full-charge shots from a long thirty-pounder—and the notion that he might have lost track of that much explosives had to be a sobering reflection. Then the captain drew a deep breath and crossed the office to take his swordbelt from the wall rack. He buckled it and settled it methodically into place, took down his hat from the same rack, and turned to his cousin.

"Come on. The simplest way to see whether it's there or not is to go take a look. Care for a walk?"

▼ ▼ ▼

"Stop," Captain Sahlavahn said as he and Mahndrayn reached a heavily timbered, locked door set into a grassy hillside.

A small, green-painted storage shed stood beside the door, and the captain opened its door.

"Here." He took a pair of felt slippers from a pigeon-holed shelf with two dozen compartments and handed them across. "These should fit, if I remember your boot size. Speaking of which—boots, I mean—they get left here."

He pointed into the shed, and Mahndrayn nodded. Both of them removed their Navy boots, setting them under the shelving, then pulled on the slippers. Despite every precaution, the possibility of loose grains of powder on the magazine floor was very real, and a spark from an iron shoe nail or even the friction between a leather sole and the floor could have unpleasant consequences.

Sahlavahn waited until Mahndrayn had his slippers on, then unlocked the magazine door.

"Follow me," he said, and led the way into a brick-walled passageway.

There was another heavy, locked door at its end, and a lighter door set into the passageway's side. Sahlavahn opened the unlocked door into a long, narrow room. Its right wall, the one paralleling the surface of the hillside into which the magazine had been built, was solid brick, but its left wall was a series of barred glass windows, and a half-dozen large lanterns hung from hooks in its ceiling. Sahlavahn drew one of the new Shan-wei's candles from his pocket, struck it on the brick wall, and lit two of the lanterns from its sputtering, hissing flame.

"That should be enough for now," he said. He waved out the Shan-wei's candle, moistened his fingertips and pinched them together on the spent stem to be sure it was fully extinguished, then stepped back out into the passageway and closed the side door behind him.

He made sure it was securely shut before he unlocked the inner door, and Mahndrayn heartily approved of his caution. The last thing anyone wanted inside a powder magazine was a live flame, which was the reason for the lantern room; the light spilling through its carefully sealed windows would provide them with illumination without actually carrying a lamp into the magazine itself. At the same time, the possibility of powder dust drifting out of the opened magazine and into the lantern room was something to be avoided. It was far less likely to happen now than it would have been just three or four years ago, of course. The new grained powder didn't separate into its constituent ingredients the way the old-fashioned meal powder had, which meant it didn't produce the explosive fog powder shipments had all too often trailed behind them. But as someone who worked regularly with explosives, Mahndrayn was in favor of taking every possible precaution where this much gunpowder was concerned.

Sahlavahn opened the inner door—this one fitted with felted gaskets—and the two of them entered the magazine proper. Barrels of powder were stacked neatly, separated by convenient avenues to facilitate handling them with all the caution they deserved. It was cool and dry, just the way it was supposed to be, and Mahndrayn stood for a moment, allowing his eyes to adjust fully to the relatively dim illumination coming from the lantern room.

"It looks pretty nearly full," he said. "How are we going to tell if—?"

His voice cut off abruptly as the point of his cousin's sword drove into the back of his neck, severing his spinal cord and killing him almost instantly.

▼ ▼ ▼

"Captain Sahlavahn!" the shift supervisor said in surprise. "I didn't expect you this afternoon, Sir!"

"I know." The captain looked a little distracted— possibly even a little pale—the supervisor thought, but he spoke with his usual courtesy. "I just thought I'd drop by." The supervisor's expression must have given him away, because Sahlavahn shook his head with a chuckle which might have sounded just a bit forced if someone had been listening for it. "Not because I think anything's wrong! I just like to look things over once in a while."

"Of course, Sir. Let me—oh, I see you already have slippers."

"Yes." Sahlavahn looked down at the felt slippers on his feet. They were a little dirty and tattered-looking, the supervisor thought. "I thought it would be simpler to leave my boots in my office, since I had these lying around in one of my desk drawers," the captain explained, and the supervisor nodded.

"Of course, Sir. Do you want an escort?"

"I believe I'm adequately familiar with the facility," Sahlavahn said dryly.

"Of course! I didn't mean—"

"Don't worry about it, Lieutenant." Sahlavahn patted him lightly on the arm. "I didn't think you did."

"Yes, Sir."

The supervisor stood respectfully to escort Sahlavahn out of his office. He accompanied the captain into the anteroom and waited until Sahlavahn had left, then turned to one of his clerks. Like everyone who worked in the powder mill proper, the clerk was already in slippers, and the supervisor twitched his head after the vanished captain.

"Quick, Pahrkyr! Nip around the side and warn Lieutenant Mahrstahn Captain Sahlavahn's on his way!"

"Yes, Sir!"

The clerk dashed out of the anteroom, and the supervisor returned to his own office wondering what bee had gotten into the Old Man's bonnet. It wasn't like the perpetually efficient, always well-organized Captain Sahlavahn to just drop by this way.

The supervisor was just settling into his chair once again when he, his clerks, Captain Sahlavahn, and the one hundred and three other men currently working in Powder Mill #3 all died in a monstrous blast of fire and fury. A chain of explosions rolled through the powder mill like Langhorne's own Rakurai, rattling every window in Hairatha. Debris vomited into the sky, much of it on fire, trailing smoke in obscenely graceful arcs as it soared outward, then came crashing down in fresh fire and ruin. It shattered barracks and administrative buildings like an artillery bombardment, setting more fires, maiming and killing. Voices screamed and stunned men wheeled towards the disaster in disbelief. Then alarm bells began a frenzied clangor and the men who'd frozen in shock ran frantically into the fire and chaos and the devastation looking for lives to save.

Eleven minutes later magazines Six, Seven, and Eight exploded, as well.

▼ ▼ ▼

"It's not looking any better, is it?" Cayleb Ahrmahk's voice was flat and hard, and Prince Nahrmahn shook his head.

The two of them sat in a private sitting room located off the room which had been Cayleb's grandfather's library. That library—added to generously by King Haarahld—had long since outgrown the chamber and been moved to larger quarters, and Cayleb had had the old library converted into a working office near the imperial suite. Now he and Nahrmahn sat looking out the windows which faced north, out across the waterfront and the blue expanse of Howell Bay in the general direction of Big Tirian Island. They didn't actually see the bay, however. Big Tirian was almost six hundred miles from where they sat, but both of them were gazing at the imagery relayed from Owl's SNARCs.

"I don't think it *is* going to look any better," Nahrmahn said quietly, looking at the shattered, smoking hole and the demolished buildings around it which had been one of the Empire's largest and most important powder mills, and shook his head sadly. "I think all we can do is bury the dead and rebuild from scratch."

"I know." It was obvious the financial cost of rebuilding was the least of Cayleb's concerns at this moment. "I just—" He shook his own head, the movement choppier and angrier than Nahrmahn's headshake had been. "We've been so lucky about avoiding this kind of accident. I just can't believe we've let something like this happen."

"We didn't," Nahrmahn said, and Cayleb looked at him sharply as he heard the iron in the Emeraldian prince's voice.

"What do you mean?" the emperor asked sharply.

"I mean this didn't just 'happen,' Your Majesty. And it wasn't an accident, either." Nahrmahn met his gaze, his normally mild brown eyes hard. "It was deliberate. An act of sabotage."

"You're not serious!"

"Indeed I am, Your Majesty." Nahrmahn's voice was grim. "We may never be able to *prove* it, but I'm positive in my own mind."

Cayleb pushed back in his armchair and regarded his imperial councilor for intelligence narrowly. No one else in Tellesberg, aside from the other members of the 'inner circle,' knew anything about the disaster at Hairatha, and no one would until sometime the next day. That rather restricted the number of people with whom they could discuss it, but Maikel Staynair, his younger brother, Ehdwyrd Howsmyn, and Bynzhamyn Raice were all listening in over their coms.

"Bynzhamyn?" the emperor said now.

"I'm not certain, Your Majesty," Baron Wave Thunder replied. "I think I see what Prince Nahrmahn is getting at, though."

"Which is?" Cayleb prompted.

"It's the delay in the magazine explosions, isn't it, Your Highness?" Wave Thunder said by way of reply.

"That's exactly what I'm thinking about," Nahrmahn agreed grimly. He looked at Cayleb. "Nobody, not even Owl, was watching when this happened. Perhaps that's an oversight we'd like to rectify in the future, although I realize we're already taxing even his capabilities with the number of SNARCs we've got deployed. Because we weren't watching, we'll never be able to reconstruct the events leading up to it—not accurately, and not anything like completely. But there was a significant delay between the main explosion in the powder mill itself and the explosions in the magazines. I'm no expert on the way powder's handled and stored in the mills or what their standard safety measures may be, but I'd be surprised if it was easy for an explosion in one magazine to touch off an explosion in another one. And if that's true, it should certainly have been difficult for an explosion in the *mill* to cause *any* of the magazines to explode, far less *three* of them. Yet that's exactly what happened, and it didn't happen *simultaneously,* which is what I would have expected if it had been a sympathetic detonation. And all of that suggests to me that the explosions were deliberately arranged with some sort of timer."

"Owl?"

"Yes, Your Majesty?" the distant AI said politely.

"I know you weren't watching Big Tirian or Hairatha, but did any of your SNARCs pick up the explosions, and if so, how close together did they come?"

"In answer to your first question, Your Majesty, yes, the com relay above The Cauldron did detect the explosions. In answer to your second question, the powder production facility itself was destroyed by seven distinct explosions occurring over a period of approximately eleven seconds. Each magazine was destroyed by a single primary explosion followed by a chain of secondary detonations. The first magazine was destroyed approximately eleven minutes and seventeen seconds after the first detonation in the powder production facility. The second magazine was destroyed thirty-seven seconds after that. The third was destroyed three minutes and nine seconds after the second one."

Cayleb and Nahrmahn looked at one another and Domynyk Staynair swore softly over the com.

"I think Nahrmahn's right, Your Majesty," Howsmyn said quietly. "It had to be some kind of timing mechanism, at least in the magazines. I don't know what *kind* of timer—it could have been something as simple as a lit candle shoved into a powder cask and allowed to burn down—but I think that's the only explanation for how they could have come that long after the main explosion but still have been sequenced that closely."

"Damn." Cayleb shoved up out of his chair and crossed to the window, folding his arms across his chest while he stared out towards the invisible island and the pall of smoke still hanging above it. "How did they get in?"

"We'll probably never know, Your Majesty," Nahrmahn told him heavily. "Obviously, our security measures weren't stringent enough after all, though."

"I don't see how we could make them much tighter, Your Highness," Wave Thunder objected. "We've always recognized the powder mills would be a priority target for any Temple Loyalist intent on seriously damaging us. We've got round-the-clock Marine sentries on the gates and every building, and the magazines themselves are kept locked except when powder's actually being transferred. Keys to the locks are held only by the mill's commanding officer and the current officer of the watch. When powder transfers are ordered, they're always overseen by a commissioned officer with a Marine security and safety detachment, and additional keys have to be signed out individually by that officer, who's also responsible for their return. And when *any* of the magazines are opened for transfers, we have sentries on all the *other* magazines, as well. Beyond that, nobody's allowed into the facility unless he actually *works* there or has clear, verified authorization for his visit. Any visitor's accompanied at all times by someone assigned to the mill, and regular and random patrols sweep the perimeter fence."

"My comment wasn't a criticism, Bynzhamyn," Nahrmahn said, "simply an observation. Whether we can make them tighter or not, they obviously weren't sufficiently tight to prevent what just happened. I do think it would be a good idea to assign at least a couple of remotes to each of our remaining powder mills, though. We might not've been able to do anything quickly enough to prevent what happened at Hairatha even if Owl had been watching and realized something was amiss before the explosions, but at least we'd be in a much better position after the fact to figure out what actually did happen and who was responsible for it. And that might put us in a better position to keep it from happening again."

"You think it's part of an organized operation?" Cayleb asked. "That they may attempt to blow up our other powder mills, as well?"

"I don't know." Nahrmahn shook his head, eyes intent as he considered the question. "All it would really take would be one truly convinced Temple Loyalist in the wrong place. For all we know, that's what happened here—the fact that some sort of timer was used may indicate we're looking at the work of a single individual or a small number of individuals. Or it may not indicate anything of the sort; perhaps it was a larger group that used timers for all four of the primary explosions so its members could get out again. If it was a larger group, that would seem to up the chances of additional, similar attempts. We just don't know. But I don't see where keeping a closer eye on the remaining mills could hurt anything, and it might just help quite a lot."

"Agreed." Cayleb nodded. "Owl, please implement Prince Nahrmahn's suggestion and assign sufficient remotes to keep all of our remaining powder mills under observation."

"Yes, Your Majesty."

"Thank you," Cayleb said, and Howsmyn sighed heavily over the link.

"What is it, Ehdwyrd?"

"I was just thinking that, terrible as this is from every perspective, it gets even worse when I think about Urvyn's having walked into the middle of it, Your Majesty," the ironmaster said heavily. "It's going to devastate Ahlfryd when he finds out. For that matter, it's hitting *me* damned hard. But that's from a purely personal, selfish viewpoint. We *needed* him, needed him pushing the envelope and constantly coming up with new ideas, like that breech-loading rifle of his."

"I know," Cayleb sighed. "I know." He shook his head. "And speaking of personal viewpoints, think about his family. They didn't lose just him, but his cousin, too." He shook his head again, his expression hard. "I want the people responsible for planning this. I want them badly."

"Then we'll just have to see what we can do about finding them for you, Your Majesty," Prince Nahrmahn said.

. III .

Shakym,
Princedom of Tanshar

"All right, you lazy bastards! On your feet! Your little pleasure cruise just came to an end!"

Sir Gwylym Manthyr's head twitched up at the raucous chorus of shouts. He could see virtually nothing in the hot, stinking tween-decks space, but he heard the thud of hammers as the wedges which secured the hatch battens were driven out. Boots clumped and thumped on the deck overhead, other voices bawled orders, and heavy chain rattled metallically in the darkness around him.

I guess I really can sleep just about anywhere, he thought. *Must be Shakym. About time, even for this tub.*

He knew very little about Shakym beyond the name; only that it was the major seaport of the Princedom of

Tanshar and that it lay across the four-hundred-and-fifty-mile-wide mouth of the Gulf of Tanshar from Gairlahs in the Duchy of Fern, the most northwesterly of Dohlar's provinces. If this was Shakym, they were officially in West Haven, little more than five hundred miles from the Temple Lands border and fourteen hundred miles from Lake Pei.

"Sir?" The voice was faint, barely audible, and his right hand gently stroked the matted hair of the head lying in his lap.

"It seems we're here, Master Svairsmahn." He kept his own voice as close to normal as he could, but it was hard when the boy's bony hand reached up and gripped his wrist. "I imagine we're going to have some light in a few minutes."

"Can't come too soon for me, Sir," the midshipman said gamely. He grunted with effort, shoving himself up into a sitting position, and Manthyr heard a retching sound. It went on for several seconds before it stopped.

"Sorry about that, Sir," Svairsmahn said.

"You're not the only one who's fouled himself down here, Master Svairsmahn," Manthyr told him. "Not your fault, either. Chain a man where he can't move and leave him there long enough, and it's going to happen."

"True enough, Sir Gwylym," Captain Maikel Krugair's voice came out of the dark. "And just think how much fun these bastards are going to have washing down all this shit—if you'll pardon the expression, Sir—once we're out of here."

The man who'd captained HMS *Avalanche* sounded positively cheerful at the thought, and Manthyr heard other laughter from men he couldn't see.

"There is that bit in the *Writ* about reaping what you sow, Cap'n," someone else observed. "An' shit fer shitheads is about right, t' my way of thinking."

There was more laughter, and then the first batten was thrown aside and bright morning sunlight streamed down into the cavernous, stinking hold.

"Hold your noise, you fucking scum!" someone shouted. "Keep shut, if you know what's good for you!"

"Why?" a Charisian voice shot back derisively. "What're you going to do? Tell the Grand Inquisitor on us?!"

Laughter hooted in the stinking hold, and Manthyr's heart swelled with weeping pride in his men.

"Think it's funny, do you?" the voice which had shouted snarled. "We'll see how you like it in a month or so!"

Manthyr looked around him, squinting his eyes against the light as more battens were heaved aside. Naiklos Vahlain lay beside him, blinking groggily. Manthyr didn't like the valet's sunken cheeks and hollow eyes. Vahlain was ten years older than he was, and he'd started without the inherent toughness a life at sea had given Manthyr. No man in the world could have more courage and spirit, but Vahlain's body was beginning to fail him.

Beyond Vahlain, as the light explored their fetid prison, he saw other scarecrows, many of them lying in pools of their own filth. Dysentery was stalking among them, taking its own toll, and his heart was grimly certain that at least some of those still lying motionless would never move again.

When he thought about it, it was almost a miracle so many of them were still alive. The six five-days since they'd left Gorath had been the most brutal and crushing of Manthyr's life, and that was saying something for a Charisian seaman. But, then, whatever men might say, the sea was never truly cruel. She simply didn't care. It took *men* to practice cruelty. Men who deliberately and knowingly gave themselves to cruelty's service, and it didn't matter whether they claimed to do it in the name of God or the name of Shan-wei herself. What mattered was the sickness and the hunger and the perversion eating away whatever it was inside them that might once have made them truly human.

Things had gotten a little better after Twyngyth. Manthyr didn't really know why, although he'd come to the conclusion they probably owed at least some of it to

Father Myrtan. The fair-haired young upper-priest seemed no less fervent in his faith than Vyktyr Tahrlsahn, and Manthyr doubted Father Myrtan would hesitate to put any heretic to the Question or to the Punishment. The difference between him and Tahrlsahn was that Tahrlsahn would *enjoy* it; Father Myrtan would simply *do* it because that was what his beliefs required of him. Manthyr couldn't decide which of those was actually worse, when he came down to it, but at least Father Myrtan didn't delight in the sort of small souled brutality which had killed almost a dozen of Manthyr's men in the first five-day and a half of this nightmare journey.

Oh, stop trying to analyze things, Gwylym, he told himself. *You know perfectly well what it really was. Even that asshole Tahrlsahn finally realized none of you were going to live the rest of the way to Zion if he kept it up. Pity he figured it out. It would've been* so *fitting for him to have to face Clyntahn and explain how he'd come to use up all of the Grand Asshole's "heretics" before he got home with them! Hell, he'd probably have gotten to take our place!*

He let himself dwell for a moment or two on the delightful image of Tahrlsahn facing his own Inquisition, then brushed it aside. Whether Tahrlsahn faced justice in this life or the next really didn't matter. Face it he would, one way or the other, and for now, duty called, and duty—and fidelity—to his men were really all he had left.

"Wakey, wakey, Naiklos!" he called as cheerily as he could, shaking the valet gently. "They say our cruise is over. Back on the road again, I suppose."

"Yes, Sir." Vahlain shook himself, struggling gamely up into a sitting position and fastidiously straightening the remaining rags of his clothing. "I'll see to making reservations at a decent hotel, Sir."

"You do that," Manthyr said affectionately, resting one hand on the older man's slight shoulder. "Nothing but the best, mind you! Clean linen and warming pans for me and Master Svairsmhan. And be sure you pick the wine; can't trust *my* judgment about that, you know."

"Of course, Sir." Vahlain managed a death's-head smile, and Manthyr squeezed his shoulder before he turned back to Svairsmahn.

The midshipman smiled, too, but it looked even more ghastly on him. Vahlain was over sixty; Lainsair Svairsmahn was not yet thirteen, and thirteen-year-old boys—even thirteen-year-old boys who were king's officers—weren't supposed to be one-legged, hollow-cheeked and sunken-eyed, half-starved, wracked by fever and nausea, and filled with the knowledge of what awaited all of them.

Three Temple Guardsmen clattered down the steep ladder from the upper deck. Manthyr was pretty sure they'd been chosen for their duty as punishment for some lapse in duty, and he heard them gagging on the stench despite the bandannas tied across their noses and mouths. Three days locked in the hold of an undersized coasting brig tended to produce quite an aroma, he thought grimly.

"On your feet!" one of them snarled. "You, there!" He kicked one of the seamen lying closest to the hatch. "You first!"

He tossed the seaman a key, then stood back, tapping the two-foot truncheon in his right hand against the side of his boot while the Charisian fumbled with the padlock. He managed to get it open, and iron grated and rattled as the chain which had been run through ring-bolts on the deck and then through the irons on every man's ankles was released. He pushed himself clumsily to his still-chained feet and staggered towards the ladder.

"Get a move on, whoreson!" the Guardsman sneered, prodding him viciously with the truncheon. "Can't be late for your date in Zion!"

The Charisian almost fell, but he caught himself on the ladder with his manacled hands and climbed slowly and painfully up it while the cursing Guardsmen kicked and cuffed and beat his fellows to their feet. They made no distinction between officer, noncom, and enlisted, and neither did the Charisians, anymore. Those distinctions had been erased in the face of their common privation, and all that remained were *Charisians*, doing whatever they could to help their companions survive another day.

Which is stupid of us, Manthyr thought as he forced himself to his feet and then bent to half assist and half lift young Svairsmahn. *All we're doing is prolonging our own punishment until we get to Zion. If we had any sense, we'd figure out how to hang ourselves tonight.*

That dark thought had come to him with increasing frequency, and he braced himself against its seduction while he slipped his arm around Svairsmahn's shoulders and helped him towards the ladder. However tempting it might be, it wasn't for him—not while a single one of his men lived. There might not be one damned thing he could do for any of them, but one thing he *couldn't* do was to abandon them. And they, the miserable, starving, sick, gutsy bastards that they were, would never give the Inquisition the satisfaction of giving up.

AUGUST, YEAR OF GOD 895

·✦·

. I .

Royal Palace,
City of Talkyra,
Kingdom of Delferahk

"I could wish they'd just go ahead and get all of this set-tled," King Zhames II grumbled across the dinner table.

The king's kingdom, despite its respectable size, was not one of the great realms of Safehold. In fact, it was on the penurious side, which was one reason his own father had arranged his marriage to one of Hektor of Cori-sande's cousins. King Styvyn had had hopes that the rela-tively wealthy island princedom would see its way to making investments in his longed-for project to turn the port city of Ferayd into the kernel for a Delferahkan mer-chant marine which, in alliance with that of Corisande, might actually have been capable of challenging Charis' maritime dominance. Alas, it had never been any more than a hope—a dream, really—although Prince Fronz and, later, Hektor had been relatively generous in loans over the years. Not that Zhames had entertained any illu-sions that it had been out of the goodness of Hektor's heart, whatever might have motivated his father. Hektor of Corisande had always invested his marks wisely, and it had been Zhames Olyvyr Rayno's distant kinship to an up-and-coming bishop of the Order of Schueler which had been the true reason for Hektor's generosity.

Not that Wyllym Rayno had ever done a damned thing for Delferahk, Zhames reflected grumpily. He'd been willing enough to use Zhames as a go-between to Hektor once or twice, and he'd helped arrange the remittance of the interest on a couple of the king's more pressing loans from the Temple, but that was about it. And now there was *this* mess.

"Sooner or later it will all blow over, I'm sure, dear," Queen Consort Hailyn said serenely from her own side of the table. The two of them dined alone together more often than not, less for any deep romantic reasons than because state dinners were expensive. At the moment, their three grown sons were elsewhere, no doubt entertaining themselves in some fashion of which a dutiful mother would not have approved. The queen consort had grown increasingly accustomed to that over the years. In fact, she'd grown accustomed to a great many things and taken most of them placidly in stride.

"Ha!" Zhames shook his head. Then, for added emphasis, he shook his finger across the table, as well. "Ha! You mark my words, Hailyn, this is going to get still worse before it gets better! And we're already stuck in the middle of it, no thanks to dear, distant Cousin Wyllym!"

"Hush."

Few things could disturb Queen Hailyn's even-tempered world, but her husband's occasional criticisms of Mother Church—and especially of the Inquisition—were among them. She looked around the dining room, then relaxed as she realized there'd been no servants to hear the injudicious remark.

"Saying things like that isn't going to help, dear," she said much more severely than she normally spoke to her royal spouse. "And I really wish you'd be a little more sparing with them. Especially"—she looked straight across the table—"these days."

Zhames grimaced, but he didn't protest, which was itself a sign of the times. Despite the distant nature of his relationship to the Archbishop of Chiang-wu, he'd never cherished many illusions about the inner workings of the vicarate. There'd been times when he'd been hard put to visualize exactly how those workings could serve the interests of God, but he'd been wise enough to keep his nose out of matters that were none of his affair.

Until, of course, his wife's cousin dumped his two surviving children into Zhames' lap and simultaneously dumped the king into the Temple's business right up to his royal neck.

It had seemed like a situation with no downside when Hektor first requested asylum for his daughter and younger son. The request had come with promises of a very attractive subsidy in return for the king's hospitality. And given the fact that Hektor had become the Temple's anointed paladin in its struggle against the Charisian heretics, it had offered Zhames an opportunity to cement his relations with that dratted distant kinsman of his, as well. It wasn't likely to make his relationship with Charis any worse, either, given that business in Ferayd. And in a worst-case situation (from Hektor's perspective, that was) it would give Zhames physical control of the rightful ruler of Corisande. Best of all, he'd had absolutely no responsibility for getting the royal refugees to Talkyra; all he'd had to do was offer them reasonable quarters (or as close to it as the old-fashioned fortress of his "palace" permitted) if they succeeded in getting there.

Then Hektor managed to lose his war against Charis. *And* to get himself assassinated.

Suddenly Zhames found himself in the middle of what looked like turning into a nasty situation. On the one hand, he was forced to recognize—or at least deal with—Prince Daivyn's Regency Council in Corisande despite the fact that it had signed a peace treaty with Cayleb and Sharleyan of Charis and sworn to abide by its terms. Vicar Zahmsyn, speaking as Chancellor Trynair, had made Mother Church's position on the legitimacy of that council abundantly clear, but at least he'd recognized certain pragmatic constraints on Zhames' position and stopped short of threatening the king for his "dealings" with the proscribed council. On the other hand, Vicar Zhaspahr, speaking as Grand Inquisitor Clyntahn, had made it equally abundantly clear Zhames dared not give any formal recognition to the Regency Council, which forced him to squirm through all sorts of convoluted hoops just figuring out how to phrase his correspondence with it. Yet, simultaneously, both Vicar Zahmsyn and Vicar Zhaspahr had informed him, speaking as Knights of the Temple Lands, that they very much desired for him to retain physical custody of young Daivyn for the fore-seeable future.

Zhames often found himself wondering exactly why that was. Surely the boy would be safer in the Temple's direct custody in Zion, where no Charisian assassin could get at him! And if the Temple intended someday to restore him to his father's throne, then wouldn't it have made more sense to see to it that he was trained up from child-hood in a spirit of proper respect for (and obedience to) Mother Church in Mother Church's own imperial city?

The contemplation of those questions had led him to certain unhappy conclusions. Indeed, to conclusions un-happy enough that he hadn't shared them even with his wife.

"I'm just saying," he said now, "that we're in a sticky situation and this squabbling and bloodshed isn't going to make it any better. Langhorne only knows how the Charisians are going to react when those prisoners Rahn-yld captured get to Zion, but it's not going to be pretty. We've had our own demonstration of that, haven't we?"

His wife frowned the way she always did whenever someone alluded to the "Ferayd Massacre." She'd never been happy about the part Delferahkan troops had played in the original incident, and despite what she'd said a moment ago, she'd had some tart words of her own for the Inquisition following the murders. The Em-pire of Charis' reprisal against the city hadn't made her one bit happier, although she recognized that the Chari-sians had actually been rather restrained in their re-sponse, however it had been reported by the Inquisition.

"We're lucky they've been too busy elsewhere to go on raiding our coasts," Zhames continued, "but that can al-ways change, especially now that they've settled things with Tarot. Everything they had committed to blockading Gorjah is available for other enterprises now, you know. And leaving that completely aside, the more settled things get in Corisande, the more . . . awkward they're likely to get for us here in Talkyra."

It was the closest he'd yet come to broaching his suspicions about who'd really murdered Prince Hektor and his older son. From the flicker in Hailyn's eyes she might have been entertaining a few of those same suspicions herself.

"This 'Regency Council' of young Daivyn's is starting to sound far too conciliatory where Charis is concerned for my peace of mind," he continued, deliberately steering the conversation to one side. "I'm not sure how much longer Vicar Zahmsyn's going to go on allowing me to correspond with them, and what do we do about Daivyn then?" He shook his head. "The most likely outcome I can see is for the Temple to take him into its direct custody."

Hailyn's eyes widened and one hand rose to the base of her throat.

"Whatever else Daivyn and Irys may be, they're my cousins," she said, "and prince or not, Daivyn's only a little boy, Zhames! He only turns eleven next five-day, and Irys isn't even nineteen yet! They need family, especially after all they've already been through!"

"I know," Zhames said more gently, "and I'm fond of them myself. But if the vicarate"—he saw her grimace slightly, proof both of them knew he was actually speaking about the Group of Four—"decide we've gotten too cozy with the Regency Council, and if they decide the Regency Council's gotten too cozy with *Charis*, that's exactly what they're likely to do. And in the meantime, they're more or less ordering me to go *on* corresponding with the Regency Council! And they're insisting on receiving true copies of every document from the Regency Council to me or to Coris. So if anyone in Manchyr commits anything . . . indiscreet to writing, *that's* likely to come home to roost here in Talkyra, as well!"

"Surely they realize that as well as you do, dear."

"Is 'they' the Regency Council, Coris, or the vicarate?" Zhames inquired just a bit caustically, and her brief, unhappy smile acknowledged his point.

"Well, I suppose all we can do is the best we can do," he continued. "I'd prefer not to've made an enemy out of Charis in the first place, but since it's a little late to do anything about that, I think we'll just concentrate on keeping our heads down and staying out of their line of fire. As far as Daivyn and Irys are concerned, we're just going to have to go on playing it by ear, Hailyn. I don't say I like it, and I don't say I'll be happy if the decision is made to take them out of our custody, but it's not as if we'll have a lot of choice if that happens."

And, he added silently as his wife nodded unhappily, *as much as I don't wish them any ill fortune, it would still be a vast relief to see them somewhere else.*

Somewhere where no one could possibly blame me *for whatever happens to them.*

▼ ▼ ▼

"So what do we do with *this* one?" Sir Klymynt Halahdrom asked dourly.

"I presume we go ahead and deliver it to the boy," Fahstair Lairmahn, Baron of Lakeland and first councilor of the Kingdom of Delferahk, replied. "Why? Does it contain anything dangerous?"

"Nothing except six of the biggest, nastiest-looking wyverns I've seen in a while," Halahdrom replied. "I went through it pretty carefully, you can be sure, but I didn't see anything else out of the ordinary about it."

As the palace's chief chamberlain, he'd seen his share of bizarre royal gifts over the years, and he'd seldom paid much attention to them, if the truth be told. That was no longer true, however, and he'd looked this one over closely.

"Wyverns?" Lakeland repeated, eyebrows arching. "All the way from Corisande?"

"All the way from Corisande," Halahdrom confirmed. "According to the cover note, they're a gift from Earl

Anvil Rock for the boy's birthday. Apparently he was just starting to fly his own wyverns for small game before his father packed him off to us." The chamberlain chuckled. "Be a few years before he's ready to fly any of *these*, though! The damned things are big enough to pick *him* up and fly away."

Lakeland shook his head with a bemused smile. Worrying about the gifts someone might send a boy for his eleventh birthday wasn't something which concerned most first councilors. Of course, most first councilors weren't in Lakeland's position. Bishop Executor Dynzail Vahsphar had made it abundantly clear that he was to be kept fully informed about *anything* which was delivered to Prince Daivyn or any other member of his household. Bishop Mytchail Zhessop, Vahsphar's intendant, had made it equally clear he intended to hold Lakeland personally responsible for the completeness of those reports.

The whole thing struck the baron as excessive, to say the least. Anybody who tried to poison the boy, for example, was unlikely to do it by sending him sweetmeats from Corisande, and that was the *most* likely threat he could imagine. Well, the most likely threat from anything anyone might openly send him, at any rate, Lakeland amended a bit more grimly.

Still, Halahdrom might have a point about this particular gift. It seemed evident the boy had to take after his mother, since by all reports Hektor of Corisande had been a tall, powerfully built fellow, and Prince Daivyn was never going to be a large man. Three days short of his eleventh birthday, he was a small, slender boy. Not *delicate*, just small, with a wiry knit frame that seemed unlikely to ever bulk up with muscle. He was smart, too, almost as smart as that sister of his, and Lakeland suspected that under normal circumstances he probably would have been a lively handful. As it was, he was quiet, often pensive, and he spent a lot of time with his books. Partly that was a natural consequence of the king wyvern's eye his sister, King Zhames' guardsmen, and the members of his own household kept on him. Given what had happened to his father and his older brother, that sort of suffocating surveillance was inevitable, but it had to have a depressing effect on a lad's natural high spirits and sense of mischief. Perhaps that was why neither Lakeland nor Halahdrom had seen any sign of a passion for hunting wyverns in him. It wasn't as if he'd had any opportunity to pursue the sport since arriving here, after all.

"Did any other gifts arrive with them?" he asked.

"No." Halahdrom shook his head, then made a face. "Most of them got here a couple of five-days ago, courtesy of that Charisian 'parole.' These just arrived today, and I think they must've been an afterthought. Either that or somebody figured the Charisians might not pass them through for some reason."

"Why do you say that?"

"Well, they're obviously from Anvil Rock—most of the correspondence is in a secretary's hand, of course, but he sent along a nice little personal note to the boy in his own handwriting, along with a list of devotional readings he'd like the lad to be studying now that he's getting older." The chamberlain shrugged. "We've seen enough of his handwriting by now to know it's really his, and the secretary's writing matches the last several sets of letters we've received, as well. But they didn't come covered by a Charisian guarantee of safe passage, the way the rest of the birthday gifts did." He chuckled. "In fact, they came upriver from Sarmouth by messenger—courtesy of a smuggler, unless I miss my guess."

"That's interesting." Lakeland rubbed his nose. "A smuggler, you say?"

"That's my best guess, at any rate." Halahdrom shrugged. "I've got the fellow waiting outside if you'd like to speak to him directly."

"That might not be a bad idea," Lakeland said, and smiled slightly. "If the fellow's a smuggler—or knows somebody who is, at any rate—we might even be able to get some decent whiskey through that damned blockade!"

Halahdrom chuckled, nodded, and departed. A few

moments later, he returned with a tall, brown-haired and brown-eyed man in the decent but nondescript dress of a seaman. If the stranger was worried as he was ushered into the first councilor's office he hid it well.

"Ahbraim Zhevons, My Lord," Halahdrom said, speaking rather more formally in the outsider's presence, and Zhevons bobbed a respectful bow.

"So, Master Zhevons," Lakeland said, "I understand you've come to deliver a birthday gift for Prince Daivyn?"

"Aye, My Lord, I have. Or so Sir Klymynt tells me." Zhevons shrugged. "Nobody told me the lad was a prince, you understand. Mind, it seemed likely he wasn't what you might be calling a *common* lad, given how much somebody was willing to pay to get his present delivered to him. And let me tell you, keeping those damned wyverns—begging your pardon—fed without losing a finger was a harder job than I'd figured on!"

There was a twinkle in the brown eyes, and Lakeland felt his own lips hovering on the brink of a smile.

"So you brought them all the way from Corisande, did you?" he asked.

"Oh, no, My Lord! I, um, made connections in Tarot, as you might say. I've just . . . helped them along the last leg."

"Smuggler, are you?" The baron allowed his expression to harden slightly. This fellow might or might not be a smuggler and he might or might not have known young Daivyn was a prince. And this struck the first councilor as an unlikely way to get an assassin into the boy's presence, for that matter. Still. . . .

"That's a hard word." Zhevons didn't sound particularly hurt by it, however. "I'm more of a . . . free-trader. I specialize in small cargoes for shippers who'd sometimes sooner avoid any unnecessary paperwork, as you might say, true, but my word's my bond. I always see to any delivery myself, you see, and my rates are reasonable, My Lord." He smiled charmingly. "*Very* reasonable."

"Somehow I suspect your definition of 'reasonable' and mine may differ just a bit," Lakeland said dryly.

"Oh, I'm sure we could come to an agreement suitable to both of us, always assuming you ever had need of my services, of course."

"Now *that* I can believe." Lakeland leaned back. "I don't imagine you'd have access to any Chisholmian whiskey, would you, Master Zhevons?"

"No, not personally, I'm afraid. Not since the Grand Inquisitor went and declared his embargo, of course. Still, I'm sure I could lay hands on someone who does. Indirectly, of course."

"Oh, of course," Lakeland agreed. "Well, if you do manage it, I think I can safely say you'd find it worth your while to deliver some of it here in Talkyra."

"I'll bear that in mind, My Lord. Ah, would it be *too* much of a disappointment to you if it was to arrive here without Delferahkan tax stamps?" Zhevons smiled winningly when Lakeland looked at him. "It's not that I'm trying to rob you or your King of any rightful revenue, My Lord; it's more a matter of principle, so to speak."

"I see." Lakeland's lips quivered. "Very well, Master Zhevons, I'm sure I'll be able to deal with my disappointment somehow."

"I'm glad to hear it, My Lord." Zhevons bowed again, politely, and Lakeland chuckled.

"If you can manage to stay unhanged long enough you'll die a wealthy man, Master Zhevons."

"Kind of you to be saying so, My Lord, but it's my aim to *live* a wealthy man, if you take my meaning."

"Indeed I do." Lakeland shook his head, then sobered a bit. "I take it that you don't know exactly how this delivery got to Tarot in the first place, though?"

"I've no certain knowledge one way or the other, My Lord, but I do know the fellow who brought it as far as Tarot is a fine seaman who somehow managed to forget to apply for his tax documents when he docked in Corisande. Well, that's what I've *heard*, at any rate."

"And would this fellow have a name?" Lakeland pressed.

It was obvious Zhevons didn't really like the thought

of passing along any additional information. Actually, that made Lakeland think the better of him, since it seemed to indicate a certain honor among thieves . . . or among smugglers, at least. But the first councilor wasn't letting him off that lightly, and he sat silently, eyes boring into Zhevons' until, finally, the smuggler shrugged.

"Harys, My Lord," he said with a slight but unmistakable emphasis, looking levelly back at the baron. "Zhoel Harys."

"Ah." Lakeland glanced quickly at Halahdrom, then nodded to Zhevons. "I realize revealing professional confidences cuts against the grain of a . . . free-trader such as yourself, Master Zhevons. Nonetheless, I'm sure you understand why we have to exercise at least a little caution where people delivering unexpected gifts to Prince Daivyn are concerned."

"Aye, I can see where that might be the case," Zhevons conceded.

"Well, I believe that's all I really needed to discuss with you," Lakeland said. "I'm serious about the whiskey, though!"

"I'll bear that in mind, My Lord," Zhevons assured him, and bowed again as Halahdrom nodded at the door.

"Wait for me in the hall for a moment, Master Zhevons," he said.

"Of course, My Lord."

"Harys, is it?" Lakeland murmured as the door closed behind the smuggler. "Interesting choice of deliveryman, don't you think, Klymynt?"

"Yes, it is," the chamberlain agreed. "I wonder why they didn't just send him all the way to Sarmouth himself?"

"Oh, come now!" Lakeland shook his head. "Cayleb and Nahrmahn've had the better part of two years on the ground in Corisande by now. I'd say there's a good chance they know exactly who Hektor used to get the Prince and his sister to the mainland. They'd probably really like the opportunity to have a few words with him, especially if Anvil Rock and Coris are still using him, too.

But they'd be looking for him here or in Corisande, not in Tarot of all places! So it would make sense for him to use somebody they've never heard of for the last leg."

"I suppose so," Halahdrom agreed. "Of course, if it *is* Harys, that makes this 'gift' a bit more suspicious, don't you think?"

"It might, and it might not. My thought, though, is that since Anvil Rock apparently had no problem getting permission to send Prince Daivyn's other birthday presents through the blockade with Charisian approval, if there's anything 'suspicious' about *this* gift, it's probably something he didn't want the *Charisians* to know about. You haven't found *anything* out of order about it?"

"Nothing." Halahdrom shook his head. "I even had the wyverns moved into another cage while I checked the bottom of the one they came in for false partitions or compartments."

They looked at one another for a moment while both of them considered the possibility of things like *spoken* messages which would leave no inconvenient written records behind.

"Well, given the thoroughness of your examination, I think we simply make sure we've got copies of all the correspondence, then report its arrival to Bishop Mytchail, send him the copies, and pass it on to Earl Coris for Prince Daivyn," Lakeland decided. He leaned back in his chair again, meeting Halahdrom's eyes. "And given the Lord Bishop's views on smugglers and the embargo, I see no need to describe our conversation with Master Zhevons to him, do you?"

▼ ▼ ▼

"A gift from Earl Anvil Rock, is it, My Lord?" Tobys Raimair cocked an eyebrow at Phylyp Ahzgood. "Would it happen the boy was *expecting* any additional gifts from him?"

"No, it wouldn't," the Earl of Coris replied. "Which is why it occurred to me that it might be as well for you and

I to accept delivery before we let it—or the deliveryman—into his presence."

"Oh, aye, I can understand that," Raimair agreed. "Would you like me to ask one of the other lads to step in, as well?"

"I doubt that will be necessary," Coris replied with a slight smile, considering the sword and dirk riding in well-worn sheaths at Raimair's side. "Not for one man who's not even getting into the same room with the boy."

"As you say, My Lord." Raimair bowed, then crossed the room to open the door.

A tall, brown-haired man stepped through it, followed by two of the palace's servants and Brother Bahldwyn Gaimlyn, one of King Zhames' junior secretaries. Between them, the wary footmen carried an ornately gilded traveling cage which contained six large wyverns. The wyverns gazed about with beady, unusually intelligent-looking eyes, and Coris frowned. It seemed an odd choice for a gift from Anvil Rock, who knew perfectly well that Daivyn had never showed the least interest in hunting wyverns. That had been his older brother's passion.

"Master . . . Zhevons, is it?" Coris asked the brown-haired man.

"Aye, Sir. Ahbraim Zhevons, at your service," the stranger replied in a pleasant tenor voice.

"And you're an associate of Captain Harys?"

"Oh, I'd not go that far, My Lord." Zhevons shook his head, but his eyes met Coris' levelly. "It's more that we're in the same line of business, so to speak. These days, at least."

"I see." Coris glanced at the footmen and Brother Bahldwyn, who were waiting patiently, and wondered which of them was Baron Lakeland's ears for this conversation. Probably all three of them, he decided. Or perhaps one was Lakeland's and one was Mytchail Zhessop's.

"Did Captain Harys pass on any messages to me?" he asked out loud.

"No, My Lord. Can't say he did," Zhevons replied. "Except that he did say as how you might be seeing me or one of my . . . ah, *business* associates with another odd delivery now and again." He smiled easily, but his eyes held Coris' gaze intently. "I think you might say the Captain's of the opinion he might've become just a bit too well known to be serving you the way he has before."

"Yes, I suppose I might," Coris said thoughtfully, and nodded. "Well, in that case, Master Zhevons, thank you for your efficiency."

He reached into his belt pouch, withdrew a five-mark piece, and flipped the golden disk to the smuggler, who caught it with an easy economy of movement and a grin. One of the footmen smiled as well, and Coris hoped the man had made note of the fact that there'd been absolutely no way for anything written to have been exchanged in the process.

"I'm sure these fellows can see you safely on your way, Master Zhevons," he continued. "And I'm sure you can imagine there's a certain young man anxiously awaiting my report on what his mysterious birthday gift might be."

"Oh, that I can, My Lord! I'd no idea he was a *prince*, of course, but I'm sure every boy that age is much the same under the skin."

The earl smiled again and nodded, and Zhevons sketched a bow and followed the footmen and Brother Bahldwyn out. Coris watched the door close behind him, then turned to Raimair.

"And what do you make of our Master Zhevons, Tobys?"

"Seems a capable sort, My Lord," Raimair replied. "Never heard as how the boy—Prince Daivyn, I mean—was all that fond of wyvern hunting, howsome ever."

"That's because he wasn't . . . and isn't," Coris murmured.

"You don't say?" Raimair observed. "Now that makes a man feel just a mite suspicious, especially arriving all unannounced this way, doesn't it just?"

"Perhaps, but Master Zhevons says Captain Harys got them as far as Tarot," Coris said, lifting his eyes to Raimair's face. "Of course, by this time it's entirely possible someone's figured out how we got here from Corisande, so the fact that Zhevons *claims* he knows Harys doesn't necessarily prove anything. It does strike me as an indicator in its favor, though. And then there's this."

He pulled out the (already opened) envelope which had accompanied the traveling cage. It contained a sheaf of correspondence, and the earl extracted the letters and showed them to Raimair.

"I recognize the handwriting—both Earl Anvil Rock's and his secretary's," he pointed out.

He looked down at them for a moment, then shrugged and walked across to his bookcase. He ran his finger down the spines of the shelved books until he found the one he wanted, then took it from the shelf, sat down at his desk, and unfolded Anvil Rock's letter to Daivyn. The chapter and verse notations Anvil Rock had included in his letter were exactly the sort to which a considerably older kinsman and a regent might want to direct a youthful charge's attention, especially if they had no opportunity for personal contact with the boy. A little somber and weighty for a lad Daivyn's age, perhaps, but the boy *was* the legitimate ruler of an entire princedom. Something a bit more serious than the sorts of verses most children memorized for catechism might well be in order, given those circumstances.

Coris wasn't particularly interested in looking up the passages indicated to check their content, however. Instead, he was turning pages in the cheap novel (printed in Manchyr) he'd taken from the shelf, selecting page numbers, then lines down the page, then words in the lines. *Langhorne* 6:21-9, for example, directed him to the sixth page, the twenty-first line, and the ninth word. He tracked down each passage's indicated words, jotting each of them down quickly on a sheet of paper. Then he sat gazing at the sheet for a moment, frowning, before he dropped it into the fire on his sitting room's hearth, stood, and crossed to the traveling cage. Its gilded bars were topped with ornamental finials, and he counted quickly around them from left to right until he got to the thirteenth. He gripped it, careful to keep his fingers out of reach of the wyverns' saw-toothed beaks, and twisted, but it wouldn't budge.

"You've got stronger wrists than I do, Tobys," he said wryly. "See if you can get this thing to screw off. It turns clock-wise to loosen, not counter-clockwise."

Raimahn raised an eyebrow, then reached out. His powerful hand closed on the finial and he grunted with effort. For a moment, nothing happened; then it yielded. Once it started turning, it went on turning easily until he'd screwed it completely off, revealing that the bar was hollow and contained two or three tightly rolled sheets of paper.

"Well, well, well," Coris murmured, reaching in and extracting the sheets.

He unrolled them and began to read, then stopped abruptly. His eyes widened in shock, and he looked quickly at Raimahn.

"My Lord?" the guardsman asked quickly.

"It's . . . just not from who I thought it would be from," Coris said.

"Is it bad news, then, My Lord?"

"No, I wouldn't say that." Coris managed a smile, beginning to come back on balance with the practice of decades as a spymaster. It was, he admitted to himself, rather harder this time than it had ever been before, however. "*Unexpected* news, yes, but not bad. At least, I don't think so."

He looked back down at the note, trying to wrap his mind around all it implied. The handwriting in the correspondence was definitely Anvil Rock's, but if the note in his hand was to be believed, Anvil Rock had never written it. Never even seen it, although exactly how the man who *had* written it—and had the sheer audacity to personally deliver it to Talkyra—had managed to forge the correspondence so perfectly *and* gained access to the code book Anvil Rock and Coris had arranged so long ago were certainly . . . interesting questions.

"Earl Coris," it began, "First, I beg your pardon for a slight deception on my part. Two of them, to be more accurate. First, I've never actually *met* Captain Harys, I'm afraid, nor has any portion of Prince Daivyn's 'gift' ever been within a thousand leagues of Corisande. And, second, I'm afraid my name isn't actually Ahbraim Zhevons. It serves me well enough when needed, however, and while I'm aware you've never heard of me, I'm an associate of someone I'm certain you *have* heard of: Merlin Athrawes. I do the occasional odd job for *Seijin* Merlin when it would be impolitic for him to handle them himself, and he asked me to deliver these wyverns to you as a gift from Earl Gray Harbor. I'm sure you've noticed they're a bit larger than most messenger wyverns, and there's a reason for that. You see—"

. II .

Tellesberg Palace
and
Tellesberg Cathedral,
City of Tellesberg,
Kingdom of Old Charis

"God, it's good to be *home!*" Sharleyan Ahrmahk sighed, curling up against her husband's side and resting her head on his shoulder. She closed her eyes, feeling as if she were expanding the pores of her skin to absorb the gentle night breeze breathing through the bedchamber's open windows. Exotic insects she hadn't heard in too many months sang in the moon-silvered darkness, the brilliant stars of the southern hemisphere hung overhead like ornaments from some cosmic glassblower, and the part of her which had been missing for far too long was back beside her.

"So Tellesberg is 'home' now, is it?" Cayleb teased gently, and she nodded.

"At the moment, at least." She raised her head long enough to kiss him on the cheek, then snuggled back down and wrapped one arm around his chest, all without ever opening her eyes again. "Don't let this go to your head, but home is wherever *you* are."

His own arm tightened around her and he pressed his cheek against the top of her head, inhaling the sweet scent of her hair and savoring its silken texture.

"Works both ways," he told her. "Except, for me, home is wherever you and *Alahnah* are."

"Correction accepted, Your Majesty."

"Thank you, Your Grace."

Sharleyan giggled.

"What's so funny?" Cayleb demanded. "You've got something against formality and courtesy?"

"Under most circumstances, no, I don't. But under *these*. . . ."

Her hand slid down under the light thistle silk sheet covering them to the waist, and Cayleb smiled.

"Courtesy is never wasted," he informed her. "I'm courteous to *every* naked lady I find in my bed. In fact—"

He broke off with a sudden twitch, and she raised her head from his shoulder to smile sweetly at him.

"I'd consider my next sentence very carefully if I were you," she said.

"Actually, my brain doesn't seem to be working very well at the moment," he replied, scooping her up and draping her diagonally across his body while he smiled up into her eyes. "I think this may be one of those moments when silence is golden."

▼ ▼ ▼

The mood was rather different as the two of them headed for the council chamber they used as a working office whenever both of them happened to be in Tellesberg at the same time.

Not the most exacting of their subjects—and not even the two of them, for that matter—could have demanded they give themselves over to official business the day before. Not after that same "official business" had separated the two of them for over four months. HMS *Dawn Star*'s arrival in Tellesberg on yesterday afternoon's tide had been greeted even more tumultuously than Cayleb's return from Chisholm. In some ways, the citizens of Old Charis had taken Sharleyan even more deeply to their hearts than Cayleb. They loved both of them, but they *adored* her, which (as Cayleb put it) indicated the soundness of their taste. And like the majority of their subjects, Charisian and Chisholmian alike, the citizens of Tellesberg were entranced by the deep and obvious love between the handsome young king and beautiful young queen who had married for reasons of state. Half the city had crowded the waterfront to watch *Dawn Star* being nudged gently up against the Royal Quay's pilings, and they'd seen Emperor Cayleb go bounding up the gangplank almost before the galleon was fully moored. And when he swept Empress Sharleyan up into his arms, tossed her over one shoulder, and carried her back *down* the gangplank while she laughed and whacked him on the back of his head, the entire huge crowd had erupted in cheers and whistles. Anyone who had suggested that the two of them should do anything besides take themselves off immediately to the palace would probably have been tarred and feathered on the spot.

It had all been most improper, of course, as Sharleyan was well aware. On the other hand, she didn't much care. And, on a more pragmatic note, she knew the short shrift she and Cayleb often gave protocol and formal state occasions was part of the legend that made them not simply respected but beloved by their subjects.

She knew Earl Gray Harbor had also decided yesterday belonged to them, not to the Empire, but that had been then. This was now, and she wasn't looking forward to the news he'd delayed giving them that first, precious day.

They reached the council chamber door, Merlin following at their heels, and Sergeant Seahamper saluted before he opened it for them and stood aside. Cayleb smiled at the sergeant, resting one hand briefly on his shoulder, then escorted Sharleyan into the chamber where the waiting ministers and councilors stood respectfully to greet them.

"Oh, sit back down." Cayleb waved them back into their seats. "We can get all formal later, if we need to."

"Yes, Your Majesty. Of course."

Gray Harbor managed to sound simultaneously patient, amused, and long-suffering, and Cayleb made a face at him while he pulled Sharleyan's chair back from the table and seated her. The first councilor smiled back, although there truly were times when he found Cayleb's informality—even by Charisian standards, which were far more flexible than most—a little disconcerting.

All in all, he vastly preferred it to the sort of ego-aggrandizing formality, bowing, and scraping with which too many monarchs (and *far* too many lesser nobles, for that matter, in his opinion) surrounded themselves. It wasn't that he had any objection to the way in which Cayleb and Sharleyan handled themselves; it was that the part of him which looked to the future worried, sometimes, about the traditions they were establishing. The two of them had the strength of will, ability, and self-confidence—and the sheer charisma—to handle their roles and responsibilities without taking refuge in strictly regulated, well-worn formality, but what happened when the Empire found itself ruled by someone without those strengths? Someone who wasn't able to laugh with his councilors without undermining his authority? Someone who lacked the confidence to pick up his wife in public or make jokes at his own expense in formal addresses to Parliament? Someone who couldn't *allow* herself to be scooped up without sacrificing one iota of her dignity when she needed it? Someone who lacked the focused sense of duty that prevented informality and tension-releasing humor from degenerating into license and frivolity?

A kingdom was fortunate to have a single monarch of Cayleb or Sharleyan Ahrmhak's caliber in a century; no realm could count on having two of them at the same time . . . still less on producing a third to follow in their footsteps. Indeed, much as Gray Harbor loved the baby crown princess, it had been his observation that the children of the towering rulers who dominated the history books had a distinct tendency to disappear in their parents' shadows. And what soul could have the hardihood to stand in the shadows of rulers like these two without feeling diminished—even angry—under the weight of their subjects' expectations? No wonder the heirs of so many great kings and queens had ended up giving their lives over to dissolution and sensuality!

You must *be feeling more confident about the outcome of this minor war of ours if you're wasting time worrying about things like* that, *Rayjhis,* he told himself dryly. *Cheerful, too. Alahnah's just turned one and you're already worrying about her having drunken orgies after her parents are gone? About the way the Empire's going to fall apart after them? Neither of them is* thirty *yet, for Langhorne's sake! It's not like* you're *going to be around for the transition.*

No, he wasn't—God willing—but it was one of a first councilor's jobs to worry about things like that. Besides, he'd been making a conscious effort to stand back and consider the long view whenever he could. It was entirely too easy to get trapped up in the day-to-day concerns of simply surviving against an opponent the size of the Church of God Awaiting, and when that happened, unhappy consequences could sneak up on someone.

And it also keeps you from thinking about what you're going to have to tell them on their very first full day together in almost five months, doesn't it? he asked himself grimly.

Cayleb sat in his own chair, laid his folded hands on the table in front of him, and glanced at Maikel Staynair, sitting at its foot.

"Maikel?"

"Of course, Your Majesty." Staynair looked once around the table, then bent his head. "Oh God, maker and keeper of the universe, author of all good things, our loving creator and father, bless these Your servants Cayleb and Sharleyan and all of their advisors. Let us all hear Your voice and be guided by Your council, and let our Emperor's and

Empress' decisions be worthy of their responsibility to the subjects who are also Your children, even as they are. Amen."

No one seemed to notice the absence of any reference to the "Archangels," Cayleb reflected as he opened his own eyes once more. Ever since he'd been elevated to archbishop, Staynair had focused even more directly upon every human being's *personal* relationship with God rather than on the intermediary role of the Archangels. By now, people scarcely noticed the subtle but deeply significant shift, and the majority of the Church of Charis' clergy seemed to be taking their own stance and practices directly from their archbishop's.

Maikel always did think in terms of long-term strategy, didn't he? And speaking of long-term thinking. . . .

The emperor looked directly across the table at Gray Harbor.

"Would you care to go ahead and share with us what you were sparing me and Sharley yesterday, Rayjhis?" he asked dryly.

"Your Majesty?" Gray Harbor raised his eyebrows, and Cayleb snorted.

"I've known you since I was a boy, Rayjhis. I don't want to get into anything about books and reading, but it was obvious to both me and Sharley that you had something on your mind yesterday. And since you didn't bring it up, it seemed equally obvious it had to be something you didn't think was going to make us happy." The emperor shook his head. "Trust me, we appreciate that. Still, it's a new morning and we might as well get down to it."

"Of course, Your Majesty."

Gray Harbor smiled involuntarily at Cayleb's tone, but it was a fleeting smile, quickly faded, and he drew a deep breath and squared his shoulders.

"I regret to inform you, Your Majesty, that we've received letters from Admiral Manthyr. One contains a complete roster of the officers and men who surrendered to Earl Thirsk—and of those who died in captivity after surrendering."

It was very quiet and still, the humor of only a moment before fading as quickly as the earl's smile. No one else spoke, and he looked steadily at his monarchs as he continued.

"There's also Sir Gwylym's formal report. It's very brief—he had none of his logs or records to consult when he prepared it, and for reasons his other letters make clear, very little time in which to write it. It confirms most of what we already knew and suspected about his final engagement . . . and also something we've all feared."

Gray Harbor's eyes flitted briefly aside to Captain Athrawes, standing just inside the council chamber's door. He'd been taking Merlin's "visions" into his calculations for years now, but not everyone in the chamber was cleared for that information. And, of course, Merlin had been away from Tellesberg for the better part of a year, during which he'd been unable to provide any updated reports on Gwylym Manthyr's situation.

"King Rahnyld has formally surrendered custody of Sir Gwylym and all of his officers and men to the Inquisition." The earl's voice was flat and harsh now. "They left Gorath overland for Zion either late in May or in the first five-day of June. Given the length of the journey and the quality of mainland roads, they must have already reached the Temple."

The stillness became absolute. Every man and woman in that chamber knew what that meant, and most of the councilors turned their heads to look at Maikel Staynair. By any traditional reckoning, he was the senior member of the Imperial Council as Charis' archbishop. His should have been the most important of the opinions offered on any subject, and especially anything touching upon the Church and religion. But Staynair had worked hard to make the Council as independent of the Church of Charis as it possibly could be in what was, after all, a religious war. His position throughout had been that the Church's proper role was to *teach*, not to enforce, and more than one of them wondered how he would react to news of this fresh atrocity decreed in God's name.

He sat motionless for several seconds, then sighed and shook his head heavily, his eyes dark with sadness.

"May God have mercy on them and gather them in arms of love," he said softly. A quiet chorus of amens ran around the table, and then the others sat respectfully waiting while the archbishop closed his eyes in brief, silent prayer, took a deep breath, sat back in his chair, and looked at his old friend.

"May I ask how these letters come into our possession after all these months of silence, Rayjhis?"

"I can't answer that question—not completely, at any rate," Gray Harbor replied. "As nearly as I can tell, they must have traveled by courier from Gorath to Silk Town, where they were handed over to one of the 'Silkiahan' merchantmen to be delivered to us here. That part's fairly obvious. What I *can't* tell you is who authorized their delivery, although I have my suspicions."

"Sir Gwylym didn't say?" Baron Ironhill asked.

"Reading between the lines, he was very careful *not* to say, Ahlvyno." Gray Harbor smiled tightly. "No doubt he knew what would happen to anyone who'd 'aided and abetted heretics' if his letters should fall into the Inquisition's hands."

"I'm sure he did," Baron Wave Thunder said. "Of the other hand, I don't think there's any doubt your 'suspicions' are accurate, Rayjhis. The only person who could have authorized it—who conceivably *might* have authorized it, from what we know of him—is Earl Thirsk."

"Agreed," Cayleb said. In fact, he and Wave Thunder knew perfectly well who'd arranged it. "I wish to God that man wasn't on the other side," the emperor continued soberly. "And I wish I hadn't been quite so hard on him after Crag Reach." He shook his head. "He deserved better, even if there wasn't any way for me to know it at the time."

"I rather hate to suggest this, Your Majesty," Prince Nahrmahn said delicately, "but if it should happen to leak back to the Inquisition that. . . ."

"No," Cayleb said flatly, and Sharleyan shook her head

firmly at his side. Then the emperor made himself sit straighter in his chair. "No, Nahrmahn," he said in a more natural voice. "Mind you, you're not thinking anything that hadn't already occurred to me. And I suppose from a proper cold-blooded, pragmatic perspective no ruler in his right mind could justify rejecting such a neat way of removing his most capable military opponent from play. But the man who risked sending us Gwylym Manthyr's final letters deserves better of us than that."

"I agree, Your Majesty." Nahrmahn nodded. "Such possibilities need to be considered; that's why I mentioned it. But not only would it be wrong to betray the Earl to the Inquisition, it would be foolish. Whatever the advantages in removing him as a military commander, the long-term consequence would be to guarantee that there were no more Earl Thirsks within the ranks of the Temple Loyalists. Zhaspahr Clyntahn's actions have blackened the Group of Four beyond redemption in the eyes of any reasonable person. The last thing we need to do is to put ourselves into that same category by being no better than he is."

"Cold-bloodedly but cogently reasoned, Your Highness," Staynair said with a crooked smile. Nahrmahn looked at him, and the archbishop smiled more naturally. "I have no objection to considering the political advantages of doing the right thing, Your Highness. I hope, however, that you'll understand that from my perspective the fact that it's the *right* thing takes precedence over the fact that it also happens to be politically expedient."

"Your Eminence, I agree with you entirely," Nahrmahn replied with a wry smile. "It's simply that the right thing and the politically expedient thing are so seldom the *same* thing that I couldn't let it pass without mentioning it."

"We're in agreement, then, that we won't be publishing these letters abroad, Your Majesties?" Gray Harbor asked.

"Why do I seem to hear a little . . . hesitation in your voice, Rayjhis?" Sharleyan looked at him shrewdly, and the first councilor grimaced.

"There are also letters from others of his officers and enlisted men, Your Grace," he sighed. "The very last letters any of them will ever write. If we don't admit we've received them, we can't deliver them to their loved ones, either."

There was silence again for several seconds. A lot of the people around the table were busy avoiding one another's eyes, and Gray Harbor wondered how many of them found it as ironic as he did that this decision should arrive so close on the heels of Staynair's and Nahrmahn's discussion of the difference between expediency and what was *right*.

"I believe there may be a solution," Staynair said finally, and the eyes which had been studying the tabletop or the paintings on the council chamber's walls swiveled to him. "By now, there's been time for this same news to have reached Silk Town from Gorath by other means, and for us to have heard of it from someone besides Sir Gwylym or Earl Thirsk. That being the case, I propose we announce it without mentioning the receipt of any formal reports from Sir Gwylym or, for that matter, *any* of the letters. Instead, in a short time—two or three five-days, perhaps—I'll announce the *Church* has come into possession of final letters from many of the prisoners who were handed over to the Inquisition. I'll refuse to say how those letters reached me, but I'm sure everyone will assume it was courtesy of some Reformist member of the mainland clergy." His lip curled, and his normally mild eyes glittered. "I rather like the thought that it may inspire the Inquisition to hunt for traitors among its own ranks."

"I think that's an excellent idea, Your Majesties," Nahrmahn agreed enthusiastically. "I'm sure Clyntahn's response will be to brand any letters which end up being made public as forgeries on our part. They won't *really* be from any of our people; we'll have made them up as another step in our efforts to discredit Mother Church and the Inquisition. He may even actually believe that himself . . . in which case it could help divert a little pressure from Earl Thirsk."

Cayleb looked at Sharleyan, who nodded, then turned back to the rest of the Council.

"Very well." He nodded. "I think you've come up with the best solution for that particular problem, Maikel. But there's still the matter of how we go about making news of this public . . . and what position we take."

"I agree." Staynair nodded gravely. "This is something to which both Crown and Church must respond strongly and clearly, with no ambiguity. Your subjects and God's children must clearly understand what this means, and where we stand in respect to it. And there's also the question of timing. We're less than a five-day from God's Day, which is about as ironic as it gets, I suppose." He raised one hand to his pectoral scepter. "Under the circumstances, I think there's only one possible venue for addressing this matter properly, Your Majesty."

▼ ▼ ▼

It was unusually quiet in Tellesberg Cathedral, especially for today. God's Day—the unnumbered extra day inserted into every year in the middle of the month of July—was *the* great high holy day of the Church of God Awaiting. Every month had its religious holidays, its saints' days, its liturgical observances, but this day, God's Day, was set aside above all others for the contemplation of one's soul and the state of God's plan for all humanity. It was a day of solemn celebration, of joyous hymns, as well as a day on which gifts were exchanged, children were baptized, weddings were celebrated, and the praise and gratitude of the entire world ascended to the throne of God.

There was always a special solemnity to the high masses celebrated in the great cathedrals of Safehold on God's Day, and never more so than in those rare instances when an archbishop had scheduled his yearly pastoral visit to coincide with the religious festival. Of course, that seldom happened; it was far more important to be in Zion, at the Temple, on this holiest of days, and the archbishoprics were usually left to their bishop executors.

But not in Tellesberg, or in places like Eraystor,

Cherayth, or Manchyr. In those places, archbishops *regularly* celebrated mass in their own cathedrals, and Tellesberg Cathedral had filled to overflowing before dawn. Thousands of additional worshippers filled the square outside and spilled down the avenues in every direction, covering every square foot of pavement, sitting in the windows and on the roofs of buildings overlooking Cathedral Square. Priests and deacons formed human chains, stretching through the crowd, waiting for Archbishop Maikel's sermon so that they could relay his words to every waiting ear.

No one knew what the archbishop intended to say, but Maikel's sermons were famous, and rightly so, for their warmth and their loving insight into the hearts and minds of human beings. They were followed even in the mainland realms—printed and distributed semi-openly in northern and eastern Siddarmark, and less openly in other lands. Indeed, they formed a major component of the Reformist propaganda so mysteriously and successfully spread across both continents despite all the Inquisition could do.

But there was no mystery about their availability in the Empire of Charis. They were regularly reprinted and distributed in the bookstores and in the Empire's newspapers, posted in broadside sheets in villages and town squares. Not because the Church or the Crown required it, but because those bookstores and newspapers' readers, the citizens of those villages and towns, demanded it.

Yet for all that, there was a special tension in the air. There were rumors, whispers, that the archbishop had something especially weighty to discuss today. The air would have been supercharged on God's Day under any circumstances, given the religious aspects of the war being waged against Charis, but there was more to it this time, and as the Cathedral Choir's voices faded, they were replaced by a silence so intense a muffled cough would have sounded like a cannon shot.

Archbishop Maikel rose from his throne and crossed to the carved and gilded pulpit. Anyone who'd ever seen the archbishop knew that purposeful stride of his, that sense of powerful forward movement and focused determination. Yet it was more pronounced, more deliberate, even than usual today, and the congregation's tension ratcheted higher.

He reached the pulpit and stood for a moment with his hand on the *Holy Writ* and his eyes closed, his head bent in silent prayer. Then he raised his head once more, looking out over the wide expanse of packed, silent pews.

"Today's Scripture is written in the fifth chapter of *The Book of Chihiro*, verses ten through fourteen," he said clearly, and opened the *Writ*. Pages whispered as he turned them, the tiny sound distinctly audible in the stillness, but when he'd found the passage he sought, he didn't even look at it. He didn't need to, and he stood with his hand resting on the huge volume, eyes sweeping the congregation, while he recited from memory.

"'Then the Archangel Langhorne stood upon Mount Heilbronn, looking down upon the Field of Sabana, where so many had fallen opposing evil, and his eyes were wet with tears, and he said, "The time must come when only the sword of justice can oppose the many swords of evil—of pestilent ambition, of greed, of selfishness and cruelty, of hatred and terror. Might may be used to destroy might, and strength may be used to oppose strength, but *justice* is the true armor of the godly. That which cannot be done with justice must not be done at all, for only the Dark cannot stand in the brilliance of God's Light. So you will abide by justice, by keeping faith with that which you know is right. You will do justice not in the heat of battle or the white fury of your anger, be that anger ever so justified. You will do justice soberly, with reverent respect for that love of one another God has placed within you. You will not condemn out of hatred, and he who uses justice for his own ends, he who perverts justice into that which he wishes it to be rather than what it truly is, that one shall be accursed in the eyes of God. Every man's hand shall be against him. As he sows, so shall he reap, and the mercy he denies to others shall be denied to him in his turn. I will not shield him from his enemies. I will not hear him when he calls to me in his extremity. And in the final judgment, when he comes before the throne of God, I will not see him. I will not speak for him, and God Himself will turn His back upon him as he is cast forever into that bottomless abyss reserved for him throughout all eternity.'''"

The stillness couldn't possibly have gotten more absolute . . . yet somehow, as Staynair spoke, it did. God's Day was a day for celebration, for joyous acknowledgment and thanks, not for the grim, harsh passages of *The Book of Chihiro* and the clashing iron of condemnation. That was true for any cathedral, any sermon preached upon this day, and to hear such words out of the gentle Archbishop of Charis only made them even more shocking.

Staynair let the stillness linger, then turned his head slowly, surveying the congregation.

"My sermon today will be brief, my children," he said then. "It is not one I relish. This is supposed to be a day of joy, of the rediscovery of God's love for His children and the expression of their love for Him, and I wish with all my heart that I could preach that message to you today. But I can't. Instead I must speak of news which has reached us here, and which will reach homes and families everywhere within the Empire of Charis all too soon."

He paused, the stillness wrapping itself around him in the smoke chains of incense and the spangled light shafts of the cathedral's stained glass. His archbishop's crown glittered in that light, his vestments gleamed with jewels and precious embroidery, and his eyes were dark, dark.

"Word has come to Tellesberg from Gorath," he said finally, and somewhere in the cathedral a woman's voice cried out indistinctly. Staynair's eyes turned in its direction, but his voice never faltered.

"King Rahnyld has chosen to yield Sir Gwylym Manthyr and all of the men under his command who were honorably surrendered to the Dohlaran Navy to the Inquisition. They were consigned to the Inquisition at the end of May. By this time, my children, they have already reached Zion. No doubt they are enduring the Question even as I stand before you."

More voices joined that first, single protest, crying out. Not in denial of Staynair's words, but in grief—and anger—as the thing they had all feared would come to pass was finally announced to them. Rage guttered in the depths of those voices, and hatred, and growing under both of them—newborn, yet already with bones of iron and fangs of steel—was vengeance.

The priests and deacons relaying Staynair's sermon to the crowds outside had repeated his words, and the same instant upwelling of anger rolled across Cathedral Square and down the avenues. That vast crowd's fury could be heard even inside the cathedral, even over the voices being raised within its walls, and Staynair raised one hand, commanding silence.

He got it, and it was a testimony to his stature, his congregation's love and respect for him, that he did. That he *could*.

It didn't come instantly, that silence. Even for him, it came slowly, limpingly, like a catamount unwillingly surrendering its prey, and it spread even more slowly to the throngs beyond the cathedral's walls. Yet it came at last, and he looked out across the pews once more.

"Our brothers and fathers and sons and husbands have been given over into the hands of torturers and murderers serving that vile corruption which sits in the Grand Inquisitor's chair," the normally gentle and loving archbishop said harshly. "They have been given over not because of anything they've done that deserves such hideous punishment, whatever Zhaspahr Clyntahn and his coterie of sycophants and butchers may claim. They've been surrendered to suffer all of those agonies and the final and culminating agony of the Punishment of Schueler because they dared—*dared*, my children!—to defend their families and their loved ones and their fellow children of God against exactly that which they themselves are even now suffering. They dared to defy the evil and corruption and the arrogance of the Group of Four, and Zhaspahr Clyntahn has perverted his office, just as he has perverted his immortal soul, to punish that defiance not of God, but of *him*.

"This is not the act of the Temple Loyalists, although many among them may be so deceived by the Group of Four's lies that they applaud it. This is not the act of the neighbor across the street from you who continues to oppose the schism, the 'heresy,' of the Church of Charis. This is not the act of someone who truly seeks to know and to understand God's will. It is not the act of someone who respects law, or justice, or truth, or *anything* in God's wide world which is more important than *himself*."

More than one of the people in that cathedral stared at him in something very like shock. Not at what they were hearing, but at who they were hearing it *from*. This was Maikel Staynair, the gentle shepherd—the archbishop who'd cried out for understanding and compassion from the very same pulpit in which he stood today with the blood of his own intended assassins splashed across his vestments. Yet there was no gentleness in him this day.

"As today's Scripture tells us, 'That one shall be accursed in the eyes of God. Every man's hand shall be against him. As he sows, so shall he reap, and the mercy he denies to others shall be denied to him in his turn.'" The archbishop's voice was ribbed with iron, and his eyes were harder yet. "The Church of Charis does not torture, does not murder, does not massacre—not even in the name of *God*, far less in the name of foul and vaunting ambition! The Empire of Charis will not strike out blindly, will not mistake the unwilling servant for the corrupt and despicable master. No doubt there will come a reckoning for King Rahnyld, in the fullness of time, yet Rahnyld is *nothing*. He is only a servant, a slave of his masters in Zion, and we know our *true* enemies. We know the hand behind this crime. We know the twisted mind and the withered soul which commanded it. We know whose hand this blood is truly on, and we will remember. We will *remember* . . . and we will call that hand to account."

Bared steel clashed in the depths of that promise, and he looked out over the shocked, silent cathedral.

"I have consulted with Emperor Cayleb and Empress Sharleyan about this matter," he said quietly, flatly. "I have urged from the beginning that we leave justice to be done by the Crown, and so I urge now. I beg all of you, as God's children, to refrain from seeking objects of vengeance. Those Temple Loyalists who live in the Empire had *nothing* to do with this! The vast, vast majority of Temple Loyalists living even in *Dohlar* had nothing to do with this. It was done not at the orders of the Dohlaran Navy or the Dohlaran Army, but at the orders of the Inquisition and of that unspeakably vile individual whose every breath profanes the vicar's robe he wears. And because it was, the Empire of Charis and the Church of Charis will not strike out at the innocent or those who had no choice but to obey corruption's orders."

He drew himself up to his full impressive height, and his voice rolled with harsh thunder.

"No doubt there are those who will argue that we should carry out reprisals against the far greater number of prisoners who lie in our hands. That we should make clear to the kings and princes who oppose us in the service of the Group of Four that we will treat their surrendered soldiers and sailors precisely as they treat ours. But we are called upon to wield the sword of *justice*, my children, not the sword of blind vengeance. Your Emperor and Empress will not dishonor themselves or stain the honor of those who serve in our Navy and our Marines and our Army with the murder of those who have done nothing but follow their officers' orders and fight honorably and openly upon the field of battle.

"But—*but*, my children!—the Inquisition has shown itself to be the enemy of all mankind. Whatever it may once have been, it has fallen into the grasp of men like Zhaspahr Clyntahn who have distorted and twisted it into something which it may never be possible to cleanse again. Its members have become not servants of God but

His enemies. God gave all men free will, the ability to choose, and they have chosen to serve the *Dark,* instead.

"So be it. 'As he sows, so shall he reap, and the mercy he denies to others shall be denied to him in his turn.' There will be no torture, but neither will there be mercy. From this day forth, Inquisitors—not simply intendants, not simply Schuelerites, but those in the direct and personal service of the Grand Inquisitor—shall receive precisely what the *Writ* promises them. As they have chosen to deny mercy to others, it will be denied to them. Soldiers and sailors may be allowed to surrender and receive the humane, honorable treatment to which their actions have entitled them; Inquisitors will not. Let the word go forth, my children. Let there be no ambiguity, no misunderstanding. Those who wish to renounce the distorted and twisted policies and commands of Zhaspahr Clyntahn are free to do so. They may still face trial and punishment for acts they have already committed, but they will be granted that trial. And for those who do not wish to renounce their allegiance to Zhaspahr Clyntahn, who continue to willingly lend themselves to his acts of murder and terrorism and torture, there will be a different policy. The only trial they will receive is to determine whether or not they truly are servants of the Inquisition, and if they are so found to be, there will be only one sentence, and that sentence will be executed upon them immediately and without appeal, just as surely as, in the fullness of time and God's good grace, it will be executed upon Zhaspahr Clyntahn himself."

. III .

Sairaih's Tavern,
City of Tellesberg,
Kingdom of Old Charis

Ainsail Dahnvahr had forgotten how good real Charisian beer tasted. His father had been willing to pay the premium for Charisian beer when Ainsail was younger, and he'd developed a taste for it. Of course, that had changed abruptly when the kingdom of Rahzhyr Dahnvahr's birth turned against Mother Church, although Ainsail was pretty sure his father would have gone ahead paying for the imported beer if that hadn't become so . . . indiscreet in the Temple Lands.

It shamed him to admit that, but there was no point trying to pretend otherwise. His father's faith was weak, no match for the fervor of Ainsail's mother's belief. Or Ainsail's, for that matter. There'd been times Ainsail had suspected that deep in the secret places of his own heart his father was still a Charisian first and a servant of God second, and that had caused him more than shame. That suspicion was the mother of *pain,* and twice Ainsail had almost mentioned his father's Charisian sympathies to one of the Inquisition's agents.

I should have, he thought now, staring down into the beer mug. *God forgive me, I should have. But I couldn't. I just couldn't.*

He took another swallow of beer, trying to wash away the sour taste in his mouth, the knowledge that he'd failed God and the Archangel Schueler. And he wasn't even positive why. He knew his mother still loved his father dearly, despite Rahzhyr's lack of conviction. That was the reason he hadn't informed the Inquisition. He was sure of it. And yet. . . .

Memories flowed through him. Memories of a time when he'd been a boy, not a young man faced with his father's weakness. Memories of riding on his father's shoulders, laughing as his father tickled him or wrestled with him. Memories of his father's hands teaching him the use of plane and miter saw and lathe. Memories of when Rahzhyr Dahnvahr was the tallest, strongest, smartest, most handsome man in all of Ainsail's world. And as those memories glowed through his mind once more, the suspicion returned. It wasn't his *mother's* love for his father which had made him too weak to do what he knew he should have done.

Well, no mortal man was perfect. Not his father, and certainly not him. But if he was as strong as he could be, and if he truly trusted in God, then he would find he had strengths as well as weaknesses, and he would learn how to use the steel in his soul to offset the soft and flabby iron. And whatever his father's faults, however badly his father might have failed or the weakness of his father's convictions, there was nothing wrong with Ainsail's faith. He'd proven that to Archbishop Wyllym's satisfaction, and Vicar Zhaspahr had personally chosen him for his mission. That was enough to awaken the sin of pride in any man, however hard Ainsail might fight against it. But perhaps God would forgive him a *little* pride. And it wasn't as if Ainsail could have accomplished his purpose without the aid of dozens of others, most of whom he'd never met and none of whom knew who he truly was.

" 'Nother round, dearie?" the plump barmaid asked him brightly.

"Yes, I think so," he replied, setting the empty mug on her tray and dropping a silver tenth-mark beside it. Her eyes widened at the size of the coin, and she started to hand it back to him, but he put his own hand on top of it. "Keep it," he said, and smiled at her. "I'm leaving on a long voyage, and I won't have anywhere to spend it anyway. Besides, you can wish me luck for it, if you like."

"Oh, that I will!" she assured him with a broad smile. "And I'll have that new beer back to you quicker than a cat lizard could lick her ear, Sir!"

"No 'sir,' " he told her. "Just a simple sailorman."

"Not to me, you're not," she assured him.

From the glow in her eye she would have been perfectly prepared to demonstrate that to him, as well, but he only smiled and made shooing motions to send her on her way. Not that it wasn't tempting, but there were other and far more important things to concentrate on at this moment. In fact, it had probably been foolish of him to give the girl such a lavish tip. It might make her remember him later, not that "later" was going to be a problem. Besides, he'd been sent on his way with plenty of cash and, as he'd told her, he wouldn't have any place to spend the rest of it.

He leaned back in the ancient, leather-upholstered booth, smelling decades of pipe smoke, of beer, of fried sausages, fish, potatoes, and spider crabs. It was a comforting, homey kind of smell that soothed his nerves. And he had to admit there was something soothing about the ebb and flow of the conversations around him, as well.

He'd never quite fitted in in the Temple Lands, with his "islander" accent. The other boys his age had been merciless about teasing him over it, and there'd been several fistfights—one of them fairly spectacular, culminating in an uncomfortable interview with the city guard—before they'd finally learned better. But no matter how hard he'd tried, he hadn't been able to rid himself of that telltale accent, and in the end that had proven a good thing. It had helped him slip seamlessly back into the land of his birth, yet he was still more than a little amused by how *right* the dialect he'd tried so hard to eradicate in himself sounded falling upon his ear from others.

Well, it's not as if they're all heretics and blasphemers, now is it? he asked himself. *There are plenty of Faithful still right here in Charis. They're just afraid to show it, that's all. Wave Thunder's damned spies are everywhere. They've managed to sniff out every organization the Grand Inquisitor's tried to establish here, so of course the Charisian Temple Loyalists are afraid to trust anyone enough to organize any kind of effective resistance!*

For that matter, he reminded himself, there *had* been Charisian Loyalists who'd dared to raise their hands against their heretical, excommunicate king and his apostate bride. They'd almost gotten that bastard Staynair in his own cathedral! And they'd come within inches of getting Sharleyan at Saint Agtha's. And then there'd been the man who'd made his own mission possible.

"Here you are, dearie," the barmaid said, sliding the fresh beer onto the table before him. She'd added a complimentary bowl of fried potato slices, and he smiled his thanks as he popped one of the fresh, piping hot slices into his mouth. In fact, it was hot enough he had to follow it rather quickly with an extinguishing swallow of beer.

"Good!" he told her, nodding enthusiastically even as he puffed out air to cool his scorched tongue and lips. "Hot, but good."

"Not the only thing here you could say that about," she told him with a saucy wink, and headed back off through the early evening crowd with an even saucier swing of her hips.

He smiled after her, but then the smile faded as he thought about how far he'd come. Not much further to *go*, though, he thought. Not much further at all.

He never would have admitted it to a soul, but he'd had more than a few reservations after his mission had been fully explained to him. Not about the mission itself, but about the complexity involved in getting him into position and preparing the way for it. The thought of returning to Charis completely on his own would have been enough to make anyone nervous. The fact that he was strictly prohibited from actually contacting any of the people who'd made his trip possible or contributed to the arrangements here in Charis had produced even more anxiety. He had to simply trust that each of the people responsible for moving him along would do his—or *her*, for all he knew, in some cases—part and that none of the details would go astray. The notion that such a complex set of arrangements could possibly work had seemed absurd, but as Archbishop Wyllym had pointed out, the Inquisition had been conducting similar operations for centuries. Perhaps not under conditions quite this extreme, but close enough to give them the expertise they needed once they'd realized what an efficient counter-spying organization they were up against here in Charis.

And there hadn't been all *that* many people involved, not really. It only seemed that way to him because he'd had to rely on them so blindly. But that very blindness had been his own best defense, because they hadn't known him, either. For that matter, they hadn't even known *why* they were doing what they'd been assigned to do. Not only that, every one of them had done his or her job exactly as Ainsail had—with no contact with *anyone* else in the service of Mother Church from the moment they or their instructions left Zion. No one would overhear any conversations or intercept any communications between them because there *were* no conversations or communications. There were only Ainsail and his fellow volunteers (none of whom had ever met, so far as he knew, even in Zion) and the detailed directions they'd been given before they were sent out.

When the Charisian powder mill blew up, Ainsail had been certain the entire operation had gone up in the same explosion. He had no idea who the Inquisition's contact inside the Charisian Navy was, yet it had been obvious there had to be one. And when he'd heard about the explosion—he'd still been in Emerald at the time, waiting for the brig to carry him for the final leg of his wearisome journey from Zion—he'd realized that whoever the contact was, he must have been unmasked somehow. And that meant he hadn't been able to complete his part of the preparations.

Ainsail had considered aborting the operation. He'd had that option, yet he'd known even as he'd considered the possibility that he wasn't going to do it. He hadn't come this far to turn back. And so he'd continued and, to his amazement, he'd found the promised supplies waiting exactly where he'd been told they'd be. Obviously, the Inquisition's contact *had* managed to complete his preparations, and Ainsail found himself wondering if perhaps the destruction of the powder mill had always been part of the plan. For that matter, *had* the contact been in the mill when it blew up? Could he have contrived the explosion with some sort of delay mechanism that let him escape before the blast?

Ainsail didn't know about that. It wasn't the way *his* part of the operation was supposed to work, but there was nothing that said other parts of it couldn't work differently. In fact, he rather hoped it had. Anyone who could have made Rakurai possible was far more valuable alive than dead.

I don't suppose I'll ever know, he reflected now, cautiously testing another of the potato slices to see if it had cooled enough. It had, and he chewed slowly, savoring the taste despite his scorched tongue. It was the best tasting fried potato he'd ever had, he thought, and then snorted in amusement. *Sure it is! Then again, maybe it's not. And maybe the beer isn't really as good as I think it is, either. Maybe it's just that knowing how close I am is making me savor everything more than I ever did before.*

He didn't know about that, and he wasn't going to waste his time worrying about it, either. He had two more five-days here in Tellesberg, and he intended to use those days wisely.

. IU .

Citadel of Schueler,
The Temple,
City of Zion,
The Temple Lands

He didn't know if it was day or night.

They were careful about that. There was no daylight, no moonlight or stars, to help keep track of time, and they deliberately fed them—if you could call it "feeding"—

at irregular, staggered intervals. No one was allowed to sleep uninterrupted, either. Buckets of ice-cold water hurled through the bars of their cells were enough to wake anyone up, although sometimes the guards varied their procedure. White-hot irons on the ends of long wooden shafts were quite effective at rousing sleepers, as well.

They'd been stripped of even the ragged remnants of their uniforms before they'd been consigned to their cages under the bowels of the Citadel of Schueler. It wasn't part of the original Temple complex, the Citadel; it had been built later, expressly for the Inquisition, and its walls were thick enough, its dungeons buried deep enough, that no one beyond its precincts could hear what happened within.

And that was where they'd been thrown into their cells, naked, deprived of any last vestige of human dignity. Beaten, starved, tortured at seemingly random and totally unpredictable intervals. Perhaps the most horrible thing of all, Gwylym Manthyr thought, was that they'd learned to sleep right through the shrieks of their tortured fellows. It wasn't that they'd become callous; it was that their bodies were so desperately starved for sleep . . . and that those shrieks had become a *routine* part of the only hellish world they had left.

He looked down at his own hands in the dim lantern light. There were no nails on those scabbed, scarred fingers now, but he was luckier than some. Naiklos Vahlain—before his valiant heart finally failed him and he escaped—had been held down by two brawny inquisitors while a third had used an iron bar to methodically break every bone in his skilled, deft hands one joint at a time.

He wanted to put it down to nothing but rabid, unthinking cruelty, yet he knew it was far worse than that. All of it had a purpose, and not simply to "punish the heretics." It was designed not simply to break them, but to *shatter* them. To stretch their souls upon the rack, not just their bodies, until their faith in themselves, the courage of their convictions, whatever it was that let them defy Zhaspahr Clyntahn, shattered into a million fragments that sifted through their broken fingers to the floors of their cells. It was designed to turn them into shambling scarecrows who would mouth whatever lies were dictated to them when they were paraded before the faithful, if only they would finally be allowed to die.

It was hard, he thought. *Hard* to maintain his faith, his trust in a God who could let something like this happen. Hard to sustain his belief in the importance of standing for what was just in defense of what he knew was true and his love for his homeland. All of that seemed far away, dream-like, from this unchanging, lantern-lit slice of hell. Not quite real, like something out of a fever delirium. Yet he clung to that faith and belief, that love, anyway, and their unlikely ally was hate. A bitter, burning, driving hate such as he'd never imagined he might feel. It filled his tortured, half-broken body with a savage determination which lifted him above himself. Which drove him onward, despite the sheer stupidity of surviving another single day, because it refused to let him stop.

He heard iron-nailed boots clashing their way across the stone floor, and the sliding sound of someone's feet trailing across it as the inquisitors hauled him along by his arms. He stepped closer to the front wall of his tiny cell, holding on to the bars despite the way the guards liked to hammer the prisoners' fingers against the unyielding steel with their truncheons, and peered through them. He heard the soft moaning as the inquisitors drew closer, and he recognized the prisoner being dragged to face whatever fresh torture had been devised for him.

"Hang on, Horys!" he called, his own voice hoarse and distorted. "Hang on, man!"

The words were pointless, and he knew it, yet Captain Braishair managed to raise his head as he heard them. It wasn't the *meaning* of the words that mattered; it was the *fact* of them. The evidence that even here there was still someone who cared, someone who knew Horys Braishair for who he *was*, not what the Inquisition was determined to make him.

"Aye, Sir Gwylym," Braishair half whispered. "I'll do that thing, and—"

He broke off with a strangled grunt, jerking spastically as the weighted truncheon slammed into his kidneys. The inquisitors didn't even bother to explain why the blow had landed; to do that would have been to acknowledge that their prisoners had some remnant of humanity that deserved explanations.

They dragged Braishair away, and a few moments later Manthyr heard fresh screams echo down the dungeon's stone-walled gut. He leaned his forehead against the bars, pressing his eyes closed, feeling the tears on his cheeks, and he was no longer ashamed of that "unmanly" wetness, for it was so utterly unimportant against what truly mattered.

The Inquisition wanted to break them all, but especially to break *him*, and he knew it. They wanted the Charisian admiral—Emperor Cayleb's own flag captain at Rock Point, and Crag Hook, and Darcos Sound—to admit his heresy. To denounce his emperor as a worshipper of Shan-wei, a liar and blasphemer, and the Church of Charis as a foul, schismatic perversion of God's true Church. They wanted that so badly they could *taste* it, and so they tortured his men even more cruelly than they tortured him. They ground his responsibility to them and his utter inability to do anything *for* them into his heart and soul and they expected that to break him in the end.

But they'd miscalculated, he thought, opening his eyes once more, staring at the stone wall opposite his cell. Even the Inquisition could do that, and it had, because they weren't going to break him. Not now, not next five-day, not next year—*never*. And the reason they weren't was what they'd done to his men. Men who would have died before the watching crowd of spectators no matter what Sir Gwylym Manthyr did or did not "confess to." Men he couldn't have saved no matter what he'd done. Duty to his Emperor, faith in his God, loyalty to his Church—all of those things mattered, even here and even now. They were still part of him. But it was love and the hate—that molten, grinding hate which burned so much hotter for what they'd done to his men than for what they'd done to him—which would carry him to the bitter end. They could kill him, they could—and had, and would again—make him scream, but they could not—*would* not—break him.

▼ ▼ ▼

"On your feet!" someone snarled, and a braided lash snaked between the bars to pop viciously against Manthyr's chest.

His head jerked up, and he shoved himself to his feet, the rough stone wall sliding against his spine as he leaned against it for support. He didn't scream, didn't even curse. He simply glared at the inquisitor beyond the bars. He didn't know the man's name; none of them *had* names, as far as he could tell. But this one wore an auxiliary bishop's ruby ring and his purple habit was trimmed in green and ecclesiastic white.

The bishop tucked his hands behind himself, considering the naked, scarred, burned, and welted man behind the bars.

"You're a stubborn bunch, aren't you?" he asked finally. "Stupid, too." He shook his head. "Surely you've realized by now that not even Shan-wei can save you from God's cleansing fire. Maybe you're so lost to God you refuse to turn back to Him even now, but why cling to the Mistress who's betrayed you the way she betrays everyone? Confess your sins and at least you can be spared further Question!"

Manthyr considered him for a moment, then spat. The spittle hit the bishop on the right cheek, and the man's hand rose slowly to wipe it off. There was something ineffably evil about his self-control, the fact that his expression never even changed. It was a statement that the cruelty he inflicted would be carefully measured, not the result of blind fury that might slip and allow its victim to escape into death too soon.

"That was foolish," he said flatly. "Do you think you're the only one who can pay for your stupidity?"

"Go to hell," Manthyr told him softly.

"Oh, no, not me." The inquisitor shook his head. "But *you* will, and by your example, you're dragging others with you."

He turned his head and nodded to someone beyond Manthyr's field of view, and two more Inquisitors dragged someone else down the passage. A third unlocked Manthyr's cell, and they hurled the barely breathing body into his cell with him. He went to his knees, staring in horror at Lainsair Svairsmahn, and the Schuelerite bishop's laugh was an icicle.

"That *boy* is clinging to your example," he said softly. "Look at what your bravado is costing *him* and see if it's still worth it."

He turned on his heel and stalked off, followed by the other Inquisitors, and Manthyr crouched over the body of his midshipman, staring at the seared and puckered wounds where the boy's eyes had been. Svairsmahn was a brittle bundle of bones and skin, so broken and scarred it was almost impossible to believe he was still alive. But that thin chest continued to rise and fall, and Manthyr laid a gentle, shaking hand on his cheek.

Svairsmahn flinched, one hand rising weakly in futile self-defense, but Manthyr gripped its wrist.

"It's me, Master Svairsmahn," he said.

"Sir Gwylym?" He could hardly hear the thready whisper and he bent closer, his ear inches from the midshipman's mouth.

"I'm here, Lainsair."

"I . . . tried, Sir. I tried." Svairsmahn's blind face turned towards him. "I tried, but . . . they made me. I . . . I told them. Told them . . . you worshipped . . . Shan-wei. I'm sorry . . . Sir. I tried. I *tried*."

"Shush, Lainsair." Manthyr's voice broke as he lifted that slight, maimed, broken body in his arms. He held the boy to his chest, cradling him as he might have a far younger child and urging his head down against his shoulder. "Shush. It's all right."

"But . . . but I lied," Svairsmahn whispered. "I lied . . . about you. About the Emperor. About . . . everybody . . . just so they'd stop."

"Don't think about that now," Manthyr said into his ear, feeling the fresh tears on his own cheeks. "You're not alone. You think no one else's told them what they wanted to hear? Look what they've done to you, Lainsair. Look what they've done. Of *course* you told them what they wanted you to."

"Shouldn't." Svairsmahn tried to shake his head again against Manthyr's shoulder. "Officers . . . don't lie, Sir."

"I know. I know, Lainsair, but it's all right."

Manthyr settled into a sitting position, Svairsmahn in his lap, and stared through the bars of his cell. The boy couldn't survive much more, yet Manthyr knew why the bishop had left him here. Because they were going to come back, and they were going to torture this broken, dying boy again in front of him until *he* told them what they wanted to hear.

But they've made a mistake, Lainsair, he thought. *This time, they've made a mistake.*

He cradled the boy's head between his half-crippled but still strong hands, thanking God with all his heart for their captors' mistake, and leaned forward until his forehead touched the midshipman's.

"Listen to me, Lainsair," he said. "This is important. Are you listening?"

"Yes, Sir Gwylym," Svairsmahn whispered.

"You've never done less than your duty as a king's officer, Master Svairsmahn," Manthyr said firmly, his voice strong and calm despite the tears. "Not in all the time I've known you. What you may have said to them, what you may have told them because they tortured you, can't change that. And it can't change who you are, who you've always been, either. I'm proud of you, Lainsair. You've done well, and I'm proud of you. It's been my highest honor to serve with you."

"Thank you, Sir." He could scarcely hear the wisp of a voice, but the boy's cracked lips moved in a ghost of a smile.

"No, Lainsair." Manthyr raised the midshipman's head far enough to kiss the boy's forehead and adjusted his grip with careful, loving firmness.

"No, Lainsair; thank *you*," he said, his voice soft . . . and his hands twisted sharply.

. U .

The Gulf of Jharas,
Desnairian Empire

"My respects to the Admiral, Master Aplyn-Ahrmahk, and inform him that Admiral Shain has hoisted the signal."

"Aye, aye, Sir. Your respects to Admiral Yairley and Admiral Shain has hoisted the signal."

Aplyn-Ahrmahk was pleased by how calm his voice sounded, under the circumstances, and as he saluted and headed for the ladder, the old saying about things changing and yet remaining the same ran through his mind. He could remember hundreds of times Midshipman Aplyn-Ahrmahk had been sent below with messages for Captain Yairley, and here he was doing it again, except that *this* message was rather more important than most of those others. Well that, and the fact that *Ensign* Aplyn-Ahrmahk was taking the message to *Admiral* Yairley, and he'd been chosen not because he happened to be conveniently available but because he'd become Admiral Sir Dunkyn Yairley's flag lieutenant.

On the face of it, he was ridiculously junior for such a post. On the other hand, he'd served under Sir Dunkyn for the better part of four years now, and the Navy was as strapped for experienced officers as it was for seamen, especially in the wake of its current expansion. It was unlikely there was a lieutenant equally familiar with the admiral's ways running around loose. And he had far more experience than his sixteen years (well, sixteen years in another couple of five-days) might have suggested. And, for that matter, he'd be a lieutenant on that birthday of his. So he supposed it all actually made sense, even though he'd discovered that even after Sir Dunkyn's intensive tutelage, the social skills that normally went with his position were not precisely his strongest suit. Well, he'd just have to make up for it by working on them still harder.

He reached the paneled door to Admiral Yairley's day cabin. It was, in fact, the same cabin which had belonged to Captain Yairley, since *Destiny* was not, unfortunately, one of the later and larger galleons which had been built with separate flag quarters.

Another example of things staying the same, he thought, nodding to the Marine sentry and then rapping sharply. For a moment he thought his knock hadn't been heard, but then a voice answered.

"Enter!"

Aplyn-Ahrmahk took off his hat, tucked it even more carefully than usual under his left arm, and ran straightening fingers through his tousled hair before he stepped through the door. Not that he was worried about the admiral's reaction to his appearance. Oh no, not *his.* . . .

Sylvyst Raigly, Sir Dunkyn's valet and steward, had become awesomely aware of his employer's exalted status the instant the brand-new admiral's streamer had been broken from *Destiny*'s mizzen. Raigly was only about thirty years old, well read, and always well dressed and carefully groomed, but when he decided to feel waspish, he was capable of the most icily polite, formal, biting, exquisitely *nasty* set downs Aplyn-Ahrmahk had ever encountered. The ensign had never heard him utter a single overtly inappropriate or discourteous word . . . which didn't prevent Raigly from vivisecting anyone unfortunate enough to rouse his ire. He was also a crack pistol shot and an excellent swordsman, and one of his shipboard duties had been to instruct the midshipmen in sword work. He'd done a great deal to improve Aplyn-Ahrmahk's combat skills, and the two of them were friends . . . which wouldn't save Aplyn-Ahrmahk's neck if he came into the admiral's presence with his tunic unbuttoned or a hat on his head below decks.

There was no sharp-eyed and ominous valet waiting for him this time, however; merely an admiral. Well, an admiral and his secretary, who was *far* less terrifying than any valet!

"Yes, Hektor?" Yairley asked, looking up from the chart he'd been contemplating while he dictated a letter to Trumyn Lywshai, his newly appointed flag secretary.

"Captain Lathyk's compliments, Sir. Admiral Shain has hoisted the signal."

"I see."

Yairley glanced back at the chart once more, then straightened. He stepped to the skylight, looked up at the wind indicator, and nodded in satisfaction.

"I suppose we should go on deck, then," he said mildly, and looked at Lywshai. "We'll finish that correspondence later, Trumyn."

"Of course, Sir Dunkyn."

Lywshai was ten years older than Raigly, although he and the valet got along well. But whereas Raigly was as Charisian-born and bred as a man came (and looked it), Lywshai's hair was so dark a black it was almost blue and his eyes had a much more pronounced epicanthic fold. His father had been born in the Harchong Empire and sold to a Harchongian merchant captain by the local baron as a "cabin boy" when he was only seven. Shaintai Lywshai seldom spoke about those years, although they'd left deep and painful scars, and not just of the body. But the captain who'd bought him had decided to dabble in piracy as a sideline and picked the wrong galleon as a prize. Which was how Shaintai had ended up in Tellesberg at the age of thirteen, adopted by the captain of the galleon his previous (deceased) owner had attempted to capture. And which also explained the ferocious loyalty of Shaintai's son Trumyn and the entire extensive Lyws-hai family to Charis and the Charisian crown.

"Do you want me to wait until you come back below?" Lywshai asked now. "Or should I start making the fair copies of your other letters for your signature?"

"Go ahead and finish up the ones I've already dictated," Yairley decided. "I don't believe we'll be able to get very much done on the rest of it until this little affair is over, though."

"Of course, Sir Dunkyn," Lywshai said again, with a small half bow, and Yairley smiled at him. He hadn't had very long to get to know the secretary, but he'd already decided High Admiral Rock Point's glowing recommendation had been right on the mark. He watched Lywshai's skillful fingers adroitly sorting through the correspondence, then raised his voice.

"Sylvyst!"

"Coming, Sir Dunkyn!" a tenor voice replied, and Raigly stepped out of the admiral's sleeping cabin carrying Yairley's uniform tunic over one arm and the admiral's sword belt over the other.

Yairley grimaced at sight of the sword belt, but he didn't argue. He only slid his arms into the offered tunic, buttoned it, and then buckled the belt around his waist. Unlike many other officers, he carried no pistols, but Raigly made up for that. Technically, the valet was a civilian, not that his lack of official martial standing seemed to cause him any undue concern. Although he wore civilian clothing, he was armed with sword and dirk and no less than four double-barreled pistols, two in holsters and the second pair shoved through his belt.

"We haven't cleared for action yet, you know, Sylvyst," Yairley observed.

"No, Sir Dunkyn, we haven't," Raigly agreed.

"Then don't you think that might be a little . . . excessive?" the admiral asked, waving at the valet's arsenal.

"No, Sir Dunkyn. Not really," Raigly replied politely, and Yairley gave up. Between the valet and Stywyrt Mahlyk he'd have the equivalent of an entire squad of Marines

keeping an eye on him. And now, no doubt, Aplyn-
Ahrmahk, relieved of ship-handling duties, would add
himself to the bodyguard corps, as well. In some ways, it
was a relief; at other times he found himself wondering a
bit plaintively why neither his valet nor his coxswain nor
(now) his flag lieutenant had figured out he was an adult
capable of looking after himself.

Best not to follow that thought up, he reminded himself again. *You probably wouldn't like where it ended.*

"Well, if you're satisfied that you're sufficiently well
armed, let's go see what the rest of the fleet is doing," he
said dryly.

"Of course, Sir Dunkyn," Raigly replied gravely, and
Yairley heard something which sounded suspiciously like
a chuckle from his flag lieutenant.

▼ ▼ ▼

"Oh, shit."

Sir Urwyn Hahltar, Baron of Jahras and Admiral
General of the Imperial Desnairian Navy, spoke quietly
but with great feeling as he looked at the semaphore message in his hand.

"They're coming?" Daivyn Bairaht, the Duke of Kholman, didn't sound any happier than his brother-in-law.

"Of course they're coming!" Jahras growled. "It was
only a matter of time." He tossed the balled-up message
slip into the trash can beside his desk with a disgusted
expression. "The only surprise is that they've waited this
long!"

He stamped his way to the window and looked out
across the Iythrian waterfront. The good news was that
there'd been time to complete almost all of the Desnairian Navy's building program. That meant he had ninety-
one fully armed galleons at his disposal. The bad news
came in two installments. First, all of his ships were
smaller than a typical Charisian galleon, with lighter armaments, less reliable guns which were prone to burst at
inconvenient moments, and crews which were far less
well trained. Second, according to the message from the

Sylmahn's Island semaphore station, something on the order of a hundred Charisian galleons, an unknown number of them armed with the new exploding "shells" which had gutted Kornylys Harpahr's fleet, were headed directly for his window at this very moment.

Some of Emperor Mahrys' senior advisers—the ones safely far away from the Gulf of Jahras and with the least responsibility for building and training the emperor's navy—had urged Jahras to adopt a mobile, aggressive strategy. The idiots in question obviously failed to grasp the difference between ships at sea and the cavalry for which the Desnairian Empire was famed. They'd seen no reason why he shouldn't have kept the enemy entirely out of the Gulf by using Howard Reach's constricted waters to tie up any Charisian assault with spoiling attacks launched by smaller, handier squadrons that could dash in, hammer the enemy, and then fall back on his main force. After all, how different could it be from using cavalry attacks to tie up and pin down a more numerous foe trying to fight his way through a mountain pass?

There were times Jahras was tempted to suggest one of *them* should become admiral general. Unfortunately, none of them were quite stupid enough to accept the job.

Especially now.

About the only thing they are *smart enough to avoid,* he told himself bitterly. *And can anyone explain to them the difference between a spirited and noble cavalry charger on a nice solid piece of ground and a galleon dependent entirely on wind and current? Or the fact that, unlike a cavalry regiment, a ship can sink, or burn, or just damned well* blow up *if someone shoots at it enough? No, of course they can't! And they're conveniently forgetting about the Charisians' new little* weapon, *aren't they?*

"I don't suppose we've had any last-minute orders from Vicar Allayn that you just neglected to mention to me?" he asked Kholman over his shoulder, never looking away from the ships in the harbor.

"If he'd said a word since your last dispatch to the Temple, I'd have told you about it." The duke's expression was as frustrated as Jahras' own. As the effective Desnair-ian naval minister he'd presided over Jahras' efforts to build the ships Mother Church had required of the empire. He knew exactly how difficult the task had been . . . and why Jahras was unwilling to face Charis at sea.

"I don't think we're *going* to get a reply from Vicar Allayn," he continued now, his tone flat. "I think he's going to wait to see how things work out, then either take credit for 'allowing us to use our own initiative' if it's anything short of a disaster, or point out our 'failure to comply with Mother Church's strategic directions' if it turns out as badly as we're afraid it will."

"Wonderful." Jahras sighed, puffing out his cheeks, his expression pensive. "I'm almost tempted to go ahead and sail," he admitted. "Assuming I didn't get blown up, shot, or drowned I could at least point out that I'd followed orders."

He turned his head, looking his brother-in-law in the eye, and Kholman nodded soberly. Anything that might lead the Grand Inquisitor or his agents to question one's determination and loyalty was contraindicated.

"Between the doomwhale and the deep blue sea," the duke said quietly.

"Exactly." Jahras nodded back, then squared his shoulders. "But if I have to do this, I'm going to do it as effectively as I can and hope for the best. Shan-wei, Daivyn! Thirsk got himself hailed as a hero for capturing four Charisian galleons, and he'd already lost one of his own! For that matter, he'd surrendered an entire *damned* fleet after Crag Hook! If we can at least bleed them when they come in here after us, maybe somebody in Zion will be smart enough to realize we did the best anyone could have."

"Maybe," Duke Kholman replied. "Maybe."

▼ ▼ ▼

"The schooners report no change in their deployment, Admiral," Captain Lathyk said, saluting as Admiral Yairley arrived on *Destiny*'s quarterdeck.

"Not surprising, I suppose, Captain," Yairley replied. A greater degree of formality had crept into his public relationship with Lathyk—inevitably, he imagined. Given his new rank, he was now a passenger in *Destiny*, not her master after God, and it was important he and Lathyk make that point clearly for the ship's company. A warship could have only one captain, and any confusion about who that warship's crew looked to for orders in an emergency could be disastrous. "I wish they *would* come out, but obviously no one in Iythria is foolish enough to do that. Barring direct orders, of course."

Lathyk nodded, and Yairley's lips quirked briefly. As High Admiral Rock Point had pointed out, to date, the Group of Four had been Charis' best allies when it came to naval matters. Rock Point had hoped, more wistfully than with any great expectation of its happening, that Allayn Maigwair might issue Baron Jahras direct, non-discretionary orders to sortie and engage the Imperial Charisian Navy at sea. Apparently even Maigwair had more sense than that, however . . . unfortunately.

"Well," the admiral said now, "if they won't come out, we'll just have to go in."

"Going to be lively, Sir!" Lathyk observed with that irritating prebattle smile of his, and Yairley shrugged.

"I suppose that's one way to describe it," he agreed with a smaller, tighter smile of his own.

Destiny's motion was a little uneasy as she lay hove-to in the Middle Ground between Sylmahn Island and Ray Island, but that didn't explain Yairley's queasiness. He knew what *did* cause it, of course. The same odd, hollow feeling which always afflicted him when battle drew near was already quivering inside him, and he suppressed a familiar sense of envy as Lathyk chuckled in response to his comment. He didn't think Lathyk was any less imaginative than he was, but somehow the captain—like so many of Yairley's fellows—seemed impervious to the sort of tension which gripped him at times like this. And even *he* wasn't all that consistent about it, he thought irritably. It made absolutely no sense for the thought of being splattered across the deck by a cannonball to . . . concern him so much when the thought of drowning in a storm didn't cause him to turn a hair. Well, not *much* of a hair, anyway.

"Signal from *Terror*, Captain!" Midshipman Saylkyrk called out. He was in the maintop with his enormous spyglass trained on HMS *Terror*, Admiral Shain's flagship. "Relayed from *Destroyer*. Our pendant number, then Number Thirty, Number Thirty-Six, Number Fifty-Five, and Number Eight." He looked down from the maintop to where Ahrlee Zhones had the signal book open, already finding the signal numbers from the grid.

"Make sail on the larboard tack, course south-by-east, and prepare for battle, Sir!" the younger midshipman announced after a handful of seconds.

"Very good, Master Zhones," Lathyk said. "Be good enough to acknowledge the signal under the squadron's number."

"Aye, aye, Sir!" Zhones was obviously nervous, but he also wore a huge grin as he beckoned to the quarterdeck signal party.

"Master Symkee!" Lathyk continued, turning to the lieutenant who'd become *Destiny*'s executive officer in parallel with his own promotion.

"Aye, Sir?"

"Hands to braces, if you please. Prepare to get the ship underway."

"Aye, aye, Sir! Hands to braces, Bo'sun!"

"Aye, aye, Sir!"

The signal had scarcely been unexpected, and the colorful bunting had already been spilled out of its canvas bags and bent to the signal halliards. The flags went soaring up while bo'sun's pipes shrilled and the ship's company went racing to its stations, and Admiral Yairley folded his hands behind him and crossed to the taffrail to gaze astern while his flag captain and his flagship's crew got about the business of translating High Admiral Rock Point and Admiral Shain's orders into action.

The other five ships of his squadron—HMS *Royal Kraken*, HMS *Victorious*, HMS *Thunderbolt*, HMS

Undaunted, and HMS *Champion*—also lay hove-to, keeping close company on *Destiny*, and High Admiral Rock Point had done him proud when he made up the squadron's numbers. *Destiny* was the oldest and smallest of the six, but all of them were purpose-built war galleons from Charisian yards, not captured prizes or converted merchantmen, and between them they mounted three hundred and forty guns. Well found, well handled, and (after the voyage from Tellesberg to Thol Bay to the Gulf of Jahras, at least) well drilled, they were a potent force. Especially since all of them carried shot lockers full of the new exploding shells. *Royal Kraken* and *Thunderbolt* also carried massive fifty-seven-pounder carronades, short-ranged compared to the new model krakens on their gun decks but capable of throwing much heavier and more destructive shells. The other four carried uniform armaments of thirty-pounders, and unlike the Battle of the Markovian Sea, all of his gunners had been given ample opportunity to train with the new ammunition.

Which is a very good thing, he thought dryly, that hollowness in his middle feeling somehow even emptier, *given our part of the battle plan.*

The wind was a stiff topsail breeze out of the northeast-by-east, blowing at a speed of perhaps twenty-four miles per hour and raising eight-to ten-foot waves. On her new heading, *Destiny* would be sailing large, with the wind almost dead on her quarter. That was just about her best point of sailing, which meant she ought to make good seven and a half or eight knots, with just under thirty miles to go. Call it four hours, he thought. Time to get all the men fed a good, solid lunch before they cleared for action, and then. . . .

"All ships have acknowledged, Sir!" Saylkyrk called from above.

"Very good, Master Saylkyrk!" Lathyk called back, then turned respectfully to Yairley.

"All ships have acknowledged receipt of the signal, Admiral."

"Thank you, Captain," Yairley replied gravely, and

glanced up at the stiffly starched signal flags himself. By hoisting the squadron's number above Admiral Shain's signal, Lathyk had repeated it to all of the squadron's units. When it was hauled down, Yairley's command would execute it, the rest of the fleet's sixteen squadrons would make sail in his wake in succession to execute their own portions of the high admiral's master plan, and the die would be cast.

My, how dramatic, Dunkyn, he thought wryly. *"The die was cast" before you ever left Tellesberg.*

"Very well, Captain Lathyk," he heard himself say calmly. "Execute."

▼ ▼ ▼

Sir Domynyk Staynair stood on HMS *Destroyer*'s quarterdeck, watching his flagship's crew scamper about making final preparations. Or that was what he looked like he was doing, at any rate. In fact, he was watching the imagery projected on his contact lenses as Dunkyn Yairley and Payter Shain began to move and the rest of the fleet started unfolding into its own component columns behind them.

The Imperial Charisian Navy had returned to the Gulf of Mathyas in strength within less than a month of *Destiny*'s damage-enforced retreat, and this time it hadn't come simply to keep an eye on the exit from the Gulf of Jahras. Admiral Shain had sent his fleet-footed schooners deep into the Gulf to reconnoiter the approaches to Terrence Bay, Port Iythria, and Mahrosa Bay. In the process, they'd swept the once-sheltered waters clear of Desnairian commerce, and, taking a page from Rock Point's own tactics in Thol Bay, Shain had used his Marines to seize control of Howard Island, well inside Staiphan Reach and right in the throat of the Howard Passage.

The island was barely thirty-five miles long, and aside from Tern Bay, at its northern end, it didn't present much in the way of decent anchorages. Even Tern Bay was little more than an open roadstead, offering no protection at all against northerlies. Still, it was a source of fresh water, always a warship's most limiting supply factor. It had taken two five-days for the heavy naval guns landed across the island's eastern beaches to batter the fortress guarding the small town of Tern Bay into submission, but they'd been time well spent, given how greatly its capture had eased Shain's logistics. The admiral had also landed enough Marines and enough artillery to make sure no Desnairian pounce was going to take it back from him, and suddenly the largely worthless island had become a cork driven firmly into the Desnairian bottle.

Operating from the (relative) security of Tern Bay, the Imperial Charisian Navy had gone basically wherever it chose in the Gulf of Jahras. Rock Point had rather hoped Baron Jahras would venture out to dispute the ICN's invasion of the Desnairian Empire's most economically vital coastal waters, but what had happened to Kornylys Harpahr had made the baron wiser than that. So the Charisian cruiser squadrons had amused themselves wiping out the Gulf's coasting trade and sending cutting-out expeditions into its lesser harbors under cover of darkness to capture or burn anything bigger than a fishing boat. And they'd also trailed their coats just beyond artillery range of the Desnairian Navy's harbor fortifications, counting noses and examining anchorages.

As a result, they'd been able to provide Rock Point with intelligence on his enemy's dispositions which was almost as good as what Owl's SNARCs delivered. Not *quite*, of course, since unlike the SNARCs they couldn't actually eavesdrop on Jahras' discussions with Kholman or his ship commanders, but they'd provided more than enough information Rock Point could openly share with his own subordinates for planning purposes. And as he'd studied and discussed those reports with Shain, Yairley, and his other flag officers and senior captains, it had become evident that Jahras realized he simply couldn't fight the Charisian Navy and hope to win. Not at sea, at any rate. Not only that, but somewhat to Rock Point's surprise, the baron had demonstrated the moral courage to tell his superiors he couldn't.

The Navy of God's shock after the Markovian Sea had been profound enough for those superiors to actually listen to him, as well. Or profound enough that they hadn't actively overruled him, at least, when he'd turned his galleons into what amounted to no more than floating batteries. Despite the importance of the Gulf's shipping to the Desnairian economy, he hadn't even tried to defend most of its ports, either. They'd had to make do with their existing coastal fortifications—which, admittedly, were more than enough to discourage any thought of widespread Charisian *landings,* especially with the Imperial Desnairian Army hanging about just in case it might be needed—because he'd refused to disperse those galleons. Iythria, with its major shipyards and dockyards, was the Gulf's largest and most important harbor and its primary naval base. It had been built up into a major node in the Church of God's shipbuilding and support system, and he'd decided he had no choice but to stake everything on protecting his fleet's supporting infrastructure, although even that much was a daunting challenge for a fleet which dared not meet its opponent under sail.

Iythria's approaches were screened by an arc of islands, extending from Sylmahn Island to the west, through Singer Island (the most northeasterly outpost of the port city), and then back to Pearl Point on the mainland. That, unfortunately, was a distance of over a hundred and fifty miles, which was far too long to protect with any sort of fixed defenses.

Sylmahn Island and Ray Island formed a second theoretical line of defense south of that, but the Middle Ground—the stretch of water between Sylmahn and Ray—was still forty-five miles across, and shallow enough in several spots to offer practical anchorages beyond the range of the island fortresses' artillery. South of the Middle Ground lay the Outer Roadstead, another thirty miles in a north-south line before one reached the Inner Harbor and the waterfront proper of Port Iythria. Taken altogether, it was one of the finest anchorages Rock Point had ever seen, and if Desnair hadn't been a primarily land-based power

with its attention firmly focused on the Republic of Siddarmark and the Harchong Empire, it would have offered
a sound base for a thriving merchant marine. Instead,
other realms' shipping—primarily Charis', before the . . .
current unpleasantness—had made use of its potential,
which meant among other things that Rock Point's charts
for Iythria and its approaches were very, very detailed.

The only way to actually reach Iythria from the sea
required an attacker to penetrate one of the two open-
ings in the shoals protecting the Inner Harbor. The West
Gate, the passage between Rocky Bank Shoal and Sickle
Shoal, was the narrower of those approaches. Navigable
by small vessels across virtually its entire width at high
water, the *deepwater* channel was unfortunately serpen-
tine and relatively narrow, which made it a much more
problematical route for blue water galleons. On the other
hand, the North Gate—the opening between Sickle Shoal
and Triangle Shoal, directly north of the city—was far
broader than the West Gate. It was also deeper, with a
twelve-mile ship channel, navigable even at low water,
with nary a twist nor a turn.

The Desnairians were well aware of just how wide the
door to Iythria's heart was, and they'd built powerful
(and expensive) fortifications on both Sickle Shoal and
Triangle Shoal. The masonry forts rose straight out of the
water, which put any sort of siege or assault landing out
of the question, but the total water gap between them was
the better part of twenty-four miles across, and the maximum reach of their artillery was no more than *three* miles.

As part of Jahras' strategy to emulate a horn lizard and
curl up into an armored ball no one could get at, he'd
blocked the West Gate by sinking ships and driving pilings into the main shipping channel. Opening it again was
going to be an incredible pain, but for now he could be
certain no Charisian galleons were going to come sneak-
ing in on him that way. Boat attacks, and possibly even
attacks by the shallow-draft schooners at high water, perhaps, but not those deep-draft galleons with their heavy
artillery.

With the West Gate closed, he'd turned his attention to the North Gate and anchored his galleons directly across the ship channel. He'd moored them in a long chain, running twelve miles from east to west, with barely fifty yards between each ship and the next in line. Under normal circumstances, the interval would have been two or three times that great in order to give the vessels room to ride to their anchors with shifting tide and wind without fouling one another. Jahras clearly wasn't particularly worried about that; besides, each ship had put out no fewer than two bow and two stern anchors, with springs rigged to each of them. Those ships weren't moving, and he'd laid buoyed hawsers between them, as well. According to Owl's SNARCs, each of those cables was a good ten inches in diameter, and there were four of them between each ship. Obviously, they were intended to keep anybody from passing through the narrow gaps Jahras had left between his galleons.

In addition to the galleons, he'd managed to throw together thirty genuine floating batteries, essentially just big rafts with heavy bulwarks. He'd run out of naval artillery, so he'd requisitioned every field piece the Desnairian Army could get to Iythria in time, which meant the rafts were armed with an incredible hodgepodge of ancient cannon on every conceivable sort of improvised carriage. Most of them hadn't even been cast with trunnions, although the Iythrian artillery works had been welding banded trunnions onto them as quickly as possible. The batteries' fire was going to be a questionable asset, but there were still a lot of them, and he'd anchored them in the shallower water at either end of his line of galleons. Obviously, he intended for them to close as much as possible of the remaining water gap between his ships and the fortifications on Sickle Shoal and Triangle Shoal.

Backing up both galleons and floating batteries were fifteen or twenty old-fashioned galleys. They didn't have much in the way of artillery, but their job was to lurk on the inner side of the galleon line and to pounce upon and board any Charisian galleon foolhardy enough to force its way between Jahras' battleships.

It was obvious the baron had paid close attention to the reports he'd received about what had happened in the Markovian Sea. His awareness of the advantage the Charisians' exploding shells bestowed upon them was probably incomplete, but it was clear enough to explain his flat refusal to lead his fleet to sea against Rock Point. And he'd done what he could to protect his ships and batteries against the new threat, as well. He'd ransacked the entire Gulf for every length of chain he could find and draped it over his galleons' sides in an effort to make them at least a little more resistant to shellfire. He didn't have enough of it and it wasn't heavy enough to stop short range fire, but it was a clear indication he was at least thinking hard about the threat he faced.

The poorly armed floating batteries were actually better protected than his galleons. He'd had their already thick bulwarks fitted with frameworks which extended three or four feet, then he'd filled the frameworks with sandbags. The weight did unfortunate things to the rafts' stability and reduced their flotation margins dangerously, but a four-foot depth of sandbags was far better armor against smoothbore shells than the chain he'd draped down the galleons' sides.

Taking everything into consideration, Rock Point had to admit Jahras' preparations were both more thorough and more competent than he'd anticipated. Obviously, the baron realized that even with exploding shells the Charisians were still going to have to come into his range if they wanted to engage him. His anchors and springs should allow him to turn his ships in place and concentrate a devastating weight of solid shot on anyone approaching his line, and he'd done everything he could to prevent his line from being penetrated and doubled. Nor had he neglected the landward defenses. The waterfront batteries had been reinforced; he'd drafted entire infantry regiments from the Imperial Desnairian Army to reinforce his Marine contingents against the possibility of boarding actions; his decision to fight only from anchor meant he wouldn't need any seamen for maneuvering and that every man of every crew would be available to serve his guns; and he had something like twenty-five thousand additional men in Iythria's garrison, from which boats could ferry replacements to his galleons and batteries as they suffered casualties.

Yet despite all that, Sir Domynyk Staynair truly was as confident as he looked. He didn't expect it to be *easy,* but then again, few things worth doing were, and he smiled slightly as he recalled a discussion with Prince Nahrmahn.

"I have to say I didn't expect Jahras to put together such a nasty reception for you, Domynyk," the little Emeraldian had said over the com. His tone had been somber, obviously concerned, but Rock Point had only chuckled grimly.

"He's worked hard at it, I'll give him that," the admiral had replied. "And given his disadvantages, this is probably about the best plan he could've come up with. But there's a big difference between 'best plan he could come up with' and 'a plan with a chance in hell of succeeding,' Nahrmahn."

"I realize this is your area of expertise, not mine, but it looks ugly enough to me," Nahrmahn had said.

"That's because you're not a professional seaman." Rock Point had shaken his head. "Oh, if we didn't have the exploding shells and Ahlfryd's 'angle-guns' it would be a lot nastier, I'll give you—and Jahras—that. But we'd still take him in the end, even with nothing but old-fashioned round shot. The butcher's bill would be a hell of a lot higher than it's going to be, but we'd still take him."

"How can you be so sure?" There'd been only honest curiosity, not disbelief, in Nahrmahn's question, and Rock Point had shrugged.

"A warship is a *mobile* gun platform, Nahrmahn, and Jahras doesn't have the kind of experience a Charisian flag officer has. He thinks he's taken mobility out of play, but he's wrong. To a landsman or an army officer, I'm sure his position looks downright impregnable. What a *sailor* sees, though, are the rat-holes in his ramparts, and I mean to shove an entire fleet right through them."

That's what I said, Your Highness, he thought now, *and that's what I meant. Now to demonstrate how it works.*

. VI .

Outer Roadstead
and
Inner Harbor,
Port of Iythria,
Empire of Desnair

The guns on Triangle Shoal opened fire first.

Stupid, Sir Dunkyn Yairley thought. *We're still at least a mile out of range, you idiots! Probably the damned Army; even Desnairian naval gunners would know you couldn't hit anything—especially with Desnairian artillery—at four miles.*

Still, he had absolutely nothing against watching enemy gunners waste powder and shot. The first, most carefully prepared and aimed salvos were always the most effective, which was the reason most captains reserved their fire until they were close enough they figured they couldn't miss. Of course, fortress guns had the advantage of nice, solid, *unmoving* firing platforms, which no naval gunner ever had. That was one of the reasons no sane naval commander *ever* fought a well-sited, well-protected shore battery.

Or that was the way things used to be, at any rate. Charisian galleons had successfully out-dueled masonry-protected harbor defenses at Delferahk, after all. Still, even the majority of Charisian naval officers regarded that as something of a fluke . . . which it undoubtedly had been. For one thing, the rickety fortifications in question had been in less than perfect condition—indeed, some of them had been about ready to fall down on their own. More importantly, however, Admiral Rock Point had confronted old-style artillery, with a rate of fire less than a quarter that of his own, and he'd had the advantage of total surprise. Not surprise at being attacked, but astonishment—and probably sheer disbelief—at the volume of fire his ships had been able to produce.

That particular surprise no longer applied, and judging by the rapidity with which the Triangle Shoal fortress was pumping out round shot, it had been equipped with updated artillery, as well. If those shore gunners had modern guns, on modern carriages, and were using bagged charges, then the stability of their footing should actually allow them to serve their pieces even more rapidly than the Charisian gunners could.

On the other hand, there's a difference between rapid fire and effective fire, Yairley reminded himself. *Blazing away and not hitting anything is just a more spectacular way to accomplish absolutely nothing, and anybody who's going to open fire at this range is unlikely to be the most accurate gunner in the world at any range.*

He stood on *Destiny*'s quarterdeck, hands once more clasped behind him, feet spread, shoulders deliberately relaxed, and concentrated on looking calm.

I wonder if one reason I'm feeling so smug about the standard of Desnairian gunnery in general is that gloating over what lousy shots they are is one way of reassuring myself that they're not going to hit anything. Like me.

The thought made him chuckle, and he shook his head at his own perversity, then looked at Lathyk. The captain was bent over the binnacle, taking a compass bearing on the smoke-spurting fortress. Then he straightened and glanced up at the masthead weathervane with a thoughtful frown.

"Well, Captain?"

"I make it about another mile and a half before we alter towards them, Sir. Perhaps thirty more minutes."

Yairley turned to gaze over the bulwarks, considering angles and rates of movement, then nodded.

"I believe you're right, Captain. I think it's time to make the signal to Captain Rahzwail."

"Aye, Sir. I'll see to it."

Yairley nodded again, then looked around at the unfolding panorama. At least all the men who were about to die had been given a lovely day on which to do it. The sky was a deep, perfect blue, with only the lightest scattering of high-altitude cloud and the water was a gorgeous blend of blues and greens, creaming in white under the galleons forefeet, in the early afternoon sunlight. The seabirds and sea wyverns who'd followed the Charisian galleons, swooping and bobbing as they hoped for garbage in the ships' wakes, seemed confused by the sudden, rolling bursts of thunder on such a perfect day. They were circling away from the ships, although they didn't really seem panicked yet. On the other hand, they were probably bright enough to realize that what was about to happen was none of *their* business.

The rest of his squadron forged along in *Destiny*'s wake, and astern of them was a moving forest of masts and canvas weathered to all different shades of gray and tan and dirty white. The imperial standard flew from mastheads throughout the fleet—some of the more enthusiastic captains had one at each masthead—and the long, thin, colorful tongues of flag officers' command streamers blew from mizzenmasts for rear admirals and commodores, from mainmasts for admirals, and from foremasts for the newly introduced rank of vice admiral. Up until the last year or two, Yairley couldn't have imagined seeing that many ships in one place, all bent on a single mission under the command of a single admiral. Even now the sheer magnitude of the spectacle seemed preposterous.

He couldn't pick *Destroyer* out of the mass of her consorts, but she was back there, sailing along in the middle of that huge sprawl, rather than leading the way as he knew High Admiral Rock Point would have preferred.

But that exposed position wasn't the proper place for a high admiral—not in something like this. No, that was more properly left to a more *expendable* flag officer . . . like one Sir Dunkyn Yairley.

"The signal to Captain Rahzwail is ready, Sir," Ensign Aplyn-Ahrmahk said respectfully, and Yairley gave himself a shake.

"Very well, Master Aplyn-Ahrmahk, let's get it sent," the admiral said with a crooked smile. "And then I think we should probably signal the squadron to reduce sail, don't you think?"

▼ ▼ ▼

"They don't seem very impressed by General Stahkail's gunnery, My Lord," Captain Mahlyk Ahlvai observed dryly.

"No, they don't, Captain," Baron Jahras agreed.

They stood on the poop deck of HMS *Emperor Zhorj*, Jahras' forty-eight-gun flagship. Unlike the majority of the Desnairian Navy, *Emperor Zhorj* was a purpose-built war galleon, with much heavier framing and planking than her converted merchant consorts. Despite that, she was considerably smaller and more lightly armed than the ships sailing steadily towards her.

Jahras had strongly considered remaining in his shore-side office. With access to the semaphore and the signal flag mast on top of the main dockyard building, he'd actually have been better able to send orders from there (at least until smoke obscured all signals), especially with *Emperor Zhorj*'s masts truncated because of his orders to send topmasts and topgallant masts ashore. It would also have been considerably safer, in a personal sense. But while Jahras had steadfastly avoided combat with the Imperial Charisian Navy, there was nothing wrong with his personal courage. If his fleet had to fight, his proper place was with it. And from a somewhat more cynical and calculating perspective, he was more likely to avoid condemnation for the debacle about to occur if he could point out to Vicar Allayn and Vicar Zhaspahr that he'd commanded from the front, in the very heart and fury of the action. He didn't know how *much* more likely to avoid condemnation he might be, but anything was worth striving for.

At the moment, however, he could only endorse Captain Ahlvai's opinion. General Lowrai Stahkail, the commanding officer of the Triangle Shoal fortress, had not been Jahras' choice for his job. He could think of at least a half-dozen officers he would have preferred to see commanding that fort, but Stahkail had friends at court and a reputation—mostly self-bestowed—as an artillerist. Jahras had never seen any evidence he deserved it, although, to be fair, he was an *Army* artillerist, not a naval gunner.

Not that the baron was interested in being any fairer to Stahkail than he had to at the moment.

He raised his telescope and picked up the white flaws of round shot skipping across the waves. Perhaps Stahkail was trying to ricochet the shot into the ships, extending his range by bouncing the projectiles the way an artillerist could sometimes do on land. If so, he didn't seem to be succeeding.

You really should be at least a little fair, Urwyn, he told himself. *There's not much chance the Charisians are going to come into his range. If he wants to hit them at all he's going to have to do it from a long way away.*

Unfortunately, Stahkail's . . . enthusiasm seemed to be contagious, and some of the floating batteries closest to Triangle Shoal were beginning to fire sporadically, as well. Their guns were much closer to the water, giving them even less range than the fortress, and he lowered the glass with an angry grimace.

"Signal to the floating batteries if you please, Captain!" he snapped. "Cease fire! Do not waste powder and shot!"

"Aye, My Lord," Ahlvai replied, then cleared his throat. "Ah, should I address the signal to General Stahkail, as well, Sir?"

"By no means, Captain." Jahras actually managed a

smile. "First, he's got a lot more powder in his magazines than any of the batteries do. Second, I don't think he quite grasps that the Navy is in charge of Iythria's defense. There seems to be some confusion in his mind as to the exact structure of the chain of command, and I'd hate to overtax his clearly overworked brain trying to explain it to him in the middle of a battle."

"I see, My Lord." Ahlvai seemed to be having a little difficulty keeping his voice level, Jahras observed. Well, it wasn't as if his opinion of Stahkail should come as any surprise to his own flag captain, although he supposed he really shouldn't be throwing more fuel on that particular fire.

The captain turned away, his shoulders quivering with what certainly looked like suppressed laughter, and beckoned to his signals lieutenant. Jahras watched Ahlvai for a moment or two, then turned back to the oncoming Charisians as they began reducing sail.

Stripping down to fighting sail, he thought. *Langhorne, I hope you and Chihiro are both keeping an eye on us down here, because I think we're going to need you.*

▼ ▼ ▼

Sir Dunkyn Yairley had little attention to spare for the line of anchored galleons and floating batteries, even though that was his own squadron's immediate objective. He was too busy watching Captain Ahldahs Rahzwail's ship and her half-dozen sisters.

HMS *Volcano* was an . . . odd-looking vessel. She was actually larger than *Destiny,* although she was rated at only twenty-four guns and showed only twelve ports on a side, and all of her guns were mounted on the spar deck, which put her ports a good twenty feet above her designed waterline. Her bulwarks were higher than most galleons', and the ports piercing them were disproportionately tall, as well. She was disproportionately beamy and massive-looking, too, although that was less evident watching her in profile the way Yairley was at the moment.

There was a reason for her odd appearance, and also a reason she'd been built at King's Harbor, rather than one of the more publicly accessible yards the Navy was using for the majority of its construction these days. No one had wanted anyone getting a close look at her or her sisters and wondering about their peculiarities. In fact, even though Yairley had seen *Volcano* herself on the ways, he'd never noticed most of the unusual features of her design until they'd been pointed out to him by High Admiral Rock Point.

The reason she carried so few guns was that each of the ones she did carry weighed more than twice as much as one of the new model krakens on *Destiny*'s gundeck. Despite that, the gun tubes looked short and stubby, and their carriages looked downright bizarre. Not too surprisingly, he supposed, since each of those guns had a ten-inch bore and those ridiculous, tall carriages were designed specifically to permit them to be elevated to absurd heights. That had required some tricky engineering, particularly given the recoil forces involved. The mammoth guns took either a hundred-and-fifty-pound solid shot or a hundred-pound shell, and the stresses when one of them fired were . . . extreme. The downward thrust engendered by their high elevations had to be absorbed by the ship's deck, which helped to explain *Volcano*'s extraordinarily massive frames and thick deck planking. All war galleons were basically mobile gun platforms, but *Volcano* and her sisters took it to ridiculous extremes.

That had been Yairley's initial reaction, at any rate. Before he'd sailed to join Admiral Shain, however, he'd had the opportunity to exercise with Captain Rahzwail's squadron, and he was rather looking forward to sharing that experience with the Desnairians.

▼ ▼ ▼

That's odd, Baron Jahras thought, watching the half-dozen or so galleons which had peeled off from the rest of the advancing line.

It was obviously a planned and deliberate maneuver. The meticulous order the Charisians were maintaining as they advanced to battle was sobering for someone who'd tried to get his own fleet organized to at least all sail in approximately the same direction on the same day. It had proven to be an exercise all too like trying to herd cat-lizards, but *those* galleons were maneuvering with the kind of precision and discipline for which Desnairian cavalry was famed. Given Jahras' unhappy experiences with his own fleet, he had altogether too good an appreciation for how difficult that was. Despite the vast size of the fleet sailing towards him, there was no sign of confusion anywhere in that mountain-range mass of canvas and masts.

Which made the antics of the ships which had caught his eye even more perplexing. Instead of bearing away from Triangle Shoal, they were actually headed *for* it, and he realized they had cutters and longboats out in front, taking soundings with lead lines to determine the depth of the water.

No, he realized as one of the longboats put a buoy over the side, *they're running* lines *of soundings, matching them with the depths on their charts to help determine their exact positions. But why? And that buoy is inside Stahkail's extreme range. He's not likely to hit anything on purpose, but if they anchor that close in and he fires enough shots, blind, dumb luck is likely to give him a chance to hurt them after all.*

It made no sense. There was no *need* for them to enter the play of Stahkail's guns!

Perhaps not, yet that was clearly what they had in mind. In fact, as he watched, the first galleon dropped a stern anchor. Her companions continued onward, and then a second ship anchored by the stern, as well. Then a third. A fourth. They were actually *anchoring*, forming a line and making themselves unmoving targets, and Jahras frowned in disbelief as he realized they had springs on their anchor cables. They were deliberately courting an artillery duel with heavy fortress guns protected by thick masonry walls!

Thin white waterspouts began to pock the surface of the waves around the anchored Charisians, but they went calmly about the business of taking in sail. Then they began adjusting their positions, using the springs to wind themselves around until they presented their broadsides directly to Stahkail's fortress. They seemed in no hurry, almost as if they were unaware of the plumes of smoke rising from the furnaces Stahkail was using to heat his round shot until they glowed cherry-red. One or two of those heated shot lodged in a ship's timbers could turn it into an inferno, yet they appeared unconcerned by the possibility. What kind of madmen—?

▼ ▼ ▼

"All guns cleared away and prepared to fire, Sir!" Ahldahs Rahzwail's executive officer informed him. "Elevation thirty-five degrees."

"Very well, Master Byrk. You may open fire."

▼ ▼ ▼

Baron Jahras' fingers tightened convulsively on the barrel of his spyglass as the first of the galleons fired. He could actually see the trajectory of their shot, and they arched impossibly high, lofting across the blue sky in a delicate arc that took them over the top of the fortress' curtain wall and dropped straight into its interior.

And then they exploded.

▼ ▼ ▼

Ahldahs Rahzwail smiled in satisfaction as *Volcano*'s first broadside slammed into its target. He couldn't see it actually hit, but that was rather the point of the exercise, and his smile turned into a fierce, savage grin as the shells exploded inside the fortress.

Rahzwail had had his doubts when Commander Mahndrayn first approached him, but he'd known Mahndrayn for several years. He'd respected the younger man's brain power, and Baron Seamount was recognized as the Navy's premier gunnery expert. When both of them insisted Seamount's new "high-angle gun" was a practical proposition, he'd agreed to become one of the officers involved in developing it as a workable weapon. It was obvious to him that the current high-angle guns (which *Volcano*'s crew had already shortened to "angle-gun"—or even just "angles"—for day-to-day use) were only a crude, very early development of what would one day be possible. On the other hand, the entire Charisian Navy had grown accustomed to being a work in progress. Looking back at the breakneck rate of change involved in the conversion from a fleet of two hundred galleys to an equally large fleet of gun-armed galleons in less than five years was enough to make a man's head spin, and there was no reason to suppose anything was going to change in that regard, whatever the Grand Inquisitor might have preferred.

Mahndrayn's death had been a tragedy in more ways than Rahzwail could count. The commander had been exactly the sort of brilliant innovator the Charisian Empire needed if it was going to survive. Rahzwail himself wasn't in the same league, and he knew it, yet he'd also realized he was going to have to step up to the plate and try anyway. He'd already started working on a couple of rough ideas for a proper *rotating* gun mount, although he was pretty sure it would have to wait for those iron-framed ships Mahndrayn had been talking about. And making it work with all the masts and spars in the way was going to be a challenge, as well. But once they'd managed to *rifle* the angle-guns, figured out how to lengthen the tubes further, and gotten them into a pivot mount that could stand the recoil, possibly figured out a way to make breech-loading work, then—*then* . . . !

For now, though, crude though they might be, *Volcano*'s guns were doing exactly what they'd been designed to do.

He turned his back on the fortress. Any hit it managed to score would be a matter of pure luck. Not only that, but *Volcano*'s scantlings and planking were almost twice the thickness of a standard galleon, and not just to resist the recoil of her own guns. Those thick sides should be the next best thing to invulnerable even to fortress guns at such extreme range. The same, alas, could not be said for fortress walls where *her* guns were concerned.

Given their sheer size, those guns would have made highly effective battering pieces in a traditional siege, hurling their hundred-and-fifty-pound round shot against those walls again and again, and the fortifications protecting Iythria were old-fashioned masonry, without the shot-absorbing earthen berms which improvements in artillery had imposed on modern fortress designers. They would have shattered quickly under the sort of pounding *Volcano* could have given them. But why pound your way *through* a wall when you could simply ignore it, instead?

He watched the gun crews reloading. It was an inevitably slow process, although he and Mahndrayn had done what they could to improve matters. The upper portion of the carriage was a separate structure which recoiled on skids cut into the lower, wheeled carriage. The lower portion was fitted with castered wheels that ran on iron rails set into the deck, arranged so that the entire piece could be pushed around in train (in calm weather, at least) by only two men, despite its massive weight. When the upper portion of the slide carriage recoiled, it did so in an angled plane, which brought the elevated muzzle closer to parallel to the deck. It was still inconveniently high for the members of the gun crew responsible for swabbing out and reloading, but it was workable. And it meant they didn't have to depress the barrel and then reelevate it between every shot. It was all still clumsy, and the rate of fire was far slower than a standard long thirty-pounder's, but Rahzwail was trying to come up with a better way to manage things. It all went back to breech-loading, he thought again. If they could ever get *that* to work . . .

Despite all their handicaps, *Volcano*'s gunners managed to sustain a rate of fire which was almost twice that of the old prebagged charge and pre-truck gun carriage days. As he watched, fresh powder bags slid down the barrels and were rammed home, followed by shells strapped to stabilizing "shoes." The "shoes"—flat wooden disks the same diameter as the shells—fixed the shells' attitude in relation to the angle-guns' bores and made sure their fuses faced away from the powder charges. They also made the shells easier to handle, which was nothing to sneer at when the things weighed a hundred pounds each!

The fuses were a significant improvement on Baron Seamount's original design, too. The new fuses burned much more consistently, and they could be adjusted for more finicky time increments. It was still something of a "by-guess-and-by-Langhorne" endeavor, but it was less a matter of guesstimating than it had been, and a little spread in detonation times wasn't going to matter much. They were dropping their fire at steep angles into the fortress' interior, and those same masonry walls were going to confine the shells—and their blast—right on top of the target. Not only that, but no fortress designer in the world had ever considered ways to deal with plunging fire like this. The interior of that fortress had no overhead protection at all, because it had never been needed before.

▼ ▼ ▼

Jahras' jaw clenched as the volume of (thoroughly useless) fire from Triangle Shoal dropped abruptly. The peculiar Charisian galleons were staggering their fire in an obviously preplanned fashion. Their steady, rolling broadsides were timed to see to it that at least one ship's shells went plunging into the fortress every few seconds. They were maintaining a cauldron of explosions inside the fort. No wonder Stahkail's fire was dropping! How in Shanwei's name had even *Charisians* come up with—?

The question chopped off with ax-like suddenness as the fortress' main magazine exploded.

▼ ▼ ▼

Rahzwail's eyes widened as the fortress suddenly emulated *Volcano*'s namesake. *That* was unexpected! The plan had been simply to drive the gun crews off their pieces and possibly disable the guns themselves, not to *blow up* the damned fortress!

Damn. They must've had even less overhead protection than we expected, he thought with an odd sense of detachment as he watched stonework, pieces of heavy wooden beams, an entire gun carriage and cannon, and (undoubtedly) bits and pieces of men launch themselves across the heavens, trailing comet tails of smoke as they arced outward. They seemed to hang at the tops of their trajectories for a long moment, and then they came plunging down into the water in explosions of white, and Rahzwail shook his head.

Looks like we're going to have to introduce some additional new ideas in fortress design, he thought as a sizable piece of one fortress wall pitched wearily outward and slid down into a white cauldron of foam. *I wonder how deep we'll have to bury a magazine to keep a ten-inch shell from reaching it? And if rifled shells are as much heavier as Baron Seamount is predicting, how deep will we have to go to protect against one of them?*

He had no idea what the answer to either of those questions might be, but he made a mental note to discuss it with Baron Seamount at his earliest opportunity. It was only going to be a matter of time before the other side figured out how to build its own angle-guns, after all. When that happened, it would probably be a good idea for Charis to be ahead of the *defensive* game, as well.

"Be so good as to send a boat close enough to the fortress to hail it, Master Byrk," he said out loud, showing his first lieutenant a bared-teeth grin as shells continued to plunge into the target and the smoke of heavy fires came belching up from its interior to join the smoke and dust plume of the explosions still lingering above it. "I imagine they might be in the mood to consider surrendering, don't you?"

▼ ▼ ▼

"Well, that's a thing, Sir Dunkyn," Rhobair Lathyk murmured, gazing back at the smoke-gushing fortress. "Can't say as I expected *that!*"

"I don't think *anyone* did," Yairley replied almost absently. "Still, I'm not going to complain."

"Oh, not me, either, Sir!" Lathyk grinned. "Matter of fact, if it takes a little starch out of those lads in front of us, I'll be just delighted!"

His flag captain had a point, Yairley thought. His squadron had slowly altered course, coming around to a heading of approximately east-by-south, almost but not quite parallel to the line of Baron Jahras' anchored galleons. They were closing only slowly now under topsails and jib alone, and here and there a Desnairian gun was beginning to thud in defiance. None of those shots were coming anywhere near *Destiny*—yet—but as the range continued to fall, that was likely to change.

"Very well, Captain Lathyk," he said. "I believe it's time."

"Aye, aye, Sir." Lathyk nodded and raised his speaking trumpet. "Man the braces!"

▼ ▼ ▼

Baron Jahras was still staring at Triangle Shoal when he heard the bellow of fresh gunfire coming from the west. At first he thought the Charisian galleons approaching his line had opened fire, but then he realized his mistake. Somewhere beyond his line of sight, another cluster of those damned . . . bombardment galleons, or whatever the hell someone wanted to call them, had opened fire on the Sickle Shoal fortress, as well. That was too far away for Jahras to see from his current position, but off the top of his head he couldn't think of any reason for that fortress to be any more successful than Stahkail's had been.

He stamped to the forward edge of the poop deck, raising his spyglass and peering through it. From this close to the water he couldn't actually see the fortress thanks to the curve of the earth, but he could make out the clouds of gunsmoke rising beyond Sickle Shoal. He knew it was pointless, but he was still trying to pick out some sort of detail when Captain Ahlvai cleared his throat.

"Beg pardon, My Lord, but it seems the heretics are about to come calling."

Jahras lowered the glass and looked across *Emperor Zhorj*'s starboard rail, and his expression tightened. The leading Charisian squadron had turned downwind once more, sailing directly into his anchored ships' broadsides. He had enough of an angle on them to see their rigged anchors and realize they, too, intended to anchor by the stern, undoubtedly on a spring. With the wind setting steadily out of the northeast and the tide making, wind and current alike would help them maintain their positions. There wasn't much subtlety to it, he thought harshly. A straight broadside duel, a pounding match. One he ought to be able to win, even if his guns were lighter, because he could bring so many more of them to bear. Except for the minor fact that unless he was sadly mistaken, every one of those galleons was about to begin firing the same sort of ammunition which had just blown the guts out of a heavy masonry fortress.

And we're just a tiny bit more likely to catch fire—or sink—than a fortress, a mental voice told him.

"Open fire, Captain Ahlvai," he said flatly.

. VII .

Inner Harbor,
Port of Iythria,
Empire of Desnair

The afternoon tore apart in thunder, lightning, smoke, and screams.

HMS *Destiny* had missed the savage battle in the Markovian Sea, but she made up for it now. The Imperial

Desnairian Navy was nowhere near the equal of the Navy of God. Its crews had less training, most of them had less motivation, and although their artillery had been manufactured to the same design, there was an enormous difference in its workmanship and quality. Most of Baron Jahras' captains refused to load their guns with full charges, given their propensity to explode unexpectedly, and the gun crews (who tended to have a closer association with them) were even more leery of their weapons. Worse, Jahras had been more or less forced to settle for dry-firing their pieces for training, since he couldn't afford to use them up before they were actually needed in battle. His gunners had mastered the motions of their drill, but it was a largely theoretical mastery, without the experience of the actual thunder of their weapons, the reek of smoke, and—certainly—without a live enemy on the far side of the gunport from them.

On the other hand, there were a *lot* of guns on those Desnairian ships, and Jahras' galleons had been in place literally for months. His crews might be nowhere near the equal of their Charisian opponents as seamen, but then very few seamen were. And the Desnairians might not have the Charisians' tradition of victory—because, again, very few navies did. But what those Desnairian crewmen did have was practice and complete familiarity with their commander's battle plan, and while they might not have mastered the gunner's trade in the brimstone reek of actual burned gunpowder, the *motions* of the evolution had been drilled into them mercilessly. They knew exactly what they were supposed to do, because their captains had explained it to them in detail and they'd practiced it over and over again. And if their fire might not be as accurate or as rapid as their opponents', it was far more accurate and rapid than it would have been at sea, maneuvering under sail while the ship moved and surged underfoot.

The crewmen assigned to the capstans had spent literally five-days practicing turning their ships, pivoting them to exactly the angles their captains wanted, and they did that now. As the Charisian line, led by HMS *Destiny*, headed for its enemies, a hailstorm of white splashes rose all about Sir Dunkyn Yairley's flagship and her consorts. It wasn't well aimed, but there was so much of it that not all of it could miss, and heavy splintering sounds announced the arrival of twelve-pound and twenty-five-pound round shot. They slammed into *Destiny*'s bow as she headed straight into the line of Jahras' anchored galleons, and Hektor Aplyn-Ahrmahk saw one of his ship's long fourteen-pounder bow chasers take a direct hit. Its carriage disintegrated, spewing out a fan of splinters that wounded three men at other guns. Half its own crew was killed by the hit, and one of the survivors was down, kicking in agony on the deck while the fingers of his right hand tried vainly to stanch the bleeding where his left arm had been. Two members of the same gun crew who seemed to be unhurt grabbed their maimed companion and started dragging him towards the hatch and the waiting healers . . . just as another broadside lashed the water around the ship and another round shot ripped through all three of them.

This time, there were no survivors.

The ensign turned away, looking for his admiral, and saw Captain Lathyk standing on top of the starboard hammock nettings, one arm through the mizzen shrouds for balance while he leaned out, trying to fix the Desnairians' position in his mind despite the solid wall of smoke their guns were belching out. As Aplyn-Ahrmahk watched, another Desnairian round shot came whimpering and whining out of the thunder. It slammed through the hammock nettings less than three feet from the captain and a flying splinter cut a deep gash in his right cheek, but Lathyk didn't even seem to notice. He only leaned farther out, as if he thought he could somehow bend down and look under the smoke, between it and the water, to see his enemy clearly.

Sir Dunkyn stood beside the binnacle, hands still clasped behind him, his head moving steadily back and forth as his gaze swept between Captain Lathyk and the masthead weathervane. Sylvyst Raigly stood two paces behind him, head cocked, watching the chaos as if he were considering how best to arrange seating for a formal dinner. Stywyrt Mahlyk stood on the admiral's other side, arms folded, head settled well down on his neck while he chewed a wad of chewleaf with the air of someone who had seen this sort of nonsense altogether too often.

Yairley seemed unaware of his henchmen's presence. His expression was calm, almost contemplative as he glanced briefly down at the binnacle compass card, and Aplyn-Ahrmahk drew a deep breath. It wasn't as if he'd never seen battle before, he reminded himself, remembering the thunder of guns, the screams, the clash of steel on steel from the Battle of Darcos Sound. But there was a difference this time, he realized. For the first time, he wasn't truly part of *Destiny*'s company. He was Admiral Yairley's flag lieutenant, with no assigned battle station, no responsibility to the ship that he could grasp in mental hands and cling to when the world went mad around him. He couldn't believe what an enormous difference that made, and yet as the recognition struck him, he also realized it had to be even worse for the admiral. Like Aplyn-Ahrmahk, Yairley was only a passenger this time. The man who'd commanded *Destiny*, who'd been ultimately responsible for every order given aboard her, found himself with absolutely no decisions to make once the order to engage had been given.

The youthful ensign stepped up beside his admiral. Mahlyk saw him coming and grinned, then spat an expert jet of brown chewleaf juice over the leeward rail. Yairley, alerted by his coxswain's grin, turned his own head, looking at the ensign, and raised one eyebrow as yet another salvo of round shot plowed the water around his flagship.

"Lively, I believe the Captain predicted, Sir?" Aplyn-Ahrmahk had to speak loudly to be heard through the tumult.

"A sometimes surprisingly apt way with words, the Captain has," Yairley replied with a nod.

"Exactly what I was thinking myself, Sir." Aplyn-Ahrmahk managed a smile. "Except I think it's going to get even more lively shortly."

"One can only hope, Master Aplyn-Ahrmahk," Yairley said. "One can only hope."

▼ ▼ ▼

Baron Jahras coughed as incredibly foul-smelling gunsmoke rolled back across *Emperor Zhorj*'s decks. Hard as he'd tried to prepare himself, he'd never imagined anything like this ear-crushing din. The sheer concussion of hundreds of pieces of artillery, the bubbles of overpressure spreading out when they fired, was unimaginable. He felt the surges of air pressure coming back, punching at his face like immaterial fists reeking of Shan-wei's own brimstone come hot from hell, and the deck planking underfoot shook to the recoil of his flagship's guns like a terrified animal. Yet for all the thunder and fury, the range from *Emperor Zhorj* to her enemies was longer than Jahras had expected . . . and her fire was proportionately less accurate as a result.

The northeasterly wind swept diagonally across his east-to-west line of anchored ships, rolling the smoke before it. It blew back into his eyes, but he could still make out the Charisian mastheads above the fog bank born of his own artillery, and something like a chill ran down his spine as he watched those implacable mastheads—the ones which had maintained their distance as they approached his line on an almost parallel course, in a long loop from the east—turn suddenly towards it.

They have to be out of their minds! he thought. *Langhorne, they're sailing straight into our broadsides!*

He'd never anticipated *that*. Sail directly into an opponent's fire, on a heading which let every one of *their* broadside guns bear when *none* of yours would? *Madness!* Yet that was precisely what the Charisians were doing, and that chill in his spine grew colder and stronger as he realized why.

As he watched, the first six ships in the Charisian line

headed directly for the six easternmost galleons in his own line. They weren't going to sail along his line, exchanging broadsides with him, after all. Had their earlier heading been nothing but a bluff to make him think they would? He didn't know, but whether they'd deliberately tried to deceive him or not was immaterial now. Their new course wouldn't allow him to concentrate the fire of multiple ships on each of theirs as they moved into position as he'd planned; instead, each of those ships was deliberately taking the fire of its own clearly preselected target end-on in order to close the range far more rapidly than Jahras had ever expected.

They're going to come to the range they want, then they're going to anchor, and they're going to pound the ever living hell out of the end of my line, he realized sickly. *They're going to get hurt doing it, but they're also going to blow a gap the ships* behind *them will be able to sail straight through.*

He watched those mastheads coming on unflinchingly, knew those ships had to be taking dozens of hits . . . and recognized that it didn't matter.

▼ ▼ ▼

More and more round shot smashed into *Destiny*'s sturdy hull. Many of them, especially from the lighter twelve-pounders, failed to penetrate, although no one aboard the Charisian ship realized that was partly because the Desnairian gunners were firing with reduced charges because they distrusted their own artillery. Even with the understrength charges, however, the twenty-five-pounders were another matter. Aplyn-Ahrmahk heard splintering crashes and the screams of wounded men from the crews on the gundeck's long thirty-pounders as those heavier shot punched through, and a four-foot section of *Destiny*'s midships bulwark exploded inward in a tornado of splinters and shredded hammocks. Then—

"Heads below! Main topgallant's coming adrift!"

The admiral and the ensign looked up in time to see the entire main topgallant yard, shot clean through right at the slings, begin its fall. The two halves of the yard slipped downward, then plunged like broken javelins, still joined by the shredded remnants of the sail. The braces, secured to the ends of the yard, stopped it before it actually hit the nettings stretched over the deck to protect against falling debris, and it dangled untidily, swinging like an ungainly pendulum in a tangle of canvas, broken wood, and cordage.

"Get aloft and secure that wreckage!" Boatswain Symmyns bellowed, and men went swarming up the rigging to capture and tame that pendulum before it could plunge the rest of the way to the deck with lethal consequences.

"Stand by to anchor!" Captain Lathyk shouted. "Hands to buntlines and clewlines! Stand by the larboard broadside!"

Seamen moved through the smoke and the turmoil with disciplined haste. The crews of the larboard guns crouched down, getting as much out of the way as they could. With only topsails and jib set, *Destiny* needed only a fraction of the men normally required to make or take in sail, which was just as well under the circumstances, Aplyn-Ahrmahk reflected. At least five of the galleon's larboard guns had already been knocked out of action, her decks were splashed with blood, he saw at least a dozen bodies lying where they'd been dragged out of their mates' way, and casualties were piling up at the healers' station on the orlop deck.

"Larboard your helm!" the captain shouted. "Take in fore and main topsail!"

Destiny turned to starboard as the wheel went over, presenting her waiting larboard broadside to the Desnairian galleon HMS *Saint Adulfo*, the fifth ship in from the eastern end of Jahras' line.

"Let go the larboard anchor!"

The sheet anchor rigged from the larboard cathead was released. It plunged instantly, but this time the cable was flaked out on the gundeck, not the upper deck, and run not from the hawsehole, but through a stern gunport.

The galleon continued past the point at which the anchor had been dropped under her jib alone, sailing out her cable while the men on the gundeck stayed carefully out of the way of the thick hawser rumbling and roaring out the gunport. Then the cable hit the stoppers, halting its run, and *Destiny* shuddered and jerked as the anchor's flukes dug into the bottom and held. The cable snapped taut, and Chief Kwayle and his waiting party pounced, nipping the bitter end of the spring to it.

"Made fast!"

The call came up from below, and Lathyk nodded.

"Take in the jib! Veer the cable, Master Symkee! Take tension on the spring!"

▼ ▼ ▼

Captain Ehrnysto Plyzyk, of the Imperial Desnairian Navy, watched the Charisian galleon stop moving. She edged a bit further to windward under bare spars as her topsails were brailed up and her jib dropped, and his stomach muscles tensed. She was veering a little more cable, he realized, and when she finished, she'd have the slack she needed for the spring she'd undoubtedly rigged to control her heading just as the springs on his own anchors controlled *Saint Adulfo*'s. And when that happened. . . .

"Pound her, boys!" he bellowed, jabbing his sword like a pointer at the Charisian half-obscured by his own gunsmoke. "If you want to live, *pound* that bitch!"

▼ ▼ ▼

"Stand by the larboard battery!" Lieutenant Tymkyn shouted.

A hurricane of round shot hammered his ship, although only HMS *Loyal Defender*, *Saint Adulfo*'s next ahead, was able to turn to lend her guns to *Saint Adulfo*'s defense. *Holy Langhorne*, astern of *Saint Adulfo*, might have assisted her as well, but she no longer had any attention to spare. Captain Bahrdahn's *Undaunted* had fetched up to windward of her, and Tymkyn heard the thunder of *Undaunted*'s artillery as the other galleon came into action.

Still, between them, *Saint Adulfo*'s and *Loyal Defender*'s broadsides mounted forty-four guns to *Destiny*'s twenty-five . . . or what would have been twenty-five if she hadn't been so heavily hit on the way in. In fact, she probably had no more than eighteen or nineteen guns, and Tymkyn peered through the smoke, waiting for the spring to bring her fully around. He wasn't going to waste that first broadside by firing one second before he was sure all of his guns bore on the target, and—

The twelve-pound shot from *Saint Adulfo*'s starboard battery struck *Destiny*'s youthful third lieutenant just below midchest and tore his body in two.

▼ ▼ ▼

Aplyn-Ahrmahk saw Tymkyn flung aside in a spray of blood and torn flesh. At almost the same instant, he realized Trahvys Saylkyrk, Tymkyn's assistant in command of the larboard battery, was down as well—wounded or dead, he couldn't tell. Up until his elevation to Admiral Yairley's flag lieutenant, that had been Aplyn-Ahrmahk's duty station when the ship cleared for action, and old reflexes took over. He didn't stop to think; he simply acted, leaping up onto the larboard gangway. His feet slid in Tymkyn's fresh blood despite the sand scattered over the decks for traction, and he clutched at the main shrouds for balance to keep himself from falling.

"As you bear, lads!" he screamed, then waited two more heartbeats.

"*Fire!*"

▼ ▼ ▼

Saint Adulfo heaved as another broadside blasted out of her smoke-streaming gun muzzles, and there was a sharper, louder report from forward as her number three gun blew up despite the reduced charge. Fortunately, the gun tube simply split lengthwise. Half its crew was killed, the ready charges being brought up for it and the number four gun were touched off in sympathetic detonation by the flame gushing from the shattered cannon, wounding four more men, but it could have been worse. Indeed, it *had* been worse the last time one of *Saint Adulfo*'s guns burst.

But that didn't change the fact that it *had* burst, and at the worst possible time, Captain Plyzyk thought bitterly. The entire forward half of his starboard battery was thrown into confusion by the sudden—and fully understandable—terror a bursting gun always produced.

"More hands to the forward guns!" he shouted. "Let's get some fresh—!"

The Charisian galleon fired at last.

▼ ▼ ▼

HMS *Destiny*'s larboard side belched flame and smoke. She'd closed to within less than fifty yards of *Saint Adulfo* before she anchored, and the air trapped between the two ships was a fiery maelstrom as her broadside fired for the first time. A quarter of her company lay dead or wounded before she fired her first shot, and even as Aplyn-Ahrmahk shouted the command, a twenty-five-pound round shot cut through her mainmast three feet above the deck. The mast toppled into the smoke like a weary tree, and rigging parted, broken ends lashing out, flailing like maddened serpents. Men who got in the way of that heavy, tarred cordage were swatted casually from their feet, usually with broken bones and torn flesh, and others scrambled madly for safety as the entire massive complex of the mainmast came thundering down. The fore topgallant mast followed it, and the galleon staggered as if she'd just lost her rudder all over again.

But the men on her larboard guns ignored the chaos and confusion. They paid no heed to the damage control parties racing to cut away the wreckage and drag the injured and dying out of the tangles of fallen cordage. They were totally focused on their guns, for this was the reason *Destiny* had taken so much damage. This was what she'd come to do, and as they heard the youthful ensign's familiar voice, they did it.

▼ ▼ ▼

Ehrnysto Plyzyk saw the Charisian mainmast start to topple and opened his mouth to cheer. But before he could, the smoke between the two ships lifted on a fresh furnace blast, and this one didn't come from *his* guns.

The deck hammered against the soles of his shoes. It was the first time he'd ever felt heavy shot striking a ship, and a corner of his mind recognized the difference between the recoil from his own guns and the sharper, lighter, and yet somehow more . . . vicious shock of enemy fire.

And then sixteen of the eighteen shells which had struck his ship exploded almost simultaneously.

▼ ▼ ▼

"Reload! *Reload!*"

Aplyn-Ahrmahk heard the gun captains' shouted commands and looked around, trying to find Lieutenant Symkee to take over the larboard battery. But then something smacked him sharply on the shoulder.

"Go, Hektor!" His head whipped around as Admiral Yairley smacked his shoulder a second time. "*Go!*" the admiral repeated, and actually smiled. "Captain Lathyk can have you back for the moment!"

"Aye, aye, Sir!"

The ensign leapt into the disciplined madness, knowing better than to disrupt the choreographed training by shouting unnecessary orders. Instead, he watched the gun crews, his eyes trying to be everywhere at once, ready to intervene if something went wrong.

But nothing went wrong. *Destiny*'s gunners had trained for two hours every day during their weary voyage from Tellesberg to Iythria. They'd polished old skills and learned new ones as they grappled with the novel concept of exploding shells, and Aplyn-Ahrmahk watched as the number two on each gun removed and pocketed the lead patch protecting the fuse before the shell was loaded.

The fuse times had been set by Payter Wynkastair, *Destiny*'s gunner, before the ship ever cleared for action, and at the *end* of the action, the number two on each gun would be required to hand over those patches as proof the shells had been properly prepared for firing.

"Run out! Run out!"

One by one the galleon's surviving guns were brought back to battery, and gun captains all along the line raised their left hands, right hands gripping the firing lanyards.

▼ ▼ ▼

Captain Plyzyk clawed his way up from his knees, shaking his head like a dazed prizefighter while he tried to make his brain work. He didn't know what had hit him, and he probably never would, but he was pretty sure whatever it was had broken his right shoulder blade.

And even at that, he realized, he was better off than his ship.

Smoke—much of it wood smoke now, not just powder smoke—streamed from shattered holes ripped through *Saint Adulfo*'s timbers and planking. Some of those holes looked big enough for a man to walk through. They weren't, of course, but they looked *huge* compared to the much smaller holes round shot punched through a ship. Splintered and broken wood was everywhere, torn canvas and severed lengths of rigging littered the deck, he heard voices screaming in mingled agony and terror, and at least half the midships upper deck twelve-pounders had been knocked over like toys. The bulwark in front of them was simply *gone*; the deck edge looked like a cliff shattered by a hurricane, and he realized three or four of the Charisians' infernal "shells" must have impacted almost together to produce that damage.

But there was plenty of other damage to go with it, and someone grabbed him, dragging him bodily out of the way as his galleon's mizzenmast came thundering down.

"Fire!" somebody screamed. *"Fire in the cable tier!"*

Plyzyk staggered back to his feet once more, wondering

who'd just saved him from being crushed by the falling mast, but it was an almost absent thought, lost in the terrifying thought that his ship was on fire.

"Away firefighting parties!" he bellowed, and the seamen who were detailed for that very purpose went rushing below with buckets of water and sand.

Langhorne! She can't take much more of this, he thought. *She—*

▼ ▼ ▼

"*Fire!*" Hektor Aplyn-Ahrmahk shouted.

Destiny's second broadside smashed into *Saint Adulfo* like an avalanche, but this was an avalanche of iron and fire and a deadly freight of gunpowder. The six-inch shells slammed through the Desnairian's planking, and this time *all* of them exploded.

▼ ▼ ▼

One of Ensign Applyn-Ahrmahk's shells exploded almost directly under Ehrnysto Plyzyk's feet, and for him, the fate of his ship became forever moot.

. VIII .

Duke Kholman's Office,
Port of Iythria,
Empire of Desnair

Daivyn Bairaht watched in stony-eyed silence as the two officers in Charisian uniform were ushered through the door of his office.

"Your Grace, Admiral Sir Dunkyn Yairley and his flag lieutenant, Ensign Aplyn-Ahrmahk," their guide, Captain Byrnahrdo Fahrya, told him. "Admiral Yairley, His Grace the Duke of Kholman."

Yairley and his ensign were immaculate, looking as if

they'd dropped by for a state dinner, Kholman thought bitterly. Fahrya was another matter. His uniform was torn and filthy, reeking of powder and wood smoke. His expression was grim, tight and strained, but he was lucky to be alive. His ship, *Holy Langhorne*, had taken fire, burned to the waterline, and sunk under the devastating Charisian assault. She was scarcely the only Desnairian galleon that had happened to, and from the look of things Fahrya had spent some time in the water before he'd been recovered by the victors. He'd obviously done what he could to straighten his hair, wash his hands, wipe the powder grime from his face, but the contrast between him and the two faultlessly attired Charisians' dress uniforms could not have been sharper.

Or more deliberate, the duke reminded himself as he realized he could even smell the Charisian flag officer's fresh cologne. *Yairley must've made damned sure the two of them would be as neat as pins. He obviously recognizes the value of setting the stage properly.*

"Admiral," he made himself say, his tone courteous but cold, and bowed very slightly in greeting.

"Your Grace," Yairley responded with an even slighter bow, and Kholman's jaw tightened at that abbreviated bow's subtle insult to his aristocratic rank. Of course, it was possible—*possible!*—it hadn't been Yairley's intention to do any insulting. Then again . . .

"Before anything else," he said, "allow me to express my personal thanks for High Admiral Rock Point's message about Baron Jahras."

"I'm sure I speak for the High Admiral when I say you're most welcome, Your Grace," Yairley said. "I regret the severity of the Baron's wounds, but my understanding is that, barring any unforeseen complications, the healers are confident he'll recover in time."

And once he learns how to write left-handed, Kholman thought harshly. *But at that, he's lucky to be alive. And maybe the fact that he's lost an arm will help protect him when Clyntahn gets word of this.*

"I hope you're right," he said out loud. "However, I

doubt you came ashore just to tell me my brother-in-law is likely to survive." He showed his teeth briefly. "Somehow I don't think you're likely to tell me the same thing about my Navy."

"With the exception of the floating batteries at the western end of Baron Jahras' line, I'm afraid all your ships have struck," Yairley said gravely, and despite the way he'd braced himself internally, Kholman flinched visibly.

At least the Charisian hadn't said "all your *surviving* ships have struck," although that would have been more accurate. According to Kholman's most recent report, nineteen galleons and twelve of the floating batteries had burned, blown up, burned *and* blown up, or simply sunk as the result of battle damage. He didn't know how many of the others were damaged, or how badly, and he didn't even want to think about the human cost, but he knew it had been huge. For that matter, he'd sent over a thousand replacements into the maelstrom before he'd accepted he was simply incurring additional casualties in a lost cause.

All the fortifications on Sickle Shoal and Triangle Shoal had also surrendered, although they hadn't hauled down their flags until they'd taken massive damage. That was what the reports said, at least, and Kholman had no reason to doubt them. Especially since only one of the four fortress commanders—General Stahkail, inevitably—was still alive and unwounded. Those accursed . . . bombardment ships were also why they'd lost so many of the floating batteries. The conventional Charisian galleons had declined to venture into the shoal water beyond the main shipping channel to engage them, but the bombardment ships had taken up positions where the batteries' guns couldn't reach them and started dropping those damned exploding shells on top of them. Their percentage of hits hadn't been high, but every hit they *had* scored had been devastating.

Of course that word—"devastating"—pretty much summed up the entire battle, didn't it? Once the eastern end of Jahras' line was blasted out of the way, the Charisians had poured galleons through the gap. They'd doubled the line of Desnairian ships, sailing along it and engaging it from both sides, pouring their accursed exploding shells into their victims. They hadn't bothered to anchor the way the ships who'd initially broken the line had. Instead they'd simply smashed one ship after another into splintered, all too often burning wreckage. By the time they'd worked their way along half the line, ships were striking their colors before they were even fired upon. Kholman didn't want to think about how Zhaspahr Clyntahn was likely to react to *that,* but no reasonable man could possibly condemn them when they'd seen half their entire Navy turned to driftwood in barely two hours by a weapon they couldn't possibly match.

"I see," he said out loud, then stiffened his spine. "May I ask what message High Admiral Rock Point has sent you to deliver to me, Admiral Yairley?"

"You may," Yairley said gravely. "Admiral Rock Point has sent me to require the surrender of all of your remaining harbor fortifications, your shipyards, sail lofts, ropewalks, cannon foundries, and naval supplies."

"That's *preposterous*!" The protest exploded out of Kholman before he could stop it, but he glared at the Charisian. "I have a garrison of over twenty thousand men in and around this city! You may have defeated— even destroyed—our Navy, but the *Army* is still fully capable of defending the soil of the Desnairian Empire!"

Neither Yairley nor the wiry young ensign standing respectfully at his side so much as turned a hair. They simply waited until he'd finished and stood glowering at them, at which point Yairley shrugged very slightly.

"First, Your Grace, your garrison may or may not be able to defend this city. I mean no disrespect to the Imperial Army, but I rather doubt it would find itself as effective against the Imperial Marines and Army battalions aboard High Admiral Rock Point's transports as it was against the Republic the last time you clashed with the Siddarmarkians. Second, however, we have no need to land troops to destroy your shipyards, at the very least. Admittedly, the foundries might be somewhat more difficult targets, but I remind you of what happened to your outer fortifications. The Imperial Charisian Navy is fully capable of carrying out the same sort of bombardment of your waterfront batteries and warehouses and, for that matter, the shipyards themselves, without putting a single Marine into Iythria. High Admiral Rock Point has instructed me to point out to you that by requiring the surrenders I've described, he's attempting to *minimize* the loss of Desnairian life and collateral damage to civilian property."

"I've had reports of what happened to the first of your ships to engage ours, Admiral," Kholman replied in a chilly tone. "And you wouldn't have the advantage of surprise this time around. No doubt you *could* destroy the shipyards—or damage them severely, at any rate—with a bombardment, but you wouldn't do it without losses of your own! And I doubt you have the range to bombard the cannon foundries and our other facilities at all."

"You might be surprised in that regard, Your Grace. Nonetheless, the High Admiral has instructed me to inform you that his terms are not negotiable." The Charisian admiral's brown eyes looked levelly into Kholman's, and if there was any bluff in them, the duke couldn't see it. "He *will* destroy those facilities—all of them—before he withdraws from Iythria, Your Grace. The degree and extent of additional damage inflicted is, in large part, up to you. Whether or not he'll succeed in his mission is not."

"He has a high opinion of himself and his capabilities, doesn't he?" Kholman inquired acidly, and Yairley surprised him with a slight smile.

"I suppose he does, Your Grace. On the other hand, he's earned the right to it, I believe. If you don't think so, you could discuss the matter with Earl Thirsk, or perhaps Bishop Kornylys or Admiral of the Broad Oceans Sun Rising. Or, for that matter"—his eyes stabbed Kholman suddenly—"Baron Jahras."

"That's an impressive catalog of defeated foes," Kholman said in a somewhat milder tone. "As it happens, I mean that sincerely. But it's not enough to convince me to simply roll over in the face of such demands. If he believes he can accomplish them by force of arms, I invite him to make the attempt."

"Your Grace," any trace of humor had vanished from Yairley's expression and voice, "I strongly suggest you reconsider that position." He raised one hand in an oddly courteous gesture before Kholman could respond. "I'm speaking for myself, not High Admiral Rock Point, when I say that, Your Grace. The High Admiral truly is trying to minimize bloodshed and destruction here in your city, but he has no intention of shedding *Charisian* blood unnecessarily in the attempt."

"I'm afraid he's going to find it *is* necessary," Kholman said coldly. "I have a duty to my Emperor . . . and to Mother Church." He suppressed an urge to bite his own tongue for the way that came out, as if the Church was only an afterthought. "I'm responsible for defending this entire city, not simply commanding the naval forces which you've already defeated, Admiral Yairley."

"Then I'm afraid I have an additional message for you, Your Grace." Yairley's voice was flat now, cold. "High Admiral Rock Point instructs me to inform you that should you choose to force him to bombard and invade your city, he will unfortunately find it necessary to free himself of the distraction of your surrendered vessels and fortresses first. In that event, he'll be forced to burn his prizes and blow up the fortresses."

This time Kholman managed not to wince physically. He doubted there was any way the Empire was getting any of those ships back, anyway. In fact, it would actually be better from his perspective if Rock Point did burn them. At least that way he could point out to the Group of Four that unlike Kornylys Harpahr's ships, none of *his* would find their way into Charisian service against Mother Church!

"The High Admiral must do as he thinks best," he said. "If he truly intends to burn all of those ships, I'll make arrangements to take off their crews. I'm sure we can arrange a proper parole for them."

"I'm afraid you didn't fully understand the High Admiral's position, Your Grace. Under the circumstances, he regrets to point out to you that it won't be possible to land any of his prisoners or remove them from their vessels before he burns their ships."

For an instant, it totally failed to register. Then it did, and Kholman's face went white as the threat sank home. There were almost thirty thousand men aboard those ships, and that didn't even count the crews of the floating batteries or the harbor fortresses which had surrendered!

"You can't be serious!" he heard his voice say.

"On the contrary, Your Grace. The High Admiral is deadly serious." There was no emphasis at all in Yairley's voice . . . which made it the most terrible voice the Duke of Kholman had ever heard.

"That's *monstrous!*"

"As monstrous as King Rahnyld's decision to hand prisoners of war over to the Inquisition to be systematically tortured and murdered?" Yairley asked softly.

"I had nothing to do with that!"

"Perhaps not," Yairley conceded. "But if we'd lost here instead of winning, and if Zhaspahr Clyntahn demanded the surrender of *your* prisoners, do you think for one moment Emperor Mahrys wouldn't hand them over?"

Kholman stared at the Charisian flag officer, sickness churning in his stomach, because he saw the truth looking back at him out of those level brown eyes. Of course the Emperor would have surrendered them to the Inquisition.

"I was under the impression it was your Empire's position that honorably surrendered prisoners of war would not be abused in that fashion," he said, instead of answering the question.

"Whenever possible, that is indeed Emperor Cayleb and Empress Sharleyan's policy," Yairley replied. "That doesn't mean their armed forces will incur unnecessary casualties avoiding . . . unfortunate consequences for those taken in arms against us, however. Unlike you, Your Grace, my Empire is fighting for its very survival, and you know perfectly well what will happen should we lose. We have no intention of losing, and however much we may regret it, we *will* do what we must.

"You talk about arranging parole for your personnel. Do you think we're foolish enough to believe for an instant those paroles would be *honored*? Of course they wouldn't! Even if you fully intended to honor them— and I'll grant you the courtesy of believing you would— the Group of Four would never permit it. Anyone who *tried* to honor a parole to the Empire of Charis would be condemned by the Inquisition and probably suffer the Punishment of Schueler as a warning to anyone else 'cowardly enough' to entertain such an arrangement. So let's be clear here. If High Admiral Rock Point returns your personnel to you, you and I both know none of our own surrendered people will ever be returned to us alive but we *will* see your people again under arms. He's under no obligation to hand them back to you under those circumstances, but he's prepared to do so in return for the surrender—and destruction—of the facilities he's listed.

"Your Emperor and your Empire have agreed to serve the Group of Four. Perhaps you believe that's the right thing to do. Perhaps you've agreed to serve only because you have no choice. In either case, however, the decision was made, and my High Admiral has instructed me to point out to you that decisions have consequences. The consequence of this decision is that you've ranged yourself with our enemies in what, for us, is a war for survival, and the price for your survival and the survival of your men is the destruction of all war-making potential in and around the city of Iythria."

Tension hissed and crackled in the office, but somehow Kholman couldn't look away from the Charisian admiral's eyes.

"That's High Admiral Rock Point's message for you, Your Grace," Yairley said flatly. "I do, however, have an observation of my own to add to it, if you'd care to hear it."

Kholman made a curt "go ahead" gesture, and the Charisian admiral smiled thinly. It was not a pleasant expression.

"I'd recommend you remember what happened in Ferayd, Your Grace. And who was in command of that punitive expedition. And, for that matter, that there are significant differences between that expedition and today.

"Unlike the situation which existed in regard to the Kingdom of Delferahk at that time, the Desnairian Empire has formally joined the Group of Four's jihad against Charis, and I invite you to remember what the *Writ* itself says about the rules of war where jihad is concerned. Many of those rules are specifically set aside under the provisions of *The Book of Schueler*, and while Charis didn't begin this jihad, we recognize that there comes a point at which the only way to deter outrages against us or our people is to threaten reprisal. As you've pointed out, my Emperor and Empress have specifically rejected the notion of applying the Punishment to any of our prisoners, but they *haven't* renounced the right to set aside the same rules of war which have been set aside against us.

"The Group of Four—excuse me, the Grand Vicar, speaking in the holy name of Mother Church in his own good judgment and with the guidance of the Archangels"—the contempt in Yairley's voice was withering—"has officially declared what's going to happen to Tellesberg and Cherayth on the day of our 'inevitable' defeat. I suggest you consider the terms of the destruction your Empire has pledged itself to help carry out when you consider High Admiral Rock Point's offer. By simple reciprocity, this entire city is subject to the same treatment. Which means that if the time comes for High Admiral Rock Point to abandon his efforts to minimize death and destruction of *Desnairian* subjects and their property, your entire city could legitimately be burned to the ground with its citizens still in it. He doesn't want to do that . . . but he will if he must. And"—the Charisian admiral's eyes bored into Kholman once more—"if he has to begin by burning your ships, then so be it."

It was very quiet and still in that office. The silence lingered for at least thirty seconds before it was broken. Then—

"Would you care to reconsider your decision, Your Grace?" Sir Dunkyn Yairley asked softly.

SEPTEMBER, YEAR OF GOD 895

·✦·

.I.

HMS *Destiny*, 54,
Tarot Channel,
and
Tellesberg Palace,
City of Tellesberg,
Kingdom of Old Charis

". . . and I have the honor to remain Your Majesties' obedient servant," Sir Dunkyn Yairley finished, leaning back in his chair with his feet propped on a footstool, long, curve-stemmed pipe in hand, while he gazed out the opened stern windows at HMS *Destiny*'s wake.

". . . remain . . . Your Majesties' . . . obedient servant," Trumyn Lywshai repeated softly, the nib of his pen scratching busily. He finished writing and looked up, one eyebrow raised.

"What does that leave us, Trumyn?" Yairley asked, turning his head to look at the secretary.

"I believe that's actually just about everything, Sir," Lywshai replied after contemplating the deckhead thoughtfully for a moment while he consulted his orderly memory. "I need to check the squadron's medical lists to make sure that portion of your report is up-to-date, but I think we've actually covered everything at this point."

"Remarkable," Yairley said dryly. He took another puff from his pipe, then clamped it between his teeth, climbed out of his chair, and walked over to the stern window, resting both hands on the windowsill as he looked out across the sternwalk at the brilliant blue waters of the Tarot Channel.

"You know," he said over his shoulder, never looking away from the water, "back when I was a mere captain, I made the sobering discovery that, contrary to the foolish and romantic belief of more junior officers, the Navy *really* sailed on paper, not water. Or that getting all of the paperwork done and the forms filled out and the returns properly—and accurately, damn their ink-stained little souls!—tallied was obviously more important than simply, oh, training your gunners or exercising aloft, at any rate." He shook his head, taking the pipe from his mouth to tamp the tobacco with a thumb while he sighed mournfully. "Little did I realize how much more paperwork was lurking in my future the instant I allowed them to give me that damned streamer."

Lywshai chuckled, and Yairley wheeled, putting his back to the windows and pointing an accusatory pipe stem at the younger man.

"Don't you laugh, Master Secretary! I know who really invented all these reports and forms! You and the rest of your kind, that's who. It's all a plot to give employ to people like you! I'm sure if I examine the *Writ* hard enough I'll find 'bureaucrat' listed somewhere as one of Shan-wei's major demon familiars!"

"Alas, you've found us out, Sir." Lywshai shook his head, expression sad. "And most of my colleagues thought simple sailors would never tumble to the truth! What gave us away? Was it the creation of the new numbers?"

"That *was* a clue," Yairley said soberly, although his lips twitched as he spoke. "Obviously just another ploy to generate even more reports for the Admiralty and—especially!—the Office of Supply!"

"I warned the others we were reaching too far with that one, Sir," Lywshai said mournfully.

"And well you should have," Yairley said roundly. "In fact—"

He paused as someone knocked on his cabin door. A

moment later, Sylvyst Raigly poked his head into the after cabin.

"Ensign—I mean, *Lieutenant* Aplyn-Ahrmahk—is here, Sir Dunkyn."

"And why is he there," Yairley inquired, pointing at the open door, "instead of *here?*" He pointed at the rug covering the after cabin's deck planking.

"Of course, Sir Dunkyn!" The steward smiled and beckoned to the young officer behind him. A moment later, Hektor Aplyn-Ahrmahk, his tunic bearing the single silver cuff star of a lieutenant, stepped into the cabin.

"I apologize for interrupting, Sir Dunkyn," he said, "but the lookout's just spotted Channel Point fine on the starboard bow. Captain Lathyk estimates we should round Cape Thol by dinnertime."

"Excellent!" Yairley smiled, then looked back at Lywshai. "It would appear we've gotten on top of your nefarious correspondence just in time, Trumyn. If Captain Lathyk's estimate is as reliable as usual, we should be anchored by this time tomorrow. Can you have fair copies of all those dratted reports ready for dispatch by then?"

"I believe so, Sir Dunkyn, although"—the secretary smiled at Aplyn-Ahrmahk—"I *may* have to requisition your flag lieutenant's assistance to get it all done in time."

"You may, eh?" Yairley snorted. "Well, in that case, put him in charge of writing up my expense report. With his handwriting, they'll never figure out how much we actually spent!"

▼ ▼ ▼

"I'm glad Hektor's made it home in one piece again, even if we did miss his birthday," Cayleb Ahrmahk said. He and his wife and daughter sat on their private terrace—still tyrannized by Princess Zhanayt's accursed parrot—enjoying an unusually cool Tellesberg evening as they watched HMS *Destiny* through Owl's SNARCs.

"He hasn't quite made it *home* yet, love," Sharleyan pointed out, and Cayleb snorted.

"You're the one who keeps telling me that anywhere

the Charisian flag flies is just as much Charisian territory as Tellesberg itself," he pointed out. "In fact, for someone who had the bad taste to be born a Chisholmian, you're almost rabid about the point! And given that Gorjah's now a subject monarch of the Empire in good standing, Tarot is certainly Charisian territory. So there!"

He stuck out his tongue, and Sharleyan shook her head mournfully.

"It always amazes me what a soul of perfect tact and unfailing courtesy you are. Just remember Alahnah's watching you. The example you set's going to come home to haunt you in just a year or two. And if there's any justice in the world, your daughter's going to grow up to be a female version of *you*."

"God, I hope not!" Cayleb shuddered in not entirely feigned dismay at the thought. "On the other hand, I'd probably deserve it. I remember Father's most deadly parental curse was always 'May you have children just like mine'!"

"Most parents feel that way, I suspect, Your Majesty," another voice said in Cayleb's earplug. "And, speaking as a parent with a little more experience than you or Her Grace have yet achieved, I can tell you you're going to find out it *always* comes true. Of course, there are good points about that, too. Especially if you've had the wisdom to pick the right spouse to contribute to the mix."

Sharleyan laughed and shook her head.

"Nahrmahn, don't try to convince me you don't dote on all of your children!" she accused.

"Of course I do," the Emeraldian prince replied from his study in Eraystor. "You can't expect me to simply go around admitting that, though. Especially not where *they're* likely to hear it! I can see why Merlin was concerned about my discovering Machiavelli—although, to be fair, I'd already figured out most of it for myself, and the man's cynicism about religion is almost worthy of Clyntahn himself—but there's never a child born who wasn't a *natural* Machiavelli where his parents were concerned. The last thing you need to do is give anyone as ruthless and self-centered as a *child* another handle to manipulate you!"

"That may be one of the most cynical things I've ever heard anyone say," Cayleb observed mildly, and it was Nahrmahn's turn to laugh.

"I didn't say they weren't lovable—or *loving*, for that matter—Your Majesty. I only said children are self-centered and ruthless, and they are. One of the harder tricks, I think, is hammering any other attitude into their brains. Worth it, in the end, but hard. I was luckier than I deserved to be with Felayz, and so far Nahrmahn Gareyt's turning out pretty well, too, I think. Of course, that's more Ohlyvya's doing than mine; I'm afraid I've been too occupied as a scheming, conniving, ruthless practitioner of real politik to contribute to civilizing them the way I really should have. Still, they *are* good kids, aren't they?"

"Yes, they are," Cayleb agreed with a smile. "And so is young Hektor, too. Although now that I think about it, he's not as young as he was, is he?"

"Lieutenant His Grace the Duke of Darcos Sound," Sharleyan repeated with a smile of her own. "I'm sure he never saw *that* coming when he sat for his midshipman's exam!"

"No, he didn't." Cayleb's smile faded as he recalled how Master Midshipman Aplyn had become a member of the Charisian royal family.

"I didn't mean to bring up an unhappy memory, Cayleb," Sharleyan said softly, and he shook his head quickly.

"We've both lost people we love, Sharley. And like Maikel always says, losing them is the price we pay for loving them in the first place. But sometimes we're fortunate enough to find something good coming out of the loss, and that's what Hektor is. I'd like to say I could take credit for raising a good 'son,' but his parents get the thanks for that. I'm just grateful he's turning out as well as he is. Assuming we can keep him alive, of course."

He and Sharleyan looked at one another, eyes momentarily dark with memories of the carnage of the Battle of Iythria's opening phases.

"We can only try, Cayleb," Nahrmahn said. "That would be easier for me to say if Nahrmahn Gareyt weren't getting close to the age when I'm going to have to think about sending *him* off to sea. But it's true, and I suspect we wouldn't be doing any of them—or any of our subjects—any favors if we tried to keep them safely at home. You already knew what naval service was like because your father sent you off to see it firsthand, and that's been incredibly valuable to all of us over the last few years. For that matter, the tradition that privilege has to be earned by service is one any ruler ought to learn early . . . and one I'm ashamed to admit I learned at a rather later point in life than you did. There's a lot to be said for that Charisian tradition of yours, when you come down to it. I don't want to see my son traumatized the way Hektor was at Darcos Sound, but I do want him to understand the reality of what war costs and what it's really all about. And if he turns into half the young man your Hektor is, I'll be proud to be his father."

Cayleb and Sharleyan looked at each other again, and this time their eyes had softened and warmed. It wasn't often, even now, that Nahrmahn Baytz let anyone far enough inside his armor to see the heart within it. There'd been a time when Cayleb would have been prepared to argue he didn't have one to *be* seen, but not anymore.

"Well," the emperor said more briskly, intentionally shifting the subject, "now that Hektor—and Admiral Yairley, of course—are this close to home, we'll be able to start taking official cognizance of what happened at Iythria. Have you had any more thoughts on that, Nahrmahn?"

"Not really, Your Majesty." There was an edge of amusement in Nahrmahn's voice as he recognized Cayleb's deliberate return to greater formality. Then his tone sobered. "The really *interesting* question is how Clyntahn and the rest of the Group of Four are going to react. Especially to Kholman's and Jahras' decision to . . . emigrate."

"That *is* going to piss him off, isn't it?" Cayleb's smile was unpleasant. "Not that he has anyone but himself to blame for it."

Sharleyan nodded in grim agreement. They still weren't going to officially "know" about that until Rock Point himself reached home, since *Destiny* had been sent off as soon as she'd been able to step a replacement mainmast. Partly that was because Staynair wanted to get his initial dispatches home as quickly as possible, but it was also because *Destiny*—like the other ships in company with her—had damage that was going to take a dockyard to put right. Yairley's flagship had been severely holed below the waterline before *Saint Adulfo* and *Loyal Defender* struck their colors and Master Mahgail and his carpenter's mates hadn't been able to find—or plug, at any rate—all of the leaks. *Destiny*'s pumps were working for over twenty minutes in each watch to keep the slow flooding under control, and he'd wanted her in dockyard hands as quickly as possible, so he'd sent her off while Duke Kholman was still struggling with the harshness of the Imperial Charisian Navy's terms.

In the end, the duke had decided against calling Domynyk Staynair's bluff. That had probably been wise of him, since Domynyk hadn't been bluffing. The high admiral's patience with those who served the Group of Four had grown increasingly thin as reports of what was happening to Gwylym Manthyr and his people leaked out of Zion. Sharleyan knew Rock Point wouldn't actually have burned his surrendered prisoners alive in their own ships (he *was* Maikel Staynair's brother when all was said), but he *would* have bombarded however much of the city he'd had to to take out his assigned targets, which would have been quite bad enough.

Fortunately, he *hadn't* had to. Kholman had bowed to the inevitable, ordered Iythria's garrison to withdraw from the city, and allowed Rock Point's Marines and Army battalions to land unopposed. In return, Rock Point had taken stringent precautions to minimize civilian casualties or injuries. There'd still been a couple of incidents with Temple Loyalists who'd attempted to ambush Charisian detachments. Desnairian casualties had been close to a hundred percent in those instances, although Rock

Point's shore commanders had kept their men under iron control to prevent things from getting out of hand.

They might have found it easier to maintain that kind of control because of the intense satisfaction their men took in the systematic destruction of anything in Iythria that could have contributed to the Desnairian war effort. Every gun had been loaded with quadruple charges and four or five round shot and fired until its tube split, then dumped into the harbor. Every battery emplacement and powder magazine had been blown up. The shipyards and sawmills and sail lofts and ropewalks which had built and rigged Baron Jahras' galleons had been put to the torch. Thousands of tons of naval supplies—seasoned timbers, acres of canvas, hundreds of thousands of feet of cordage, endless barrels of turpentine, paint, pitch, varnish, linseed oil, oakum, thousands of bags of biscuit and tons of preserved meat and vegetables—had gone up in thick, choking columns of dense black smoke. Huge stocks of muskets, cutlasses, pikes, and pistols had been seized and lightered out to the waiting Charisian transport galleons. Several hundred thousand round shot had been loaded aboard barges and hulks, towed into deep water, and then sent to the bottom. All five of the cannon foundries around the city had been blown up, most of the waterfront warehouses had been burned to the ground, and every one of the surviving fortresses on the islands dotted about the Gulf had been thoroughly demolished. The millions upon millions of marks the Church of God Awaiting and the Desnairian Empire had invested in turning Iythria into one of the anchors of the Group of Four's naval power had disappeared in those roaring flames and rivers of smoke, and Kholman had realized what that meant for him personally.

When Sir Domynyk Staynair landed his prisoners (without even attempting to secure the paroles he knew they would never be allowed to honor), the Duke of Kholman and every member of his immediate family had joined Baron Jahras aboard HMS *Destroyer*. Along with the rest of Staynair's fleet, the fugitives were perhaps a five-day and a half behind *Destiny*.

"You know they're never going to admit Kholman and his family were *driven* into seeking asylum because of Clyntahn's vindictiveness," Sharleyan said. "And it won't matter what Kholman and Jahras have to say, either."

"Not as far as the *Group of Four*'s propaganda is concerned, no," Cayleb agreed. "On the other hand, that's not the only propaganda circulating in Haven."

"No, Your Majesty," Nahrmahn agreed cheerfully. "And I'll bet Clyntahn's frothing at the mouth trying to figure out where those 'heretical printing presses' are! To be honest, one of the things I most regret about Merlin's inability to put SNARCs inside the Temple is the fact that I can't actually watch his blood pressure rise when Rayno makes his reports on that front."

All three of them laughed, but he had a point, Cayleb thought. The Inquisition was searching with grim determination for the printers distributing the propaganda broadsheets which somehow mysteriously kept circulating throughout the various mainland realms. Unfortunately for the Inquisition, while there truly were a handful of mainland Reformists running very small presses, the stealthed remotes which actually distributed the overwhelming majority of the offending broadsheets were just a *bit* hard to spot. Every day, the Inquisition ripped those broadsheets down from one wall or another in virtually every mainland city; every night Owl's remotes put them back up on different walls in completely different neighborhoods.

And no one ever saw a thing.

The one place they were careful about *not* distributing propaganda like that was the Republic of Siddarmark. Siddarmark had by far the largest community of Charisian expatriates, and the situation there was becoming increasingly tense. No one in Charis wanted to add any additional sparks to such a potentially incendiary mixture. Which, unfortunately, didn't prevent a growing number of people *inside* Siddarmark from distributing their own propaganda. Worse, the Reformist movement was steadily gathering strength in the Siddarmarkian church, and no one this side of God had any idea where *that* was going to lead!

"I'm sure those mysterious, shameless propagandists and vile enemies of Mother Church will capitalize on these defections," Cayleb continued with a pious expression. "And I suspect that's going to have a greater effect than Clyntahn or the Inquisition want to think about. But I'm more interested in what it's going to do from *our* perspective." His expression turned much more serious. "I know it sounds mushy-headed and softhearted, but I've always wanted Charis to be a genuine refuge, a place that welcomes people fleeing from intolerance or oppression or persecution. That's got to be the real basis for everything we're trying to build—the foundation for human freedom and human dignity—and to stand against something like the Church and someone like Clyntahn, that foundation has to be *firm*. It has to have roots sunk into bedrock, deep enough to weather *any* storm.

"And for that to really work, Charisians have to see *themselves* that way. Our people have to define themselves as *welcoming* refugees from persecution if we don't want those refugees to become—what was that word Merlin used? *Ghettoized*. That was it. Unless we want those refugees to settle in isolated, undigested chunks instead of being integrated into the society and the church around them, we need to embrace them. And we need that foundation set *now,* before we have to start dealing with telling the entire world the truth about Langhorne and the other 'Archangels.' People like Madame Dynnys, or Father Paityr's family, are a visible proof to everyone, including our own people, that that's the way it works, the way we really think, at least here in Charis, by God! And for that matter, you and Gorjah are proof we're even willing to welcome old *enemies* and actually integrate them into our own society and government if they're willing to stand up beside us against people like the Group of Four, Nahrmahn. Now we've got a chance to do the same thing with Jahras and Kholman, and I damned well want to see it handled the right way!"

Sharleyan nodded, leaning closer to rest her head on

his shoulder while they watched Alahnah scurrying around the terrace on hands and knees.

"We're working on it, love," she told him. "We're working on it."

. II .

Gray Wyvern Avenue, City of Tellesberg, Kingdom of Old Charis

It was a handsome freight wagon, if he did say so himself, Ainsail Dahnvahr thought. He'd spent a lot of effort on it, and the fact that he was a skilled carpenter and wagon-maker had played a prominent part in the planning for his part of Operation Rakurai. He was sure others among the Grand Inquisitor's Rakurai had skills of their own which had been factored into Archbishop Wyllym's planning and orders, although no one had ever told him that. He understood why that was, of course. What he didn't know couldn't be tortured out of him if he had the misfortune to be captured alive by the heretics.

To be fair—which he didn't really want to do—he had to admit he'd seen no overt evidence the heretics hadn't meant it when they promised not to torture their enemies, but what happened in the open wasn't always the same as what happened in secret, and the heretics' success in picking off every effort to build some kind of effective organization against them certainly suggested they were forcing people to talk *somehow*. But however they were managing it, it wouldn't do them any good if he didn't have the information they wanted in the first place.

And it wasn't going to matter a great deal longer one way or the other, he reminded himself.

"It'd be a lot simpler if we could just go ahead and

unload the wagon, Master Gahztahn," the wheelwright said, surveying the broken wheel and cracked axle. "Get the weight off of it, and we could jack it up a lot easier."

"I know it would," the man who called himself Hiraim Gahztahn agreed with a nod. "And if you see some place to park another wagon this size while we shift the load to it, I'm all for it!"

He waved his hands with an exasperated expression, and the wheelwright grimaced in acknowledgment. Gray Wyvern Avenue was one of the busiest streets in Tellesberg, a city famous for the density of its traffic. "Gahztahn" had been doing well to get his eight-wheeled articulated wagon dragged to the side of the street after the right front wheel broke. To accomplish even that much, he'd had to crowd up onto the sidewalk, and the foot traffic's need to flow around it wasn't doing a thing to ease the congestion. Now the hill dragon between the shafts stood patiently, head down while it rummaged through the feed bag hung from its head, ignoring the even more constricted traffic oozing past the obstruction. The City Guard had already made it clear they wanted this particular wagon fixed—quickly!—and out of the way before the traffic jam got any worse.

"Well," the Charisian said now, turning with his hands on his hips to watch as his apprentice managed to squeeze their work wagon in behind "Gahztahn's" stalled vehicle, "I reckon we'll just have to do the best we can." He shook his head. "I'm not sure how well it's going to work if that axle's as bad as it looks, but I *think* we've got a spare wheel we can change out at least long enough to tow you out of the middle of all this damned traffic."

"Good!" Ainsail said, nodding enthusiastically, and rolled his eyes. "If I have one more irritated Guardsman wander by to ask me 'How much longer do you think you'll be?' I think I'll just go ahead and cut my throat right here."

"Seems a mite drastic to me," the wheelwright told him with a grin. "Still and all, you're close enough to the

Cathedral you could probably get in line with the Archangels pretty quick."

He laughed, and Ainsail made himself laugh back, although there wasn't anything funny about the blasphemous reference as far as *he* was concerned. And he noticed
the heretic didn't sign himself with the scepter when he
mentioned the Archangels, either. Well, it was hardly a
surprise.

He stepped back and watched the wheelwright and his
assistant get to work. They were good, he admitted, as
Charisian workmen tended to be, but they were in for a
surprise. Well, two surprises, if he was going to be accurate, although they probably wouldn't have time to appreciate the second one. But that spare wheel of theirs wasn't
going to fit. Ainsail had taken some pains to make *sure* no
standard Charisian wheel hub was going to fit that axle,
just as he'd very carefully arranged for the wheel to break
precisely where—and when—it had. Fortunately no one
had noticed the sharp rap with the hand sledge which had
been required to knock out the wedge he'd fitted to keep
the wheel rim properly tensioned against the steel tire until
he reached exactly the right spot. Hopefully, the wheelwright wasn't going to notice that the "break" was suspiciously straight edged and clean, either. Ainsail was a little
worried about that, but only a little.

God wouldn't have let him come this far only to fail at
this point.

▼ ▼ ▼

"You worry too much, Rayjhis," Bishop Hainryk Waignair
said teasingly. "If it weren't the Gulf of Jahras, it would
just be something else. Admit it! You're a *fussbudget!*"

The white-haired, clean-shaven Bishop of Tellesberg
leaned forward to tap an index finger on Earl Gray Harbor's chest, brown eyes gleaming with amused challenge.
He and Gray Harbor had known one another almost as
long as Gray Harbor had known Maikel Staynair, and
Waignair, as the second-ranking prelate of the Church of

Charis, often sat in for the archbishop on meetings of the Imperial Council when Staynair—as today—was otherwise occupied with the responsibilities of his own ecclesiastic office.

"I am *not* a 'fussbudget,' " Gray Harbor said with immense dignity as the carriage moved steadily along the street. "I'm simply a conscientious, thoughtful, insightful—don't forget insightful!—servant of the Crown. It's my *job* to worry about things, just like it's *your* job to reassure me that God is on our side."

" '*Insightful!*' " Waignair snorted. "Is *that* what you call it?"

"When I don't feel an even stronger term is appropriate, yes," Gray Harbor said judiciously, and the bishop laughed.

"I guess there might be a little something to that," he said, holding up the thumb and forefinger of his right hand perhaps a quarter of an inch apart. "A *little* something!" His eyes glinted at his old friend. "Still, with Domynyk in command and *Seijin* Merlin's visions assuring us everything went well, can't you find *something* better to worry about than the Gulf of Jahras?"

Gray Harbor considered for a moment, then shrugged.

"Of course I can. In fact, I think probably one reason I'm worrying about the Gulf is that we do know it worked out well." Waignair looked perplexed, and Gray Harbor chuckled. "What I mean is that 'worrying' about something I know worked pretty much the way we had in mind distracts me from worrying about the *other* somethings out there that we *don't* know are going to work out the way we have in mind. If you take my meaning."

"You know, the frightening thing is that I *do* understand you," Waignair said. "Probably says something unhealthy about my own mind."

Gray Harbor chuckled again, louder, and the bishop shook his head at him. The truth was, of course, that both of them knew about the good news Gray Harbor was going to be able to announce in the next five-day or so. Waignair, as a member of the inner circle, had actually watched the battle through Owl's remotes for several hours. He'd spent most of that time praying for the thousands of men who were being killed or maimed in that cauldron of smoke and fire and exploding ships, and he knew exactly what price Domynyk Staynair's fleet had paid to purchase that victory. Gray Harbor hadn't been able to watch personally, but the first councilor was an experienced naval officer, with firsthand experience of what that sort of carnage was like. And he'd long since grown accustomed to taking Merlin's "visions" as demonstrated fact. He'd been planning how best to use the destruction of the Desnairian Navy ever since the battle had been fought, and he was looking forward to putting those plans into motion as soon as the news officially reached Tellesberg.

"The problem's not with your *mind*, Hainryk," Gray Harbor told him now. "The *problem's* with—"

▼ ▼ ▼

Ainsail stood on the narrow, constricted space of open sidewalk beside his wagon, between it and the building he'd managed to park alongside, and watched the traffic flow past while the wheelwright and his apprentice swore with feeling and inventiveness. They'd just discovered the non-standard dimensions of the wagon axle, and as soon as the two of them got done expressing their feelings, Ainsail was sure they'd get around to working out ways to deal with the problem.

Or they would have if they'd had time, he thought as he finally spotted the vehicle he'd been waiting for. It was a good thing he *had* made sure the repairs were going to be more time-consuming than the wheelwright had originally thought, since the carriage making its way slowly along the crowded street was substantially behind its regular schedule. And, as it drew closer, Ainsail felt his mouth tighten in disappointment. It was unaccompanied by the guardsmen in the orange-and-white livery of the archbishop who normally escorted it.

Why today? he demanded silently. *Today, of all days!*

Would it have been too much to ask for the bastard to keep to his own—?

He cut that thought off quickly. The fact that God and Langhorne had seen fit to bring him this far, grant him the degree of success he'd achieved, was more than any man had a right to demand. He had no business complaining or berating God just because he hadn't been given still more!

Forgive me, he prayed humbly as he opened the small, carefully concealed panel he'd built into the side of the wagon bed. *It's not my place to set my wisdom above Yours. I'm sure it's all part of Your plan. Thank You for the opportunity to be part of Your work.*

He reached into the hidden compartment and cocked the flintlock. Then his hand settled around the pistol grip and he stood, shoulders relaxed, watching with a calm tranquility he was a little surprised to realize was completely genuine, as the carriage rolled steadily closer.

"We're going to have to go back to the shop, Master Gahztahn," the wheelwright was saying. "It looks like we'll need to—"

He went on talking, but Ainsail tuned him out. He nodded, pretending he was listening, but his attention was on another voice. His mother's voice, reciting the catechism with a much younger Ainsail as he sat on her lap in her kitchen. And then there was Archbishop Wyllym's voice, and other voices, all with him at this moment, bearing him up on their strength. He listened to them, embraced them, and as the carriage drew even with the wagon, Ainsail Dahnvahr smiled joyously and squeezed the trigger.

Tellesberg Palace,
City of Tellesberg,
Kingdom of Old Charis,
and
Cathedral Square,
City of Eraystor,
Princedom of Emerald

"I came as quickly as I could, Cayleb," Maikel Staynair said as a stone-faced Edwyrd Seahamper escorted him into the royal couple's private chambers. The archbishop crossed the room quickly and knelt beside Sharleyan, who sat hunched in a chair, clasping her daughter in her arms while tears ran down her cheeks.

Cayleb only nodded curtly as Staynair put a comforting arm around Sharleyan's shoulders. There were no tears in his eyes, only fury, and the archbishop hid a stab of concern as he recognized his emperor's rage.

There's only so much provocation any man can take before he starts forgetting he's not the kind of animal his opponents are, Staynair thought quietly. *Please, Cayleb. Please! Step back from this. Draw a deep breath. Don't lash out in some way you'll regret in days to come.*

"We should've taken more precautions," the emperor grated. "We were too predictable. They knew where to find you and Rayjhis, Maikel. That's what this is all about—the only reason they managed to pull it off. They *knew* where to find you because we let you use the same route every time you come to the palace."

"Cayleb—" Staynair began, but Cayleb cut him off.

"No, it's not *your* fault." The emperor glared at him. "No, you didn't tell your driver or your escort to take alternate routes, but neither did anyone else. Neither did

Merlin and neither did I, and we damned well *should* have. Damn it to hell, Maikel! We know Clyntahn thinks assassination's a perfectly acceptable tool. And unlike you, Nahrmahn," he said to the distant Prince of Emerald, "he doesn't give a spider-rat's *ass* how many innocent bystanders he kills along the way. Hell, there *aren't* any innocent bystanders! Either they're fucking heretics who deserve whatever the hell they get, or else they're noble martyrs to God's plan! Either way, he can kill however the hell many of them he wants 'in God's name' and feel nothing but the satisfaction of a job well done!"

Staynair winced. Not because he disagreed with a single thing Cayleb had just said, but because of the magma-like fury that filled every syllable.

"Cayleb—" he began again, only to be stopped by a choppy wave of the emperor's hand. Cayleb turned away, fists clenched at his sides as he glared out a window and fought for self-control. His eyes didn't see the peaceful garden outside his window; they were watching the imagery projected on his contact lenses as Merlin and a party of Imperial Guardsmen worked their way through the bloody wreckage of Gray Wyvern Avenue.

There must've been at least a ton of gunpowder in that wagon, he thought bitterly. *Where the fuck did they get their hands on that? And how in hell did they get it into Tellesberg? And how did* none *of us spot them at it?*

He already knew Merlin was going to blame himself for it, just as he blamed *himself*, but his brain, unlike his emotions, knew both of them would be wrong. They weren't the only ones with access to Owl's SNARCs, and responsibility for surveillance here in Old Charis lay primarily with Bynzhamyn Raice, with Prince Nahrmahn as his backup. Both of them were undoubtedly already savaging themselves over what had happened, but Cayleb knew exactly what their procedures were, the sort of information they had access to, and he couldn't think of a single thing they could have done differently.

"What's the latest death toll estimate?" he said out loud, his voice flat, never turning from the window.

"I don't think anyone knows," Staynair replied quietly. "Bynzhamyn is at Saint Marzhory's. It's chaos there, of course. And I ought to be there, not here."

Cayleb turned his head just long enough to stab a single glance at the archbishop, then returned to the window again. There was no way in the universe he was going to allow Maikel Staynair outside the confines of Tellesberg Palace until they had a far better handle on what had just happened. Staynair looked at his rigid, unyielding spine for a long moment, then sighed.

"As I say, it's chaos," he continued. "So far, they've admitted over three dozen patients, and they're sending the less badly hurt to some of the smaller hospitals. How many of the ones they're keeping are going to live. . . ."

He shrugged helplessly. Saint Marzhory's Hospital was the main hospital of the Order of Pasquale in Tellesberg. Only six blocks from Tellesberg Palace, the savage attack had happened almost outside the enormous complex's front door. That was the one mitigating aspect of this entire murderous day, because Saint Marzhory's had the finest healers and the best surgeons in all of Old Charis. But despite all the medical knowledge and "healing liturgies" tucked away in *The Book of Pasquale*, Saint Marzhory's was no trauma center. Those healers would do the best they could, but they were going to lose a heartbreaking percentage of the maimed and broken bodies which had inundated them.

"Merlin says they've already confirmed at least two hundred dead on-site," Nahrmahn Baytz said from Eraystor. He and Princess Ohlyvya had been visiting his uncle Hanbyl, the Duke of Salomon, when the attack occurred. Now their carriage was on its way back to their palace, and Ohlyvya was pressed tightly against his side, her face resting on his shoulder.

"I don't want to distract him by pestering him with questions at the moment," the chubby little Emeraldian continued flatly, "so I don't have a better count than that. I'm sure there are more bodies—or parts of them, anyway—waiting to be found, though. Midday on Gray

Wyvern Avenue?" He barked a harsh, angry laugh that was more than half snarl. "We're going to be lucky if the final count doesn't top *three* hundred! And you're right, Cayleb; they couldn't have pulled this off if we hadn't let ourselves get too predictable."

"I don't think that was the only reason they got away with it," Sharleyan said, raising her head as she cuddled a silent, big-eyed Alahnah against her shoulder. The little girl didn't have a clue what was going on, but she was obviously sensitive to the emotions of the adults around her.

"What do you mean?" Cayleb asked, raising an eyebrow at her.

"I mean our own confidence turned around and bit us in the ass, as Merlin might put it," she said. "We know what an advantage we have with the SNARCs and with Owl to manage them for us. Oh, we also know things can leak through—like what happened in Manchyr, for example. But despite that, we know we still have better security than anyone else in the entire world. Right?"

"You're saying we let ourselves be lulled into overconfidence." Cayleb shrugged. "That's the same reason we let ourselves get too predictable, Sharley."

"No, that's not what I'm saying. Or it's not *everything* I'm saying, anyway." Sharleyan drew a deep breath. "I guess what I really meant is that *we* know what an advantage we have, but sometimes we forget the other side's figuring it out, too. They're finding ways to work around it, and we didn't expect them to."

There was silence for a moment, and then Nahrmahn nodded as his carriage began making its way through the heavier traffic in Cherayth.

"Like they did with that misinformation about which way Harpahr was actually going to be sent with his fleet, you mean?" he asked.

"I think, yes," she replied. "But this goes further than that." She was obviously working her way through her own analysis as she spoke, and Cayleb folded his arms across his chest, watching her intently. "That was more . . .

passive. Or defensive, perhaps. It was *misinformation*, as you said, Nahrmahn; this is something a lot more active. They managed to get whoever put that wagon in position into Tellesberg, and they managed to provide him with the gunpowder he needed, and we never saw a thing. Not a *thing!* How did they do that? How could they build an organization that could coordinate something like that without us seeing a thing?"

"They couldn't," Cayleb said slowly, and she nodded.

"Which is why I don't think they did anything of the sort," she said flatly. "I don't know how, but God knows the Inquisition's been managing spies and informants and agents provocateurs forever, and Clyntahn already proved in Manchyr that he could engineer the assassination of a reigning *prince* without anyone catching him at it! They managed to get *this* assassin and his weapon into position somehow, too, and the only way I can think of for them to've done that without our catching them at it is to organize it the same way they must have organized their misinformation gambit before the Markovian Sea."

"They planned it and put it together inside the Temple, where we can't get SNARCs in to snoop on them," Nahrmahn said. "That's what you're saying. And because they've figured out our spies are better than theirs, even if they don't have a clue why that's true, they sent their man in unsupported."

"Unsupported by anyone he had to contact *here,* anyway," Sharleyan corrected. "I don't think there's any way anyone could have set this all up on his own after he was here. There *had* to be some spadework before they sent him in. But I'll bet you any contact with anyone here in Tellesberg or Old Charis went through the Temple, not through anyone else here."

"Limiting themselves to communications channels that go directly from one person back to the Temple and then from the Temple back to that one person?" Cayleb could have sounded dismissive, but he didn't, and his expression was thoughtful. "How in hell could they pull that off?"

"That depends on how willing they'd be to use things like the semaphore system and ciphers," Nahrmahn responded. "We're still using it to communicate with Siddarmark and Silkiah. In fact, we're allowing greater access to it than the Church ever did, so if they feel confident of their cipher system, they could be sending their correspondence back and forth that way easily enough. For that matter, we're not the only people with messenger wyverns, Cayleb." The Emeraldian shook his head. "That'd be slow and cumbersome and not very responsive, but they could have set up a system that would do the job without ever going near the sempahore.

"The key point isn't how they get messages back and forth, though. It's the point Sharley's raised: the probability that they're sending out solo operatives. Our ability to detect them depends in large part on Owl's ability to recognize key words in conversation and direct our attention to the people who used them, or on our ability to identify one agent and then work outward until we've found all the members of his network. A single assassin, especially one who's prepared or even eager to die in the attempt, the way this fellow certainly was, is going to be one hell of a lot harder to spot and stop."

"That's true," Cayleb agreed, rubbing his chin thoughtfully. "On the other hand, a single assassin's going to be able to do a lot less damage than a full-blown conspiracy *if* we can keep the bastard away from wagonloads of gunpowder. And nothing anyone's brought up so far suggests how they got that big a load of explosives through our customs inspections. If they're avoiding building or working with a large organization, then surely they wouldn't have tried to bribe the inspectors, and I doubt they'd use *smugglers* if they're worried about the potential for being betrayed to the authorities! So how—?"

He broke off suddenly, eyes narrowing in thought. Then he grunted angrily and slammed his right fist into his left palm.

"Hairatha," he said flatly. "That's what that damned explosion was about! They didn't smuggle the gunpowder into Tellesberg from one of the mainland realms; they used *our* gunpowder!"

"Wait. Wait!" Nahrmahn objected. "I'm not saying you're wrong, Cayleb, but how do we jump from what just happened in Tellesberg to Hairatha?"

"I don't know," Cayleb admitted. "I don't *know*, all right? But I'm right, I *know* I am! Call it a hunch, call it instinct, but that's what happened. Somebody at Hairatha with the authority—or the access, at least—to doctor shipping manifests diverted gunpowder from our own powder mill. And they blew the damned place up to keep anyone from realizing they'd done it! To get rid of any paper trail that might have led back to them or to who they sent the powder to." His expression was murderous. "My God, Hairatha shipped gunpowder in thousand-ton lots on a regular basis, Nahrmahn! We could have *dozens* of wagonloads of it sitting out there!"

"But how could they coordinate something like that without that organization you all seem to be agreeing they don't have?" Staynair asked quietly.

"All they'd really need is what the intelligence organizations back on Old Terra used to call a 'bagman.'" Nahrmahn's tone was unhappy, as if he was unwillingly coming to the conclusion Cayleb might have a point. "If somebody did manage to divert a quantity of gunpowder from Hairatha to someone else in Old Charis—possibly somebody he'd never even met or contacted in any way himself, but whose address was supplied to him by a controller in Zion—then that person could have distributed it to a dozen other locations which had been set up exactly the same way. Or, for that matter, he could have kept it all in a single location and these lone assassins we're hypothesizing about could have been given the address before they ever left Zion. I can't begin to count the number of potential failure points in something like that, but all the ones I can think of would be much more likely to simply cause someone to not get to where he needed to be than to give the operation away to the other side. And look at it from Clyntahn's perspective. What does he lose if it doesn't work? But if it *does* work, he gets something like he just got today. He kills important members of Cayleb and Sharleyan's government, and he does it very, very publicly. With lots of other bodies to go around. It's a statement that even if the Group of Four can't beat us at sea, they can still reach out into the very heart of Tellesberg and hurt us. Do you think for a moment that wouldn't seem like a win-win situation for someone like him, Maikel?"

"But if you and Cayleb are right, how many other 'lone assassins' are out there?" Staynair's expression was troubled.

"I have no idea," Nahrmahn admitted frankly. He glared out the carriage window in frustration as it crossed into Cathedral Square, less than four blocks from the palace. "There could be scores of them, or this could have been the only one. Knowing Clyntahn, though, I doubt he'd have settled for one when he might have been able to get dozens into place. Why settle for a little bit of carnage when he could have a lot?"

"You're probably right about that," Cayleb said bitterly.

"And he'd want to underscore his 'statement' as strongly as possible, too," Sharleyan added. Staynair and Cayleb looked at her, and she shrugged. "I think Nahrmahn's right. He's going to have been thinking in terms of as many attacks as he could contrive, within the limitations of whatever coordination system he had. And he's going to want to concentrate them in terms of timing, too—get them in in the most focused window of time he can. He's the kind who thinks in terms of hammer blows when he goes after his opponents' morale."

"Some kind of timetable?" Cayleb's expression was suddenly strained once more. "You mean we're probably looking at additional attacks scheduled to occur simultaneously?"

"Over a short period of time, anyway," Sharleyan said, nodding unhappily. "There's no way he could count on their being *simultaneous,* but they don't have to be. Don't forget the communications problem. We can talk back and forth instantaneously, but he doesn't know that. As far as he's concerned, word is going to have to spread before anyone can know to start taking precautions, and we can't get warnings out any more rapidly than by semaphore. That means he only has to achieve approximate coordination, because he'd still be inside what Merlin calls our communications loop."

"You may have a point," Nahrmahn conceded. "On the other hand, I could see some advantages—from his perspective—to stretching things out, hitting us with a series of attacks to demonstrate we couldn't stop him from getting through to us. So—"

He paused suddenly, staring out the window. Then—

"Stop the carriage!" he shouted. *"Stop the carriage!"*

The carriage came to a sudden halt, and the commander of its mounted escort wheeled his horse, trotting back towards it with a puzzled expression. He had no idea what was happening, but like most of Nahrmahn Baytz' armsmen, he had a lively respect for the prince's instincts.

"Out!" Nahrmahn said to Ohlyvya. *"Out, now!"*

She stared at him in confusion and a sudden sparkle of fear. She'd never seen his expression like that, but the crack of command in his voice had her moving before she even realized it. He pushed her towards the carriage's left-hand door, already reaching out, turning the handle. She hesitated for a moment as the door swung open, then cried out in sudden panic as her husband put his shoulder into her back and literally *heaved* her out the door.

It was a three-foot drop to the paving, and Ohlyvya Baytz cried out again, this time in pain, as she landed off-balance and her ankle broke. But there was no time for her to think about that. Nahrmahn was already plunging out of the carriage behind her, pinning her down, covering her with his own body.

And that was when the wagon parked by the Cathedral Square exit closest to the palace—the wagon that wasn't supposed to be there—exploded.

Royal Palace,
City of Eraystor,
Princedom of Emerald

"Leave us," Ohlyvya Baytz said flatly, her expression terrible.

It was night outside the bedchamber's window—a beautiful moonlit night, sprinkled with the stars that were God's own jewels. A gentle breeze stirred the window drapes, night wyverns whistled sweetly, and the harsh, agonized breathing of the semi-conscious man in the bed filled her heart with grief.

"But, Your Highness—" the senior healer, a Pasqualate bishop, began.

"*Leave us!*" she snapped. The bishop looked at her, his expression worried, his eyes dark with sympathy, and she made herself draw a deep breath.

"Is there anything else you can do for him, My Lord Bishop?" she asked more quietly. "Can you save him?"

"No, Your Highness," the bishop admitted, his voice sad but unflinching. "To be honest, I don't understand how he's lived this long. The best we can do is what we have, to ease his pain."

"Then leave us," she repeated a third time, tears welling in her eyes, her voice far softer than it had been. "This is my husband. He will die with his hand in mine in this room we have shared for twenty-seven years. And I will be alone with him, My Lord. I will bear him company, and I will witness his death, and if he speaks again before the end, what he says will be for my ears and no others. Now leave us, please. I have little time with him, and I refuse to lose any of it."

The bishop looked at her for a moment longer, then bowed his head.

"As you wish, Your Highness," he said softly. "Shall I send in Father Zhon?"

"No," Princess Ohlyvya said, staring down at her husband's face and holding his remaining hand in hers.

The bishop started to argue, then made himself stop. Father Zhon Trahlmahn, the royal household's official confessor, was actually more of a tutor to Nahrmahn and Ohlyvya's children than the keeper of the prince's conscience. The prince, the bishop thought, had never been as observant a man as the Church might have wished. The bishop was a man of strong Reformist beliefs himself, and Prince Nahrmahn's courage and willingness to speak in the cause of reforming Mother Church's faults and healing her wounds had won his admiration and gratitude, yet he could wish that at this moment. . . .

It wasn't his decision, he reminded himself. It was Princess Ohlyvya's. Father Zhon had already administered extreme unction, and presumably heard the prince's confession, before the princess had sent him to comfort the children. But who would comfort *her* in this terrible hour, the bishop wondered. Who would hold *her* hand as she held her dying husband's?

"Very well, Your Highness," he said very quietly. "If you should decide you need me, send word."

"Thank you, My Lord, but I think that will be unnecessary," she told him with heartbreaking serenity. "I'm sure you're needed by the other victims of this attack. Go, do what you can for them with my thanks and my blessing."

The bishop bowed, then gathered up the lesser clergy with his eyes. The door closed behind them, and Ohlyvya leaned closer to the bed, resting her head on the pillow with her forehead touching Nahrmahn's cheek.

"I'm here, love," she said softly. "I'm here."

His left eye was covered in a thick dressing, but his right eye opened. He blinked slowly, the tiny movement of his eyelid heavy with effort, then turned his head and looked at her.

"Ear . . . plug?" he got out, and Ohlyvya astonished herself with a soft, weeping laugh.

"Oh, Nahrmahn!" She cupped the uninjured side of his face with her free hand. "Oh, my love, who but you would worry about that at a time like this?!"

He said nothing, but there was a flicker of something almost like amusement under the pain and the drug clouds in his eye, and she shook her head.

"I don't know what happened to your earplug," she told him. "No one found anything when the healers examined you, anyway. Maybe they just had other things on their mind than looking in your ears. I don't know."

"Make . . . sure, later," he whispered.

"I will," she promised. "I will. Now hush, my love. Don't worry about anything, not now."

"Love . . . you," he said. "Always have. Never . . . told you so . . . enough."

"You think I didn't know?" She smoothed hair from his brow. "I knew. I always knew. And you saved me today, Nahrmahn." She managed a wavering smile. "I know you've never thought you were a properly heroic figure, but you were always hero enough for me. And never more than today."

His answering smile was heartbreaking but his eye slipped slowly shut once more, and her grip on his hand tightened. Had he heard her? Did he understand? Her ankle was broken, the left side of her face was one enormous bruise, and it had taken fourteen stitches to close the gash on her left shoulder, but not a single member of their escort had survived. Neither had the coachmen. And if Nahrmahn hadn't protected her with his own body, *she* would be dead or dying, too. It was important that he know that, and—

She heard a foot on the marble bedchamber floor behind her, and her head jerked up, her eyes flashing with sudden, grief-fueled fury as she wheeled.

"How *dare* you intrude—?!" she began, then stopped abruptly.

"I came as soon as I could, Ohlyvya," Merlin Athrawes

said. "I couldn't risk it before dark, and getting away from Tellesberg under the circumstances. . . ."

He shrugged, crossing to the bed, and sank to one knee beside her chair. He held out his arms to her, and she threw herself into them, weeping on his mailed shoulder as she'd refused to let anyone else see her weep.

"Take him to your cave, Merlin!" she sobbed. "Take him to your cave! Let Owl save him!"

"I can't," Merlin whispered into her ear, stroking her hair with a sinewy hand. "I can't. There's not enough time. We'd lose him before I ever got him there."

"No!" She struggled against his embrace, striking his unyielding cuirass with her fists. It was as if his arrival had offered her the hope of a last-minute reprieve and the destruction of that hope was more than she could bear. "No!"

"Maybe, if I'd been able to get here sooner, then . . . maybe," Merlin said, holding her with implacable strength. "But I couldn't. And Owl's been monitoring, Ohlyvya. I don't think we would've been able to save him even if I had been able to get here sooner. It's only the nanotech keeping him alive now, and it's burning out, using itself up."

"Then why are you here?" she demanded, furious in her sorrow. "Why are you even here?"

"Because Sharleyan and Cayleb and I love you," he said. "And because I can at least give you this."

She stared at him as he put his hands on her shoulders and very gently settled her back into her chair before he stood once more. He reached into his belt pouch and extracted a lightweight headset of silvery wire and gently adjusted it on Nahrmahn's head. Nothing happened for a moment, but then the eye which had closed opened once more.

"Merlin?" Nahrmahn's voice was stronger than it had been, clearer, and Merlin nodded.

"More of your magic?" Nahrmahn asked.

"No more 'magic' than the rest of me, Nahrmahn," Merlin told him. "I'm sorry I couldn't get here sooner."

"I guess . . . when you're a thousand years old . . . you tend to . . . lose track of time," Nahrmahn managed, and Ohlyvya laughed through her tears, covering her mouth with both hands.

"It's not much," Merlin told her, his sapphire eyes deeper and darker than the sea, "but it's all I can do right now."

"What—?"

"The headset will keep his mind clear, and I programmed it to shut down the pain centers." Merlin managed a smile of his own. "I don't think you have much time, Ohlyvya, but the time you do have will be clear . . . and it will be *yours*."

He touched her face very gently, then looked back down at Nahrmahn.

"It's been an interesting trip, Nahrmahn," he said, laying his hand on the dying prince's shoulder. "And it's been a privilege working with you. Thank you for everything you've done. But now, I think I'll leave you with your wife. God bless, Nahrmahn. Hopefully we'll have a chance to talk again someday."

He squeezed Nahrmahn's shoulder and looked at Ohlyvya.

"I'll be out in the garden, listening, if you should need me," he said gently, and vanished back through the window by which he'd arrived.

Ohlyvya Baytz looked after him for a moment, tearful eyes shining with gratitude, and then she turned back to her husband and reached for his hand once more.

Plaza of Martyrs,
The Temple,
City of Zion,
The Temple Lands

"Rhobair, you *have* to come," Zahmsyn Trynair said flatly.

"No, Zahmsyn. Actually, I don't."

Rhobair Duchairn looked steadily back at the Chancellor. Trynair's expression was an odd mixture of anxiety, frustration, distaste for what he himself was saying, and anger, but the Treasurer's face was calm, his eyes almost—not quite, but *almost*—tranquil.

"This is *not* a time to be suggesting there's division between us, Rhobair," Trynair said.

"Anybody who's worrying about whether or not there's 'division' between me and Zhaspahr Clyntahn on this issue has either already figured out there *is* one, or he's such a drooling idiot he probably can't put on his own *shoes* without assistance!" Duchairn replied. "And, frankly, if someone does realize I'm . . . at odds, let's say, with Zhaspahr Clyntahn over this . . . this ritualized *butchery* of his, that's fine with me. Even *The Book of Schueler* reserves the full Punishment for genuine, unrepentant *heretics*, Zhamsyn—not for people who simply happen to have pissed Zhaspahr off by having the audacity to survive when he ordered them to lie down and die!"

He'd been wrong, Trynair realized. Duchairn's eyes weren't tranquil; they were those of a man who didn't *care* any longer. A chill went through the Chancellor as he realized that, and he felt something altogether too much like panic fluttering somewhere inside his chest.

"You told Zhaspahr—and me—you wouldn't oppose him on this if we wouldn't oppose you on the matters that were important to you," he said carefully.

"And I have no intention, to my shame, of openly opposing him. There are, however, limits to the stains I'm prepared to accept upon my soul. This is one of them. You and I both know any 'confessions' of heresy or blasphemy or—God help us all!—Shan-wei worship were gotten out of those men only by torture, and eight in ten of them *died* rather than perjure themselves to suit Zhaspahr's purposes. Do you truly have any concept at all of the courage it took to *defy* that kind of savagery?! They may be schismatics, but they are *not* blasphemers, idolaters, or demon-worshippers, and they *damned* well haven't sacrificed any children to Shan-wei, and you know that as well as I do! So if my refusal to participate in his vengeance upon men whose only *true* crime was to defeat his unprovoked attack on their families and their homeland incenses him so completely that he chooses to make our breach public, so be it."

"Rhobair, you can't *survive* if that happens. If he openly turns against you, denounces you, you'll go exactly the same way these Charisians are about to!"

"I could be in worse company," Duchairn said flatly, his voice cold. "In fact, I'm inclined to think I couldn't be in *better* company. Unfortunately, I'm no longer as certain as I once was that my *eternal* destination is going to be the same as theirs. I can only pray it will."

Trynair's blood ran cold. He'd known Duchairn was becoming ever more embittered, ever more sickened, by Clyntahn's policies, but this was the harshest, most unyielding denunciation of the Grand Inquisitor Duchairn had dared to voice even to him. And if the Treasurer really pushed this, if it did result in an open break between him and the Grand Inquisitor, Trynair knew which of them would survive. In some ways, that might almost be a relief, yet with Duchairn gone, the Chancellor would be alone against Clyntahn with only the effective nonentity of Allayn Maigwair as a potential ally. Which meant. . . .

"Don't *say* things like that!" he pled, waving both hands in calming motions. "I know you're angry, and I know this whole thing makes you sick at heart, but if you push Zhaspahr far enough and *you* go down, there'll be nobody left to oppose him even slightly." The Chancellor grimaced, his expression more than half-ashamed. "*I* won't be able to, and I know it. Not now."

"He has rather saddled the whirlwind for all of us to ride, hasn't he?" Duchairn said sardonically. "Why did we let him get away with it, do you think?" His eyes suddenly stabbed the Chancellor to the heart. "Because the notion of doing what we knew was right didn't matter enough for us to bestir ourselves out of our luxurious little lives? Because we didn't give a single good goddamn about our responsibilities to Mother Church? Was *that* the reason, Zahmsyn?"

"Don't you dare try that with me!" Trynair snapped. "Maybe that was the reason, but you were right there in the middle of it with the rest of us, Rhobair! You could've said 'Stop!' anytime you wanted to. Maybe it wouldn't have accomplished anything, but you could have at least made the attempt, and you didn't, did you? You didn't even *try!* So now you've rediscovered your conscience. Fine! I'm happy for you! But don't you take your new-found piety and try to cram it down *my* throat! You're so fucking proud of how *noble* you've become? Well, that's fine. But if you think you're going to *shame* me into standing beside you when Zhaspahr decides to have *you* put to the Question to 'prove' you're just as heretical as Samyl Wylsynn ever was, you've got another think coming!"

"So you do have a little spine left," Duchairn said with a thin, cold smile. "Pity it didn't turn up earlier. And before you start in again, no, I'm not trying to pretend I wasn't just as spineless and just as blind to the consequences as you were when Zhaspahr launched us on this little disaster. I've never pretended I *wasn't* those things. The difference between us is that, yes, I *am* ashamed of myself, and there are limits to the additional complicity I'm willing to assume. And, frankly, I don't really care if the thought of finding yourself all alone with Zhaspahr after I'm gone makes you feel threatened. I'm not looking for martyrdom, Zahmsyn. It might be better for my soul if I were, but I'm not prepared to go that far . . . yet, anyway. And I'm not going to have any public shouting matches with Zhaspahr. I undoubtedly should, but you and I both know it would be a futile gesture. So you just run along back to him and Allayn. The three of you go and eat your fried potato slices at the spectacle this afternoon. Drink your beer and enjoy the entertainment. But I'm not going to be there, because I've got something a lot more pressing to spend my time on. I'm sure that if Zhaspahr and that loathsome slime toad Rayno want to know where I am, they can ask Major Phandys. No doubt he'd be *delighted* to tell them. And if *you* want to tell him where I am, that's fine with me too, because where I'll be, Zahmsyn, is in the Temple praying for God's forgiveness for *not* being out in that plaza denouncing Zhaspahr Clyntahn for the foul, sadistic murdering *bastard* he is!"

Rhobair Duchairn gave the Chancellor of the Church of God Awaiting one more cold, stony glare and slammed out of the office. Trynair stared after him, shocked and stunned by the power of the Treasurer's denunciation, and listened to the boots of Duchairn's "personal guard," clattering down the hallway behind Major Khanstahnzo Phandys as the lot of them tried to keep up with the furiously striding Treasurer.

▼ ▼ ▼

"Well, I see Zahmsyn has finally deigned to join us," Zhaspahr Clyntahn said, watching from the central platform as the Chancellor slipped unobtrusively into the silent, watching ranks of the Church's vicars. "Better late than never, I suppose. And where do you think our good friend Rhobair might be, Wyllym?"

"Somewhere else, Your Grace," Wyllym Rayno replied with a sigh. "I'm afraid his absence is going to be remarked upon."

"Of course it is." Clyntahn spoke from the corner of his mouth, lips scarcely moving as he looked out across the packed approaches to the Plaza of Martyrs. "That's why the bastard's *doing* it!"

"I agree, Your Grace, but I trust we're not going to make the mistake of underestimating him."

"Underestimate *Rhobair Duchairn*?" Clyntahn snorted. "That would be extraordinarily difficult to do, Wyllym! Oh, I'll grant you he's got more guts than Trynair, not to mention five or six times as much brains as Maigwair ever had. In fact, let's be honest—if there's one of the other three who'd ever have the courage and the willingness to speak out against the jihad, it would have to be Duchairn. But he's not ready for an open break. And the truth is that whatever he may think, he never *will* be."

"I'm . . . inclined to agree with you in most regards, Your Grace," Rayno said, choosing his words with some care. "All the same, I can't help thinking Vicar Rhobair has . . . changed a great deal over the last few years. I don't think we can afford to overlook the possibility that he may change still further."

"You mean grow big enough balls to consider an open confrontation with me?" Clyntahn asked calmly, turning to look directly at the Archbishop of Wu-shai for the first time. Rayno was obviously a bit nonplussed by the question, and the Grand Inquisitor chuckled coldly. "If it were just a matter of screwing up his nerve, he'd already have done it, Wyllym," he said flatly. "Whatever I may think of him, I'm willing to admit he's no coward. It's not *fear* holding him back—not anymore, anyway. And I don't need any spies to tell me he hates my guts, either. For that matter, I don't need any Bédardists to tell me that somewhere down inside he's come to hate himself, as well, for not 'standing up to me,' and that kind of hate can eat at a man until it finally drives him into doing something he'd never do otherwise. All of that's true, but he's still not going to push it to the point of an open break."

"May I ask why you're so certain of that, Your Grace?" Rayno asked cautiously.

"It's very simple, really." Clyntahn shrugged. "If he pushes me into having him . . . removed, there won't be anyone left to argue with me. You think Trynair or Maig-wair are going to draw any lines and dare me to step across them?" The Grand Inquisitor's laugh was a short, contemptuous bark. "Not in a thousand years, Wyllym. Not in a thousand years! And Rhobair knows that. He knows all his precious projects, all his 'kinder, gentler' plans and pious aspirations, any possibility of 'restrain-ing my excesses,' will go straight into the crapper with him, and he's not going to let that happen. The way he sees it, the only chance he has for redemption is to do some good in the world to make up for all those years when he was just as committed as any of the rest of us to the *practical* side of maintaining Mother Church's author-ity. He can't do that if he's dead, and that, more than any fear of the Question or the Punishment, is what's going to stop him. He'll always be able to find some way to ratio-nalize not coming directly at me because it's up to him to do whatever he can to minimize the 'damage' I'm doing."

Rayno simply looked at him. For once, even the Schue-lerite adjutant was at a loss for words, and Clyntahn chuckled again, more naturally.

"Rhobair, unfortunately, is one of those people who believe man actually has a better nature. He genuinely thinks he can appeal to that 'kinder, gentler' side he's sure most everyone really has. He doesn't recognize that the reason God gave Schueler authority to decree the disci-pline of Mother Church is that, thanks to Shan-wei, man *has* no better nature. Not any longer, anyway. God and Langhorne tried Rhobair's idea of loving gentleness, of begging men to do the right thing, and mankind repaid them by embracing Shan-wei's foulness. What? Rhobair thinks he's greater than Holy Langhorne? Greater than God *Himself*? That mankind is going to suddenly dis-cover a 'better nature' it hasn't had since the very dawn of Creation just because he, the great Rhobair Duchairn, is determined to appeal to it?"

The Grand Inquisitor's lips worked as if he wanted to spit on the ground, but he made himself draw a deep breath, nostrils flaring.

"Whatever may be going through his mind, he's simply incapable of understanding that man *won't* embrace God's will and accept God's authority without the iron rod of discipline. Humans have demonstrated again and again that unless they're *made* to do what they know God wants them to do, they *won't* do it. They have neither the wit, nor the will, nor the understanding to do it, and they're too dull-witted even to recognize their own stupidity without us to make God's will plain to them!

"That's why Rhobair doesn't understand the Inquisition's job, its responsibilities—its *duty*. He's not willing to admit what has to be done, so he pretends it doesn't have to be. He's willing to condemn *us* for doing it, as long as *his* hands are clean, and he genuinely believes we're unnecessarily harsh. That we *could* renounce that iron rod if we were only willing to. Well, we can't, unless we're prepared to see everything Mother Church stands for go down in ruin, but that's all right. Because as long as he believes he can continue to do things 'behind the scenes' to mitigate our 'excesses,' he'll go right on preserving his ability to do them. He'll make whatever compromises with his own soul he has to in order to accomplish that. And what that means, Wyllym, is that it would be almost impossible to drive him to a point where he decided he had nothing left to lose and came at us openly, because he'll go right on clinging to that responsibility to do good to offset our 'evil.' "

Rayno glanced away for a moment, looking up at the sky above Zion, touched with a colder, brighter autumn blue. The last blossoms had fallen from the elaborate gardens beyond the Plaza of Martyrs' spectacular fountains, and fall color was creeping into the foliage. It would be winter again all too soon, and snow and ice would close in around the Temple once more. He thought about that, then looked back at his superior.

"I hope you're right, Your Grace," he said.

There was an unusual edge of doubt in his voice, however. Not disagreement, simply a note of . . . reservation. Clyntahn heard it, but he chose to let it pass. One of the things that made Rayno valuable to him was that the adjutant was perhaps the only person left who would argue with him if he thought Clyntahn was wrong.

"I *am* right," the Grand Inquisitor said instead. "And if I'm not, I've got you and Major Phandys keeping an eye on him, don't I? We'll know if he starts to become a genuine threat. As for his absence this afternoon, I'll let him have that much. It's not as if anyone else is going to ignore today's lesson, is it? Besides," Clyntahn smiled suddenly, the smile of a slash lizard scenting blood, "it's useful in its own way."

"I beg your pardon, Your Grace?"

"Wyllym, Wyllym!" Clyntahn shook his head, still smiling. "Think about it. First, he's such a convenient focus for anyone who might disagree with us. All we have to do is watch for anyone who seems inclined to suck up to him instead of to me and we'll know where the real weak links are. And, second, Trynair and Maigwair are so busy trying to stay out of the line of fire between me and Rhobair that neither one of them is even going to *consider* doing something to make me think they're choosing his side instead of mine. Oh, they may side with him over some purely technical issues, like how we balance the books and pay for the jihad, but not on anything *fundamental*. From that perspective, it's far better to have him right where he is, driving them into *our* arms in their desperation to make it clear they're not rushing into *his*."

Rayno was still thinking about that when the bells began to ring.

▼ ▼ ▼

Sir Gwylym Manthyr could hardly stay on his own feet, yet he wrapped his right arm around the man beside him, draping the other Charisian's left arm across his own shoulders and somehow supporting the shambling, stumbling weight. The two of them staggered along, two more "penitents" in the rough, scratchy burlap robes that covered their savagely scarred, emaciated nakedness. For now, at least.

It was a beautiful day, Manthyr thought, listening to the magnificent, silver-throated bells of Zion as he looked around at the handful of his men who'd survived this long. There weren't many. He didn't have a definite count, but there couldn't be more than thirty, and he was amazed the number was that high.

Tough, those Charisian seamen, he thought. *Too tough and too stupid for their own good. The smart ones gave up and died. But that's all right, because I'm not very smart either, I guess.*

He knew every one of those thirty shambling, broken wrecks of human beings had been given the option: confess their heresy, admit their blasphemies and all of the hellish crimes to which they had set their hands in the service of their accursed emperor and empress, and they would face the garrotte, not the Punishment. Some of his men—a handful—had taken that offer, and Manthyr couldn't find it in his heart to condemn them for it. As he'd told Lainsair Svairsmahn a seeming eternity ago, there was only so much any man could endure, and there was no shame in breaking under the savagery of the Question.

But if there was no shame in breaking, there was pride in *not* breaking, and his heart swelled as he looked around at those stumbling, crippled, tormented ruins and knew exactly what they'd already endured without yielding. As long as one of them—*one* of them—was still on his feet, still defiant, Sir Gwylym Manthyr would stand beside him at the very gates of Hell. They were his, and he was theirs, and he would not—*could* not—break faith with them.

They marched across the plaza, and he saw the heaps of wood, the charred wooden posts arranged on the marble flags—many of them cracked now with the heat of past fires—between the fountains and the Temple's soaring colonnade. They marked where others of Clyntahn's victims had already died, those posts, and he watched his men being separated from one another, dragged to those heaps of wood, chained to those grim, scorched posts. He watched inquisitors coating their bodies with pitch that would take the flame and cling to them even as it offered their flesh a brief, transitory protection that would make their dying even longer and harder. He saw leather gloves, knuckles reinforced with steel studs, striking anyone who didn't move fast enough, who showed any trace of fight. They had to use those weighted fists quite often, he thought, watching, taking it all in. When it was his turn to appear before the Throne of God he wanted to be certain he had it all straight as he gave his testimony against the men who had twisted and perverted everything God stood for.

Then all of his men were chained, fastened atop their pyres, and there was only him. A pair of inquisitors started to drag him past his men, but he found the strength to shake off their hands and walk—slowly, but steadily, under his own power, making eye contact for one last time with every man he passed—towards the platform which had been reserved for him. The platform with the wheel and the rack, the white-hot irons waiting in their nests of glowing coals.

He longed for one final opportunity to defy the Inquisition, to speak for his men, to ridicule the charges against them, but they'd taken that from him when they cut out his tongue. He could still scream—they'd proven that to him—but they'd silenced his ability to deny the "confession" they were going to read and attribute to him. He'd held out, he'd never admitted or signed a single damned thing, but that wasn't the story they were going to tell. He knew that. They'd explained it to him in smirking detail in a last-ditch effort to break him into actually signing, and it grieved him that he could never set the record straight. Not so much for himself, but because it meant he couldn't speak out for his men, either.

It doesn't matter, he thought as he climbed the steps to the platform, eyes hard with hate and defiance as they met Zhaspahr Clyntahn's in person at last. *Anybody who'd believe Clyntahn's lies in the first place would never believe anything I said. And anyone who knows the truth about Clyntahn already knows what I would have said if*

I could. Those people, my Emperor and my Empress and my Navy, they know, *and the time will come when they will* avenge every one of my men.

He saw the torches, flames pale in the cool autumn sunlight, as the inquisitors strode towards his chained and helpless men, and his belly tightened. They were going to burn the others first, let him listen to their screams and watch their agonizing deaths, before it was his turn. It was the kind of "refinement" he'd come to expect out of Zhaspahr Clyntahn's Inquisition.

Two more inquisitors seized his arms, stretching them out, chaining them to the rack, and Zhaspahr Clyntahn stepped closer to him. The Grand Inquisitor's face was studiously calm, set in stern lines of determination as he prepared to play out the final line of this carefully scripted farce.

"You have heard the judgment and sentence of holy Mother Church upon you for your blasphemy, your heresy, your wanton defiance of God and allegiance to Shan-wei, Gwylym Manthyr," he said, his voice carrying clearly. "Have you anything to say before that sentence is carried out?"

Clyntahn's eyes glittered with satisfaction as he asked the question he knew Manthyr couldn't answer. There was no way for his victim to voice his defiance, demonstrate his rejection of the judgment and sentence which had been pronounced upon him, yet there was also no way for anyone in that watching crowd to *know* his voice had been taken from him before the question was even asked. They would see only the terrified heretic, too cowed by the onrushing approach of the eternal damnation he'd earned to say a single word.

Sir Gwylym Manthyr looked back at the gloating Grand Inquisitor as Clyntahn savored his triumph . . . and then he spat squarely into the vicar's face.

· VI ·

Saint Bailair's Church
and
Madam Aivah Pahrsahn's
Townhouse,
Siddar City,
Republic of Siddarmark

"I don't like it, Father," Stahn Mahldan said unhappily as he knelt in the closed booth of the confessional. "I don't like it at all. Where's it *coming* from?"

"I don't know, Brother," Father Lharee Traighair, the rector of Saint Bailair's Church, replied, although he wasn't as sure of that as he would have liked.

"It's all so . . . wrong," Mahldan said, his eyes anxious, and Traighair smiled affectionately at him.

Brother Stahn was in his late fifties, thinning hair going steadily white, and there wasn't a malicious bone in his entire body. There wasn't an ambitious one, either, as far as Traighair could tell, which probably explained why Brother Stahn was still only a sexton of the Order of the Quill at his age. It certainly wasn't because of lack of ability, faith, or industry!

A librarian by training and inclination alike, Mahldan was an absentminded, otherworldly sort who was always happiest puttering about in the histories he was responsible for maintaining and updating. He had a sharp, analytical brain, but one which was altogether too poorly suited for considering ugly truths outside the covers of his beloved histories. He was inclined to assume that since he wished ill to no one, no one could possibly wish ill to him, which, unfortunately, was no longer true even in the Republic, if it ever had been.

At least the old fellow's had the sense to keep his feel-

ings mostly to himself, Traighair thought. *Or I hope to Langhorne he has, at any rate!*

"I agree it's wrong, Brother Stahn," he said. "But I'm afraid it's also fairly inevitable, as well." He shook his head, his expression sad. "Men who are afraid do ugly things. And one of the things they do first is to strike out at and try to destroy whatever frightens them."

Mahldan nodded, although Traighair was pretty sure the sexton's understanding was more intellectual than emotional. The priest wished he were a more inspired speaker, better able to explain what he saw so clearly, but he was a teacher more than a preacher, without the gift of language which God had given so generously to some other priests. He tried not to envy their greater gifts and to appreciate the ones *he'd* been given, but that was harder to do in times like these.

"All I can tell you, Brother, is that I urge you to go home. Go about your business and do your best to . . . well, keep your head down." Traighair's smile was fleeting. "I don't know where the fellows you're talking about are likely to go in the end, but I advise you to keep yourself out of their sights."

"But they're *threatening* people, Father!" Mahldan protested. "And they're claiming it's what God and Langhorne want them to do!"

"I *understand* that, Brother," Traighair said as patiently as he could. "But there's nothing you can do about it, and if you confront them, you only run the risk of pouring oil on the flames. Trust me, men who say the things you say they said aren't going to respond well to reasonable argument!"

He gazed into the sexton's eyes, willing Mahldan to simply take his word for it. He didn't want to have to tell the gentle librarian that if he confronted the Temple Loyalist toughs he'd described he was only going to bring their violence down on his own head. And he didn't want to have to explain that he was beginning to fear no amount of "reasonable argument" could head off what he was afraid was coming.

"Are you sure, Father?" Mahldan shook his head. "The

Writ says we're supposed to stand up for what we know is right and denounce what we know is wrong."

"Yes, we are. And you *have*—to me," Traighair said firmly. "You'll just have to trust me when I say I'll bring it to the attention of the proper ears. That's *my* responsibility, not yours."

Mahldan still looked unhappy and distressed, but he finally nodded.

"Good, Brother Stahn. Good!" Traighair patted the older man on the arm. "Now, about those 'sins' of yours." He shook his head and smiled. "I believe I can safely say they're all scarcely even venal, this time. So light a candle to the Holy Bédard, leave an extra silver in Pasquale's Basket this Wednesday, and say ten 'Hail Langhornes.' Understood?"

"Yes, Father," Mahldan agreed obediently, and the young priest stood and began escorting him down the nave.

"I know you're worried," he said quietly as they reached the front steps. "To be honest, so am I, because these are worrying times. But you're a good man and, if you'll forgive my saying so, a gentle one. I think you'll best serve by lending your prayers to those of all good and God-fearing people. And"—he looked the sexton firmly in the eye—"by staying home, keeping out from underfoot, and not making things *worse*. Understand me?"

"Yes, Father." Mahldan managed a wry smile and nodded again, more firmly.

"Good!" Traighair repeated. "Now, go home!"

He pointed like a stern grandfather, and the white-haired Mahldan laughed and obeyed the imperious gesture. The priest watched him until he turned the corner, then turned and walked briskly back into his church. It would be tight, but he had time to talk to those "proper ears" he'd promised Mahldan he'd speak to between now and afternoon mass if he hurried.

▼ ▼ ▼

"I can see why Father Lharee was upset, Your Eminence," Aivah Pahrsahn said.

She stood gazing out her windows at North Bay once more. The Navy of God galleons had long since departed for Hsing-wu's Passage, and the blue water sparkled under the September sun, busy with the weathered, tan sails of Siddar City's teeming commerce. It would be winter again soon enough, she thought, with icy snow, rain, and the bay the color of a polished steel blade. She wasn't looking forward to that. In fact, there were several things she wasn't looking forward to, and she was frankly surprised they'd held off this long.

"What worries me most is Father Lharee's fear that he *knows* these men," Zhasyn Cahnyr said unhappily.

"Surely that doesn't come as a surprise, Your Eminence?" Aivah turned to face him, and her expression was a strange mix of compassion and exasperation. "Did you truly believe this was all purely spontaneous? Something just naturally bubbling up out of Siddarmark's burning loyalty to Mother Church and the people currently controlling her policies?"

"I . . ." Cahnyr looked at her for a moment, then shrugged unhappily. "No, of course not," he said. "I mean, in some ways I'd *like* to believe it's purely out of loyalty to the Church, even if a mob mentality is a dangerous thing. Mobs can do horrible things, and I've seen it. But if Father Lharee is right, if these men Brother Stahn is talking about really do come out of Bishop Executor Baikyr's or Father Zohannes' offices, then we may be looking at something a lot worse than some kind of spontaneous vigilantism!"

"Of course we are," Pahrsahn told him flatly. "And Father Lharee *is* right, Your Eminence. I already had the names of four of the men he's talking about, and at least one of them works directly for Father Saimyn."

Cahnyr looked at her sharply, and his expression tightened. Father Zohannes Pahtkovair, the Intendant of Siddar for the last sixteen months, was about as ardent as even a Schuelerite came. Cahnyr couldn't be positive, but unless he was sadly mistaken, Pahtkovair had been handpicked by Zhaspahr Clyntahn for his current post specifically because of that ardency. The Inquisitor General would have made it his business to be certain he had a reliable intendant in a place like Old Province, the original heartland of the Republic of Siddarmark, under any circumstances. These days, with the upsurge in Reformist sympathies throughout the Republic, Clyntahn was going to be more focused on his intendants' reliability than ever. Especially since Bishop Executor Baikyr Saikor was apparently at least a little more sympathetic to the Reformists than Archbishop Praidwyn Laicharn, his immediate superior. Of course, Saikor was also a bishop executor of the old school—a bureaucrat first and foremost, not someone likely to succumb to a sudden rush of piety. He'd follow his superiors' instructions to the letter whatever his personal views might be. Still, it was obvious to Cahnyr that the bishop executor wasn't going out of his way to stamp on peaceful, process-oriented Reformists, which probably explained why he'd been assigned a more . . . activist intendant last year.

Father Saimyn Airnhart, however, worried the Archbishop of Glacierheart even more than Pahtkovair. Zohannes Pahtkovair was zealous about keeping a close eye on the reliability of the local clergy, but Airnhart was even more zealous. Which undoubtedly explained why he'd been assigned as Pahtkovair's immediate subordinate for what was euphemistically termed "special functions." In effect, Airnhart was responsible for managing the Inquisition's covert operations. Not information gathering, not observation, but active operations—*offensive* operations, one might better say—intended to identify, unmask, and destroy the enemies of God and Mother Church . . . no matter where or who they might be. And no matter what he had to do to accomplish his mission, which had to suit Airnhart just fine. As Schueler had written in the very first chapter of his book, after all, "Extremism in the pursuit of godliness can never be a sin." Cahnyr wasn't at all convinced Saimyn Airnhart had ever bothered to read any of the rest of *The Book of Schueler*.

"You really didn't know, did you, Your Eminence?" Pahrsahn said quietly.

"About Airnhart?" Cahnyr pursed his lips and exhaled heavily, then shrugged. "I knew about him, of course. We've been . . . keeping an eye out for him. But I hadn't realized Bishop Executor Baikyr was working that directly with him. Or vice versa."

"To be honest, I'm not sure how directly involved the Bishop Executor actually is," Pahrsahn said. "I know Pahtkovair has both his hands in the pie right up to the elbow, and Airnhart's his chief kitchen assistant. On the other hand, I know where both of them are. I can keep an eye on them, and"—her voice turned grimmer, her eyes harder—"if I have to, I can put my *hand* on them anytime I need to, as well. I know you don't want to hear that sort of thing, Your Eminence, but I'm afraid I've become rather addicted to that aphorism about the Archangels helping those who help themselves."

She looked at Cahnyr, who nodded. She was right; he didn't want to hear about "that sort of thing," but what he wanted and what he needed were two different things.

"The thing that bothers *me* most about Father Lharee's report," Pahrsahn continued, "is what Brother Stahn had to say about Laiyan Bahzkai. He's been turning into a really nasty piece of work, Your Eminence, and until today, I genuinely thought he was a 'spontaneous' bigot."

"What do you mean?"

"Bahzkai's an . . . interesting fellow, Your Eminence. He's a Temple Loyalist, but he's also a Leveler. And he's been getting more active as an organizer over the past several months. More visible and more vocal. And he's been moving steadily further and further towards their violent wing ever since Clyntahn declared his embargo against Charisian trade."

Cahnyr's mouth tightened. He'd never heard Bahzkai's name before, but he was more familiar with the Levelers than he wanted to be. In truth, he was more than a little sympathetic to at least three-quarters of their platform. He was less than convinced about the need for the complete and total *destruction* of capitalism, yet he was certainly willing to admit the system as it existed—especially in the Temple Lands, where senior churchmen used their privileged positions, entrenched corruption, and cronyism to amass staggering fortunes while squeezing out any competition—could and did create huge inequities. That was the main reason the Levelers had originated in the Temple Lands, and many Reformists were at least mildly sympathetic to the Levelers' core arguments.

These days the Levelers were more active in the Republic of Siddarmark than anywhere else, however, which was precisely because the Republic's level of tolerance was so much higher than that of most other mainland realms. As far as he was aware, they had virtually no representation in Charis, but that was understandable enough given the general Charisian enthusiasm for trade and individual self-betterment. Charisians *liked* capitalism—a lot—and they weren't especially interested in hearing from people who disapproved of it.

It was ironic, perhaps, that the realm in which the movement operated most openly was the one where the inequalities against which it inveighed were least pronounced, but that didn't make it something the Republic's civil authorities embraced with open arms, either. In Cahnyr's opinion, though, the Levelers' position that all men and women were equally children of God and therefore should take equal care of one another was straight out of the *Holy Writ*. There was nothing the least objectionable about *that!* And the majority of Levelers advocated peaceful means of pursuing their platform, although strikes and work stoppages had a tendency to turn violent at the best of times, especially in places like the Temple Lands or quite a few of the Border States between them and the Republic. And God only knew what would happen to a batch of Levelers who tried "civil disobedience" someplace like the Harchong Empire!

A growing number of Levelers did advocate a more . . . proactive stance, however. What Pahrsahn had just called their "violent wing" was tired of peaceful remonstrance and petitions for redress. Its members had come increasingly to the view that no one would ever take them seriously until they convinced the rest of the world they *were* serious, and that would require violence. Personally, Cahnyr thought they were out of their minds if they believed they could reform society into genuine egalitarianism by killing anyone who disagreed with them, although he supposed that when the rest of the world was busy going insane anyway, they might be excused for thinking they saw an opportunity to implement some of their own reforms. But still. . . .

"A Leveler working hand in glove with the Inquisition?" he said. "That sounds suitably bizarre!"

"They don't usually find one another congenial company, do they?" Pahrsahn agreed. "That's what bothers me about this. Bahzkai's a printer and a pamphleteer, and he's produced some fairly inflammatory stuff for several years now. The Republic's authorities've known exactly who he was and where to find him, but however inflammatory he may have been, he was always careful to stay away from advocating any form of violence. Only that emphasis of his has been changing over the last year or so. Since shortly after Pahtkovair was assigned to the Siddar archbishopric, in fact. And he's been focusing more and more of his complaints about the unfair, unequal distribution of wealth on the Empire of Charis and Charisians in general."

"Not Reformists? Charisians?"

"Well, in some ways an anti-Charisian bias from somebody like a Leveler is understandable enough," Pahrsahn pointed out. "If there's any city in the entire world whose society is further from the Leveler ideal than Tellesberg's, it could only be Shang-mi, and that's heading in the *opposite* direction!"

Despite himself, Cahnyr chuckled at her disgusted expression. Shang-mi, the capital of the Harchong Empire, made *Zion* seem like a hotbed of reform!

"But Bahzkai's been concentrating on how damned rich Charis is supposed to be getting out of this war," Pahrsahn continued, her expression becoming much more somber once more, "what with 'sucking the lifeblood' out of 'legitimate Siddarmarkian businesses' because of the embargo and the way the trading houses are evading it. As nearly as I can tell, he buys into the theory that what this is really all about is greed and that Charis, rather than needing every single mark to pay for the navy it needs to survive, is deliberately siphoning the Republic's wealth into its own purse out of sheer avarice. Its 'indecently wealthy plutocrats' are actively pushing a deliberately aggressive, militant foreign policy to *promote* the war in order to fill their purses with more of the *deserving* world's marks. If it weren't for their greed, this whole thing could've been settled ages ago by a simple appeal to the Grand Vicar's justice."

"That's ridiculous!"

"Forgive me, Your Eminence, but it's always seemed to me that the very first thing that happens with any zealot is that he removes his brain just in case any thoughts that might challenge his zealotry should happen to stray into it. Present company excepted, of course."

"Ouch." Cahnyr winced. "Do you really think of me as a *zealot*?"

"For certain definitions of the word, I certainly do," Pahrsahn replied calmly. "On the other hand, *I'm* a zealot. For that matter, there's zealotry and then there's zealotry, and while I may be prejudiced by my own perspective, I don't think of you as a fanatic zealot. Just a . . . *zealous* zealot."

"Thank you for your exquisite tact, my dear."

"Don't mention it, Your Eminence." She smiled at him, but then her expression sobered again. "Anyway, the reason Bahzkai came to my attention had less to do with his excoriation of the Empire of Charis than it did with his growing hostility towards Charisians in *general*. In particular, he's been focusing on how Charisian refugees here in the Republic have been taking employment away from *Siddarmarkians*. He's scarcely the only one doing that, as I'm sure you're at least as well aware as I am, but he's been a lot more organized about it than most of the loudmouths and hotheads. And now we have this suggestion that he's associated with Airnhart somehow. And apparently he's been accepting some printing jobs from people who're putting up broadsheets attacking the Reformists, as well. I knew he wasn't a huge admirer of the Reformists—which always struck me as a little odd, since the Reformists are a lot more sympathetic to the kind of world the Levelers want to build than someone like Clyntahn or Trynair could ever be—but it hadn't occurred to me that Airnhart might be steering some of those printing jobs to him."

"I don't think I like where you're going with this," Cahnyr said slowly.

"Neither do I."

She turned to look out the window once more, reaching up to slowly coil and uncoil a lock of hair around her right index finger while she thought. She stood that way for several minutes, then looked back over her shoulder at the fugitive archbishop.

"The Temple Loyalist rhetoric and invective against the Reformists have been growing steadily stronger, Your Eminence. We both know that. And in the last month and a half or so, I've been hearing more and more clearly vocalized anger against the Charisians, as well. The thing that's occurring to me—and Father Lharee's report isn't the only reason I'm thinking this way, either—is that somebody may actually be deliberately orchestrating that growth in anger and invective. That particular nasty suspicion was already running through my brain, but if Bahzkai, who I know is involved in it, is working directly with Airnhart, I think we have to very seriously consider the possibility that this extends a lot further than I thought it did. I was operating on the assumption that it was primarily an *urban* phenomenon, something which was strongest in the cities where the Reformists and Charisians are most concentrated and political opinions are always likely to ferment more . . . energetically than in the countryside. But if the Inquisition's the one stirring the pot, they may be nursing it along in places I hadn't even considered yet."

"You think this is some sort of Republic-wide . . . plot,

for want of a better word?" Cahnyr could have wished
his own tone was more incredulous. Pahrsahn's slow nod
of agreement didn't make him feel any better, either.
"That's . . . well, I don't want to call it preposterous, but it
sounds awfully ambitious even for someone like Clyntahn."

"Our illustrious Grand Inquisitor's done something
in the last three or four years to convince you he doesn't
think in 'ambitious' terms?" Pahrsahn asked just a bit
derisively.

"Of course not. I just meant—"

"You meant that the Republic of Siddarmark is huge
and that organizing anything like this as a workable
proposition would be an enormous undertaking, especially in the middle of a war?"

"Well, yes. Pretty much."

"At first sight I might be inclined to agree with you,
Your Eminence," she said very seriously, "but consider
three things. First," she held up her left fist, index finger
extended, "the Inquisition, like Mother Church herself,
is everywhere. And, two," her second finger joined her
index finger, "at this moment Zhaspahr Clyntahn's concentrated more power in his hands than probably any
other Grand Inquisitor in the history of Mother Church.
And, third," her ring finger joined the other two, "we
are in the middle of a war, which means he and Rayno
are in a position to argue convincingly that the Church
is fighting for her very survival. Your Eminence, even
priests who fundamentally disagree with many of the
things Clyntahn's doing right now are acquiescing because of the Church's frightened, defensive mindset.
And to be honest, the Charisians' string of victories
only makes that fear still stronger. Worse, Clyntahn's
made it abundantly clear what he's willing to do to anyone he might even remotely consider an opponent or an
enemy. So added to the fear for Mother Church's survival we have the personal fear that anyone who gets
in the Inquisition's way is going to suffer for it—suffer
severely.

"So we have the Inquisition's feelers and tentacles threaded throughout not just the Republic but all of the mainland realms, and we have a Grand Inquisitor with a genuine iron fist and a taste for using it, and a priesthood—not just in the Inquisition, but *everywhere* in Mother Church—frightened by the combined challenge of the Church of Charis from without and the Reformists from within *and* frightened of that iron fist of his. Do you really think under those circumstances that someone like Zhaspahr Clyntahn and Wyllym Rayno wouldn't see the potential to . . . destabilize a Republic of Siddarmark they've hated and distrusted literally for decades? I know the very thought is revolting, but try to put yourself inside their minds for a moment. From their perspective, would there really be any conceivable downside to tearing the entire Republic apart and simultaneously getting their hands around the throat of the Reformist movement here in Siddarmark?"

Zhasyn Cahnyr looked at her grim, lovely face for the better part of a minute and a half in silence. And then, slowly, he shook his head.

. VIII .

Lord Protector Stohnar's Residence and the Charisian Embassy, Siddar City, Republic of Siddarmark

"The temperature seems to be rising awfully sharply for September," Greyghor Stohnar said sourly, looking around the handsome, inlaid table in the richly appointed library of the Lord Protector's personal residence.

He could have held this meeting in his public office in

the Lord Protector's Palace off Constitution Square, but public offices were just that: public. Not even Henrai Maidyn's agents could be sure there weren't spies in his own staff, although it *seemed* unlikely. He was almost certain the Group of Four would have taken much more strenuous action against him long before now if Zhaspahr Clyntahn had managed to get a spy that close to him. On the other hand, he hadn't survived this long by taking anything for granted.

"Temperatures tend to do that when someone starts blowing on the flames," Maidyn said unhappily.

"You're sure that's what's happening, then?" Lord Samyl Gahdarhd asked, his expression acutely unhappy. Maidyn looked back at him, and the Keeper of the Seal grimaced. "I realize you're not in the habit of just casually dropping unsubstantiated rumors on us, Henrai, but if you're right about what's going on under the surface, we're about to land in a sea of trouble."

"Then I recommend we all learn how to swim," Daryus Parkair, the Republic's Seneschal, said harshly. Gahdarhd's eyes moved to him, and Parkair shrugged. "Every one of my agents is reporting exactly the same thing Henrai's are. Or, the ones I'm sure haven't been suborned by Paht-kovair or Airnhart, anyway." He showed his teeth briefly. "Frankly, there aren't as many of those as I wish there were."

Stohnar ran his right hand through his hair, his expression rather more harried than he ever allowed it to look in public. It wasn't as if they hadn't seen this coming for quite some time, he reminded himself. There was, however, a difference between anticipating something at some unspecified future date and actually seeing it rumbling towards you like Shan-wei's salt grinder.

"All right," he said after a moment, "I think we just answered the question of whether or not they're up to something. So it seems to me that the ones still before us are how soon they intend to move, how *widely* they intend to move, and exactly how they plan on all of this coming down in the end."

"I hope no one minds my pointing out that those are rather *broad* questions," Gahdarhd observed dryly.

"I agree." Maidyn nodded crisply and turned to the Lord Protector. "I don't think we can answer any of them in any definitive sense. What does seem probable, though, is that they've been working on whatever they have in mind ever since Clyntahn sent us Pahtkovair. I wouldn't be surprised if they've had contingency plans basically forever, and when Charis declined to lie down and die they decided to dust one off and update it to fit the new circumstances.

"I also think we can assume they'd really like for whatever they have in mind to happen before the snow starts flying. That would explain why their agitators are ratcheting the 'temperature' up right now—they've only got about another month or a month and a half before winter closes in."

"You're probably right, Henrai," Parkair said, "but let's not invest too much confidence in that timing. If we're looking at some widespread operation directed at the Republic as a whole, then, yes, they'd probably prefer to have it out of the way before winter starts cutting down on their mobility. If what they're planning is a more focused operation, something like seizing control of Siddar City and the government in a quick coup rather than some popular general uprising by our 'outraged citizenry'—with no outside provocation at all, of course!—they might see winter weather as their ally. If they don't succeed in the first rush, bad weather would make it more difficult for us to bring in reinforcements from outlying regions that decided to remain loyal to us."

"A valid point," Stohnar said. "On the other hand, we're talking about Zhaspahr Clyntahn. He's not the sort to think small, and we've got reports of the same sorts of propaganda and 'spontaneous' organizations from at least a dozen other cities and towns. To me, that suggests he's thinking in terms of your 'widespread operation,' Daryus."

"I think we have to assume he is, anyway," Maidyn

agreed. "We'll be a lot better off planning against a bigger threat than we actually end up facing than underestimating the danger and getting our heads handed to us when the shit really starts flying."

"Granted," Parkair agreed, and Stohnar nodded.

"All right, we'll think in terms of an execution date on their part sometime in the next two months. If it turns out we've got longer, so much the better."

"Have we heard anything from Cahnyr or the lovely and devious Madam Pahrsahn?" Gahdarhd asked wryly, and Stohnar chuckled.

"Not directly, no. Then again, we're officially trying to arrest Cahnyr—as soon as we can find him, of course—and Madam Pahrsahn doesn't know—officially, at least—we're even aware of her activities. That makes it just a tiny bit difficult for them to openly share information with us. On the other hand, I suspect at least some of Henrai's informants are really part of Madam Pahrsahn's network. I think she's making sure we find out about certain things she's discovered. What I'm a lot less sure of is whether or not she's telling us *everything* she's discovered." The Lord Protector shook his head. "The lady has an agenda of her own, and while I'm prepared to welcome just about any ally if this turns out as badly as we're afraid it could, I'm not about to assume she isn't feeding us selected information. I don't think she'd actually *lie* to us to get us to do what she wants, if only because she's foresighted enough to realize how badly that could hurt her with us down the road, but I'm positive she wouldn't be above . . . manipulating information in order to prod us into doing what she wants. Whatever it turns out *that* is."

"The lady *is* a force to be reckoned with," Parkair agreed. "She and my wife have become quite close, you know. I've warned Zhanaiah to be cautious, and you all know Zhany's no fool, but she obviously approves of Madam Pahrsahn. She thinks she's one of the smartest people she's ever met, too."

"That's Tymahn and Owain Qwentyn's view, as well," Maidyn agreed.

"I know." Parkair nodded. "But what the Qwentyns may not know is that Madam Pahrsahn's purchasing agents—purchasing agents she seems to have been very careful to keep well away from the House of Qwentyn and her official, legal investments—have now taken possession of something over eight thousand rifled muskets. Which have all mysteriously disappeared since."

"*What?!*" Gahdarhd stared at him, and the Seneschal chuckled sourly.

"Hahraimahn did tell us she was investing in rifles," he pointed out. "And *we* told *him*—unofficially, of course—to go ahead and sell them to her as a way to finance some additional manufactory capacity without any investment on our part." He shrugged. "Obviously I'd prefer to be doing the investing and stockpiling the weapons ourselves, but if there's one thing Clyntahn's agents have to be looking for it's evidence we're involving ourselves in some major rearmament program without mentioning it to Mother Church."

"I understand all that," the Keeper of the Seal said a bit impatiently. "I was part of the discussion, remember? But *eight thousand* rifles?!"

"It would appear Madam Pahrsahn had rather more to invest than we thought when we told Hahraimahn to sell her whatever she ordered," Parkair said a bit whimsically. "I wonder what she would have done if he'd offered to make *artillery* for her?"

"What in hell, if you'll pardon my language, does she plan to do with that many rifles?" Gahdarhd asked Stohnar, and the Lord Protector shrugged.

"Something Clyntahn won't like, I hope. In the meantime, though, unless we want to take official cognizance of her and ask her if she'd be so kind as to hand them over to us, I think we need to plan on the basis of what we know *we* have and what we're *afraid* Pahtkovair and

Airnhart may have managed to make available on their side of the hill. Suggestions, anyone?"

▼ ▼ ▼

". . . the honor to be, et cetera, et cetera," Sir Rayjhis Dragoner said, looking out across the city of Siddar, drowsing peacefully under a golden September afternoon sun. He sighed, then turned and stood with his back to the window, watching Wynai Thyrstyn's busy pen jot down the last few words. "I'll trust you to finish it up properly," he said with a smile which was only slightly forced.

"Yes, Ambassador." Wynai looked up with a smile of her own. It wasn't much of a smile, but Dragoner was glad to see it anyway. She hadn't smiled very often since losing not simply her brother but her favorite cousin, as well, in the Hairatha powder mill explosion. "I'm sure I can come up with a properly respectful closing."

"I knew I could count on you. Zheryld was right about how useful you've been, and not just taking dictation and dealing with the correspondence. I've valued your input on a lot of issues, Wynai. You realize that, I hope?"

"I've tried to be useful, Sir Rayjhis," she said with a small bob of her head, but the fleeting smile had disappeared again. "I only wish I thought it was really going to do some good."

"All we can do is the best we can do." Dragoner's tone was firmer and more optimistic than he truly felt, and he was pretty sure Wynai knew it.

He truly was glad Zheryld Mahrys, his secretary of many years, had managed to find Madam Thyrstyn for him, and not just because she was a skilled stenographer and secretary. He could always use more people with that set of skills, but she was also *smart,* and it was that, coupled with the many years she'd lived here in the Republic, which made her truly valuable to him. She *understood* Siddarmarkians in ways he simply didn't, despite how long he'd been posted as the Charisian ambassador to the Republic.

And you might as well admit it, Rayjhis, he told himself now, turning back to the window. *You value her be-cause she's your window into the Charisian Temple Loyalists here in the city, too.*

"Do you really think it's as bad as some people seem to be saying, Sir Rayjhis?" she asked now, and he shrugged.

"I think it's not as *good* as I wish it were," he said. "Let's just put it that way." He shrugged again. "All we can do is warn people to be careful, to avoid provocations, and for any of them who can to return to Charis."

"I've lived here almost half my entire life, Sir Rayjhis!" Wynai said with an unusual flash of fire. "I'm not going to just run away from my neighbors and my friends—and my family!—and all the rest of my life because some people are letting their mouths run away with *them!*"

"I hope that's all it is," he said, turning back around to look at her. "You've seen the dispatches I'm sending home, though. You probably know more about what's happening here in the capital than *I* do, when it comes down to it. And you know I'm trying hard not to be alarmist and make a bad situation worse. But I'd be derelict in my duties if I didn't warn the Charisian community about the rumors we're picking up."

"Why did we ever have to start all this?" she asked, her eyes pained. "It's all . . . all just *crazy*, Sir Rayjhis!"

"In some ways I agree with you," he said heavily. In fact, he agreed with her in a lot more ways than he was prepared to admit. His personal balancing act as a loyal son of Mother Church and the ambassador of the heretical Empire of Charis had become nothing but more difficult as the Church moved steadily towards an official declaration of jihad. Over the last year, since that declaration had actually come, it had gotten even harder, and deep inside himself he wondered what he was going to do if worse came to worst in the Republic. Only his overriding sense of duty to the House of Ahrmahk had kept him at his post this long, and he didn't know if even that could have done the trick if he hadn't seen so many indications Mother Church was striving to keep the Republic as close to neutral territory as it could. He'd had enough clear signs—signals that could only have come from Vicar Rhobair and Chancellor Trynair—that Mother Church actually *wanted* the embargo to continue "leaking" in Siddarmark's case. That had been enough to keep him in his office, still able to serve both of the causes which were so dear to his heart. But if that balance was shifting, if Mother Church was changing her mind, what did he do then?

"In some ways I agree with you," he repeated, "but we live when we live, and all any of us can do is pray for guidance to get through all this without trading away any more of our souls than we have to. And if we get an opportunity to do something which may make it even a little better—or at least less bad—than it would have been otherwise, then we give thanks on our knees."

"Yes, Sir." Wynai lowered her eyes, seeming a bit abashed at having spoken out, and he inhaled deeply.

"Go ahead and get clear copies of those written up," he told her in a gentler tone. "And tell Zheryld we're going to have a special dispatch bag for Tellesberg."

"Of course, Sir."

"And, Wynai, if you'd like to send any messages home to Charis, feel free to use the dispatch bag." She looked up at him, and he smiled at her. "I know you don't abuse the privilege, and at least this way they'll get home a little quicker."

"Thank you, Sir Rayjhis. I appreciate it."

Wynai gathered up her notepad and her pen and headed down the hall to her own little cubbyhole of an office. The door closed quietly behind her, and Dragoner returned his attention to the window, looking across those sunlit roofs at North Bay's sail-dotted azure water and thinking about the homeland which lay so far beyond it.

▼ ▼ ▼

Wynai Thyrstyn closed her office door behind her and sat in the creaky, slightly rickety chair at her desk. She laid her shorthand notes on the blotter and stared down at them, thinking about them, wondering what she should do. Then she leaned back, closed her eyes, and covered her lids with her hands while she tried not to weep.

There were times she felt almost unbearably torn by guilt as she sat in Sir Rayjhis' office, taking down his words, working on his correspondence, answering his questions about the Charisian and non-Charisian communities here in Siddar City. It was wrong of her to feel that way, she knew that. She wasn't doing anything she shouldn't be doing, and Sir Rayjhis was a good man, one who needed her help. She could see how he was aging before her, the way his hair was going progressively whiter, the lines carving themselves more and more deeply into his face. He'd revealed more of his own spiritual turmoil than he thought he had—she was pretty sure of that—and she wondered how much longer he could bear it. And how he was going to react when the inevitable happened.

And it *was* inevitable. She lowered her hands again, staring at the icon of the Archangel Langhorne hanging on the wall above her desk. God couldn't permit any other outcome, but why did it have to be so *hard*? Why did so many people—*good* people, and there *were* good people, on *both* sides—have to die?

The tears came despite her efforts to stop them as she thought of her brother Trai and her cousin Urvyn. Sir Rayjhis had tried so hard to comfort her when the terrible news came, tried to tell her it had all been some horrible accident, but Wynai knew better. She couldn't be *certain,* of course, but . . . she knew better. If only Urvyn had been able to see the truth the way she and Trai had! But he hadn't, and they'd lost him to the heresy, and she'd still loved him so much, and, O Sweet Bédard, but it *hurt* so much to be so sure Trai had killed him . . . and himself.

Forgive him, she prayed now, staring at the image of the Archangel on the wall before her, not entirely certain if she were praying for her heretical cousin or the brother who'd violated divine law by taking his own life. But then she shook herself. God couldn't possibly condemn Trai for giving up his life in His own service! Yet even so—

Forgive all of them, please! I know Urvyn and the others are wrong, I know it's all so horribly wrong, but they're not really evil. They're doing what they think they have to do, what they think you and God want them to do. Do they really have to spend all of eternity paying for that?

The icon didn't answer her, but she hadn't really expected it to, and she drew a deep breath. A decisive breath.

She'd wanted to do more from the very beginning, but Trai had convinced her—no, be honest, he'd *ordered* her—not to. She remembered that first letter of his, the one which had filled her with mingled fear and elation. It was so like her big brother to take charge, to know exactly what to do, and she'd taken his warnings seriously. She'd never said a single word to anyone, not even her own priest and confessor, about the "personal letters" to her which she relayed to her husband's aunt in Zion. The letters which went from there directly to the Office of the Inquisition . . . and the replies to which were transmitted to him in her own "personal letters." She had no idea what information and what instructions had passed back and forth, because Trai had been very clear about that, as well. At his request, the Inquisition had sent him a code book by an entirely separate route—she didn't know what it had been—and he and whoever he was actually writing to had buried their messages in the word puzzles and acrostics he and Wynai had shared regularly by mail ever since her marriage had taken her to the Republic so many years before.

But he'd been very specific in that first letter. She was to do nothing *but* relay letters. That was the most important thing she could possibly do, and she mustn't do *anything* that could compromise her ability to perform that task. So she'd had no contact at all with the Inquisition here in Siddar. She'd spoken as calmly and reasonably as she could when the inevitable debates erupted between Temple Loyalists and adherents of the Church of Charis, avoiding anything which could have gotten her labeled an extremist by either side. And she'd never, not once, used her privileged position here inside the embassy to provide information to Mother Church.

In a lot of ways, she'd been grateful Trai's instructions had precluded her from doing that. But Trai was gone now, and Urwyn, both of them sacrificed to the war impious man had declared upon God Himself, and that meant she was free. It would be a betrayal of Sir Rayjhis' trust, and she regretted that deeply, yet she had no choice but to serve God and the Archangels in any way she could.

She drew another deep breath and began transcribing her notes in the beautiful, clear handwriting she'd been taught as a child in Tellesberg. She had the dispatch bag to catch, and she would. But this time, instead of destroying her original notes the way she always had before, she would take them with her when she left.

It was very quiet in the tiny office, with only the soft, purposeful scratching of her pen to break the silence.

. VIII .

The Temple, City of Zion, The Temple Lands

"God *damn* them! God damn *all* of them!"

Zhaspahr Clyntahn threw the entire file across the sitting room of his luxurious personal suite. It hit the outer wall's unbreakable transparent crystal with a thump and flew back, scattering pages across the thick, rich carpets, and the Grand Inquisitor snarled. His heavy-jowled face was purple with fury as he snatched up a priceless glass paperweight that was over three hundred years old and hurled it across the room, directly into a glass-fronted cabinet of crystal decanters. It struck with an ear-shattering crash and the sharp scent of expensive brandies and whiskeys as paperweight, glass, and bottles exploded in fragments.

Spectacular as it was, the destruction had no apparent effect on Clyntahn's rage, and he bent and snatched up the bronze coffee table. It had to weigh a hundred pounds, Wyllym Rayno thought, but the Grand Inquisitor didn't even seem to notice. He only hurled it after the paperweight with an explosive grunt of effort, demolishing the entire wet bar in a cascade of shattered snifters, goblets, liqueur bottles, and exquisite—and exquisitely *expensive*—cabinetry.

The Archbishop of Chiang-wu made himself as small and inconspicuous as he possibly could. It wasn't the first time he'd seen Clyntahn explode in all but incoherent fury, but it was never a pleasant experience. And he'd seldom seen the Grand Inquisitor *this* angry. In fact, it was entirely possible he'd *never* seen Clyntahn this angry.

Not even Zhaspahr Clyntahn in the grip of a monumental rage could throw something as heavy as that coffee table without consequences. He stumbled, nearly falling, and kept himself on his feet only by grabbing the back of a couch. He snarled, shoved himself back upright, and kicked the couch halfway across the room. It knocked over a display pedestal, and a marble bust of the Archangel Chihiro—carved from life by the second-century master Charkain—toppled to the floor in a crunching, face-first impact that sent fragments of white stone flying. He looked around, as if seeking something else expensive to destroy, then stomped out of the sitting room, kicking heirloom furniture out of his way, and Rayno heard more shattering sounds from the adjacent bedchamber.

Fortunately, Clyntahn hadn't ordered the archbishop to accompany him, and Rayno breathed a quiet prayer of thanks as he tucked his hands into the sleeves of his cassock and prepared to wait out his superior's rage.

From the sounds of things, it was going to take a while.

▼ ▼ ▼

"All right," Clyntahn said flatly, the better part of two hours later. "Give me the details."

He and Rayno had withdrawn to the small conference room attached to the Grand Inquisitor's suite. The door had opened at their approach and then closed silently behind them, cool air whispered through the overhead ducts, and the conference room's soundproofing guaranteed that none of the white-faced servants creeping about while they dealt with the wreckage littering the wake of Clyntahn's rage would hear a word they said.

Rayno considered pointing out that all "the details" he possessed had been contained in the file, but he didn't consider it very hard. He'd quietly gathered up the file's scattered contents and brought them with him, but reminding Clyntahn he'd cleaned up behind him probably wouldn't be a good idea.

"I'm afraid there's not a great deal to add to what I've already told you, Your Grace," he said just a bit cautiously. "The destruction appears to be effectively total. Jahras' entire fleet seems to have been sunk, burned, or taken. All the navy yard facilities were burned. The artillery foundries in and around Iythria were all destroyed, and the port's batteries were blown up. As nearly as I can tell, Your Grace, the Imperial Desnairian Navy now consists solely of the twenty-one galleons in Desnair Bay. And, in all honesty, Your Grace, I'll be astounded if the heretics don't move against Desnair the City very soon now." His mouth twisted. "They made it clear enough at Iythria that they're not afraid to confront heavy fortifications *or* our galleons, and I don't think there's anything at Desnair that could stop them if Jahras couldn't stop them at Iythria."

"No?" Clyntahn glared at him, jowls tinged with just a hint of the purple which had suffused them earlier. "What about a fucking commander with at least a little *guts?*" he snarled. "What about a goddamned navy that remembers it's fucking fighting for *God?!*"

Rayno started to reply, then paused. From the casualty reports he'd read (and which Clyntahn hadn't gotten to before he'd launched off into his paroxysm of fury), the Desnairian Navy had fought—and died—hard before its final surrender. He thought about pointing out that of the ninety-plus ships with which Jahras had begun the action, the Charisians had kept only thirty-five or forty as prizes. The others had been so badly damaged Rock Point had ordered them burned. That didn't strike him as the sort of damage a fleet that gave up easily suffered. And Jahras' after battle report had pulled no punches about the devastating advantage the Charisians' new ammunition had provided them.

No, there'd been nothing wrong with the fighting spirit of Iythria's defenders. Not until after Jahras' surrender, at least. But pointing that out would be . . . impolitic.

"I trust we have both of those things at Desnair the City, Your Grace," he said instead. "It *is* the Empire's capital city, after all, and the added motivation of fighting under Emperor Mahrys' own eye should help to stiffen their spines, as well. I know!" He raised a hand quickly as Clyntahn's eyes flashed. "The fact that they're fighting under *God's* eye should be motivation enough for any man. But you've always told me, Your Grace, that we have to allow for men's inevitable weaknesses, the way their fallen nature leads them to fall short of their duty. I've dispatched instructions to Archbishop Ahdym and Bishop Executor Mahrtyn to do all in their power to strengthen the faith and determination of the capital's defenders, and I'm sure they will. At the same time, though, if there are any purely secular . . . motivators we can apply, I'm in favor of using them, as well."

The incipient glare in Clyntahn's eyes eased slightly under Rayno's reasonable tone. He continued to stare at the archbishop for a long, simmering moment, but then he shoved himself back in his chair with a choppy nod.

"Point taken," he said, his own voice once again flat and controlled. "I want Jahras and Kholman, though. They've failed Mother Church—*betrayed* Mother Church—and they have to pay the price."

"I agree entirely, Your Grace, and I'm already considering possible ways to see that they do. The fact that they've cravenly fled to Charis like the cowards they are is going to make it difficult, however."

In fact, Rayno thought, Baron Jahras and Duke Kholman had displayed prudence, not cowardice, in removing themselves from Clyntahn's reach. And unless he was mistaken, before their departure they'd done their best to report honestly and accurately—and warningly—on what they'd faced when the Charisian Navy came to call. Best not to make *that* point just yet, either, though.

"Our inability to operate with any degree of flexibility in Charis is going to work against us, as well," he continued instead. "At the moment, I don't think it would be possible to send in any of our agents to deal with them. Getting to them is going to require something like Operation Rakurai, and until we know exactly where the heretics are keeping them, even beginning to plan that kind of mission is going to be . . . impractical, I'm afraid."

Clyntahn growled something under his breath, but he also gave another of those jerky nods. In fact, his color seemed to improve a little, and Rayno congratulated himself on having brought up Operation Rakurai. There'd been too little time for any reports to reach Zion yet, so it was impossible to say how well the Rakurai had fared. Clyntahn anticipated a high degree of effectiveness, however, and contemplating that seemed to take at least the worst edge off his fury over Iythria. Of course, if it turned out Operation Rakurai had been a *failure*, and not a success, his rage would simply return in redoubled force, but as the *Writ* said, sufficient unto the day was the evil thereof.

"All right," the Grand Inquisitor said again, after a moment. "I'll accept that—for now. But I want every member of their families who didn't flee with them. I want them *here*, in Zion, Wyllym. *All* of them, you understand me?"

"Of course, Your Grace." Rayno bowed slightly across the conference table. "In fact, I'd already anticipated your wishes. I've detailed a team of our most reliable inquisitors to oversee the process of taking them into custody."

"Good," Clyntahn grunted, then reached out and dragged the battered file away from Rayno.

He opened it, and the archbishop unobtrusively held his breath. This time, however, the Grand Inquisitor didn't explode. His lips tightened and his brows lowered as he turned through the pages, yet he had himself back under control, and his eyes darted over the sentences of the various reports.

Clyntahn was a very fast reader. Even so, it took him the better part of twenty minutes to work through the file, during which Rayno sat quietly, his expression one of calm, attentive patience. Finally, the Grand Inquisitor finished, slapped the file shut again, and shoved it away from him.

"Well, that's a fine pile of dragon shit," he observed in something very like a calm voice. "Jahras was obviously trying to cover his own ass, but I notice his report's dated before Kholman's decision to just hand over the entire fucking city. That probably means there's at least a *trace* of accuracy in it somewhere."

"That was my own impression, Your Grace."

"Well, if there *is*, we obviously need to push our own development of these 'shells' harder. Remind me to kick Allayn in the ass and find out how he's coming."

"Of course, Your Grace."

Clyntahn sat silent for another two or three minutes, lips pursed, eyes focused on something only he could see. Then he stirred in his chair once more and refocused his attention on Rayno.

"You know, one of the things that occurs to me is that they went after Iythria, not Desnair the City. I know Jahras had a lot bigger fleet based there, so I suppose it makes sense for them to have gone after it, but Desnair's only—what?—five hundred miles farther from Tarot than Iythria, and it's the Desnairians' *capital*. And let's be honest, Wyllym—Desnair's fortifications aren't any tougher than Iythria's were. So surely they had to have been at least tempted to go after the capital first. Think of what a fist in the eye *that* would have been!"

"I hadn't really considered that aspect of it, Your Grace."

Rayno considered adding that one reason he hadn't was that Iythria had represented well over three-quarters of Desnair's total shipbuilding capacity. And, for another, the Gulf of Jahras was—or had been, at least—far more important than Desnair Bay from any commercial perspective. With the Gulf under Charisian control, the Desnairian Empire's internal economy had taken a significant blow which was going to have major consequences in the not so distant future. The psychological impact of an attack on Desnair the City might have been profound, but from a hard-boiled military and economic perspective, there was no comparison between that and the value of the attack the Charisians had actually executed.

And the defection of two of the Empire's most prominent nobles—one of whom just happened to be the Navy Minister and the other of whom just happened to be the Navy's commanding officer—is probably a fairly adequate "psychological" substitute for attacking the capital, he reflected sourly.

"Well, it's obvious to *me*," Clyntahn emphasized the pronoun, "that they went after Iythria first because it's closer to Silkiah and Siddarmark."

Rayno managed not to blink. It had been painfully obvious for years that the Charisians had no intention of drawing the Church's attention any more forcefully than it could avoid to the Silkiahan and Siddarmarkian evasion of the Grand Inquisitor's embargo. Clearly, they'd wanted to do *nothing* to imperil that highly lucrative trade. In fact, as far as he could see, they'd probably

decided to attack Iythria because of its military importance *despite* its proximity to Silkiah, rather than because
of it.

"What do you think they're trying to accomplish, Your
Grace?" he asked cautiously.

"Oh, it's obvious, Wyllym!" Clyntahn retorted impatiently. "From the moment Harpahr blundered straight
into disaster last year, the heretics've seen the opportunity to completely neutralize Mother Church's naval
power in eastern waters. They're probably planning on
getting around to Desnair the City sometime soon, and
then, eventually, they'll go around the tip of Howard and
demonstrate how gutless *Thirsk* is when the pressure's
really on." His jaw tightened. "We're going to have to
seriously consider putting somebody from the Navy of
God in command of *all* our naval forces, since it's obvious our secular commanders aren't up to the task. Of
course, *Harpahr* didn't exactly cover himself with glory,
either, now did he?"

Rayno nodded silently, his mouth prudently shut, and
Clyntahn grunted like an angry boar. Then he shook himself.

"But, back to my point. It's obvious that now they've
cleared all our naval power out of eastern waters, from
the Sea of Justice to the Icewind Sea, they'll take advantage of that to establish still closer economic ties with
Siddarmark. Hell, there's not even a frigging *rowboat*
left now to see what they're really sending in and out of
that bastard Stohnar's harbors, is there? We don't have
squat in the way of an eastern naval presence after this!
You think somebody like Stohnar—or like Cayleb, for
that matter—won't take advantage of that? They've just
blown the embargo completely out of their way, and
trust me, that son-of-a-bitch Stohnar's just waiting for
the 'Reformist' movement in the Republic to get strong
enough before he opens the door and invites in a military Charisian presence. He especially wants those new
rifles and fieldpieces of theirs—think what the Siddarmarkian Army could do with *those* added to its arsenal!

You think he doesn't just lie awake at night drooling over the possibility?

"Of course he does, and the Charisians know it, too. *That's* why they went after Iythria. Because it's closer to Siddarmark—and to Silkiah, of course—and it's going to have more impact in *Siddarmark*. They could care less what the effect in Desnair is! They want to show the Republic that they can go anywhere the hell they want and do anything the hell they choose to encourage the 'Reformists' to turn against Mother Church openly and to reassure Stohnar that they can assist him militarily when he seizes the opportunity to finally bury his dagger in Mother Church's back."

Rayno started to reply, then stopped and considered. He wasn't at all sure he shared the logic process which had led the Grand Inquisitor to his conclusion, and he was even less confident that the possibility of a direct military alliance with Siddarmark had played any part in the Charisian decision to attack Iythria. As far as he could see, that had been purely an example of their going after the most immediately valuable—and most immediately threatening—military objective they could strike.

Yet none of that meant their triumph wasn't going to have exactly the effect Clyntahn had just described. Not instantly, perhaps, but in the fullness of time. And while Rayno had always been less than convinced that Greyghor Stohnar was simply biding his time until the moment was ripe to move against the Border States and the Temple Lands, that had been when the entire world wasn't already at war. Not only that, it had been before the Inquisition began preparing the Sword of Schueler against the Republic. Unless the Lord Protector was far, far stupider than Rayno could bring himself to believe, Stohnar had to have become at least partially aware of the Sword. It was unlikely he realized everything Clyntahn and Rayno had in mind, and even if he did, it was even less likely he'd be able to survive. But he was almost certainly picking up at least *some* warning signs, and if he did decide what had happened at Iythria strengthened his hand—and especially if it encouraged the Siddarmarkian Reformists—he probably would begin cautiously exploring options with Charis.

"I see your thinking now, Your Grace," he said. "Of course, it's unlikely Stohnar will be able to act on the opportunity before the Sword strikes."

"I know that's the plan," Clyntahn said. "And hopefully, Rakurai's going to have knocked the bastard Charisians back on their heels, at least for a little bit, too. But they surprised us with this one, Wyllym. Let's not pretend they didn't. And everything we're hearing suggests the 'Reformists' are gaining ground steadily in Siddarmark. At least some of those bastards are likely to come out openly in support of Stohnar when the coin finally drops. For that matter, they're gaining ground in *other* places, too."

He glowered at Rayno across the table, and the archbishop nodded. Despite what the Church was reporting, the truth—which had a nasty tendency of leaking out through the producers of those accursed anti-Church broadsheets the Inquisition *still* couldn't run to ground—was that the Church of Charis *wasn't* being "heroically and defiantly resisted" in the "conquered territories."

That was to be expected in Old Charis itself, and probably to some extent in Emerald, as well, if only due to the princedom's proximity to the original source of the contagion. Yet the truth was that Chisholm, which definitely *wasn't* right next door to Old Charis, had reacted with appalling calmness to its renegade queen's decision to actually *marry* the heretic King of Charis. Still worse, in some ways, Zebediah had done the same. In fact, from all reports, Zebediah was actively *embracing* the Charisian Empire, and if that meant accepting the Church of Charis as well, its subjects seemed perfectly willing to do that, too. No doubt that was largely an inevitable reaction to how cordially hated Tohmys Symmyns had been, but that wasn't keeping it from happening. And, worst of all. . . .

"You're thinking about Corisande, Your Grace?"

"I'm thinking about everywhere the goddamned Charisians *go*," Clyntahn said sourly, "but, yes, Corisande was the other major ulcer I had in mind. I know our reports from Manchyr are always out of date by the time they get here, and I know you've been trying to put the best face on the ones we do get," he shot Rayno a moderately frigid look, "but the goddamned 'Reformists' are obviously gaining ground in Corisande. And the dog-and-lizard show that bitch Sharleyan put on when she was down there's only pushing that process along. The damned Corisandians are going over to Charis, just like the Chisholmians and the Zebediahans, and you know it, Wyllym."

Unfortunately, Rayno *did* know it. And he *had* been trying to "put the best face on" his reports from Corisande, for that matter. It would have been nice if there'd been some actual good news in any of them, though.

It seemed evident to him (although even now he didn't propose to point it out to Clyntahn) that there'd always been a much greater Reformist sentiment in Corisande than anyone in Zion had realized. That sentiment hadn't extended—initially, at least—to actually embracing schism and heresy, yet it had been there. And it had grown only stronger after Clyntahn broke the Reformist Circle in Zion itself. Rayno understood why the Grand Inquisitor had done it, yet there was no point pretending Corisande—insulated from the object lesson by all of the salt water between it and the mainland—hadn't reacted with revulsion and anger. That had helped push more Corisandians into the arms of the Church of Charis, and the careful way in which Cayleb and Sharleyan had handled their occupation, coupled with Sharleyan's display of mercy in pardoning so many who'd been convicted of treason, had drastically undermined the purely secular anger evoked by Hektor's murder. Especially when she'd gone right on displaying mercy after she'd so nearly been killed on her throne! For that matter, the original outrage engendered by Hektor's assassination had begun to fade even before Northern Conspiracy's leaders had been arrested, far less convicted.

So, yes, the "damned Corisandians" *were* going over to Charis.

"The other thing we have to face here, Wyllym," Clyntahn continued flatly, "is that we're getting our ass kicked every time we go up against the Charisians at sea. Don't think anybody inclined to consider heresy's missing *that* point, either. Hopefully, the Rakurai are going to have demonstrated by now that we're not powerless when it comes to striking back, but the *military* momentum's clearly on the heretics' side for right now, and that's giving them the impetus where morale's concerned, as well. We need to grab that momentum back, regain the upper hand psychologically, the way we had it after we snuffed out the Wylsynns' conspiracy. Finally getting around to Punishing those bastards Thirsk captured was a start. Rakurai's going to be another step on the same journey, too, and the Sword's going to be a huge stride in the right direction. But I want to hit them in as many places as possible. I think it's time to poke up the fire in Corisande."

"Prince Daivyn?" Rayno asked, tilting his head while he considered options and possibilities.

"Exactly. And I want it to coincide with the Sword. I want those bastards in Tellesberg to take as many good, heavy kicks in the balls, from as many directions as we can manage, in the shortest time period possible."

"If you actually want to coordinate the two operations, Your Grace, we're going to have to tinker with the timing."

"What do you mean, 'tinker'?"

"Forgive me, Your Grace. That was the wrong word. I should have said we're going to have to consider the timing carefully. If we hold to our current planning and send in a team of 'Charisian' assassins, it's going to take at least a few five-days—possibly an entire month—to get them into position in Delferahk, so the question becomes how closely we want the assassination to coincide with the Sword. Do we want to delay events in Siddarmark in order to coordinate them with the assassination, or do we want to move as quickly as possible in Siddarmark and settle for *approximate* coordination between the Sword and the assassination?"

"I want them to happen as close to simultaneously as possible," Clyntahn said after a moment's thought. "I want Cayleb and Sharleyan to *know* we timed them to happen that way." He smiled unpleasantly. "After all, *they're* going to know they didn't kill Daivyn, no matter what happens. So let's just underscore the statement for them and see how they like that!"

"Of course, Your Grace." Rayno bowed across the table again. "I'll get started on that immediately."

. IX .

Queen Frayla Avenue, City of Tellesberg, Kingdom of Old Charis

"I have a priority alert, Lieutenant Commander Alban."

Merlin Athrawes' head snapped up as Owl's voice spoke calmly over his built-in com. He stood in the window of his palace bedchamber, looking out into the steadily gathering twilight, and his expression was grim. Tellesberg—even Tellesberg, the city which never slept, which was never quiet—seemed hushed and somber. Lanterns and lamps were already beginning to illuminate the oncoming night, and his enhanced vision could see the longshoremen and the ships still loading and unloading cargo along the waterfront. But the city's tempo had clearly dropped, and people went about their business more quietly than usual, with a degree of fearfulness which grieved his heart.

The Gray Wyvern Avenue attack wasn't the only one Tellesberg had endured, although it had been the most costly of them all.

Another wagon loaded with explosives had been intercepted as it rolled through the gates of the Tellesberg dockyard. In the wake of Gray Wyvern Avenue, an alert

Marine sentry had taken it upon himself to question all incoming deliveries unless the driver was known to him personally. His initiative had irritated the dockyard authorities immensely, since it had resulted in confusion and delays in the dockyard's always bustling movement of supplies and deliveries. In fact, his company commander had dispatched a sergeant with orders for him to cease and desist. Fortunately, the sergeant hadn't arrived yet when the officious sentry stopped an articulated freight wagon almost as large as the one used in Gray Wyvern Square. *Unfortunately*, that wagon driver had arranged one of the flintlock pistol-based detonators where he could reach it from his high box seat.

The explosion had killed another fifty-six people, including the sentry, and wounded over a hundred more, but it would have been far worse if the driver had managed to reach his intended destination.

Two more, similar explosions had racked Tellesberg in the next twelve hours. Fortunately, they'd been smaller, but they'd created something entirely too much like panic for Merlin's taste. They'd also led to the declaration of martial law and a decree freezing all wagon traffic until the authorities could put some sort of security system into place.

The attackers' tactics had been shrewdly chosen to hit Tellesberg where it was most vulnerable, Merlin thought grimly. Not only had they targeted the leaders of the Empire's government—what had happened to Gray Harbor, Waignair, and Nahrmahn was proof enough of that—but Tellesberg's commerce was its very life's blood. The city's coat of arms, quartered with galleon and freight wagon, was nothing but accurate in that regard, and the grating, rumbling roar of those heavy wagons was both the bane of Tellesberg's repose and the source of a perverse pride.

Now those wagons had become a source of fear, not civic pride, for who knew which of them might be yet another bomb rolling towards its destination?

Cayleb and Sharleyan had seen no option but to impose unprecedented controls on the movement of freight through the city. No system could be perfect, but they'd moved quickly to begin issuing permits and licenses which were to be carried at all times and displayed upon demand. Moreover, every cargo load would now have to be documented, with a detailed bill of lading that would be inspected before it was allowed into the waterfront area or access to any cathedral, church, or public building.

Fortunately, the majority of the capital's freight was moved by professional drayage firms, all of which were already required to be bonded and inspected twice a year. Given those records' existence, they'd been able to move far more rapidly than someone like Clyntahn probably would have expected, and at least limited wagon traffic had been allowed to resume within two days of the initial attack. The smaller independents, who hadn't been in the records, were another matter, and some of them were suffering severe economic hardship while they tried to get the documentation and licensing which had never before been required. Baron Ironhill, aware both of the hardship for them and the consequences for the city's economic sector in general, had already set aside a fund to help reimburse some of those independent drayers' losses.

Even under the best circumstances, however, all the new inspections and regulations and licenses had begun imposing a significant drag on the Tellesberg economy. The cost of stationing City Guardsmen and Marines to do the inspecting was going to be a non-trivial budget item, as well. Yet even worse was the pervasive apprehension, the fear that yet another attack was inevitable. Tellesbergers refused to be cowed, and their anger at the indiscriminate slaughter of men, women, and children far eclipsed their fear, yet that fear was there, and Merlin was sadly certain it wasn't going away anytime soon.

"What sort of priority alert?" he asked Owl tersely now.

"A wagon has just entered one of the primary surveillance zones," the AI replied in that same calm tone. "As per your standing instructions, I have placed a parasite sensor in the wagon bed. It confirms the presence of high concentrations of gunpowder."

▼ ▼ ▼

Tailahr Ahndairs suppressed a highly inappropriate urge to swear as he turned the wagon down Queen Frayla Avenue and one wheel bumped jarringly over the cut-granite curb between the roadway and the sidewalk.

He'd been selected for his mission because of his religious fervor and his Charisian accent, both of which were completely genuine. Unfortunately, he was a tinker by trade, not a drayman, and there'd been less time to teach him the rudiments of managing a heavy freight wagon than he might have wished. The traffic in Tellesberg was also far, far heavier than he'd ever really anticipated, which only made things worse, but at least there were some advantages to the controls on movement the heretics had slapped down. Operation Rakurai's planners hadn't counted on their being able to do that as quickly as they had, and Tailahr was unhappily aware that he had neither permit nor license. If he was stopped, there was no way he could pretend to be anything but what he was. On the other hand, there was far less traffic than there had been, so even if he had no license, he also had fewer other wagons to contend with and—hopefully—his own poor driving would be less of a problem.

It had been so far, at least, and he didn't have much farther to go.

He looked along the street ahead of him. Quite a few heads turned, eyes watching him warily as he rumbled past, and he exulted inside at that proof the heretics had been hurt. They were *afraid* now, and well they should be! It bemused him that they should go through their lives showing so little concern for the eternity of punishment their actions were storing up in Shan-wei's hell, yet react so strongly—exactly as Archbishop Wyllym and Vicar Zhaspahr had predicted they would—to a threat to their merely mortal, transitory bodies. He didn't—couldn't—understand that sort of thinking, but he didn't have to understand to recognize the effect, and he smiled grimly at the proof of what he and his fellows had already accomplished.

Lights were beginning to glow in the establishments around him. Most of them were shops or eateries, and he saw couples and families gathering around the tables of the open-air cafés in the comfort of the cool, breezy evening. The traffic around him was primarily pedestrian, with a smattering of private vehicles and an occasional dragon-drawn streetcar. There were very few freight wagons in the area, however, which made Tailahr's wagon stand out even more. That was also the reason his wagon was so much smaller than the others had been, because there was nothing here to justify the presence of one of the huge, articulated vehicles. The fact that he only had to manage a simple pair of draft horses instead of one of the dragons was an additional plus, but mostly it was because he needed to appear as unthreatening as possible until the moment came. He was simply one more driver, obviously there to drop off deliveries of fresh vegetables for the restaurants, and he reminded himself to smile and wave reassuringly at the pedestrians who stopped as they saw him passing.

Ahead of him, on the left, he saw the sentry box and the Imperial Charisian Marines standing guard at the open wrought-iron gate of his target. He wasn't going to be able to get as close as he would have liked, but that had been factored into his plan. His wagon wasn't loaded just with gunpowder; it had been packed with bits and pieces of scrap iron, old nails, cobblestones, and anything else he could find to use as projectiles. When he set off the charge, it would turn the vehicle into an enormous shotgun, hurling its improvised grapeshot for hundreds of yards—inaccurately, but with lethal power.

He felt the tension coiling tighter at his center as the moment approached. To be chosen for this particular attack had been an enormous honor. His chances of successfully killing his primary target were probably less than even, given how far from the building he'd be when he detonated his weapon, but he could always hope. And according to their best information, the apostate traitor's office faced on the street and he normally worked far later into the night than this. So there was at least a chance, and even if he missed Wylsynn, he'd get scores of the bastard's assistants. He was about to strike a devastating blow at the center of all those accursed perversions of the Proscriptions, and that—

Tailahr's thoughts broke off abruptly as a man materialized out of nowhere. One instant he wasn't there; the next he was reaching up, catching the driver's seat's grab rail, and vaulting up beside Tailahr with impossible, fluid speed.

Tailahr flinched away, instantly and automatically, instead of immediately reaching for the cocked and ready pistol grip concealed in the seat beside him, and before he could even begin to recover, a hand moving with blurring speed had caught his left wrist. He screamed as that same hand effortlessly twisted his arm up until the back of his wrist pressed his shoulder blades; then another demonically strong hand gripped the nape of his neck, and Tailahr screamed again as his captor stood upright on the wagon seat, dragging him with him.

Even through the pain in his arm and shoulder, the anguish of the iron vise locked around the back of his neck, Tailahr's eyes bulged in disbelief as he realized the man who'd leapt into the wagon with him was actually holding him at arm's length with his toes an inch in the air. Then, without even a grunt of effort, the monster who'd sprung upon him leapt effortlessly down from the high seat.

Tailahr's scream was a shriek this time. Something crunched noisily and agonizingly in his shoulder socket, sending lightning bolts exploding through his entire body, as they hit the ground and his hand was wrenched abruptly even higher. And then the hand on his neck was driving him down. He found himself flat on the paving stones, his useless left arm thumping down beside him with a fresh stab of agony, as if it belonged to someone else, and a knee slammed painfully into his spine while his right arm was captured and twisted up behind him as casually as the other one had been.

Voices were beginning to shout in alarm, and he heard the clatter of boots as at least one of the Marine sentries ran towards them, shouting a challenge, but he managed somehow to turn his head. He looked up, and his entire body jerked in disbelief and terror as he saw the sapphire eyes, gleaming in the glow of his own wagon's driving lights, and recognized the livery of the Imperial Guard.

"I think you and I have a lot to talk about," Captain Merlin Athrawes told him coldly.

OCTOBER, YEAR OF GOD 895

·✦·

.I.

Tellesberg Palace,
City of Tellesberg,
Kingdom of Old Charis

"I, Nahrmahn Gareyt Baytz, do swear allegiance and fealty to Emperor Cayleb and Empress Sharleyan of Charis," the young man said, kneeling before the side-by-side thrones with his hand on the cover of the *Holy Writ*, "to be their true man, of heart, will, body, and sword. To do my utmost to discharge my obligations and duty to them, to their Crowns, and to their House, in all ways, as God shall give me the ability and the wit so to do. I swear this oath without mental or moral reservation, and I submit myself to the judgment of the Emperor and Empress and of God Himself for the fidelity with which I honor and discharge the obligations I now assume before God and this company."

Cayleb and Sharleyan looked down at him, seeing the unshed tears behind those brown eyes, hearing the grief in the young voice which refused to remain completely steady despite all its owner could do. Cayleb felt his own throat closing, and he glanced at Sharleyan, saw the tears glistening in her eyes, as well, as they stretched out their hands to cover the boy's.

"And we, Sharleyan Ahdel Alahnah Ahrmahk and Cayleb Zhan Haarahld Bryahn Ahrmahk," Sharleyan said, her voice clear but soft, "do accept your oath. We will extend protection against all enemies, loyalty for fealty, justice for justice, fidelity for fidelity, and punishment for oath-breaking. May God judge us and ours as He judges you and yours."

There was a moment of intense silence as the three of them gazed into one another's eyes, their hands still joined atop the *Writ*. Then Cayleb cleared his throat.

"There was a day," he told the young prince kneeling before him, "just over three years ago this month, when another Prince of Emerald named Nahrmahn knelt where you are today, Your Highness. He came as a defeated foe, making the best terms he could for his House and his people, knowing my wife and I, as his sworn enemies, might well have demanded his head in return. He came anyway, despite that danger, and knelt on the same cushion and swore the same oath you've sworn this day. I'd been raised all of my life knowing Emerald was the enemy of Charis. There'd been decades of spying and maneuvering for position and—finally—war between us. We had every reason to hate one another, and very little reason not to.

"Last month, that prince died." Cayleb had to pause and clear his throat again, and despite himself his voice was husky when he continued. "He died protecting his wife—and your mother—with his own body. He died at the hands of an assassin who murdered thirty-seven other people with the same bomb. He died having fought with all his marvelous intelligence and wisdom, at my side and Sharleyan's, for three years. Having fought for that in which he believed, for that which he loved . . . and for that for which he gave his life. And my lifelong enemy died not simply as our vassal, but as my friend, my ally, and my brother. In a few more years, my younger brother will wed your older sister, but know this—our Houses are already joined, and while Sharleyan and I weep at bidding your father go with God, we rejoice at welcoming you to the throne you now assume. I know how much your father loved you, Nahrmahn Gareyt, and I know how much you loved him. Remember him, as we will, and follow the example he set for you. If you do that you'll become not simply a prince to be respected and obeyed, but a *man* to be loved and celebrated."

The young man who would be sixteen Safeholdian

years old—fourteen and a half, in the years of Old Terra—in four more five-days gazed up at his emperor and empress. Then he bent his head, his forehead on their clasped hands until Sharleyan withdrew hers and rested it on his dark, curly hair. Nahrmahn Gareyt's shoulders quivered, ever so slightly, and the empress' smile trembled as she stroked his hair. Then she drew a deep breath.

"Rise, Prince Nahrmahn Gareyt, Nahrmahn III of Emerald. You are summoned to our Imperial Council, and we have much of which to speak."

▼ ▼ ▼

Nahrmahn Gareyt was already taller than his father had been. He was also athletic and muscular, without Nahrmahn the Elder's undeniably portly physique. His eyes were much the same, however—dark and sharp. It remained to be seen if the brain behind them was the equal of his father's, but the signs were hopeful, Sharleyan thought. The young man had never expected or wanted to take a throne so young, yet his parents had trained him well, both as a potential ruler and as a boy growing steadily into manhood, and those sharp eyes drank in every detail of the council chamber.

He was also clearly aware of his youth as he sat in the chair which had belonged to his father. There was a definite nervousness in the ever so slightly too erect posture, in the way he watched whoever was speaking. There was still too much grief in that youthful face, as well, and every so often his left hand touched the black mourning band on his right arm. Yet he showed far more composure than many a man twice his age might have, and Sharleyan remembered a girl child, even younger than he, who'd also come to a throne untimely because her father had been assassinated. She'd always felt close to Nahrmahn Gareyt, and now that common bond of murder had drawn them closer still.

"I meant what I said in the throne room, Nahrmahn Gareyt," Cayleb said, looking down the table to where Nahrmahn Gareyt sat at its foot. "I didn't expect even to *like* your father before we met, but both of us were rulers, both of us knew the survival of our realms and our people required us to find an accommodation. I never anticipated how much we'd come to treasure one another, or how valuable his wisdom and counsel would be. I'm sure you know Sharleyan and me well enough by now to realize how sincerely attached we were—and are—to your entire family, little though any of us expected that outcome. And despite your youth, you're a full voting member of the Imperial Council. You *are* the Prince of Emerald, the second ranking noble of the Charisian Empire, and we'll value your input and opinions. I'm sure you'll be more hesitant than your father was to *offer* an opinion." Despite the solemnity of the moment, Cayleb's lips twitched. "God knows Nahrmahn was never shy about offering *opinions!*"

A mutter of laughter ran around the council chamber, and even Nahrmahn Gareyt smiled at the emperor's wry expression.

"That hesitancy is only to be expected, given the combination of your age and how recently come to your throne you are," Cayleb continued more seriously as the moment's humor ebbed. "When you do wish to speak, however, you have not only the right but the responsibility to do so. I trust you understand I mean every word I've just said?"

"I do, Your Majesty. And Your Grace," Nahrmahn Gareyt said, bowing down the length of the table to Sharleyan. His voice hadn't yet settled completely into its adult register, but he met his monarchs' eyes steadily. "And you're right. For at least a while I'm going to take my mother's advice."

"Oh?" Sharleyan cocked her head. "And what advice did Princess Ohlyvya give you, Your Highness?"

"To keep my mouth shut in official settings even if I think people are going to assume I don't know what they're talking about rather than open it and *prove* I don't," Nahrmahn Gareyt told her with something approaching his normal grin. "She, ah, *suggested* it would be wise of me to mostly listen until I actually have a clue what the people around me are discussing."

"A wise woman, your mother, Your Highness," Cayleb observed with an answering smile.

"I think so most of the time myself, Your Majesty. Although there *have* been times when her idea of 'wisdom' and mine weren't exactly the same."

"I can imagine," Cayleb said feelingly. Then he shook his head and looked around at the other councilors seated at that table, and his amusement—welcome though it had been—disappeared.

Some of the faces had changed. Nahrmahn's left a painful gap, but much as Cayleb would miss the plump little Emeraldian, the gap where Sir Rayjhis Yowance had sat for so long was even more painful to him. And yet, as bitterly as he missed the man who'd been his friend, mentor, unofficial uncle, adviser, and, finally, servant, he felt no qualms when he looked at the man who'd replaced him.

Trahvys Ohlsyn, the Earl of Pine Hollow, had been Prince Nahrmahn's first councilor for many years, but he would be unavailable to Prince Nahrmahn Gareyt in that role, because Cayleb and Sharleyan had stolen him for the Empire. Quite a few Charisian noses had been put out of joint by their decision to name Pine Hollow to succeed Gray Harbor, yet no one had complained too loudly. Partly that was because the people who might have done the complaining suspected how little patience the emperor and empress would have shown their protests. Perhaps equally importantly, however, was the irreproachable job Pine Hollow had done managing Emerald's affairs while Nahrmahn was distracted by his responsibilities as Sharleyan and Cayleb's imperial councilor for intelligence.

In the process of doing that job, Pine Hollow had also spent a great deal of time in Tellesberg, conferring with Gray Harbor and the council members permanently based there. He'd gotten along particularly well with Gray Harbor himself, and they'd carried on a lively correspondence even when he wasn't in Tellesberg. As a result, he was very much a known quantity, with a command of the issues he would confront in his new position which very few of his new colleagues on the council could have matched and none could have excelled.

There were other reasons to name him to that position as well, of course. One was to demonstrate Cayleb and Sharleyan's willingness to step outside their own realms of Old Charis and Chisholm to fill such a vital position. It was another proof they'd genuinely meant it when they declared that the Empire of Charis was to be an empire of *all* its peoples. In addition, Pine Hollow had the advantage of having understudied one of the most skilled, cunning, and devious rulers in Safehold's history, which would undoubtedly prove valuable. And, finally, in the wake of Nahrmahn's death, the Brethren of Saint Zherneau had finally (if tardily) accepted the Emeraldian's recommendation that Pine Hollow be added to the inner circle.

Cayleb would have given literally anything to have Gray Harbor still sitting in that chair, but if he couldn't have that, at least he had someone who was every bit as determined and every bit as intelligent as Gray Harbor had been himself. And one who knew the full truth about the struggle they confronted . . . and who had access to Owl and the coms which tied the inner circle together.

Now if we could only get those lovable old fossils to let us bring Ironhill *fully on board,* Cayleb thought. Then he snorted mentally. *Just like you, isn't it, Cayleb? Never content, never satisfied! Why don't you just concentrate on the things the Brethren have managed to do* right *and contemplate some of the things they may have kept* you *from doing* wrong, *instead?*

"Bynzhamyn," he said out loud, turning to where Bynzhamyn Raice sat next to Nahrmahn Gareyt, "I suppose we should start with you."

"Of course, Your Majesty."

Baron Wave Thunder looked as weathered and solid as

ever, yet it was clear he'd taken the suicidal attacks hard. His expression was grim, and the mood of the entire council darkened perceptibly as its members turned their attention to him. All of them knew they weren't going to like what he had to report, but only those who were also members of the inner circle knew there was even worse he *couldn't* report yet.

"As of my most recent figures," he said, "the death toll from all of the attacks stands at one thousand seven hundred and sixteen. Over half of those were from the Gray Wyvern attack. In addition, according to the Order of Pasquale, we have at least another twenty-five or thirty in hospital who may yet succumb to their injuries. And over ninety who are expected to live, although some of them have lost limbs."

His voice was harsh, and his eyes met Cayleb's. Both of them knew those numbers were low, although neither could say so, since no reports had come in as yet from Chisholm. That meant there was no acceptable way for them to know another three hundred plus people had died in Sharleyan's kingdom. Baron Green Mountain, her own first councilor and beloved mentor, might still be one of them, too, although the healers seemed to have him stabilized.

"The only good news is that we did manage to take at least one of Clyntahn's agents alive," Wave Thunder continued. "It was only blind luck, of course." In fact, it had been Owl's SNARCs and Merlin Athrawes' ability to sprint halfway across Tellesberg under cover of darkness at superhuman speeds, but, again, that was something he couldn't very well explain to the council at large. "We were all lucky Captain Athrawes happened to be outside the Patent Office to notice the wagon approaching the building. If he hadn't become suspicious and overpowered the driver before he could reach the detonating mechanism—"

"Captain Athrawes does seem to have a talent for that sort of thing, doesn't he?" Sharleyan observed, deliberately pitching her voice to lighten the mood as she turned her head to smile at the sapphire-eyed Guardsman standing just inside the council chamber door.

"He *has* proved a moderately useful fellow upon occasion, I suppose," Cayleb agreed in a judicious tone.

"One tries, Your Majesty," Merlin replied respectfully, and the entire council laughed. A mere bodyguard might not have been expected to reply to an emperor that way in most realms, but this was Charis, the bodyguard was Merlin Athrawes, and they *needed* that cleansing laughter.

"At any rate, Your Majesties," Wave Thunder said, "the one man we've managed to capture hasn't been the least bit reticent about who he is or why he's here, or even who sent him. In fact, Master Ahndairs is *proud* to have been personally selected by the Grand Inquisitor as one of his 'Rakurai.' His only regret seems to be that he was captured before he killed himself blowing up the Patent Office and as many people who worked in it as possible—and Father Paityr, in particular—and he's boasted to anyone who would listen that he and his companions were only the first wave of the attacks Clyntahn intends to launch."

There was no laughter this time, and faces hardened all around the table.

"I suppose something along these lines was only to be expected, eventually, given how uniformly unsuccessful they've been in regular military confrontations with us," Pine Hollow said quietly. "Given the timing, it was probably the Markovian Sea that actually pushed Clyntahn into this strategy, I expect."

"I agree, Your Majesties," Baron Ironhill said, his expression grim. "Granted, it never occurred to any of us, since we tend to think of wars as something in which you try to *minimize* carnage among civilians and innocent bystanders. We should have remembered that as far as Clyntahn's concerned, there *are* no 'innocent bystanders' in Charis. He doesn't give a *damn* who he slaughters."

His voice went hard and ugly with the last sentence, and not just because of the carnage Clyntahn's "Operation Rakurai" had wreaked. The official report of the murder of Sir Gwylym Manthyr and his remaining men had reached Tellesberg, as well. In fact, the version of their deaths the Inquisition was trying hard to suppress across Haven and Howard had come to Tellesberg, courtesy of the tiny, highly stealthy, purely passive remote Merlin Athrawes had deployed to within visual range of the Plaza of Martyrs. That remote had seen Gwylym Manthyr's final gesture of defiance, and the propaganda broadsheets going up throughout the mainland realms contained a detailed etching of Manthyr's spittle hitting Clyntahn in the face to give the lie to the Grand Inquisitor's claim that Manthyr had confessed to all of the crimes and blasphemies charged against him.

Yet that remote had also recorded the agony in which those Charisians had died. Ironhill hadn't seen it, but he didn't need to. Cayleb and Merlin *had* seen it, driven by their loyalty to Gwylym Manthyr, and wished with all their hearts they hadn't. Sharleyan—wiser, perhaps, than either of them—had refused to look. She honored Manthyr's dauntless courage, yet she preferred to remember him as he had been, unshadowed and unmarred by the hideous death he'd died.

"You're right, of course, Ahlvyno," Cayleb said now. "And we'll be watching for similar attempts, I assure you. I just pray we can protect ourselves against this kind of thing without turning into some kind of suppressive tyranny ourselves."

"I'm afraid we're going to have to put at least some additional precautions in place, Your Majesty," Wave Thunder replied unhappily. "They succeeded in large part because we weren't expecting it, and I think future attacks on the same scale are unlikely. I doubt they're going to be rolling around the city with wagonloads of gunpowder again, for example, especially with our new licensing and inspection systems in place. No system's perfect though, and we obviously can't guarantee they don't have the men and materials in place to keep testing it for weak spots when we still don't even know how they got the gunpowder into the assassins' hands to begin with!"

"We still don't have *any* clues about that, My Lord?"

one of the other councilors asked, and Wave Thunder grimaced in disgust.

"No," he admitted flatly. "And I'm reasonably certain the one 'Rakurai' we managed to capture doesn't know how they did that, either. No one's going to torture any confessions out of him, but we haven't been especially gentle and understanding about questioning him." He smiled thinly. "He's told us where he went to collect *his* explosives, but they were delivered to him by another of Clyntahn's agents—the one who detonated the Gray Wyvern Avenue bomb, unless I'm mistaken. *He* got the gunpowder from a source—a pickup point—here in Old Charis, but our prisoner doesn't know where that was. What we do know, unfortunately, from examining the wagon Merlin kept him from blowing up in Queen Frayla Avenue is that the powder originally came from us."

"*What?!*" the other councilor demanded, sitting up sharply in his chair, and Wave Thunder grimaced.

"Forty pounds of it were still in its original kegs," he said, "and they carried the markings of the Hairatha Powder Mill. I think we have to assume that's why the powder mill was blown up. My current theory is that Commander Mahndrayn, Baron Seamount's assistant at King's Harbor, noticed a discrepancy somewhere in one or more of the shipping manifests from Hairatha. Most of you may not know that Captain Sahlavahn, the commanding officer at Hairatha, was Commander Mahndrayn's cousin. It would have made a certain degree of sense for him to take any suspicions to his cousin in an effort to handle things as quietly as possible, and it seems likely that whoever was responsible somehow realized Commander Mahndrayn and Captain Sahlavahn had become aware he'd diverted powder from the mill. I don't know how that happened, how the Commander and Captain Sahlavahn might have given away their suspicions, but if I'm right about what happened, he blew up the entire powder mill to conceal his actions."

"That's speculative," Cayleb observed, "but it does make sense. And it suggests that getting large quantities of gunpowder into the Empire isn't going to be as easy for Clyntahn as simply sending in lunatics willing to blow themselves up as long as they get to kill as many Charisians as possible. Of course, the reverse side of that mark is that we don't know how *much* powder was diverted from Hairatha. There could still be tons of it sitting around somewhere."

"Indeed there could, Your Majesty." Wave Thunder nodded. "Which is why I have my best agents and all of our resources looking for it." He didn't add that "all of our resources" included Owl's SNARCs. "In addition, we're trying to make all City Guardsmen aware of the need to look for *anything* out of the ordinary. They don't have to use *wagons* to get bombs into position, especially if they can work out some reliable way to set them off with a delayed timer of some kind, and even a fairly small explosion in a crowded market square will inflict a lot of casualties. This time around, Clyntahn ordered his 'Rakurai' to specifically target senior clergy and secular leaders; all the dead and maimed civilians were simply a happy side effect of that, according to Master Ahndairs. Next time, the bastards may simply choose to go for as much death and destruction as they can inflict.

"At the same time, we have to be on the lookout for completely different techniques. For example, if they could get their hands on our own gunpowder, they may manage to get access to our grenades, as well. For that matter, they could make grenades or similar small explosive devices of their own without much trouble. An attack like that couldn't kill anywhere near as many people as their . . . wagon bombs, but they'd also be harder to detect, and they'd probably be better at penetrating any security we set up."

Heads nodded soberly, and Cayleb's expression was grim. He wondered how the rest of his councilors were going to react when they discovered that a "Rakurai" with four grenades under his tunic had entered Cherayth Cathedral less than twenty-six hours before this very meeting, waited for Archbishop Pawal Braynair to arrive to celebrate mass, and then seized one of the processional candles and used it to light the fuse. He'd managed to kill only three people . . . but that was only because Braynair and two other men had tackled him and smothered most of the explosion with their own bodies.

"I'm afraid one of the precautions we're going to have to take—and you're not going to like it, Maikel," Wave Thunder, who *did* know about Braynair's death, said, looking directly at Maikel Staynair, "will be stationing guardsmen outside all public buildings, *including* cathedrals and churches, and requiring anyone entering to demonstrate he's not carrying a bomb under his tunic."

"I won't have armed guards outside God's house," Staynair said flatly, but then even the redoubtable archbishop jerked in his chair as Cayleb's open palm slapped the tabletop like a gunshot.

"Perhaps *you* won't, Maikel," the emperor said even more flatly, "but *I* will!" Their eyes locked, and the index finger of the hand which had slapped the table tapped it in emphatic time with Cayleb's words as he continued. "You may choose to risk your life in the service of God, and I'll respect you for it, even as I cringe inside every time I think about how readily you expose yourself to murderers like these 'Rakurai' of Clyntahn's. That's your option, though, Maikel, and I won't dictate to you. But you have no right to expose *other people* to that same risk. We're not talking about three men with knives this time—we're talking about people who blow up entire *city squares*! I am *not* opening the doors of God's house to that kind of wholesale murder and massacre. Don't fight me on this one, Maikel; you'll lose."

Silence hovered tensely for long, still moments. Then, finally, Staynair bowed his head.

"I . . . hadn't thought of it exactly that way," he admitted. "I still don't like it. In fact, I hate the very thought, but you're right, I suppose."

"We don't like the thought either, Maikel," Sharleyan said gently. "And if we can find a better way, we will. But for now, it has to be this way."

Staynair nodded silently, and Cayleb inhaled deeply as the council chamber's tension eased perceptibly.

"We'll look forward to hearing anything more you turn up on this front, Bynzhamyn. In the meantime, though, we can't afford to let our concern over these murders divert us from other problems. I'm sure that's at least partly what Clyntahn hopes to accomplish. So since we're not going to let that bastard have *anything* he wants, I suggest we turn our attention elsewhere. For one thing, I'd like to hear anything you and Trahvys can tell us about the situation in Siddarmark."

"Of course, Your Majesty," Pine Hollow said, after a glance at Wave Thunder. "Bynzhamyn and I have been looking at reports from certain of our sources in the Republic." Pine Hollow hadn't yet had as much experience as his predecessor in not looking at Captain Athrawes when he made comments like that, and his eyes flicked briefly in Merlin's direction. It was only a *very* brief glance, however, and he continued calmly. "We don't have anything like detailed information, I'm afraid, but it would appear the Group of Four intends to strike at the Republic very soon now."

Expressions turned grave once more, and the new first councilor shrugged.

"It seems evident from the reports that someone—almost certainly agents of the Inquisition—is skillfully fanning public unrest and anger directed first and foremost at the Charisian community in Siddar City and the other eastern provinces, but also at Reformists in general. The most telling aspect, in my opinion, is that the propaganda we've become more recently aware of directly links Lord Protector Greyghor and his government to the 'support and protection' of 'heretics and blasphemers' throughout the Republic. And you may find this of particular interest, Ahlvyno," he said, glancing at Ironhill, "but they're also emphasizing the way in which the Charisian immigrants are 'taking food out of our babies' mouths' and somehow managing to simultaneously make the consequences of Clyntahn's embargo *our* fault."

"That's insane," the Charisian Keeper of the Purse said, and Pine Hollow chuckled harshly.

"And you were of the opinion propaganda has to make sense to be *effective?*"

"No, I suppose not," Ironhill sighed.

"And what happened at Iythria—especially the destruction of the port—is going to play into their propaganda efforts, as well," Sharleyan observed. "I'm not sure how, but no doubt they'll figure out a way to suggest we're about to do the same thing to the *Republic*—with Stohnar's connivance!—for some nefarious reason of our own."

"Probably," Cayleb agreed. "And that being the case, what *do* we do?" He looked around the council table. "Suggestions, anyone?"

. II .

Royal Palace,
City of Talkyra,
Kingdom of Delferahk;
Tellesberg Palace,
City of Tellesberg,
Kingdom of Old Charis;
and
HMS *Destiny*, 54,
Thol Bay,
Kingdom of Tarot

"What is it, Phylyp?" Irys Daykyn asked, looking up from the flowers she'd been arranging to greet the Earl of Coris with a welcoming smile as he entered the library.

Spring was coming on apace, and the early-season wildflowers crowning the hills around the castle above Lake Erdan reminded her—fleetingly—of the brilliant blossoms of her homeland. They were a pallid substitute, yet they echoed at least the ghost of Corisande, and she'd spent several hours collecting them that morning, escorted by Tobys Raimair and one of his men. She'd been arranging them ever since, and singing softly—something she seldom did, since her father's death—as she worked.

Phylyp Ahzgood knew that, which was one of the reasons he hated having to disturb her . . . especially with this.

"I'm afraid something's come up, Irys," he said. "Something we need to talk about."

Her smile faded as his tone registered. She laid the flowers on the table beside the trio of vases she'd been filling and wiped her hands on the apron she wore over her gown.

"What is it?" she repeated in a very different tone.

"Sit down," he invited, pointing at one of the well-upholstered but worn-looking chairs. "This may take a while."

"Why?" she asked, sitting in the indicated chair and watching him with intent hazel eyes as he turned another chair backwards and sat straddling it, forearms propped on the top of its back.

"Because we have to discuss something we've both been avoiding," he said gravely. "Something you've been dancing around, and that I've *let* you dance around."

"That sounds ominous." Her effort to inject a light note into her voice failed, and she folded her arms across her chest. "But in that case, I imagine the best way to do this will be for you to come straight to the point," she said.

In that moment, she looked very like her father, Coris thought. She had her mother's eyes and high yet delicate cheekbones, but that hair came straight from her father, and so did the strong chin—softened, thank God, into a more feminine version in her case. And the look in those eyes came from Hektor Daykyn, as well. It was the look Hektor had worn when the time came to set aside theories and nuanced understandings. When it was time to make decisions by which men lived or died. It grieved Coris, in many ways, to see that look in Irys' eyes, but it was a vast relief, as well.

"All right, I *will* come to the point," he replied, and inhaled deeply.

"Irys, I know you blamed Cayleb Ahrmahk for your father's death. We haven't discussed it in some time, but it's seemed to me your confidence that he was responsible for it may have . . . waned a bit over the past year or so."

He paused, one eyebrow arched. After a moment, she nodded ever so slightly.

"I've . . . entertained the possibility that there could be other explanations."

"I thought that was what was happening," Coris said. "I haven't pushed you on it, for a lot of reasons, but one of them, frankly, was that if my suspicions were correct, then having you publicly and vocally suspicious of Cayleb was your best protection. Unfortunately, it doesn't look like it was protection enough."

"What do you mean?"

Those eyes were even more like her father's, and he sighed.

"Irys, Cayleb and Sharleyan of Charis didn't have your father murdered. Zhaspahr Clyntahn did."

For a moment, her expression didn't even flicker. Then her eyes widened, less in disbelief than in surprise at the flat confidence in his tone, he thought. She looked at him in silence, and then it was her turn to draw a deep, slightly shaky breath and sit back in her chair.

"You have proof of that?"

"Proof that he personally ordered your father's assassination, no," Coris admitted. "Very strong suggestive evidence that he planned it, yes."

"What sort of evidence?" she asked in a cold, dispassionate voice which had no business coming from a young woman who wouldn't be twenty years old for another month yet.

"First, let's think about his possible motives for doing

something like that," Coris responded. "Your father was losing, Irys. No, he wasn't losing; he'd *lost,* and he knew he had. I wasn't there, because he'd sent me away with you and Daivyn, but I have reports from trustworthy agents which all confirm Cayleb and Earl Anvil Rock are telling the truth when they say Prince Hektor had contacted Cayleb to open surrender negotiations. I'm not going to tell you Cayleb of Charis is a saint, because I don't really believe in saints. And I won't argue that your father wouldn't still be alive today if Cayleb hadn't invaded Corisande, since that almost certainly created the circumstances which led to his murder. But I will tell you Cayleb Ahrmahk was about to get everything he'd invaded to get, and that he's clearly smart enough to know that killing your father in that fashion at that time would have been the worst, stupidest thing he could possibly have done.

"But the things that would have made it stupid from *Cayleb's* perspective would all have been positive outcomes from *Clyntahn's* viewpoint."

Coris held up his index finger.

"One. If your father had reached an accommodation with Cayleb, even if he'd planned on denouncing it as non-binding at the first opportunity, since any promises would have been made to an excommunicate, it would have made him another Nahrmahn in Clyntahn's view. That would have been enough by itself to drive him into a frenzy but there was even worse from his perspective. The way he would have seen it, it wouldn't simply have been a case of the prince the Group of Four had anointed as Mother Church's champion against the 'Charisian blasphemer' cutting a deal with the blasphemer in question to save his own crown, it would have encouraged others to do exactly the same thing."

He extended the second finger of the same hand.

"Two. If your father reached an accommodation with Cayleb and decided, for whatever reason, that he had no choice but to abide by it, Charis' conquest—or control, at least—of Corisande would have been enormously simplified."

He extended his third finger.

"Three. If Cayleb *assassinated* your father, however, or if someone else did and Cayleb simply ended up blamed for it, then instead of becoming another traitor to the Group of Four and another example of someone reaching an accommodation with Charis, your father became a martyr of Mother Church."

His fourth finger rose.

"Four. Your father may not have been much beloved outside Corisande, but he was remarkably popular with his own subjects. If Cayleb had him murdered, it would arouse intense resentment among those subjects. That would lead to unrest, which would require substantial numbers of Charisian troops to suppress, and that would almost certainly lead to incidents between those troops and the people of Corisande, which would only strengthen your people's resentment and anger. Violent confrontations and incidents would increase, bloodshed would rise, and Corisande would become a sinkhole for the Charisian military resources that would be tied down there and not available for use against the Group of Four anywhere else. Of course, hundreds or even thousands of Corisandians would have been killed in the process, but from Clyntahn's perspective that would simply have been the cost of doing business."

He paused for a moment, and then, slowly, extended his thumb, as well.

"And five. By killing your father after he'd sent you and Daivyn out of Corisande to keep you safe, and by making sure your brother died at the same time, Clyntahn created a situation in which the legitimate heir to the throne of Corisande was a minor child, outside the princedom, and under the Church's direct or indirect control. Daivyn's exile from Corisande *guaranteed* the fragmented authority and legitimacy that led to the 'Northern Conspiracy,' Irys. It contributed directly to the bloodshed and executions in Corisande. And it left Daivyn conveniently parked where the Group of Four could make whatever future use of him seemed most valuable."

He let his hand fall, and Irys sat, gazing at him silently. From her expression, he was confident he hadn't told her anything which hadn't already crossed her own mind. But still she sat looking at him, then cocked her head.

"That's not proof, Phylyp. It's a description of why it might have made sense to a man like Clyntahn to murder Father and Hektor. A very convincing description—I'll grant that. And after watching what he did to the Wylsynn family and his other rivals in the vicarate, I'm certainly not prepared to argue that the fact that he's a vicar of God would have slowed him down for a moment! The man's a butcher, a tyrant, a murderer, and a monster." The flat, almost emotionless detachment of her voice only made it even more terrible, Coris thought. "Yet none of that constitutes 'proof' he had Father and Hektor killed. I'm willing to admit it's time to consider the possibility that *Cayleb* didn't do it, but that's a long way from deciding Clyntahn *did*."

"Your father taught you well," Coris said with a small, sad smile. "Always look for the other possibility, the less obvious one. Never decide something must be the truth simply because you *want* it to be."

"Father also taught me never to trust anyone completely," she said, looking into his eyes. "That was his very first rule, his most important single axiom. But he set it aside in your case, and I'm willing to do the same. Only I'm not prepared to accept that simply because I trust you, you have to be right."

Coris' heart swelled with pride as he looked at her, and he nodded.

"My God, what a queen you would have made," he said softly. "Your father and I talked about that once. He hated Sharleyan, you know, though it wasn't really personal. She was just . . . in the way, and he knew she'd never rest until she'd avenged her father's death. But he admired her, too—deeply—and I think he'd seriously considered trying to change the law of succession in Corisande." The earl shook his head with a smile. "Only he told me he'd decided against it because he didn't think

Safehold could survive you and Sharleyan at the same time unless you were both on the same side, and that wasn't going to happen."

Irys' eyes softened and her mouth trembled ever so slightly, but then she shook her head and unfolded her arms to point a finger at him.

"No courtier's tricks, Phylyp! You're not going to distract me that easily. You said you had 'strong suggestive evidence.' Show it to me."

"Of course." Coris gave her a seated bow, then turned his head towards the closed library door. "Rhobair, Tobys!"

The door opened a moment later and Tobys Raimair and Coris' valet, Rhobair Seablanket, walked through it. Seablanket was a thin man, with stooped shoulders and a long nose. His brown hair, touched with white, was beginning to thin, but the neatly trimmed beard he favored to hide the scar on his jaw was still dark and full. Irys had always thought he was one of the most lugubrious men she'd ever seen, and she'd never really warmed to him.

"I'm sure you recall my hiring Master Seablanket when we passed through Shwei on our way here," Coris said, turning back to Irys as Seablanket and Raimair crossed the library and halted behind him. "I was fortunate to find a Corisandian suitable to my requirements that far from home, wasn't I?"

"The thought had crossed my mind, yes," she replied slowly. "And, if you'll pardon my saying so, it seemed a little suspicious." She looked across the earl's shoulder at Seablanket. "It struck me that if someone wanted to plant a spy on you, that might've been one way to go about it. On the other hand, I've known you since I was a little girl. It seemed . . . unlikely that same possibility wouldn't have occurred to you."

"I'm afraid there are times even I can be a bit gullible and overly trusting," Coris said with a sigh. "And this, alas, was one of them. In fact, Irys, Rhobair is an agent of the Inquisition." He watched the young woman's eyes widen in sudden alarm but continued unhurriedly. "He was, in fact, specifically assigned to worm his way into my employment by Wyllym Rayno himself. Unfortunately for Archbishop Wyllym, however, when Rhobair first entered the Grand Inquisitor's personal service, he already had an employer . . . your father."

Despite her formidable self-control, Irys' jaw dropped. She stared at Coris for a moment, then whipped her eyes back to the valet, who suddenly looked much less lugubrious. In fact, he smiled at her, eyes touched by an amused light she'd never seen in them before, and bowed deeply.

"He worked for *Father?!*" she more than half blurted.

"Exactly." Coris shrugged. "It's an interesting thing about the Inquisition, Irys. They plant spies and agents everywhere, and they're very good at finding disaffected people to inform on others, yet until at least very recently, it never seems to have occurred to them that anyone else might plant spies on *them*. I think it has to do with the arrogance of power. They're so busy dealing with all the things they're doing to other people that they never consider the possibility of what other people might do to *them*. Or what steps those other people might take to protect themselves against the Inquisition's spies. And they did make a minor recruiting error in Rhobair's case."

"They did?" she asked in a fascinated tone.

"Oh, indeed they did," Coris practically purred, yet there was an odd, icy edge under his obvious satisfaction. "You see, Rhobair *is* a Corisandian, born and raised, but his mother was born in Harchong . . . where his grandfather was beaten to death on the very steps of his village church while the local inquisitor looked on. And his crime?" Coris looked into her eyes. "The squire beating him to death had wanted to bed his youngest daughter. She'd refused, he'd ignored her refusal, and her father had had the unspeakable temerity to protest his thirteen-year-old daughter's rape. That daughter was Rhobair's mother."

Irys' eyes flitted back to Seablanket and saw the truth as cold, bitter memory—and hate—quenched the humor which had flickered in his eyes.

"I won't bother you with the details of how his mother

and her two sisters managed to reach Corisande, Irys. That's not really my story to tell, anyway. But they did get to Manchyr, eventually, where your grandfather employed all of them on the palace staff and she married one of his armsmen. So when Rhobair came to your father and told him he'd been approached by an inquisitor about becoming a spy inside your grandfather's household, your father told him to agree.

"That was over thirty years ago. They soon realized what a prize he was and pulled him out of Corisande to use other places before I ever came into your father's service. He became very valuable to them over the years—valuable enough that it took very little effort on his part to plant the notion that he be sent to Shwei to 'infiltrate' Daivyn's court in exile. After all, he certainly knew enough about Corisande and about Corisandian politics to be perfect for the job. And he'd been a trusted agent of the Inquisition since long before I became your father's spymaster, so even though he'd grown up in your grandfather's palace, I wouldn't recognize him when I saw him. It was, alas, childishly easy for him to worm himself into my confidence . . . and he's been reporting exactly what I wanted him to report ever since."

Irys leaned back, shaking her head slowly. Not in denial, but in surprise.

"Phylyp, I'm trying, but it's a little hard to believe even you could be audacious enough to plant—what? A *double agent*?—on the Office of the Inquisition!"

"I did nothing of the sort, Your Highness! First, he's not a double agent; technically he's a *triple* agent," Coris protested with a smile, raising both hands in an eloquent gesture of innocence. "Besides, I had nothing to do with his original recruitment by the Inquisition. Your *father* did . . . when he and Rhobair were both about your age, in fact."

His smile disappeared, replaced by a far sadder expression.

"I learned a great deal from your father, Irys. I'd like to think he learned a few things from me in return, too. Yet the one lesson neither of us learned until it was too late is that some things in this world are genuinely more important than the 'Great Game.' The truth is, I don't think your father ever did learn that, but watching what happened to him, seeing what's happening to this entire world, has taught *me* there are. Your father made mistakes, Irys. Even the smartest man can do that, especially when he's blinded by ambition, and—forgive me—he was. I speak with a certain degree of experience, because I *helped* him make a lot of those mistakes and shared a lot of those ambitions. But your father wasn't simply my Prince. He was my *friend,* and that bastard in Zion had him and his son—my *godson*—butchered on the streets of his own capital just so he could blame it on someone else. And now he wants to murder Daivyn, too."

"*Daivyn?!*" Irys gasped. She jerked up out of her chair, her face pale, and one hand rose to the base of her throat.

"That's my 'strong suggestive evidence,' Irys. I've been sent orders to help clear the way for a party of assassins to murder Daivyn. What my orders don't tell me is that after Daivyn is dead, I'm going to be killed, as well. That will both remove any unfortunate witnesses who might know a little too much about how the tragedy came to occur and allow Clyntahn to argue that—just like your cousin Anvil Rock and his friend Tartarian—I've betrayed Corisande in return for some promised reward from Cayleb and Sharleyan Ahrmahk. Unfortunately for Clyntahn, the man who's been charged with denouncing me to King Zhames and the Inquisition is none other than my valet, who will—unfortunately—have become aware of my treasonous intentions just too late to prevent your brother's murder. Oh, and as a crowning touch, the murderers—all of whom will either perish in the attempt or die under the Inquisition's urgent interrogation—will be Charisians. Or, at least, all of them were *born* Charisians, although most of them have grown up and spent most of their lives here on the mainland. That's a nice refinement, don't you think?"

Irys sank slowly back into the chair, eyes huge, and Coris shrugged.

"I could be making all of this up, lying to you, but I think you know I'm not. And even though I can't show you a written order from Clyntahn to have your father and young Hektor murdered, I think the pattern we're seeing is clear enough, don't you?"

"We can't let him kill *Daivyn*, Phylyp!" For once, Irys Daykyn looked as young as her years, her eyes filling with tears. "*Please.* He's all I have *left,* all the family I have! And he's such a *little* boy. He doesn't deserve any of this!"

"I know." He reached out and took her hand. "I know, Irys, and Rhobair and Tobys and I will do anything we can to protect him—and you. But we're going to need help, and lots of it, or all we'll be able to do is to die in your defense. And I hope you'll forgive me for saying it," he smiled a small, crooked smile, "but I'd really prefer *not* to do that. Especially not if there's a chance of getting away alive in a way that will piss Zhaspahr Clyntahn off badly enough pure apoplexy might just kill the son-of-a-bitch. Pardon my language."

"Help?" she repeated, ignoring the last three words, her expression confused. "Who's going to be able to help us *now*?"

"Well, it happens that if you're willing to let me ask for assistance, I have a . . . friend who might just be able to do a little something for us after all."

▼ ▼ ▼

"You're joking!" Trahvys Ohlsyn said, looking back and forth between Merlin Athrawes and Bynzhamyn Raice. "Aren't you?"

"Does he *look* like he's joking?" Baron Wave Thunder demanded, jabbing a thumb in Merlin's direction.

"No, but. . . ." Earl Pine Hollow's voice trailed off, and Wave Thunder chuckled.

"All this new information access takes some getting used to, doesn't it?"

"You can say that again!" Pine Hollow shook his head. "And, to be honest, the fact that I'm still playing catch-up in so many areas doesn't help. I haven't had as much time to practice with this 'com' as I should have because I'm so busy discovering all the balls Earl Gray Harbor had in the air." He shook his head again. "I always respected the Earl, but I hadn't even begun to guess everything he'd been up to!"

"You do have a hard example to live up to, My Lord," Merlin agreed soberly. "I think you'll do well, though. And I hate to say it, but having you as a member of the inner circle's going to help a great deal in the long run."

"I'll grant you that it's not going to *hurt* any," Pine Hollow said with an off-center smile. "I do wish I'd known about it while Nahrmahn was still alive, though. And I wish I could tell Baron Shandyr about it now." The Emeraldian earl chuckled. "Hahl *still* hasn't figured out why your counter-espionage efforts here in Old Charis were so damned effective!"

"Hopefully someday we'll have the chance to explain that to him," Merlin said with an answering smile. "For right now, though, there's this other minor matter . . . ?"

"Of course there is!" Pine Hollow gave himself a shake. "I'm still having a little trouble believing it, though!"

"Well, the messenger wyvern's on its way right now." Merlin shrugged. "The SNARC Owl has keeping an eye on Irys and Coris picked up on the key words 'Charis,' 'Cayleb,' 'Clyntahn,' and 'assassination' when they discussed what to do. That was enough to flag the entire conversation to me and Bynzhamyn. I'll ask Owl to shoot the visual and the audio over to you later tonight, but the key point is that they're asking for asylum. I don't think Irys is quite prepared to promise she or Daivyn will swear fealty to Cayleb and Sharleyan or accept Corisande's permanent incorporation into the Empire, but from what I can see she's at least confident we won't murder her baby brother. From her perspective, that's a major step up from the situation they're in."

"I can see where that might be true," Pine Hollow said feelingly. "The question is what we do about it."

"I think the first order of business is probably to discuss

it with Cayleb and Sharleyan," Merlin replied. "On the other hand, I've discovered there are times when a little preparation work before you get around to the '*first* order of business' is indicated. Having a policy ready to suggest strikes me as an especially good idea in this case."

"And you want *me* to do the suggesting. I see." Pine Hollow smiled. "Do you really expect them to react that adversely?"

"On the contrary, I expect them to endorse the suggestion wholeheartedly. I just thought that as the Empire's brand-new first councilor, with this opportunity to demonstrate your mettle coming along, you might want to take advantage of it."

"That's Merlin for you," Wave Thunder snorted. "Always looking out for opportunities by which we can advance ourselves. Remind me to tell you about the first opportunity he gave *me* someday, My Lord."

"Now, Bynzhamyn! Let's not be bringing up the past," Merlin said severely, and turned back to Pine Hollow. "What I've been thinking, My Lord—"

▼ ▼ ▼

"Sir Dunkyn?"

"Yes, Hektor?" Admiral Sir Dunkyn Yairley looked up from the captains' reports in front of him as Lieutenant Aplyn-Ahrmahk stepped into his day cabin.

"A messenger from the Port Admiral's just come aboard, Sir. He has a dispatch for you."

"And I presume there's some reason you haven't already handed it to me?"

"As a matter of fact, Sir, I'm afraid you'll have to sign for it. Personally."

Yairley's eyebrows rose. He considered his young flag lieutenant for a moment, then shrugged.

"Very well, I suppose you should ask this messenger to step into the cabin."

"Aye, Sir."

Aplyn-Ahrmahk disappeared for a few seconds, then returned escorting a full commander.

"The plot thickens," Yairley murmured at sight of the "messenger's" seniority.

"Commander Jynkyns, Sir Dunkyn," Aplyn-Ahrmahk said.

"I see. You have a dispatch for me, Commander?"

"Yes, Sir. I do." Jynkyns saluted, then opened an attaché case and extracted a heavy canvas envelope. A paper label was stitched across the open end to hold it closed, and he laid it on Yairley's desk.

The admiral looked at it for a moment, then dipped his pen in the inkwell and scribbled his name across the label.

"Very good, Sir Dunkyn. Thank you," Jynkyns said, retrieving the envelope and examining the signature briefly but closely. Then he drew a small knife and carefully slit the stitches which had closed the envelope. There was another smaller envelope inside, and he withdrew it and handed it to Yairley before returning the outer envelope to his attaché case.

"I was instructed to inform you, Sir Dunkyn, that Admiral White Ford requests an estimate of your readiness to deal with this matter within the next two hours."

"I see." Yairley weighed the envelope in his fingers. It didn't seem all that heavy, but then again, orders never did . . . until the time came to carry them out.

"Hektor, would you please see Commander Jynkyns back to his boat?"

"Of course, Sir Dunkyn."

"Thank you. And, Commander," Yairley's gaze moved back to Jynkyns—"inform Admiral White Ford that I'll report to him as quickly as possible."

"I will, Sir Dunkyn. Thank you."

The commander saluted again and withdrew, escorted by Aplyn-Ahrmahk. Yairley watched them go, and when the cabin door closed behind them, opened the second envelope, extracted the half-dozen sheets of paper, and began to read.

▼ ▼ ▼

"Yes, Sir Dunkyn?" Aplyn-Ahrmahk said, stepping back into the day cabin ten minutes later. "Sylvyst said you wanted to see me?"

The lieutenant, Yairley observed with some amusement, was clearly on fire with curiosity about the mysterious dispatch. It was equally obvious that nothing on earth could have prevailed upon Aplyn-Ahrmahk to *admit* his curiosity.

"I did," he acknowledged. "I think we're going to be a bit busy for the next hour or so, Hektor."

"Of course, Sir. How?"

"I am requested and required to report to Admiral White Ford within no more than two hours' time the squadron's readiness state and whether or not we can depart Thol Bay with the evening tide."

Aplyn-Ahrmahk's eyes widened slightly. *Destiny* had only officially left dockyard hands the day before, and—as always happened these days—she'd hemorrhaged manpower while she was being repaired. Captain Lathyk was almost seventy men short of a full complement, and the chance of his coming up with that many men in the next six hours ranged from non-existent to something somewhat less than that. Then there was the minor problem of how they provisioned and stored the ship in that same six hours . . . which, frankly, sounded impossible to him. There could, however, be only one possible response from any king's officer to such an order.

"Of course, Sir," Lieutenant Aplyn-Ahrmahk said calmly. "I'll just go and find the Flag Captain, shall I?"

NOVEMBER, YEAR OF GOD 895

✦

. I .

HMS *Destiny*, 54,
Schueler Strait,
and
Tellesberg Palace,
City of Tellesberg,
Kingdom of Old Charis

"Gentlemen, thank you for coming."

Most of the faces around the polished wooden table in Sir Dunkyn Yairley's day cabin were worn with weariness, grooved with lines of fatigue, and adorned with at least a day or two of stubble. Yairley, however, was clean-shaven and brisk, his eyes bright, without any sign of exhaustion, which was something of a miracle under the circumstances.

Somehow (and most of his captains didn't know how, really, even now) his squadron had made its departure time, sailing on the evening tide almost exactly five five-days earlier. Since then, for reasons none of them knew, Yairley had driven them as if Shan-wei herself were in pursuit and gaining steadily. He'd informed them that he intended to be off Schueler Strait within twenty-eight days, which most of them had regarded as an outright impossibility. Instead, he'd done it in only twenty-*six*, which had required him to maintain an *average* speed of almost eight and a half knots. Topgallants, royals, staysails, studding sails—he'd set every scrap of canvas that would draw, and refused to reduce sail until he absolutely had to. He'd even ignored the Navy tradition of "reefing down," reducing sail and taking a precautionary reef in his topsails every night, lest some squall, unseen in the darkness, overtake a ship under too much canvas and rip the masts out of her or even drive her bodily under.

He hadn't told them why, he'd only told them *how* and then driven them like a slave master, and to their total astonishment, they'd actually done it. Now the squadron's ships lay hove-to in the mouth of the strait, their crews sunning on deck despite the brisk, chill weather while they luxuriated in the brief, well-earned (and badly needed) respite and all his captains repaired aboard *Destiny* where, just perhaps, they might finally learn what all of this was about.

One captain was missing. Captain Daivyn Shailtyn's *Thunderbolt* had lost her main topgallant and royal masts when she'd been hit by a sudden gust before she could reduce sail. Some of Yairley's officers had expected him to take Shailtyn's head off for letting that happen, but the admiral wasn't a fool. He knew whose fault it was, and so he'd simply signaled Shailtyn to continue at his best speed to a rendezvous point fifty miles south of Sarm Bank in the approaches to Sarmouth Keep, although why anyone in his right mind would want to go there was something of a puzzle.

Hopefully, they were about to discover that puzzle's answer.

"I'm sure all of you have wondered what could have possessed me to push our people this hard," Sir Dunkyn said, as his steward and flag lieutenant silently and efficiently provided each captain with a snifter of brandy. "I can now tell you at least part of the reason, although there are other portions of our orders which must remain confidential for a while longer."

The captains glanced at each other. Secret orders weren't exactly unheard of, but they *were* more heard of than actually seen. And orders whose contents couldn't be shared aboard vessels hundreds of miles from anywhere in particular were even rarer. Who was going to overhear any careless talk out *here,* after all?

Yairley watched those thoughts go through his officers' minds, then cleared his throat gently, recalling their attention to him.

"The squadron is ordered to attack, seize, and destroy Sarmouth Keep," he told them. "This isn't simply a raid, Gentlemen; it's an all-out attack which will leave nothing but rubble where the fortifications are now. In addition, it will include the seizure of any shipping we may encounter in Sarmouth itself *and* the destruction of the city's docks, wharves, and warehouses."

There was silence for a moment, and then Captain Lathyk took a sip of brandy and broke it.

"Excuse me, Sir Dunkyn, but may we know *why* we're to destroy Sarmouth?"

His tone could not have been more respectful, yet his expression made it clear he couldn't think of any conceivable reason for the operation. Sarmouth, in the Earldom of Charlz, was, admittedly, the second-largest seaport of the Kingdom of Delferahk, but that wasn't saying much. The Sarm River, which emptied into the Southern Ocean at Sarmouth, was over three hundred miles long, flowing all the way from the Sarman Mountains in the Duchy of Yarth. It was navigable (by anything larger than a rowboat, at any rate) for only about a third of its length, however, and Sarmouth itself was little more than a sleepy fishing port with occasional delusions of grandeur when a particularly ambitious Earl of Charlz started trying (usually with a depressing lack of success) to attract trade away from Ferayd. At the moment, it was probably even more of a ghost town than Ferayd, thanks to the systematic Charisian destruction of the Delferahkan merchant marine and Clyntahn's embargo. Nor was Sarm Keep any more impressive than the "city" it had been built to protect.

"I can't answer that question completely at this time, Rhobair," Yairley said after a moment. "I will tell you, however—and this is *not* to be discussed aboard your ships, even with your first officers—that the primary purpose of the attack is to serve as a distraction. While everyone's attention is hopefully focused on our noisy efforts to properly wreck everything in sight, we'll be sending a small party up the Sarm River in boats. The reason I say this isn't to be discussed outside this cabin is that I want none of our men who might be going ashore during the raid itself to know anything about it. I trust their hearts completely; I'm a little less confident about their tongues." He smiled briefly. "I want no careless comments ashore to alert any Delferakhan that we might be hanging about to recover those boats."

The captains glanced at each other again. It was amazing how gaining additional information hadn't left them any less in the dark.

"I realize you're all puzzled by the purpose of our orders," Yairley continued. "I promise I'll inform you more fully as soon as my own instructions permit. In the meantime, however, it's vital that we carry out our attack no later than twelve days from today." One or two sets of eyes widened, and he smiled thinly. "Perhaps you can see now why haste has been so imperative."

"I think you could safely say that, Sir Dunkyn, yes," Lathyk said dryly, and two of the others chuckled. Even at the insane rate of speed Yairley had maintained, it would require another six or seven days just to reach Sarmouth, and there was no guarantee they'd be able to maintain that speed. In fact, the odds were against it.

"I thought I could," Yairley said in an equally dry tone. "Still, I believe we can probably spend the time to properly enjoy the dinner Sylvyst promises me will be the high point of our entire voyage before we get back underway. I've taken the liberty of informing your first officers by signal that you'll be remaining aboard to dine, and I'm confident they'll take the opportunity to see to it that your people are properly fed, as well. Of course, we'll be driving as hard as ever as soon as you've returned to your ships. I'm sure—Charisians being Charisians—that there'll be quite a bit of grumbling among your ships' companies when the people realize that. However, you may inform them that Their Majesties have graciously consented to pay head money for every member of the garrison taken into temporary custody and to pay prize money for destroyed vessels and warehoused goods, based upon a fair valuation." It was his turn to chuckle. "I know it won't be much, but I also know Charisian seamen. Telling them they'll have a few extra marks rattling around in their pockets if they do well always seems to cheer them up, doesn't it?"

▼ ▼ ▼

"What is it, Merlin?"

Cayleb Ahrmahk's question was broken in the middle by a prodigious yawn. He pushed himself up in bed, careful to avoid disturbing Sharleyan, and grimaced as he looked out the bedchamber window.

"What *time* is it?" he demanded in a mildly ominous tone.

"It'll be dawn in another hour," Merlin replied over the com earplug.

"I'm going to assume there's a good reason I'm not still blissfully asleep," Cayleb remarked, climbing out of bed and shrugging into a light robe as he walked across the room and sat on the windowsill, looking out at the peaceful predawn garden. "I don't think I'm quite as ready to assume there's a good reason *you're* not still blissfully asleep, however. Correct me if I'm wrong, but aren't we in the middle of that 'compulsory down time' you're supposed to take every night? Do I have to go ahead and sic Owl on you to report you when you don't take it?"

"Actually, we're not halfway through it," Merlin replied with scrupulous accuracy. "We're closer to *two-thirds* of the way through it, if you want to be persnickety about it."

"Oh, that's *much* better." Cayleb's lips twitched, but he firmed them back up in a disapproving frown. "There was a reason I promulgated that particular arrogant imperial decree, if you'll recall, *Seijin* Merlin. And it just happens we have several other people now who can cover things while you 'sleep.'"

"That's true," Merlin admitted. "In rebuttal, however, I'll just point out that all of them happen to be in the same time zone at the moment. So I told Owl that if anything urgent comes up in the middle of the night, he's supposed to give it to me rather than wake up one of you flesh-and-bloods—who need *actual* sleep, not just the opportunity to rest your diodes. Besides, I've gotten quite a bit of rest since I got back to the Cave, you know. In fact, I'm getting too damned *much* rest at the moment."

Cayleb folded his arms and glowered at the garden, looking for some logical way to attack Merlin's reasoning. Unfortunately, none occurred to him.

"All right," he said finally. "You got me. This time. Now, what's so damned urgent you decided to wake *this* flesh-and-blood up at this godforsaken hour? I could've gotten at least another solid hour of sleep, you know."

"Owl's just spotted what looks an awful lot like it must be Clyntahn's assassination team." Any trace of humor had disappeared from Merlin's tone, and Cayleb sat up straighter, his eyes narrowing. "I'm not absolutely positive, but we've planted a couple of parasites on them. If these are the people we're looking for—and I can't think of why anyone else would be traveling to Delferahk from the Temple Lands this time of year, especially with snow all over the roads in both Havens—they're bound to say *something* to confirm it."

"What makes Owl think this could be them? Aside from the fact that they're riding through the snow and ice, that is?"

"There are fifteen of them, all in a single party, and twelve of them have Charisian accents. They're making it a point to stop at Church hostels along the way, and when they do, they make sure the staff hears those accents of theirs. And they're dropping the occasional Charisian mark when they pay their tab before they head on down the road. And, just as another little indicator that they're probably the people we're looking for, they're being very careful to let people know—or think, anyway—that they came out of the Republic. Obviously Clyntahn's decided that suggesting active collusion between Lord Protector Greyghor and Charis may give his operation there an extra boost. Unfortunately, whatever they may be suggesting to the people they meet along the way, Owl has the same crew getting off a Harchong-registry ship—whose immediately previous port of call was in Malansath, *not* the Republic—in the Duchy of Malikai two five-days ago. Now, I suppose really sneaky Siddarmarkian assassins *might* have decided to travel a couple of thousand miles west overland to get aboard a ship in the Harchong Empire and then sail back east for fifteen hundred miles before they head *south* for their real destination, but . . . I don't know, Cayleb. It seems a little roundabout to me."

"Was Nimue Alban as much of a smartass as you are?" Cayleb inquired pleasantly.

"Probably not. She was a lot more junior than I am, of course."

"Oh, of course," Cayleb agreed with a nod, and rubbed his chin for a moment, thinking.

"How did you put all of that together?" he asked after a moment. "I'm not complaining, you understand, but . . . ?"

He let his voice trail off and sensed Merlin's distant shrug.

"It's not really all that surprising. I've had Owl conducting continual reconnaissance of all three continents. I don't want him wasting processor power trying to actually *monitor* that much area on any real-time basis, but he's got a sub-routine set up to store the imagery in *Romulus'* computer core as it comes in. That way it's available for us to backtrack just about anything we want to if it turns out there's a reason we should. Things like individual horsemen don't even show up in the raw imagery, but once he starts enhancing and manipulating it, he can turn up a surprising amount of detail and do a lot about backtracking targets once they've been pointed out to him.

"He's beginning to show more initiative within his assigned parameters, too. Bynzhamyn and I instructed him to cover inns and hostels in Delferahk with parasites and listen for key words that might identify the assassins, and he decided on his own to place parasites in the Temple hostels on the main roads into Delferahk from Sodar and the Desnairian Empire, as well. Then he started moving farther back up the line without mentioning it to us. One of the ostlers in a hostel he'd wired for sound waited until this particular group had left and then described them as 'Langhorne-damned Charisians, probably heretics the lot of them,' to one of his coworkers. That popped through Owl's filters and he started going through the data—including what he had of the group this fellow was describing talking to each other from his other parasites—until he could locate and positively ID them. Once he had them, he simply ran back through the recorded imagery, backtracking them until the first time he picked them up. Which, as I say, was in Malikai. He was able to track the *ship* back to Malansath, but it looks like they must have gone aboard during one of the blizzards that rolled through there last month."

"It sounds to me like we got lucky," Cayleb said.

"We got lucky because Owl's getting better. Still, you're right. On the other hand, we've got a lot denser fence along the Delferahkan border, and Owl's keeping a real-time watch over Talkyra itself. If we hadn't picked them up now, we'd have picked them up then. I think."

"You *hope*, you mean," Cayleb snorted. He thought again for several more seconds. "So what does this imply for your plans?" he asked after a moment.

"My biggest concern is the fact that they're moving sooner than we thought they would—or faster, anyway," Merlin pointed out. "By my calculations, they'll reach Talkyra sometime around the fifteenth, a good two days earlier than we'd allowed for. For that matter, Yairley's squadron isn't even supposed to hit Sarm Keep until the *thirteenth*. I realize he's a little ahead of schedule, but whether or not the wind will let him *stay* that way is another question. And then there's the minor fact that nobody in Talkyra's heard back from us yet." Cayleb sensed another of those distant shrugs. "I think I'm going to have to go ahead and move down to the Sunthorns to be a little closer to the scene, just in case. And it's probably time I went and had that conversation with Earl Coris, too. In a manner of speaking, of course."

. II .

Royal Palace,
City of Talkyra,
Kingdom of Delferahk

Phylyp Ahzgood was a light sleeper.

He always had been, and his tendency to sleep less soundly than most had only grown stronger over his years as a spymaster. Hektor Daykyn had teased him about it, once upon a time, pointing out that it was probably the result of an increasingly guilty conscience. The Earl of Coris had responded that it had far less to do with guilty consciences than with a growing familiarity with—and appreciation for—the versatility of assassins.

Whatever the reason, he tended to wake up quickly and completely . . . and without moving.

Now he lay very still and let one hand steal slowly, slowly under his pillow. Its fingers settled around the dagger hilt, and his nostrils flared as he drew a deep, silent breath and prepared to fling himself out of the bed and away from the direction from which he thought the slight sound had come.

"I do hope you're not planning to do anything hasty with that dagger, My Lord," a voice said politely out of the darkness. "This is a new tunic. I'd hate to have to have it patched so soon."

Coris froze, eyes narrowing. There was something about that voice. He couldn't quite put a finger on it, but he knew he'd heard it before somewhere. . . .

"If you don't mind, My Lord, I'm going to strike a light," the voice continued as pleasantly as if it held conversations in someone else's bedchamber in the middle of the night on a regular basis.

"Go ahead," the earl invited, trying to match the voice's conversational tone.

"Thank you, My Lord," the voice replied.

There was a scratching sound, and then sudden, painful light smote Coris' eyes as something flared and guttered blindingly. He smelled a stink of brimstone, and despite himself, flipped out of bed and landed in a half crouch on its other side, dagger ready.

The intruder paid him no attention. He simply lifted the glass chimney from a lamp, lit the wick, and then blew out the flaming sliver of wood he'd used to do the lighting.

"What in Langhorne's name was *that*?" Coris demanded, his voice considerably more shaken than he would have liked.

"The Charisians call it a 'Shan-wei's candle,'" the other man said in an amused tone. "Personally, I think they could've come up with a more tactful name, given Vicar Zhaspahr's current attitude towards the Empire and the Church of Charis." He shrugged. "On the other hand, given how . . . enthusiastically it takes fire—and the stink—it *is* an appropriate name, don't you think? Besides, I don't think they're especially concerned by the thought of hurting the Grand Inquisitor's tender feelings these days."

"Zhevons," Coris said, eyes going wide as his orderly memory put a face—and a name—together with the oddly familiar voice. "Ahbraim Zhevons."

"At your service," Zhevons acknowledged with a bow. It was clearly the same man and the same voice, but the accent and dialect had changed completely. Unlike the smuggler Coris had met earlier, this man could have stepped straight off a street—an *expensive* street—in Zion itself.

"What are you doing here? And how the *hell* did you

get into my bedroom?" the earl demanded, his dagger still raised between them.

"As to how I got in, let's just say King Zhames' guards aren't the most alert lot in the world. In fact, they're pretty pathetic," Zhevons said in a judicious tone. "Sergeant Raimair's lads are *much* better than that, but there aren't very many of them. And, frankly, I'm a lot better at creeping around in the shadows than anyone else they're likely to meet."

"You are, are you?" Coris straightened from his crouch, lowering the dagger. "Given the fact that you're here, I'm inclined to take your word for that. On the other hand," his eyes narrowed, "that doesn't explain *why* you're here."

"You sent a message to Earl Gray Harbor last month," Zhevons said, his voice suddenly flat and serious, without the edge of humor which had marked it. "I'm the response."

The tip of an icicle ran down Coris' spine. It was an instant, instinctive reaction, born of his awareness of just how precarious his position truly was. But he pushed the instant hollowness of his stomach aside quickly. If Zhevons were an agent of the Inquisition, there'd be no point in any sort of elaborate charade designed to entrap him. And he *was* the man who'd delivered the messenger wyverns in the first place.

"As it happened, I was in a position to get to Talkyra rather more quickly than anyone else could have done it," Zhevons continued. "So *Seijin* Merlin asked me to deliver the reply to your message."

"Merlin?" Coris repeated.

He'd collected a great deal of information about Merlin Athrawes over the last three or four years. Most of it was preposterous and obviously grossly exaggerated. On the other hand, there was so *much* of it he'd been forced to accept that as ridiculous as it seemed, Athrawes truly was a *seijin*. Of course, no one seemed to be exactly sure what a *seijin* really was, and the old fairy tales about them didn't help a lot in that regard, so simply pinning a label on Athrawes didn't accomplish a great deal. On the other hand, the fact that this Zhevons had slipped—apparently effortlessly—through not simply Zhames of Delferahk's admittedly inferior guardsmen but also past Tobys Raimair's sentries, suggested—

"Should I assume you're a *seijin*, too, Master Zhevons?"

"People keep *asking* me that," Zhevons replied with an edge of exasperation. "They keep asking Merlin, too, I'm sure. And I think his response is probably the same as mine. I wouldn't call *myself* a *seijin*, but I have to admit that Merlin and I both have some of the abilities legend ascribes to *seijins*. So if you absolutely have to have a label, I guess that one's as good as any."

"I see." Coris smiled thinly, only too well aware of the surreal quality of this entire conversation. "On the other hand, according to my research, very few supposed *seijins* have ever called themselves *seijins* during their own lifetimes."

"So I've heard," Zhevons agreed pleasantly. "Now, about that message I'm here to deliver—?"

"By all means." Coris tossed the dagger onto the bed, where it settled into the soft mattress, then seated himself in his dressing-table chair and crossed his legs as urbanely as a man surprised in his nightshirt could manage. "I'm all ears."

"So I see." Zhevons smiled briefly, but then his expression sobered. "First, the bad news: Earl Gray Harbor is dead." Despite himself, Coris jerked upright, his mouth opening, but Zhevons continued speaking. "He was assassinated, along with several other members of the Imperial Council and prominent churchmen. Bishop Hainryk in Tellesberg, Archbishop Pawal in Cherayth, Bishop Stywyrt in Shalmar . . . they almost got Archbishop Fairmyn in Eraystor, too. And they *did* kill Prince Nahrmahn."

Coris inhaled deeply, unable to hide his shock. He'd never met any of those men, but he'd corresponded frequently with Nahrmahn, back in the days when he and

Hektor had been so consistently underestimating the little Emeraldian.

"How in God's name—?"

"God had very little to do with it, although that probably won't be Clyntahn's version. Let's just say there were several very large explosions—explosions that killed well over fifteen hundred men, women, and children in addition to the men I've just mentioned." Zhevons' expression was cold and bleak now. "The youngest victim we've identified so far was eighteen months old. Or would have been, if she'd lived another five-day."

"Langhorne." Revulsion twisted Coris' face. "The man's completely mad!"

"I'm afraid he's just getting started, My Lord," Zhevons said grimly. "Which is rather the point of this dramatic little visit, when you come down to it."

"Yes, of course." Coris gave himself a shake. "You say Earl Gray Harbor was killed. Obviously someone's stepped into his shoes. May I ask who?"

"Earl Pine Hollow."

"Ah!" Coris nodded. "An excellent choice, I think. I was always impressed by his correspondence."

"My impression is that he's more than competent," Zhevons replied with a slight, amused smile. "At any rate, he's read your message to Earl Gray Harbor, and he's prepared to offer you, Princess Irys, and Prince Daivyn asylum. Obviously, there are going to be a few strings attached."

"*Obviously,*" Coris agreed rather sourly, and Zhevons chuckled.

"It's only reasonable, My Lord," he pointed out.

"Knowing a tooth has to be pulled doesn't make the trip to the dentist enjoyable, however 'reasonable' it may be," Coris responded, then inhaled. "What would the 'few strings' be in this instance?"

"First, Their Majesties will require you to 'go public,' as I believe Emperor Cayleb put it, about Clyntahn's involvement in the effort to assassinate Prince Daivyn and hand over any evidence you might have implicating him in Prince Hektor's assassination." He looked sharply at the earl. "Earl Pine Hollow and Their Majesties are assuming that since you've seen fit to request their protection for Irys and Daivyn against *Church* assassins you've come to the conclusion they didn't have Hektor murdered after all."

"To be honest," Coris admitted with a sigh, "I've never thought Cayleb was behind that assassination. For a time I thought it might have been someone—a particularly *stupid* someone—trying to curry favor with him, but the more I thought about it, the more unlikely even that seemed. And I know Anvil Rock and Tartarian. There's no way they would have been party to Hektor's murder, whatever the Church's propagandists have said about them since they agreed to sit on Daivyn's Regency Council. Which only left one suspect, really, when it came down to it." He shrugged. "I'm afraid, though, that I don't have any *evidence* he ordered Hektor's assassination. I do have the orders to . . . facilitate *Daivyn*'s murder which my valet, Rhobair Seablanket, and I were sent by Archbishop Wyllym. They're a bit obliquely phrased, but their meaning's clear enough if you read between the lines. Of course, Rayno and Clyntahn are obviously going to denounce them as forgeries and us as paid liars."

"Of course." Zhevons shrugged. "On the other hand, given the way they've just assassinated over a dozen Charisians and murdered almost two thousand more of them, whereas Hektor is the *only* person Cayleb's been accused of assassinating, I think you might say the preponderance of the evidence is going to be on Charis' side in the court of public opinion."

"It damned well is for anybody with a working brain, anyway," Coris agreed grimly. "Very well, I can agree to that 'string' readily enough. And the next?"

"Cayleb and Sharleyan personally undertake to guarantee Irys' and Daivyn's safety. In fact, they propose to place both of them in the personal care of Archbishop Maikel. I think you know that, despite all the lies told about him by the Group of Four, Maikel would die himself before he permitted anyone under his protection to be harmed."

Coris nodded silently.

"Whether or not Irys and Daivyn—especially Daivyn—will be allowed to *leave* Tellesberg is going to depend on a lot of different factors," Zhevons continued. "According to the information I've received from Merlin, Their Majesties, Earl Pine Hollow, and Archbishop Maikel would all vastly prefer to see Daivyn returned to his father's throne in accordance with the terms of the peace settlement signed in his name by his Regency Council." His eyes met the earl's. "If he can't accept that in good conscience, no one will attempt to compel him to do so. However, under those circumstances he'll remain Their Majesties' 'guest' in Tellesberg indefinitely. I've been told to assure you he'll be treated with all the respect his birth and title command, and that his person will be sacrosanct, but I'm afraid that stipulation is non-negotiable."

"I assumed it would be," Coris said heavily. "And I won't pretend I'm delighted to hear it. Irys won't like it, either. I think she's genuinely accepted that Cayleb didn't order her father killed, but in many ways, she still holds him responsible for Hektor's death. If Charis hadn't invaded Corisande, he'd still be alive, after all. That's how she sees it, at any rate. I think she's probably even prepared to admit—intellectually, and only under duress, possibly, but to admit—that Cayleb didn't have much choice about invading, but what the head understands is sometimes difficult for the heart to accept, especially when you're only twenty years old."

"Trust me, if there's anyone in this world who understands that, it's Empress Sharleyan," Zhevons said quietly. "I won't presume to speak for the Empress, but I believe she'll be as gentle with both Irys and Daivyn as she possibly can."

"Despite our anti-Sharleyan propaganda in Corisande, that's what I'd expect, as well," Coris admitted. "To be honest, it's one reason I was prepared to approach her and Cayleb in the first place. Although, if I'm going to be *completely* honest, the fact that they were the only people in the world who *might* be able to protect my Prince and his sister from the people bent on murdering both of them was an even bigger factor in my thinking." He smiled humorlessly. "What's that old saying about any port in a storm? Especially if it's the *only* port available?"

"Then I should assume you—and Irys—are willing to accept the conditions I've just described?"

"You should," Coris affirmed. "I'd already warned Irys that Cayleb and Sharleyan would require what you've just described at a *minimum*. Her brother's all she has left, Master Zhevons. She's prepared to swallow far worse than that as the price of keeping him alive. In fact—"

He broke off, waving one hand in a dismissing gesture, and Zhevons cocked an eyebrow at him.

"You were about to say something, My Lord?"

"I was going to observe," Coris said after a long, thoughtful moment, "that from everything I've ever learned of Empress Sharleyan, she and Irys have a great deal in common, including an absolute, unswerving determination to avenge their fathers' murders. I don't say Irys is going to be prepared to accept Charisian dominion over Corisande, because, frankly, she *is* her father's daughter and she's thinking in terms of protecting her brother's birthright. But I will say that in so far as she can without prejudicing Daivyn's claim to the Corisandian throne, she's probably at least as hungry to see Clyntahn's blood as any Charisian could possibly be. I think there's at least the possibility of an . . . understanding in that."

"That would be most welcome, My Lord," Zhevons said frankly. "On the other hand, within the conditions I've already described, Their Majesties' decision stands, whether she and Daivyn are ever prepared to accept an accommodation with the Charisian Crown or not."

"And, to be honest, those conditions are more generous than I would have anticipated," Coris admitted. "I'm beginning to suspect that honesty, compassion, and fairness are much more dangerous weapons than most of us duplicitous diplomats have begun to realize even now. Probably because until Emperor Cayleb and Empress Sharleyan came along, we'd had so little exposure to them. It's going to take a while for us to develop proper immunity to them."

"Their Majesties do seem to have that effect on people, My Lord," Zhevons acknowledged with a grin. Then he turned serious again.

"The other message I'm here to deliver is that your proposed plan for getting Irys and Daivyn out isn't going to work."

"I realize it's a little risky," Coris began, "but I've done some preliminary spadework, and—"

"I'm aware of that, My Lord. I'm afraid, however, that both Duke Perlmann and Earl Ashton have been more thoroughly infiltrated by the Inquisition than they realize. I'm also aware that neither of them knows at this point that they're actually dealing with you or that the 'two Delferahkan nobles' you're trying to sneak out are Irys and Daivyn. Once the hue and cry goes up after you disappear from Talkyra, however, it isn't going to take either of them long to realize who you—and the children—really are, and at that point even if *they* don't decide to hand you over to the Inquisition—which, frankly, I think they probably would—you're bound to be spotted by the Inquisition and taken into custody."

"But—" Coris began, his expression worried.

"My Lord, I said your original plan wouldn't work, not that we can't get you out," Zhevons said calmly, and the earl closed his mouth abruptly.

"At this time, a Charisian naval squadron is on its way to Sarmouth," the *seijin* continued. "When it arrives there, it will seize the port and spend some time wrecking it from one end to the other. While it's doing that, a party of Charisian seamen and Marines will take advantage of the confusion and general hullabaloo to head up the Sarm by boat. They should be able to make it all the way to Yarth, and a lot faster than they could make the same trip overland. You'll meet them in the Sarman Mountains, then travel downriver to the naval squadron, which will deliver you to Tellesberg."

"That . . . might work," Coris said slowly, his eyes thoughtful. "It's, what, about two hundred and fifty miles from Talkyra to Yardan, isn't it?"

"By road, yes," Zhevons agreed. "It's only about a hundred and eighty miles in a straight line, though. And, frankly, if you try to go by road, they'll run you down long before you get there. For that matter, they'll simply send word ahead to Bishop Chermahk in Yardan by semaphore and have him—or Duke Yarth's armsmen—waiting when you get there." He shook his head. "You'll have to go cross-country."

"That's going to be hard with a boy Daivyn's age," Coris pointed out. "He was a good horseman for his age before we left Corisande, but he's had very little opportunity to ride since we got here. I think we can deal with that, but none of us know the terrain between here and Yarth." His expression was worried. "I don't like the thought of having to recruit a guide on such short notice."

"That won't be necessary, My Lord." Zhevons smiled. "I'm afraid *I'm* going to be occupied elsewhere, but Their Majesties have decided getting you, Daivyn, and Irys safely to Tellesberg takes precedence over almost anything else. That being the case, they're prepared to commit whatever resources it takes, and *Seijin* Merlin's been on his way here almost since the moment your message arrived in Tellesberg. In fact, he's probably a lot closer already than you'd believe he could be. You'd be astonished by how quickly he can cover ground when he needs to."

"*Merlin* will be our guide?" Coris repeated very carefully.

"Among other things, My Lord. Among other things." Zhevons smiled oddly. "I think you'll find he's a handy fellow to have around in a lot of ways . . . and"—the smile disappeared—"he has a remarkably short way with assassins."

. III .

Sarmouth Keep
and
HMS *Destiny*, 54,
Sarmouth,
Kingdom of Delferahk

"Shit!"

Colonel Styvyn Wahls, Royal Delferahkan Army, clutched wildly at the railing as the entire fortress of Sarmouth Keep seemed to buck under a fresh wash of explosions. He smelled stone dust, powder smoke, wood smoke, blood, and fear, and he shook his head, trying to clear his brain and figure out what the Shan-wei was happening.

He managed to stay on his feet and dragged himself the rest of the way up the internal stair while those infernal guns were reloading. He reached the top of the elevated battery covering the Sarm River estuary and crouched low as he scuttled out towards the dubious shelter of the crenellated battlements.

The sky was salmon and rose in the east, still dark blue in the west, and streaked with blue-gray clouds which hadn't yet caught the sunlight overhead. The predawn twilight made the blinding fury of the long tongues of flame spurting from the broadsides of the Charisian galleons even more terrifying, and he wondered if that was one of the reasons for their timing.

Bastards have more guts than sense to sail straight up the estuary in the dark, he thought as their royal masts began to catch the dawn light, gleaming golden above the low-lying fog bank of gunsmoke rolling slowly north on the wind blowing in from the sea. The galleons had just enough sail set to hold them motionless against the river's current while they flailed his fortress with their guns.

Damned Charisians! Think they can go any damned where they've got three inches of water to sail in!

The thought would have been more comforting if the Charisian Navy didn't regularly demonstrate that it *could* go anywhere it had three inches of water to sail in. And Charisian arrogance or not, they were damned well here now.

Another salvo rippled down the side of the third galleon in the Charisian line, each gun obviously individually laid and fired, and Wahls ducked instinctively, trying to ooze out flat on the gun platform behind the battlements' protection as the exploding shot streaked towards the fortress. An artillerist himself by training, the colonel was almost as astonished by the elevation of the ship's guns as by what they were firing at him. Their damned, incredible exploding shot arced upward, tracing lines of fire across the half-dark, and dropped neatly over the top of the curtain wall. He kept his head down and prayed the rest of his men were doing the same. He'd already almost gotten himself killed gawking at the round shot skittering around the parade ground like Shan-wei's bowling balls while sparks and flame spat from them. He'd realized those sparks had to be coming from fuses of some sort barely in time and flung himself to the ground just as they began exploding.

At least fifty of Sarmouth Keep's understrength garrison had been less fortunate . . . or slower to react. Half his total manpower had to be out of action by now, and the fury of the Charisian bombardment was only mounting.

He'd tried to man his own artillery and return fire, but Sarmouth Keep wasn't—or hadn't been—considered a likely target. King Zhames' purse was shallower than usual these days, and Wahls' garrison was made up of old men past their prime, young men who didn't yet have a clue, and gutter-scraping mercs the Crown could pick up cheap. He did have a reasonably solid core of noncoms, but the total surprise when the first Charisian ship opened fire had panicked most of his men. He didn't suppose he could blame them for that, since he'd felt pretty damned panicked himself, yet he'd been in the process of restoring order when that first broadside of exploding shot came over the curtain wall and exploded . . . just as his sergeants had gotten them fallen in on the parade ground. They'd gone down like tenpins—except, of course, that tenpins didn't roll around on the grass screaming while they tried to hold their own ripped-out guts in place.

The handful of men who'd actually gotten to their guns and tried to man them had fared almost worse than the ones on the parade ground as the Charisians swept in close and hammered the battery embrasures with storms of grapeshot. Sarmouth Keep's artillery had never been updated, and Colonel Wahls had never encountered the new-style guns the Charisians had introduced. Now he had, and none of the reports he'd heard about them had done them justice. He couldn't *believe* the rapidity of those galleons' fire or the tempest of grapeshot which had silenced his own guns in such short order.

"Sir!" his second-in-command shouted in his ear, shaking him by the shoulder. "Sir, this is *useless!* The second barracks block's on fire, and it's right next to the main magazine! We're not even getting a shot off, and *they're* blowing *us* to hell!"

The colonel stared at the other man, unwilling to accept what he was saying. But then another wave of exploding shot slammed into his command and he heard fresh screams. His jaw tensed, and he nodded once, choppily.

"Haul down the flag," he grated. "Then get our people into the best cover we can find—*if* we can find any!—until they stop shooting at us."

▼ ▼ ▼

"Well, that was using a hammer to crack an egg, wasn't it?" Sir Dunkyn Yairley said mildly as the flag above the battered, smoking, burning keep came down like a shot wyvern.

"Personally, I'm in favor of doing just that, Sir Dunkyn," Captain Lathyk replied, grinning fiercely. "Not any more eager to kill people than the next fellow, you understand,

Sir. But if somebody's got to get killed, I'd a lot rather it was the other fellow's people!"

"I can't argue with that, Rhobair. And Captain Rahzwail did us proud, didn't he?" the admiral continued, turning to look at HMS *Volcano* as her crew began securing her guns.

"He did, indeed, Sir. A useful fellow to have along."

"Agreed." Yairley gazed at the bombardment ship for a moment, then beckoned to his flag lieutenant. Aplyn-Ahrmahk crossed the quarterdeck and stood waiting respectfully while the admiral examined him.

"I assume you're ready and—like every young lieutenant who's yet to develop a working brain—eager to go, Hektor?" he said finally.

"I wouldn't say *eager*, Sir," Aplyn-Ahrmahk replied, "but my boat crew's waiting. Well, actually I suppose, *your* boat crew."

"They're yours for the moment," Yairley reminded him. "And keep an eye on that rascal Mahlyk. Don't let him damage my paintwork!"

"I'll make sure he behaves himself, Sir," the flag lieutenant promised.

"See that you do. Now, go! I believe you have a little trip to make."

"Aye, aye, Sir!"

The lieutenant touched his chest in salute, first to Yairley, then to Captain Lathyk, and headed for the boat hooked onto *Destiny*'s main chains. He didn't look back, and Yairley watched him go, then shook his head.

"Young Hektor will do just fine, Sir Dunkyn," Lathyk said quietly, and Yairley cocked his head at his flag captain.

"That obvious, was I?"

"Well, we've served together for a while now, you and I, Sir. And young Hektor, for that matter." Lathyk shrugged. "I don't think *everyone* in *Destiny*'s guessed how you feel about the lad, though. Why, I'm sure there's some assistant cook's mate who hasn't noticed at all!"

"I see why the men think so highly of your sense of

humor, Captain," Yairley said dryly, but Lathyk only smiled, saluted, and turned away to see to conning his ship the rest of the way up the estuary to the town of Sarmouth itself.

Yairley watched him go, and the truth was that the flag captain's humor *had* helped . . . a little, at least. On the other hand, if anything happened to Aplyn-Ahrmahk, the admiral knew he'd spend the rest of his life second-guessing himself. He'd had no specific orders to send the youngster upriver, and he was quite certain any number of other captains and flag officers would have been horrified by his decision to detail a member of the imperial family— even an *adoptive* member of the imperial family—to such a risky venture. But the Charisian Navy's tradition was that neither birth nor rank exempted a man from the risks everyone else ran, and trying to wrap the boy—the young man, now—in cotton silk to protect him would have done no one any favors. All the same, he wondered sometimes if some perverse streak inside him kept goading him into sending Aplyn-Ahrmahk into danger in an effort to prove, possibly only to himself, that he was willing to do it. Or as some sort of bizarre counterweight for how fond of the boy he'd become.

In this case, however, given who the boat party was supposed to pick up, Aplyn-Ahrmahk was actually a logical choice. In some ways, at any rate. And as long as one could overlook the probability of getting a member of the imperial family killed, of course. Not likely to enhance a flag officer's future career, that.

Oh, stop it, Dunkyn! The boy's in no more danger than anyone else you're sending with him! The experience will do him good, and Lieutenant Gowain's a good, competent officer. He'll keep Hektor out of trouble.

Sir Dunkyn Yairley took a deep breath, clasped his hands behind him, put Lieutenant Aplyn-Ahrmahk firmly out of his mind, and began to pace slowly up and down the weather hammock nettings while he watched his squadron advance on the hapless little town they'd come to destroy.

Siddar City,
Republic of Siddarmark

"*Kill* the heretics! Burn the bastards out!"

The raucous shout went up from somewhere deep inside the mob, and other voices took up the refrain, bellowing the words in an ugly, hungry rhythm. It sounded like the snarl of some huge beast, not something born of human throats. It was still several blocks away, but Byrk Raimahn's heart plummeted as he heard it coming.

"Come *on*, Grandfather!" he said, reaching out and actually grasping Claitahn Raimahn's arm as if to drag him bodily out of the courtyard.

The old man—he was in his sixties, his hair shining like snow in the cold winter sunlight—was still powerfully built, and he jerked his arm out of his grandson's grasp.

"Damn it, Byrk!" he snarled. "This is our *home!* I'm not handing it over to a mob of street scum!"

For a moment, Byrk seriously contemplated knocking him unconscious and simply hauling his limp body down the street. Claitahn might still be a fit, muscular man, but Byrk had spent the last five years sparring with some of the finest boxing coaches available in Tellesberg's and now Siddar City's gymnasiums. A quick jab to the solar plexus to bring his grandfather's hands down, then a right hook to the jaw would do the trick, he thought grimly.

But he couldn't do that, of course. Not to his *grandfather*. And because he couldn't, he stepped back, drew a deep breath, and made his voice come out flat and hard.

"We've got to *go*. Go now, while there's still time."

"This is our *home*," Claitahn repeated, "and it's a lot safer place to be than getting caught in the street by those thugs! The City Guard's bound to turn up soon, and when it does—"

"The Guard isn't going to get here—not in time to do any good," Byrk said, hating himself for the words as he saw the look in his grandfather's eye. Yet they had to be said. "And we're in the richest part of the Quarter. Those bastards out there will make burning us out a priority. I know you don't like the thought, but we've got to go."

"And where do you propose we go *to?*"

"I know a place. A place where we'll be safe—or, at least, if we're not safe there, we won't be safe anywhere in Siddar City!"

"Then go!" Claitahn snapped. "Take your Grandmother and *go.* But I didn't give up everything in Tellesberg just to let gutter trash and street scum drive me out of my home *here!*"

"Grandfather, they may be street scum," Byrk said as reasonably as he could, "but there are *hundreds* of them. You wouldn't stand a chance of stopping them. All you'd manage to do is get yourself killed."

"And if I choose—" Claitahn began, but for the first time since he'd been a passionate, adolescence-driven fifteen-year-old, Byrk cut him off in midsentence.

"And if you choose to stay here and get yourself killed, Grandmother will stay *with* you! There's no way she'll run away and leave you ... and neither will I, you stubborn, stiff-necked, *obstinate*—!"

He made himself stop and glared at his grandfather. Eyes of Raimahn brown locked with eyes of Raimahn brown, and after a brief, titanic moment, it was Claitahn's which fell.

"I. . . ."

"Grandfather, I *understand.*" Byrk reached out again, resting his hands on Claitahn's shoulders. "You've never run from anything in your life, and giving ground before a mob comes hard. I know that. But I don't want to see you die, and I know you don't want to see Grandmother die, so, *please,* can we get out of here, you stubborn old ... gentleman?"

Claitahn stared at him for a moment, then surprised himself with a harsh laugh. He put his right hand over the younger, stronger hand resting on his left shoulder, just for a moment. Then he nodded sharply.

"My legs aren't as young as they used to be," he said. "So if we're going to be running away, what say we see if we can't get a good head start?"

▼ ▼ ▼

Samyl Naigail gave a yell of delight as he used the smoldering slow match to light the rag stuffed into the neck of the bottle of lamp oil and threw the incendiary through the display window. Glass shattered, and a moment later he smelled smoke and saw the spreading pool of fire flickering in the depths of the shop. Racks of dry goods and bolts of cloth began to smolder, taking flame quickly, and Naigail's eyes glowed.

This was better even than bedding a woman! There was a *power*—a wild fierce freedom—in finally freeing the anger which had boiled inside him for so long. Smoke rose from other shopfronts all around him as the mob rampaged through the Charisian Quarter, torching everything in sight. Fortunately, the wind was out of the northwest. It would blow the wind and cinders away from the central part of the city, and if they happened to set fire to the harborside tenements where the filthy Charisians lived like so many spider-rats in a city garbage dump, so much the better!

He turned away from the burning shop, reaching into his satchel, and heard a shrill scream. He looked up just in time to see three or four more young men—his age or a little older—run down a girl who couldn't have been more than fifteen. They trapped her against the wall of a building, and she cowered back against it, head darting around frantically, looking for any escape. Then she made a desperate dash for an alley mouth, but one of her pursuers caught up with her first. She cried out again, in mingled terror and pain as he wrapped his hand in her hair and jerked her off her feet. Naigail heard her crying out—begging, pleading, imploring anyone to help her— and he smiled. He watched them dragging her by the hair down the alley where the little Charisian bitch had thought she might find safety, and then he drew another bottle from his satchel, lit the rag, and threw it through another shop window.

▼ ▼ ▼

"Behind me—*now!*" Sailys Trahskhat snapped.

Myrahm Trahskhat looked up, then gasped and stumbled back behind her husband. She clutched three-year-old Sindai, their youngest in her arms, while seven-year-old Pawal clung to her skirts, their eyes huge with terror as the bedlam thundered around them. Thirteen-year-old Mahrtyn pushed himself in front of her, behind his father, his face white and frightened but determined. Behind the boy, Myrahm darted her head around, looking for any escape, but with two small children, outdistancing pursuit was out of the question.

Trahskhat knew exactly what was going through his wife's mind, and his own terror was as deep as her own. Not for himself, but for her and the children. Only he couldn't let that terror paralyze him, and he glared at the three men sauntering arrogantly towards them. He knew two of them—longshoremen, like himself, but definitely not Charisians, and both of them with knives thrust through their belts. The third was a stranger, but he carried a sword and there was a cruel, eager glitter in his eyes.

"Stay with your mother, Mahrtyn," he said quietly, his voice iron with command, never taking his own eyes from the other men. "Whatever else happens, look after your mother and the babies."

"Well, well, well," the sword-armed man called mockingly. "What *do* we have here?"

"Pretty wife you've got there, Trahskhat," one of the longshoremen said, reaching down and rubbing his crotch suggestively while his fellow leered and drew the foot-long knife from his belt, testing its edge with a gloating thumb. "Gonna enjoy showing her a really *good* time."

Trahskhat's face tightened, and he brought up the

baseball bat. He'd had that bat for more years than he could remember. He'd broken plenty of others over the years, but never this one. It had always been his lucky bat, and he'd brought it with him from Tellesberg when he left the Krakens behind with the rest of his heretical homeland.

Somehow, he didn't feel lucky today.

"Ooooh! What's he gonna do with the big bad baseball bat?" the sword-armed man taunted in a high-pitched falsetto. He raised his own weapon, smoky light gleaming on its point. "Come on, baseball man! Show us what you've got."

"Sailys?" Myrahm's voice was frightened, and he heard his younger children weeping in terror. But he never took his eyes from the men in front of him.

"*Now!*" the swordsman shouted, and the hunting pack charged.

Sailys Trahskhat had a lifetime professional batting average of .302. He'd always been a strong man, but not especially fast, so he'd been forced to hit for power rather than rely on speed on the bases. Over the years, he'd developed rather amazing bat speed, and the longshoreman with the drawn knife made the mistake of getting a little in front of the others.

The same bat which had hit twenty-three home runs in Sailys Trahskhat's last season with the Tellesberg Krakens hit him squarely in the forehead with a terrible crunching, crushing, *squashing* sound. He didn't even scream; he simply flew backward, knife spinning away through the air, blood spraying from his shattered forehead, and Trahskhat stepped to his left.

The baseball bat slashed over and around in a flat, vicious figure-eight. The other longshoreman saw it coming. His eyes flared with sudden panic as his right hand fumbled frantically at the hilt of his knife and the other arm rose to fend off the blow. But he was too slow, and the panic in his eyes disappeared as they went unfocused and forever blank as the end of the bat caved in his right temple with contemptuous ease.

That quickly, that suddenly, Trahskhat found himself facing only one opponent, and the swordsman looked down at the two corpses sprawled untidily in the street. His eyes darted back up to Trahskhat and the blood-dripping bat poised in the big Charisian's powerful hands, and Trahskhat smiled at him.

"That's what I'm going to do with the big bad baseball bat, you *bastard,*" he said, all the resentment and anger he'd felt since coming to Siddar City roaring up inside him with his terror for his family's safety. "You want a piece of me? A piece of my *family*? You bring it on, god-damn you! *You bring it on!*"

The swordsman stared at him, then stepped back, re-treating. But it was only a feint. The instant Trahskhat's bat started to dip, the man threw himself forward again.

Yet he wasn't the only one who'd been capable of feinting. As he came forward, the bat which had been waiting the entire time came up again, arcing from below belt level, catching his sword on the flat of the blade and flinging it to one side, then crunching into the underside of his jaw. The swordsman screamed, teeth and blood fly-ing. He dropped the sword, clutching at his shattered face with both hands as he stumbled the rest of the way forward, and Trahskhat stepped out of his path. The man lurched, starting to go to his knees, and that terrible baseball bat slammed into the back of his skull like the Rakurai of Langhorne.

He hit the pavement in a puddle of blood, and Trahs-khat looked down at him, breathing hard.

"Threaten *my* family, will you?" he hissed, and kicked the dead man in the ribs. Then he looked at his wife and children. "Are you all right?" he demanded.

Myrahm nodded mutely, her eyes huge, shaking with terror and reaction. Mahrtyn, he saw, had already pounced on the knife his first victim had lost, and if the foot of steel shook in his hand, his eyes were grim and determined. Those eyes were shocked by what they'd just seen, but they met his father's levelly, and Trahskhat's heart filled with pride.

And then young Pawal, still clinging to his mother's skirt with one hand, pointed with the other.

"Daddy," he said, seven-year-old voice quivering with fear and yet reaching for some comforting familiarity in a world which had gone insane. "Daddy, you broke your bat!"

▼ ▼ ▼

"Come on!" Major Borys Sahdlyr barked. "We're behind schedule already!"

"So what?" Kail Kaillyt shot back. He waved his sword at the smoke belching from burning shops and tenements, the motionless bodies littering the streets and sidewalks, and laughed drunkenly. "This is the most fun we've had in years! Give the lads a little slack!"

Sahdlyr glared at him, but Kaillyt only looked back at him unrepentantly. The major's second-in-command was intoxicated with violence and the release of long-held hatred, and in some ways that was worse than anything wine or whiskey might have produced.

Damn Father Saimyn! Sahdlyr thought bitterly, even though he knew he shouldn't. But still. . . .

He made himself draw a deep breath of smoky air. As one of the handful of Inquisition Guardsmen who'd been smuggled into Siddar City as part of the planning for the Sword of Schueler, Sahdlyr had done his best to instill some sort of discipline into the volunteers Father Saimyn and Laiyan Bahzkai were recruiting. Unfortunately, his superiors had been too enthralled by Father Saimyn's reports to listen to his own warnings that the loyal sons of Mother Church were far more enthusiastic than organized . . . or experienced. It was one thing to smuggle in weapons; it was quite another to train civilians in their use. Even people like Kaillyt, who'd served as a member of the Capital Militia, had strictly limited training compared to their regular army counterparts.

Nor had it been possible for Sahdlyr to rectify those shortcomings. Actually *training* any large body of men required space and time, and it wasn't something which could be done in secret in the middle of a Shan-wei-damned city. He'd done his best, but the unfortunate truth was that he'd been largely restricted to lecturing Father Saimyn's "officers" on theory, and that was no substitute for hands-on time working with their weapons and their troops. He'd deeply envied his fellows who'd been sent to less citified parts of the operation. Scattered around the estates of Temple Loyalists in the Republic's central and western provinces, where farmers, foresters, miners, and rural craftsmen already resented the wealth of the eastern provinces' urban populations, *they'd* been able to actually *drill* the men they were responsible for leading. They'd been able to put them together and train them as *units*, accustomed to taking orders and obeying them.

Sahdlyr had warned Father Saimyn—and even Father Zohannes—that without the same opportunity, he and his subordinate commanders were unlikely to retain control of their units here in the capital when the day finally came. It wasn't the men's motivation he mistrusted. It wasn't even their *willingness* to take orders; it was their . . . reliability. They'd never been given the chance to acquire the habit of obeying their officers when the violence actually began.

But had Father Saimyn listened? Of course he hadn't! And neither had Father Zohannes. Or Sahdlyr was confident neither of them had allowed it to color any of their reports to Archbishop Wyllym or the Grand Inquisitor, at any rate. And Father Saimyn was probably—*probably*—right that it wasn't going to matter in the end.

It had become apparent over the last few five-days that the government had started to realize, at least dimly, that trouble was brewing. They obviously hadn't guessed how deep their danger truly was, however, or they'd have taken more precautions. True, Daryus Parkair's decision to empty most of the Capital Militia's arsenals and send the weapons to be held under guard at Fort Raimyr, the main Army base north of the city, had deprived the insurgents of arms Father Saimyn had assumed would be available. But Fort Raimyr was fifteen miles from the capital and the Army was understrength at the moment. Despite a few belated troop movements, there couldn't be more than five thousand men stationed at Raimyr, and they were peacetime soldiers with a peacetime mentality. They'd need time to get themselves organized and move, and they'd be badly outnumbered if even two-thirds of the men Father Saimyn had promised would join the insurgency actually turned up.

There was time, Sahdlyr told himself, and so far the uprising's sheer suddenness and ferocity were carrying everything before them, but it was messy. And it was throwing him behind schedule. He should already have reached Constitution Square and the Lord Protector's Palace, and here he was instead, trying to drag his men away from the arson and looting—and, undoubtedly, rape, he thought bleakly, looking at a half-naked young woman lying sprawled in death almost at his feet—going on throughout the Charisian Quarter.

Damn it, Father Saimyn and Bahzkai had other groups poised and ready for that part of the operation, and they were *doing* it. The smoke and screams—and bodies—were proof enough of that! *He* was supposed to be making certain Stohnar and his accursed minions didn't manage to escape. The last thing they needed was for those bastards to get away to someplace like Charis and try to foment trouble back here on the mainland from their safe, comfortable exile!

"They can have all the slack they want once we've got Stohnar and his Council in the bag!" he snapped now, glaring at Kaillyt. "Are they here to do God's will, or simply to steal anything they can't burn?!"

The question came out with deliberate, sneering contempt, and Kaillyt's eyes flashed with anger. Which was exactly what Sahdlyr had wanted.

"We're not just a bunch of thieves!" he shot back furiously.

"No?" Sahdlyr matched him glare for glare for a moment, then allowed his own expression to soften . . . slightly. "I don't think you are," he said, "but that's what we're *acting* like, and we've got more important things to do!" He held the other man's eyes for another heartbeat, then hardened his voice again. "So let's get them moving again, shall we?"

Kaillyt looked around, as if truly seeing the confusion and the chaos for the first time. Then he gave himself a visible shake and looked back at Sahdlyr.

"Yes, Sir!" His sword flipped up in salute. "I'll do that little thing."

He turned away and started bellowing orders at their smaller unit commanders, and Sahdlyr nodded in satisfaction.

▼ ▼ ▼

"Langhorne!" Greyghor Stohnar muttered, standing on the balcony of one of the Lord Protector's Palace's ornate towers.

The official seat of the Republic's government had never been designed as a serious fortification. Its defense was the Siddarmarkian Army and its pikemen, not stone and mortar. Now, as he watched smoke rising over the city—and not just over the Charisian Quarter, any longer—he found himself wishing its architects had given just a little more attention to stopping blood-maddened street mobs short of the Chamber of the Senate and the Hall of Records.

And don't forget about short of your own hide, Greyghor, he reminded himself grimly.

"Where the hell are they all *coming* from?" he demanded.

"I don't know," Henrai Maidyn admitted. The Chancellor pointed out across the city at the scores of smoke columns rising from the Charisian Quarter. "I didn't think they had enough manpower to do that *and* come after the Palace." He shook his head, and his expression was grim.

Stohnar nodded. Part of him wanted to lash out at Maidyn and point out that it had been his *job* to determine what was actually coming, but it would have been pointless. It would have been unfair, too, for that matter. The Chancellor had brought Stohnar regular reports, and the Lord Protector had agreed with his conclusions. Only it appeared they'd both been wrong.

"We should have detailed more troops to protect the Palace," Maidyn continued. "It's my fault. I'm the one who—"

"It's not 'your fault,' Henrai," Stohnar interrupted. "I agreed with you and Samyl that we had to give priority to protecting the Quarter." He laughed harshly. "Not that it appears we're doing a lot of good over *there,* either!"

"Where the hell is Daryus?" Maidyn demanded, wheeling to glare towards the north. "What the hell is taking him so *long*?"

"Probably more of *that,*" Stohnar replied, gesturing disgustedly at the burning tenements of the Charisian Quarter. "Or more crap like it." He shrugged angrily. "I was wrong not to go ahead and muster the Regulars right here in the city and the hell with keeping them out at Raimyr."

"Without a better indication the wyvern was about to take flight, you couldn't risk warning—"

"Spare me the excuses," Stohnar said wearily.

Unlike Maidyn, the Lord Protector had risen to regimental command before he left the Army, returned to his native Siddar City, and entered politics. He should have remembered, he told herself. Whatever the arguments in favor of making certain Clyntahn was clearly guilty of the first move, he should have paid more attention to Daryus Parkair's argument that it was even more important they hang on to the capital in the first place. They could always argue over who'd started what later— assuming they survived to do the arguing—the Seneschal had observed acidly. And nobody who was inclined to believe Clyntahn in the first place would be impressed by any claims the Republic was an innocent victim of the Grand Inquisitor's lust for vengeance, no matter how truthful they were.

And I shouldn't have detailed so many of the troops we do have in the city to protect the Quarter, he told himself even more grimly. He hated to even think thoughts like that, yet there was a cold, bitter edge of truth to it. *You wanted to prevent massacres? Well, holding on to the damned capital would have helped a lot in that little endeavor! Instead, you parceled your troops out in tenth-mark packets trying to protect the Charisians, and look at it! Accomplished one hell of a lot, didn't you? Now you're going to lose both of them!*

He forced himself to straighten his shoulders as he looked down into Constitution Square at the single regiment of pikemen deployed to cover the approaches to the Palace. There weren't enough of them to cover all the entrances into the square, so they'd been stationed along the huge plaza's eastern edge to protect the enormous arched gate through the Palace's ornamental outer wall. The wall would probably help some, but that regiment simply wasn't big enough to cover its entire length, and then there was that damned, wide-open gate. If enough rioters came storming across the square—

It's not as bad as you think it is, Greyghor, he told himself harshly. *You don't have a single reliable report about what's going on out there. Daryus could be a lot closer than you think he is, and all that smoke is bound to make the situation in the Quarter look worse than it really is. And however many men they may have in the streets, most of the population's staying home and keeping its head down. It's not like the entire damned city is really up in arms, so if you can just hang on long enough for Daryus to get here. . . .*

▼ ▼ ▼

Byrk Raimahn looked back and swore with bitter, savage venom. They'd been lucky so far, but their luck had just run out.

The outriders of the mob had spotted the small band of refugees he and his grandfather had collected on their flight towards the docks. Part of him had never wanted to slow down for a moment, but he'd been unable to harden his heart enough to ignore the tattered drifts of terrified people—more often than not women or children—who'd clustered around them. He suspected they'd been drawn by his grandparents' well-to-do appearance and the general aura of composure and command they couldn't help projecting even in the middle of a murderous riot. But perhaps it had simply been the fact that the Raimahns were obviously *going* somewhere, not simply fleeing. It certainly couldn't have been because of how well armed and numerous they were!

He'd realized immediately that the larger their group got, the slower it would become . . . and the more likely it would be to attract the human slash lizards rampaging through the streets. But his grandparents would never have forgiven him for trying to shake off those terrified fugitives, and another part of him had been glad it was so. He knew he would never have forgiven *himself* later . . . not that it seemed he was likely to have the opportunity to worry about that after all.

He looked around quickly. There were perhaps a half-dozen other men his age or a few years older in their group. Fathers, most of them, he thought sickly, seeing how their wives and children clung to them. Another three or four were somewhere between them and his grandfather's age. That was it, and there had to be at least a hundred men in the mob spilling into the avenue behind them.

He stood for just a moment, then turned to his grandfather.

"Give me your sword," he said.

Claitahn Raimahn's hand fell to the hilt of the old-fashioned cutlass at his side. The one he'd carried as a young man on long-ago galleon decks—twin to the one hanging from the baldric slung over his grandson's shoulder.

"Why?" he demanded, and managed a strained smile. "Looks like I'm going to *need* it in a minute or so!"

"No, you're not," Byrk said flatly. "You're going to take Grandmother—and all the rest of these women and children—to Harbor Hill Court. Number *Seven*, Harbor

Hill Court." Claitahn's eyes widened as he recognized Aivah Pahrsahn's address. "There are . . . arrangements to protect them there." Byrk stared into his grandfather's eyes. "And you're going to get them there, Grandfather. I'm depending on you for that."

"Byrk, I can't—" Claitahn's voice was stricken, but there was no time for that, and Byrk reached out and drew the older man's cutlass from its scabbard.

"I love you, Grandfather," he said softly. "Now go!"

Claitahn stared at him for a moment longer, then dragged in a ragged breath and turned to his weeping wife.

"Come with me," his voice frayed around the edges. "He's . . . he's right."

Behind him, Byrk was looking at the other men in their small group.

"Who's with me?" he demanded. Two of the men about his own age looked away, their expressions shamed. They refused to meet his eyes, and he ignored them, looking at the others.

"I am," a roughly dressed fellow in his forties said, hefting a truncheon he'd picked up somewhere along the way. He spat on the paving. "Legs're getting tired, anyway!"

Someone actually managed a laugh, and the others looked at Byrk with frightened, determined faces.

"Here," he offered his grandfather's cutlass to a stocky, roughly dressed man carrying a badly cracked baseball bat crusted with blood. There was more dried blood on the fellow's tunic, although it was obvious none of it was his. Byrk had no idea whether or not the other man had a clue about how to use a sword, but he was obviously determined enough to make a good try.

The man looked at his bat. He hesitated for a moment, then grimaced.

"Thanks." He dropped the bat and took the cutlass, and Byrk's eyebrows rose as he took two or three practiced cuts, obviously getting the weapon's feel. "Militia-man back home," he explained.

"Good. Glad to meet you, by the way. Byrk Raimahn." Byrk tapped his chest, and the other man snorted.

"Sailys, Sailys Trahskhat," he said, then glanced down the street, where the mob had clearly finished coalescing and was beginning to flow towards them. "Pleased to meet you."

"Likewise." Byrk drew a deep breath and looked around at his small band. "It's pretty simple," he told them. "We slow them down, right?"

"Right," the fellow with the truncheon said with a grim smile. "And we take as many of the bastards with us as we can!"

The others snarled in agreement and drew into a tighter knot around Byrk in the center of the street.

Byrk's heart thundered and his hands felt sweaty. Despite all the songs, he'd never really believed battle and killing were glorious, and the truth was that he wanted nothing in this world so much as to run away. Well, either run away or throw up, he thought. But he couldn't . . . and, he realized, he wouldn't have if he could have.

Something else rose up inside him to join the terror and the determination. Something hot and angry and bitter tasting that seemed to quiver in his limbs. There were a lot of things he'd intended to do in his life, and regret flowed through him as he realized he wasn't going to get them done after all, yet that savage eagerness to get *on* with it was stronger still.

"Wait for it," he heard a stranger saying with his own calm voice as the front of the mob accelerated towards them. "Let *them* come to *us*. And stay together as long as we can."

"Die hard," the truncheon-armed man growled. "Die *hard*, boys!"

The mob swept towards them, baying its blood hunger, and the tiny knot of Charisians settled even more solidly in place. Byrk watched the Siddarmarkians moving from a walk into a trot, and from a trot into a run, and—

"*Fire!*" another voice shouted suddenly, and the mob's howls of fury turned into sudden shrieks of terror as something exploded deafeningly behind Byrk and twenty-five rifled muskets poured fire into them. Men went down, screaming and twisting on the pavement, blood erupting, as the heavy bullets plowed furrows through them.

"Second rank—*fire!*" the same voice shouted, and more thunder erupted. Byrk spun towards the sound and saw a double line of men in civilian dress—one kneeling; the other standing—all armed with bayoneted rifles. Smoke spewed from the standing line's weapons, and more of the mob went down. The musketeers were still outnumbered at least three or four to one, but that commanding voice never hesitated.

"*At the charge, boys!*" it shouted, and the musketeers howled—howled the terrifying war cry of the Charisian Marines—as they lunged forward in a compact, deadly mass behind their bayonets.

The mob was too tightly packed to evade them, and the hungry, hating shouts which had whipped it along only seconds before turned into screams of panic as it disintegrated into individual terrified men desperately trying to get out of the way of those lethal, glittering bayonets.

Bayonets that ran red moments later.

"Well, Byrk?" the voice of command shouted. "Going to just stand there all day?" Byrk looked at the man who'd shouted, and Raif Ahlaixsyn grinned fiercely at him, then pointed at the fleeing mob with his ornately chased, blood-dripping rapier. "Get a move on, man!"

▼ ▼ ▼

"Kill the heretics!"

"Death to all traitors!"

"Holy Langhorne and no quarter!"

"Down with tyranny!"

"Kill the bloodsuckers!"

"Kill the Charisian lackeys!"

"*God wills it!*"

Well, it would've been nice if Daryus had made it in time, Greyghor Stohnar thought as the mob began to pour into Constitution Square from the west behind the yammering thunder of its shouted slogans. There were at least five or six thousand of them, he judged with the eye of an ex-military officer who knew what five or six thousand men standing in one place really looked like. There were quite a few men in cassocks and priest's caps, as well. He couldn't make out colors very well from this distance, but he was willing to bet most of them were badged with the purple of the Order of Schueler.

He saw pikes and halberds waving here and there, but mostly swords, clubs, some pitchforks . . . weapons which could be easily concealed or improvised when the moment came. Maybe that was the reason he and Maidyn had underestimated the potential numbers available to Pahtkovair and Airnhart. They'd had their agents focused on looking for stores of heavier, more sophisticated weapons.

Should've remembered they can kill you just as dead with a cobblestone as a pike, Greyghor, he told himself. *Of course, it* is *basically a mob, not an army. No telling how good their morale is. They may not have the stomach for it when they come up against formed troops. Then again,* he thought as the screaming tide of humanity reoriented itself, coalesced, flowed together, and started across the square, *maybe they will.*

He glared at that accursed, ornamental gate in the Palace's outer wall. What he wanted was a massive portcullis, preferably with murder holes and huge cauldrons of boiling oil and naptha waiting for the torch; what he *had* was nothing at all. It had always been the Republic's boast that its citizens had access to the center of its government without let or hindrance, which meant there *was* no gate set into that gleaming, sculpted archway. The damned thing was so wide it took an entire company of pikemen just to cover it, too, and that was an entire company who'd had to be taken off the wall itself.

The mob obviously recognized just how undermanned that wall was, and it seemed to be under at least rudimentary control by its leaders. Its center hung back slightly, threatening the gate arch but keeping its distance while its flanks flowed forward. It was gradual, at first, but the flanking groups moved more and more rapidly, charging for the extreme ends of the wall in an obvious effort to spread the single defending regiment even thinner.

The bastards are coming over it, he told himself, resting one hand on the hilt of the Republic's Sword of State, hanging from the baldric looped across his right shoulder. That sword had belonged to Lord Protector Ludovyc Urwyn, the Republic's founder. He'd carried it through a dozen campaigns and at least twenty battles, and despite all the gold and cut gems that had been added to it over the last four centuries, it was still a fighting man's weapon. If it had been good enough for the Republic's first Lord Protector, it would be good enough for the Republic's *last* Lord Protector when someone pried it from his dead hand.

Best be getting down there, Greyghor. You'll get a chance to kill more of them at the wall than you will once they're inside and—

His thoughts broke off as a sudden crashing roll of thunder exploded from the southern edge of the square.

▼ ▼ ▼

Borys Sahdlyr whipped around in shocked disbelief as the unmistakable sound of a musket volley crunched down on the mob's baying shouts like an iron boot. Gunsmoke spurted, rising all along the south side of Constitution Square, and for just an instant, the shattering, totally unexpected concussion of at least a couple of hundred muskets seemed to stun the mob into silence.

Then the screams began again, but they were different this time.

Sahdlyr looked around, unable to see over the men packed between him and that wall of smoke. Then he turned and bulled his way through the shocked, motionless bodies around him until he reached the towering bronze equestrian statue of Ludovyc Urwyn. The complex tracery of its elaborate fountains hadn't been turned off for the winter yet, and he ignored their icy coldness as he hurdled the wall around the catch basin. He splashed through the knee-deep water, then clambered up onto the base of Urwyn's statue, getting his head high enough to look across the square.

He was only halfway there when the second volley roared out, and he'd just reached the knees of Urwyn's horse when a *third* volley exploded.

Impossible! he thought, listening to that thunder of gunfire. *We know exactly how many muskets they had in the city arsenals, and they sent* all *of them to Fort Raimyr! They can't have* that many *of the damned things!*

But they did, and his blood ran cold as he finally got high enough to see.

At least a thousand men had poured into Constitution Square from the south while the mob's attention was concentrated on the Lord Protector's Palace. There wasn't a single pike among them, either—every one of them was armed with a musket, and Sahdlyr's belly twisted with sudden nausea as he realized they weren't matchlocks. They were the new model *flintlocks,* and they had the new bayonets, as well, and that was just as impossible as all the rest of it. Mother Church had forbidden the Republic to purchase more than five thousand of the new weapons, and Father Saimyn's agents knew where all five thousand of those weapons had gone. Over three thousand were at Fort Raimyr, but that wasn't where *these* had come from. The men carrying them were no Army musketeers; they wore civilian clothing of every imaginable color and cut, but every single one of them also wore an identifying white sash from right shoulder to left hip.

Sahdlyr clung to his vantage point, and his eyes went cold and bleak as a *fourth* volley crashed out. There were only three ranks of the newcomers, which meant the first rank had fired and then reloaded in no more than twenty or twenty-five seconds, and that was vastly better than matchlocks could have done. Worse, the successive, deafening, smoky cracks of thunder had carpeted a sixth part of the square with dead, dying, and wounded men.

The newcomers were still outnumbered—badly—but

they were a formed, cohesive unit, with all the organization his own mob lacked. Worse, they were far better armed, and their sudden, totally unanticipated appearance had stunned his own men. However willing the "spontaneous" mob might have been when it started out, no amount of willingness could armor it against *that* kind of surprise.

And once a mob like this breaks, Schueler himself couldn't get it back together again, Sahdlyr thought numbly. *If it breaks once, it'll turn into a* rabble *forever, and then—*

A fifth volley roared, and then came an even more dreadful sound—the unmistakable high, baying howl of the Imperial Charisian Marines.

No! Sahdlyr shook his head in wild denial. *Those can't be Marines! There's no way they could have gotten here, even if the Charisians had figured out what was coming, and—!*

But it didn't matter whether or not Charisian Marines could be in the heart of Siddar City. What mattered was that the mob, already worse than simply decimated by those deadly, crashing volleys, recognized the Marines' war cry when they heard it. And they knew what they and their fellows had already done to the Charisian Quarter . . . and how Charisian Marines would react to that.

Four hundred and seventeen of the "spontaneous rioters" were trampled to death by their fellows trying to get out of Constitution Square in time.

Little more than half of them made it.

▼ ▼ ▼

Greyghor Stohnar passed through the Lord Protector's Palace's gate with a guard of thirty pikemen. They had to pick their way carefully over Constitution Square's corpse-littered, blood-slick paving stones. No one had even begun to count the bodies yet, but there had to be at least a couple of thousand of them.

He approached the command group of the mysterious musketeers who'd appeared in the proverbial nick of time, and his eyebrows rose as a slender figure stepped forward to meet him. Slim hands rose, pushing back the hood of a heavy coat, and he inhaled deeply. They'd never been introduced, but he recognized her without any trouble at all.

"Madam Pahrsahn, I see," he said as calmly as he could.

"Lord Protector," she replied with a masculine bow some people might have criticized as scandalously abbreviated and informal, given Stohnar's exalted position. Considering the circumstances under which he was alive to receive it, however, *Stohnar* had no bone to pick with it.

"This is a surprise," he observed, and she laughed as if they were at one of her soirées rather than knee-deep in bodies in the heart of the Republic's capital.

"I'm sure Lord Henrai's been keeping you apprised of most of my activities, My Lord," she replied. "All of the ones he knew about, anyway." She gave him a dimpled smile. "Obviously, he didn't know about quite *all* of them."

"We were aware you'd acquired a ... modestly substantial number of rifled muskets, My Lady," he responded. "Obviously we didn't know everything we should have, of course. For example, none of us realized you'd somehow managed to train men to *use* them without anyone's noticing."

"Well, just buying guns and not learning how to use them properly would be pretty silly, don't you think?" She smiled again. "I'm sure Master Qwentyn told you I've been heavily invested in agriculture for years now, as well. An interesting thing about a big, commercial farm, My Lord—it's got a lot of empty space. Plenty of room for five or six retired Charisian Marines to train men one company or so at a time without drawing a great deal of attention. Especially if you've taken pains over the years to turn any ears that might overhear them into friends of yours by seeing to it that the local freeholders and their families are treated well."

"I suppose that's true," Stohnar said. "And it would appear to be fortunate the Group of Four clearly underestimated you even more badly than we did."

"They've had more experience underestimating me than you might expect, My Lord," she agreed, and this time her smile was cold and ugly. "This isn't the first time I've crossed swords, so to speak, with the Grand Inquisitor."

"No?" He considered her for a moment, head cocked, then barked a laugh. "Somehow I find that easy to believe, My Lady! Might I assume that your opportune rescue of myself and my government indicates you intend to *continue* 'crossing swords' with him?"

"Oh, I think you could, My Lord." She smiled that cold, ugly smile again. "I think you could."

. U .

Sarm River,
Kingdom of Delferahk

"Easy," Lieutenant Aplyn-Ahrmahk said quietly as the boat moved slowly towards the riverbank in the dim predawn gloom. The water gleamed faintly as the first blush of yellow and rose touched the eastern horizon, and a wyvern whistled querulously from somewhere ahead of them.

"Over the side and find the bottom, Braisyn!" he continued. "Can't be too deep this close in."

"Easy for you to say, if you don't mind me sayin' so, Sir," Braisyn, a tall young topman who'd been part of Mahlyk's boat crew for over two years, replied feelingly.

"Oh, nonsense! Pretend it's beer—I know *that'll* make you feel better about it!"

Several members of the boat crew chuckled, and Braisyn grinned at the lieutenant.

"Does that mean you're buying when we get back to the ship, Sir?" he asked, and Aplyn-Ahrmahk laughed.

"For *you?*" The lieutenant shook his head. "I'd rather buy water for fish at *whiskey* prices. It'd cost me less!"

Braisyn's grin got even bigger, and then he slipped over the side of the boat, hanging on to the gunwale while his feet felt for the bottom.

"Don't like my beer quite this cold, Sir," he informed Aplyn-Ahrmahk. "And it's a mite—*Ow!*" He yelped, hauling himself higher in the water and shaking his head. "Found the bottom, Sir. Little rocky for my taste!"

"Then next time, keep your *shoes* on, you stupid bugger!" Stywyrt Mahlyk suggested helpfully.

"Don't like squelching around in soggy shoes, Cox'in," Braisyn replied cheerfully.

"Just take us in, Mahlyk," Aplyn-Ahrmahk said in a tone of exaggerated patience. "Lieutenant Gowain wants us hidden again before sunrise."

"Aye, aye, Sir," Mahlyk said. "Give way all. And you, Braisyn—keep your damned delicate tootsies out of the rocks so you don't bruise 'em!"

"Keep that in mind I will, Cox'in," Braisyn assured him with another grin.

Aplyn-Ahrmahk shook his head, yet the banter between Mahlyk and the members of his boat's crew was the best possible (and welcome) proof that the men's morale was doing just fine.

They were just over a hundred and eighty miles up the Sarm River, two-thirds of the way across the sparsely populated Earldom of Charlz, and that was a long, twisty way from the salt water that was a Charisian sailor's natural element. True, rivers *were* full of water, but they were also full of rocks, bugs, and shallows where boats had to be dragged across sandbars or portaged around rapids. Fortunately, they hadn't encountered any waterfalls—yet, at least—but they'd done extraordinarily well to average three miles per hour during the fourteen or fifteen hours of darkness and twilight available to them each day. He was glad they weren't doing this later in the spring, when the days would be longer, but there were downsides to rowing and sailing your way up an unknown river in the dark . . . especially for the boat Lieutenant Gowain had decided should scout ahead for the others. They seemed to spend a lot of time hopping in and out of it when it went aground, for example.

Still, everyone seemed cheerful enough so far, and unusually (in Aplyn-Ahrmahk's experience) everything was actually going according to plan and more or less on schedule.

Which obviously means something's bound to go wrong sometime soon, he reflected, glancing over his shoulder at the silhouettes of the other, larger boats behind them.

No one had noticed them when they first started upriver. The sun still hadn't risen when they went rowing past the Sarmouth waterfront, and given the dozens of other boats from the squadron which had been headed *towards* the waterfront with fell intent, it probably wasn't too surprising no one had paid *them* any attention.

As an added touch, Admiral Yairley had ordered the boats repainted in mismatched shades of dirty white, gray, and black, and then scuffed the new paint in ways no Navy boatswain would ever have tolerated. They'd passed several small towns and isolated farms as they headed upstream from Sarmouth, and every time they'd shouted their warning that the Charisian heretics were attacking up the river. Sarmouth was on fire! Sarmouth Keep had been reduced to rubble! Run! Run for your lives, *the Charisians are coming!*

Frankly, Aplyn-Ahrmahk had thought that particular touch would be too much when Sir Dunkyn came up with it. In fact, it had worked beautifully. It had allowed them to row straight through the daylight hours for the first day and a half and get over a hundred miles upriver without anyone wondering what six ship's boats were doing that far north of the port.

After that, they'd restricted themselves to the night hours and progress had slowed, but even so—

His thoughts chopped off as something flashed blindingly in the shadows ahead of them. There was a solid, meaty thumping sound and Braisyn grunted explosively, then turned his head and looked up at Aplyn-Ahrmahk with an incredulous expression. He opened his mouth as if to speak, but all that came out was a gush of blood and then he disappeared into the river as his hands released the gunwale.

"Out of the boat!" Aplyn-Ahrmahk heard his own voice bark even before the topman lost his grip. "Cutlasses and tomahawks! No muskets! *Move, damn you!*"

He was talking to an empty boat by the time he got to "move," and he heard another bullet "thunk" into the wood as he snatched up his own sword baldric, then rolled over the side into the icy water. They'd gotten closer to the shore, and the water was less than armpit deep, but he crouched, keeping just his head above the surface as he hurriedly slung the baldric over his shoulder.

"Stywyrt, hang on to the painter—don't you *dare* lose this boat!" he hissed at the coxswain. "The rest of you—with me!"

More gunshots exploded out of the darkness ahead of them, and he swore silently as he heard screams from farther out on the river. He had no idea who was behind those shots or what in God's name *anyone* was doing out here on the riverbank in the middle of nowhere an hour before dawn. What mattered was that the boats on the open river were far more visible than the men hiding in the impenetrable shadows under the willows, alders, and conewood along the bank.

"Stay low!" he commanded, pitching his voice as low as possible. "Keep in the water as long as you can and follow me!"

Wading through ice-cold, neck-deep water would have been a slow, exhausting process even without the current. They couldn't possibly move as quickly as he wanted to, and with gunshots continuing to crack from the darkness, it seemed to be taking even longer. Then someone in one of the boats managed to begin returning fire, which added the delightful possibility of being shot in the back by their own people. The good news—for Aplyn-Ahrmahk and *his* people, at least—was that there seemed to be at least three times as many bullets headed out from the bank at the other boats and away from *them*.

He felt the river bottom underfoot smoothing as it shallowed, more sand mixed among the rocks and gravel, and breathed a silent prayer of thanks as the footing improved. He'd picked his destination more by instinct than by anything resembling deliberate thought, but that instinct had served him well, he realized. He and his boat crew were coming up on the river side of a huge, fallen conewood trunk that screened them completely from anyone on shore.

He stopped for a moment, looking around, making sure the rest of his people were with him. There were only ten of them, and he bared his teeth while the muskets continued to fire out of the darkness. He saw the blink-lizard glow of slow matches scattered under the trees, and his eyes narrowed.

"Matchlocks, boys," he told them in a low voice. "Nice little lights to help us find the bastards, and it sounds like they're loading loose powder. They're going to be *slow*. Get in close and rip their guts out, got it?"

A chorus of growls answered him, and he nodded sharply.

"And while you're at it, howl like you're all damned Marines!" he said with a savage grin. "Now—*after me, lads!*"

His boat crew exploded out of the water, vaulting over the conewood trunk with naked steel in hand. Aplyn-Ahrmahk carried his sword in his right hand and a wicked, spike-backed boarding tomahawk in his left, and the high, baying warcry of the Imperial Marines came with him. It sounded as if there were at least fifty of them, he thought wildly, and then a figure loomed up in front of him.

A cavalryman, he thought, taking in the dimly seen helmet. But armed with a matchlock. That meant a dragoon, not a lancer or a hussar, probably, and Delferahkan dragoons didn't have breastplates, and *that* meant—

Charisian cutlasses had chisel points, as well adapted to thrusting as to slashing, and Aplyn-Ahrmahk felt the jerking quiver of someone else's muscles transmitted up the blade as he drove a foot of steel into the man's chest. The dragoon shrieked, clutching at the impaling blade, but Aplyn-Ahrmahk kicked him away and went charging past him, screaming like a madman just like the rest of his boat crew.

The dragoons who'd been waiting in ambush reared up from their firing positions, turning towards the demons who'd suddenly materialized in their midst, and shocked astonishment turned almost instantly into panic. It was impossible for either side to know how many enemies it actually faced, and surprise—and fear—didn't lend themselves well to making accurate estimates.

Aplyn-Ahrmahk hacked down another opponent. A third man came at him desperately, matchlock clubbed, completely forgetting the sword at his own side in his panic. The lieutenant ducked under the musket, but the dragoon was on the wrong side for his cutlass. The tomahawk lashed out, coming up from below, driving its sharpened, spur-like hook up through the man's jaw and into the roof of his mouth. The Delferahkan's scream chopped off in a hot spray of blood, and Aplyn-Ahrmahk lost his grip on the suddenly slippery tomahawk as the body fell.

Another dragoon loomed up—this one an officer who'd remembered his sword. It was several inches longer than Aplyn-Ahrmahk's cutlass, but the lieutenant had served under Sir Dunkyn Yairley. That meant every midshipman (and ensign) spent a solid hour at sword drill every single day, and the instincts Sylvyst Raigly had helped pound into Aplyn-Ahrmahk's muscle memory took over. He twisted away from the Delferahkan's frantic, clumsy thrust and his left hand lashed out, capturing the wrist of the dragoon's sword arm. The Delferahkan was bigger, taller, and broader-shouldered than Aplyn-

Ahrmahk, but the lieutenant's wiry strength and the advantage of surprise were enough to shove the other man's arm almost straight up as they slammed together, chest-to-chest. At which point Aplyn-Ahrmahk's cutlass drove into his belly with all the elegance of a meat ax.

The officer went down with a bubbling scream, and suddenly there was no more fighting. Instead, there were only moans, sobs, and—in the distance—the thud and thunder of galloping hooves disappearing into the darkness.

"Anybody with a prisoner, hang on to him!" Aplyn-Ahrmahk barked, and then turned back to the river.

▼ ▼ ▼

"That's the best I can do, Sir," Lywys Taibor said. The healer's mate looked drawn and weary, and well he should. The ambush had cost the boat party heavily, with five dead and twice that many wounded. Now he stood up, rubbing his back, and looked glumly down at Lieutenant Fairghas Gowain, who lay unconscious on the rough pad made of captured Delferahkan saddle blankets.

"How soon is he going to wake up?" Aplyn-Ahrmahk asked. He felt as tired as the healer's mate looked, but he couldn't afford to admit it.

"Dunno, Sir," Taibor said honestly. "Head wound like that, he may *never* wake up. Or he could come to in the next ten minutes. If you want me to guess, probably not for a day or two. And I don't know if his wits're going to be wandering when he does come to or not."

"I see." Aplyn-Ahrmahk gazed down at the lieutenant for several moments, then patted the healer's mate on the shoulder. "Thank you," he said sincerely. "And not just for the prognosis. The lads are lucky they had you along."

"Did what I could, Sir," Taibor replied in an exhausted voice. "But I'd be lying if I said I was happy about 'em. Got at least four we need to get to a proper healer fast as we can, or we'll lose them sure as Shan-wei."

"Understood."

Aplyn-Ahrmahk patted him on the shoulder again, then walked to the riverbank and stared out across the cold, clear water.

Lieutenant Gowain, HMS *Victorious'* first lieutenant, was in command of the entire operation. But now he was unconscious indefinitely, and Lieutenant Bryndyn Mahgail, the senior Marine, was dead. Which left Lieutenant Aplyn-Ahrmahk—all sixteen years old of him—in command and the next best thing to two hundred miles from the nearest senior officer.

At least they'd taken three of the dragoons alive, and the Delferahkans had been so shocked by the abrupt reversal of their ambush that their tongues had wagged freely. It was also possible the sight of Stywyrt Mahlyk contemplatively sharpening a knife as he smiled evilly in their direction might have had some bearing on their loquaciousness, of course.

Aplyn-Ahrmahk had kept them separated from one another to deprive them of any opportunity to coordinate their stories, yet all three of them had told basically the same tale.

Word of the attack on Sarmouth had spread even faster than Admiral Yairley's plan had allowed for. Worse, some idiot upriver from the port had actually believed the boat expedition's warnings that the horrible Charisian heretics were sending an entire invasion fleet up the miserable Sarm River! Aplyn-Ahrmahk couldn't understand how anybody with the sense to pour piss out of a boot, to borrow one of Mahlyk's favorite phrases, could have credited *that* story, but according to all three of their prisoners, one of the Earl of Charlz' bailiffs had actually believed the Charisians were burning both banks of the river as they advanced deep into the heart of Delferahk. He'd sounded the alarm and sent out parties of dragoons to scout for the invaders.

The one good aspect of the entire comic-opera farce was that the dragoons in question were militiamen, not regulars. The bad news was that this particular lot of them had spotted the Charisian boats the previous evening and shadowed them from shore. Working against the current, the boats were actually slower than the horsemen, which was how the Delferahkans had been able to get into position for the ambush. And an unknown number of them had gotten away. By now, they had to be raising the alarm, and Aplyn-Ahrmahk doubted the number of "Charisian invaders" was going to decline when they started explaining how they'd gotten their asses kicked. Which meant every man the Delferahkans could scrape up would be hunting for his people by late afternoon.

So what did he do? If there were more dragoons available, it wouldn't be hard for them to repeat this bunch's tactics. And even if there weren't, the word had to be going out by semaphore (if it was available) and by runner and courier (if the semaphore wasn't available) even as he stood here. He knew how important this mission was, but if he continued, the odds were overwhelming that he'd simply lead his own pursuers straight to the people he was *supposed* to be rescuing. And that didn't even consider those badly wounded men Taibor had mentioned.

He looked out at the slowly flowing water and tried to think.

. VI .

**Sunthorn Mountains
and
Royal Palace,
City of Talkyra,
Kingdom of Delferahk**

Lazy wings of snow drifted almost silently on the wind sighing among the peaks of the Sunthorn Mountains ninety-odd miles northwest of the city of Talkyra. The temperature hovered at a brisk six degrees below zero on the old Fahrenheit scale, and the stars showing through the cloud rifts overhead were huge and bright . . . and icy. Technically, it was spring south of the equator, but at these elevations that meant very little, especially in the small, still hours of the morning just after Langhorne's Watch.

The single Imperial Charisian Guardsman sat in a lotus position atop an ice-crusted boulder. He'd been sitting there for three days now, ever since his conversation with Baron Coris, and there was snow drifted on his hair—and on his skin, for that matter—but he seemed unaware of it. Because he *was* unaware of it. He'd allowed his body temperature to drop to that of the air about him, and after he'd caught up on some of the SNARC reports he'd been unable to give proper attention to when they first came in and spent a day or so contemplating future possibilities, he'd actually put himself on standby and taken the equivalent of a lengthy nap. It wasn't as if anyone was going to be wandering around four thousand feet above the permanent snow line to stumble across him while he was "asleep," and it would probably make Cayleb happy.

And if it didn't, at least it would offer him a handy bit of ammunition to toss back at the emperor the next time Cayleb decided to lecture him about the need for "down time."

It wasn't often Merlin Athrawes had the opportunity to simply sit and think, which made him value those rare chances even more when one of them came along. For the most part, he was far too visible (aside from those "retreats to meditate" which had become a more frequent part of his life of late) for something like this. If "*Seijin* Merlin" dropped out of sight, even briefly, people started wondering where he was and what he was up to and, as a general rule, he tried very hard to avoid having people wonder about things like that.

In this instance, however, it was going to be necessary to explain how Captain Athrawes had gotten to the city of Talkyra. Or, to be more accurate, it was going to be necessary to allow time for him to have made the trip. Everyone knew *seijins* moved in mysterious ways and at speeds few other mortals could match, so the exact details of his travel arrangements could be glossed over. But it still took them at least *some* time to make a journey of over six thousand miles, which was why he'd left Tellesberg five five-days earlier.

He'd spent most of that time in Nimue's Cave, going over reports, discussing the events racing towards a violent confrontation in the Republic of Siddarmark with the rest of the inner circle, refining the propaganda Owl's remotes were distributing across all three continents, catching up on some reading, and working with Owl on a couple of private projects he'd been unable to give proper attention before.

In particular, he and the AI had the Class II VR unit almost up and running. Owl still didn't have the specifications he needed to build another PICA, and Merlin was no more enthusiastic than he had been about letting the computer take apart his own cybernetic housing to find out how it worked. But at least if he had to, he now had a refuge for his and Nimue's memories and personality. A Class II VR wasn't as big and capable as the massive virtual reality computers the Terran Federation had used as "homes" for electronic iterations of their top R&D, military analysts, and pure researchers. It simply didn't have the memory and the processing power to maintain two or three dozen fully aware personalities in detailed virtual environments indistinguishable (from the inside) from reality. A Class II could handle no more than three or, at the outside, four virtual personalities if it was going to give the VPs a fully developed world in which to live. There'd be plenty of room for Nimue/Merlin, though. If worse came to worst, he could set up housekeeping in there even if "Seijin Merlin" became totally inoperable, and at least one other possible use had occurred to him, although he still wasn't at all certain that one was going to work out.

In addition, he'd decided it was time to take advantage

of Commander Mahndrayn's work with his breech-loading rifle and the percussion caps he'd developed for it, and he and Owl had used some of the free time to re-design his own sidearms. Those were going to come as a nasty surprise to someone—possibly sometime soon—he thought, and they wouldn't violate a single clause of the Proscriptions. Father Paityr had already made that abundantly clear, although none of the Empire's gunsmiths had yet come up with the design he and Owl had built.

The truth was, though, that as much as he'd enjoyed having time to tinker and putter, he'd gotten bored. Unfortunately, he'd had no choice but to go on marking time for at least another five-day or two if he didn't want to raise all sorts of eyebrows about the truly miraculous, not simply mysterious, speed with which *Seijin* Merlin could cover distances of six or seven thousand miles. That was why he'd landed here in the mountains after Zhevons' chat with Coris, sent the recon skimmer back to Owl, ordered his nannies to regrow *Seijin* Merlin's hair, and then gone to standby mode for fifty minutes of every hour.

Of course, even with that, if anyone ever started adding up times, they were bound to come to the conclusion that *seijins* must know some magic spell to give them command of wind and wave.

In theory, he'd sailed from the Earldom of West Harding, the Island of Charis' westernmost headland, rather than Tellesberg, which had at least reduced the length of his supposed voyage to the Desnairian Empire's Crown Lands from over ten thousand miles to "only" fifty-seven hundred. He'd actually turned up in West Harding, publically (and noisily) "borrowed" a forty-foot single-masted schooner, and put to sea in order to make sure everyone "knew" how he'd gotten where he was going in the fullness of time.

That schooner, unfortunately, was now on the bottom of the Parker Sea. He regretted that. It had been a sweet little craft, and Nimue had always loved single-handing her sloop back on Old Terra whenever she'd had the chance. In fact, he was increasingly irked with himself for having abandoned the schooner as quickly as he had. With so much time to kill, he might as well have spent some of it doing something he'd always enjoyed so much before.

You need a vacation, he told himself. *Well, to be fair, I guess you needed a vacation. You'd really have to call the last month or so something like a vacation, after all, but you're just too damned contrary to actually take time off, aren't you? Always have to be doing something. Everything depends on you.* He snorted mentally. *You need Sharley or Cayleb closer to hand to kick you in the butt when you get too full of your own importance.*

It was amazing how comforting it was to be able to think that. The loss of so many colleagues left a special aching wound at the center of the theoretically immortal *"seijin's"* heart, yet the inner circle had survived, even continued to grow. Best of all, *he* wasn't indispensable any longer, and that was a greater relief than he'd ever imagined it might be. If something happened to him, the others would still have access to Owl and the technology hidden away in Nimue's Cave. Not that he planned on anything happening to him, of course. It was just—

"Excuse me, Lieutenant Commander Alban."

Merlin twitched internally, although his physical body never moved, as Owl's voice invaded his thoughts.

"Yes?"

"The sensor net deployed to cover Talkyra has reported a situation which programming parameters require me to call to your attention."

"What sort of situation? No, scratch that. I assume you have the raw take from the sensors for me, yes?"

"Affirmative, Lieutenant Commander Alban."

"Then I suppose you'd better show it to me."

▼ ▼ ▼

"Tobys."

Tobys Raimair looked up from the dagger edge he'd been carefully honing and cocked an eyebrow at the man who'd just poked his head into his spartan little bedchamber. Corporal Zhak Mahrys was one of his small guard force's noncoms. Normally a calm, almost phlegmatic sort, he looked more than a little anxious at the moment.

"What is it, Zhakky?"

"There's something going on," Mahrys said. "You know Zhake Tailyr?"

"Sure." Raimair nodded; Tailyr was one of King Zhames' guardsmen. He was also a drinking buddy of Mahrys', and Raimair and Earl Coris had encouraged the corporal to pursue the friendship. "What about him?"

"He says there's been a lot of going back and forth between Colonel Sahndahl's office and Father Gaisbyrt's office since lunchtime. A *lot*, Tobys."

Raimair's face stiffened. Father Gaisbyrt Vandaik was a Schuelerite upper-priest attached to Bishop Mytchail's office in Talkyra.

"What kind of back and forth?" Raimair asked.

"Dunno. He said it was Brother Bahldwyn mostly, though . . . and Vandaik came back to the castle with him about an hour ago."

Better and better, Raimair thought. Bahldwyn Gaimlyn was attached to the king's household—technically as a "secretary," although there was precious little evidence King Zhames had requested his services.

"Did Tailyr have any idea what it was about?" he asked.

"If he did, he wasn't telling me." Mahrys looked even more concerned. "He's somebody to hoist a few beers with, Tobys, not my blood brother. He may know—or suspect—a lot he's not telling me. On the other hand, at least he dropped some warning on me."

Raimair nodded, although he had to wonder if Tailyr's decision to "warn" Mahrys had really been his own. Raimair could think of a couple of scenarios in which a particularly devious Schuelerite—and they were *all* devious, sneaky, underhanded bastards—might arrange to have a "warning" passed in order to manipulate someone he suspected into incriminating himself.

"Thanks, Zhakky," he said now, standing and sliding the dagger into its belt sheath. "Pass the word to the rest of the lads. No one makes any moves, no one does anything to suggest we're worried, but check your equipment and be sure you keep it handy. I want them ready to move fast and hard if we have to. Got it?"

"Got it." Mahrys nodded and disappeared, and Raimair walked down a short hallway, up a half-flight of stairs, and knocked on another door.

"Yes?" a voice responded.

"Could I have a minute of your time, My Lord?"

▼ ▼ ▼

"I don't know, Irys," Phylyp Ahzgood said, looking out the turret window into the darkness. "*I* can't think of any good reason for Vandaik to be talking to Colonel Sahndahl. Or not any reason that would be good for *us,* anyway."

"Can we go ahead and run now?" Irys asked, watching his back, seeing the tension in his shoulders.

"Maybe. But we weren't *supposed* to run for another two days, and we don't even know for sure what's happening. Making a break for it now might be the worst thing we could do!" The frustration in his voice was evident, and he turned to her with a sour expression. "I'm not used to having things like this sneak up on me."

"I know you're not," Irys said with a lopsided smile. "And I count on it not happening. But you're only human, Phylyp, and the truth is—"

"And the truth is," a much deeper voice neither of them had ever heard before said calmly, "that everyone makes mistakes occasionally. Even me."

Irys and Coris whipped back around to the window just as a tall man with blue eyes, fierce mustachios, and a dagger beard swung lightly over the windowsill and into the room. The fact that they were three stories up and that the wall fell sheer from the window would have made that astonishing enough, but to make bad worse, the stranger wore the livery of the Charisian Imperial

Guard in the middle of the capital of the Kingdom of Delferahk.

The earl and the princess gaped at the apparition, and he bowed gracefully.

"Please excuse my unceremonious arrival," he said, straightening from the bow and stroking his mustache. "Captain Merlin Athrawes, at your service."

"But . . . but how—?"

The imperturbability of even a Phylyp Ahzgood had its limits, and the Earl of Coris couldn't seem to get the question finished. He only stared at the newcomer, and Merlin chuckled. Irys Daykyn was made of sterner stuff, though.

"Captain Athrawes," she acknowledged, bending her head in a gracious nod. "I won't say the Empire of Charis is especially near and dear to my heart, but at this moment, I'm *most* happy to see *you*."

"Thank you, Your Highness." He bowed more deeply. "And please accept Their Majesties' greetings. They look forward to seeing you safely out of Delferahk."

"And *into* Tellesberg, of course," she riposted in a slightly barbed tone.

"Well, of course, Your Highness, but I'm trying not to be tacky," Merlin murmured with a slight smile, and Irys' lips quivered for just a moment. Then she cleared her throat.

"It would appear you've arrived at an opportune moment, *Seijin* Merlin," she said then. "Of course, we don't know *why* it's an opportune moment or how you've managed to arrive at it, now do we?"

"In answer to the second half of your question, Your Highness, everyone insists on calling me a *seijin*, so it's only reasonable I should act like one on occasion, including arriving at opportune moments. If I recall my fairy tales correctly, *Seijin* Kody did a *lot* of that sort of thing." He smiled more broadly, but then his expression sobered. "And in answer to the question you and Earl Coris were discussing when I arrived—I hope you don't mind that I spent a moment or two listening outside your window before I intruded—it turns out Master Seablanket wasn't the only spy planted on you by the Inquisition, after all."

"He wasn't?" Coris came back to life, his eyes narrowing. He sounded more than a little affronted by Merlin's explanation, and Merlin smiled at him.

"It's not really your fault, My Lord," he said. "As you may know from your discussion with my friend Ahbraim, we *seijins* have our own means of gathering intelligence. That's how I discovered Bishop Mytchail had decided to insert one of his own agents into King Zhames' household to keep an eye on you. He wasn't instructed to, and his agent reports only to him, not to Rayno or Clyntahn, but I'm afraid he's come to the conclusion that you're ... well, up to something. He doesn't know *what,* but he's decided it's probably something you shouldn't be doing. So he's sent Father Gaisbyrt to order Colonel Sahndahl to take your own armsmen into custody and replace them with members of King Zhames' Guard ... under Father Gaisbyrt's direct command. Just for your own safety, of course."

"And the King?" Irys asked, gazing at Merlin intently. "Is he party to all this?"

"No, and so far as I'm aware, neither is Baron Lakeland or Sir Klymynt," Merlin told her. "On the other hand, none of them will attempt to overrule Bishop Mytchail, Your Highness. And, to be honest, you can't really blame them, can you?"

"My *heart* certainly can, *Seijin* Merlin!" she said tartly, but then she shook her head. "My head, unfortunately, can't. Not knowing what that butcher Clyntahn would do to anyone who helped us slip out of his clutches."

"Slip out of his clutches *alive,* Your Highness," Merlin corrected gently.

"Correction accepted, *Seijin* Merlin."

"How much time do we have before Sahndahl moves?" Coris demanded.

"None," Merlin replied calmly. "There are forty Royal

Guardsmen on their way right now, along with half a dozen inquisitors. And their instructions are to use whatever force is necessary to make sure none of you go anywhere."

"*Forty!*" Coris exclaimed in dismay.

"All we have to do is get out of the castle, reach the stable where you've had those horses waiting for a week, and then ride for the rendezvous," Merlin replied with a shrug, as if he were discussing a simple picnic outing.

"Past *forty* Royal Guardsmen?"

"And the inquisitors, My Lord," Merlin reminded him. The earl glared at him, and the *seijin* shrugged. "Sergeant Raimair has his people ready, My Lord," he pointed out, "and they're all good, solid men. They'll take care of twenty or twenty-five of Zhames' armsmen if they have to, I'm sure."

"And the *other* twenty armsmen and the half-dozen inquisitors?" Coris inquired more than a bit acidly.

"Ah, them." Merlin shrugged again. "Well, for *them*, My Lord, you have me."

. UII .

Royal Palace,
City of Talkyra,
Kingdom of Delferahk

"Father, are you *sure* this is something we want to do?" Colonel Fraimahn Sahndahl asked.

"Are you questioning the Inquisition, my son?" Father Gaisbyrt Vandaik asked in a gentle, silky tone.

"Never, Father," Sahndahl replied as calmly as he could. "I simply don't have any orders from His Majesty, and it would only take an hour or so to send a messenger after him."

"*My* orders are from Bishop Mytchail," Vandaik

pointed out. "And were His Majesty here, I'm sure he would remind you secular forces are required to assist Mother Church's Intendant when he calls upon them."

Sahndahl did his best not to glare at the smiling Schuelerite. He'd met priests like Vandaik before, more often than he might have wished, and he knew exactly how Vandaik's report to his own superiors would be written if Sahndahl didn't do exactly what he wanted. Yet the colonel's oaths hadn't been sworn to the Inquisition; they'd been sworn to King Zhames of Delferahk, and he wasn't at all certain the king would have approved of the notion of seizing his own relatives and handing them over to the Inquisition "for their own safety."

Especially when he'd been ordered to do the seizing by force. And extra especially when Vandaik had told him—orally—that this mission was important enough to risk endangering Princess Irys' or Prince Daivyn's lives . . . and declined to include that in his written instructions.

The colonel was a simple soldier, disinterested in politics, and a loyal son of Mother Church, but he wasn't stupid, and he'd served as the second in command of King Zhames' Guard for almost seven years. Whether he'd wanted to or not, he'd developed political feelers over those years, and every one of them quivered with warning now. The waters around him had suddenly become deep and murky, and he found himself much more seriously considering a ridiculous suspicion which had crossed his mind some time ago when he pondered who might have assassinated Prince Hektor if it *hadn't* been Cayleb Ahrmahk.

"Of course I realize His Majesty's Guard is obligated to assist Mother Church in time of need, Father," he said with all the dignity he could summon up. "I'm sure you can understand that as King Zhames' man, I'd really prefer to get his instructions, as well, however."

"If there were time for that, I would have no objections at all," Vandaik assured him. "Unfortunately, I don't believe there *is* time. And in that regard, Colonel, I'm afraid I have to point out that we're *wasting* time discussing this."

He glanced pointedly out Sahndahl's office window at the tower in which the Corisandian exiles were housed, and the colonel's jaw tightened. There were limits to what he could ignore, however, and he gave the Inquisitor a jerky nod.

"Point taken, Father," he said, then raised his voice. "Captain Mahgail!"

"Sir?" a tall but stocky officer replied, opening the office door and stepping through it.

"Get them ready, Byrt," Sahndahl said.

"Yes, Sir!"

Mahgail saluted and disappeared, and Sahndahl heard him giving orders in a loud, clear voice. Mahgail was a good man, but he was a bit too prone (in Sahndahl's opinion) to take a churchman's word at face value. If the Inquisition said Princess Irys and Prince Daivyn were in danger from their own retainers, then Mahgail was perfectly prepared to kill as many of those retainers as necessary to "rescue them." He obviously wasn't going to lose one bit of sleep over his orders, either . . . unlike Sahndahl. The colonel had recognized the kind of man Tobys Raimair was the moment he laid eyes on him, and he knew that kind of man would die in defense of his prince or princess. The thought that he might somehow *threaten* them was ludicrous.

But no one was interested in Fraihman Sahndahl's opinion . . . except, perhaps, for his liege lord, who he wasn't going to be allowed to ask about it.

I'm sorry, Your Majesty, he thought now, rising heavily and reaching for his own swordbelt. *I knew I should've drowned that little weasel Brother Bahldwyn months ago when I realized why Zhessop planted him on you. Secretary—ha!*

Unfortunately, he hadn't, and he buckled the swordbelt, settled it in place, and strode slowly and deliberately out of his office.

▼ ▼ ▼

"The good news is that over half the regular Palace Guard detachment is off with the King and Queen tonight," Tobys Raimair said to the tall, blue-eyed Charisian guardsman.

Right offhand, Raimair couldn't think of anything he'd ever done that felt . . . stranger than taking orders from a Charisian when it was the Charisian Empire which had conquered his own homeland. And the man had to be crazy as a Harchong serf drunk on that incredibly vile rice-based "whiskey" they distilled to go wandering around the middle of the Kingdom of Delferahk in Charisian livery. He *had* heard about the Ferayd Massacre and why most Delferahkans believed it had happened, hadn't he?

On the other hand, "*Seijin* Merlin" was obviously accustomed to being obeyed. And crazy or not, something about him—something that spoke to Raimair's well-honed noncom's instincts—made Raimair grateful he was here.

Hell, some of the best combat officers I've ever known were bug-ass crazy, come to that, he reflected. *Not necessarily the safest ones to serve under, maybe, but the kind who always seemed to get the job done somehow. And that's what it's all about tonight, isn't it? The job.*

He glanced over his shoulder at the tall, slender young woman with her arm around her brother's shoulders, her own expression calm and confident because that was what the boy needed her to be. Then he looked back at the Charisian Imperial Guardsman and saw those blue eyes watching him.

"Don't worry, Sergeant," Merlin said quietly, voice pitched for only Raimair's ears, and his expression was far more sober than it had been. "I know it's . . . complicated, but I give you my word. You can't possibly want those two to reach safety more than I do, and between us, that's exactly where we're going to get them."

"If you say so, Captain."

"I do say so," Merlin replied, resting one hand lightly on the sergeant's shoulder for a moment. "And you remind me of another sergeant I met a couple of years ago—a fellow by the name of Seahamper. I think you'll like him when you meet him. And do me a favor."

"Favor?" Raimair asked just a bit suspiciously.

"Stay alive and in one piece," Merlin said very seriously. "Prince Daivyn and Princess Irys need you. Unless I'm mistaken, *she* needs you more than he does at the moment, as a matter of fact, and I think she's already lost enough people she needed. Don't you?"

Raimair stared at him for a moment, then nodded slowly, his expression one of wonderment.

"Aye," he said after a moment. "Aye, that she has."

"Then let's not make any more holes in her life." The hand on Raimair's shoulder tightened, and then the reckless, confident grin reappeared under the waxed mustachios. "Now, you were saying about the opposition?"

"So I was, Sir." Raimair gave himself another shake. "There's no more than half the usual detachment here tonight. The Colonel could call up reinforcements from the local militia, and there's a full regiment of militia dragoons in Talkyra. Take a while to get them rousted out of bed and pulled away from their dinners, though. And, to be honest, I don't see any reason he'd be thinking he needed 'em, come to that." The sergeant shrugged. "These are good lads I've got here, but there's only a dozen of 'em, when all's said. Even with only half the detachment, he's four times that many."

"Understood." Merlin's expression turned serious again. "You do realize that the instant they see me, you're all going to be guilty of treason and consorting with heretics in both Mother Church and King Zhames' eyes?"

"Thought had crossed my mind," Raimair replied with sour irony. "Don't suppose I could convince you to change out of that armor of yours?"

"Sergeant, it's not going to make one bit of difference in the long run." Merlin chuckled. "The moment Grand

Inquisitor Zhaspahr discovers Irys and Daivyn have slipped through his fingers alive, we're all dead men if he ever gets his hands on us. That being the case, I prefer to fight in my own colors."

"And if seeing you in them causes Colonel Sahndahl's lads to come at us harder, my own lads are going to find any bridges burned behind them," Raimair said.

"A point which *had* occurred to me," Merlin acknowledged. "Of course, that's another way of saying it's going to get them focused on staying alive and keep them there, isn't it?"

"Sounds better that way, anyhow," Raimair said, then laughed. "And truth to tell, we've burned our bridges already."

"That's fortunate," Merlin told him, raising his head and cocking it to one side, "because unless I'm mistaken, Colonel Sahndahl's on his way right now."

▼ ▼ ▼

Fraihman Sahndahl walked across the paved courtyard with a grim, determined stride. Three squads of Guardsmen followed him, and he sensed the men's confusion. They had no idea why they'd just been ordered to arrest—and, if necessary, kill—men they'd been drinking beer with only that afternoon. The presence of half a dozen Schuelerites, including Bahldwyn Gaimlyn, who'd been one of King Zhames' secretaries for almost a year, discouraged any speculation on their part, however. And with those damned inquisitors watching, there was no doubt in Sahndahl's mind his men would do whatever they were ordered to do.

God, I hope Raimair and Coris are smart enough to surrender for the kids' sake, he thought. Yet even as he told himself that, another thought ran deeper down, counter pointing it. Given what Zhaspahr Clyntahn was capable of, if he were one of the men in that tower and he believed the Inquisition had come for *him,* they'd take his weapons only out of his cold dead hands . . . and the last thing he'd do before he died was cut both of Prince

Hektor's children's throats to keep *them* out of the Inquisition's hands, as well.

Stop that! he told himself sternly. *It's not doing a bit of good and it's not going to change a thing.*

"Wait here," he told Mahgail, and continued across the courtyard to the steep flight of steps leading up to the tower's open door.

He climbed the steps heavily. A pair of lanterns burned at its top, one on either side of the massively timbered door set deep into the tower's ancient stonework, and he was acutely aware of the archer's slits in the wall above him. He allowed no sign of that awareness to cross his expression, however, as Rahskho Mullygyn—who would have been Sergeant Mullygyn, if Tobys Raimair had dared to be open about the nature of the "footmen" and "servants" he'd assembled around Irys and Daivyn Daykyn—met him in the doorway.

"Evening, Colonel," Mullygyn said calmly, glancing past him at the block of Guardsmen in the courtyard. "Can I help you, Sir?"

"I need to speak to Earl Coris, Rahskho," Sahndahl said.

" 'Fraid he's already turned in for the evening, Sir." Mullygyn smiled slightly. "Said something about not feeling too well."

"Then I'm afraid you're going to have to go and get him up," Sahndahl said flatly, and looked Mullygyn straight in the eye. "It's official, Rahskho, and I'm under orders. Let's not make this any messier than it has to be."

"Messy, Sir?" Mullygyn had many virtues; thespian talent was not among them, and his lack of surprise was all the confirmation Sahndahl needed that Tobys and his men had at least sensed what was coming. That was going to make things ugly, given their position inside the tower's thick walls. Nonetheless. . . .

"Just go get him, Rahskho," the colonel said in that same flat voice. "And you might ask Tobys to step out here, too. I need to talk to both of them."

"See what I can do, Sir," Mullygyn replied, and stepped back inside the tower.

Sahndahl was tempted to follow him, but he suppressed the temptation easily. He doubted Mullygyn had been the only occupant of the guardroom just inside the doorway, and he wondered if it might not have been wiser to just go ahead and rush the place without warning anyone inside he was coming.

No, you were right the first time, he told himself. *Too good a chance the girl or the boy'd get killed in the confusion, even if you got inside on the first rush. And if they really have figured out you're coming, trying to "rush" a tower like this would be a good way to get half your men killed at the outset. So—*

His thoughts broke off in an abrupt mental hiccup as someone else stepped out of the tower door. Not Mullygyn, and sure as hell not Earl Coris! The man in front of him was taller than either of them—a good two or three inches taller even than Captain Mahgail—with sapphire eyes, black hair, and a scarred cheek. Sahndahl had never seen him before in his life, which would have been cause enough for surprise in itself, but finding himself face-to-face with someone in the livery of the Charisian Imperial Guard hit him like a punch in the belly.

"I'm afraid Earl Coris and Sergeant Raimair are . . . occupied," the impossible stranger said. "Perhaps I might be of assistance, Colonel?"

"Who . . . who—?" Sahndahl realized he sounded entirely too much like a stupefied owl, and he gave himself a sharp, tooth-rattling jerk.

"Captain Merlin Athrawes, Charisian Imperial Guard, at your service." The man bowed, apparently blissfully unaware of the insanity of what he'd just said. "And I'm afraid, Colonel, that Prince Daivyn and Princess Irys have requested asylum in Tellesberg. It seems"—those blue eyes looked past the colonel and into the dumbstruck brown eyes of Father Gaisbyrt—"Vicar Zhaspahr has ordered that they be killed, much as he did their father, and they'd prefer to avoid that outcome. Undutiful of them, I know, but"—his smile could have frozen Lake Erdan in mid-summer—"I'm sure you can understand their viewpoint."

"That's . . . ridiculous," Sahndahl managed, feeling his hand creep to the sword at his side.

"Oh, come now, Colonel!" Athrawes chided gently. "You know I'm telling you the truth. Clyntahn's decided murdering Daivyn may destabilize Corisande again. Especially if he can blame it on Charis . . . again."

Those blue eyes were even colder than his smile, a fragment of Sahndahl's mind observed.

"Lies! *Lies!*" Vandaik shouted suddenly from behind Sahndahl. "This man is an acknowledged heretic and blasphemer—an enemy of God Himself! How can you even *consider* the possibility he might be telling the truth?!"

"Ah, now there's the problem, isn't it, Father Gaisbyrt?" Athrawes asked, and the Schuelerite stiffened at the revelation that the Charisian knew his name. "And a bit of a problem for Father Zhames and Father Arthyr and Brother Bahldwyn and Brother Zhilbyrt, too, isn't it?" the heretic continued, naming each of the inquisitors in turn. "Because you know they *are* considering it, don't you, Father? Thanks to that butcher in Zion you serve, *everyone's* considering it, aren't they, *Father?*"

"*Lies!*" Vandaik screamed. "Yield now, heretic, or die!"

"Let me see." Athrawes tilted his head to one side, eyes contemptuous. "Surrender, and be tortured to death later for Clyntahn's amusement, or die now, seeing how many of his inquisitors—and their flunkies I'm afraid, Colonel," he added, eyes flitting back to Sahndahl, "I can kill first. Let me see, let me see. Which one should I choose . . . ?"

"Heretic *bastard!*" Vandaik screamed. "Do your duty, Sahndahl! *Seize him!* Seize him and all the others, as well, or answer to Mother Church!"

"I—" Sahndahl half drew his sword, then froze as Athrawes waved an index finger at him like a chiding tutor.

The Charisian Guardsman's sheer force of will seemed to freeze all of Sahndahl's men. It certainly froze the colonel himself!

"If you try to execute that order, or to seize Prince Daivyn or Princess Irys, or to prevent them in any way from leaving this castle of their own free will, Colonel, a lot of people are going to die." There was no humor at all in Athrawes' voice. "Most of them will be yours." He looked very levelly into Sahndahl's eyes. "I have no desire to kill any man simply because he has the misfortune to serve a corrupt and evil master, but the choice is yours. Stand aside, or try to take us. Live or die, Colonel. Make the choice."

▼ ▼ ▼

"He's *insane!*" Irys Daykyn whispered, watching from the third-floor window, listening to the conversation with Earl Coris' arm around her shoulders. "My God, he's out of his mind!"

"Maybe he is," the earl replied, shaking his head, but there was something very like admiration in his tone. "Maybe he is, but, *Langhorne*, it feels good to hear someone take on one of those sanctimonious pricks in public!"

Irys' head turned. She looked up at Coris' profile, and her eyes widened as she saw the fierce, triumphant grin on her guardian's face.

"You *like* him!" she said almost accusingly.

"Like him?" Coris cocked his head consideringly. "Maybe. I don't know about that, Irys, but by God you've got to admire his *style!*"

▼ ▼ ▼

"That's bold talk for one man alone standing in front of fifty," Sahndahl replied at last.

"There're good men enough standing behind me," Athrawes said evenly, "and *you're* standing in *front* of me. If you want to survive this night, Colonel, be somewhere else. Now."

Sahndahl stared at him, ice crawling through his veins as he digested the total certitude in the Charisian's voice and remembered all the fantastic tales about "*Seijin* Merlin." But the colonel was a veteran. He recognized tall tales and impossible legends when he heard them. And he was no coward. It was entirely possible Athrawes might kill *him*, especially at such a short range, but not even a *seijin* could defeat forty-five Royal Guardsmen plus the inquisitors with them.

And better to die cleanly fighting someone like Athrawes than answer to the Inquisition if the Prince or the Princess get away, a small, still voice said deep at his core.

"I thank you for the warning, Captain Athrawes," he heard his voice say, "but I think not." He drew a deep breath.

"Take them!"

▼ ▼ ▼

Sahndahl's sword came out of its sheath.

That, unfortunately, was the first—and last—thing that happened the way he'd planned, because Merlin Athrawes' hands moved.

Phylyp Ahzgood, watching from the window above the tower door, hissed in disbelief. No one could move that quickly—no one! One instant the *seijin*'s hands were at his side, his shoulders relaxed, his eyes locked with Colonel Sahndahl's. The next instant there was a pistol in each hand, as if they'd magically materialized there and not been drawn from the holsters at his side.

And then they began to fire.

It was hopeless, of course. One man, with only two pistols, against fifty? Even if he was a crack shot who never missed, the most he could hope for would be to fell four of them before the others charged up the stairs and swarmed him under. But Merlin Athrawes seemed unaware of that, and the blinding brilliance of a muzzle flash ripped holes in Coris' vision.

The *seijin* fired from the hip with both hands, and the measured "CRACK," "CRACK," "CRACK" of his fire pounded the ear like a hammer. Yet even as he fired, Coris realized something was wrong. There were no flashes from the pistols' pans. No up-flash of igniting primer, no sparks as chipped flint struck the frizzen. There were only the long, stabbing flashes from the muzzles, more brilliant than ever against the night's darkness as they spewed flame, smoke, and death.

And they went right *on* spewing all three of those things.

Impossible! Coris thought as the *seijin* fired his fifth shot. Then his sixth. His seventh! *His eighth!*

Sahndahl had been the first to fall. He sat at the top of the stairs, both hands pressing at the blood-gushing wound in his abdomen, head shaking in either disbelief or denial while his eyes glazed their way into death. Captain Mahgail screamed in rage as his commander fell and charged the stairs, sword in hand. Behind him, forty-five more men hurled themselves towards the single figure in the blackened armor standing at their head.

But each time Merlin Athrawes squeezed one of those triggers, another man went down—screaming, unconscious, or dead—*and he went right on firing.*

Courage that might have brushed aside his fearsome reputation was no match for the drumbeat of death and destruction thundering and flashing from his hands. The cloud of gunsmoke was so dense they could scarcely even see him through it, but *still* he fired, each muzzle blast illuminating the cloud of smoke like Langhorne's Rakurai, and the heavy bullets plowed through them like the sword of Chihiro himself. As their formation tightened to charge up the steps, some of those bullets tore through two or even three bodies, and King Zhames' Guardsmen broke.

They fell back, stampeding into the darkness, and the Inquisitors who'd launched them gaped at the demonic apparition at the top of the stairs.

Merlin Athrawes had downed thirteen Delferahkan guardsmen with ten shots, and he raised his right hand deliberately.

"My regards to Vicar Zhaspahr, Father!" he called, even his deep voice sounding somehow high-pitched and frail after the thunder of so much gunfire. "He'll be along shortly!" he added, and an eleventh thunderbolt leapt from the pistol. Gaisbyrt Vandaik was almost fifty yards from the tower stairs, but the heavy, soft lead bullet struck him squarely in the center of his chest and punched cleanly through his heart.

"And I haven't forgotten *you*, Brother!" the *seijin* called, and Bahldwyn Gaimlyn squealed in sudden terror before the pistol in Merlin's left hand ended his squeal forever.

. VIII .

Royal Palace, City of Talkyra, and Sarman Mountains, Kingdom of Delferahk

Merlin stood on the front steps, shrouded in a cloud of powder smoke, slowly fraying on the breeze. He surveyed the body-littered courtyard with ice-cold blue eyes and holstered his left-hand pistol, then heard a sound behind him.

Human ears battered by that much gunfire would have been unable to hear it, but Merlin Athrawes' ears weren't human. He turned towards the soft noise and found himself facing Tobys Raimair. The ex-sergeant's sword was drawn, his face tight, and his eyes were hard.

"I'm thinking all those tales about you being a demon or a wizard aren't so far-fetched after all!" the sergeant grated.

"I can see where that might occur to you," Merlin replied calmly. "On the other hand, there's nothing at all demonic or magic about my pistols, Tobys."

"Oh, aye, I can *see* that!" Raimair said caustically. "Why, just *anyone* could shoot for an hour or two out of one wee little gun like that!"

"No, not for an hour," Merlin corrected in that same calm voice. "Just six shots, Tobys. Only six."

"Six?!" Raimair glared at him. "Why not ten? Langhorne, why not *thirty?!*"

"Because they wouldn't fit into the cylinder," Merlin told him, and Raimair looked down as he heard a metallic clicking sound. His sword never wavered, but his eyes widened as he realized the *seijin*'s pistols weren't like any other firearm he'd ever heard of. For one thing, they seemed to be made entirely out of steel, except for the wooden handgrips. For another, some sort of heavy cylinder had just come out of the center of the thing to rest in the palm of the *seijin*'s left hand. It left a queer, squared-off gap or opening in the middle of the rest of the weapon, and Merlin held it up where he could see it.

"It's actually a simple concept," he said. "A friend of mine—I call him Owl—made it for me. He calls it a 'revolver,' because the central cylinder here"—he waved his left hand gently—"*revolves* when you cock the hammer. If you look, you'll see it has six holes drilled in it. Each of those is big enough to hold one charge of powder and one bullet. The bullets are a bit smaller than the ones most of the Guard's pistols fire, but to make up for it, the charge is about a fourth again as large, so they hit a lot harder. And it doesn't need a priming pan because a very clever Charisian officer—another friend of mine, named Mahndrayn—invented something called a 'percussion cap' that flashes over when you hit it with a hammer. If you look here," he reversed the cylinder, showing Raimair the back end, which was solid but had six raised, odd-looking bumps of some sort, "you'll see where the caps fit over the nipples here so the hammer can strike them as they rotate and each shot lines up with the barrel." He shrugged. "It's just a way to carry more firepower, Tobys, and I promise you it violates none of God's laws.

When we get to Tellesberg, you can discuss it directly with Father Paityr, our Intendant, if you like."

Raimair held out his free hand, and Merlin smiled slightly as he dropped the cylinder into it. The sergeant turned it, held it up to one of the door lanterns in order to see it better, then raised it to his nose and sniffed the scent of burnt gunpowder. He lowered it again, looking down at it for several seconds, then drew a deep breath, lowered his sword, and handed it back over.

"I'm sure you know your own business best, *Seijin*," he said, "but you might want to *warn* people before you do things like that. Could save yourself a peck of trouble . . . not to mention a sword in the ribs, now I think about it."

"Tobys, you're a good man," Merlin told him, "and if you can get a sword into my ribs, I'll figure I must have deserved it."

Raimair looked at him suspiciously, obviously trying to figure out if he'd just been complimented or insulted, and Merlin smiled. Then he looked past the sergeant as Earl Coris appeared behind Raimair.

"That was certainly impressive," the earl said just a little tartly. "Was it really necessary, though, *Seijin* Merlin? Once they stop running, they'll spread the tale of your 'demon weapons' all over the Kingdom! If they might've had any trouble getting together the manpower to chase us before, they certainly won't now—especially with two Inquisitors dead, to boot!"

"Finding the manpower was never going to be a problem, My Lord," Merlin replied calmly, reaching into his belt pouch and extracting a cylinder identical to the one in Raimair's hand, except that this one was still loaded and capped. He slipped it into the revolver frame and slid the central locking pin back into place to hold it. Then he holstered the reloaded weapon, drew its twin from the other holster, and replaced its cylinder, as well.

"The Inquisition can—and will—rouse the entire countryside," he continued as he worked. "Whether or not I had any 'demon weapons' won't matter a solitary damn as far as that's concerned! But if you'll notice, the entire Royal Guard has temporarily decamped. I figure they'll be back shortly—whatever else they may be, they aren't cowards, and as soon as they get over the shock, they'll come back. They'll be cautious, but they'll come. In the meantime, however, we can get a bit of a head start. And it's occurred to me that the best horses in the entire Grand Duchy of Talkyra are right here in King Zhames' stables. I realize you have some nice ones waiting for you at that livery stable outside town, but I doubt they're the equal of the ones in the *royal* stables. Not only that, but depriving our pursuers of horses that good strikes me as an excellent idea, as well. And while I'm thinking about things that might discourage or hamper pursuit, I think I'll just take the opportunity while you and Tobys here go acquire our transportation to leave a few little . . . incendiary calling cards here and there around the castle. Places like, oh, the magazine, for example."

He smiled beatifically and looked at Raimair.

"Do try to get them moving, Tobys," he said. "Those Guardsmen may come back sooner than I thought, and I'd just as soon be on our way."

He swept the stunned-looking earl a bow and headed down the stairs.

▼ ▼ ▼

Irys Daykyn managed not to groan as she swung down out of the saddle. The sun was working its way towards evening overhead, although that was difficult to tell at the moment. The mature growth forest they were passing through had been only thinly invaded by imported terrestrial species, and even the towering Safeholdian* pines seemed small and dwarfed under the shadows of the titan oaks. Most of those titan oaks had probably been growing here since the Day of Creation itself, she thought. Some of them were as much as fifteen feet in diameter at the base, and each individual tree would probably have produced enough wood to build an entire war galleon. Even this early in the spring, they wove a solid, green canopy overhead, and the dense shade of their branches had almost completely choked out any underbrush. It was already dim, bordering on outright dark, under that twiggy roof, but at least the absence of undergrowth had allowed the fugitives to make excellent speed.

They'd maintained an alternating trot and walk for the last twenty-two hours, pausing only to rest the horses occasionally . . . or to swap their saddles to fresh mounts. Merlin had been right about that, she reflected. Not only had King Zhames' stables had the best horses available, but there'd been enough of them to provide each member of their party with no less than three mounts apiece. Not all were equally good, but even the worst was well above average, and the spare mounts had allowed Merlin to set a pace they could never have maintained with only a single horse each.

And he had—oh, but he *had!* Irys was grateful her father had had scant patience with the more scandalized ladies of Manchyr who'd insisted his daughter had to ride sidesaddle. She would have been even more grateful if she'd been able to stay in practice after her arrival here in Delferahk. Although, to be fair, she'd thought she *had* stayed in practice . . . until she'd spent the better part of an entire day in the saddle.

But by her estimate, they'd traveled almost eighty miles—something closer to sixty, probably, as a wyvern might have flown—and they'd left the foothills of the Sunthorns three hours ago. Which meant they still had somewhere around another hundred and fifty miles— again, in that mythical straight line—to go.

"He's a remarkable man, isn't he, Phylyp?" she asked quietly as the earl took her reins. The princess loosened her saddle girth and patted the weary horse's neck affectionately, then took the reins of both horses while Coris performed the same service for his own mount.

"I assume you're referring to the redoubtable *Seijin* Merlin?" he said, smiling at her tiredly. He'd done more hard riding than she in the last couple of years, but he was also better than twice her age.

"Of course I am." She smiled back and shook her head, then twitched it to indicate the *seijin*. "Look at him."

Prince Daivyn sat on an outcrop of rock, looking up at Merlin with an almost worshipful expression. Irys could have counted the number of times she'd seen him that relaxed since leaving Corisande on the fingers of one hand, yet she knew Daivyn was only too well aware that somewhere behind them they were being vengefully pursued. It didn't seem to matter to him, though, and she wondered how much of that stemmed from the aura of competence and . . . well, invincibility that clung to the *seijin*. Certainly it would make sense for a terrified little boy to take comfort from the presence of an armsman who was renowned throughout Safehold as the most deadly bodyguard in the world. And while she wished Daivyn hadn't had to see the bodies and blood littering the palace courtyard, knowing all that carnage had been wreaked by a single man who was now dedicated to getting *him* to safety had to be reassuring.

Yet that wasn't the whole story, and she knew it. Unlike her, Daivyn's instruction in horsemanship had been far from complete when they fled Corisande, and King Zhames had discouraged him from pursuing it in Delferahk. There were times Irys suspected the king had been instructed to do exactly that by the Inquisition—it wouldn't have done for the boy to be capable of escaping them, after all. But whatever the reason, Daivyn definitely wasn't equal to the brutal, bruising pace Merlin had been setting.

Fortunately, he hadn't had to be. Merlin had simply taken him up before him on his own saddle, wrapped one arm around him, and told him one fantastic fairy tale after another as they rode along. Irys had never even heard of half or more of the stories the *seijin* produced effortlessly, and in between tales she'd heard his murmuring voice calmly answering Daivyn's questions without a hint of patronization. And then there'd been the intervals when she'd looked across and seen her brother sleeping peacefully, despite the horse's motion, held safe in the crook of that apparently tireless arm.

No wonder Daivyn looked at him that way!

And either Merlin had the homing instincts of a messenger wyvern, or else they were hopelessly lost and he simply wasn't going to admit it. He'd never hesitated, never taken a false turn, never stopped and looked for landmarks. It was as if he had some internal sense which knew exactly where he was at every instant and exactly where he needed to go next. And he had an equally uncanny ability to find the easiest, fastest going. Irys had been on hunting expeditions in Corisande with guides intimately familiar with the area of the hunt, and she'd *never* seen anyone thread so effortlessly through such difficult terrain. In fact, she was beginning to wonder if there was anything the *seijin* couldn't do.

"I agree he's remarkable, Irys," Coris said softly, his eyes, too, on Daivyn as the *seijin* passed him a wedge of cheese and the boy smiled up at him. "And it does my heart good to see him with Daivyn. But don't forget—he's a Charisian, and his loyalty's to Cayleb and Sharleyan."

"Oh, I'm not forgetting," she told him, a hint of bleakness shadowing her hazel eyes. "But I don't think he's *pretending* to be a good man, Phylyp. Daivyn's got very good instincts in that regard, and look at how he's opened up to Merlin! And I can't see a man like that offering his sword to a monster. Or"—she looked back at Coris, meeting his gaze levelly—"to someone who'd murder a defeated foe who'd offered to negotiate an honorable surrender."

"I agree," Coris said, after a moment. "And I think Cayleb and Sharleyan are probably about as honorable as rulers get. But they're still *rulers,* Irys. Even the best of them have to be willing to do what's required to protect their subjects and their realms. And Daivyn's a prize of enormous potential value."

"I know, Phylyp. I know."

▼ ▼ ▼

Merlin drew rein as his weary horse topped out on the long ridgeline and he gazed to the east, down the valley of the Sarm River. The Sarman Mountains stretched away on either hand ahead of them, rising in endless green waves like an ocean frozen in earth and stone. It was the second day since they'd left King Zhames' palace, the western sky was deep copper behind the mountain summits over his right shoulder, and despite the extra mounts, their pace had slowed as the horses grew increasingly weary.

"What is it, Merlin?" the boy in front of him asked, looking trustingly up at him. He was eleven now, which made him not quite ten by the calendar of murdered Old Terra, and he was obviously worn-out from the pace Merlin had set. For that matter, all the flesh-and-bloods were feeling the strain, and he knew it. But they were within less than thirty miles of the rendezvous point now.

That was the good news. The bad news. . . .

"I think it's time for another rest, Daivyn," he told the prince. "And I need to discuss some things with Earl Coris, Tobys, and your sister." He swung down from the saddle, carrying the boy with him, then set Daivyn on his feet.

"See if Corporal Zhadwail can find you something a little easier to chew than hard tack while I talk to them, all right?"

"All right." Daivyn nodded, then stretched and yawned and started off towards Zhadwail. Merlin watched him go, then crossed to Coris and Irys.

"We've got a problem," he said quietly.

"What sort of 'problem'?" The earl's eyes narrowed, and Merlin shrugged.

"Whoever's in charge of chasing us is better at his job than I'd like," he replied. "We've left anyone from Talkyra well behind, but unless I miss my guess, whoever they had tracking us initially had messenger wyverns with him. Between that and the semaphore, they've managed to figure out roughly where we were headed and get around in front of us."

"What makes you think that, *Seijin* Merlin?" Irys asked.

"There's someone on the other side of the valley ahead of us with a signal mirror," Merlin replied. "I caught the flash from it just as we topped the ridge."

"You did?" Coris' tone sharpened. "Do you think *they* saw *us*?" he demanded, and Merlin shrugged again.

"Trust me, my eyes are better than most, and *we* weren't deliberately reflecting sunlight at anyone the way they were." He shook his head. "No, I don't think they could've seen us . . . yet. The problem is they're down-valley from us, which means they're directly between us and where we have to go. And even though the ones I spotted may not've seen us, I'm reasonably sure there are additional parties sweeping the area. I don't know if they've realized who we're out here to meet or if they simply figure this is the valley we're going to follow to get through the Sarmans, but that doesn't really matter, does it?"

"No, it doesn't," Coris said slowly, eyes slitted as he thought hard.

"I know you don't *claim* to be a *seijin*, Merlin," he said after a moment, "but do you think you can pick a way through for us without our being spotted?"

"Maybe yes and maybe no," Merlin replied after a moment. "I'm positive I'd be able to spot any of them before *they* spotted *us*, but that's not the same as saying we could evade them all. If they've got the manpower to really sweep the valley, it's likely we'd end up eventually with one—or more—search parties hard on our trail. And good as these horses are, they're worn out. If they catch scent of us, they'll be able to run us down before we can reach the rendezvous."

There was silence, then Irys reached out and laid a hand on his forearm.

"You've got something in mind, Merlin," she said softly, gazing up into his face. "What is it?"

"Well, the simplest way to keep them from chasing *you* is to give them something *else* to chase, Your Highness."

"Such as?" she asked slowly, hazel eyes locked with his.

"Such as me," he told her with a smile. "I leave you

with the best, most rested of our horses, then I take all the others, ride off into the mountains, attract their attention, and lead them over hill and dale until they're thoroughly lost . . . and you've reached the rendezvous."

"I thought you just said their horses were going to be better than ours?" Irys said sharply, and he shrugged.

"True, but the ones I take with me won't have anyone in their saddles, and without the weight of a rider, they'll do pretty well."

"'Pretty well' isn't good enough if there are enough other horses that *do* have people in their saddles chasing you!" she snapped.

"You really *are* going to get along with Sharleyan," he observed with a crooked smile.

"Don't make silly jokes!" She stamped her foot at him. "I don't care how mighty a warrior a *seijin* is. It's not going to matter if enough of them catch up with you!"

"And they're not *going* to catch up with me, Your Highness," he assured her. She glared at him, and he shrugged. "You might ask Earl Coris about the visit my friend Ahbraim paid him. For that matter, you might think about the first time you and I met, Your Highness." He shook his head. "Trust me, once it gets fully dark—especially in this kind of terrain—I'll be able to slip away from them on foot without any problem. All they'll catch up with in the end is a bunch of worn-out horses with no riders. In fact, I'd *love* to see their expressions when they do. I wonder if I can hang around close enough to actually watch?"

She glared at him, obviously unhappy with his airy assurance, and he looked at Coris over her head.

"She's your Princess, My Lord," he said. "Personally, I'm not going to be all that impressed if she decides to throw a tantrum. If she does, though, are you going to be able to handle her?"

"I'm not a piece of luggage to be handled!"

"No, but at the moment you're not thinking very much like a princess, either," Merlin pointed out, his tone suddenly much more serious than it had been. "Even assuming they were going to catch me—which they aren't—it would be my job to lead them away and *your* job to make sure your brother gets to safety. Now, are you and I going to have to argue about this?"

She locked eyes with him for another moment. Then her shoulders slumped, and she sighed.

"No." She shook her head unhappily. "No, we're not going to have to argue about it. But be *careful,* Merlin. Please!"

"Oh, I'm always careful, Your Highness!" He leaned forward and, before she realized what he had in mind, gave her a quick peck on the cheek. She reared back in surprise, and he grinned unrepentantly. "Just for luck, Your Highness," he assured her, and nodded to Coris, who was trying very hard not to laugh.

"Take care of her, My Lord."

"I will," Coris promised. "Well, Tobys and I will. And while we're doing that, she'll take care of Daivyn."

"Are you going to tell him goodbye?" Irys asked quietly. He looked at her, and her smile trembled just a bit. "He's lost most of the stability in his world, Merlin. Don't just disappear."

"A good point, Your Highness," he acknowledged, and looked back at Coris.

"Straight down the river, My Lord. There's a waterfall about twenty-five miles downstream. The boats are supposed to be waiting just below it."

"And if they're not there?"

"If they're not there, my advice is to continue downriver, anyway. If they're not at the rendezvous by the time you get there, they're probably still on their way. Charisian seamen don't turn back easily, you know. So if you just keep going, you'll probably run into them."

"'Probably' isn't one of my favorite words when applied to desperate escapes," Coris observed dryly. "Despite which, that sounds like the best advice."

"One tries, My Lord." Merlin bowed, then straightened, looking past him at Daivyn. "And now, if you'll forgive me, I have to go tell a young man goodbye."

▼ ▼ ▼

"Is *Seijin* Merlin *really* going to be all right, Irys?" Prince Daivyn whispered urgently. He was mounted in front of Irys now, since hers was the freshest horse and she weighed the least of any of the experienced riders. He twisted slightly, looking up at her, his expression hard to see in the rapidly fading light. "Tell me the truth," he implored.

"The truth, Daivy?" She looked down at him and hugged him tightly. "The truth is that I don't know," she admitted. "But if anybody in the whole wide world can do this, it's probably him, don't you think?"

"Yesssssss," he said dubiously, then nodded. "Yes!" he said more firmly.

"That's what I thought, too," she told him with another hug.

"But how is he going to make sure they follow *him*?" Daivyn demanded. "I mean, it's getting awful dark. What if they don't even *see* him?"

"I don't know what he has in mind, Daivy, but from what I've seen of *Seijin* Merlin, I think we can predict it's going to be something fairly . . . spectacular."

▼ ▼ ▼

Sergeant Braice Mahknash stood in the stirrups so he could massage his posterior. Hardened cavalryman that he was, he'd spent long enough in the saddle over the last two or three days to last him for months. But that was all right with him. He *wanted* the traitorous bastards who'd massacred so many of the Royal Guard. And the news that Earl Coris had betrayed his trust—actually taken Cayleb of Charis' bloodstained gold and sold his own prince and princess to their father's murderer—filled Mahknash with rage. He hoped Bishop Mytchail was wrong, that Coris and the so-called "*Seijin* Merlin" wouldn't really cut the prince's and princess' throats rather than allow them to be rescued, yet surely even that would be better than letting them be handed over to the heretic emperor and empress to be tortured into proclaiming their allegiance to Prince Hektor's killers.

And that wasn't the only reason Mahknash wanted them. Delferahk had suffered enough at Charisian hands without accepting the insult of an attack on the king's very castle! Not enough to massacre the Royal Guards who'd thought they were there to protect Prince Daivyn, the treacherous sons-of-bitches had actually blown up two-thirds of the castle and set fire to the rest! King Zhames had taken Prince Hektor's orphans in out of the goodness of his heart and a kinsman's love, and his reward was to have his armsmen slaughtered and his home itself destroyed? No, that couldn't be allowed to stand, and it wouldn't. Not with the pursuit so close upon them.

And the bastards don't know their ride isn't coming, either, he thought with grim satisfaction.

The discovery that the fugitives were headed for the Sarm Valley, where the West Sarm flowed through the gap between the Trevor Hills and the Sarman Mountains proper, had made sudden sense out of the mysterious boats which had clashed with a troop of Earl Charlz' dragoons two days ago. Clearly this plot had been organized far in advance, with plenty of forethought, but that didn't mean it was going to work. Especially not when the boats they were counting on to rescue them had turned back the day before yesterday.

Mahknash smiled in satisfaction. The dragoons had suffered heavy casualties, but the Charisians had been even more badly hurt. Their boats had been observed headed back downriver, heaped with wounded, running with their tails between their legs. Moving with the current, they'd easily outdistanced any pursuit, unfortunately, and it wasn't like there were any warships or galleys on the river between them and Sarmouth, so their escape was virtually certain. But they'd managed it only by cravenly abandoning the people they'd come to meet.

Still, what more could you expect out of heretics and blasphemers? Out of people who cut children's throats as blood sacrifices to Shan-wei? Mahknash had read every word of the confessions the Inquisition had wrung out of the Charisians the Earl of Thirsk had handed over for their rightful punishment, and he'd been horrified by their crimes and perversions, but not surprised. After all, *Delferahk* knew what Charisians were like. In fact, Delferahk knew better than anyone else, given what the bastards had done to Ferayd!

I wonder if they've got any sort of fallback plan? he mused. *I don't know where they expected to meet those boats, but assuming they manage to get past the patrols—Ha! As if that were going to happen!—they're bound to realize eventually that they've been left high and dry. So what do they do then? Try to head cross-country all the way down to Sarmouth on horseback? Fat chance! We'd be on them in—*

Sergeant Mahknash's thoughts were interrupted by the arrival of a forty-five caliber bullet launched from one of the first two cap-and-ball revolvers ever manufactured on the planet of Safehold. It struck him squarely at the base of the throat at approximately eleven hundred feet per second, driven by sixty grains of black powder, and blew out the back of his neck, knocking him back across his horse's rump. He hung there for a moment, then thumped heavily to the ground, and his companions shouted in confusion as more gunfire rang out through the darkened mountain woods.

There had to be at least a dozen attackers. Obviously the collision had been as unexpected for them as for Sergeant Mahknash's patrol. The shots came in rapid succession, but they'd have come in a single, concentrated volley if the traitors had realized they were about to run into the pursuit.

Three more of Mahknash's troopers were hurled off their horses, and a fourth swayed, wounded but sticking to his saddle, and they heard voices shouting to one another in alarm. Then they heard the thunder of hooves as the fugitives turned, spurring their weary horses away from the patrol.

"Nyxyn, see to the wounded!" Corporal Walthar Zhud

shouted, reasserting command. "Zhoshua, you're on courier! Get your ass back to the Colonel! Tell him we're in contact and pursuing to the northwest. It looks to me like they're breaking back the way they came!"

"On my way, Corp!" Private Zhosua responded as he wheeled his horse around and slapped his spurs home.

"The rest of you—after me!"

▼ ▼ ▼

"Mite showy, My Lord," Tobys Raimair said judiciously, watching the lurid stab of pistol fire on the far side of the valley.

"Perhaps a *little*," Coris allowed, holding one hand out palm down and waggling it from side to side. "Effective, though."

"Wonder how many he winged this time?" Raimair said. "I mean, shooting from a horse—critter has to be spooked, what with guns going off in its ear for the first time—and in the dark, and all, with no lanterns. Has to be less accurate than he was back at the Palace, wouldn't you say, My Lord?"

"I'm not prepared to wager against the *seijin* under any circumstances, Tobys," Coris replied dryly.

"Will you two *stop* it?!" Irys demanded. "They're probably chasing him over there right this minute!"

"Well, of course they are, Your Highness," Raimair acknowledged, turning in the saddle to face her. "Whole point of the exercise."

"But what if he was wrong about being able to sneak away from them?" Daivyn demanded, his voice tight with anxiety, and Raimair reached out and ruffled the boy's hair with his hand.

"You ever hear the story about the hunting hound that caught the slash lizard, Your Highness?" he asked. The prince looked up at him without speaking for a second or two, then nodded slowly, and the sergeant shrugged. "Well, there's your answer. I'm sure they're doing their damnedest—pardon my language, Your Highness," he apologized to Irys, "to catch up with him this very minute. And if they're dead unlucky, they will."

▼ ▼ ▼

"We've got them now, Sir!"

"You think so?" Colonel Aiphraim Tahlyvyr looked up from the map to arch one eyebrow at his aide. The young man was holding the bull's-eye lantern so the colonel could see the map, and he looked astounded by his superior's question.

"Well . . . yes, Sir," he said after a moment. "Don't you?"

"I think we've got an excellent *chance* to catch up with them now," Tahlyvyr replied. "On the other hand, we *ought* to have caught them well before now. Traitors or not, and heretics or not, this is an elusive fish, Brahndyn. I'm not going to count it as caught until I've netted it and got it in the boat."

Lieutenant Maigowhyn nodded. His colonel's passion for fishing was something he'd never understood, but the metaphor made sense, anyway.

"The thing I'm wondering," Tahlyvyr said meditatively, tapping himself on the chin while he thought, "is whether all that gunfire was really a surprise reaction."

"I beg your pardon, Sir?"

"Well, whether running into our patrol was a surprise or not, it was pretty spectacular, wasn't it? Would you care to bet a silver that every single picket and patrol out there isn't headed in the same direction right now? If you were leading one of those patrols, wouldn't *you* have headed straight for the gunfire?"

"Of course, Sir!"

"Spoken like a good officer in training, Brahndyn. 'Ride to the sound of the guns'—that's what we teach you. And it's *usually* the right thing to do, too. But suppose it wasn't really all gunfire to begin with? Remember, these bastards blew up a sizable chunk of King Zhames' palace, according to the wyvern messages. What if they brought along a supply of firecrackers? One man with three or four of those double-barreled 'pistols' the Charisians seem so fond of and a couple of dozen firecrackers to go off in the underbrush, and all of a sudden every man we've got scattered around the hills is haring off like slash lizards that smell blood. And meanwhile—?"

He arched both eyebrows at Maigowhyn this time, and the lieutenant frowned. Then his eyes widened.

"And meanwhile the rest of them sneak right past us to the river and meet up with their boats, Sir! You really think that's what's *happening?*"

"Frankly, what I think is almost certainly happening is exactly what Corporal *Zhud* thinks is happening, and even if it isn't, their boats turned back two days ago, so there's no one to meet them anyway," Tahlyvyr replied. "But I didn't get to be a colonel by not hedging my bets."

"So what do you want to do, Sir?"

"Given that anyone who can see lightning or hear thunder knows about that gunfire, and that all of our good, aggressive, competent junior officers and sergeants are going to be riding to the sound of the guns"—the colonel smiled at his aide—"there's not a whole lot we *can* do. About the only people we have who aren't already off wandering through the woods, hopefully overhauling the miscreants even as we speak, are Lieutenant Wyllyms and his detachment."

"Yes, Sir," Maigowhyn said with a slight but discernible lack of enthusiasm, and Tahlyvyr chuckled.

"Not the sharpest pencil in the box, I'll grant, although I really shouldn't say it," he admitted. "That's why I put him in command of our reserves and the extra horses. It let me keep him out of trouble. Now, unfortunately, it also means he's the only one I can be sure isn't off chasing gunfire in the gloaming."

"Yes, Sir."

Tahlyvyr gazed back down at the map for several seconds, then sighed.

"It's a pity he doesn't have more men, but we *are* talking about a fairly unlikely eventuality. Take him a message, Brahndyn. He's to leave half his men to look after the remounts. I want him to take the rest downstream as far as this waterfall." He tapped the map. "I think it's the first real fall in the stream, so wherever they were supposed to make rendezvous with those boats that aren't coming after all, it has to be on the far side of that, which means they have to get past it one way or the other. Tell him I want his men posted at the *foot* of the fall. And, Brahndyn—try to make him feel that I'm trusting him with this because of his competence, not because he's the only person I can send, all right?"

"Yes, Sir." Maigowhyn tried hard not to smile, and the colonel shook his head at him.

"You're a wicked young man, Brahndyn. I foresee a great future for you."

"Thank you, Sir."

"You're welcome." Tahlyvyr started to wave the lieutenant on his way, then paused. "Oh, and while you're at it, remind him that the King and Mother Church would really like to have the Prince and Princess back alive. Tell him I don't want any shooting unless he's positive he knows what he shooting *at*."

▼ ▼ ▼

Full night had fallen long since, and the moon was sliding steadily up the eastern sky as Tobys Raimair picked his cautious way down the steep hillside to the brink of the river. The rumbling, rushing, pulsing sound as it poured smoothly over the lip of the waterfall to the basin forty feet below was loud in the darkness. In fact, it was a lot louder than Raimair liked. He would have preferred to be able to hear something besides moving water.

Oh, don't be an old woman, Tobys! he told himself. *It's worked exactly the way the* seijin *said it would so far, so don't go borrowing trouble at this point!*

He snorted quietly, then turned in the saddle to wave to the others before he started his horse down the rough footpath beside the river. If *Seijin* Merlin's description was as accurate as everything else he'd told them, their ride should be waiting for them at the end of the steep switchbacks.

▼ ▼ ▼

"By God!" Lieutenant Praiskhat Wyllyms blurted. "By God, the Colonel was right, Father!"

"Yes, it would appear he was, my son," Father Dahn-yvvn Schahl agreed. "We shouldn't take God's name in vain, however," he continued in a gently scolding tone.

"Yes, Father. I'm sorry, Father," Wyllyms said quickly, and Schahl hid a smile at the lieutenant's well-trained response. He'd often found the kindly tutor's role most effective in controlling younger men. Especially younger men who weren't particularly smart, which described young Wyllyms quite well.

But then the temptation to smile disappeared. To be honest, he'd been almost certain Colonel Tahlyvyr was sending Wyllyms off on a wild wyvern chase. Still, there'd been the possibility he wasn't, and the sad truth was that Schahl was in no position to influence whatever happened when the colonel's dragoons caught up with the fugitives in the middle of the woods. He could only be in one place at a time, when all was said, and there was no telling which of the pursuers would actually bring their quarry to bay in the end. It would have been nice if Bishop Mytchail had authorized him to tell the colonel what was really going on, although there was clearly a potential downside to such a revelation. Tahlyvyr was likely to balk at simply cutting the throats of a twenty-year-old girl and an eleven-year-old boy, no matter who told him to do it. And explaining why Irys and Daivyn Daykyn had to die would have been getting into waters it was best to keep laymen well out of. For that matter, Schahl rather doubted Bishop Mytchail had told *him* everything.

Under the circumstances, he'd decided it made sense to attach himself to Wyllyms. However unlikely, it was still *possible* Wyllyms would encounter their prey, and the inquisitor felt confident of his ability to manipulate Wyllyms into doing what he wanted, especially given his status as

Bishop Mytchail's special representative. That was how he'd planned on explaining his thinking to the bishop afterward, at any rate. No need to mention the fact that he rode like a sack of potatoes and that his buttocks felt scraped raw and treated with salt.

And now it looked like he'd rolled treble sixes, after all.

"What do you intend to do, my son?" he asked.

"I'm going to let them get most of the way down, then catch them on the trail, Father," the lieutenant explained. "We've got the matches shielded as well as we can, so I don't *think* anyone's going to see them as long as we stay well back in the trees, but I'd just as soon keep them from getting too close before we move. And it's so damned dark—pardon my language, please—down here in the valley that nobody'd be doing any accurate shooting. But if I catch them spread out on the trail in the moonlight, they won't have any choice but to surrender."

"I think, perhaps, it might be better to let them get all the way to the base of the fall before you pounce, my son," Schahl said.

"Excuse me, Father?" It was impossible to see the lieutenant's expression in the dark, but Schahl heard the confusion in his voice. "The shadows are far darker below the fall, Father," Wyllyms pointed out respectfully after a moment, "and the moonlight isn't getting to the bottom the way it is on the trail. That'd make any kind of accurate shooting even harder. And if we let them get off the trail, down here where the going is better, they might actually try to ride right through us. Frankly, with my men already dismounted to use their matchlocks, there'd be a chance they'd get away with it, too."

Schahl nodded gravely, revising his estimate of Wyllyms' mental prowess upward . . . slightly.

"Those are excellent points, my son," he said. "And I'm a simple priest, of course, not a soldier. Still, it seems to me that if we let them reach the bottom, they'll have a sense of confidence at having passed the obstacle. That means the shock of suddenly discovering we're already down here waiting for them will hit even harder. I believe that's more likely to paralyze their will to fight *or* flee. And if they do try to break past us, your men can catch them in a crossfire as they go. I think by far the most likely outcome, however, would be that they'd realize they couldn't possibly escape back up that steep trail and, with an unknown number of troopers between them and escape on the downriver side, they'd surrender. Assuming they'd be willing to surrender under *any* circumstances, at least."

"I see," Wyllyms said slowly. It was obvious to Schahl that the lieutenant's instincts were at war with his advice. That was unfortunate. Still, Wyllyms had already demonstrated his deference to the cloth, and Schahl reached up and casually adjusted his priest's cap.

"As I say, my son, I'm no soldier, but I'm afraid I really must insist in this instance." Wyllyms stiffened slightly, and Schahl patted him on the shoulder with a fatherly air. "There are elements of the situation of which you're not aware, my son. Please, just trust me in this."

"Of course, Father," Wyllyms said after a moment, and began whispering orders to his sergeants.

Schahl stood back, listening and nodding in approval while his right hand crept into the side pocket of his cassock and touched the smooth, curved wooden grip of the pistol Bishop Mytchail had provided.

▼ ▼ ▼

Tobys Raimair reached the bottom of the trail and dismounted. The basin below the fall was much larger than he'd thought it was looking down into the darkness from above. It extended well away from the rumbling smother of foam where the water crashed down into it, and he led his weary horse to the edge of the wind- and current-ruffled pool, enjoying the blowing mist and letting the beast drink but keeping one eye on it to make sure it didn't drink too much. His other eye was on the trail, watching the others make their way down it—slowly and carefully, despite the moonlight—and he allowed himself a sense of cautious optimism.

Still, something didn't quite smell right. He couldn't put his finger on what it was, but there was *something*. . . .

You really are an old woman tonight, aren't you? he asked himself sardonically. *You'll find something to worry about, no matter what!*

That might very well be true, but it didn't do anything about that itch he couldn't quite scratch. Perhaps it was just that the Charisians didn't seem to have reached the rendezvous point. Well, *Seijin* Merlin had warned them how far the boats had to come, so it was hardly surprising they hadn't arrived yet. In fact, the truth was that even with Merlin being forced to lead off the pursuit, this entire operation had gone far more smoothly than Raimair would have believed possible after a lifetime in the Army. *Something* always went wrong. That was the soldier's wisdom, and it had never yet failed him.

He grinned, shaking his head, then looked up as Princess Irys reached the bottom with Daivyn before her. Earl Coris was right behind her. The rest of the men followed in single column, with Zhak Mahrys, Rahzhyr Wahltahrs, and Traivahr Zhadwail bringing up the rear.

"Go ahead and dismount, Your Highness," he said quietly as the princess reached him. "We should probably rest the horses again before we head on downriver. Besides, I'd like to let the moon get a little higher. It's pretty rocky down here, and the horses'll need all the moonlight we can get if they're not going to break a leg."

"Won't that make us more visible?" Irys asked. It was a question, not an argument or a criticism, Raimair observed, and nodded back to her.

"Aye, Your Highness, it will," he agreed. "Still and all, I think we're probably past them now, given the *seijin*'s diversion. And, truth be told, I think it's a lot more likely a tired horse is going to put a foot wrong in bad light than that we're suddenly going to be ambushed by a batch of Delferahkan dragoons."

"Sounds sensible to me, Tobys," Coris agreed, dismounting as he reached the sergeant's side. "And—"

"*Stand where you are!*" a voice shouted suddenly out of the darkness. "Throw down your weapons!"

▼ ▼ ▼

Young Wyllyms had really done quite well, Schahl observed. It was a pity, in so many ways, that Bishop Mytchail's instructions left him with no alternative.

"—down your weapons!" the lieutenant shouted, and Schahl heard his two sergeants ordering their men to advance cautiously. The Corisandians were frozen, standing as if struck to stone by the totally unexpected ambush. They obviously had no idea how many men Wyllyms had. If they'd realized how understrength the lieutenant's platoon actually was, they might have shown more fight. As it was, Wyllyms' ambush was about to become a brilliant success.

And that, unfortunately, could not be permitted.

The Schuelerite quietly drew the pistol from inside his cassock. He'd never used one of the Charisian-invented weapons before, but it wasn't all that complicated, and he cocked it as he stepped up close behind the lieutenant.

"It worked, Father!" Wyllyms said exuberantly. "You were right—this is *perfect!*"

"I'm happy for you, my son," Schahl said, and then pressed the muzzle of the pistol against the back of the young man's skull and pulled the trigger.

▼ ▼ ▼

Tobys Raimair stood frozen by the shock of the sudden shout, cursing himself for not having listened to that inner instinct. He should have *listened!* And how had he missed spotting the damned slow matches? They were coming out into the open now, glowing like blink-lizards, but he'd never even seen a thing before they did! He hadn't paid even *that* much attention to his job, had he? Oh, no, not him! Instead, he'd let the girl and her brother walk straight into it, and now—

Then the gunshot roared in the darkness, and the blinding muzzle flash and echoing report jerked him out of his funk. He turned towards Irys, both arms reaching out, gathered her and her brother to his chest, and flung all three of them not to the ground, but into the pool below the waterfall.

▼ ▼ ▼

"They've shot the Lieutenant!" Schahl bellowed, tossing the empty pistol into the river and grimacing distastefully at the blood and bits of brain matter which had blown back over his cassock. "They've shot the Lieutenant!" He drew a deep breath. *"Kill the heretics!"*

▼ ▼ ▼

"Down! Everybody down!" Phylyp Ahzgood shouted as he heard the three-word command and knew—somehow he *knew*—it had come from an inquisitor's throat. Worse, the troopers out there in the dark would know the same thing, and the bone-deep reflex of obedience to the voice of Mother Church would finish what confusion had begun.

A matchlock flashed, thundering in the darkness. Langhorne only knew where the ball had gone, but another fired, and then another. Inaccurate at the best of times, it would take a special miracle for one of them to hit someone at this range under these conditions, but matchlocks weren't the only weapons dragoons carried, and Coris knew what was coming.

Why God? a voice demanded bitterly deep inside him. *Why did You let us come this far only to fail* now?

God didn't reply. Or not immediately, at any rate. But then—

"Take 'em, lads!" another voice shouted, and someone cried out in alarm, then screamed in anguish.

"Zhaksyn, make sure none of them get past us!" that same voice shouted—an extraordinarily young voice, Coris realized, but one which carried a hard ring of command.

Another matchlock fired, and then there was a different sound—a flintlock. A fresh muzzle flash stabbed the night, and suddenly half a dozen flintlocks went off almost as one, firing from the hillsides, upslope from and on either side of the dragoons who'd been hidden in the woods.

"Bayonets!" that voice yelled out of the darkness. "Up and in, boys! *Up and in!*" it shouted, and the night was abruptly ugly with the clash of metal, the terrible wet sounds of steel driving into human flesh, with screams and curses.

"Quarter!" someone bawled suddenly. "Quarter! Sweet Langhorne! *Quarter!*"

And then, that abruptly, it was over.

Silence fell, broken only by the crash and surge of the waterfall and the whimpers of the wounded, and Coris stood very slowly in the fragile stillness. Other sounds began returning to the night, as if creeping cautiously back into it, and he heard rough, sharp voices ordering surrendered men to their feet, herding them together, taking their weapons. It would, he decided, be prudent to remain where he was and avoid any . . . misunderstandings until that process was completed, and his eyes narrowed as someone stepped out of the darkness into the moonlight.

It was difficult to be certain in such poor light, but the newcomer certainly looked as if he wore the uniform of a Charisian naval officer, although it was obviously somewhat the worse for wear. He paused and cleaned his sword on the tunic of a fallen dragoon, then sheathed the weapon with smooth, economical grace. Coris was still staring at him when he heard a splashing sound.

"If you don't mind, Phylyp," Irys Daykyn said tartly, her teeth chattering slightly, "I'd really appreciate a hand."

He turned quickly, reaching down to take Daivyn as she and Raimair boosted the shivering, obviously frightened boy out of the icy mountain water. The prince flung his arms around Coris' neck, clinging tightly, and the earl patted his back reassuringly.

"It's all right, Daivyn. It's all right now," he said soothingly.

"I know," Daivyn said in a tight voice, and nodded once, convulsively, but he never relaxed his hold, and Coris looked helplessly down at Irys over her brother's shoulder.

"Allow me, Your Highness," someone else said in a pronounced Charisian accent, and the newcomer in the naval uniform was suddenly beside him, reaching down both hands to Irys. She looked up at him for a moment, then reached to take the offered hands. The Charisian wasn't especially tall or broad-shouldered, but he boosted her effortlessly out of the water. Then he reached down again and hoisted Tobys Raimair out, as well.

"That was quick thinking, getting them below ground level that way when the shooting started," he congratulated the sergeant. It was still a ridiculously young-sounding voice, Coris decided, but it was also crisp and decisive. A very *reassuring* voice, all things taken together.

"Excuse me," its owner continued, turning back to Coris, Irys, and Daivyn. He bowed gracefully. "Lieutenant Aplyn-Ahrmahk, Imperial Charisian Navy, at your service. If you're ready to go, I have two boats waiting about a mile downstream from here. It'll be a little crowded," teeth gleamed faintly in the moonlight which was finally probing into the darkness at the foot of the waterfall, "but I believe you'll find the accommodations preferable to these."

"I believe you're right, Lieutenant," Coris said gratefully. "In fact—"

"Beg pardon, Sir," another voice interrupted, and Aplyn-Ahrmahk—and did that name indicate this youngster was who Coris *thought* he was?—turned towards the interruption with a frown.

"What is it, Mahlyk?" he asked in a no-nonsense tone.

"Beg pardon for interrupting, Sir," the other voice belonged to what could only be a professional Charisian petty officer, "but I think this is important."

"And what, exactly, is 'this'?" Aplyn-Ahrmahk prompted.

"Well, Sir, Zhaksyn put the arm on this priest here when he tried to scamper off downstream," the petty officer said, dragging a prisoner into the moonlight. "And we found the officer in command of this here ambush, too, Sir. Seems *somebody*"—the petty officer kicked the prisoner to his knees, and Coris saw the priest's cap and cassock—"blowed the poor bastard's—beg pardon for the language, Your Highness"—he bobbed Irys a brief bow—"blowed the poor bastard's brains out. 'Twasn't any of us, because from the powder burns, whoever it was shot him from behind and real up close and personal, like. And a funny thing, Sir, but this here priest? He's got blood and brains splashed all over his right arm."

"Does he now?" Aplyn-Ahrmahk said in a deadly soft voice.

"I'm a priest of Mother Church!" the captive thundered suddenly, surging up as he started back to his feet. "How *dare* you—?!"

He went back down again, this time squealing in pain, as the petty officer casually, and with brutal efficiency, stamped down—hard—on the back of his right knee.

"A priest, are you?" Aplyn-Ahrmahk said in that same deadly voice. "And a servant of the Inquisition, no doubt?"

"A priest of any order is still a priest of God!" the prostrate cleric shouted furiously, both hands clutching at the back of his knee. "And he who lays a hand on *any* priest of God is guilty of blasphemy!"

"An inquisitor, all right," Aplyn-Ahrmahk said, and looked past the petty officer still standing over the Schuelerite. "Zhaksyn, go find me the senior prisoner. Bring him here."

"Aye, Sir."

"I tell you, you're all—!" the priest began again, and Aplyn-Ahrmahk looked at the petty officer.

"Mahlyk?" he said quietly.

"My pleasure, Sir," the petty officer said, and kicked the priest none too gently in the belly. The inquisitor doubled up into a ball with a shrill, whistling cry of pain and then lay grunting and gasping for breath while the petty officer watched him with a mildly interested air.

The priest was just starting to get his breath back when the man named Zhaksyn returned with a Delferahkan dragoon. The man had been wounded, and a rough dressing around his upper left arm was stained black with blood in the moonlight, but the shock of such abrupt defeat when victory had seemed certain was obviously more debilitating than any sword cut.

"This here's the senior sergeant, near as I can tell, Sir," Zhaksyn said.

"Thank you." Aplyn-Ahrmahk turned to the Delferahkan. "*Are* you the senior prisoner?" he asked.

"Aye, that I am . . . Sir," the Delferahkan said. "Leastwise, I am if the Lieutenant's really dead."

"Oh, he's dead, mate," the petty officer said. "Shot in the back of the head, and from real close, too."

"What?" The Delferahkan looked back and forth between Aplyn-Ahrmahk and the petty officer. "That don't make no sense . . . Sir. The Lieutenant, he was behind us. And the Father said he was dead before any of you lot started shooting from the hills! I thought the shot had to come from here."

He jabbed the index finger of his good hand at the rocky edge of the pool.

"That's exactly what you were supposed to think, Sergeant," Aplyn-Ahrmahk said grimly. "This Schuelerite bastard murdered your lieutenant in order to turn what should have been an orderly surrender into a massacre. And it would have *worked* if we hadn't already been here keeping an eye on things—and you—when your lot first arrived, wouldn't it?"

"Well, I don't know as how—" the sergeant began uncomfortably, then stopped. "Aye, Sir," he admitted in a lower voice. "Aye, it would've, that it surely would."

"This is all lies!" the priest sputtered suddenly, still more than a little breathless from that kick in the belly. "Lies by heretics and blasphemers—by excommunicates!

Sergeant, you can't take *their* word for this! Why, it probably *was* one of them, deliberately shooting poor Lieutenant Wyllyms down from ambush without warning, just to discredit me! Is it *my* fault I was standing so close to him I was splashed with his blood when *they* killed him?!"

The sergeant looked down at the priest for a moment, then met Aplyn-Ahrmahk's eyes in the moonlight.

"He weren't the very smartest officer nor I ever served under, the Lieutenant," he said, "but he were a good lad, an' he always tried to do what was right. Didn't always manage it, but he *tried*, Sir. And in a fair fight, all the holes would've been in the front, not the back like this. It ain't right, Sir." He shook his head, his voice stubborn. "It ain't *right*."

"No, it isn't, Sergeant," Aplyn-Ahrmahk agreed. "So I have only one more question for you."

"Sir?" the Delferahkan said a bit cautiously.

"This man is obviously a Schuelerite," Aplyn-Ahrmahk said. "Can you confirm that he's also an inquisitor?"

"Aye, Sir," the Delferahkan replied. "That he is. Attached to Colonel Tahlyvyr special by Bishop Mytchail. Heard him telling the Colonel myself, I did."

"Think what you're doing, Sergeant!" the priest snapped. "By God, I'll see you put to the Punishment for collaborating with heretics! I'll—"

The Delferahkan flinched, but then his shoulders hunched stubbornly and he glared down at the priest.

"He's an inquisitor, Sir," he said firmly. "Sure as sure."

"Thank you, Sergeant." Aplyn-Ahrmahk nodded to the Delferahkan, then looked at the petty officer. "Stand him up, Mahlyk," he said flatly.

"Waste of good sweat, Sir," the petty officer said. "He'll only be back down in a minute or two."

"Even an inquisitor should have the chance to die on his feet, Stywyrt," Aplyn-Ahrmahk replied in a voice of iron.

"What?" The priest stared up at him in shock. "What did you just say?"

"You and your friend Clyntahn should pay more attention to proclamations coming out of Tellesberg," Aplyn-Ahrmahk said coldly. "Some of those men you tortured and butchered in Zion were friends of mine, and every damned one of them was innocent. Well, the blood on your cassock says you're *not,* and my Emperor and Empress' policy where inquisitors are concerned is very clear."

"You can't be—I mean, I'm a *priest!* A priest of Mother Church! You can't just—"

"I know priests," Aplyn-Ahrmahk told him as Stywyrt Mahlyk hauled him to his feet by the collar of his cassock. "I even know a *Schuelerite* priest—a good one, the kind who truly serves God. And that's how I know you *aren't* one, whatever that fat, greedy bastard in Zion might say." He drew a pistol from his belt and cocked it. "If you want to make your peace with God, you have thirty seconds."

"*Damn* you! Who do you think you *are* to threaten a consecrated priest of God! You wouldn't *dare*—!"

"You don't want to make peace?" Aplyn-Ahrmahk said. "Fine."

His hand rose, his finger squeezed, and Dahnyvyn Schahl's eyes were just starting to widen in disbelieving terror when his head disintegrated. The body dropped like a sring-cut puppet, and Aplyn-Ahrmahk turned to Earl Coris and Princess Irys.

"I apologize for the delay," he said as the muzzle smoke of his pistol wisped away on the cool, damp breath of the fall. "Now, I believe those boats are still waiting for us."

FEBRUARY, YEAR OF GOD 896

✦

. I .

Nimue's Cave,
The Mountains of Light,
The Temple Lands,
and
Tellesberg Palace,
City of Tellesberg,
Kingdom of Old Charis

"So just exactly how was it you were planning to get home again without raising any eyebrows?" Cayleb Ahrmahk asked, leaning back in the rattan lounge and gazing up at a spectacular sunset.

His daughter lay curled on his chest, her nose pressed into the angle of his neck while she slept with the absolute limpness possible only for small children and cat-lizards, and Empress Sharleyan's crochet hook moved busily as she looked across at him and smiled.

"Why should I get home without raising any eyebrows?" Merlin responded over the com plug in his ear. "I'm a *seijin*—the mysterious, deadly, probably magical *Seijin* Merlin!" There was a clearly audible sniff. "I come and go, and no man sees me pass."

"You're getting remarkably full of yourself, aren't you?" Sharleyan inquired sweetly.

"Well, I think I've done fairly well the last few five-days," he pointed out.

"That's true, I suppose," Cayleb said judiciously. "I especially liked the bit with the voices shouting to each other there at the end, on top of the gunshots. No wonder they thought all of you were right in front of them!"

"If you've got a programmable vocoder for a voice box, you might as well use it," Merlin replied smugly, but then he sighed. "Actually, though, I think I'm blowing my ego out of my ears because I'm bored and I want to come home."

Sharleyan looked across at Caleb, and her expression softened.

"We're looking forward to *seeing* you at home," Caleb assured him, speaking for them both. Then he shrugged—very gently, so as not to disturb the sleeping child next to his heart. "I agree sending you personally to oversee Irys and Daivyn's rescue was the right move, but having you operate openly that far away's inconvenient as hell in a lot of ways."

"I've noticed that myself," Merlin said dryly. "I'm thinking about adding a few extra members to Master Zhevons' ensemble cast. It can be a pain covering for absences on my part while Zhevons—or someone else, for that matter—runs around in the middle of Howard, but it saves us from having to account for all of this damned 'transit time'!"

"I see your point, but I think it was a good thing you were 'running around in the middle of Howard' this time," Sharleyan said soberly, and Merlin shrugged.

"I'm inclined to agree, given my own modest contribution to getting them out of Talkyra and delivering them to the rendezvous, but Hektor did pretty well himself, didn't he?"

"Yes," Caleb agreed. "Yes he did. Especially for someone as young as he is."

"This from the gray-bearded septuagenarian sitting on the throne of Charis, I see," Merlin replied, and Sharleyan giggled.

"All right, so I was only a couple of years older than he is now when you took me in hand," Caleb acknowledged. "But he still did a *damned* good job."

"No question about that," Merlin acknowledged, and there wasn't.

Faced with the loss of all of the expedition's senior officers, Aplyn-Ahrmahk had decided to continue the mission, despite the risk of additional encounters with the Delferahkan militia. So he'd transferred all his wounded into four of the six boats and sent them back downstream with orders to remain in the middle of the current as much as possible. The Sarm wasn't an enormous river, but it was broad enough that troops armed with the relatively short-barreled, smoothbore matchlocks dragoons carried would play hell trying to hit a target in midstream. Artillery would have been a different matter, but the Royal Delferahkan Army had no new model field artillery. For that matter, it didn't have very much artillery at *all*, and the cumbersome, slow-firing pieces it did possess lacked the mobility to intercept boats moving at the better part of twelve miles an hour under sail and oars while the river's current worked *for* them instead of against them.

He'd also ordered the boats to travel in daylight to make it abundantly clear to any observer that they were straggling back to Sarmouth in disorder as quickly as they could get there. As he'd hoped, the Delferahkans had pursued the retreating boats with their cargo of wounded and clearly dispirited passengers as vigorously as they could all the way back downriver. Meanwhile, he and the remaining two boats had continued upstream unnoticed, moving only under cover of darkness, and with Stywyrt Mahlyk's cutter towing the second boat all but empty. Proceeding with barely thirty men was an obvious risk, but it had let him save room in the second boat for the passengers he'd intended to collect.

It had also left him far shorter-handed than he could have wished when he encountered the unfortunate Lieutenant Wyllyms' dragoons. Luckily, he'd arrived at the rendezvous fifteen hours before Colonel Tahlyvyr's regiment moved into the area and he'd posted pickets well out from his carefully hidden boats. They'd spotted

Wyllyms' troopers moving into position early enough for Aplyn-Ahrmahk to arrange his own counter-ambush. Even so, he'd had to wait for the dragoons—who'd still substantially outnumbered his own people—to emerge from the woods and bunch up before he could pounce. In the end, he'd ordered the attack with impeccable timing, and, frankly, the cold-blooded patience with which he'd waited for exactly the right moment was even more surprising out of someone his age than the initiative, in Merlin's opinion.

"What do you think about Bishop Mytchail's reaction to what happened to that poisonous piece of work Schahl?" Cayleb asked after a moment.

"I think it was inevitable." Merlin shrugged. "I happen to agree with the policy, but it was obvious from the get-go the inquisition was going to take the view that all of its inquisitors were purer than the new fallen snow, the blameless, stainless victims of those vicious, vile, Shan-wei-worshipping, baby-murdering Charisian heretics." His mouth twisted in distaste. "The farther away people are from where the atrocities take place, the more likely they are to buy that line of dragon shit, too. Owl's remotes are still getting our version tacked up on convenient walls all over both continents, but the Church is going to have the inside track when it comes to convincing the faithful for quite a while. Look at the way they're handling that business in Siddarmark!"

Cayleb made a harsh sound in his throat, and Sharleyan kicked him gently on the outside of his right thigh.

"You wake her up," she said, twitching her head in their daughter's direction, "and you get to sing her back to sleep, Cayleb Ahrmahk!"

"I'll be good," he promised with a penitent smile. "But it's Merlin's fault for bringing up things like that."

"Tell me you're not going to be discussing it with Trahvys, Bynzhamyn, and Maikel first thing tomorrow morning," Merlin challenged.

"But that's then, not now," Cayleb retorted.

"True." Merlin nodded, leaning back in his own chair

deep under the far-off Mountains of Light. "It's going to be ugly, however it finally works out," he said somberly, and it was Cayleb's turn to nod.

"What I'm most worried about at this point, to be honest, is food," he said. "Clyntahn timed it entirely too well from that respect, damn him to hell."

"Agreed. But if Stohnar can hold out through the winter, our good friend the Grand Inquisitor may just find the wheels coming off his little wagon." Merlin's expression was no less somber, yet there was a note of grim satisfaction in his voice. "I think he actually expected to sweep the board, and it didn't quite work out that way, did it?"

"Thanks in no small part to your friend Ahnzhelyk. Or I suppose we should call her Aivah, now." Cayleb smiled in simple admiration. "I'll guarantee you none of Clyntahn's agents guessed for a moment that she had fifteen hundred trained riflemen right there in Siddar City. Which doesn't even count the *sixty-five hundred* rifles hidden aboard those ships of hers on North Bay. She more than doubled the total number of modern firearms available to Stohnar."

"Not to mention rescuing the Lord Protector's august posterior on the very first day," Merlin agreed. "Without her, they probably would have taken the capital, you know."

"And massacred every Charisian and Reformist they could get their hands on," Sharleyan put in grimly, her eyes shadowed. "It was bad enough even with her preparations, and I get sick to my stomach every time I think of what happened in so many other places."

"I know," Merlin said softly.

Siddar City's Charisian Quarter was the largest, richest, and most densely inhabited in the entire Republic, but almost all of Siddarmark's coastal cities had boasted their own Quarters. For that matter, even the larger inland towns had been home to expatriate Charisians who'd married Siddarmarkians or simply located in the Republic because of the financial opportunities.

Outside the capital, most of those Charisian communities had been effectively wiped out. Even in Siddar City, despite Aivah Pahrsahn's preparations and Lord Protector Greyghor's decision to divert over half his own available strength to protecting its Charisian inhabitants, over two thousand people had been killed. Rape and torture had run rampant as the rioters slaked their hatred in the blood of their victims. Nor had they restricted their activities to Charisians. Reformist churches had been burned throughout the Republic. Reformist priests had been murdered—in some cases burned to death inside their own churches—and Reformist congregations had been killed or driven into headlong flight from towns in which their families had lived for centuries.

It had been worst in the Republic's western provinces, partly because of those provinces' deep, often bitter resentment of the *eastern* provinces' greater wealth, but also because Clyntahn and Rayno had devoted the most attention to making sure they would succeed in the provinces closest to the Temple Lands. There'd been some notable exceptions, however. In Glacierheart and Cliff Peak, the militia had turned on the insurrectionists and rabble-rousers in its own ranks and crushed the uprising within days. The same thing had happened in Icewind Province, although the situation looked much grimmer there. No one was moving any troops now that winter had closed down, but the provinces of Tarikah, New Northland, and Westmarch were all firmly in the hands of Temple Loyalists who'd denounced the Republic's elected government as a "lackey, tool, and minion of the accursed and excommunicate Charisian heretics." Between them, those provinces formed a blade thrusting into the Republic's heart, and Icewind was completely isolated from the rest of the country.

The outcome was still very much in doubt in Hildermoss Province, as well, and what happened there might well be critical. If Hildermoss remained loyal to the Lord Protector, it would shield Glacierheart from any attacks out of Westmarch and protect Old Province from attacks out of Westmarch and Tarikah. More to the point, Mountaincross Province was one of the eastern provinces which had gone over to Clyntahn. If Hildermoss held, a counter-attack out of Northland and Old Province could almost certainly retake Mountaincross; if Hildermoss fell, the rebels would be able to strike directly at the capital all along Old Province's northern frontier by early summer, at the latest.

Farther south, the Southmarch Lands were a nightmare. Clyntahn and Rayno had devoted special attention to the huge, sparsely populated area, but they'd been less successful than they'd hoped in bringing the regular Army units over to their side. The entire "province" was actually one huge military district, divided into regional commands and administered by Army officers. Indeed, one of the grievances Rayno and Laiyan Bahzkai's agitators had appealed to was the Southmarch's resentment that it hadn't yet been organized into provinces with representation in the Chamber of the Senate. At least a third of the Southmarch commands had remained staunchly loyal to the Lord Protector and the central government, however, and the fighting was turning increasingly vicious.

The rebels had also managed to seize control of the southwestern portion of Shiloh Province, although it seemed unlikely they'd be able to hold on to it if Stohnar survived the winter. Unfortunately, the rebels appeared to be aware of that, and the pogroms and killings in Shiloh were brutal almost beyond belief. If southwestern Shiloh was retaken by the government, it was going to be mostly one huge sea of gutted farms and burned-out ruins.

For the moment, Southguard, Transhar, and Windmoor Provinces were at least provisionally in the Lord Protector's column, although the situation in Southguard was confused and turning increasingly bloody. Atrocity begat atrocity, and bushwhackers and arsonists stalked one another mercilessly through the cold, rainy winter. The hate those attacks and counter-attacks were generating was going to grow nothing but uglier, Merlin thought sadly. Indeed, it was the kind of violence and brutality that were likely to bequeath a multi-generational legacy of hatred among the survivors and their children.

Malitar Province had gone against the pattern for most of the rest of the Republic—the insurgents inside Marik, Malitar's provincial capital and Siddarmark's second largest seaport, had seized control of the entire city, and it had been the militias from the surrounding countryside which had fought their way back into Marik and crushed the rebels. Unfortunately, the city's entire Charisian Quarter had been burned to the ground before the militias could retake Marik. There'd been very few survivors, and the Reformist churches had suffered almost equally severely.

Markan and Transhar had held successfully for the Lord Protector and the government, and things were actually fairly quiet there. The same was true in Rollings Province, in the extreme northeast, although the coastal area of Midhold Province, between Rollings and Old Province, had been the scene of some ugly fighting. The extreme western portion of Midhold was dominated by the successful rebels in Mountaincross, at the moment, as well, which had to be causing a certain amount of anxiety in Siddar City.

As far as anyone could tell, almost two-thirds of the regular Army had honored its oath to the constitution and the Lord Protector. Several of those units which had remained loyal had been overwhelmed by the insurgency, unfortunately, and very few of those men had survived, since the Temple Loyalists weren't very interested in taking prisoners. Between defections, desertions, and combat losses it was unlikely Stohnar could call on more than a third—possibly as little as a quarter—of the once mighty Siddarmarkian Army. Worse, the Grand Vicar had proclaimed Mother Church's support for the "valiant children of God warring against evil and corruption" in the Republic and extended the jihad to anyone who supported "the apostate and accursed Greyghor Stohnar and his minions." As a consequence, "volunteers" were prepared to pour into the western Republic from the Border States as soon as weather permitted. For that matter, it was only a matter of time before actual contingents of the Temple Guard turned up.

And, as Cayleb had pointed out, Clyntahn had timed his uprising to coincide with the final stages of the Siddarmarkian harvest. The southern provinces harvested later, of course, but his attack had come before the produce from the agrarian west had been shipped east for the winter, and part of his strategy had included the deliberate destruction of foodstuffs—warehouses, farms, granaries—throughout the eastern provinces, as well. By Owl's estimates, those provinces had lost almost half the food which would normally have carried them through the winter months. And at the very time the food supply had been interrupted, Reformist and Charisian refugees from the west were pouring east in a desperate search for safety.

"Do you think Stohnar's going to make it through the winter, Merlin?" Sharleyan asked after a moment.

"I think he's got a good chance," Merlin replied. "I don't know what's going to happen come spring, though. We're seeing an awful lot of orders from Maigwair to the Border States and the various Temple Lands military commands. I imagine he's planning on moving east to steamroller Stohnar as soon as he can put an army in the field. And I expect Clyntahn's going to be 'suggesting' to the Silkiahans that they'd better toe the line on the embargo from here on out if they don't want the same treatment the Republic just got."

"What's driving me and Domynyk, Trahvys, and Bynzhamyn crazy is the fact that we still 'don't know' what's going on up north!" Cayleb growled. "We can't do a thing—can't even establish contact with Stohnar about this!—until we 'find out' it's happening!"

"It won't be much longer, love," Sharleyan said, reaching out to lay a comforting hand on his shoulder. "We're already starting to 'hear rumors,'" she pointed out, "and all the world knows what a wonderful spy network we have!"

"I know." Cayleb smiled crookedly at her. "That's what Trahvys and Bynzhamyn and I are going to be talking about tomorrow morning. We're going to haul Ahlvyno in, as well, and begin assembling relief shipments of food 'as a precaution' at Maikel's suggestion." He grimaced. "Our economy's going to have the crap kicked out of it by the loss of so much Siddarmarkian trade, and if Silkiah does decide it has to start paying attention to Clyntahn's embargo, that's only going to get worse. On the other hand, we'll suddenly have a lot of spare merchant galleons we can snap up to help ship in food and medical supplies."

"Maybe it won't be quite that bad," Merlin said encouragingly. "I've got a feeling something may turn up, despite the embargo. And if Stohnar *does* make it through the winter—and next spring—we may finally have the mainland ally we need."

"And if he *doesn't* make it through the winter—and next spring—it's going to be at least ten years before any *other* mainland realm is willing to stand up with us," Cayleb said sourly. "Assuming, of course, that those 'returning Archangels' give us that long."

"My, you are in a testy mood," Merlin observed mildly.

"I've got a lot to be testy *about*," Cayleb shot back. "This hasn't exactly been the easiest year we've ever had, you know."

"Yes, I do know," Merlin said more gently. "But Hektor has Irys, Daivyn, and Coris safely back aboard *Destiny*. They'll be headed home soon, and it should be interesting to see how Corisande reacts when Coris and Irys tell them it was *Clyntahn* who had Hektor murdered . . . and tried to murder Daivyn, as well. And for better or worse, Clyntahn's come out into the open on the mainland. This isn't just an overseas war for Howard and the Havens anymore, and that was his decision, not ours. In the long run, I think it's going to come home to roost with a vengeance, as long as Stohnar does manage to hold. And Ehdwyrd and Seamount have the new rifled guns in production, not to mention Mahndrayn's breechloaders. I know we all miss Mahndrayn, but that was a brilliant design approach, and the Church isn't going to like it one bit when it runs into them in the field. Kynt Clareyk's about to suggest infantry mortars, as well, and that's going to come as an unpleasant surprise to our friend Clyntahn, too. And then there's Ehdwyrd's first steam engine. *That's* going to be a game-changer, especially since we won't have to waste all that time tinkering and experimenting to improve it into a working proposition like they did back on Old Terra."

"Are you trying to cheer me up by pointing out that the momentum is on our side?" Cayleb asked dryly. "Because, if you are, allow me to point out that for the next several months, at least, the momentum's going to be rather solidly on *Clyntahn's* side in Siddarmark. And if he knocks off the Republic, we'll be a long time looking for another opportunity to establish a foothold anywhere on the mainland."

"You *are* determined to be gloomy," Merlin said in a gently teasing voice. "And, no, I wasn't trying to tell you the *momentum* was on our side. I'm not even going to argue at this point that *history* is on our side, although I think it probably is. No, I'm just thinking about something you said a while back, Cayleb. This *has* been a bad year in a lot of ways . . . but we're still here, and we're stronger than we were the year before. And the reason we are is that you and Sharley and Maikel *have* laid a foundation here in Charis that someone like Zhaspahr Clyntahn will never be able to appreciate or match. Charis *understands* what this is about, and that's our strength, the bedrock that Clyntahn doesn't even begin to understand. These people—*your* people—recognize evil when they see it, and they're not willing to let it triumph. They *refuse* to see it triumph. They may not know all that we know, and they've damned well never heard of the Terran Federation or the Gbaba, but they're ready to pay the price to buy their children's and their children's children's freedom from what Clyntahn represents, whatever that price is. And when you come down to it," Merlin smiled crookedly, "we can work with that, you know."

"You do have a way of finding a bright side, don't you? What was it they called that back in the old days—a Pollyanna, I think?" Cayleb replied, but he was looking at his wife as he spoke, and he, too, smiled. He cupped one hand over the back of his sleeping daughter's head and hugged her gently, and then he nodded.

"But you're right, Merlin," he said softly. "We *can* work with that."

Characters

ABYLYN, CHARLZ—a senior leader of the Temple Loyalists in Charis.

AHBAHT, CAPTAIN RUHSAIL, IMPERIAL DESNAIRIAN NAVY—commanding officer HMS *Archangel Chihiro*, 40; Commodore Wailahr's flag captain.

AHBAHT, LYWYS—Edmynd Walkyr's brother-in-law; XO, merchant galleon *Wind*.

AHBAHT, ZHEFRY—Earl Gray Harbor's personal secretary. He fulfills many of the functions of an undersecretary of state for foreign affairs.

AHDYMSYN, BISHOP ZHERALD—previously Erayk Dynnys' bishop executor for Charis, now one of Archbishop Maikel's senior auxiliary bishops.

AHLAIXSYN, RAIF—well-to-do Siddarmarkian poet and dilettante; a Reformist.

AHLBAIR, LIEUTENANT ZHEROHM, ROYAL CHARISIAN NAVY—first lieutenant, HMS *Typhoon*.

AHLDARM, MAHRYS OHLARN—Mahrys IV, Emperor of Desnair.

AHLVAI, CAPTAIN MAHLYK, IMPERIAL DESNAIRIAN NAVY—CO, HMS *Emperor Zhorj*, 48. Baron Jahras' flag captain.

AHLVEREZ, ADMIRAL-GENERAL FAIDEL, ROYAL DOHLARAN NAVY—Duke of Malikai; King Rahnyld IV of Dohlar's senior admiral.

AHLWAIL, BRAIHD—Father Paityr Wylsynn's valet.

AHNDAIRS, TAILAHR—a Charisian-born Temple Loyalist living in the Temple Lands recruited for Operation Rakurai.

AHRDYN—Archbishop Maikel's cat-lizard.

AHRMAHK, CAYLEB ZHAN HAARAHLD BRYAHN—Duke of Ahrmahk, Prince of Tellesberg, Prince Protector of the Realm, King Cayleb II of Charis, Emperor Cayleb I of Charis. Husband of Sharleyan Ahrmahk.

AHRMAHK, CROWN PRINCESS ALAHNAH ZHANAYT NAIMU—infant daughter of Cayleb and Sharleyan Ahrmahk; heir to the imperial Charisian crown.

AHRMAHK, HAARAHLD VII—King of Charis.

AHRMAHK, KAHLVYN—Duke of Tirian (deceased), Constable of Hairatha; King Haarahld VII's first cousin.

AHRMAHK, KAHLVYN CAYLEB—younger son of Kahlvyn Ahrmahk, deceased Duke Tirian, King Cayleb's first cousin once removed.

AHRMAHK, RAYJHIS—Duke of Tirian; Kahlvyn Ahrmahk's elder son and heir.

AHRMAHK, SHARLEYAN ALAHNAH ZHENYFYR AHLYSSA TAYT—Duchess of Cherayth, Lady Protector of Chisholm, Queen of Chisholm, Empress of Charis. Wife of Cayleb Ahrmahk. See also Sharleyan Tayt.

AHRMAHK, ZHAN—Crown Prince Zhan; King Cayleb's younger brother.

AHRMAHK, ZHANAYT—Queen Zhanayt; King Haarahld's deceased wife; mother of Cayleb, Zhanayt, and Zhan.

AHRMAHK, ZHANAYT—Princess Zhanayt; Cayleb Ahrmahk's younger sister; second eldest child of King Haarahld VII.

AHRMAHK, ZHENYFYR—Dowager Duchess of Tirian; mother of Kahlvyn Cayleb Ahrmahk; daughter of Rayjhis Yowance, Earl Gray Harbor.

AHRNAHLD, SPYNSAIR—Empress Sharleyan's personal clerk and secretary.

AHRTHYR, SIR ALYK, CORISANDIAN GUARD—Earl of Windshare; Sir Koryn Gahrvai's cavalry commander.

AHSTYN, LIEUTENANT FRANZ, CHARISIAN ROYAL GUARD—the second-in-command of King Cayleb II's personal bodyguard.

AHZGOOD, PHYLYP—Earl of Coris; previously spymaster for Prince Hektor of Corisande; currently legal guardian for Princess Irys Daykyn and Prince Daivyn Daykyn.

AIMAYL, RAHN—a member of the anti-Charis resistance in Manchyr, Corisande. An ex-apprentice of Paitryk Hainree's.

AIRNHART, FATHER SAIMYN—Father Zohannes Pahtkovair's immediate subordinate. A Schuelerite.

AIRYTH, EARL OF—see Trumyn Sowthmyn.

AIWAIN, CAPTAIN HARYS, IMPERIAL CHARISIAN NAVY—CO, HMS *Shield*, 54.

ALBAN, LIEUTENANT COMMANDER NIMUE, TFN—Admiral Pei Kau-zhi's tactical officer.

ANVIL ROCK, EARL OF—See Sir Rysel Gahrvai.

APLYN-AHRMHAK, ENSIGN HEKTOR, IMPERIAL CHARISIAN NAVY—Duke of Darcos; ensign, HMS *Destiny*, 54; later promoted to lieutenant and serves as Sir Dunkyn Yairley's flag lieutenant. Cayleb Ahrmahk's adoptive son.

ARCHBISHOP MAIKEL—see Archbishop Maikel Staynair.

ARCHBISHOP PAWAL—see Archbishop Pawal Braynair.

ARTHMYN, FATHER OHMAHR—senior healer, imperial Palace, Tellesberg.

ATHRAWES, CAPTAIN MERLIN, CHARISIAN IMPERIAL GUARD—King Cayleb II's personal armsman; the cybernetic avatar of Commander Nimue Alban.

AYMEZ, MIDSHIPMAN BARDULF, ROYAL CHARISIAN NAVY—a midshipman, HMS *Typhoon*.

BAHLTYN, ZHEEVYS—Baron White Ford's valet.

BAHNYR, HEKTOR—Earl of Mancora; one of Sir Koryn Gahrvai's senior officers; commander of the right wing at Haryl's Crossing.

BAHR, DAHNNAH—senior chef, Imperial Palace, Cherayth.

BAHRDAHN, CAPTAIN PHYLYP, IMPERIAL CHARISIAN NAVY—CO, HMS *Undaunted*, 56.

BAHRDAILAHN, LIEUTENANT SIR AHBAIL, ROYAL DOHLARAN NAVY—the Earl of Thirsk's flag lieutenant.

BAHRMYN, ARCHBISHOP BORYS—Archbishop of Corisande for the Church of God Awaiting.

BAHRMYN, TOHMYS—Baron White Castle; Prince Hektor's ambassador to Prince Nahrmahn.

BAHRNS, KING RAHNYLD IV—King of Dohlar.

BAHZKAI, LAIYAN—a Leveler and printer in Siddar City; a leader of the Sword of Schueler.

BAIKET, CAPTAIN STYWYRT, ROYAL DOHLARAN NAVY—CO, HMS *Chihiro*, 50; the Earl of Thirsk's flag captain.

BAIKYR, CAPTAIN SYLMAHN, IMPERIAL CHARISIAN NAVY—CO, HMS *Ahrmahk*, 58. High Admiral Lock Island's flag captain.

BAILAHND, SISTER AHMAI—Mother Abbess Ahmai Bailahnd of the Abbey of Saint Evehlain.

BAIRAHT, DAIVYN—Duke of Kholman; Emperor Mahrys IV of Desnair's Navy minister; Sir Urwyn Hahltar's brother-in-law.

BAIRZHAIR, BROTHER TAIRAINCE—treasurer of the Monastery of Saint Zherneau.

BANAHR, FATHER AHZWALD—head of the priory of Saint Hamlyn, city of Sarayn, Kingdom of Charis.

BARCOR, BARON OF—see Sir Zher Sumyrs.

BAYTZ, FELAYZ—Prince Nahrmahn of Emerald's youngest child and second daughter.

BAYTZ, HANBYL—Duke of Solomon; Prince Nahrmahn of Emerald's uncle and the commander of the Emeraldian Army.

BAYTZ, MAHRYA—Prince Nahrmahn of Emerald's oldest child.

BAYTZ, NAHRMAHN GAREYT—second child and elder son of Prince Nahrmahn of Emerald.

BAYTZ, NAHRMAHN HANBYL GRAIM—see Prince Nahrmahn Baytz.

BAYTZ, PRINCE NAHRMAHN II—ruler of the Princedom of Emerald; Cayleb and Sharleyan Ahrmahk's Imperial Councilor for Intelligence.

BAYTZ, PRINCESS OHLYVYA—wife of Prince Nahrmahn of Emerald.

BAYTZ, TRAHVYS—Prince Nahrmahn of Emerald's third child and second son.

BÉDARD, DR. ADORÉE, PH.D.—chief psychiatrist, Operation Ark.

BISHOP EXECUTOR WYLLYS—see Bishop Executor Wyllys Graisyn.

BISHOP ZHERALD—see Bishop Zherald Ahdymsyn.

BLACK WATER, DUKE OF—see Sir Adulfo Lynkyn.

BLACK WATER, DUKE OF—see Admiral Ernyst Lynkyn.

BLAHNDAI, CHANTAHAL—an alias of Lysbet Wylsynn in Zion.

BLAIDYN, LIEUTENANT ROZHYR, ROYAL DOHLARAN NAVY—second lieutenant, galley *Royal Bédard*.

BORYS, ARCHBISHOP—see Archbishop Borys Bahrmyn.

BOWAVE, DAIRAK—Dr. Rahzhyr Mahklyn's senior assistant, Royal College, Tellesberg.

BOWSHAM, CAPTAIN KHANAIR, ROYAL CHARISIAN NAVY—CO, HMS *Gale*.

BRADLAI, LIEUTENANT ROBYRT, ROYAL CORISANDIAN NAVY—true name of Captain Styvyn Whaite.

BRAIDAIL, BROTHER ZHILBYRT—under-priest of the Order of Schueler; a junior Inquisitor in Talkyra.

BRAISHAIR, CAPTAIN HORYS, IMPERIAL CHARISIAN NAVY—CO, HMS *Rock Point*, 38. POW of Earl Thirsk surrendered to the Inquisition.

BRAISYN, AHRNAHLD, IMPERIAL CHARISIAN NAVY—a member of Stywyrt Mahlyk's boat crew.

BRAYNAIR, ARCHBISHOP PAWAL—Archbishop of Chisholm for the Church of Charis.

BREYGART, COLONEL SIR HAUWERD, ROYAL CHARISIAN MARINES—the rightful heir to the Earldom of Hanth. Becomes earl 893.

BREYGART, FRAIDARECK—fourteenth Earl of Hanth; Hauwerd Breygart's great-grandfather.

BROUN, FATHER MAHTAIO—Archbishop Erayk Dynnys' senior secretary and aide; Archbishop Erayk's confidant and protégé.

BROWNYNG, CAPTAIN ELLYS—CO, Temple galleon *Blessed Langhorne*.

BRYNDYN, MAJOR DAHRYN—the senior artillery officer attached to Brigadier Clareyk's column at Haryl's Priory.

BYRK, FATHER MYRTAN—upper-priest of the Order of Schueler; Father Vyktyr Tahrlsahn's second-in-command.

BYRK, MAJOR BREKYN, ROYAL CHARISIAN MARINES—CO, Marine detachment, HMS *Royal Charis*.

BYRKYT, FATHER ZHON—former abbot and current librarian of the Monastery of Saint Zherneau.

CAHKRAYN, SAMYL—Duke of Fern, King Rahnyld IV of Dohlar's first councilor.

CAHMMYNG, AHLBAIR—a professional assassin working for Father Aidryn Waimyn.

CAHNYR, ARCHBISHOP ZHASYN—fugitive Archbishop of Glacierheart; a Reformist member of Samyl Wylsynn's Circle; a major spiritual leader of the Reformists in Siddar City.

CHAHLMAIR, SIR BAIRMON—Duke of Margo; a member of Prince Daivyn's Regency Council.

CHAIMBYRS, LIEUTENANT ZHUSTYN, IMPERIAL DESNAIRIAN NAVY—second lieutenant, HMS *Archangel Chihiro*, 40.

CHALMYR, LIEUTENANT MAILVYN, ROYAL CHARISIAN NAVY—first lieutenant, HMS *Tellesberg*.

CHALMYRZ, FATHER KARLOS—Archbishop Borys Bahrmyn's aide and secretary.

CHARLZ, CAPTAIN MARIK—CO, Charisian merchant ship *Wave Daughter*.

CHARLZ, MASTER YEREK, ROYAL CHARISIAN NAVY—gunner, HMS *Wave*, 14.

CHERMYN, MATHYLD—Hauwyl Chermyn's wife.

CHERMYN, RHAZ—Hauwyl Chermyn's oldest son.

CHERMYN, VICEROY GENERAL HAUWYL, IMPERIAL CHARISIAN MARINES—CO, Charisian occupation forces in Corisande. Cayleb and Sharleyan Ahrmahk's regent in Corisande; later Grand Duke of Zebediah.

CHERYNG, LIEUTENANT TAIWYL—a junior officer on Sir Vyk Lakyr's staff; he is in charge of Lakyr's clerks and message traffic.

CLAREYK, GENERAL KYNT, IMPERIAL CHARISIAN ARMY—

Baron of Green Valley. Ex-brigadier, Imperial Charisian Marines.

CLYNTAHN, VICAR ZHASPAHR—Grand Inquisitor of the Church of God Awaiting; one of the so-called Group of Four.

COHLMYN, ADMIRAL SIR LEWK, IMPERIAL CHARISIAN NAVY—Earl Sharpfield, second-ranking officer, Imperial Charisian Navy. Ex-Royal Chisholmian Navy.

CORIS, EARL OF—see Phylyp Ahzgood.

CRAGGY HILL, EARL OF—see Wahlys Hillkeeper.

DAHNVAHR, AINSAIL—Charisian-born Temple Loyalist living in the Temple Lands recruited for Operation Rakurai.

DAHNVAHR, RAHZHYR—Ainsail Dahnvahr's father.

DAHNVAIR, CAPTAIN LAIZAHNDO, IMPERIAL CHARISIAN NAVY—CO, HMS *Royal Kraken*, 58.

DAHNZAI, LYZBYT—Father Zhaif Laityr's housekeeper at the Church of the Holy Archangels Triumphant.

DAHRYUS, MASTER EDVARHD—an alias of Bishop Mylz Halcom.

DAIKHAR, LIEUTENANT MOHTOHKAI, IMPERIAL CHARISIAN NAVY—XO, HMS *Dart*, 54.

DAIKYN, GAHLVYN—King Cayleb's valet.

DAIVYS, MYTRAHN—a Charisian Temple Loyalist.

DARCOS, DUKE OF—see Hektor Aplyn-Ahrmahk.

DARYS, CAPTAIN TYMYTHY, IMPERIAL CHARISIAN NAVY—CO, HMS *Destroyer*, 54. Sir Domynyk Staynair's flag captain.

DAYKYN, DAIVYN—Prince Hektor of Corisande's youngest child. Prince of Corisande in exile following his father's assassination.

DAYKYN, HEKTOR—Prince of Corisande, leader of the League of Corisande. Assassinated 893.

DAYKYN, HEKTOR (THE YOUNGER)—Prince Hektor of Corisande's second oldest child and heir apparent. Assassinated 893.

DAYKYN, IRYS—daughter of Prince Hektor of Corisande; older sister of Prince Daivyn.

DAYKYN, RAICHYNDA—Prince Hektor of Corisande's deceased wife; born in Earldom of Domair, Kingdom of Hoth.

DEEP HOLLOW, EARL OF—see Bryahn Selkyr.

DEKYN, SERGEANT ALLAYN—one of Kairmyn's noncoms, Delferahkan Army.

DOBYNS, CHARLZ—son of Lyzbyt Dobyns; an adolescent Corisandian convicted of treason as part of the Northern Conspiracy.

DOBYNS, EZMELDA—Father Tymahn Hahskans' housekeeper at Saint Kathryn's church.

DOYAL, SIR CHARLZ, CORISANDIAN GUARD—former artillery commander in Prince Hektor's field army; now chief of staff and senior intelligence officer for Sir Koryn Gahrvai.

DRAGONER, CORPORAL ZHAK, ROYAL CHARISIAN MARINES—a member of Crown Prince Cayleb's bodyguard.

DRAGONER, SIR RAYJHIS—Charisian ambassador to the Republic of Siddarmark.

DRAGONMASTER, BRIGADE SERGEANT MAJOR MAHKYNTY ("MAHK"), ROYAL CHARISIAN MARINES—Brigadier Clareyk's senior noncom during Corisande Campaign.

DUCHAIRN, VICAR RHOBAIR—Minister of Treasury, Council of Vicars; one of the so-called Group of Four.

DYMYTREE, FRONZ, ROYAL CHARISIAN MARINES—a member of Crown Prince Cayleb's bodyguard.

DYNNYS, ADORAI—Archbishop Erayk Dynnys' wife.

DYNNYS, ARCHBISHOP ERAYK—Archbishop of Charis. Executed for heresy 892.

DYNNYS, STYVYN—Archbishop Erayk Dynnys' younger son, age eleven in 892.

DYNNYS, TYMYTHY ERAYK—Archbishop Erayk Dynnys' older son, age fourteen in 892.

EASTSHARE, DUKE OF—see Ruhsyl Thairis.

EDWYRDS, KEVYN—XO, privateer galleon Kraken.

EKYRD, CAPTAIN HAYRYS, ROYAL DOHLARAN NAVY—CO, galley King Rahnyld.

EMPEROR CAYLEB—see Cayleb Ahrmahk.

EMPEROR MAHRYS IV—see Mahrys Ohlarn Ahldarm.

EMPEROR WAISU VI—see Waisu Hantai.

EMPRESS SHARLEYAN—see Sharleyan Ahrmahk.

ERAYK, ARCHBISHOP—see Erayk Dynnys.

ERAYKSYN, LIEUTENANT STYVYN, IMPERIAL CHARISIAN NAVY—Sir Domynyk Staynair's flag lieutenant.

ERAYKSYN, WYLLYM—a Charisian textiles manufacturer.

FAHRMAHN, PRIVATE LUHYS, ROYAL CHARISIAN MARINES—a member of Crown Prince Cayleb's bodyguard.

FAHRMYN, FATHER TAIRYN—the priest assigned to Saint Chihiro's Church, a village church near the Convent of Saint Agtha.

FAHRNO, MAHRLYS—one of Madam Ahnzhelyk Phonda's courtesans.

FAHRYA, CAPTAIN BYRNAHRDO, IMPERIAL DESNAIRIAN NAVY—CO, HMS *Holy Langhorne*, 42.

FAIRCASTER, SERGEANT PAYTER, CHARISIAN ROYAL GUARD—one of Emperor Cayleb's personal guardsmen. A transferee from Crown Prince Cayleb's Marine detachment.

FAIRYS, COLONEL AHLVYN, IMPERIAL CHARISIAN MARINES—CO, First Regiment, Third Brigade, ICMC.

FALKHAN, LIEUTENANT AHRNAHLD, ROYAL CHARISIAN MARINES—CO, Crown Prince Cayleb's personal bodyguard. Later CO, Prince Zhan Ahrmahk's bodyguard.

FATHER MICHAEL—parish priest of Lakeview.

FAUYAIR, BROTHER BAHRTALAM—almoner of the Monastery of Saint Zherneau.

FERN, DUKE OF—see Samyl Cahkrayn.

FHAIRLY, MAJOR AHDYM—the senior battery commander on East Island, Ferayd Sound, Kingdom of Delferahk.

FHARMYN, SIR RYK—a foundry owner/ironmaster in the Kingdom of Tarot.

FOFÃO, CAPTAIN MATEUS, TFN—CO, TFNS *Swiftsure*.

FORYST, VICAR ERAYK—a member of the Reformists.

FRAIDMYN, SERGEANT VYK, CHARISIAN ROYAL GUARD—one of King Cayleb II's armsmen.

FUHLLYR, FATHER RAIMAHND—chaplain, HMS *Dreadnought*.

FURKHAL, RAFAYL—second baseman and leadoff hitter, Tellesberg Krakens.

FYSHYR, HARYS—CO, privateer galleon *Kraken*.

GAHDARHD, LORD SAMYL—keeper of the seal, Republic of Siddarmark.

GAHRBOR, ARCHBISHOP FAILYX—Archbishop of Tarot for the Church of God Awaiting.

GAHRDANER, SERGEANT CHARLZ, CHARISIAN ROYAL GUARD—one of King Haarahld VII's bodyguards.

GAHRMYN, LIEUTENANT RAHNYLD—XO, galley *Arrowhead*, Delferahkan Navy.

GAHRNAHT, BISHOP AMILAIN—deposed Bishop of Larchros.

GAHRVAI, GENERAL SIR KORYN, CORISANDIAN GUARD—Prince Hektor's army field commander; now CO, Corisandian Guard, in the service of the Regency Council. Son of Earl Anvil Rock.

GAHRVAI, SIR RYSEL—Earl of Anvil Rock; Prince Daivyn Daykyn's official regent; head of Daivyn's Regency Council in Corisande.

GAHZTAHN, HIRAIM—Ainsail Dahnvahr's alias in Tellesberg.

GAIMLYN, BROTHER BAHLDWYN—under-priest of the Order of Schueler; assigned to King Zhames of Delferahk's household as an agent of the Inquisition.

GAIRAHT, CAPTAIN WYLLYS, CHISHOLMIAN ROYAL GUARD—CO of Queen Sharleyan's Royal Guard detachment in Charis.

GAIRLYNG, ARCHBISHOP KLAIRMANT—Archbishop of Corisande for the Church of Charis.

GALVAHN, MAJOR SIR NAITHYN—the Earl of Windshare's senior staff officer; Corisande Campaign.

GARDYNYR, ADMIRAL LYWYS, ROYAL DOHLARAN NAVY—Earl of Thirsk and King Rahnyld IV's best admiral.

GARTHIN, EDWAIR—Earl of North Coast; one of Prince Hektor's councilors, now serving on Prince Daivyn's Regency Council.

GHATFRYD, SANDARIA—Ahnzhelyk Phonda's/Nynian Rychtair's personal maid.

GORJAH, FATHER GHARTH—Archbishop Zhasyn Cahnyr's personal secretary.

GORJAH, SAHMANTHA—Father Gharth Gorjah's wife.

GORJAH, ZHASYN—firstborn child of Gharth and Sahmantha Gorjah.

GOWAIN, LIEUTENANT FAIRGHAS, IMPERIAL CHARISIAN NAVY—XO, HMS *Victorious*, 56.

GRAHSMAHN, SYLVAYN—employee in city engineer's office, Manchyr, Corisande; Paitryk Hainree's immediate superior.

GRAHZAIAL, LIEUTENANT COMMANDER MAHSHAL, IMPERIAL CHARISIAN NAVY—CO, schooner HMS *Messenger*, 6.

GRAISYN, BISHOP EXECUTOR WYLLYS—Archbishop Lyam Tyrn's chief administrator for the Archbishopric of Emerald.

GRAIVYR, FATHER STYVYN—Bishop Ernyst's intendant, Ferayd, Delferahk.

GRAND VICAR EREK XVII—secular and temporal head of the Church of God Awaiting.

GRAY HARBOR, EARL OF—see Rayjhis Yowance.

GREEN MOUNTAIN, BARON OF—see Mahrak Sandyrs.

GREEN VALLEY, BARON OF—see General Kynt Clareyk.

GREENHILL, TYMAHN—King Haarahld VII's senior huntsman.

GUYSHAIN, FATHER BAHRNAI—Vicar Zahmsyn Trynair's senior aide.

GYRARD, CAPTAIN ANDRAI, ROYAL CHARISIAN NAVY—CO, HMS *Empress of Charis*.

HAARPAR, SERGEANT GORJ, CHARISIAN ROYAL GUARD—one of King Haarahld VII's bodyguards.

HAHLEK, FATHER SYMYN—Archbishop Klairmant Gairlyng's personal aide.

HAHLMAHN, PAWAL—King Haarahld VII's senior chamberlain.

HAHLMYN, FATHER MAHRAK—an upper-priest of the Church of God Awaiting; Bishop Executor Thomys Shylair's personal aide.

HAHLMYN, MIDSHIPMAN ZHORJ, IMPERIAL CHARISIAN

NAVY—a signals midshipman aboard HMS *Darcos Sound*, 54.

HAHLMYN, SAIRAIH—Sharleyan Ahrmahk's personal maid.

HAHLTAR, ADMIRAL GENERAL SIR URWYN, IMPERIAL DESNAIRIAN NAVY—Baron Jahras; commanding officer, Imperial Desnairian Navy; Daivyn Bairaht's brother-in-law.

HAHLYND, ADMIRAL PAWAL, ROYAL DOHLARAN NAVY—the Earl of Thirsk's senior subordinate admiral.

HAHLYND, FATHER MAHRAK—Bishop Executor Thomys Shylair's personal aide.

HAHRAIMAHN, ZHAK—a Siddarmarkian industrialist and foundry owner.

HAHSKANS, DAILOHRS—Father Tymahn Hahskans' wife.

HAHSKANS, FATHER TYMAHN—a Reformist upper-priest of the Order of Bédard in Manchyr; senior priest, Saint Kathryn's Church.

HAHSKYN, LIEUTENANT AHNDRAI, CHARISIAN IMPERIAL GUARD—a Charisian officer assigned to Empress Sharleyan's guard detachment. Captain Gairaht's second-in-command.

HAHVAIR, COMMANDER FRANZ, IMPERIAL CHARISIAN NAVY—CO, schooner HMS *Mace*, 12.

HAIMLTAHN, BISHOP EXECUTOR WYLLYS—Archbishop Zhasyn Cahnyr's executive assistant in the Archbishopric of Glacierheart.

HAIMYN, BRIGADIER MAHRYS, ROYAL CHARISIAN MARINES—CO, Fifth Brigade, RCMC.

HAINREE, PAITRYK—a silversmith and Temple Loyalist agitator in Manchyr, Princedom of Corisande.

HALCOM, BISHOP MYLZ—Bishop of Margaret Bay.

HALMYN, ARCHBISHOP—see Halmyn Zahmsyn.

HANTAI, WAISU—Waisu VI, Emperor of Harchong.

HANTH, EARL—see Tahdayo Mahntayl. See also Sir Hauwerd Breygart.

HARMYN, MAJOR BAHRKLY, EMERALD ARMY—an Emeraldian army officer assigned to North Bay.

HARPAHR, BISHOP KORNYLYS—Bishop of the Order of Chihiro; Admiral General of the Navy of God.

HARRISON, MATTHEW PAUL—Timothy and Sarah Harrison's great-grandson.

HARRISON, ROBERT—Timothy and Sarah Harrison's grandson; Matthew Paul Harrison's father.

HARRISON, SARAH—wife of Timothy Harrison and an Eve.

HARRISON, TIMOTHY—Mayor of Lakeview and an Adam.

HARYS, CAPTAIN ZHOEL, ROYAL CORISANDIAN NAVY—CO, galleon *Wing*; responsible for transporting Princess Irys and Prince Daivyn to safety from Corisande.

HARYS, FATHER AHLBYRT—Vicar Zahmsyn Trynair's special representative to Dohlar.

HASKYN, MIDSHIPMAN YAHNCEE, ROYAL DOHLARAN NAVY—a midshipman aboard *Gorath Bay*.

HAUWYRD, ZHORZH—Earl Gray Harbor's personal guardsman.

HENDERSON, LIEUTENANT GABRIELA ("GABBY"), TFN—tactical officer, TFNS *Swiftsure*.

HILLKEEPER, WAHLYS—Earl of Craggy Hill; a member of Prince Daivyn's Regency Council; also a senior member of the Northern Conspiracy.

HOLDYN, VICAR LYWYS—a member of the Reformists.

HOTCHKYS, CAPTAIN SIR OHWYN, ROYAL CHARISIAN NAVY—CO, HMS *Tellesberg*.

HOWSMYN, EHDWYRD—a wealthy foundry owner and shipbuilder in Tellesberg.

HOWSMYN, ZHAIN—Ehdwyrd Howsmyn's wife.

HUNTYR, LIEUTENANT KLEMYNT, CHARISIAN ROYAL GUARD—an officer of the Charisian Royal Guard in Tellesberg.

HWYSTYN, SIR VYRNYN—a member of the Charisian Parliament elected from Tellesberg.

HYLLAIR, SIR FARAHK—Baron of Dairwyn.

HYNDRYK, COMMODORE SIR AHLFRYD, IMPERIAL CHARISIAN NAVY—Baron Seamount. Imperial Navy's senior gunnery expert. Effectively CO, Imperial Charisian Navy R&D.

HYNDYRS, DUNKYN—purser, privateer galleon *Raptor*.

HYRST, ADMIRAL ZOHZEF, CHISHOLMIAN NAVY—Earl Sharpfield's second-in-command.

HYSIN, VICAR CHIYAN—a member of the Reformists.

HYWSTYN, LORD AVRAHM—a cousin of Greyghor Stohnar, and a midranking official assigned to the Siddarmarkian foreign ministry.

HYWYT, COMMANDER PAITRYK, ROYAL CHARISIAN NAVY—CO, HMS *Wave*, 14 (schooner). Later promoted to captain as CO, HMS *Dancer*, 56. Later promoted to commodore; CO of squadron escorting Empress Sharleyan to Zebediah and Corisande.

IBBET, AHSTELL—a blacksmith convicted of treason as part of the Northern Conspiracy in Corisande.

ILLIAN, CAPTAIN AHNTAHN—one of Sir Phylyp Myllyr's company commanders.

IRONHILL, BARON—see Ahlvyno Pawalsyn.

JAHRAS, BARON OF—see Admiral General Sir Urwyn Hahltar.

JYNKYN, COLONEL HAUWYRD, ROYAL CHARISIAN MARINES—Admiral Staynair's senior Marine commander.

JYNKYNS, BISHOP ERNYST—Bishop of Ferayd.

KAHBRYLLO, CAPTAIN AHNTAHN, IMPERIAL CHARISIAN NAVY—CO, HMS *Dawn Star*, 58, Empress Sharleyan's transport to Zebediah and Corisande.

KAHNKLYN, AIDRYN—Tairys Kahnklyn's older daughter.

KAHNKLYN, AIZAK—Rahzhyr Mahklyn's son-in-law; a senior librarian with the Royal College of Charis.

KAHNKLYN, ERAYK—Tairys Kahnklyn's oldest son.

KAHNKLYN, EYDYTH—Tairys Kahnklyn's younger daughter.

KAHNKLYN, HAARAHLD—Tairys Kahnklyn's middle son.

KAHNKLYN, TAIRYS—Rahzhyr Mahklyn's married daughter; a senior librarian with the Royal College of Charis.

KAHNKLYN, ZHOEL—Tairys Kahnklyn's youngest son.

KAHRNAIKYS, MAJOR ZHAPHAR, TEMPLE GUARD—an officer of the Temple Guard and a Schuelerite.

KAILLEE, CAPTAIN ZHILBERT, TAROTISIAN NAVY—CO, galley *King Gorjah II*.

KAILLYT, KAIL—Major Borys Sahdlyr's second-in-command in Siddar City.

KAIREE, TRAIVYR—a wealthy merchant and landowner in the Earldom of Styvyn, Kingdom of Charis.

KAIRMYN, CAPTAIN TOMHYS—one of Sir Vyk Lakyr's officers, Delferahkan Army.

KAITS, CAPTAIN BAHRNABAI, IMPERIAL CHARISIAN MARINES—CO, Marine detachment, HMS *Squall*, 36.

KEELHAUL—High Admiral Lock Island's rottweiler; later Baron Seamount's.

KESTAIR, AHRDYN—Archbishop Maikel's married daughter.

KESTAIR, SIR LAIRYNC—Archbishop Maikel's son-in-law.

KHAILEE, MASTER ROLF—a pseudonym used by Lord Avrahm Hywstyn.

KHAPAHR, COMMANDER AHLVYN, ROYAL DOHLARAN NAVY—effectively, the Earl of Thirsk's chief of staff.

KHARMYCH, FATHER AHBSAHLAHN—Archbishop Trumahn Rowzvel's intendant in Gorath. A Schuelerite.

KHATTYR, CAPTAIN PAYT, EMERALD NAVY—CO, galley *Black Prince*.

KHOLMAN, DUKE OF—see Daivyn Bairaht.

KHOWSAN, CAPTAIN OF WINDS SHOUKHAN, IMPERIAL HARCHONGESE NAVY—Count of Wind Mountain, CO, IHNS *Flower of Waters*, 50. Flag captain to the Duke of Sun Rising.

KING GORJAH III—see Gorjah Nyou.

KING HAARAHLD VII—see Haarahld Ahrmahk.

KING RAHNYLD IV—see Rahnyld Bahrns.

KING ZHAMES II—see Zhames Olyvyr Rayno.

KLAHRKSAIN, CAPTAIN TYMAHN, IMPERIAL CHARISIAN NAVY—CO, HMS *Talisman*, 54.

KNOWLES, EVELYN—an Eve who escaped the destruction of the Alexandria Enclave and fled to Tellesberg.

KNOWLES, JEREMIAH—an Adam who escaped the destruction of the Alexandria Enclave and fled to Tellesberg, where he became the patron saint of the Brethren of Saint Zherneau.

KOHRBY, MIDSHIPMAN LYNAIL, ROYAL CHARISIAN NAVY—senior midshipman, HMS *Dreadnought*.

KRAHL, CAPTAIN AHNDAIR, ROYAL DOHLARAN NAVY—CO, HMS *Bédard*, 42.

KRUGAIR, CAPTAIN MAIKEL, IMPERIAL CHARISIAN NAVY—CO, HMS *Avalanche*, 36. POW of Earl Thirsk surrendered to the Inquisition.

KRUGHAIR, LIEUTENANT ZHASYN, IMPERIAL CHARISIAN NAVY—second lieutenant, HMS *Dancer*, 56.

KWAYLE, TYMYTHY, IMPERIAL CHARISIAN NAVY—a senior petty officer and boatswain's mate, HMS *Destiny*, 54.

KWILL, FATHER ZYTAN—upper-priest of the Order of Bédard; abbot of the Hospice of the Holy Bédard, the main homeless shelter in the city of Zion.

LAHANG, BRAIDEE—Prince Nahrmahn of Emerald's chief agent in Charis before Merlin Athrawes' arrival there.

LAHFAT, CAPTAIN MYRGYN—piratical ruler of Claw Keep on Claw Island.

LAHFTYN, MAJOR BRYAHN—Brigadier Clareyk's chief of staff.

LAHMBAIR, PARSAIVAHL—a prominent Corisandian greengrocer convicted of treason as part of the Northern Conspiracy.

LAHRAK, NAILYS—a senior leader of the Temple Loyalists in Charis.

LAHSAHL, LIEUTENANT SHAIRMYN, IMPERIAL CHARISIAN NAVY—XO, HMS *Destroyer*, 54.

LAICHARN, ARCHBISHOP PRAIDWYN—Archbishop of Siddar; the ranking prelate of the Republic of Siddarmark. A Langhornite.

LAIMHYN, FATHER CLYFYRD—Emperor Cayleb's personal secretary, assigned to him by Archbishop Maikel.

LAINYR, BISHOP EXECUTOR WYLSYNN—Bishop Executor of Gorath. A Langhornite.

LAIRAYS, FATHER AWBRAI—under-priest of the Order of Schueler; HMS *Archangel Chihiro*'s ship's chaplain.

LAIRMAHN, FAHSTAIR—Baron of Lakeland; first councilor of the Kingdom of Delferahk.

LAITEE, FATHER ZHAMES—priest of the Order of Schueler; assistant to Father Gaisbyrt Vandaik in Talkyra.

LAITYR, FATHER ZHAIF—a Reformist upper-priest of the

Order of Pasquale; senior priest, Church of the Holy Archangels Triumphant; a close personal friend of Father Tymahn Hahskans'.

LAKYR, SIR VYK—SO, Ferayd garrison, Kingdom of Delferahk.

LANGHORNE, ERIC—chief administrator, Operation Ark.

LARCHROS, BARON OF—see Rahzhyr Mairwyn.

LARCHROS, BARONESS OF—see Raichenda Mairwyn.

LATHYK, LIEUTENANT RHOBAIR, IMPERIAL CHARISIAN NAVY—XO, HMS *Destiny*, 54. Later promoted to captain and CO, HMS *Destiny*.

LAYBRAHN, BAHRYND—Paitryk Hainree's alias.

LAYN, MAJOR ZHIM, ROYAL CHARISIAN MARINES—Brigadier Kynt's subordinate for original syllabus development. Now the senior training officer, Helen Island Marine Base.

LEKTOR, ADMIRAL SIR TARYL—Earl of Tartarian; CO, Royal Corisandian Navy under Prince Hektor during Corisande Campaign; Earl Anvil Rock's main ally since Hektor's death, another member of Prince Daivyn's Regency Council.

LOCK ISLAND, EARL OF—see High Admiral Bryahn Lock Island.

LOCK ISLAND, HIGH ADMIRAL BRYAHN, IMPERIAL CHARISIAN NAVY—Earl of Lock Island; CO, Imperial Charisian Navy. Cayleb Ahrmhak's cousin.

LORD PROTECTOR GREYGHOR—see Lord Protector Greyghor Stohnar.

LYAM, ARCHBISHOP—see Archbishop Lyam Tyrn.

LYNDAHR, SIR RAIMYND—Prince Hektor's keeper of the purse; now serving on Prince Daivyn's Regency Council.

LYNKYN, ADMIRAL ERNYST, CORISANDIAN NAVY—Duke of Black Water; CO, Corisandian Navy; KIA, Battle of Darcos Sound.

LYNKYN, SIR ADULFO—Duke of Black Water; son of Sir Ernyst Lynkyn, killed at the Battle of Darcos Sound.

LYWKYS, LADY MAIRAH—Empress Sharleyan's chief lady-in-waiting. She is Baron Green Mountain's cousin.

LYWSHAI, TRUMYN—Sir Dunkyn Yairley's secretary.

NAVY—CO, Experimental Board. Commodore Sea-mount's senior assistant.

MAHNDYR, EARL—see Gharth Rahlstahn.

MAHNTAIN, CAPTAIN TOHMYS, IMPERIAL DESNAIRIAN NAVY—CO, HMS *Blessed Warrior*, 40.

MAHNTAYL, TAHDAYO—usurper Earl of Hanth.

MAHNTEE, LIEUTENANT CHARLZ, ROYAL DOHLARAN NAVY—XO, HMS *Rakurai*, 46.

MAHNTYN, CORPORAL AILAS—a scout-sniper assigned to Sergeant Edvarhd Wystahn's platoon.

MAHRAK, LIEUTENANT RAHNALD, ROYAL CHARISIAN NAVY—first lieutenant, HMS *Royal Charis*.

MAHRLOW, BISHOP EXECUTOR AHRAIN—Archbishop Halmyn Zahmsyn's executive assistant, Archbishopric of Gorath, Kingdom of Dohlar.

MAHRLOW, FATHER ARTHYR—priest of the Order of Schueler; assistant to Father Gaisbyrt Vandaik in Talkyra.

MAHRTYN, ADMIRAL GAHVYN, ROYAL TAROTISIAN NAVY—Baron of White Ford. Senior officer, Royal Tarotisian Navy.

MAHRTYNSYN, LIEUTENANT LAIZAIR, IMPERIAL DESNAIR-IAN NAVY—XO, HMS *Archangel Chihiro*, 40.

MAHRYS, CORPORAL ZHAK—Tobys Raimair's junior non-com.

MAHRYS, ZHERYLD—Sir Rayjhis Dragoner's senior secretary and aide.

MAHZYNGAIL, LIEUTENANT HAARLAHM, IMPERIAL CHARI-SIAN NAVY—High Admiral Rock Point's new flag secretary.

MAIDYN, LORD HENRAI—Chancellor of the Exchequer, Republic of Siddarmark.

MAIGEE, CAPTAIN GRAYGAIR, ROYAL DOHLARAN NAVY—CO, galleon *Guardian*.

MAIGEE, PLATOON SERGEANT ZHAK, IMPERIAL CHARISIAN MARINES—senior noncom, Second Platoon, Alpha Company, 1/3rd Marines, ICMC.

MAIGOWHYN, LIEUTENANT BRAHNDYN, ROYAL DELFERAH-KAN ARMY—Colonel Aiphraim Tahlyvyr's aide.

MAIGWAIR, VICAR ALLAYN—Captain General of the Church of God Awaiting; one of the so-called Group of Four.

MAIK, BISHOP STAIPHAN—a Schuelerite auxiliary bishop of the Church of God Awaiting; effectively intendant for the Royal Dohlaran Navy in the Church's name.

MAIKEL, CAPTAIN QWENTYN, ROYAL DOHLARAN NAVY—CO, galley *Gorath Bay.*

MAIKELSYN, LIEUTENANT LEEAHM, ROYAL TAROTISIAN NAVY—first lieutenant, *King Gorjah II.*

MAIRWYN, RAHZHYR—Baron of Larchros; a member of the Northern Conspiracy in Corisande.

MAIRWYN, RAICHENDA—Baroness of Larchros; wife of Rahzhyr Mairwyn.

MAIRYDYTH, LIEUTENANT NEVYL, ROYAL DOHLARAN NAVY—first lieutenant, galley *Royal Bédard.*

MAITLYND, CAPTAIN ZHORJ, IMPERIAL CHARISIAN NAVY—CO, HMS *Victorious*, 56.

MAITZLYR, CAPTAIN FAIDOHRAV, IMPERIAL DESNAIRIAN NAVY—CO, HMS *Loyal Defender*, 48.

MAIYR, CAPTAIN ZHAKSYN—one of Colonel Sir Wahlys Zhorj's troop commanders in Tahdayo Mahntayl's service.

MAKAIVYR, BRIGADIER ZHOSH, ROYAL CHARISIAN MARINES—CO, First Brigade, RCMC.

MAKFERZAHN, ZHAMES—one of Prince Hektor's agents in Charis.

MAKGREGAIR, FATHER ZHOSHUA—Vicar Zahmsyn Trynair's special representative to Tarot.

MALIKAI, DUKE OF—see Faidel Ahlverez.

MANTHYR, ADMIRAL SIR GWYLYM, IMPERIAL CHARISIAN NAVY—Cayleb Ahrmahk's flag captain at battles of Crag Hook, Rock Point, and Darcos Sound; later admiral; CO, Charisian expedition to Gulf of Dohlar; senior Charisian POW surrendered to Inquisition by Kingdom of Dohlar.

MARGO, DUKE OF—see Sir Bairmon Chahlmair.

MARSHYL, MIDSHIPMAN ADYM, ROYAL CHARISIAN NAVY—senior midshipman, HMS *Royal Charis.*

MATHYSYN, LIEUTENANT ZHAIKEB, ROYAL DOHLARAN NAVY—first lieutenant, galley *Gorath Bay*.

MAYLYR, CAPTAIN DUNKYN, ROYAL CHARISIAN NAVY—CO, HMS *Halberd*.

MAYSAHN, ZHASPAHR—Prince Hektor's senior agent in Charis.

MAYTHIS, LIEUTENANT FRAIZHER, ROYAL CORISANDIAN NAVY—true name of Captain Wahltayr Seatown.

MHULVAYN, OSKAHR—one of Prince Hektor's agents in Charis.

MULLYGYN, RAHSKHO—Tobys Raimair's second-ranking noncom.

MYCHAIL, ALYX—Rhaiyan Mychail's oldest grandson.

MYCHAIL, MYLDRYD—one of Rhaiyan Mychail's married granddaughters-in-law.

MYCHAIL, RHAIYAN—a business partner of Ehdwyrd Howsmyn and the Kingdom of Charis' primary textile producer.

MYCHAIL, STYVYN—Myldryd Mychail's youngest son.

MYLLYR, ARCHBISHOP URVYN—Archbishop of Sodar.

MYLLYR, SIR PHYLYP—one of Sir Koryn Gahrvai's regimental commanders, Corisande Campaign.

MYLS, BRIGADIER GWYAHN, IMPERIAL CHARISIAN MARINES—CO, Second Regiment, Third Brigade, ICMC.

MYRGYN, SIR KEHVYN, ROYAL CORISANDIAN NAVY—CO, galley *Corisande*. Duke Black Water's flag captain. KIA, Battle of Darcos Sound.

NAIGAIL, SAMYL—son of a deceased Siddarmarkian sailmaker; Temple Loyalist and anti-Charisian bigot.

NAIKLOS, CAPTAIN FRAHNKLYN, CORISANDIAN GUARD—CO of Sir Koryn Gahrvai's headquarters company; later promoted to major.

NARTH, BISHOP EXECUTOR TYRNYR—Archbishop Failyx Gahrbor's executive assistant, Archbishopric of Tarot.

NETHAUL, HAIRYM—XO, privateer schooner *Blade*.

NOHRCROSS, BISHOP MAILVYN—Bishop of Barcor for the Church of Charis; a member of the Northern Conspiracy in Corisande.

NORTH COAST, EARL OF—see Edwair Garthin.

NYLZ, ADMIRAL KOHDY, IMPERIAL CHARISIAN NAVY—senior squadron commander, ICN; previously commodore, Royal Charisian Navy.

NYOU, GORJAH ALYKSAHNDAR—King Gorjah III, King of Tarot.

NYOU, MAIYL—Queen Consort of Tarot; wife of Gorjah Nyou.

NYOU, PRINCE RHOLYND—Crown Prince of Tarot; infant son of Gorjah and Maiyl Nyou; heir to the Tarotisian throne.

NYXYN, DAIVYN, ROYAL DELFERAHKAN ARMY—a dragoon assigned to Sergeant Braice Mahknash's squad.

OARMASTER, SYGMAHN, ROYAL CHARISIAN MARINES—a member of Crown Prince Cayleb's bodyguard.

OHLSYN, TRAHVYS—Earl of Pine Hollow; Prince Nahrmahn of Emerald's first councilor; later first councilor of Charis.

OLYVYR, AHNYET—Sir Dustyn Olyvyr's wife.

OLYVYR, SIR DUSTYN—a leading Tellesberg ship designer; chief constructor, Royal Charisian Navy.

OWL—Nimue Alban's AI, based on the manufacturer's acronym: Ordoñes-Westinghouse-Lytton RAPIER Tactical Computer, Mark 17a.

PAHLMAHN, ZHULYIS—a Corisandian banker convicted of treason as part of the Northern Conspiracy.

PAHLZAR, COLONEL AHKYLLYS—Sir Charlz Doyal's replacement as Sir Koryn Gahrvai's senior artillery commander.

PAHRAIHA, COLONEL VAHSAG, IMPERIAL CHARISIAN MARINES—CO, Fourteenth Marine Regiment.

PAHRSAHN, AIVAH—Nynian Rychtair's public persona in the Republic of Siddarmark.

PAHSKAL, MASTER MIDSHIPMAN FAYDOHR, IMPERIAL CHARISIAN NAVY—a midshipman assigned to HMS *Dawn Star*, 58.

PAHTKOVAIR, FATHER ZOHANNES—Intendant of Siddar. A Schuelerite.

PARKAIR, LORD DARYUS—seneschal, Republic of Siddarmark.

PARKAIR, ZHANAIAH—Daryus Parkair's wife.

PARKYR, GLAHDYS—Crown Princess Alahnah's Chisholmian wetnurse and nanny.

PAWAL, CAPTAIN ZHON, IMPERIAL CHARISIAN NAVY—CO, HMS *Dart*, 54.

PAWALSYN, AHLVYNO—Baron Ironhill, keeper of the purse (treasurer) of the Kingdom of Old Charis.

PEI, KAU-YUNG, COMMODORE, TFN—CO, Operation Ark final escort; husband of Dr. Pei Shan-wei.

PEI, KAU-ZHI, ADMIRAL, TFN—CO, Operation Breakaway; older brother of Commodore Pei Kau-yung.

PEI, SHAN-WEI, PH.D.—Commodore Pei Kau-yung's wife; senior terraforming expert for Operation Ark.

PHALGRAIN, SIR HARVAI—majordomo, Imperial Palace, Cherayth.

PHANDYS, MAJOR KHANSTAHNZO—an officer of the Temple Guard. Promoted to major; CO of Vicar Rhobair Duchairn's personal security detachment.

PHONDA, AHNZHELYK—an alias of Nynian Rychtair; one of the most successful courtesans in the city of Zion; an agent and ally of Samyl Wylsynn.

PINE HOLLOW, EARL—see Trahvys Ohlsyn.

PLYZYK, CAPTAIN EHRNYSTO, IMPERIAL DESNAIRIAN NAVY—CO, HMS *Saint Adulfo*, 40.

PRINCE CAYLEB—see Cayleb Ahrmahk.

PRINCE DAIVYN—see Daivyn Daykyn.

PRINCE HEKTOR—see Hektor Daykyn.

PRINCE NAHRMAHN—see Nahrmahn Baytz.

PRINCE RHOLYND—see Rholynd Nyou.

PRINCESS IRYS—see Irys Daykyn.

PROCTOR, ELIAS, PH.D.—a member of Pei Shan-wei's staff and a noted cyberneticist.

PRUAIT, CAPTAIN TYMYTHY, IMPERIAL CHARISIAN NAVY—newly appointed captain of prize ship *Sword of God*.

QUEEN CONSORT HAILYN—see Hailyn Rayno.

QUEEN MAIYL—see Maiyl Nyou.

QUEEN SHARLEYAN—see Sharleyan Tayt.

QUEEN YSBELL—an earlier reigning queen of Chisholm

who was deposed (and murdered) in favor of a male ruler.

QWENTYN, COMMODORE DONYRT, ROYAL CORISANDIAN NAVY—Baron of Tanlyr Keep, one of Duke of Black Water's squadron commanders.

QWENTYN, OWAIN—Tymahn Qwentyn's grandson.

QWENTYN, TYMAHN—head of the House of Qwentyn, a powerful banking and investment cartel in the Republic of Siddarmark.

RAHLSTAHN, ADMIRAL GHARTH, IMPERIAL CHARISIAN NAVY—Earl of Mahndyr, third-ranking officer, Imperial Charisian Navy. Ex-Royal Emeraldian Navy.

RAHLSTYN, COMMODORE ERAYK, ROYAL DOHLARAN NAVY—one of Duke Malikai's squadron commanders.

RAHSKAIL, COLONEL BARKAH, IMPERIAL CHARISIAN ARMY—Earl of Swayle, a senior supply officer, Imperial Charisian Army.

RAHZMAHN, LIEUTENANT DAHNYLD, IMPERIAL CHARISIAN NAVY—Sir Gwylym Manthyr's flag lieutenant.

RAICE, BYNZHAMYN—Baron Wave Thunder, royal counselor for intelligence, Kingdom of Old Charis.

RAICE, LEAHYN—Baroness Wave Thunder; wife of Bynzhamyn Raice.

RAIGLY, SYLVYST—Sir Dunkyn Yairley's valet.

RAIMAHN, BYRK—Claitahn and Sahmantha Raimahn's grandson; musician and Reformist.

RAIMAHN, CLAITAHN—wealthy Charisian expatriate and Temple Loyalist living in Siddar City.

RAIMAHN, SAHMANTHA—Claitahn Raimahn's wife and also a Temple Loyalist.

RAIMAIR, TOBYS—ex-sergeant Royal Corisandian Army; commander of Prince Daivyn and Princess Irys' unofficial guardsmen in Delferahk.

RAIMYND, SIR LYNDAHR—Prince Hektor of Corisande's treasurer.

RAISAHNDO, CAPTAIN CAITAHNO, ROYAL DOHLARAN NAVY—CO, HMS *Rakurai*, 46.

RAISLAIR, BISHOP EXECUTOR MHARTYN—Archbishop

Ahdym Taibyr's executive assistant, Archbishopric of Desnair.

RAIYZ, FATHER CARLSYN—Queen Sharleyan's confessor.

RAIZYNGYR, COLONEL ARTTU, ROYAL CHARISIAN MARINES—CO, 2/3rd Marines (Second Battalion, Third Brigade).

RAYNAIR, CAPTAIN EKOHLS—CO, privateer schooner *Blade*.

RAYNO, ARCHBISHOP WYLLYM—Archbishop of Chiang-wu; adjutant of the Order of Schueler.

RAYNO, HAILYN—Queen Consort of the Kingdom of Delferahk; wife of King Zhames II; a cousin of Prince Hektor of Corisande.

RAYNO, ZHAMES OLYVYR—King Zhames II of Delferahk. A kinsman by marriage of Irys and Daivyn Daykyn.

RAZHAIL, FATHER DERAHK—senior healer, Imperial Palace, Cherayth. Upper-priest of the Order of Pasquale.

RHOBAIR, VICAR—see also Rhobair Duchairn.

ROCK POINT, BARON OF—see Sir Domynyk Staynair.

ROHSAIL, CAPTAIN SIR DAHRAND, ROYAL DOHLARAN NAVY—CO, HMS *Grand Vicar Mahrys*, 50.

ROHZHYR, COLONEL BAHRTOL, ROYAL CHARISIAN MARINES—a senior commissary officer.

ROPEWALK, COLONEL AHDAM, CHARISIAN ROYAL GUARD—CO, Charisian Royal Guard.

ROWYN, CAPTAIN HORAHS—CO, Sir Dustyn Olyvyr's yacht *Ahnyet*.

ROWZVEL, ARCHBISHOP TRUMAHN—new Archbishop of Gorath. A Langhornite.

RUSTMAYN, EDMYND—Baron Stonekeep; King Gorjah III of Tarot's first councilor and spymaster.

RYCHTAIR, NYNIAN—Ahnzhelyk Phonda's birth name; adopted sister of Adorai Dynnys.

SAHBRAHAN, PAIAIR—the Earl of Thirsk's personal valet.

SAHDLYR, LIEUTENANT BYNZHAMYN, ROYAL CHARISIAN NAVY—second lieutenant, HMS *Dreadnought*.

SAHDLYR, MAJOR BORYS, TEMPLE GUARD—a guardsman of the Inquisition assigned to Siddar City as part of the Sword of Schueler.

SAHLAVAHN, CAPTAIN TRAI—cousin of Commander Urwyn Mahndrayn; CO, Hairatha Powder Mill.

SAHLMYN, SERGEANT MAJOR HAIN, ROYAL CHARISIAN MARINES—Colonel Zhanstyn's battalion sergeant major.

SAHNDAHL, COLONEL FRAIMAHN, DELFERAHKAN ROYAL GUARD—XO, Delferahkan Royal Guard.

SAHNDYRS, BISHOP STYWYRT—Bishop of Solomon, Princedom of Emerald.

SAHNDYRS, MAHRAK—Baron Green Mountain; Queen Sharleyan of Chisholm's first minister.

SAHRKHO, FATHER MOHRYS—Empress Sharleyan's confessor.

SAIGAHN, CAPTAIN MAHRDAI, ROYAL CHARISIAN NAVY—CO, HMS *Guardsman*, 44.

SAIKOR, BISHOP EXECUTOR BAIKYR—Archbishop Praidwyn Laicharn's bishop executor. A Pasqualate.

SAITHWYK, ARCHBISHOP FAIRMYN—Archbishop of Emerald for the Church of Charis.

SALTAIR, HAIRYET—Crown Princess Alahnah's second nanny.

SARMAC, JENNIFER—an Eve who escaped the destruction of the Alexandria Enclave and fled to Tellesberg.

SARMAC, KALEB—an Adam who escaped the destruction of the Alexandria Enclave and fled to Tellesberg.

SAWAL, FATHER RAHSS—an under-priest of the Order of Chihiro; the skipper of one of the Temple's courier boats.

SAWYAIR, SISTER FRAHNCYS—senior nun of the Order of Pasquale, Convent of the Blessed Hand, Cherayth.

SAYLKYRK, MIDSHIPMAN TRAHVYS, IMPERIAL CHARISIAN NAVY—senior midshipman, HMS *Destiny*, 54.

SCHAHL, FATHER DAHNYVYN—upper-priest of the Order of Schueler working directly for Bishop Mytchail Zhessop; attached to Colonel Aiphraim Tahlyvyr's dragoon regiment.

SEABLANKET, RHOBAIR—the Earl of Coris' valet.

SEACATCHER, SIR RAHNLYD—Baron Mandolin, a member of King Cayleb's Council.

SEAFARMER, SIR RHYZHARD—Baron Wave Thunder's senior investigator.

SEAHAMPER, SERGEANT EDWYRD—Charisian Imperial Guardsman; Sharleyan Ahrmahk's personal armsman since age ten.

SEAMOUNT, BARON—see Sir Ahlfryd Hyndryk.

SEAROSE, FATHER GREYGHOR, NAVY OF GOD—CO, NGS *Saint Styvyn*, 52. Senior surviving officer of Kornylys Harpahr's fleet. A Chihirite of the Order of the Sword.

SEASMOKE, LIEUTENANT YAIRMAN, IMPERIAL CHARISIAN NAVY—XO, HMS *Dancer*, 56.

SEATOWN, CAPTAIN WAHLTAYR—CO of merchant ship *Fraynceen*, acting as a courier for Prince Hektor's spies in Charis. See also Lieutenant Fraizher Maythis.

SELKYR, AHNTAHN, IMPERIAL CHARISIAN NAVY—a boatswain's mate, HMS *Destiny*, 54.

SELKYR, BRYAHN—Earl of Deep Hollow; a member of the Northern Conspiracy in Corisande.

SELLYRS, PAITYR—Baron White Church, Keeper of the Seal of the Kingdom of Charis; a member of King Cayleb's Council.

SHAIKYR, LARYS—CO, privateer galleon *Raptor*.

SHAILTYN, CAPTAIN DAIVYN, IMPERIAL CHARISIAN NAVY—CO, HMS *Thunderbolt*, 58.

SHAIN, CAPTAIN PAYTER, IMPERIAL CHARISIAN NAVY—CO, HMS *Dreadful*, 48. Admiral Nylz' flag captain. Promoted admiral; flag officer commanding ICN squadron based on Thol Bay, Kingdom of Tarot.

SHAJOW, ADMIRAL OF THE BROAD OCEANS CHYNTAI, IMPERIAL HARCHONGESE NAVY—Duke of Sun Rising, senior officer afloat, Imperial Harchongese Navy.

SHANDYR, HAHL—Baron of Shandyr, Prince Nahrmahn of Emerald's spymaster.

SHARGHATI, AHLYSSA—greatest soprano opera singer of the Republic of Siddarmark; friend of Aivah Pahrsahn's.

SHARPFIELD, EARL OF—see Sir Lewk Cohlmyn.

SHAUMAHN, BROTHER SYMYN—hosteler of the Monastery of Saint Zherneau.

SHOWAIL, LIEUTENANT COMMANDER STYV, IMPERIAL CHARISIAN NAVY—CO, schooner HMS *Flash*, 10.

SHUMAKYR, FATHER SYMYN—Archbishop Erayk Dynnys' secretary for his 891 pastoral visit; an agent of the Grand Inquisitor.

SHUMAY, FATHER AHLVYN—Bishop Mylz Halcom's personal aide.

SHYLAIR, BISHOP EXECUTOR THOMYS—Archbishop Borys' executive assistant in the Archbishopric of Corisande.

SMOLTH, ZHAN—star pitcher for the Tellesberg Krakens.

SOMERSET, CAPTAIN MARTIN LUTHER, TFN—CO, TFNS *Excalibur*.

SOWTHMYN, TRUMYN—Earl of Airyth; one of Prince Hektor's councilors, now serving on Prince Daivyn's Regency Council.

STAHKAIL, GENERAL LOWRAI, IMPERIAL DESNAIRIAN ARMY—CO, Triangle Shoal Fort, Iythria.

STANTYN, ARCHBISHOP NYKLAS—Archbishop of Hankey in the Desnairian Empire.

STAYNAIR, AHRDYN—Archbishop Maikel Staynair's deceased wife.

STAYNAIR, ARCHBISHOP MAIKEL—head of the Church of Charis; was senior Charisian-born prelate of the Church of God Awaiting in Charis; named prelate of all Charis by then-King Cayleb.

STAYNAIR, SIR DOMYNYK, IMPERIAL CHARISIAN NAVY—Baron of Rock Point and High Admiral of the Imperial Charisian Navy; brother of Archbishop Maikel Staynair.

STOHNAR, LORD PROTECTOR GREYGHOR—elected ruler of the Siddarmark Republic.

STONEKEEP, BARON OF—see Edmynd Rustmayn.

STORM KEEP, EARL OF—see Sahlahmn Traigair.

STYWYRT, CAPTAIN AHRNAHLD, IMPERIAL CHARISIAN NAVY—CO, HMS *Squall*, 36.

STYWYRT, CAPTAIN DAHRYL, ROYAL CHARISIAN NAVY—CO, HMS *Typhoon*.

STYWYRT, SERGEANT ZOHZEF—another of Captain Kairmyn's noncoms, Delferahkan Army.

SUMYR, FATHER FRAHNKLYN—Archbishop Failyx Gahrbor's intendant, Archbishopric of Tarot.

SUMYRS, SIR ZHER—Baron of Barcor; one of Sir Koryn Gahrvai's senior officers, Corisande Campaign; later member of Northern Conspiracy.

SUN RISING, DUKE OF—see Admiral of the Broad Oceans Chyntai Shaiow.

SUWYL, TOBYS—an expatriate Charisian banker and merchant living in Siddar City; a Temple Loyalist.

SUWYL, ZHANDRA—Tobys Suwyl's wife; a moderate Reformist.

SVAIRSMAHN, MIDSHIPMAN LAINSAIR, IMPERIAL CHARISIAN NAVY—a midshipman, HMS *Dancer*, 56; youngest of Charisian POWs surrendered to Inquisition by Kingdom of Dohlar.

SWAYLE, EARL OF—see Colonel Barkah Rahskail.

SYMKEE, LIEUTENANT GARAITH, IMPERIAL CHARISIAN NAVY—second lieutenant and later XO, HMS *Destiny*, 54.

SYMMYNS, SENIOR CHIEF PETTY OFFICER MAIKEL, IMPERIAL CHARISIAN NAVY—boatswain, HMS *Destiny*, 54.

SYMMYNS, TOHMYS—Grand Duke of Zebediah; senior nobleman of Zebediah; a member of the Northern Conspiracy in Corisande.

SYMYN, LIEUTENANT HAHL, ROYAL CHARISIAN NAVY—XO, HMS *Torrent*, 42.

SYMYN, SERGEANT ZHORJ, CHARISIAN IMPERIAL GUARD—a Charisian noncom assigned to Empress Sharleyan's guard detachment.

SYNKLYR, LIEUTENANT AIRAH, ROYAL DOHLARAN NAVY—XO, galleon *Guardian*.

TAHLAS, LIEUTENANT BRAHD, IMPERIAL CHARISIAN MARINES—CO, Second Platoon, Alpha Company, 1/3rd Marines, ICMC.

TAHLBAHT, FRAHNCYN—a senior employee (and actual owner) of Bruhstair Freight Haulers; an alias of Nynian Rychtair.

TAHLYVYR, COLONEL AIPHRAIM, ROYAL DELFERAHKAN

THOMPKYN, HAUWERSTAT—Earl of White Crag; Chisholm's Lord Justice.

THOMYS, FRAIDMYN—Archbishop Zhasyn Cahnyr's valet.

THORAST, DUKE OF—see Aibram Zaivyair.

THYRSTYN, SYMYN—a Siddarmarkian merchant; husband of Wynai Thyrstyn.

THYRSTYN, WYNAI—Trai Sahlavahn's married sister; secretary and stenographer in Charis' Siddar City embassy.

TIANG, BISHOP EXECUTOR WU-SHAI—Archbishop Zherohm Vyncyt's bishop executor.

TILLYER, LIEUTENANT COMMANDER HENRAI, IMPERIAL CHARISIAN NAVY—High Admiral Lock Island's chief of staff; previously his flag lieutenant.

TIRIAN, DUKE—see Kahlvyn Ahrmahk.

TOHMYS, FRAHNKLYN—Crown Prince Cayleb's tutor.

TOHMYS, FRAIDMYN—Archbishop Zhasyn Cahnyr's valet of many years.

TRAHLMAHN, FATHER ZHON—Order of Bédard; Prince Nahrmahn Baytz' palace confessor.

TRAHSKHAT, MAHRTYN—Sailys and Myrahm Trahskhat's older son.

TRAHSKHAT, MYRAHM—Sailys Trahskhat's wife and also a Temple Loyalist.

TRAHSKHAT, PAWAL—Sailys and Myrahm Trahskhat's younger son.

TRAHSKHAT, SAILYS—Charisian longshoreman and Temple Loyalist living in Siddar City; former professional baseball player.

TRAHSKHAT, SINDAI—Sailys and Myrahm's Trahskhat's daughter and youngest child.

TRAIGAIR, SAHLAHMN—Earl of Storm Keep; a member of the Northern Conspiracy in Corisande.

TRAIGHAIR, FATHER LHAREE—rector of Saint Bailair's Church, Siddar City; Order of Bédard; a Reformist.

TRYNAIR, VICAR ZAHMSYN—Chancellor of the Council of Vicars of the Church of God Awaiting; one of the so-called Group of Four.

TRYNTYN, CAPTAIN ZHAIRYMIAH, ROYAL CHARISIAN NAVY—CO, HMS *Torrent*, 42.

TRYVYTHYN, CAPTAIN SIR DYNZYL, ROYAL CHARISIAN NAVY—CO, HMS *Royal Charis*.

TYMKYN, LIEUTENANT TOHMYS, IMPERIAL CHARISIAN NAVY—fourth lieutenant and later third lieutenant HMS *Destiny*, 54.

TYMKYN, ZHASTROW—High Admiral Rock Point's secretary.

TYOTAYN, BRIGADIER BAIRAHND, IMPERIAL CHARISIAN MARINES—CO, Fifth Brigade, ICMC. Sir Gwylym Manthyr's senior Marine officer.

TYRN, ARCHBISHOP LYAM—Archbishop of Emerald.

TYRNYR, SERGEANT BRYNDYN, CHISHOLMIAN ROYAL GUARD—a member of Queen Sharleyan's normal guard detail.

TYRNYR, SIR SAMYL—Cayleb's special ambassador to Chisholm; was placed/supplanted/reinforced by Gray Harbor's arrival.

UHLSTYN, YAIRMAN—Sir Koryn Gahrvai's personal armsman.

URBAHN, HAHL—XO, privateer galleon *Raptor*.

URVYN, ARCHBISHOP—see Urvyn Myllyr.

URVYN, LIEUTENANT ZHAK, ROYAL CHARISIAN NAVY—XO, HMS *Wave*, 14.

URWYN, LUDOVYC—first Lord Protector of Siddarmark; founder of Republic of Siddarmark.

USHYR, FATHER BRYAHN—an under-priest, Archbishop Maikel's personal secretary and most trusted aide.

VAHLAIN, NAIKLOS—Sir Gwylym Manthyr's valet; one of the Charisian POWs surrendered to Inquisition by the Kingdom of Dohlar.

VAHNWYK, MAHRTYN—the Earl of Thirsk's personal secretary and senior clerk.

VAHSPHAR, BISHOP EXECUTOR DYNZAIL—Bishop Executor of Delferahk. An Andropovite.

VANDAIK, FATHER GAISBYRT—upper-priest of the Order of Schueler; an inquisitor working directly for Bishop Mytchail Zhessop in Talkyra.

VELDAMAHN, BYRTRYM—High Admiral Rock Point's personal coxswain.

VRAIDAHN, MISTRESS ALYS—Archbishop Maikel Staynair's housekeeper.

VYKAIN, LIEUTENANT MAHRYAHNO, IMPERIAL CHARISIAN NAVY—XO, HMS *Ahrmahk*, 58.

VYNAIR, SERGEANT AHDYM, CHARISIAN ROYAL GUARD—one of King Cayleb II's armsmen.

VYNCYT, ARCHBISHOP ZHEROHM—primate of Chisholm.

WAHLDAIR, LIEUTENANT LAHMBAIR, IMPERIAL CHARISIAN NAVY—third lieutenant, HMS *Dancer*, 56.

WAHLS, COLONEL STYVYN, ROYAL DELFERAHKAN ARMY—CO, Sarmouth Keep.

WAHLTAHRS, RAHZHYR—Tobys Raimair's senior noncom.

WAIGAN, FRAHNKLYN, IMPERIAL CHARISIAN NAVY—chief petty officer and senior helmsman, HMS *Destiny*, 54.

WAIGNAIR, BISHOP HAINRYK—Bishop of Tellesberg; senior prelate (after Archbishop Maikel) of the Kingdom of Old Charis.

WAILAHR, COMMODORE SIR HAIRAHM, IMPERIAL DESNAIRIAN NAVY—a squadron commander of the Imperial Desnairian Navy.

WAIMYN, FATHER AIDRYN—intendant for Church of God Awaiting, Archbishopric of Corisande.

WAIMYS, ZHOSHUA, ROYAL DELFERAHKAN ARMY—a dragoon assigned to Sergeant Braice Mahknash's squad.

WAISTYN, BYRTRYM—Duke of Halbrook Hollow; Queen Sharleyan's deceased uncle and army commander.

WALKYR, EDMYND—CO, merchant galleon *Wave*.

WALKYR, GREYGHOR—Edmynd Walkyr's son.

WALKYR, LYZBET—Edmynd Walkyr's wife.

WALKYR, MIDSHIPMAN FRAID, IMPERIAL CHARISIAN NAVY—midshipman in HMS *Shield*, 54.

WALKYR, MYCHAIL—Edmynd Walkyr's youngest brother; CO, merchant galleon *Wind*.

WALKYR, STYV—Tahdayo Mahntayl's chief adviser.

WALKYR, ZHORJ—XO, galleon *Wave*. Edmynd Walkyr's younger brother.

WALLYCE, LORD FRAHNKLYN—Chancellor of the Siddarmark Republic.

WAVE THUNDER, BARON OF—see Bynzhamyn Raice.

WAVE THUNDER, BARONESS OF—see Leahyn Raice.

WAYST, CAPTAIN ZAKRAI, IMPERIAL CHARISIAN NAVY—CO, HMS *Darcos Sound*, 54.

WHAITE, CAPTAIN STYVYN—CO, merchant ship *Sea Cloud*, a courier for Prince Hektor's spies in Charis. See also Robyrt Bradlai.

WHITE CASTLE, BARON—see Tohmys Bahrmyn.

WHITE CRAG, EARL OF—see Hauwerstat Thompkyn.

WHITE FORD, BARON OF—see Gahvyn Mahrtyn.

WIND MOUNTAIN, COUNT OF—see Captain of Winds Shoukhan Khowsan.

WINDSHARE, EARL OF—see Sir Alyk Ahrthyr.

WYLLYM, ARCHBISHOP—see Wyllym Rayno.

WYLLYMS, LIEUTENANT PRAISKHAT, ROYAL DELFERAHKAN ARMY—one of Colonel Aiphraim Tahlyvyr's junior platoon commanders.

WYLLYMS, MARHYS—the Duke of Tirian's majordomo.

WYLSYNN, ARCHBAHLD—younger son of Vicar Samyl and Lysbet Wylsynn; Father Paityr Wylsynn's half brother.

WYLSYNN, HAUWERD—Paityr Wylsynn's uncle; a Reformist member of the vicarate; ex Temple Guardsman; a priest of the Order of Langhorne.

WYLSYNN, LYSBET—Samyl Wylsynn's second wife; mother of Tohmys, Zhanayt, and Archbahld Wylsynn.

WYLSYNN, PAITYR—a priest of the Order of Schueler and the Intendant of Charis. He served Erayk Dynnys in that capacity and has continued to serve Archbishop Maikel.

WYLSYNN, SAMYL—Father Paityr Wylsynn's father; the leader of the Reformists within the Council of Vicars and a priest of the Order of Schueler.

WYLSYNN, TANNIERE—Samyl Wylsynn's deceased wife; mother of Erais and Paityr Wylsynn.

WYLSYNN, TOHMYS—older son of Vicar Samyl and Lysbet Wylsynn; Father Paityr Wylsynn's half brother.

WYLSYNN, ZHANAYT—daughter of Vicar Samyl and Lysbet Wylsynn; Father Paityr Wylsynn's half sister.

WYNDAYL, MAJOR BRAINAHK, IMPERIAL CHARISIAN MARINES—CO, First Battalion, Fourteenth Marine Regiment.

WYNKASTAIR, MASTER PAYTER, IMPERIAL CHARISIAN NAVY—gunner, HMS *Destiny*, 54.

WYNSTYN, LIEUTENANT KYNYTH, ROYAL CORISANDIAN NAVY—first lieutenant, galley *Corisande*.

WYSTAHN, AHNAINAH—Edvarhd Wystahn's wife.

WYSTAHN, SERGEANT EDVARHD, ROYAL CHARISIAN MARINES—a scout-sniper assigned to 1/3rd Marines.

YAIR, FATHER AIRWAIN—chaplain and confessor to Rahzhyr Mairwyn, Baron Larchros.

YAIRLEY, CAPTAIN ALLAYN, IMPERIAL CHARISIAN NAVY—older brother of Captain Sir Dunkyn Yairley.

YAIRLEY, CAPTAIN SIR DUNKYN, IMPERIAL CHARISIAN NAVY—CO, HMS *Destiny*, 54, and acting commodore; later promoted to admiral.

YOWANCE, EHRNAIST—Rayjhis Yowance's deceased elder brother.

YOWANCE, RAYJHIS—Earl Gray Harbor, First Councilor of Charis.

YUTHAIN, CAPTAIN GORJHA, IMPERIAL HARCHONG NAVY—CO, galley IHNS *Ice Lizard*.

ZAHCHO, FATHER DAISHAN—an under-priest of the Order of Schueler. One of Father Aidryn Waimyn's Inquisitors in Corisande.

ZAHMSYN, ARCHBISHOP HALMYN—Archbishop of Gorath; senior prelate of the Kingdom of Dohlar until replaced by Trumahn Rowzvel.

ZAHMSYN, VICAR—see Zahmsyn Trynair.

ZAIVYAIR, AIBRAM, DUKE OF THORAST—effective Navy minister and senior officer, Royal Dohlaran Navy, brother-in-law of Admiral-General Duke Malikai (Faidel Ahlverez).

ZEBEDIAH, GRAND DUKE OF—see Tohmys Symmyns.

ZHADAHNG, SERGEANT WYNN, TEMPLE GUARD—Captain Walysh Zhu's senior noncom.

ZHADWAIL, TRAIVAHR—one of Tobys Raimair's guardsmen.

ZHAKSYN, LIEUTENANT TOHMYS, IMPERIAL CHARISIAN MARINES—General Chermyn's aide.

ZHANDOR, FATHER NEYTHAN—a Langhornite lawgiver accredited for both secular and ecclesiastic law. Assigned to Empress Sharleyan's staff.

ZHANSAN, FRAHNK—the Duke of Tirian's senior guardsman.

ZHANSTYN, BRIGADIER ZHOEL, IMPERIAL CHARISIAN MARINES—CO, Third Brigade, ICMC. Brigadier Clareyk's senior battalion CO during Corisande Campaign.

ZHARDEAU, LADY ERAIS—Samyl and Tanniere Wylsynn's daughter; Father Paityr Wylsynn's younger full sister; wife of Sir Fraihman Zhardeau.

ZHARDEAU, SAMYL—son of Sir Fraihman and Lady Erais Zhardeau; grandson of Vicar Samyl Wylsynn; nephew of Father Paityr Wylsynn.

ZHARDEAU, SIR FRAIHMAN—minor Tansharan aristocrat; husband of Lady Erais Zhardeau; son-in-law of Vicar Samyl Wylsynn.

ZHASPAHR, VICAR—see Zhaspahr Clyntahn.

ZHASTROW, FATHER AHBEL—Father Zhon Byrkyt's successor as Abbot of the Monastery of Saint Zherneau.

ZHASYN, ARCHBISHOP—see Zhasyn Cahnyr.

ZHAZTRO, COMMODORE HAINZ, EMERALD NAVY—the senior Emeraldian naval officer afloat (technically) in Eraystor following Battle of Darcos Sound.

ZHEFFYRS, MAJOR WYLL, ROYAL CHARISIAN MARINES—CO, Marine detachment, HMS Destiny, 54.

ZHEPPSYN, CAPTAIN NYKLAS, EMERALD NAVY—CO, galley Triton.

ZHERMAIN, CAPTAIN MAHRTYN, ROYAL DOHLARAN NAVY—CO, HMS Prince of Dohlar, 38.

ZHESSOP, BISHOP MYTCHAIL—Intendant of Delferahk. A Schuelerite.

ZHESSYP, LACHLYN—King Haarahld VII's valet.

ZHEVONS, AHBRAIM—alias and alternate persona of Merlin Athrawes.

ZHOELSYN, LIEUTENANT PHYLYP, ROYAL TAROTISIAN NAVY—second lieutenant, King Gorjah II.

ZHONAIR, MAJOR GAHRMYN—a battery commander in Ferayd Harbor, Ferayd Sound, Kingdom of Delferahk.

ZHONES, MIDSHIPMAN AHRLEE, IMPERIAL CHARISIAN NAVY—a junior midshipman in HMS *Destiny*, 54.

ZHORJ, COLONEL SIR WAHLYS—Tahdayo Mahntayl's senior mercenary commander.

ZHU, CAPTAIN WALYSH, TEMPLE GUARD—senior officer of military escort delivering Charisian POWs from Dohlar to the Temple.

ZHUD, CORPORAL WALTHAR, ROYAL DELFERAHKAN ARMY—Sergeant Braice Mahknash's assistant squad leader.

ZHUSTYN, SIR AHLBER—senior minister for intelligence, Kingdom of Chisholm.

Glossary

Abbey of Saint Evehlain—the sister abbey of the Monastery of Saint Zherneau.

Angora lizard—a Safeholdian "lizard" with a particularly luxuriant, cashmere-like coat. They are raised and sheared as sheep and form a significant part of the fine textiles industry.

Anshinritsumei—"the little fire" from the *Holy Writ*; the lesser touch of God's spirit and the maximum enlightenment of which mortals are capable.

Ape lizard—ape lizards are much larger and more powerful versions of monkey lizards. Unlike monkey lizards, they are mostly ground dwellers, although they are capable of climbing trees suitable to bear their weight. The great mountain ape lizard weighs as much as nine hundred or a thousand pounds, whereas the planes ape lizard weighs little more than a hundred to a hundred and fifty pounds. Ape lizards live in families of up to twenty or thirty adults, and whereas monkey lizards will typically flee when confronted with a threat, ape lizards are much more likely to respond by attacking the threat. It is not unheard of for two or three ape lizard "families" to combine forces against particularly dangerous predators, and even a great dragon will generally avoid such a threat.

Archangels, The—central figures of the Church of God Awaiting. The Archangels were senior members of the command crew of Operation Ark who assumed the status of divine messengers, guides, and guardians in order to control and shape the future of human civilization on Safehold.

Blink-lizard—a small, bioluminescent winged lizard. Although it's about three times the size of a firefly, it fills much the same niche on Safehold.

Borer—a form of Safeholdian shellfish which attaches itself to the hulls of ships or the timbers of wharves by boring into them. There are several types of borer, the most destructive of which continually eat their way deeper into any wooden structure, whereas some less destructive varieties eat only enough of the structure to anchor themselves and actually form a protective outer layer which gradually builds up a coral-like surface. Borers and rot are the two most serious threats (aside, of course, from fire) to wooden hulls.

Briar berries—any of several varieties of native Safeholdian berries which grow on thorny bushes.

Catamount—a smaller version of the Safeholdian slash lizard. The catamount is very fast and smarter than its larger cousin, which means it tends to avoid humans. It is, however, a lethal and dangerous hunter in its own right.

Cat-lizard—a furry lizard about the size of a terrestrial cat. They are kept as pets and are very affectionate.

Chewleaf—a mildly narcotic leaf from a native Safeholdian plant. It is used much as terrestrial chewing tobacco over much of the planet's surface.

Choke tree—a low-growing species of tree native to Safehold. It comes in many varieties and is found in most of the planet's climate zones. It is dense-growing, tough, and difficult to eradicate, but it requires quite a lot of sunlight to flourish, which means it is seldom found in mature old-growth forests.

Church of Charis—the schismatic church which split from the Church of God Awaiting (see below) following the Group of Four's effort to destroy the Kingdom of Charis.

Church of God Awaiting—the church and religion created by the command staff of Operation Ark to control the colonists and their descendants and prevent the re-emergence of advanced technology.

Commentaries, The—the authorized interpretations and doctrinal expansions upon the *Holy Writ*. They represent the officially approved and Church-sanctioned interpretation of the original Scripture.

Cotton silk—a plant native to Safehold which shares many of the properties of silk and cotton. It is very lightweight and strong, but the raw fiber comes from a plant pod which is even more filled with seeds than Old Earth cotton. Because of the amount of hand labor required to harvest and process the pods and to remove the seeds from it, cotton silk is very expensive.

Council of Vicars—the Church of God Awaiting's equivalent of the College of Cardinals.

Dagger thorn—a native Charisian shrub, growing to a height of perhaps three feet at maturity, which possesses knife-edged thorns from three to seven inches long, depending upon the variety.

Deep-mouth wyvern—the Safeholdian equivalent of a pelican.

Doomwhale—the most dangerous predator of Safehold, although, fortunately, it seldom bothers with anything as small as humans. Doomwhales have been known to run to as much as one hundred feet in length, and they are pure carnivores. Each doomwhale requires a huge range, and encounters with them are rare, for which human beings are just as glad, thank you. Doomwhales will eat *anything* . . . including the largest krakens. They have been known, on *extremely* rare occasions, to attack merchant ships and war galleys.

Dragon—the largest native Safeholdian land life-form. Dragons come in two varieties: the common dragon (generally subdivided into jungle dragons and hill dragons) and the carnivorous great dragon.

Fallen, The—the Archangels, angels, and mortals who followed Shan-wei in her rebellion against God and the rightful authority of the Archangel Langhorne. The term applies to *all* of Shan-wei's adherents, but is most often used in reference to the angels and Archangels who followed her willingly rather than the mortals who were duped into obeying her.

Five-day—a Safeholdian "week," consisting of only five days, Monday through Friday.

Fleming moss—an absorbent moss native to Safehold which was genetically engineered by Shan-wei's terraforming crews to possess natural antibiotic properties. It is a staple of Safeholdian medical practice.

Forktail—one of several species of native Safeholdian fish which fill an ecological niche similar to that of the Old Earth herring.

Gbaba—a star-traveling, xenophobic species whose reaction to encounters with any possibly competing species is to exterminate it. The Gbaba completely destroyed the Terran Federation and, so far as is known, all human beings in the galaxy aside from the population of Safehold.

Golden berry—a tree growing to about ten feet in height which thrives in most Safeholdian climates. A tea brewed from its leaves is a sovereign specific for motion sickness and nausea.

Grasshopper—a Safeholdian insect analogue which grows to a length of as much as nine inches and is carnivorous. Fortunately, they do not occur in the same numbers as terrestrial grasshoppers.

Gray-horned wyvern—a nocturnal flying predator of Safehold. It is roughly analogous to a terrestrial owl.

Great dragon—the largest and most dangerous land carnivore of Safehold. The great dragon isn't actually related to hill dragons or jungle dragons at all, despite some superficial physical resemblances. In fact, it's more of a scaled-up slash lizard, with elongated jaws and sharp, serrated teeth. They have six limbs and, unlike the slash lizard, are covered in thick, well-insulated hide rather than fur.

Group of Four—the four vicars who dominate and effectively control the Council of Vicars of the Church of God Awaiting.

Hairatha Dragons—the Hairatha professional baseball

team. The traditional rivals of the Tellesberg Krakens for the Kingdom Championship.

Hake—a Safeholdian fish. Like most "fish" native to Safehold, it has a very long, sinuous body but the head does resemble a terran hake or cod, with a hooked jaw.

High-angle gun—a relatively short, stubby artillery piece with a carriage specially designed to allow higher angles of fire in order to lob gunpowder-filled shells in high, arcing trajectories. The name is generally shortened to "angle-gun" by the gun crews themselves.

Hill dragon—a roughly elephant-sized draft animal commonly used on Safehold. Despite their size, hill dragons are capable of rapid, sustained movement. They are herbivores.

Ice wyvern—a flightless aquatic wyvern rather similar to a terrestrial penguin. Species of ice wyvern are native to both the northern and southern polar regions of Safehold.

Insights, The—the recorded pronouncements and observations of the Church of God Awaiting's Grand Vicars and canonized saints. They represent deeply significant spiritual and inspirational teachings, but as the work of fallible mortals do not have the same standing as the *Holy Writ* itself.

Intendant—the cleric assigned to a bishopric or archbishopric as the direct representative of the Office of Inquisition. The intendant is specifically charged with ensuring that the Proscriptions of Jwo-jeng are not violated.

Journal of Saint Zherneau—the journal left by Jeremy Knowles telling the truth about the destruction of the Alexandria Enclave and about Pei Shan-wei.

Jungle dragon—a somewhat generic term applied to lowland dragons larger than hill dragons. The gray jungle dragon is the largest herbivore on Safehold.

Kercheef—a traditional headdress worn in the Kingdom of Tarot which consists of a specially designed bandana tied across the hair.

Knights of the Temple Lands—the corporate title of the

prelates who govern the Temple Lands. Technically, the Knights of the Temple Lands are *secular* rulers who simply happen to also hold high Church office. Under the letter of the Church's law, what they may do as the Knights of the Temple Lands is completely separate from any official action of the Church. This legal fiction has been of considerable value to the Church on more than one occasion.

Kraken—(1) generic term for an entire family of maritime predators. Krakens are rather like sharks crossed with octopi. They have powerful, fish-like bodies, strong jaws with inward-inclined, fang-like teeth, and a cluster of tentacles just behind the head which can be used to hold prey while they devour it. The smallest, coastal krakens can be as short as three or four feet; deep-water krakens up to fifty feet in length have been reliably reported, and there are legends of those still larger.

Kraken—(2) one of three pre-Merlin heavy-caliber naval artillery pieces. The great kraken weighed approximately 3.4 tons and fired a 42-pound round shot. The royal kraken weighed four tons. It also fired a 42-pound shot but was specially designed as a long-range weapon with less windage and higher bore pressures. The standard kraken was a 2.75-ton, medium-range weapon which fired a 35-pound round shot approximately 6.2 inches in diameter.

Kyousei hi—"great fire" or "magnificent fire" from the *Holy Writ*. The term used to describe the brilliant nimbus of light the Operation Ark command crew generated around their air cars and skimmers to "prove" their divinity to the original Safeholdians.

Langhorne's Watch—the 31-minute period which falls immediately after midnight. It was inserted by the original "Archangels" to compensate for the extra length of Safehold's 26.5-hour day. It is supposed to be used for contemplation and giving thanks.

Master Traynyr—a character out of the Safeholdian entertainment tradition. Master Traynyr is a stock character in Safeholdian puppet theater, by turns a bumbling conspirator whose plans always miscarry and the puppeteer who controls all of the marionette "actors" in the play.

Messenger wyvern—any one of several strains of genetically modified Safeholdian wyverns adapted by Pei Shan-wei's terraforming teams to serve the colonists as homing pigeon equivalents. Some messenger wyverns are adapted for short-range, high-speed delivery of messages, whereas others are adapted for extremely long range (but slower) message deliveries.

Monastery of Saint Zherneau—the mother monastery and headquarters of the Brethren of Saint Zherneau, a relatively small and poor order in the Archbishopric of Charis.

Monkey lizard—a generic term for several species of arboreal, saurian-looking marsupials. Monkey lizards come in many different shapes and sizes, although none are much larger than an Old Earth chimpanzee and most are considerably smaller. They have two very human-looking hands, although each hand has only three fingers and an opposable thumb, and the "hand feet" of their other forelimbs have a limited grasping ability but no opposable thumb. Monkey lizards tend to be excitable, *very* energetic, and talented mimics of human behaviors.

Mountain spike-thorn—a particular subspecies of spike-thorn, found primarily in tropical mountains. The most common blossom color is a deep, rich red, but the white mountain spike-thorn is especially prized for its trumpet-shaped blossom, which has a deep almost cobalt-blue throat, fading to pure white as it approaches the outer edge of the blossom, which is, in turn, fringed in a deep golden yellow.

Narwhale—a species of Safeholdian sea life named for the Old Earth species of the same name. Safeholdian narwhales are about forty feet in length and equipped with twin horn-like tusks up to eight feet long. They live in large pods or schools and are not at all shy or retiring. The adults of narwhale pods have been known to fight off packs of kraken.

Nearoak—a rough-barked Safeholdian tree similar to an Old Earth oak tree. Found in tropic and near tropic zones. Although it does resemble an Old Earth oak, it is an evergreen and seeds using "pinecones."

NEAT—Neural Education and Training machine. The standard means of education in the Terran Federation.

New model—a generic term increasingly applied to the innovations in technology (especially war-fighting technology) introduced by Charis and its allies. (See "new model kraken," below.)

New model kraken—the standardized artillery piece of the Imperial Charisian Navy. It weighs approximately 2.5 tons and fires a 30-pound round shot with a diameter of approximately 5.9 inches. Although it weighs slightly less than the old kraken (see above) and its round shot is twelve percent lighter, it is actually longer ranged and fires at a higher velocity because of reductions in windage, improvements in gunpowder, and slightly increased barrel length.

Nynian Rychtair—the Safeholdian equivalent of Helen of Troy, a woman of legendary beauty, born in Siddarmark, who eventually married the Emperor of Harchong.

Offal lizard—a carrion-eating scavenger which fills the niche of an undersized hyena crossed with a jackal. Offal lizards will take small living prey, but they are generally cowardly and are regarded with scorn and contempt by most Safeholdians.

Operation Ark—a last-ditch, desperate effort mounted by the Terran Federation to establish a hidden colony beyond the knowledge and reach of the xenophobic Gbaba. It created the human settlement on Safehold.

Pasquale's Basket—a voluntary collection of contributions for the support of the sick, homeless, and indigent. The difference between the amount contributed voluntarily and that required for the Basket's purpose is supposed to be contributed from Mother Church's coffers as a first charge upon tithes received.

Persimmon fig—a native Safeholdian fruit which is extremely tart and relatively thick-skinned.

Prong lizard—a roughly elk sized lizard with a single horn which branches into four sharp points in the last third or so of its length. They are herbivores and not particularly ferocious.

Proscriptions of Jwo-jeng—the definition of allowable technology under the doctrine of the Church of God Awaiting. Essentially, the Proscriptions limit allowable technology to that which is powered by wind, water, or muscle. The Proscriptions are subject to interpretation by the Order of Schueler, which generally errs on the side of conservatism, but it is not unheard of for corrupt intendants to rule for or against an innovation under the Proscriptions in return for financial compensation.

Rakurai—literally "lightning bolt." The *Holy Writ*'s term for the kinetic weapons used to destroy the Alexandria Enclave.

Reformist—one associated with the Reformist movement. The majority of Reformists outside the Charisian Empire still regard themselves as Temple Loyalists.

Reformist movement—the movement within the Church of God Awaiting to reform the abuses and corruption which have become increasingly evident (and serious) over the last hundred to one hundred and fifty years. Largely underground and unfocused until the emergence of the Church of Charis, the movement is attracting increasing support throughout Safehold.

Round Theatre—the largest and most famous theater in the city of Tellesberg. Supported by the Crown but independent of it, and renowned not only for the quality of its productions but for its willingness to present works which satirize Charisian society, industry, the aristocracy, and even the Church.

Saint Evehlain—the patron saint of the Abbey of Saint Evehlain in Tellesberg.

Saint Zherneau—the patron saint of the Monastery of Saint Zherneau in Tellesberg.

Sand maggot—a loathsome carnivore, looking much like a six-legged slug, which haunts Safeholdian beaches just above the surf line. Sand maggots do not normally take living prey, although they have no objection to devouring the occasional small creature which strays into their reach. Their natural coloration blends well with their sandy habitat, and they normally conceal themselves by digging their bodies into the sand until they are completely covered, or only a small portion of their backs show.

Sea cow—a walrus-like Safeholdian sea mammal which grows to a body length of approximately ten feet when fully mature.

Seijin—sage, holy man, mystic. Legendary warriors and teachers, generally believed to have been touched by the *anshinritsumei*. Many educated Safeholdians consider *seijins* to be mythological, fictitious characters.

Shan-wei's War—the *Holy Writ*'s term for the struggle between the supporters of Eric Langhorne and those of Pei Shan-wei over the future of humanity on Safehold. It is presented in terms very similar to those of the war between Lucifer and the angels loyal to God, with Shan-wei in the role of Lucifer.

Slash lizard—a six-limbed, saurian-looking, furry oviparous mammal. One of the three top land predators of Safehold. Its mouth contains twin rows of fangs capable of punching through chain mail and its feet have four long toes, each tipped with claws up to five or six inches long.

Sleep root—a Safeholdian tree from whose roots an entire family of opiates and painkillers are produced. The term "sleep root" is often used generically for any of those pharmaceutical products.

Slime toad—an amphibious Safeholdian carrion eater with a body length of approximately seven inches. It takes its name from the thick mucus which covers its skin. Its bite is poisonous but seldom results in death.

SNARC—Self-Navigating Autonomous Reconnaissance and Communications platform.

Spider-crab—a native species of sea life, considerably larger than any terrestrial crab. The spider-crab is not a crustacean, but more of a segmented, tough-hided, many-legged seagoing slug. Despite that, its legs are considered a great delicacy and are actually very tasty.

Spider-rat—a native species of vermin which fills roughly the ecological niche of a terrestrial rat. Like all Safeholdian mammals, it is six-limbed, but it looks like a cross between a hairy gila monster and an insect, with long, multi-jointed legs which actually arch higher than its spine. It is nasty-tempered but basically cowardly. Fully adult male specimens of the larger varieties run to about two feet in body length, with another two feet of tail, for a total length of four feet, but the more common varieties average only between two or three feet of combined body/tail length.

Spike-thorn—a flowering shrub, various subspecies of which are found in most Safeholdian climate zones. Its blossoms come in many colors and hues, and the tropical versions tend to be taller-growing and to bear more delicate blossoms.

Steel thistle—a native Safeholdian plant which looks very much like branching bamboo. The plant bears seed pods filled with small, spiny seeds embedded in fine, straight fibers. The seeds are extremely difficult to remove by hand, but the fiber can be woven into a fabric which is even stronger than cotton silk. It can also be twisted into extremely strong, stretch-resistant rope. Moreover, the plant grows almost as rapidly as actual bamboo, and the yield of raw fiber per acre is seventy percent higher than for terrestrial cotton.

Surgoi kasai—"dreadful" or "great fire." The true spirit of God. The touch of His divine fire, which only an angel or Archangel can endure.

Swivel wolf—a light, primarily anti-personnel artillery piece mounted on a swivel for easy traverse. (See "wolf.")

Teak tree—a native Safeholdian tree whose wood contains concentrations of silica and other minerals.

Although it grows to a greater height than the Old Earth teak wood tree and bears a needle-like foliage, its timber is very similar in grain and coloration to the terrestrial tree and, like Old Earth teak, it is extremely resistant to weather, rot, and insects.

Tellesberg Krakens—the Tellesberg professional baseball club.

Temple, The—the complex built by "the Archangels" using Terran Federation technology to serve as the headquarters of the Church of God Awaiting. It contains many "mystic" capabilities which demonstrate the miraculous power of the Archangels to anyone who sees them.

Temple Loyalist—one who renounces the schism created by the Church of Charis' defiance of the Grand Vicar and Council of Vicars of the Church of God Awaiting. Some Temple Loyalists are also Reformists (see above), but all are united in condemning the schism between Charis and the Temple.

Testimonies, The—by far the most numerous of the Church of God Awaiting's sacred writings, these consist of the firsthand observations of the first few generations of humans on Safehold. They do not have the same status as the Christian gospels, because they do not reveal the central teachings and inspiration of God. Instead, collectively, they form an important substantiation of the *Writ*'s "historical accuracy" and conclusively attest to the fact that the events they describe did, in fact, transpire.

Wire vine—a kudzu-like vine native to Safehold. Wire vine isn't as fast-growing as kudzu, but it's equally tenacious, and unlike kudzu, several of its varieties have long, sharp thorns. Unlike many native Safeholdian plant species, it does quite well intermingled with terrestrial imports. It is often used as a sort of combination hedgerow and barbed wire fence by Safehold farmers.

Wolf—(1) a Safeholdian predator which lives and hunts in packs and has many of the same social characteristics as the terrestrial species of the same name. It is warm-blooded but oviparous and larger than an Old Earth wolf, with adult males averaging around two hundred to two hundred and twenty-five pounds.

Wolf—(2) a generic term for shipboard artillery pieces with a bore of less than 2" and a shot weighing one pound or less. They are primarily antipersonnel weapons but can also be effective against boats and small craft.

Wyvern—the Safeholdian ecological analogue of terrestrial birds. There are as many varieties of wyverns as there are birds, including (but not limited to) the homing/messenger wyvern, hunting wyverns suitable for the equivalent of hawking for small prey, the crag wyvern (a small—wingspan ten feet—flying predator), various species of sea wyverns, and the king wyvern (a very large flying predator with a wingspan of up to twenty-five feet). All wyverns have two pairs of wings, and one pair of powerful, clawed legs. The king wyvern has been known to take children as prey when desperate or when the opportunity presents, but they are quite intelligent. They know that man is a prey best left alone and generally avoid areas of human habitation.

Wyvernry—a nesting place and/or breeding hatchery for domesticated wyverns.

The Archangels:

Archangel	Sphere of Authority	Symbol
Langhorne	law and life	scepter
Bédard	wisdom and knowledge	lamp
Pasquale	healing and medicine	caduceus
Sondheim	agronomy and farming	grain sheaf
Truscott	animal husbandry	horse
Schueler	justice	sword
Jwo-jeng	acceptable technology	flame
Chihiro (1)	history	quill pen
Chihiro (2)	guardian	sword
Andropov	good fortune	dice
Hastings	geography	draftsman's compass

Fallen Archangel	Sphere of Authority
Shan-wei	mother of evil/evil ambition
Kau-yung	destruction
Proctor	temptation/forbidden knowledge
Sullivan	gluttony
Ascher	lies
Grimaldi	pestilence
Stavraki	avarice

The Church of God Awaiting's Hierarchy:

Ecclesiastic rank	Distinguishing color	Clerical ring/set
Grand Vicar	dark blue	sapphire with rubies
Vicar	orange	sapphire
Archbishop	white and orange	ruby
Bishop executor	white	ruby
Bishop	white	ruby
Auxiliary bishop	green and white	ruby
Upper-priest	green	plain gold (no stone)
Priest	brown	none
Under-priest	brown	none
Sexton	brown	none

Clergy who do not belong to a specific order wear cassocks entirely in the color of their rank. Auxiliary bishops' cassocks are green with narrow trim bands of white. Archbishops' cassocks are white, but trimmed in orange. Clergy who belong to one of the ecclesiastical orders (see below) wear habits (usually of patterns specific to each order) in the order's colors but with the symbol of their order on the right breast, badged in the color of their priestly rank. In formal vestments, the pattern is reversed; that is, their vestments are in the colors of their priestly ranks and the order's symbol is the color of their order. All members of the clergy habitually wear either cassocks or the habits of their orders. The headgear is a three-cornered "priest's cap" almost identical to the eighteenth century's tricornes. The cap is black for anyone under the rank of vicar. Under-priests' and priests' bear brown cockades. Auxiliary bishops' bear green cockades. Bishops' and bishops' executor bear white cockades. Archbishops' bear white cockades with a broad, dove-tailed orange ribbon at the back. Vicars' priests' caps are of orange with no cockade or ribbon, and the Grand Vicar's cap is white with an orange cockade.

All clergy of the Church of God Awaiting are affiliated with one or more of the great ecclesiastic orders, but not all are *members* of those orders. Or it might, perhaps, be more accurate to say that not all are *full* members of their orders. Every ordained priest is automatically affiliated with the order of the bishop who ordained him and (in theory, at least) owes primary obedience to that order. Only members of the clergy who have taken an order's vows are considered full members or brethren/sisters of that order, however. (Note: there are no female priests in the Church of God Awaiting, but women may attain high ecclesiastic rank in one of the orders.) Only full brethren or sisters of an order may attain to rank within that order, and only members of one of the great orders are eligible for elevation to the vicarate.

The great orders of the Church of God Awaiting, in order of precedence and power, are:

The Order of Schueler, which is primarily concerned with the enforcement of church doctrine and theology. The Grand Inquisitor, who is automatically a member of the Council of Vicars, is always the head of the Order of Schueler. Schuelerite ascendency within the Church has been steadily increasing for over two hundred years, and the order is clearly the dominant power in the Church hierarchy today. The order's color is purple, and its symbol is a sword.

The Order of Langhorne is technically senior to the Order of Schueler, but has lost its primacy in every practical sense. The Order of Langhorne provides the Church's jurists, and since Church law supersedes secular law throughout Safehold that means all jurists and lawgivers (lawyers) are either members of the order or must be vetted and approved by the order. At one time, that gave the Langhornites unquestioned primacy, but the Schuelerites have relegated the order of Langhorne to a primarily administrative role, and the head of the Order lost his mandatory seat on the Council of Vicars several generations back (in the Year of God 810). Needless to say, there's a certain tension between the Schuelerites and the Langhornites. The Order of Langhorne's color is black, and its symbol is a scepter.

The Order of Bédard has undergone the most change of any of the original great orders of the Church. Originally, the Inquisition came out of the Bédardists, but that function was effectively resigned to the Schuelerites by the Bédardists themselves when Saint Greyghor's reforms converted the order into the primary teaching order of the church. Today, the Bédardists are philosophers and educators, both at the university level and among the peasantry, although they also retain their function as Safehold's mental health experts and councilors. The order is also involved in caring for the poor and indigent. Ironically, perhaps, given the role of the "Archangel Bédard" in the creation of the Church of God Awaiting, a large percentage of Reformist clergy springs from this order. Like the Schuelerites, the head of the Order of Bédard always holds a seat on the Council of Vicars. The order's color is white, and its symbol is an oil lamp.

The Order of Chihiro is unique in that it has two separate functions and is divided into two separate orders. The Order of the Quill is responsible for training and overseeing the Church's scribes, historians, and bureaucrats. It is responsible for the archives of the Church and all of its official documents. The Order of the Sword is a militant order which often cooperates closely with the Schuelerites and the Inquisition. It is the source of the officer corps for the Temple Guard and also for most officers of the Temple Lands' nominally secular army and navy. Its head is always a member of the Council of Vicars, as Captain General of the Church of God Awaiting, and generally fulfills the role of Secretary of War. The order's color is blue, and its symbol is a quill pen. The Order of the Sword shows the quill pen, but crossed with a sheathed sword.

The Order of Pasquale is another powerful and influential order of the Church. Like the Order of Bédard, the Pasqualates are a teaching order, but their area of specialization is healing and medicine. They turn out very well-trained surgeons, but they are blinkered against pursuing any germ theory of medicine because of their religious teachings. All licensed healers on Safehold must be examined and approved by the Order of Pasquale, and the order is deeply involved in public hygiene policies and (less deeply) in caring for the poor and indigent. The majority of Safeholdian hospitals are associated, to at least some degree, with the Order of Pasquale. The head of the Order of Pasquale is normally, but not always, a member of the Council of Vicars. The order's color is green, and its symbol is a caduceus.

The Order of Sondheim and the Order of Truscott are generally considered "brother orders" and are similar to the Order of Pasquale, but deal with agronomy and animal husbandry respectively. Both are teaching orders and they are jointly and deeply involved in Safehold's agriculture and food production. The teachings of the Archangel Sondheim and Archangel Truscott incorporated into the

Holy Writ were key elements in the ongoing terraforming of Safehold following the general abandonment of advanced technology. Both of these orders lost their mandatory seats on the Council of Vicars over two hundred years ago, however. The Order of Sondheim's color is brown and its symbol is a sheaf of grain; the Order of Truscott's color is brown trimmed in *green*, and its symbol is a horse.

The Order of Hastings is the most junior (and least powerful) of the current great orders. The order is a teaching order, like the Orders of Sondheim and Truscott, and produces the vast majority of Safehold's cartographers and surveyors. Hastingites also provide most of Safehold's officially sanctioned astronomers, although they are firmly within what might be considered the Ptolemaic theory of the universe. The order's "color" is actually a checkered pattern of green, brown, and blue, representing vegetation, earth, and water. Its symbol is a compass.

The Order of Jwo-jeng, once one of the four greatest orders of the Church, was absorbed into the Order of Schueler in Year of God 650, at the same time the Grand Inquisitorship was vested in the Schuelerites. Since that time, the Order of Jwo-jeng has had no independent existence.

The Order of Andropov occupies a sort of middle ground or gray area between the great orders of the Church and the minor orders. According to the *Holy Writ*, Andropov was one of the leading Archangels during the war against Shan-wei and the Fallen, but he was always more lighthearted (one hesitates to say frivolous) than his companions. His order has definite epicurean tendencies, which have traditionally been accepted by the Church because its raffles, casinos, horse and/or lizard races, etc., raise a great deal of money for charitable causes. Virtually every bookie on Safehold is either a member of Andropov's order or at least regards the Archangel as his patron. Needless to say, the Order of Andropov is not guaranteed a seat on the Council of Vicars. The order's color is red, and its symbol is a pair of dice.

▼ ▼ ▼

In addition to the above ecclesiastical orders, there are a great many minor orders: mendicant orders, nursing orders (usually but not always associated with the Order of Pasquale), charitable orders (usually but not always associated with the Order of Bédard or the Order of Pasquale), ascetic orders, etc. All of the great orders maintain numerous monasteries and convents, as do many of the lesser orders. Members of minor orders may not become vicars unless they are also members of one of the great orders.

Turn the page for a preview of

MIDST TOIL AND TRIBULATION

DAVID WEBER

✦

Available in September 2012 from
Tom Doherty Associates

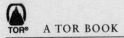

Gray Wall Mountains, Glacierheart Province, Republic of Siddarmark

Snow veils hung in the clear, icy air, dancing on the knife-edged wind that swirled across the snowpack, and the highest peaks cast blue shadows across the snow as they towered as much as a mile higher than his present position.

It looked firm and inviting to the unwary eye, that snowpack, but Wahlys Mahkhom had been born and raised in the Gray Walls. He knew better, and his eyes were hard and full of hate behind the smoked glass of his snow goggles as his belly snarled resentfully at him. Accustomed as he was to winter weather, even here in the Gray Walls, and despite his fur-trimmed parka and heavy mittens, Mahkhom felt the ice settling into his bones and muscles. It needed only a momentary carelessness for a man to freeze to death in these mountains in winter, even at the best of times, and these were far from the best of times. The Glacierheart winter burned energy like one of Shan-wei's own demons, and food was scarcer than Mahkhom could ever remember. Glacierheart's high, stony mountainsides and rocky fields had never yielded bountiful crops, yet there'd always been at least something in the storehouses to be eked out by hunters like Mahkhom himself. But not this year. This year the storehouses had been burned—first by one side, then by the other in retaliation—and the fields, such as they were, were buried beneath the deepest, bitterest snow anyone could remember. It was as if God Himself was determined to punish innocent and guilty alike, and there were times—more times than he liked to admit—when Wahlys Mahkhom wondered if there would be anyone left alive to plant the next year's crops.

His teeth wanted to chatter like some lowland dancer's castanets, and he dragged higher the thick scarf his mother had knitted for him years ago. He laid the extra layer of insulation across the snow mask covering his face, and the hatred in his eyes turned harder and far, far colder than the winter about him as he touched that scarf and, with it, the memory of why his mother would never knit another.

He raised his head cautiously, looking critically about himself once more. But his companions were as mountainwise as he was. They were just as well hidden under the white canopies of the sheets they'd brought with them, and he bared those edge-of-chattering teeth in hard, vengeful satisfaction. The snowshoe trek to their present positions had been exhausting, especially for men who'd cut themselves dangerously short on rations before they ever set out. They knew better than that, of course, but how did a man take with him the food he really needed when he looked into the eyes of the starving child who would have to go without if he did? That was the question Wahlys Mahkhom couldn't answer—not yet, at any rate—and he never wanted to be able to.

He settled back down, nestling into his hole in the snow, using the snow itself for insulation, watching the trail below him that crept through the mountains like a broken-backed serpent. They'd waited patiently here for one entire day and half of another, but if the target they anticipated failed to arrive soon, they'd be forced to abandon the mission and return empty-handed. The thought woke a slow, savage furnace of fury within him to counterpoint the mountains' icy cold, yet he made himself face it. He'd seen hate-fired determination and obstinacy kill too many men this bitter winter, and he refused to die stupidly. Not when he had so many men still to kill.

He didn't know exactly what the temperature was, although the planet Safehold had remarkably accurate thermometers, a gift of the Archangels who'd created Mahkhom's world. He didn't have to know exactly, of course. Nor did he have to know that he was nine thousand feet above sea level on a planet with an axial inclination eleven degrees greater and an average temperature seven degrees lower than a world called Earth, of which he had never heard. All he had to know was that a few moments carelessness would be enough to—

His thoughts froze as a flicker of movement caught his eye. He watched, scarcely daring to breathe, as the flicker repeated itself. It was far away, hard to make out in the dimness of the steep-walled pass, but all the fury and anger within him had distilled itself suddenly into a still, calm watchfulness, focused and far colder than the mountains about him.

The movement drew closer, resolving itself into a long line of white-clad men, slogging along the trail on snowshoes like the ones buried beside Mahkhom's hole in the snow. Half of them were bowed under heavy packs, and no less than six sleds drawn by snow lizards accompanied them. Mahkhom's eyes glittered with satisfaction as he saw those sleds and those lizards and realized their information had been accurate after all.

He didn't bother to look around for the other men buried in the snow about him, or for the other men hidden in the dense stands of evergreens half a mile farther down that icy trail from his icy perch. He knew where they were, knew they were as ready and watchful as he himself. The careless ones, the rash ones, were already dead; those who remained had added hard-learned lessons to the hunter's and trapper's skills they'd already possessed. And like Mahkhom himself, his companions had too much killing to do to let themselves die foolishly.

No Glacierheart miner or trapper could afford one of the expensive firearms the lowlanders used. Even if they could have afforded the weapons themselves, powder and ball came dear. For that matter, even a steel-bowed arbalest was hideously expensive, over a full-month's income for a master coal miner, but a properly maintained arbalest lasted for generations. Mahkhom had inherited his from his father, and his father from his father, and a man could always make the ammunition he needed. Now he rolled over onto his back under his concealing sheet. He removed his over-mittens and braced the steel bow stave against his feet while his gloved hands cranked the windlass. He took his time, for there was no rush. It would take those men and those snow lizards the better part of a quarter hour to reach the designated point, and the mountain air was crystal clear. Better to take the time to span the weapon this way, however awkward it might be, then to risk skylining himself and warning his enemies of their peril.

He finished cranking, made sure the string was securely latched over the pawl, and detached the windlass. Then he rolled back over, setting a square-headed quarrel on the string. He brought the arbalest into position, gazing through the ring sight, watching and waiting with his heart as cold as the wind while those marching figures crept closer and closer below him.

For a moment, far below the surface of his thoughts, a bit of the man he'd been only three or four months earlier stared aghast at what was about to happen here on this high, icy mountain trail. That tiny fragment of the Wahlys Mahkhom who'd still had a family knew that many of those men had families, as well. It knew that those families were as desperately dependent upon the food on those lizard-drawn sleds as the families he'd left huddling around stoves and fireplaces in the crudely built cabins and huts where they'd taken shelter when their villages were burned about their ears. It knew about the starvation, and the sickness, and the death that would stalk other women and other children when this day's work was done. But none of the rest of him listened to that tiny, lost fragment, for it had work to do.

The center of that marching column of men reached the base of the single pine, standing alone and isolated as a perfect landmark, and under the ice and frost-clotted snow mask protecting his face, Mahkhom's smile was the snarl of a hunting slash lizard. He waited a single heartbeat longer, and then his hands squeezed the trigger and his arbalest spat a sunlight-gilded sliver of death through that crystal mountain air.